# of love & life

ISBN 978-0-276-44113-4

www.readersdigest.co.uk

The Reader's Digest Association Limited, 11 Westferry Circus, Canary Wharf, London E14 4HE

# of love & life

Three novels selected and condensed
by Reader's Digest

The Reader's Digest Association Limited, London

CONTENTS

Maeve Binchy

WHITETHORN WOODS

Father Brian Flynn, the well-meaning curate of St Augustine's Church in Rossmore, has always been privately sceptical about the legendary healing power of St Ann's Well in nearby Whitethorn Woods.

But now that developers are poised to demolish the shrine, he finds many of his parishioners are up in arms—and all have a story to tell . . .

CHAPTER 1

The Road, the Woods and the Well—1

FATHER BRIAN FLYNN, the curate in St Augustine's Rossmore, hated the feast day of St Ann with a passion that was unusual for a Catholic priest. But then, as far as he knew, he was the only priest in the world who had a thriving St Ann's Well in his parish: a holy shrine of dubious origin. A place where parishioners gathered to ask the mother of the Virgin Mary to intercede for them in a variety of issues, mainly matters intimate and personal. Areas where a clodhopping priest wouldn't be able to tread, such as finding them a fiancé, or a husband, and then blessing that union with a child.

Rome was, as usual, unhelpfully silent about the well.

Well, Rome was probably hedging its bets, Father Flynn thought grimly, over there they must be pleased that there was *any* pious practice left in an increasingly secular Ireland, and not wish to discourage it. Yet had not Rome been swift to say that pagan rituals and superstitions had no place in the Body of Faith? It was a puzzlement, as Jimmy, that nice young doctor from Doon village, a few miles out, used to say. He maintained it was the same in medicine: you never got a ruling when you wanted one, only when you didn't need one at all.

There was a ceremony on July 26 every year where people came from far and wide to pray and to dress the well with garlands and flowers. Father Flynn was invariably asked to say a few words, and every year he agonised over it. He could not say to these people that it was very near to idolatry to have people battling their way towards a statue in the back of a cave beside a well in the middle of the Whitethorn Woods.

From what he had read and studied, St Ann and her husband, St Joachim, were shadowy figures, quite possibly confused with stories of Hannah in the Old Testament, who thought herself to be forever childless, but who eventually bore Samuel. Whatever else St Ann may have done in her lifetime, 2,000 years ago, she had *not* visited Rossmore in Ireland, found a place in the woods and established a holy well that had never run dry. That much was definite.

But try telling it to some of the people in Rossmore and you were in trouble. So Father Flynn stood there every year mumbling a decade of the rosary, which couldn't offend anyone, and preaching a little homily about goodwill and tolerance and kindness to neighbours.

He often felt he had quite enough worries of his own without having to add St Ann and her credibility to the list. His mother's health had been an increasing concern to them all, and the day was approaching when she could no longer live alone. His sister Judy had written to say that although Brian might have chosen the single, celibate life, she certainly had not. Everyone at work was either married or gay. Dating agencies had proved to be full of psychopaths, evening classes were where you met depressive losers; she was going to come to the well near Rossmore and ask St Ann to get on her case.

His brother Eddie had left Kitty, his wife, and their four children to 'find himself'. Father Flynn had gone to look for Eddie—had found him nicely installed with Naomi, a girl twenty years younger than the abandoned wife—and had got little thanks for his concern.

'Just because you're not any kind of a normal man at all, it doesn't mean that the rest of us have to take a vow of celibacy,' Eddie had said, laughing into his face.

Father Flynn had felt a great weariness. He thought that he *was* in fact a normal man. Of course he had desired women, but he had made a bargain. The rules, at the moment, said if he were to be a priest then there must be no marriage, no children, no good normal family life.

He had always told himself that this was a rule that would one day change. The Vatican could not stand by and watch so many men leave the ministry over a rule that was made by Man, not by God.

There were hardly any vocations to the priesthood nowadays. Brian Flynn and James O'Connor had been the only two ordinations in the diocese eight years back. And James O'Connor had left the Church because he had been outraged by the way an older, abusive priest had been protected and allowed to escape either treatment or punishment by a cover-up.

Father Brian Flynn was hanging in there, but only just. His mother had forgotten who he was, his brother despised him and now his sister was making a trip from London to visit this pagan well.

His parish priest was a gentle elderly man, Canon Cassidy, who always praised the young curate for his hard work.

'I'll stay on here as long as I can, Brian, then you'll be considered old enough and they'll give you the parish,' Canon Cassidy often said. He meant very well and was anxious to spare Father Flynn from the indignity of having some arrogant and difficult parish priest brought in over the curate's head. But at times Father Flynn wondered would it be better to let nature take its course, to hasten Canon Cassidy to a home for the elderly religious, to get someone, almost anyone, to help with the parish duties. Admittedly attendance at church had died off a great deal since he was a young man, and people did not automatically respect the Church and Churchmen any more. Far from it. But people still had to be baptised, given first communion, have their confessions heard; they still needed to be married and buried.

Not long ago he had been in the junior school at St Ita's and had asked if any of the pupils wanted to become nuns when they grew up. Not an unreasonable question to ask little girls in a Catholic school. They had been mystified. No one seemed to know what he meant.

Then one of them got it. 'You mean like the movie *Sister Act*?'

Father Flynn felt that the world was definitely tilting. Sometimes, when he woke in the morning, the day stretched ahead of him, confused and bewildering. Still, he had to get on with things, so he would have his shower and try to pat down his red hair, which always stood in spikes around his head. Then he would make a cup of milky tea and a slice of toast and honey for Canon Cassidy.

The old man always thanked him so gratefully that Father Flynn felt well rewarded. He would open the curtains, plump up the pillows, and make some cheerful comment about how the world looked outside. Then he would go to the church and say a daily Mass for an ever-decreasing number of the faithful. He would make a call to his mother's house, heart in his mouth about how he would find her.

Most probably she would be sitting at her kitchen table looking lost and without purpose. He would explain, as he always did, that he was her son, a priest in the parish; and he would make her a breakfast of porridge and a boiled egg. Then he would walk down Castle Street with a heavy heart to Skunk Slattery's newsagent's, where he would buy two newspapers: one for the canon and one for himself. This usually involved some kind of intellectual argument with Skunk about free will or predestination or how a loving God could allow the tsunami, or a famine.

By the time he got back to the priests' house, Josef, the Latvian carer, had arrived and got Canon Cassidy up, washed and dressed him and made his bed. The canon would be sitting waiting for his newspaper. Later, Josef would take the old man for a gentle walk to St Augustine's Church, where he would say his prayers with closed eyes.

Canon Cassidy liked soup for his lunch and sometimes Josef took him to a café, but mainly he took the frail little figure back to his own house, where his wife, Anna, would produce a bowl of something homemade, and in return the canon would teach her more words and phrases in English.

He was endlessly interested in Josef and Anna's homeland, asking to see pictures of Riga and saying it was a beautiful city. Josef had three other jobs: he cleaned Skunk Slattery's newsagent's; he took the towels from Fabian's hairdressers to the Fresh as a Daisy launderette and washed them there; and three times a week he took a bus out to the Nolans' place and helped Neddy Nolan look after his father.

Anna had many jobs too: she cleaned the brasses on the doors of the bank, and on some of the office buildings that had big important-looking notices outside; she worked in the hotel kitchens at breakfast time doing the washing up; she opened the boxes of flowers that came from the market to the florists and put them in big buckets of water. Josef and Anna were astounded by the wealth and opportunities they found in Ireland. A couple could save a fortune here.

They had a five-year plan, they told Canon Cassidy. They were saving to buy a little shop outside Riga.

'Maybe you'll come to see us there?' Josef said.

'I'll look down on you and bless your work,' the canon said in a matter-of-fact tone, anticipating the best in the next world.

Sometimes Father Flynn envied him. The old man still lived in a world of certainties, a place where a priest was important and respected, a world where there was an answer for every question asked. In Canon Cassidy's time there were a hundred jobs a day for a priest to do, and not enough hours to do them in. The priest was wanted, expected and needed at all kinds of happenings in the lives of the parishioners. Nowadays you waited to be asked. Canon Cassidy would have called uninvited and unannounced to every home in the parish. Father Flynn had learned to be more reticent. In modern Ireland, even in a town like Rossmore, there were many who would not welcome the appearance of a Roman collar on the doorstep.

So, as Father Brian Flynn set out down Castle Street, he had half a dozen things planned to do. He had to meet a Polish family and arrange the baptism of their twins the following Saturday. They asked him, could the ceremony take place at St Ann's Well? Father Flynn had tried to control his annoyance. No, it would take place at the baptismal font in the Church of St Augustine.

Then he went to the jail to visit a prisoner who had asked for him. Aidan Ryan was a violent man whose wife had finally broken the silence of years and admitted that he had beaten her. He showed no sorrow or remorse, he wanted to tell a rambling tale about it all being her fault, as many years ago she had sold their baby to a passer-by.

Father Flynn took the Blessed Sacrament to an old people's home outside Rossmore, which had the ridiculous name of Ferns and Heathers. The owner had said it was nicer in a multicultural Ireland not to have everything called by a saint's name. They seemed pleased to see him and showed him their various gardening projects. Once upon a time all these homes were run by religious orders, but this woman, Poppy, seemed to be making a very good fist of it.

Father Flynn had an old battered car to take him on his travels. He rarely used it within the town of Rossmore itself, since the traffic was very bad and parking almost impossible. There had been rumours that a great bypass would be built to take the heavy trucks. Already people were in two minds about it. Some were saying that it would take the life out of the place, others claimed that it would return to Rossmore some of its old character.

Father Flynn's next call was to the Nolans' house. They were a family that he liked very much. The old man, Marty, was a lively character full of stories about the past; he talked about his late wife as if she were still here, and often told Father Flynn about the miracle cure she had once got from St Ann's Well that gave her twenty-four years more of a good life. His son was a very decent man and he and the daughter-in-law, Clare, always seemed pleased to see him. Father Flynn had assisted the canon at their marriage some years back.

Clare was a teacher in St Ita's and she told the priest that the school was full of gossip about the new road that was coming to Rossmore. In fact she was asking her class to do a project on it. The extraordinary thing was that, from what you heard or could work out, the road would be going right through here, through their own property.

'Wouldn't you get great compensation if it did go through your land?' Father Flynn said admiringly. It was pleasing to see good people being rewarded in this life.

'Oh, but, Father, we'd never let it go through *our* land,' Marty Nolan said. 'Not in a million years.'

Father Flynn was surprised. Usually small farmers prayed for a windfall like this. A small fortune earned by accident.

'You see, if it came through here it would mean they'd have to tear up Whitethorn Woods,' Neddy Nolan explained.

'And that would mean getting rid of St Ann's Well,' Clare added. She didn't have to say that this was the well that had given her late mother-in-law another quarter-century of life. That fact hung there unspoken.

Father Flynn got back into his little car with a heavy heart. Yet again this well was going to become a divisive factor in the town. There would be still more talk about it, more analysing its worth, claims and counter-claims. With a deep sigh he wished that the bulldozers had come in overnight and taken the well away. It would have solved a lot of problems.

He went to call on his sister-in-law, Kitty. He tried to visit at least once a week, just to show her that she hadn't been abandoned by the whole family. Only Eddie had left her.

Kitty was not in good form. 'I suppose you'll want something to eat,' she said ungraciously.

Father Brian Flynn looked around the untidy kitchen with its unwashed breakfast dishes, the children's clothes on chairs and a great deal of clutter. Not a home to welcome anyone. 'No, I'm great as I am,' he said, searching for a chair to sit on.

'You're better not to eat, I suppose. They feed you like a prize pig in all these houses you visit—it's no wonder you're putting on weight.'

Father Flynn wondered, had Kitty always been as sour as this? He couldn't recall. Perhaps it was just the disappearance of Eddie and his taking up with the sexy young Naomi that had changed her.

'I was in with my mother,' he said tentatively.

'Had she a word to throw to you?'

'Not many, I'm afraid, and none of them making much sense.' He sounded weary.

But he got no sympathy from Kitty. 'Well, you can't expect me to weep salt tears over her, Brian. When she did have her wits, I was never good enough for her marvellous son Eddie, so let her sit and work that one out for herself. That's my view.' Kitty's face was hard. She wore a stained cardigan and her hair was matted.

For a fleeting moment, Father Flynn felt a little sympathy for his brother. If you had the choice of all the women around, which apparently Eddie had, Naomi would have been an easier and more entertaining option. But then he reminded himself of duty and children and vows, and banished the thought.

'My mother can't manage much longer on her own, Kitty. I'm think-ing of selling up her house and moving her into a home.'

'Well, I never expected anything out of that house anyway, so go ahead and do it, as far as I'm concerned.'

'I'll talk to Eddie and Judy about it, see what they think,' he said.

'Judy? Oh, does her ladyship ever answer the phone over there in London?'

'She's coming over here to Rossmore in a couple of weeks' time,' Father Flynn said.

'Well, she needn't think she's staying here.' Kitty looked around her possessively. 'This is *my* house. It's all I have. I'm not letting Eddie's family have squatters' rights in it.'

'No, I don't think for a moment that she'd want to . . . to . . . um . . . put you out.' He hoped his voice didn't suggest that Judy would *never* stay in a place like this. 'She'll stay in one of the hotels, I imagine, as she can't stay with me and the canon.'

'Well, Lady Judy will be able to pay for that, unlike the rest of us,' Kitty sniffed.

'I was thinking about Ferns and Heathers for our mother. I was there today and the people all seem very happy.'

'That's a Protestant home, Brian. The priest can't send his own mother to a Protestant place.'

'It's not a Protestant home, Kitty.' Father Flynn was mild. 'It's for people of all religions or no religions.'

'Same thing,' Kitty snapped.

'Not at all, as it happens. I was there yesterday bringing some of the residents Holy Communion. They are opening a wing for Alzheimer's patients next week. I thought maybe if any of you would like to go and look at it . . .' He sounded as weary as he felt.

Kitty softened.

'You're not a bad person, Brian, not in yourself. It's a hard old life, what with no one having any respect for priests any more or anything.' She meant it as a kind of sympathy, he knew this.

'Some people do have just a little bit of respect,' he said with a watery smile, getting up to leave.

'Why do you stay in it?' she asked as she came to the door.

'Because I joined up, signed on, whatever, and very occasionally I do something to help.' He looked rueful.

'I'm always glad to see you anyway,' said the charmless Kitty Flynn, with the heavy implication that she was probably the only one in Rossmore who might be remotely glad to see him.

He had told Lilly Ryan that he would call and tell her how her husband Aidan was getting on in prison. She still loved him and had often regretted that she had testified against him. But it had seemed the only thing to do; the blows were so violent now that she had ended up in hospital and she had three children to care for.

He didn't feel in the mood to talk to her, but since when was all this about feeling in the right mood? He drove into her little street.

The youngest boy, Donal, was in his last year at The Brothers School. He would not be at home.

Lilly was delighted to see him. 'Aren't you a reliable man, Father?'

Even though he had no good news for Lilly it was at least consoling to be considered reliable. Her kitchen was so different to the one he had just left. There were flowers on the windowsill and gleaming copper pans. She had a plate of shortbread on the table.

'I'd better not,' he said regretfully, eyeing the plate. 'I heard in the last place that I was as fat as a pig.'

'I bet you did not.' She took no notice of him. 'Anyway, can't you walk it all off you in the woods above? Tell me, how was he today?'

And with all the diplomacy that he could muster, Father Flynn tried to construct something from his meeting with Aidan Ryan that morning into a conversation that would bring even a flicker of consolation to the wife he had once beaten and now refused to see. A wife that he seriously believed had sold their eldest baby to a passer-by.

Father Flynn had looked up newspaper accounts of the time that the Ryan baby girl had been taken from a pram outside a shop in town over twenty years ago. She had never been found. Alive or dead.

Today, he managed to keep the conversation optimistic by delivering a string of clichés: the Lord was good; one never knew what was going to happen; the importance of taking one day at a time.

'Do you believe in St Ann?' Lilly asked him, breaking the mood.

'Well, yes, I mean, of course I believe that she existed and all that . . .' he began blustering and wondering where this was leading.

'But is she there listening at the well?' Lilly persisted.

'Everything is relative, Lilly. I mean, the well is a place of great piety over centuries and that in itself carries a certain charge. And, of course, St Ann is in heaven and, like all the saints interceding for us, . . .'

'I know, Father, I don't believe in the well either,' Lilly interrupted. 'But I was up there last week and, honestly, it's astonishing. In this day and age all the people coming there, it would amaze you.'

Father Flynn tried, unsuccessfully, to assemble a look of pleased amazement on his face.

'I know, Father, I felt the same as you do, once. I go up there every year, you know, around Teresa's birthday. That was my little girl, who disappeared years before you came to the parish. Usually it's just meaningless, but somehow last week I looked at it differently. It was as if St Ann really was listening to me. I told her all the trouble that had happened as a result of it all, and how poor Aidan had never been right since. But mainly I asked her to tell me that Teresa was all right wherever she is. I could sort of bear it if I thought she was happy somewhere.'

Father Flynn looked mutely at the woman, unable to summon any helpful reaction.

'But, anyway, Father, I know people are always seeing moving statues and holy pictures that speak, and all that kind of nonsense, but there was something, Father, there really was something.'

He was still without words but nodding so that she would continue.

'There were about twenty people there, all sort of telling their own story. A woman saying so that anyone could hear her, "Oh, St Ann, will you make him not grow any colder to me, let him not turn away from me any more . . ." But none of us were *really* listening to her business. We were all thinking about ourselves. And suddenly I got this feeling that Teresa was fine, that she had a big twenty-first birthday party a couple of years ago and that she was well and happy. It was as if St Ann was telling me not to worry any more. Well, I *know* it's ridiculous, Father, but it did me a lot of good and where's the harm in that?

'I just wish that poor Aidan could have been there when she said it all, or thought it or transferred it to my mind, or whatever she did. It would have given him such peace.'

Father Flynn escaped with a lot of protestations about the Lord moving in mysterious ways, then he left the little house and drove to the edge of Whitethorn Woods.

As he strolled through the woods he was greeted by people walking their dogs, joggers in track suits getting some of the exercise he obviously needed himself, according to his sister-in-law. Women were wheeling prams and he stopped to admire the babies. The canon used to say that a playful greeting of 'Who have we here?' was a great get-out when you came across a child in a pram. It covered both sexes and a failing memory for names. The mothers would fill you in and you could take it up from there: 'grand little fellow', or 'isn't she a fine little girl?'

He met Cathal Chambers, a local bank manager, who said he had come up to the woods to clear his head. He had been flooded by people wanting to borrow money to buy land round here so that they could sell it at a huge profit once the new road was given the OK. Head Office had said he was the man on the ground so he should have a feel for what was going to happen. But how could you have a feel for something like that?

Cathal said that Myles Barry, the solicitor, was in the same predicament. Three different people had come in asking him to make an offer to the Nolans for that smallholding they had. It was pure greed. Speculation and greed, that's what it was.

Father Flynn said it was refreshing to meet a banker who thought in such terms, but Cathal said that was not at all the way they looked at things in Head Office.

Skunk Slattery was walking his two bony greyhounds and came up to sneer at Father Flynn. 'There you go, Father, coming up here to the pagan well to hope that the gods of olden times will do what today's Church can't do,' he taunted the priest, while his greyhounds quivered with what seemed like annoyance as well.

'That's me, Skunk, always one for the easy life,' Father Flynn said through gritted teeth. He nailed the smile to his face for the few minutes it took before Skunk moved the trembling dogs onwards.

Father Flynn also walked on, his face grim as he headed, silently resentful and confused, for St Ann's Well. He had been there as part of parish activities, but never before on his own.

A few wooden signs carved by pious local people over the years pointed to the well. At the end of the path leading to a cave stood a pair of old wooden gates. The rocky, cavernous grotto was damp and cold. A little stream ran down the hill behind and round the well and it was muddy where many of the faithful had reached in to take scoops of the water with an old iron ladle. Since it was a weekday morning, he thought that there wouldn't be many people there.

The whitethorn bushes outside the grotto were festooned—yes, that was the only word Father Flynn thought suitable—literally festooned with bits of cloth and notes and ribbons, and there were medals and holy cures, some of them encased in plastic or cellophane. These were petitions to the saint, requests for a wish to be granted.

Sometimes there were thanks for a favour received: *He's off the drink for three months, St Ann. I thank you and beg you to continue to give him strength . . .* or *My daughter's husband is thinking of getting the marriage annulled unless she gets pregnant soon . . .* Father Flynn stood and read them all, his face getting redder. This was the twenty-first century in a country that was fast becoming secular. *Where* did all this superstition come from? Was it a throwback to a simpler time?

But it wasn't just the old people who came here. Many of the people he had met this very morning were young and they felt the well had powers. His own sister was coming back from England to pray here for a husband; the young Polish couple wanted to have their babies baptised here; Lilly Ryan, who thought she heard the statue tell her that her long-disappeared daughter was all right, was only in her early forties.

He went inside the grotto, where people had left crutches and walking sticks and even pairs of spectacles as a symbol of hope that they would be cured and able to manage without them. There were children's bootees and little socks—meaning who knew what? The desire for a child? A wish to cure a sick baby?

In the shadows stood the statue of St Ann. It had been painted and restored over the years, making the apple cheeks even pinker, the brown cloak richer, the wisp of hair under the cream-coloured veil even blonder. If St Ann had indeed existed she would have been a small dark woman, from the land of Palestine and Israel. She would *not* have looked like an Irish advertisement for some kind of cheese spread.

And yet, kneeling there in front of the well were perfectly normal people. They got more by coming here than they ever did in St Augustine's Church in Rossmore.

It was a sobering and depressing thought.

The statue looked down glassily at him, which was a bit of a relief to Father Flynn. If he had begun to imagine that the statue was addressing him personally he would really have given up. Oddly, though, even though the saint was not speaking to him, Father Flynn felt an unexpected urge to speak to her. Instead, though, he looked around and saw the young troubled face of Myles Barry's daughter, a girl who had failed to get into law school to her father's great disappointment. *What* could she be praying for with her eyes closed and her face so concentrated?

He saw Jane, the very elegant sister of Poppy who ran the old people's home. She was dressed in what seemed to be high-fashion designer clothes and was mouthing something at the statue. A young man who ran an organic vegetable stall in the marketplace was there too, his lips moving silently.

As he turned to look back at what he considered an entirely inappropriate representation of the mother of the mother of Jesus, he wished he could ask the saint, through the statue, whether any of these prayers were ever heard and ever answered. And what did the saint do if two people were seeking conflicting favours? But this way fantasy lay, and madness. And he was not getting involved.

He stroked the damp walls of the cave—walls with messages carved on them—as he left the grotto. He made his way past the whitethorn bushes crowding the entrance. No one had cut them back to give easier access because they felt the hopes and prayers and petitions of so many people were attached to them.

Even on the old wooden gates there was a note pinned: *St Ann, hear my voice.*

All around him Father Flynn could almost hear the voices calling and begging and beseeching down the years. He heard himself make up a little prayer: *Please let me hear the voices that have come to you and know who these people are. If I am to do any good at all here let me know what they are saying and what they want us to hear and do for them* . . .

CHAPTER 2

The Sharpest Knife in the Drawer
Part 1—Neddy

I'VE HEARD PEOPLE SAY about me, 'Oh, Neddy Nolan! He isn't the sharpest knife in the drawer . . .' But, you see, I never *wanted* to be the sharpest knife in the drawer. Years ago we had one sharp knife in the kitchen and everyone was always talking about it with fear.

'Will you put the sharp knife up on a shelf before one of the children cuts the hands off themselves,' my mam would say, and, 'Make sure the sharp knife has the blade towards the wall and the handle out, we don't want someone ripping themselves apart,' my dad would say. They lived in fear of some terrible accident, and the kitchen running with blood.

I was sorry for the sharp knife, to tell you the truth. It wasn't its fault. It didn't set out to frighten people, that's just the way it was made. But I didn't tell people how I felt, they'd just say again that I was being soft.

Soft Neddy, they called me.

Because I couldn't bear to hear a mouse squealing in a mousetrap, and I had cried when the hunt came near where we lived and I saw the eyes of the fox as it fled by and I shooed it into Whitethorn Woods. Yes, I suppose other fellows thought it was soft, but the way I looked at it, the mouse hadn't asked to be born in the scullery instead of out in a field, where he might have lived peacefully to be an old happy mouse. And the red fox hadn't done anything to annoy all those hounds and horses and people dressed up in red who galloped after him.

But I'm not quick and clear at explaining things like that, so often I don't bother. And nobody expects too much from Soft Neddy.

I thought it would be different when I grew up. Adults didn't get all silly about things and sorry for them. I was sure this would happen to me too. But it seemed to take a very long time.

When I was seventeen, a crowd of us—me, my brother Kit and his pals—all went off from Rossmore in a van to a dance, oh, miles away beyond the lakes, and there was this girl. And she looked very different to the others, like they were wearing dresses with straps over their shoulders, and she was wearing a polo-necked jumper and skirt, and she had glasses and frizzy hair, and no one seemed to be asking her to dance.

So I asked her up, and then when the dance was over she shrugged and said, 'Well, at least I got one dance out of tonight.'

So I asked her again, and then again; and then I said at the end, 'You got fourteen dances out of tonight now, Nora.'

And she said, 'I suppose you want the going home.'

'The going home?' I asked.

'A court a ride,' Nora said in flat resigned tones. This would be the price she would pay for having been asked to dance fourteen times.

I explained that we were from the other side of the lakes, from near Rossmore, and we'd all be going home together in a van. I couldn't work out whether she was relieved or disappointed.

Four months later Nora and her dad turned up at our place and said that I was the father of the baby she was carrying.

I could not have been more shocked.

Nora didn't look at me, she just looked at the floor. All I could see was the top of her head. Her sad frizzy perm. I felt a great wave of pity for her when Kit and my other brothers laid into Nora and her dad.

There was no way, they said, that their Neddy had spent ten seconds alone with Nora. They had a hundred witnesses for this. Red-faced, they confronted Nora's dad and swore that I hadn't even kissed the girl goodbye when they were bundling me into the van.

'I never made love with anyone,' I said to Nora's dad. 'But if I had, and it resulted in a child being conceived, then I'd certainly live up to my responsibilities and I would be honoured to marry your daughter, but you see . . . that's not the way things happened.' And for some reason everyone believed me. Everyone. And the situation was over.

And poor Nora raised her red, tear-stained face and looked at me through her thick glasses. 'I'm sorry, Neddy,' she said.

I never knew what happened to her. Somebody once said that it was all the fault of her grandfather, but because he was the money of the family, nothing had been done about him. I didn't know if her child got born and if she brought it up. Her family lived so far away from Rossmore, there was never anyone to ask.

Not long after this, I left Rossmore and went off to London in England to work on the buildings with my eldest brother Kit, who had found a flat over a shop. There were three of them there already and I made the fourth. It wasn't very clean or tidy or anything but it was near the Tube station and in London that's all that mattered.

At first I just made the tea and carried things for people on the site, and they had such cracked, broken old mugs that on the day I got my first wages I went to a market and got a dozen brand-new ones. And they were all a bit surprised at how I washed the mugs properly and got a jug for the milk and a bowl for the sugar.

'A real gent is Neddy,' they said about me.

I'm never quite sure whether people are praising me or not. I think not. But it's not important anyway.

But there was this way they had of doing things on the site, like every sixth dustbin wasn't filled with rubbish at all—there were bags of cement and bricks and spare tools. Apparently it was some kind of system, an arrangement, but nobody told me, so naturally I pointed out to the foreman that perfectly good stuff was being thrown away. I thought everyone would be pleased. But they weren't. Far from it. And Kit was the most annoyed of all.

I was ordered to stay in the flat the next day.

'But I'll be sacked if I don't go into work,' I begged him.

'You'll be flayed alive by the other fellows if you *do* go in.' Kit was very tight-lipped. It was better not to argue with him.

'What will I do here all day?' I asked.

'Jesus, I don't know, Neddy. Clean the place up a bit. Anything. Just don't come near the site.'

The other lads didn't speak to me at all, which made me realise how serious this whole dustbin thing had been. I sat down to think. I had been planning to save lots of money in London, so that I could get my mam a holiday and my dad a good overcoat with a leather trim. And here I was being ordered not to go into work. It wasn't turning out nearly as well as I had thought it would.

'Clean the place up a bit,' Kit had said. But with what? We had no bleach for the sink or the bath. No polish for the furniture. No detergent to wash any sheets. And I only had nine English pounds left.

Then I got an idea and I went down to the shop where the Patels worked hard day and night. I picked out cleaning stuff and a tin of white paint worth ten pounds in all, then I spoke to Mr Patel.

'Suppose I was to clear up your yard for you, sweep it, stack all your boxes and crates. Would you give me those cleaning things as a wage?'

He looked at me thoughtfully, as if adding up and weighing the cost and the amount of work I would do.

'And would you clean the shop window as well?' he bargained.

'Certainly, Mr Patel,' I said with a big smile.

And Mr Patel smiled too. A slow unexpected smile.

Then I went to the launderette and asked them if I could paint their door, which looked a bit scruffy.

'How much?' Mrs Price, the woman who ran the place and, they said, had many gentlemen friends, was wise in the ways of the world.

'I want to have two loads of washing and extra drying,' I said.

It was a done deal.

When Kit and the lads came back from the site they couldn't believe the transformation. They had clean beds, the shabby linoleum on the floor was polished, the steel sink was gleaming. I had painted the cupboards in the kitchen and the bathroom.

There were more jobs I could do for the Patels next day, I told them, and they would give me a thing that restored the enamel on baths. And there was more painting to be done in the launderette and that meant we could have loads of things washed there—shirts, jeans, anything—and I'd take the bags of stuff and pick them up again, what with not being able to go to the site and everything.

And because they all seemed to have calmed down and become so admiring of the nice new clean flat, I felt I could dare to ask them about the other business. Had the foreman cooled off any?

'Well, he has apparently,' Kit said. 'He can't believe that you would shop me, your own brother! I put it to him that no one would do a thing like that, nor the lads we lived with. That he'd have to look elsewhere for the culprits. So now he is looking elsewhere.'

'And do you think he'll find them?' I asked, excited.

It was like living in a thriller.

They looked at each other, confused. There was a silence.

'Probably not,' Kit said after a time.

'And will I come back to work next week?' I wondered.

Another silence. Then Kit said, 'You know, you're doing such a great job here, Neddy, making this a real smart place for us to live, maybe *this* is what you should do.'

'But how will I earn my living, my deposit on a house, if I don't have a job?' I asked in a low voice.

Kit leaned towards me.

'I think we should regard ourselves as a company, Neddy, and you could be our manager.'

'Manager?' I said, feeling overawed.

'Yeah, suppose if you were to cook us a breakfast, even make us a packed lunch and keep this place looking shipshape. And of course handle our finances, put our money in the post office for us. Then you'd be taking a load off our backs and we'd all kick in with a wage for you. What do you think, lads? Nice clean place for us to live in, we could even bring people back here once Neddy puts his mark on it.'

And they all thought it was a great idea and Kit ran out for fish and chips for everyone to celebrate the day I became their manager.

It was a great job altogether and much less confusing really than working on the site, because I made my own arrangements and knew what I was doing. I wrote all this on my weekly letter home and I thought Dad and my mam would be pleased. But they sent me warning letters telling me to be sure that Kit and the others didn't work me too hard and make use of me.

'You're such a decent, gentle boy, Neddy,' my mam wrote, 'you must look out for yourself. You'll promise me that, won't you?'

But actually it wasn't hard at all because everyone was so nice and I could make everything fit in. After serving a good, cooked breakfast for the lads, I'd take the Patel children to their school. When I got back, I'd open up the launderette because Mrs Price, who had a lot of men friends, wasn't good in the early morning.

Then I'd go back to the Patels and help them stack shelves and take their rubbish down to a dump. Afterwards, I'd get to work on the flat, clean it all up, and every day I tried to do something new for them, like put up a new shelf or do a bit of cleaning in the television repair shop in exchange for a second-hand telly. Kit found a video that had fallen off a lorry but hadn't got broken so it was like having our own cinema in the kitchen–sitting room.

I'd pick up the Patel children from school, do the shopping for Christina, an old Greek lady who made our curtains in return.

And every year I would organise the tickets back to Ireland, when Kit and I went back home to the farm outside Rossmore to see the family.

The place changed all the time, the town was growing and spreading out. There was even a bus now that came to the corner of our road. I never heard a word about that poor girl Nora and her problems.

I always did a bit of work in the house when we came home for the two weeks. Well, Kit would be out at dances, and he didn't really notice the place needing a coat of paint here, a few shelves there. Dad was out with the cattle and he hadn't the time or the energy to do it.

I would suggest to Kit that we get them a nice television set or maybe even a washing machine, but Kit said we weren't made of money and to stop pretending we were returned millionaires.

I used to worry about our mam. She had been delicate always, but she said that St Ann had given her those extra years to watch her family grow up and she was very grateful. One summer I thought she looked very frail, but she said that I was not to worry about her as everything was fine now that Dad had sold off a field and had fewer cattle so he was at home more often. She had no worries about anything except would Dad be all right when she did go.

And then Kit and I went back for Mam's funeral.

And all our friends in London sent flowers because I had told them about Mam. People said that Kit must be very well thought of over in London to have so many friends. Actually they were *my* friends, but it didn't matter. Poor Dad looked like a bloodhound. His face was all set in lines of sadness as he waved us goodbye.

'You look after young Neddy now,' he instructed Kit at the railway station. Which was odd really as I did all the looking after.

'Wouldn't you think he'd have given us our fare,' Kit grumbled. But I had our fare so it didn't matter.

And then because I fixed up all Mr Patel's outhouses for him to give him more storage, the Patels let us have another entire room included in the same rent. One of the lads had moved out to live with a girl-friend, so now we were only three in the flat and we had a room each. The others brought girls back sometimes, and they'd have breakfast and be very nice to me.

And it was all so very busy that the time just passed by and I was thirty-seven years old, but I'd been saving for a house for nearly twenty years so I had a fortune in the building society. I mean, if you're putting away twenty pounds a week at first and then that goes up to thirty and fifty, well, it all adds up. The reason I was able to save was because I didn't drink. I bought my clothes in Oxfam and anyway I worked so many hours that I didn't have time to go out and spend money.

I managed to get Kit to come back home with me every year, which wasn't always easy. He said being in Rossmore was like spending time with the living dead. So this particular year, anyway, when we went back home our dad really wasn't well. He'd grown very in on himself and wasn't keeping the place right at all. I said to Kit that he couldn't live much more on his own like this. Kit said that he'd hate to be sent to the County Home. As if I'd send our dad there! No, I said. I thought I should come back and try to run the place for him.

'And take our inheritance for yourself?' Kit said in a horrible voice.

'Oh, no, Kit, I'd get someone to value the place, maybe Myles Barry the solicitor in town, and then give you and the others your share.'

'You'd live here with Dad?' Kit was open-mouthed.

'Someone has to,' I explained, 'and, anyway, I might get married soon if I could find a nice girl.'

'Buy this house? Give us all a share? In your dreams,' Kit laughed.

But I could buy it and I did, the very next day, and my dad was delighted but Kit wasn't pleased at all. He had no savings, he said, and yet I, who'd never done a day's work in my life, was able to put my hand in my pocket and draw out enough to buy a farmhouse. It was a strange state of affairs.

'But what do you mean I've never done a day's work in my life, wasn't I your manager?' I cried, very upset at the false accusation. 'I *was* your manager,' I insisted. Because I was. I had been a great manager, made a smashing flat for them all to live in. I would have put their money away every week like I put my own, if they'd only have given it to me. But I couldn't snatch the money from them on a Friday if they were going up west to clubs or taking girls out.

I told all this to Kit patiently and explained it to him carefully in case he hadn't understood. I watched his face and he stopped being angry.

'I'm sorry, Neddy. I spoke out of turn. Of course you were our manager and a very good one. And I don't know how we'll replace you if you come back here. But then we'll have a lump sum from this place and we'll know Dad's being looked after and that will be a great relief.'

I smiled. It was all going to be all right again.

'You know, the getting married bit might be harder, Neddy. Women are very difficult to understand. Hard to work out. You're a great fellow but you're not the sharpest knife in the drawer and you wouldn't be up to what women want these days.'

Kit was being kind so I thanked him as I always thanked people for advice, whether I understood it or not. And I set about finding a girl to marry. It took seven months. Then I met Clare. She was a schoolteacher. I met her when she came home to our parish church outside Rossmore for her father's funeral. I thought she was very nice indeed.

'She's too bright for you,' they all said.

Well, my dad didn't say that because he loved living with me, and he didn't want to say anything that would annoy me. I made him porridge every morning, and I employed a man to look after the few cows we now had. I minded the chickens and the ducks and I went for walks with Dad up to the woods to keep his legs mobile. Sometimes he went to the well to thank St Ann for all those extra years he'd had with my mam. And I brought him to the pub every day to meet his friends and have a pint and a hot lunch.

Dad used to say about me, 'Neddy's not soft as you all think . . .'

And Dad thought Clare would be fine for me. He said I should spend money on a few nice shirts and get my hair properly cut.

Clare was ambitious, she told me this from the start. She wanted to get on in teaching and maybe become a principal, and I said that would be fine because the way I saw it I could be the manager in the house and have everything done when she got home. And suppose, just suppose, we had a little baby, I could look after the baby while Clare went out to work. And to my delight she said it all sounded very good and very restful and she'd be honoured to be my wife.

Kit wasn't able to come to the wedding, because he was in jail in England over some misunderstanding. The real culprits weren't found this time either.

Dad was much stronger and better now. All it had been really was loneliness and neglect that had him feeling so low.

So we got in a great builder and fixed a price and he did a marvellous job dividing up the house so that Clare could feel that, when she came to live here when we were married, she would have her own home for herself and myself and not that she had come to live with Dad and me.

I encouraged Dad's friends to come and see him of an evening. And I bought him a big television which they all loved when sport was on.

Our wedding day in Rossmore was just great. Canon Cassidy did the actual wedding bit, but Father Flynn, the new curate, was very helpful too. And we had a reception in the hotel where people made speeches.

My dad said that, as far as he was concerned, his beloved wife, who had been cured by St Ann, was in this room with us to celebrate the day and I was the best son in the world and would be the best husband.

I made a short speech and said that I wasn't the sharpest knife in the drawer—I wanted people to know that I *knew* that's what they said—but I was the luckiest knife. I had got everything I wanted.

And Clare said that she knew it wasn't usual for the bride to speak but there was something she wanted to say. She stood up in her beautiful dress and said to everyone in the room that the drawers were full of sharp awful knives. So many that she had almost despaired of opening a drawer again. But then she had found me and her whole life had changed. And as I looked round I saw everyone was half crying as they clapped and cheered, and it was simply the happiest day of my life . . .

Part 2—Gold Star Clare

WHEN I WAS AT SCHOOL at St Ita's, Rossmore, I used to get the gold star every week.

Once, when I had flu, another girl, my friend Harriet Lynch, got it, but otherwise it was always mine. I used to take it off my school tunic every Monday morning and lay it back on the principal's desk, and then an hour later, when the gold stars in each class were being read out, I would get it back again.

It was a reward for a combination of good marks, good behaviour and school spirit. You couldn't just get one for studying hard. No, you had to be an all-rounder, a balanced person, as they saw it.

And it was easy, really, to make them see it like that. Because I liked being at school. I was in early and I left late. They had plenty of time to see me and my good school spirit in their environment. I mean, if you came from *my* home, any environment was preferable. Who wouldn't prefer to be at school than at home?

It wasn't entirely my mother's fault. Not entirely.

Women were different then, they did literally everything not to rock the boat, no matter how dangerous and unpleasant that boat was. Any marriage was better than no marriage, any humiliation was better than the ultimate humiliation of being an abandoned wife. They went up to St Ann's Well to pray that things might get better, but they didn't try to make them better themselves.

And I wasn't the only child in the school who had trouble like that at home. There was a poor girl—Nora Something—who was a bit soft in the head. In her case it was her grandfather who bothered her. And she got pregnant and said that it was some fellow she'd met at a dance, but apparently the fellow brought all his brothers and proved that he was never with her alone. And poor Nora went to the nuns, had her baby and gave it up for adoption, and her grandfather went on living in that home. And they all knew. All the time. And said nothing.

Like they knew about my Uncle Niall in our home. And said nothing. I put a lock on my bedroom door and no one asked me why. They knew too well that my father's brother fancied me. But he owned most of the farm, so what could they do?

I asked God a lot if he could stop Uncle Niall from trying to do these things. But either God was busy back in those days, or there were a lot of cases worse than mine. The really hard thing was that the family knew and did nothing. They knew why I did my homework up at the school, lest he approach me when the house was empty, and why I didn't come back until I was certain that my mother had come back from the creamery where she worked, and that my father was in from the fields.

I was both proud and ashamed when I was a schoolgirl. Proud that I was able to stay out of my uncle's messy clutches. Ashamed because I came from a family that wouldn't look after me but left me to fight my own battles against things I didn't understand.

And I suppose it did make me grow up quickly. When I passed my exams I announced firmly that I was going to university miles away.

Where would they get the money to pay for this? my father wondered.

Why couldn't I stay at home and do a secretarial course and mind my sister? my mother said, as well she might.

My sister Geraldine *did* need to be minded and I would warn her well before I left. Maybe I'd go to the bad in a big city? Uncle Niall said, even though he knew and I knew and my parents knew.

But I was really quite grown up for my years and much tougher than they all thought. I'd survive, I told them. I'd get a job to pay for a flat and my fees. I was a gold star girl. I could turn my hand to anything.

And I did. I went to Dublin two weeks before term started and I fixed myself up in a flat with three other girls, and got a job in an early-morning breakfast place. It was terrific because I had nearly a day's work done and a huge breakfast eaten by the time I went to my 10 a.m. lectures, and then I worked a shift in a pub from six to ten every night.

And because of Uncle Niall, I wasn't all that keen on fellows like my flatmates were, so I could put my mind to my studies as well. And at the end of the first year I was in the top five of the whole group.

I never told anyone any of this when I went back home to Rossmore. Except for my sister Geraldine, because I wanted her to know we could do anything, *anything*, if we wanted to.

Geraldine told me that she was well able to deal with Uncle Niall now by shouting aloud, 'Oh, *there* you are, Uncle Niall, what can I do for you?' at the top of her voice, alerting the whole house, and he would slink away. And she had announced one day that she was putting a giant padlock on her door.

And then, in the middle of my second year at university, a lot of things went wrong. My mother got cancer and they said they couldn't operate. My father coped with it all by drinking himself senseless every night. Since there was no one to protect her, my sister went to stay with my friend Harriet Lynch's younger sister in order to study and to get away from Uncle Niall.

Back in Dublin they put up the rent on our flat. And just then I met Keno, who ran a nightclub, and he asked me to dance there. I said, no, I couldn't dance, and wouldn't flaunting yourself at people and then not letting them touch you be dangerous? But Keno said there was nothing to it and he had bouncers who looked after that sort of thing.

And then my mother died.

I tried to mourn her properly, but I could never forget that she had turned aside and left Geraldine and me to our fate. Shortly after the funeral, Uncle Niall sold the farm over my father's head and Geraldine hadn't done any work at school because she was so upset about everything. If I did do the dancing it meant I could have my own flat in Dublin, finish my university degree, put Geraldine into one of those sixth-form colleges and keep an eye on her. So I said OK to Keno and wore this ludicrous thong and danced round a pole every night. The music would sometimes do your head in, but the tips were enormous, and the bouncers were great and there was always a taxi home at 3 a.m.

I told Geraldine that it was a gambling club, and I was a croupier taking in the money, and that the law said she was too young to come in, and that was fine. And then one night, wouldn't you know, Harriet Lynch's father and some friends were there and recognised me.

I went to their table to have a drink and said very sweetly that everyone earned their living and took their pleasures in an individual way and I didn't see any need to inform Harriet Lynch's mother or daughters back in Rossmore of the nature of these business trips to Dublin.

They got the message and Keno told me afterwards that I was the brightest girl he'd ever had in his stable. I didn't like the word 'stable'. I felt we were all like performing prancing horses or something. But I did like Keno. A lot. He was very respectful to us all and he was doing all this because he had a very poor family who needed support back in Morocco. He would really like to have been a poet but there was no money in poetry. His sisters and brothers wouldn't have had an education if he were busy writing verses so he had this club instead.

I understood so well.

Sometimes we'd have a coffee, Keno and myself—my friends from college thought he was gorgeous. He always talked about poetry so they thought he was some kind of student. He never told any actual lies, I noticed, but he never told the whole truth either. I didn't want him to tell my friends from the BA honours group that he knew me from my pole-dancing nearly naked five nights a week in his club.

I didn't fancy Keno and he didn't fancy me, but we often talked about love and marriage and what it might be like. He said he had a child, a daughter in Marrakesh. But she was being brought up by her grandmother. Her mother was an exotic dancer in a club there.

'You're a great girl, Clare,' he said to me often. 'A real star.'

'I was a gold star at school,' I explained, and he thought that was very endearing.

'Little Gold Star Clare! Give up this nonsense of becoming a teacher and manage my club for me instead,' he begged. But I told him that when I did become a teacher I'd give up the club.

He came to my graduation and I smiled as I took my parchment in my hand. If the others knew that the girl with the first-class honours was a pole-dancer . . . A year later I was a fully-fledged teacher and I got into exactly the kind of school I wanted to. I took Keno out to lunch to say goodbye. He didn't believe it when I told him how little I was going to be earning, but for me it was plenty.

Geraldine had won a scholarship, I had my savings and hardly any outgoings. I thanked Keno for having made it possible. 'Over the years, Keno, if there's anything I can do to help you I will,' I promised.

I didn't hear from him for three years, and by the time he got in touch again a lot had changed.

After years of drinking my father eventually died and at the funeral I met a nice old man in a wheelchair called Marty Nolan, who had known my father a long time ago. His son, who was pushing the chair, was a really good-natured fellow called Neddy. Neddy had worked in England on the buildings, he said, well, more as manager for his brother and their friends, and now he had come home and looked after his father. He was an oddly restful person and I liked talking to him.

Harriet Lynch said to me, I should see his elder brother Kit, a real hunk, but apparently he was banged up in jail for something. Neddy was the one who had the decent streak in that family.

Not the brightest mind, a bit slow, a minute late, Harriet said. She would always be sorry she had volunteered this information to me. Very sorry.

I saw Neddy again because I came back to Rossmore over and over to get what I considered were Geraldine's and my just portions of my father's estate—if you could use a word like 'estate' to describe what was owing to a drunk who had died in the County Home. Over the years I had tried to contribute to my father's keep from my earnings in Keno's club, but the doctor told me that my father didn't know where he was and would only spend any money that came his way on cider.

I faced my Uncle Niall after the funeral, when he was busy accepting sympathy about his unfortunate poor brother. I asked for his attention for a moment.

'What can I do for you on this sad day, Clare?' he said, witheringly.

'Just a third of what you got for the family farm,' I said to him pleasantly. 'I have written down the bank account number.'

'And what makes you think I am going to give you one single euro?' he asked.

'Let me see, I think you won't want Geraldine and myself to tell the local doctor, the priest, half of Rossmore and, even more important, a top lawyer, the reason why she and I had to leave home,' I said.

He looked at me, unbelieving, but I met his stare. 'It will be no problem. There's a young curate, Father Flynn, here who would give Canon Cassidy the courage to stand up to you. Mr Barry would get us a hotshot barrister from Dublin, the doctor will confirm that I asked his help to get Geraldine away from your clutches. The world has changed, you know, Niall. The days are gone when the uncle with the money can get away with anything he likes.'

He spluttered at me. I think my calling him Niall was the clincher.

'If you think for one moment—' he began.

I interrupted him. 'One week from now, and a decent gravestone for my father,' I said. It was blackmail, of course, but I didn't see it as that.

I started to go out with Neddy. He came to Dublin once a week to see me, and I went down to see him once a week. We hadn't slept together because Neddy wasn't like that, but he was very restful indeed.

And then I heard from Keno. They really needed me back at the club. He needed someone reliable there, dancing, yes, and keeping an eye on the girls for him. He wouldn't ask if he wasn't desperate.

I explained how impossible it was for me, or I tried to explain. I even told Keno about Neddy and the kind of man he was.

I shouldn't really have told Keno about Neddy. When he put the pictures down on the table, he mentioned Neddy. I hadn't realised that pictures had been taken, but the girl was definitely me, and the positions were very suggestive indeed. It was sickening, just looking at them. It didn't bear thinking what the board of the school or dear innocent Neddy would make of them.

'This is blackmail,' I said.

'I don't see it as that,' Keno said, shrugging.

'Give me a week,' I said. 'You owe me that.'

'Right.' Keno was always agreeable. 'But you owe me too. For your start in life.'

During the week, wouldn't you know, Neddy asked me to marry him.
'I can't,' I said. 'Too much baggage.'
'I don't care about the past,' Neddy said.
'It's not just the past. It's the future,' I said.
And I told him. Everything. Every single thing—like my awful Uncle Niall, and Geraldine, and how tiring the dancing had been. I had left the envelope of pictures on the table and he just threw it into the fire without opening it.
'I'm sure you are very beautiful in the pictures,' he said, 'and why shouldn't people pay to look at you?'
'He'll have more,' I said in a despairing kind of voice.
'Yes, of course he will, but it won't matter.'
'Ah, come on, Neddy, these are nice respectable girls I teach—do you think anyone would let me near them if they saw those pictures?'
'Well, I was hoping that if you married me you'd come back to Rossmore and teach near by.'
'But he could still show them here,' I said.
Neddy looked at me with his honest blue eyes. 'Would you have said yes and married me if it weren't for this little problem?' he asked.
'It's a *big* problem, Neddy,' I said wearily.
'Would you, though, Clare?'
'Well, yes, I would, Neddy. I would have been honoured to marry you.'
'Right, then. We'll sort it out,' he said.
He came with me to Keno's that night. We walked right through the dancers and the punters to the office at the back. To say Keno was surprised is putting it mildly.
I introduced them formally and then Neddy spoke. He told Keno that he sympathised with his situation, and thought it must be hard running a business with all the staff problems and everything, but it wasn't fair to take away my dream. I had *always* wanted to be a teacher ever since I was a schoolgirl.
'Clare was a gold star at school,' Keno said, more to make conversation, I think, than anything else.
'I'm not at all surprised,' Neddy said beaming at me proudly. 'So, you see, we can't make Clare do anything else except concentrate on her teaching. Neither of us can.'
Keno pulled a big brown envelope from his desk drawer.
'The pictures?' he said to Neddy.
'They're very beautiful. Clare showed them to me earlier tonight.'
'She did?' Keno was amazed.
'Of course. If we are to be married we must have no secrets. I have

told Clare all about my brother Kit who has been and still is in prison. You can't keep quiet about things that are part of you. And Clare is very, very grateful for the start you gave her. So that's why we are here. To ask was there any *other* way we could help you?'

'Like what way, in God's name?' Keno was totally bewildered.

'Well, I have a great friend who does wrought iron. He could do you really nice windows outside, which would look good and also be strong against unwelcome visitors. And, let me see, if the dancing girls were tired and wanted somewhere to stay, it's very peaceful by the woods where we live . . . they could come to stay with us for a restful holiday. There's lots to see in Rossmore. There's even a wonderful well in the woods. People can make a wish there.'

I begged God not to let Keno mock him, or tell me I was marrying a simpleton. I spoke to God strongly in my mind. 'I never bothered you about things, did I, God? I didn't go up to that well rabbiting on to your grandmother, St Ann, now did I? No, I sorted out my own problems and looked after my little sister. I didn't go round doing much sin, unless the dancing is a sin? But now I want to escape from all that and marry this good man. That's the kind of thing you're meant to be *for*, isn't it, God?'

And God listened. This time.

Keno turned on the shredder and put the negatives into it.

'There aren't any more pictures,' he said. 'Get your wrought-iron man to give me a ring, Neddy. And now get the hell home, the two of you, to plan your wedding. I have an ailing business to run here.'

And we walked out of the club together hand in hand and down the cobbled street.

CHAPTER 3

The Plan
Part 1—Becca

MOTHER WAS ALWAYS SAYING to me, 'Becca, you could do anything in this world if you had a proper plan.' She would say this as we walked down Castle Street doing the shopping together, or waited for the sheets and towels to dry at the Fresh as a Daisy Launderette.

Mother did have lots of plans as life went on. Like when I was twenty-one and Father wouldn't hear of paying for a big party, Mother

developed a plan. She went to the new hotel in Rossmore and showed them our guest list with lots of important people on it. She insisted to the manager that they should give her half-price because of all the introductions she was giving them over her daughter Becca's party. And she eked this bit of money out of Father and that bit. And there you were. A stunning twenty-first! Just because she had a plan.

Dear Mother was not entirely right about Father, of course. But then, you'd need to have been some kind of mystic to have known what he was going to do. Father went off with Iris, this perfectly awful, common woman, when I was twenty-five and Mother was fast approaching fifty. The awful Iris wasn't even young. She wore a cardigan and walked through the Whitethorn Woods with a mongrel dog. Mother said it wouldn't have been so bad if she had been a silly young girl with a huge bosom. But no, she was the same age as both of them. Humiliating.

I foolishly suggested to Mother that she might go to St Ann's Well, a lot of people got their wishes answered there. She was horrified at the very thought of it. A place of pagan superstition where maids and women from the cottages went? I wasn't even to mention it again.

Mother said that if she had the energy, she would kill Iris.

I had begged her not to. 'Please, Mother, don't kill Iris. You'll get caught and arrested, and go to jail.'

'Not if I did it properly,' Mother said.

'But you wouldn't do it properly, Mother, and suppose for a moment that you did. Think how terrible that would be.'

Grudgingly, Mother agreed. 'If I were younger and could make a proper plan, then I could easily have killed Iris,' she said calmly. 'But, Becca darling, I should have started much earlier and it would all have been fine. I think you are right and that I'd be wiser to leave it now.'

Father didn't really stay in touch. He wrote from time to time to say that Mother was bleeding him dry. Mother said that he and that Iris had taken every penny she was entitled to—all she had left was the falling-down house in Rossmore. She sighed and sighed, and said that to hire yet another lawyer on top of Myles Barry was like throwing good money after bad.

'When you grow older, Becca darling, I beg you to have a plan. Do nothing without a plan, and do it sooner rather than later.'

And it seemed a very good idea, because everything Mother did later, having waited around, had gone belly up, while all the things that had been done sooner had been fine. She must have been right about striking when the iron was hot.

So I tried to have a plan about most things. I worked in Rossmore's

new fashion boutique that catered for rich clients, and I planned to get to know these people socially. Sometimes it worked, sometimes it didn't. I also made a friend of Kevin, the van driver, who drove a taxi-cab on the side, and he often gave me lifts to places.

Kevin was nice. He had a terrible cough and he was a frightful hypochondriac, but he was very fond of me and said that I could always ask him to come out and collect me on a wet night and he would. I never abused it but I did ask him sometimes.

Mother was in bad form a lot, but to be honest I didn't get too involved with her and her problems because there was so much going on in my own life. I'd just met Franklin and everything had changed.

You know the way people find it impossible to describe some huge event in their life, like seeing the Queen of England, or the Pope, or the President of the United States, or something earthshaking? You can remember all kinds of unimportant details but not the thing itself. It was just like that when I met Franklin.

I remember the dress I was wearing: a red silk dress with a halter neck that I had got at a thrift shop. I remember the perfume I wore: it was Obsession by Calvin Klein. I couldn't afford it myself, but amazingly a customer had left it behind her in the boutique.

I can't remember why I went to that particular party. It was to launch a new restaurant in Rossmore. The town was so big now and so different to the way it was when Mother was young. New restaurants, hotels, art galleries opening all the time. I hadn't been invited or anything but I knew that if you turned up at one of these parties looking well dressed they always let you in. So two or three times a month I would show up at a party and mingle. Well, you never knew who you might meet.

Up to now I had only met a lot of frogs and was beginning to despair of ever meeting a prince at any of these dos, and then that night I met Franklin. It was at 7.43 p.m. on the pink neon-lit clock. I had been thinking I might go home at eight. I wouldn't call Kevin tonight, there was a bus stop outside the door . . . and just then Franklin said hello.

He was startlingly good-looking, with blond tousled hair, blue eyes and perfect teeth. And so nice and easy. It began almost immediately between us. We discovered we had literally everything in common. We both loved Greece and Italy, Thai food and skiing, and re-runs of old movies on television. We liked big dogs, tap-dancing, and long brunch on a Sunday.

Mother had been going through a depressive stage at the time and she was very doubtful about my new romance. 'Everyone likes those things, Becca, you silly girl. Do stop getting your hopes up, darling.

He's only stating the obvious. Imagine anyone *not* liking Italy, or *Sergeant Bilko*, or *Dad's Army*, or skiing! Be sensible, darling. Please!'

Then she met Franklin and like everyone else she was bowled over. He was charming to her and she loved everything that he said.

'I see where Becca gets her wonderful cheekbones.' 'You must be fearfully intelligent to play bridge so well.' 'You *must* let me call you Gabrielle, you're much too young for me to call you "Mrs King".'

Now if I had been cynical, I could have said that it was just a line, he knew what to say to older ladies. But I'm not cynical—I'm sunny and optimistic and I said nothing. Just smiled.

And because Franklin had nowhere proper to stay, he came to stay with us. For a while he stayed in the guest room, but we soon needed that room for all his gear so he moved into mine.

Franklin didn't have a job, not as such, but he and another man called Wilfred, a friend of his, were developing an idea, a concept. They were going into business together. It had to do with mobile phones and was very hard to explain and, indeed, to understand. But Franklin and Wilfred were like two bright schoolboys with a project. Their enthusiasm carried them along.

Mother said many times that I should have a plan to keep him because treasures like Franklin didn't come along every day. I should be more domestic for one thing, and cook for him. Also I should dress up more, borrow clothes from the boutique, get them dry-cleaned and give them back. Show him what an asset I was and could be in life.

We were all so happy together. Mother taught the three of us, Franklin and Wilfred and me, how to play bridge, and then I would make us supper. It was a wonderful four months.

Franklin and I had a terrific understanding. We were both twenty-nine years old so, naturally, we both had a bit of a past. But neither of us had ever loved anyone else one-tenth as much as we loved each other. And if for any reason our love began to diminish or we met someone else, there would be no deceit, no lies. We would tell each other straight out. We pealed with laughter at the very idea!

Then one evening Franklin told me that he had met this girl called Janice at a bridge party, and that they had feelings for each other, so true to our promise and our understanding he was telling me immediately. He had a look on his face as if he should somehow be *praised* for telling me about this damn Janice. As if his honesty and trustworthiness had somehow been proved. I gritted my teeth and forced a smile.

'Maybe you only think you have feelings for her,' I said. 'Possibly, when you get to know her, you'll find it quite different.'

I admired myself for staying so calm.

But then he explained that he did know. He was very sure.

'Shouldn't you wait till you've slept with her to be so sure?' I was proud of how I was handling this.

'Oh, I have,' he said.

'That wasn't exactly part of our understanding, having sex before telling each other, was it?' I hoped my voice didn't sound quite as steely outside as it did from within.

'But you weren't there, so I couldn't ask you,' he said, as if it was the most reasonable thing in the world.

'Wasn't where exactly?' I asked.

'In the Rossmore Hotel. Wilfred and I were there meeting some investors and there happened to be a bridge session on, so we joined it and that's where I met Janice.'

I realised that my own mother had delivered the weapon of destruction herself. Why couldn't she have left Franklin ignorant of how to play bridge? If she had, then he would never have met this Janice.

I knew that I must have a plan, and that, until I did, I must remain calm. 'Well, if that's the way it is, that's it, Franklin,' I said with a huge smile. 'I hope that you and Janice will be very happy together.'

'You are marvellous!' he cried. 'You know, I told Janice that you and I had this understanding but she said you'd never honour it. But I knew you would, and I was right.' He stood there, beaming at me.

Was he insane? Could he not see what had happened to me—that the light had left my life? Did he not hear the sound that went click in my head and the rush like a great wind that seemed to be blowing all around me? Maybe it was shock. Or a breakdown. Or the beginning of madness. It was as if the world was advancing to and receding from me.

But I couldn't faint, I must not show any signs of weakness. This was a turning point in my life. He must have no idea how my world was crashing down around me. I had to work out a plan to get him back.

I told Franklin I had to rush, there was a late-night crisis at the boutique. I wished him every happiness with this Janice and I fled. I hadn't smoked for five years but I bought a packet of cigarettes. Then I let myself into the boutique and sat down at a table and cried and cried.

Kevin was there. Always a heavy smoker, he joined me at the table and patted my hand. Before I could tell him what was wrong he started to tell me his troubles. 'I'm not in great form myself, Becca,' he said and I noticed that his face was haggard and gaunt.

'What's wrong, Kevin?' I asked politely, even though I couldn't give a damn. Something wrong with the van probably, not much work in the cab business, only two numbers off winning the Lotto—who cared?

'I've got really bad cancer, Becca. No point in operating, they say. I've got two months at the most.'

'Oh, Kevin, I'm so very sorry,' I said and I was. For thirty whole seconds I forgot Franklin and Janice and the plan. 'They're very good in hospitals nowadays,' I reassured him.

'I'm not going to wait, Becca, I couldn't wake up every day wondering, is it going to happen today?'

'So what will you do?'

'I'll drive the van straight into a wall. Splat,' he said. 'No waiting, no worrying, no hanging about waiting for it to happen.'

And that's where I got my plan.

Suddenly my brain was working overtime—I felt I could cope with a hundred things at the same time. It was a daring, mad plan. But it had a great deal going for it. It would solve everything in a stroke.

If he was going to kill himself, then he could take Janice with him. If he was going to die anyway, and he was afraid of waiting, well, then, why couldn't they both leave this life together? I must be very, very clever. He must never have an inkling of what I was thinking.

'I think you're quite right, Kevin. That's just what I'd do if it were me. Well, it will be me one day, of course . . . And I'll do just that. Leave at my own time, not someone else's.'

He was completely surprised. He had expected me to beg him not to.

'But do you know what I think, Kevin? I think you should do it in a taxicab rather than your own van. Cabs are always crashing. It would look more natural when people investigate it, better for your life insurance policy. For your mother or whatever.'

'I see,' he said slowly. 'So they wouldn't pay up if they thought it was suicide?'

'Apparently not.'

'You're kind to be so interested, Becca, but what has *you* so upset?'

'Oh, nothing, compared to your problems, nothing at all, Kevin, a silly quarrel with my mother. It will blow over.'

'But everything's all right with you and Franklin?' he asked.

I think Kevin was always a little bit in love with me. Not, of course, that I showed any sign of noticing that. But he must never know what Franklin had done.

I reassured him. 'Oh, Franklin and I are fine, not a cloud on the horizon,' I said. Just thinking that made me stop crying. Kevin gave me a tissue and I wiped my eyes. It was all going to be all right.

I could afford to spend time being kind to Kevin. 'Come on, Kevin,

I'll take you out for a Chinese supper,' I said, and he looked so pathetically grateful.

'Won't Franklin mind?' he asked.

'Franklin lets me do what I want to do,' I said.

'If you were mine, I'd be just the same,' Kevin said.

And we went and had a long and terribly depressing Chinese meal,
where he told me about his diagnosis and his wish to end it all. I
nodded sympathetically and told him he was absolutely right, but I
didn't listen to one word of what he said. I just sat there thinking about
my plan. Kevin would do it for me. Kevin would see it through.

I would pretend to be enthusiastic about this awful Janice, I would
become her friend. Then I would give her Kevin's number as a reliable
taxi driver. Of course, Kevin wouldn't want to take a perfectly innocent
passenger with him to kill her, so to speak. So I'd have to tell him some
story that Janice was also suffering from a terrible incurable disease and
she had asked me to arrange a swift exit from the world. It was going to
be a challenging role for me. It was if I had to write it and act it. But it
had to be done. It was the perfect plan. No one would ever suspect me
because I was going to be Ms Nice Guy, full of human kindness.

'I don't know what I'd do without you, Becca,' Kevin said to me a
dozen times during the meal.

'And I don't know what I'd have done without you, Kevin,' I said to
him truthfully.

Wilfred, who was Franklin's friend and business partner, was
astounded by me.

'You're really full of surprises,' he said. 'I thought we'd have the full
"hell hath no fury" bit, but I was totally wrong.'

I laughed a tinkling laugh. 'Franklin and I always had an understanding, Wilfred.' And, as I saw him looking at me in awe, I gave him a
smile that I hoped would break his heart as well as Franklin's.

My mother was astonished when I told her that there was no point
whatsoever in trying to hold on to Franklin if he didn't want to be held.
She shook her head in wonder and said that I had always been even
more unbalanced than she was, so it was amazing to see me so rational.

I told Franklin that he must be in no hurry to move out. But that, of
course, he would sleep in the guest room now that things were different. I went out a lot myself. Often with Kevin. It seemed only fair. But
of course the real part of the plan was getting to know Janice.

The first blow was that she was only nineteen.

The second was that she wasn't interested in clothes, so I couldn't
offer her cheap things from the boutique. She didn't care about cookery

either, so I couldn't give her recipes. *How* was I to get to know her?

As so often in life, the solution was to be found in the game of bridge. I asked the loathsome Janice to do me a favour and be my bridge partner at a ladies' social evening for charity. Since I'd been so nice to her, and so desperately decent about handing her Franklin without any grumbling, there was really nothing she could do but accept.

We got on fine that first night, and several times she told me that she admired me and my generation for our attitude to love. Some day she hoped she would be as mature as that.

I resisted choking her to death at the bridge table with my own hands. After all, I had a much better plan.

We actually won the competition and agreed to play together again the next week at another charity function at the Rossmore Hotel. In many ways she was a fairly pleasant companion. A university student with far too much money and time for her own good, but she had nice manners and, I have to say, she was a good bridge player. Very young and silly of course, like a niece or a neighbour's child.

And, naturally, I had a few pangs, a little remorse, a concern, I suppose you'd call it, about sending a nineteen-year-old girl to her death. I mean, I am human. But then she had come between me and my one true love, and there was no way he could be talked out of her or she of him. So it was this or nothing.

On and on we played, Janice and I. We had been out together several times before I chose the night.

Franklin was talking about moving out of our home but I begged him to stay for a few more days. 'You can always go and spend nights with Janice,' I purred at him. 'But don't move all your gear yet.'

The plan would only work if he was still living with us when she died.

Kevin was very troublesome these days. He was beginning to have second thoughts. He had become most concerned about taking another passenger with him. He thought he should discuss it with her first, ask her what preferences she had. Maybe she would like to be sedated before the crash?

As Kevin and I went through the details over and over again, the same thing was always his sticking point: suppose she changed her mind at the last moment? He wouldn't be able to stop. It would be too late.

I said that I thought that she would definitely not change her mind. I explained that Janice had this terrible illness that was already beginning to take its toll, the pain would become unbearable. And in addition to the illness she was developing a personality disorder. She had asked me to arrange everything so that she wouldn't have to think about it or discuss it. Well, he only wanted to do what was best, Kevin said. He really was such a kind and considerate man.

Sometimes I allowed myself to think how much easier life would have been to love someone like him. But I didn't waste time going down that road. Since the incident when Franklin had told me about Janice I had become very focused.

During this time, Mother, Franklin, Wilfred, people at work and even poor Kevin himself told me I was not looking myself. Wild, somehow. Unhinged, Mother said. But I put on more make-up and smiled a nightmarish grin.

The night of the accident came at last. I had met Kevin earlier that day and reassured him that he was doing the right thing for himself, and that we were both doing the right thing about Janice. He turned up, just as we had planned, outside the door of the hotel where the charity bridge function was taking place.

'Oh, here's a taxi for you, Janice!' I said, sounding pleased.

'You are marvellous, Becca, everyone else is rushing about looking for them and you find one immediately.' She looked admiring.

Kevin got out of the driver's seat and came to open the passenger door. He and I gripped each other's hands.

Janice was going back to her flat where Franklin would join her later. He and Wilfred were out at yet another business meeting. I said that I must run now as my bus was just coming and we were going in different directions.

'Bye, lovely Becca,' Kevin said.

'See what I mean, Becca, everyone's mad about you,' Janice said enviously as she waved me goodbye.

I went home and talked to my mother for a long time and then went to bed. Franklin telephoned to find out what time we had all left the bridge function because Janice wasn't back at her flat. I said lots of people had seen her getting into a cab hours ago, so I couldn't understand it. In the morning he telephoned again and said she hadn't come home all night. I was sympathetic but said I had no idea what could have happened.

In the afternoon he rang to say that poor lovely little Janice had been killed and the taxi driver too. They had ploughed into a wall. Everyone was shocked. Franklin didn't move out because he was so shattered, and soon he began to love me again. The whole thing should have been perfect, it *would* have been perfect, if it hadn't been for Kevin.

I was right. He had loved me. And he had insured his life in my favour: I was going to get a small fortune. This, of course, destroyed my whole plan. No one would have connected the accident with me if it hadn't been for this policy. That, and the letter Kevin had left, thanking me for all I had done for him.

Now everyone is investigating the deaths. Insurance people, police, everyone. And the whole of Rossmore is talking about me. They say that Janice's mother and sisters went up to that ridiculous well in the woods and a kind of procession went after them. As if that was going to bring her back!

Of course I may not get charged with anything. But Franklin is nervous of me. He hasn't said this, but he's started to move his things out.

It was such a perfect plan—if only Kevin hadn't tried to be generous. Tried to give me something as he ended his life. Instead of which he managed to take my whole life away.

Part 2—Gabrielle

ALL MY FRIENDS at the bridge club have been very kind. Very kind indeed. They glare at each other if someone accidentally mentions prison, or murder, or convicts. They think I am very brave to go to visit Becca in jail every week and to hold my head up everywhere I go in Rossmore. It's not all that hard to have confidence, actually. It depends on how you look. I always knew that really, but I never had the money to look well-dressed.

My ex-husband, Eamon, left me penniless when he went off with that appalling, vulgar woman, Iris. The upkeep of the house was enormous, so I was always stuck for cash when it came to clothes. Which, of course, was why I was so grateful to the tabloids.

Now I know we have to pretend to think they are terrible and that we only let them into the house for the maid to read, sort of thing, but they were hugely interested in what poor Becca had done and in fact I was secretly delighted with them. One of them bought the story of Becca's childhood and the 'What Made Her the Woman She Became' angle. Another bought stuff about her life in a chic fashion boutique. I bet I doubled the owner's business.

Then there was a piece about how Becca had changed after her father had left home. I enjoyed helping to write that. Nowhere did they say that I was collaborating but I gave them all the information and all the pictures. It made a magnificent set of articles.

Of course I didn't like titles like 'In the Mind of the Murderess', but it did sell papers. Every time I visited, Becca would ask how had the reporters found out all these details. I reassured her that I had told them nothing new, they knew it all already. What they didn't know, they made up. Like that business about poor Becca going to the well in Whitethorn Woods to pray to St Ann that Franklin would love her.

'I never did, Mother, you know that,' she had wept at me.

I soothed her and patted her down. Of course everyone knew it was nonsense, I told her.

Actually, I had been very well paid for that particular story. It gave the newspapers freedom to take pictures of the terrible shrine. And did that sell papers! Obviously Becca knew nothing of this and I reassured her and reminded her that I *had* managed to keep Franklin out of the story and she was naturally very grateful. When she comes out of jail she will marry him, of course. Meanwhile, she doesn't want to be the cause of any unpleasant media attention.

She had begged him to come and visit her until I told her that the reporters were outside the jail all the time and they would spot him and the careful privacy we had all been keeping would be blown. She saw the sense in that.

They're quite nice in the jail, really. Basically out for the prisoners' good—which must be hard when you think of the kind of people they have to deal with. Of course, Becca is different, and they see that, naturally. She's a lady for one thing and she hasn't the *mind* of a criminal for another. She's so far above everyone in the place and yet gets on with them all, which is a true sign of good breeding.

She's learning embroidery at recreation time, from one of the warders, a nice woman called Kate. Becca says it's very restful, therapeutic even. She gave me a perfectly horrid little cushion cover she had made and I told her it has pride of place in the sitting room. Poor dear Becca! She thinks she'll be home any day to see it. She has risen above her whole terrible situation by refusing to acknowledge it. It's a way of coping and for Becca it's working very well.

She has started a huge coverlet for her bed with the words 'Franklin' and 'Rebecca' intertwined.

I have to remember not to wear my best finery going to see her because Becca can spot a designer outfit at half a mile. She would know I couldn't ordinarily afford Prada or Joseph jackets. I have what I call my prison visiting outfit, so that she won't make the connection between the publishing of the tabloid stories and my new wardrobe.

Becca herself looks a lot better as the weeks and months go by. She walks straighter, she doesn't fuss about her hair and sort of twiddle with it like she used to. It's just straight now and classy looking. One of the warders, Gwen, who is a friend of Kate (the nice one teaching her embroidery), trained as a hairdresser and gives them all a regular trim. She still works part-time in a beauty parlour apparently.

Becca seems less anxious these days, much calmer. She's very interested in shading and matching threads, and whether she'll be chosen for a netball team. Becca! Interested in sports and embroidery! Who would have thought it? Well, who would have thought any of it really?

Sometimes the tabloid people ask me, do I have any sympathy for poor Janice who went unsuspecting to her death because of Becca? I remind them that I cannot be quoted; my opinions and my natural, deep sorrow cannot be entered into. And then before they start to turn against me I feed them another picture of Becca or a titbit about the parties she used to go to—the launches and receptions—and they run another story describing her as a good-time party girl.

Imagine!

You know the way they talk about people becoming institutionalised? Well, I think it's absolutely true. Becca has few interests now outside the terrible place where she is. The only thing that unites her to the world outside is her future with Franklin.

It's marvellous, of course, that she is so positive about everything, but then she does seem to have lost touch with reality since she doesn't understand how long she is going to be in there. Nor does she ever refer to the enormity of what she has done. She sort of waves it away.

And yet it was a terrible thing. Killing Franklin's fiancée—or getting her killed, which was just as bad. 'A deliberate and cold-blooded killing,' as the judge said when he sentenced her after a unanimous verdict from the jury. Becca's never once spoken of Janice or, indeed, that sad chap, Kevin, who did the driving, or anything about that night.

Poor lamb, her life hasn't turned out at all as she had hoped. So when at first she talked about Franklin and the future I did nothing to discourage her. Once she realised that he couldn't come to see her, she stopped asking about him and what he was doing.

This was a great relief. It had been getting more and more difficult to field her questions about him. I tried to tell her about the bridge club but Becca had lost all interest—she hardly reacted when I told her about the grand slam that I had got. I think even now she barely takes on board that Wilfred and Franklin and I still play regularly together, getting a fourth where we can find one. But then I suppose bridge might be a bit of a sore subject, what with Janice's having met Franklin playing bridge, and her being his bridge partner and everything. So maybe better not mention bridge.

Trouble is that there are so many things it's better not to mention. I just talk on about whether this thread is cerise or fuchsia, and how hard it is for that warder, Kate, to support two children on her wages. I listen to stories about women who are prostitutes, or drug dealers, or who have murdered their husbands in self-defence. It's such an unreal sort of an existence.

That bloody Eamon asked would Becca like him to visit? I said certainly not. He had been no help to his daughter before all this business and he would only upset her further now.

Kate draws me aside from time to time when I visit and tells me that Becca is adapting very well and is popular with the other prisoners. As if I would somehow be pleased that these terrible women liked my Becca or not! But Kate means well. She can't help it if she had no advantages when she was growing up, and from what Becca said, Kate too has been a victim like I was. Her husband left her too.

So I've taken to bringing Kate little presents when I visit—nothing huge, just a nice bar of soap or a glossy magazine. She is very kind to my Becca.

Franklin was relieved that I had sorted out that he shouldn't visit. Very relieved, I imagine. But Wilfred, who was so polite and always tried to do the right thing, asked, should he come and see Becca? I said, not really, what would there be for him to say? And he too was frightfully relieved. I could see it. I didn't want Wilfred in there anyway, blabbing and saying the wrong thing.

He is still Franklin's partner in this mysterious mobile phone service they've been doing. Downloading or uploading or offloading something onto people's cellphones, impossible to understand.

In the early days, the mother of that poor Janice asked could she visit Becca, but I told Kate to tell the authorities that this would be the wrong thing. The poor woman was Born Again or something, and she thought Becca would find peace if she went to tell her she had forgiven her, but I think Becca has forgotten about Janice, to be honest.

Life continued in the funny way it always does, everything changed and yet some things remained the same. I continued to play bridge with Franklin and Wilfred two nights a week. Becca's father, bloody Eamon, telephoned me every time there was something new in the tabloids—his frightful wife apparently reads nothing else.

'How do they know these things?' he would cry into the phone.

I had no idea, I told him. I never saw bloody Eamon so he wouldn't know that I had smart clothes and that I had bought a sports car. Or that there was a cleaner at the house every day now and a gardener once a week. It was none of his business anyway.

I would take a taxi to the prison each week, and ask it to wait at the bus stop round the corner and then join the rest of the prison visitors, opening my bag for examination and accepting a body search before visiting my own daughter. I didn't want anyone to tell Becca that I kept a taxi waiting. She would wonder where I got the funds. And in the end it was all for her own good, for her peace of mind, and enabled me to visit her every week without too much stress and strain.

'Kate is very good to me, Mother,' she said one day.

'Yes, indeed.' I was wondering where this was leading.

'I was wondering if you could ask her for tea some time on her day off?' she asked.

'No, darling, that wouldn't do at all,' I said. Becca had lost touch with the real world. How could I ask such a sad, poor woman, who lived in a council flat and worked as a prison warder, to my house? 'Sorry, Becca, it's out of the question.'

Becca was very disappointed. I could see by her face. But she said no more, just resumed her stitching at a feverish pace. I wondered, as I got back into my taxi, why I had bothered to come to see her at all. She was really so ungrateful for all I had done. Wasn't it enough that I had bought all these little gifts for Kate? Maybe the woman had never told her. Imagine Becca thinking I could entertain her at home. I couldn't possibly let her see how we lived.

As the taxi pulled away, I thought I saw Kate standing there looking at me, but it must have been my imagination. If she had seen me she would have come over and talked, not just stood there watching as she did. I hoped that she wouldn't say anything to Becca about my taking a taxi. But then I shook myself and told myself not to be fanciful.

When I got home the chaps were waiting for me with a Scotch and ginger. Such dear boys. They always ask about Becca and I always say that it's too dreadful to talk about and that I must go and have a long bath. Just the very fact of *being* in that place makes you feel defiled. I lay in the warm scented bubbles and drank my long cool Scotch and ginger. Life was a great deal better than it used to be. Amazing, really, how having enough money can take the edge off things.

Tonight I would wear the really smart dress that had cost what we spent on our first car. I put it on. It looked nice, certainly, but I needed better shoes. Perhaps I could come up with another little story for the ghastly papers. Something like 'Stitching Her Way to the

Future' and a description of the counterpane Becca is making.

I looked at myself in the mirror. Not bad at all for my age. New shoes would make it perfect.

Franklin stood at the bottom of the stairs. Wilfred had gone ahead to be at the table to greet us. A special dinner out in a new restaurant. My treat. Always my treat. But then don't be all bitter and twisted, Gabrielle, I told myself. The boys' business is still in the foothills, it hasn't risen to great heights yet. They don't have any real money yet, poor darlings.

'You look lovely,' Franklin said. It really was a pleasure to get dressed for people who appreciated it. Bloody Eamon wouldn't notice what I was wearing.

'Thank you,' I purred at him.

'Does Becca not ask about me at all?' he said unexpectedly.

'No, well, you know, we all agreed that it was better for her not to get in touch until . . . you know . . . until she comes out.'

'But, Gabrielle . . .' he looked at me astonished. 'She's not going to get out for years and years.'

'I know,' I said. 'But you'd be amazed at how strong she is. You and I would go under in a place like that, but not Becca, she's brave as a lion.'

He looked at me affectionately. 'You make all this so much easier for me,' he said, his eyes full of gratitude.

'Come on, Franklin, let's not be late,' I said, and we walked down the steps of our home, past the new wrought-iron railings with the sweet peas and honeysuckle entwined.

Just before we got into the car I thought I saw that Kate in our road. But it must have been a hallucination. What could she have been doing in our neighbourhood?

And then next day I thought I saw her there again. It couldn't have been, of course. But it made me uneasy for some reason and I decided to get her a little present and have a chat with her on my next visit. Possibly foolish Becca had already invited her to tea in my house. And now she was annoyed because the invitation had not been followed up.

I brought Becca some roses from the garden, and some sweet peas for that Kate, together with a little lace-trimmed handkerchief with a letter 'K' on it. I found her in her office. She accepted the flowers and hand-kerchief silently with a nod of her head.

'Is everything all right, Kate?'

'Never better, thank you,' she said, reaching to the back of the door for her overcoat and leaving immediately. It was very mystifying.

That day, Becca looked just as usual but there was something watch-ful, wary about her. It was as if she were examining me.

'We are always talking about me,' she said. 'And really nothing much changes here. Tell me all about your days and nights, Mother,' she said.

I was a bit wrong-footed here. I hadn't expected this. Up to now I had been vague and she had never wanted to know.

'Oh, you know me, Becca, darling, drifting from this to that, a little bridge here, a little reminding your bloody father to give me some support there. The days pass.' She reached for my hand and lifted it to admire my nails.

'Some of them must pass at the beauty parlour,' she said.

'Oh, I wish, darling, just cheap enamel I put on myself.'

'I see. Like your hair. Do it yourself with the kitchen scissors, do you?'

I was very annoyed. These were things I couldn't hide from her, the expensive styling and shaping of my hair every five weeks with Fabian. The weekly manicure at Pompadours.

'What are you saying?' I asked.

'Not very much, Mother. You learn not to say anything here until you're quite sure what it is you are trying to say.'

'That would make the world a very silent place,' I twittered at her.

'Not really, no, just a more certain place.'

I tried to change the subject. 'Kate seemed in a hurry today, she almost brushed past me.'

'It's her half-day,' Becca said.

'Yes, and I know that you did want me to invite her to afternoon tea, darling, but you're a little out of touch, Becca. It would be so inappropriate. I hope you don't mind.'

'No, that's all right. I understood, and so did she.'

'Well, that's good,' I said doubtfully.

'Do you get lonely at all, Mother? What with Father having left you and my being in here and everything?'

I couldn't imagine why she was asking this. 'Well, lonely isn't the right word. I don't ever think about that bloody Eamon these days. I miss you, darling, and wish you were at home. One day you will be.'

'Not for years and years, Mother.' She was matter-of-fact.

'I'll be there for you,' I said firmly.

'I doubt it very much, Mother, I really do.'

She still looked totally calm but this wasn't the way she normally spoke. A little silence fell between us. Then after what seemed a long, long time Becca spoke.

'Why did you do it, Mother?' she asked.

'I don't know what you're talking about,' I began. And I didn't really— there were so many things it could have been. Was it the taxi? Had that really been Kate in the road who would have told her about the house being all painted up? That there were definitely signs of money, ill-gotten money around the place? Or had she told her anything else?

I stood up as if to leave, but her hand shot out and pinned my wrist to the table between us. One of the warders moved towards us but Becca smiled and reassured her that everything was fine.

'My mother is just about to tell me something. She's finding it a bit difficult, but she will find the words.'

I rubbed my wrist. 'Well, you see . . .' I began.

'No, I don't see, Mother. I hear that you are living with Franklin. That's what I hear.'

I began to bluster a little.

'But I'm doing it for you, Becca darling. Wilfred and Franklin had to live somewhere. I live in a big falling-down house—why shouldn't they have rooms there?'

'Not so falling-down now, I hear,' Becca said.

'But, darling, they just have rooms there—don't be so silly.'

'Do you sleep with Franklin?' she asked calmly.

'Now how can you ask that?' I began.

'Because Kate told me, and Gwen told me.'

'Gwen?'

'One of the warders here. You go to her every week for a manicure. Dressed very differently than you are dressed today . . .'

For once I was speechless. Becca wasn't speechless, however.

'It's disgusting, he's thirty years younger than you.'

'Nineteen,' I said with spirit.

'He'll move on,' she said.

'Maybe,' I agreed. 'One day, yes, maybe.'

'Sooner than you think,' my daughter said.

And Becca told me her plan. She reminded me that I had said every-one should have a plan. Becca's plan was to put Kate in touch with the tabloid papers. Kate and Gwen didn't think that it was fair, the way Becca had been treated, and had alerted tabloid photographers to lie in wait for Franklin and myself.

'Murderess Betrayed by Her Own Mother' was going to be a much, much better story than anything that I had sold them so far. They would really pay Kate well for this.

She looked very calm and in control as she spoke to me. I wondered suddenly whether, if I had put aside all my principles and invited the damn woman to afternoon tea, all this would never have happened. But we'll never know . . .

CHAPTER 4

The Last Word
Part 1—Dr Dermot

I KNOW EVERYONE in the place, that's a fair enough thing to say. If they're thirty-five or under, then I delivered them into the world, and if they're any other age I listened to their chests and coughs and cured their measles and mumps, took glass out of their cut knees.

Doon is only a small place, twenty miles from Rossmore, along a narrow, bumpy road, but we don't need to go into the big town much. We have everything we want here. It's just a small quiet country place where I know the story of every man, woman and child.

I've closed the eyes of their mothers and fathers and grandparents, I've told them good news and bad news, I've found the words that others don't find. These people owe me. That's why I was so betrayed and let down over the way they all flocked to this new young doctor.

Dr Jimmy White.

A young whippersnapper who called me Dermot as soon as looked at me. Everyone here calls me Dr Dermot but, oho, that's not good enough for Dr Jimmy White. Oh, very eager and anxious to please he is, running here and there. Of course he does house calls any time of the day and the night, and of course he has a mobile phone so you can find him anywhere. And he's thorough, sending people halfway across the country for scans, blood tests for everything, X-rays. These are simple people, they think that's a kind of magic in itself.

Even the hospital in Rossmore isn't good enough for Dr Jimmy White. He sends them to specialists, to teaching hospitals in Dublin, no less. Rather than relying on years of experience, and someone like myself who has known the patients inside and out for generations.

Not that I let them see I was upset or anything. No, indeed. I always spoke well of Dr Jimmy White. Very bright young man, I said, plays it by the book and, indeed, consults his medical books. He won't have to do that when he's older and more experienced, but very thorough, of course, always checking things out when he's not sure.

People thought I liked and admired him while I managed to sow the seeds of doubt, like why he was checking books, getting second opinions, sending blood to be tested and people to have scans.

There was an over-talkative American man called Chester Kovac—staying in the hotel, must have been made of money. His grandfather was called O'Neill, came from round here once, not that anyone remembers him. Sure, the country's coming down with O'Neills. I told him several times that the young doctor had to learn his trade somewhere, but in a way it was hard to see him make his mistakes on the people of this parish. Chester said, surely he had to be a qualified medical man and I said yes, but there was qualified and there was experienced. Chester nodded a lot as if the idea had sunk in.

Then he told me he was buying land in Doon and going to build. He wanted my advice about what services this little town needed. What were we lacking? Where were the gaps? He had an over-concerned look on his face. It would sicken you. All that kind of sensitive stuff that has no place here. I pretended to be interested. Some rambling on about social housing, affordable housing. You know the kind of thing they go on with, moaning over the past, saying that if his poor grandfather had only owned a house, then he wouldn't have had to emigrate.

I nodded and sipped my pint. And I thought to myself, if his grandfather hadn't got up off his arse and gone out to somewhere where he could find a living, Chester wouldn't be wearing designer suits and handmade shoes. But better not to say that. Let them live their dream. Oh, and he was going to build a hall, and a centre of some sort. Here in Doon, no less! Terrific, I used to say to him, before going back to the subject of Dr White and the gaps in his learning.

For a while my way of coping with my rival worked and there was enough business for both of us. Well, for me anyway. But then things took a turn for the worse.

It was all to do with that stupid woman, Maggie Kiernan, who was having a baby, and let me tell you there was no baby ever born in the world except to Maggie. Her pregnancy was endless, no mammoth could have had a longer gestation period. She was in twice a week—she was sick and then she wasn't sick, the baby was moving—Was that natural? Or it wasn't moving—Did that mean it was dead? What she wanted was a private team of gynaecologists and obstetricians standing by in her own home.

Three weeks before she was due, she rang at two in the morning to say that the baby was arriving. So I told her to have a nice cup of tea and we'd talk about it in the morning. She kept on and on that the baby was definitely coming and wouldn't I come out? Four miles out, halfway up a mountain! Was she mad? I was soothing but she just slammed down the phone.

It wasn't until halfway through the next morning I heard the story: she had called Dr Jimmy White and of course he went out there. And wouldn't you know? The child was half born and there were complications and he got an ambulance up that mountainy road and if he hadn't accompanied her to Accident and Emergency in Rossmore, then the baby would have died, and Maggie would have died, and half the population hereabouts would have died out of sympathy.

I must have heard it fifteen times that morning: poor Maggie Kiernan and how frightened she must have been, and was it not the mercy of God that young Dr White had been able to attend her. And always the unspoken words that I had let Maggie Kiernan down.

I was annoyed, of course, but I didn't show it. Instead I showered praise on Dr Jimmy White and showed concern about Maggie, and said several times that babies had minds of their own and wouldn't life be easy if they'd only let us know. I never explained, never apologised. And I thought that eventually the message was getting over to them. I was still their wise, good Dr Dermot.

Now, every Saturday at lunchtime, Hannah Harty, a single lady, comes to do the books for me. She is a qualified bookkeeper, the soul of discretion, and does books for a lot of people in town. Just five Saturdays after all Maggie Kiernan's shenanigans, Hannah cleared her throat and told me straight out that I was losing a great many patients to the new young Dr White. And therefore a fair amount of income.

At first I didn't believe her. Hannah has always been a bit of a gloom merchant. Word was that she had set her cap at me, long, long ago. But I don't think that can be true. I certainly never gave her any encouragement. I had looked after her old mother for years. Well, actually, Hannah had looked after her old mother, but I would call and reassure them a lot, and if they were eating a supper I was made part of it.

I myself had never married. I had my heart set on a woman once but she told me I was too easy-going, and that she could never settle down with a small-town doctor. Well, I am who I am. I'm not going to change for anyone. So I spent little time thinking back on what she had said.

I listened carefully to Hannah as she spoke and, indeed, less than half an hour after she had told me about my takings being down, I had begun to take action.

I called on the Foley family for a chat. Their old father was on his last legs; he wouldn't last much longer. But I was full of cheer about him, said he had the heart and constitution of a lion and that he was in fine fettle. When I left them the Foleys all felt vastly cheered. And I told myself, as I so often do, that *this* is what a doctor is meant to do, cheer people, buoy them up, carry them along. Not frighten the wits out of them with statistics and tests and scans.

On my way home I met the young Dr White.

'All that business about Maggie Kiernan . . .' he began awkwardly.

'Yes?' My voice was cold.

'Well, I wouldn't want you to think I was muscling in on your territory or anything like that . . .' he said, shifting from foot to foot.

'Do you feel you were?' I was still icy.

'Well, technically, of course she is your patient but I had to decide whether it was an emergency or not. And, well, I decided it was.'

'So you feel you did the right thing, Dr White?'

'I do wish you'd call me Jim, I call you Dermot.'

'I know, I've noticed,' I said, with one of my smiles.

'There's plenty of work for both of us, Dermot,' he said with a familiar kind of leer. 'Neither of us will go hungry in this place.'

'I'm very sure of that, Dr White,' I said, and went on my way.

When I got back home I sat and thought further and deeper. Hannah Harty telephoned and suggested that she bring me over a steak and kidney pie she had made. Since her mother died, she had not asked me to supper in her house, which I missed, especially at weekends, which can get lonely.

I do have a housekeeper, a weary-looking woman, but she just keeps the place clean, washes and irons. She shops, of course, and prepares the vegetables but there's never anything tasty like Hannah makes. I said that I'd be honoured to eat the pie with her and would produce a bottle of claret.

When Hannah came in bearing her dishes of food it was clear that she had been to the hairdresser since we had met in the morning. She was wearing a smart white blouse and a cameo brooch. She had even put on make-up, which was most unusual. Could it possibly be true that she still had notions about the two of us?

Best thing possible was to ignore all the finery in case that was what was at the back of it all. No point in complimenting her or anything. That would be just asking for trouble. We talked about the famous Rossmore bypass and would it ever happen? It had been talked about for years. Would it make any difference to our quiet little backwater, or would they just ignore our bumpy road to Rossmore?

We had a pleasant meal, and since Hannah had brought a plate of rather good cheeses I opened a second bottle of wine.

'What in God's earth are you going to do about young Dr White, Dermot?' she asked me straight out. Her face was anxious. She really cared what was going to happen to me when most of the town had gone over to the opposition. I reached forward and patted her hand.

'I wouldn't worry at all, Hannah, my dear,' I reassured her. 'It's important to stay calm in a situation like this and wait until it all blows over.'

'But it might not blow over, Dermot. You know, I work in several different establishments around the place, and a lot of them are moving. Mr Brown in the bank is going to consult Dr White because of his father's pneumonia. Mr Kenny is worried about his mother not being able to walk properly and he thinks young Dr White might get her some newer, more modern drugs. You can't just sit here, Dermot, and watch all your hard work trickle away.' She looked really upset on my behalf. Or maybe on her own behalf, if she really saw a future with me.

'No, indeed, I won't sit here and watch, Hannah. I was thinking actually that I might take a little holiday.'

'A holiday? Now, Dermot? In the middle of this crisis?' she gasped.

But I just smiled at her. 'I know what I'm doing, Hannah,' I said.

And over the next week I made several house calls. I decided that old man Foley had about two weeks to live; that Mr Kenny's mother should be allowed to live out her last months peacefully without any new medication; that Mr Brown's father was entering his last bout of pneumonia, which would take him peacefully away from this world.

Then I announced that I was taking a little holiday. I encouraged the Browns, the Foleys and the Kennys to attend that nice young Dr White while I was away. No, of *course* I didn't mind, what was life about except give and take, and the young man was extremely well qualified.

Then I put my golf clubs into the back of the car and drove 150 miles to a nice quiet hotel by the sea.

It was easy to find a four-ball so I played eighteen holes a day. Every night I played bridge in the lounge and at breakfast each morning, with my second cup of tea, I turned the pages to the Deaths column.

First I read of the death of old man Foley, then of Mrs Kenny, and finally of Mr Brown. I said a swift goodbye to my new golfing and bridge friends and drove straight back home to Doon.

I called on the homes of the bereaved, shaking my head in bewilderment over their great losses. I said I couldn't understand it—there had been plenty of life in old man Foley when I left; and in Mrs Kenny and Mr Brown. How sad and ironical that they should all die when I, who had known them for so much of their lives, was far away. Then I would shake my wise old head again and say it was a total mystery.

It didn't take long. In fact it all happened much quicker than I had expected. People began to talk.

They said that it was very odd that three perfectly well people had died during the ten days that Dr Dermot was on holiday. They said it was a pity to be hasty and to run to the new instead of staying with the tried and tested. With the man who had known them young, old, well and sick, all their lives.

Little by little they came back to me, even those who had asked for their medical records to take to Dr White. Some of them had been annoyed about the scrappy nature of the records and had not accepted that it was all in my head. I knew which child had had mumps and which had had measles, for heaven's sake. No need for computers and print-outs in my case.

I was very generous, talking to them. I showed no hurt, not even a trace of sulking in my face. They were all so relieved that I was taking them back, they wanted to denounce Dr White. But here again I was noble. I wouldn't hear a word against the boy. I called him a boy, as I smiled about him forgivingly, and said he was very young and that he had to make his mistakes somewhere. They marvelled at my generosity.

He called on me before he left town, Dr White did. A courtesy call, he said, to tell me that he was moving on. I knew already but I pretended to be surprised. I wished him well and said I would be sorry to lose him as a colleague.

'You'll find somewhere more suitable,' I said.

'Yes, I'm sure I will,' he said.

'And you have a nice manner, which is what it's all about,' I added.

'Which is what *some* of it's about, certainly, Dermot,' he said.

I winced as I did every time he was familiar like that. But I don't think it showed. I offered him a drink but he refused.

'It won't last, of course, Dermot, it can't. Would you like a little bit of advice from me before I leave?'

To humour him I said that I would. After all I had run him out of town. I could afford to be gracious.

'When the next young fellow comes in, Dermot, make him your partner, sell this house and take a room in Chester's clinic, go into semi-retirement, marry Hannah Harty, go and live in that big house of hers. It's better that way than a big malpractice suit or one of your old friends thinking you had been negligent.'

He stood up, impudent young pup, and left without looking back.

I thought for a little while about what he had said. There was no wisdom in it. None at all. And what was this that he was babbling about—Chester's clinic? Chester had been organising some kind of a medical centre, a ludicrous place with expensive machinery where people could waste time and money. They were even going to have rooms for aromatherapy or some kind of New Age nonsense. And what a mad time he had chosen to do it! Just when a new road would come to take the patients straight into Rossmore from here. As a project, it was doomed before it even began.

That was nothing for me to worry about. People round here had their feet on the ground, they wouldn't go for this nonsense all in the name of Danny O'Neill, some loser who none of them could remember. But one thing was clear and was much more important: my name was definitely up with poor Hannah Harty's. That was something that must be nipped in the bud. She was meant to be making me some fancy salmon dish tomorrow. Better ring her now and tell her I wasn't free. Everything was going so well now, it would be a pity to complicate things.

Part 2—Chester's Plan

I HAD ALWAYS PROMISED my Irish grandpa Danny O'Neill that I would go to Ireland, but I didn't make it while he was alive. He used to tell tales of his home in Doon, which was some miles from Rossmore. And of the huge Whitethorn Woods and how there was a holy well there where miracles had happened. But somehow I never got to Ireland. There was too much else to do like get an education, and make a living.

My own father, Mark Kovac from Poland, had been a carpenter but he had TB and was never strong, and so as the eldest I had to support the family. I used to say to my mom that life would have been a bit easier if they hadn't felt it necessary to have nine children. But she only laughed and asked which of them would I send back? We worked hard, got good grades at school, and we each got a job from the moment we were tall enough to stack shelves in a supermarket.

And I had a bit of luck and met a banking guy who offered me money to start my own building contractor's business, and then I was able to give jobs to all my brothers and sisters, and I put my father on the board. He was so delighted to see MARK KOVAC & FAMILY BUILDING CONTRACTORS on the trucks.

I didn't need to put my own name on the company, I *knew* it was mine, and it looked more established somehow to have the father of the family on it anyway. Gave us credibility, a pedigree.

My father's people had all left a village in Poland that didn't exist any more, but my mother's father went on and on about this lovely place in Ireland. So when I was fifty I decided to reward myself with three months' vacation.

I had never married. No time really. It sounds a bit hopeless, I suppose, but I never thought of it like that. I was too busy getting everything up and running in the business and now that was done I found I had left it a bit late. My brothers and sisters were all well married with children and so I had plenty of family life around me if I needed it.

But then my doctor said that I was suffering from hypertension and should take it easy. After Grandpa died, and there was all the Irish music at his funeral and the chat about Rossmore and the woods and everything, I got thinking about his country and I decided it might be a good time to go to Ireland and have a rest, away from the business.

But at the same time, since I wasn't a person who was used to doing nothing, I could investigate this idea I had of building a tribute to Grandpa O'Neill. Something that would show to the people of his native place that his life and his travelling to America had all been worthwhile.

Everyone thought this was a good idea, and they assured me that Mark Kovac & Family Building Contractors could manage without me.

'And maybe you might even find an Irish colleen over there,' my mother said. I thought she'd have to be a fairly long-in-the-tooth colleen to fancy me, but I said nothing like that. Over the years I'd got used to smiling at people and agreeing with them rather than having to have the last word. The last word isn't all that important really.

And so I came here to my grandpa Danny O'Neill's place, but nobody in Doon remembered him, which was disappointing. They knew the line of cottages he came from, but these had all been long knocked down because they had fallen into disrepair. And it was all so long ago, and O'Neill was a common name in Ireland anyway.

So I decided that he *would* be remembered. I would see to this. I would make a monument to him. Not something vain, but something that would be of great use in his home town. I asked around for suggestions. They were many and varied. People thought of a little theatre. Or an art gallery. Or maybe a small park where the children could play and the old people sit in the evening. Or a church hall or a museum. There were as many ideas as there were people offering them.

One old lady said I should go to pray at the well in the woods outside Rossmore and then I would see as clear as daylight what I should do. So I drove in and parked my car near the edge of the woods and went in. I met a big friendly dog that accompanied me and seemed to know his way to the well as he made the correct turning at every little wooden signpost. Then he sat outside respectfully while I went into the damp dark cave.

The well was extraordinary. That was the only word. I'm as religious as the next man. I mean, as the son of an Irish Catholic mother and a Polish Catholic father, I wouldn't have much chance of escaping it, would I? But this was beyond anything I had ever seen. People had put their petitions on the walls of the cave for all to see, they had left children's tiny shoes and socks with notes attached, praying for a recovery from rheumatic fever, or rosary beads with notes begging for the recovery of a beloved mother.

It was grotesque in many ways and yet so touching in others. Such a collection of frail hopes all gathered in one little space. It didn't give me any sense of well-being, holiness. There was no wisdom coming towards me from that statue. Instead I felt uneasy and wanted to be away from there.

As I came out I found the big dog again—a kind of sheepdog or a collie—he had been waiting for me as if I were his long-lost friend. I scratched his ears and walked back through the woods deep in thought.

Then an idea formed in my mind.

I would build a health centre so that the people of this area wouldn't have to be on their knees in this cold wet place praying to a saint, who was 2,000 years dead, that a cure would be found for a loved one. Maybe, I thought to myself, this is the way the well worked: you got your problem solved once you left it.

The dog trotted along beside me happily. He was never going to leave me now. I took him to the nearest Garda station. They looked at him thoughtfully. He had no collar and he wasn't well kept. Someone had brought him to lose him in the woods.

I was shocked. A lovely, friendly dog like that.

'You might give him a home yourself?' suggested the young Garda.

'Come on, then,' I said to the dog and he leaped eagerly into the car.

I decided to call him Zloty. It was the old Polish currency. He answered so readily that you'd think it was his original name.

Back home again in Doon, I was determined that the place would have some kind of medical centre. If anyone needed specialist treatment, or a scan, or an X-ray, they had to take the bumpy road into Rossmore. Yes, I had heard all about this bypass road that was meant to be built. But it could all be just dreams for the next decades. And, anyway, in Rossmore they didn't have all the facilities that patients needed—sometimes they had to make the long journey to Dublin. Wouldn't it be great to have all these opportunities on their doorstep?

The people in this place were all very nice and easy to talk to. I stayed in the local hotel, and Zloty slept in a big outhouse. I met Ciaran Brown from the bank, and Sean Kenny the local attorney, and the Foley family, and Maggie Kiernan, who told everyone how desperately she wanted to have a baby and eventually she did. There was a very ladylike woman, Hannah Harty, who was a bookkeeper and the soul of discretion in a very gossip-prone place. So when I bought a plot of land through Sean Kenny, he suggested that I should ask Hannah to look after the paperwork for me, and nobody would know my business.

And there were two doctors in the town, a very crabby sort of fellow, Dermot, and a much younger smarter lad called Jimmy White. Unfortunately I had registered with Dr Dermot before Jimmy White came to town so I had to stick with him. He was a slow, lazy guy, just looked at my prescribed medication and told me to continue with it. Then he went off on a vacation. After a bit I felt short of breath. I consulted Jimmy White, who sent me for a stress test and an ultrasound. Then a heart specialist changed my beta blockers and I was fine again.

That was a bad time for everyone. Old man Foley died, then Sean Kenny's mother and Ciaran Brown's father died, all within ten days. We had a path worn to the churchyard for funerals.

Poor Jimmy White was distraught.

'It would have to happen on my watch,' he confided to me one night. 'The people here think that the sun shines out of Dermot's arse and that those old folk wouldn't have died if he had been here.'

'That was certainly bad timing,' I sympathised.

'Yeah, or maybe—as I think in my more paranoid moments—it was planned,' he suggested.

I gave him a look and Jimmy White said hastily that no, of course it wasn't possible. Even Dr Dermot couldn't have killed them off by voodoo from his vacation. I thought about it myself for a while. Maybe that weaselish little doctor did actually wait to go away until he knew those old folk were going to take their last journeys.

Was I becoming as paranoid as Jimmy?

Anyway I had plenty to keep me occupied. I had a building firm in Ireland, which was fairly relaxed. Very relaxed. The foreman, Finn Ferguson, often said that when God made time he made plenty of it. Planning permissions were a nightmare; assembling a team was very different from back home. Everyone seemed to be running several jobs in tandem, I would sigh to that nice Hannah Harty sometimes, and she was always very positive and full of practical advice.

Perhaps I should tell Finn Ferguson that if his wife liked to go to America on a shopping trip, my sisters would look after her and take her to the right stores? It worked like a dream. The woman came back with three suitcases of merchandise and the news that Mark Kovac & Family Building Contractors were huge in the USA.

After that, Finn Ferguson stopped treating me just as bumbling old Chester and called me 'sir'. He would still have a beer with me now and then, and often brought a bone for Zloty as well. He would tell me of his worries about the new bypass that might or might not be built around Rossmore.

Once one of the huge construction firms got the contract for building the bypass and established themselves in the town of Rossmore, then a little company like Finn Ferguson's would be edged out of the jobs he already had. People would be seduced by big companies with huge earth movers and cranes, and his living would go down the plughole. I assured him that the thing to do was to specialise. To get a name for doing one kind of building very well. When the Danny O'Neill Centre opened there would be a beautiful glossy brochure about it, which of course Finn could use to get himself more clients.

This galvanised Finn to take a less leisurely attitude to the building, I was very relieved to observe.

'You're a very decent skin, you know, Chester, I mean, sir,' he said. 'A lot of people say that about you. I heard Miss Harty telling Canon Cassidy when he came over here last week, she said you were the angel this place has always been looking out for.'

I liked Hannah and was disappointed that she seemed to fancy Dr Dermot. I asked her once if she had ever been in love, and she said no, but at the age of fifty-two she didn't think it was a luxury that might come her way. Her mother had always said that Dr Dermot would make a good catch and she had invested a lot of time in trying to realise that. But he was a man independent and set in his ways.

'Or a little selfish maybe?' I suggested. Wrong way to go, Chester.

Hannah Harty defended him. He had worked tirelessly for this place. Nobody could think he was selfish.

I said I was just an outsider; I didn't really know. But I did know. And he was selfish. I saw this more and more. He would accept a drink from me in the hotel, but never buy the other half. I heard from Hannah how she would make him a steak and kidney pie or cook him a roast chicken because men were so hopeless. But the hotel had a perfectly good dining room where he could have entertained her and yet he never did. He was certainly very arrogant to young Jimmy White, so much so that the young man told me he would have to fold his tent and steal away. There was no living for him here.

Meanwhile my own plans were going ahead. Finn had recruited people from all over the country to build the Danny O'Neill Health Centre in Doon. It was growing like a mushroom every day.

The people could hardly believe that there would be X-ray facilities, heart-monitoring machines and a therapeutic swimming pool, all on their own doorsteps, with a dozen or more treatment rooms planned for those who might want to rent them. It was the medicine of the future, the newspapers said. Already there had been enquiries from a dental practice, a Pilates class, and a yoga class, as well as several specialists interested in the possibility of having a clinic there twice a week. It was all a matter of bringing health care to the people rather than letting patients travel great distances, adding to their distress. I had been hoping Jimmy White would be part of it, but no, he was gone before it was up and running.

Hannah Harty had obviously handed over the bulk of my work to a firm of accountants by now but she still did my own personal books for me. I enjoyed our sessions together.

Finn would come for a Friday drink at the hotel around six and bring me up to date with what had happened during the week, then Hannah Harty would join us, countersign some cheques for Finn, after which she and I would have dinner.

She always had her hair done at the beauty parlour for our meetings. She liked to talk about Dr Dermot and because I'm basically easy-going I let her chatter on. She used to meet him on a Saturday, so I think the fancy hairdo was really in his honour. But I noticed that there were more and more excuses why Dr Dermot wasn't going to be able to make their Saturday meeting.

Hannah had begun to wonder whether Dr Dermot might be avoiding her. I tutted and said surely not.

'And of course you still do his books for him?'

'Well, yes, but he just leaves the material there in a tray nowadays. He's not there himself.' She was very troubled.

'Maybe he's busy, on urgent cases.'

'Ah, Chester, you know Dermot,' she said. 'There's never anything very urgent. I think he's afraid our names are being linked.'

'But he should be proud of that, surely?' I said.

She bit her lip, her eyes filled with tears and she shook her head sadly. I wanted to go down and take that annoying Dr Dermot by his thin shoulders and shake the life out of him. Why should he upset a decent woman like Hannah Harty? She was much too good for that little weasel. And as that thought went across my mind, it was followed by another one. She was the kind of woman that I would be happy to spend much more time with. I wondered why I hadn't seen this before.

I hoped that she didn't think she had confided too much in me and therefore could never learn to see me as a person. Well, I would never know unless I moved things on a bit. So I suggested that when she had picked up Dr Dermot's papers tomorrow, she and I might take a drive.

'That's if he's not there, of course,' Hannah said.

He wasn't there, so we drove off to see an old castle that had a waterfall in the grounds. And the next week we went to an art exhibition, and the week after that we went together to the wedding of Finn Ferguson's daughter. By now Hannah was talking a lot less of Dr Dermot, and her name was most definitely up with mine or linked with mine or whatever the expression they used around here.

The three months' visit had turned into six months. And, despite the best efforts of Finn the foreman, the health centre seemed to be taking for ever. I thought less and less about going back to Kovac's in America and I told my brothers that I probably saw this as a permanent position. They were pleased for me and assured me that they could manage without me and they had long realised that I had found a life that involved me deeply back in Ireland. They didn't realise how much I was involved. And they hadn't heard of Hannah Harty.

She was such a help to me. She found a designer to do a restful décor for the health centre, she got Finn's new son-in-law to do the landscaping, she gave little dinner parties and invited Ciaran Brown from the bank, and his wife, and Sean Kenny, the attorney, and his wife. And Maggie Kiernan and her husband when they could get a baby sitter.

She did ask Dr Dermot from time to time but he was never free to accept. And then she didn't ask him any more. One day he cornered me about the new centre. He had heard it was going to be opened by a government minister. He was laughing at the thought. Had they so little to do with their time?

I reminded him that on several occasions I had invited him to take rooms there. I thought that if he had all the referral places on the premises, he might actually start sending people for the tests and scans they needed. But he had ridiculed the idea, saying that he had his own perfectly good surgery, thank you very much.

I explained that I would then be offering the rooms to other doctors, and he said he wished me luck taking money from eejits and losers. But of course I hadn't done that. The Danny O'Neill Health Centre was going to make sure that the people of this place got proper medical treatment, not like my grandpa and a great number of his brothers and sisters scattered all over the globe, each one of them setting off in poor health as they headed for a new life in a new land.

It was only now, when he realised that a real live government minister was going to come and open the premises, that Dr Dermot had shown any interest in it.

'I suppose that place will be a licence to print money for you, Chester,' he said to me with his usual sneer.

It was hardly worth arguing with him. He wasn't the kind of man who would understand that I had put my own money into it, invited others to contribute, and gathered a team. The notion that I wasn't in it for a profit would have been beyond his grasp.

'Ah, you know the way it is.' I shrugged. I had learned a few of these meaningless phrases since coming to this land.

'I don't at all know the way it is. I'm the last to know anything around here,' the doctor snapped. 'And a patient told me this morning that you have notions about Miss Harty. That was news to me too.'

'I am a great admirer of Hannah Harty, that is true. Your patient was not wrongly informed,' I said pompously.

'Well, as long as it's only admiring from afar, no one would quarrel with that.'

He was actually warning me off. Staking his claim to a woman who he had ignored and humiliated.

I felt bile rise in my throat. But I had got as far as this in life by keeping my temper. I would not give anger its head.

'I have to go now, Dr Dermot,' I said in a voice that I knew sounded choked.

He smiled his superior and hugely irritating smile. 'Well, sure you do,' he said, raising his glass at me. 'Sure you do.'

Shaking, I walked across the square. Zloty came with me to keep me company or to give me courage—I didn't know which. I had never felt so hostile to a man before. So that meant that I had never felt so strongly about a woman either. But I had no idea whether Hannah felt anything remotely similar.

I found myself walking straight towards the elegant ivy-covered house where she lived alone. Her grandparents would have lived in that house when my poor grandpa was packing his few belongings to leave. She was surprised to see me. I had never called unannounced before. But she welcomed me in and poured me a glass of wine. She looked pleased rather than annoyed to see me. So that was good.

'I was wondering, Hannah . . .' I began.

'What were you wondering now?' She held her head on one side.

I'm *hopeless* at this sort of thing. There are men who just know what to say, who have words at will. I could only be honest, straightforward.

'I was wondering if you would ever see a future with a person like me.' I'd said it, straight out.

'Someone *like* you, Chester—or you?' She was teasing me now.

'Me, Hannah,' I said simply.

She walked away from me in her elegant drawing room. 'I'm much too old for you,' she said sadly.

'You're two and a half years older than me,' I said.

She smiled as if I were a toddler who had made an endearing remark.

'Ah, yes, but before you were born I was waddling around here taking notice.'

'Maybe you were waiting for me to come and join you?' I asked hopefully.

'Well, if I was waiting for you, Chester, then I waited a long time,' she said.

And then I knew it was going to be all right. And the rage I had for Dr Dermot died down in me. What had I to be enraged about? If it hadn't been for him I might have let Hannah slip away from me.

'Will I have to go and live in America?' she asked.

'No, I'd prefer to live here. I'd like to see the centre up and running, I want to know if the big road around Rossmore ever gets built, if the St Ann's Well is taken down. I'm fascinated by this place now, and to live here with you would be better than I ever dreamed.'

She seemed very pleased.

'But I hope you'll come over and meet my family,' I said. 'My mom said that maybe I'd find a colleen over here.'

'Oh, a bit of an ageing colleen,' she said, nervously patting her hair.

'Please, Hannah . . .' I began and she went to draw the curtains of her big bay window that looked out on the square.

Before she closed them I saw Dr Dermot coming out of the hotel. He paused and looked at Hannah's house and then turned and went back to his own lonely place. He had only a short working life ahead of him. Once the Danny O'Neill Health Centre opened in Doon, there would be little demand for Dr Dermot's old-fashioned, blundering medicine.

And now he had lost the woman who might have made his last years bearable. I know that everyone always said about me that I was over good-natured, and always thought the best of everyone. But truly I felt sorry for the guy.

CHAPTER 5

The Road, the Woods and the Well—2

FATHER BRIAN FLYNN went to the station to meet his sister Judy. She hadn't been home for ten years and the time showed very definitely on her face. He was shocked at how pale and drawn she looked. Judy must only be thirty-nine or forty. She could have been in her late fifties.

She saw him and waved. 'Aren't you very good to come and meet me!' She gave him a hug.

'I'm only sorry that I can't offer you somewhere to stay. It seems terrible for you to have to pay for a hotel when you have a mother and two brothers in Rossmore.'

'Will Mam recognise me at all, Brian?'

'Ah, she will in her own way,' he said.

'What does that mean exactly?'

He had forgotten how direct Judy could be. 'I don't know what it means, Judy, it's just something I say to avoid saying anything, I suppose.'

She squeezed his arm affectionately. 'You were always a pet,' she said. 'I'm sorry I stayed away for so long. There was always one foolish thing or another keeping me over there.'

'But didn't you always write, and you were very good to our mother,' Father Flynn said.

Judy cheered up. 'Now, take me on a tour of Rossmore showing me all the changes and point me to the best hairdresser.'

'There's a very smart place called Fabian's, though that's not his name at all—I was at school with him, and he was called something else altogether, but apparently they go to him from far and near.'

'Good. I'll remember that. You see, as well as relying on St Ann to find me a husband, I think I should bring up the second line of attack and get some new clothes and a hairstyle as well. A bit of grooming, as one might say.'

'You're looking for a husband *here*?' Father Flynn was astounded.

'Well, yes. Why not? I didn't do too well in over ten years in London.'

'You got a career for yourself,' he said. Judy was an illustrator of children's books.

'Yes, but I'm not asking St Ann for a career.' Judy was brisk. 'Lord, would you look at the traffic—it's like Hyde Park Corner.'

'It might not be for much longer. There's great talk of a new road, to take all the trucks and lorries out of the town, and let the through traffic pass without clogging up our little streets.'

'And will it happen or is it only talk?'

'I think it will happen, but there's a lot of debate about it—people coming down heavily on one side or the other.'

'And is it a good thing or a bad thing in your opinion?'

'I don't know, Judy, I really don't. The road's meant to be going through the Whitethorn Woods and possibly through St Ann's Well.'

'So I got here just in time,' said Judy, with a sense of grim resolution that made her brother feel very uneasy.

They parked the car and walked along a crowded Castle Street towards the Rossmore Hotel. Judy was astounded at the way every second person seemed to greet her brother as they passed.

A woman came down the steps of the local newspaper office and her face lit up in a smile.

'There you are, Lilly,' Father Flynn said.

'This must be your sister, Father,' Lilly Ryan said, pleased.

'It's just as well he hasn't a fancy woman,' Judy said. 'They'd have her identified in ten seconds.'

'No fear of that, isn't Father Flynn a walking saint?' said Lilly, shocked.

And then Judy recognised her. She was the woman whose baby had disappeared all those years ago. Judy remembered how hundreds of people had gone into the Whitethorn Woods to hunt for a body or to pray at the well. There had been no result from either quest. She felt awkward and she supposed it must have shown on her face. But Lilly Ryan would be used to this after twenty years. Two decades of people shuffling and being unable to mention the great loss for fear of saying the wrong thing.

'I'm trying to get up the courage to visit my mother,' Judy confided. 'I'm afraid our family leaves all the hard work to Brian here.'

'Do it before you do anything else,' Lilly advised. 'If you face the hard thing first it makes it easier.'

'You might well be right,' Judy agreed. 'Brian, can you leave my case in the hotel? I'll go and see her now.'

'I'll come with you,' he said.

'No, I'll do this on my own. Good luck to you, Lilly.'

They watched as Judy turned into the small side street where her mother lived.

'I'd better go after her,' Father Flynn began.

But Lilly reminded him that Judy wanted to do this alone. So he shrugged and carried his sister's suitcase into the hotel. He would wait in one of their big armchairs until she came back and then he would buy her the stiff drink she would undoubtedly need.

Mrs Flynn had no idea who Judy was, and no amount of reminding seemed to bring any recognition. She thought that Judy was a health visitor and was anxious for her to leave.

Judy looked around in desperation but there were no photographs on the walls or in frames on the old desk. Poor Brian had done his best to keep the place in some kind of order and would take his mother's washing to the Fresh as a Daisy once a week, but Judy noticed that the place still smelt bad and her mam was very uncared for. Every month for years now Judy had sent a cheque to her brother Brian, and she knew he had spent it on items for their mam. But the iron sat there unused, the easy chair was half hidden under a pile of newspapers. Mrs Flynn didn't believe in making herself comfortable.

'You must remember me, Mam, I'm Judy. I'm the middle one. Younger than Eddie, older than Brian.'

'Brian?' Her mother's look was blank.

'You remember Brian, surely? He comes in every morning to give you your breakfast.'

'No, he does not, that's from the Meals on Wheels.' Her mother was definite.

'No, Mam, they come at lunchtime. Brian comes and gives you an egg every morning.'

'That's what he says.' Her mother wasn't convinced.

'Do you remember Eddie?'

'Of course I do, do you think I'm cracked or something? He wouldn't be told, married that Kitty, no good she was, nor any of her family. No wonder what happened happened.'

'What happened was that Eddie left her for a young one.'

'May God forgive you, whoever you are! Saying such things about my family! It was Kitty who threw my son out and kept his house, you'll note.' Her mother's mouth was set in a hard line.

'And what does Brian say about that?'

'I don't know any Brian.'

'Don't you have a daughter?'

'I do, a young one over in England doing drawings of some sort, she never gets in touch.'

'I'm your daughter, Mam, I'm Judy, you must know me.'

'Would you get away out of that, my daughter's a young girl—you're a middle-aged woman like myself.'

As Judy walked back to the hotel she decided that a visit to this smart hairdresser called Fabian's might be well overdue. She even paused outside a beauty shop called Pompadours. A course of facials and manicures might not go amiss either.

Her brother Brian was a splendid guide. As well as going with her while she made appointments in Fabian's and Pompadours, he showed her a very smart boutique.

'Didn't Becca King work there?' Judy asked.

'For God's sake, don't mention Becca King,' he said, looking left and right.

'Why on earth not?'

'She's in jail. She got one of the van men in the shop to murder her boyfriend's new lover.'

'God, and they say you take risks living in London!' Judy said in amazement.

Father Flynn brought his sister back to meet Canon Cassidy. Josef and Anna had made little sandwiches in honour of the guest, and he introduced Judy to Josef, who kept everything in the priests' house gleaming and the old man himself looking pink and clean. Unlike Judy's mother, he remembered her well. He had been there for her first communion, had looked on when the bishop came to confirm the girls of St Ita's.

'I haven't had the pleasure of assisting at your marriage yet,' Canon Cassidy said as he drank his tea and ate his dainty sandwiches.

'No, but it won't be long now,' Judy said. 'I'm going to do a novena to St Ann. I'm going to pray at her shrine for nine days so that she will find me a good husband.'

'And no better woman for doing that than St Ann,' the canon said, his simple faith and certainties all intact.

Father Flynn envied him with all his soul.

'I'd better go and see the sister-in-law,' Judy said with a sigh.

'Don't raise your hopes too high,' Father Flynn warned her.

'What would annoy her least, do you think, as a gift?' Judy wondered.

'Let me see, flowers would be a woeful waste of money, sweets would rot the children's teeth. Magazines are full of rubbish, a book could have been got in the library. Get her a loaf of bread and a half-pound of ham, she might make you a sandwich.'

'As bad as that, is it?' Judy asked.

'Worse,' said Father Flynn.

He was not in a good humour. He had discovered that there was going to be a public meeting in ten days' time, a big protest meeting, and he was going to be invited to address it. But he couldn't find it in his heart to stand up and condemn a possible scheme that would improve traffic and the quality of life for many people just because it would mean taking down a perfectly awful statue that was beginning to produce dangerously idolatrous feelings among the parishioners.

Still, with his usual optimism, he comforted himself that it was still only a rumour about the road, and he still had ten days before the meeting. There was plenty of time to work out what to say. In the meantime there were a lot of problems to be faced nearer home.

Like how to deal with Judy if St Ann didn't come up with a husband. Like how they should face up to their mother's failing health. Like how much longer Canon Cassidy could reasonably be expected to stay in the priests' house with the title of parish priest. Or how he could go to see Aidan Ryan yet again in the jail tomorrow and try to persuade him that his wife Lilly was not a villainous person who had sold their baby. And, most immediately, what was going to happen at the meeting this afternoon between the anger-filled Kitty and the tense, strained Judy.

He sighed a heavy sigh and ran his hands through his red spiky hair until it stood up around his head like a mad punk halo.

As it happened, Kitty and Judy got on perfectly fine. Eventually.

Judy decided to offer her the gift of a hairdo at Fabian's. At first Kitty laughed a sneering laugh and said Fabian's wasn't for the likes of them. Then Judy said she was asking her to come for solidarity.

'Just to patronise me, you mean,' Kitty had scoffed.

'Not at all. Just because Eddie treated you disgracefully it doesn't mean that Brian and I would. I haven't been back here in years and I wanted to give you a big box of chocolates, then I thought you might just think that they would be bad for the children's teeth, so I decided to get you something you wouldn't go out and buy for yourself.'

'You must be made of money.' Kitty was still grudging.

'No, I'm not, but I do work hard and I saved hard for this trip home.'

'And what brought you home?' Kitty was not yet won over.

'I want to get married, Kitty. It's as simple as that. I can't find anyone in London except married men, and I don't have to tell you what a foolish road that is to go down. You've experienced it from the other side. So I was hoping that maybe if I went for nine days and did a novena to St Ann at the well . . .' She let her voice trail away.

'You're making fun of me—you're just having a jeer at us, you and your London ways.'

'I'm not as it happens, but honestly, life is too short. If that's the way you want to see it, then there's nothing I can do.'

For some reason it worked. Kitty said in a tone that she hadn't used for a long time, 'If the offer's still open I'd love a hairdo. It would give me a great boost altogether . . .'

Father Brian Flynn had another deputation waiting for him when he got back to the priests' house. A request for support from the other side of the increasingly great divide. A group of concerned citizens were going to have a candlelit procession through the town, campaigning for the rumoured new road that would bring an end to the dangerous traffic that roared through Rossmore. They wanted Father Flynn to march at their head.

Great, he said to himself, absolutely great, and I haven't even answered the other lot yet.

Then his brow cleared. Maybe this was the answer. He would say that the Church must not be seen to enter local politics. Was this the wisdom of Solomon or was it in fact the refuge of a weak man? He might never know.

In a way he wished the whole thing were out in the open. These shadowlands of rumour and counter-rumour were very disturbing. Each day new fuel was being added to the flames of speculation. People said that big builders had been seen dining in the Rossmore Hotel. That meant that the road had been agreed—it was simply a matter of who would build it.

Farmers with land adjoining the woods were giving themselves airs. The land from which they had once scraped a living might now be worth something in the end. The trick would be to sell now to some speculator. Especially if you had a few acres that might not come under the compulsory purchase order when it happened but would be highly valuable for access. It seemed that everywhere you went, you heard voices. Voices with something to say.

A woman who had a small guest house on the edge of the town was reported to be thinking of putting in new bathrooms and extending her breakfast room, once the new road was given the go-ahead. There would be an unending line of engineers, advisers and consultants looking for accommodation near the site.

Places like the Fresh as a Daisy launderette just couldn't wait for the road to arrive. They had never got any business from visitors anyway. And Fabian's the hairdressers thought they would do better if their clients had room to park their cars.

But the garden centre on the edge of town didn't want the new road. They had a nice little business where travellers from east to west would stop, stretch their legs, visit the café and maybe fill the car with bedding plants or gift-wrapped azaleas for whoever they were visiting. If the new road came no one would need to pass this way any more.

And there were the hundreds who had been helped by St Ann. They couldn't believe that their fellow countrymen and women were prepared to turn their backs on the saint and allow her shrine to be dismantled. There was talk of people lying down in front of the bulldozers if they came to the woods, and obstructing all the earth-moving machinery. It was the least they could do to thank their saint for all the miracles that had been worked through her well. It didn't actually matter that these miracles had not been recognised as such by Rome. People round here knew. And people from far, far away knew. Didn't they come in droves from miles across the sea? And still, greedy, money-loving people were prepared to ignore this great blessing, which had given so much to so many, just to get traffic moving faster and earn even more money than they already had.

The canon said only that we must pray for guidance in these as in all matters. Josef and Anna confided in Father Flynn and said they thought that the old man needed full-time care.

'It's not that I am looking for more hours, Father,' Josef said. 'It's just that you should know. And of course I am always afraid that one day you will tell me he is going to a nursing home and there will be no job for me. I hope I am not being selfish but I want to be prepared.'

Father Flynn said he understood very well and it was indeed a grey area. The canon seemed very happy where he was and it would be a pity to move him. His life had no purpose if he wasn't in the priests' house. Yet, if he really needed more care, then he would have to have it.

'It's just I was thinking of getting a job helping to build the road,' Josef said.

'You mean it's really going to happen?' Father Flynn was astounded.

'I have Polish friends and they say that it will. They are going to stay with Anna and me, and, Father Flynn, you would not believe the great money they will earn building it.' Josef's face was full of hope and dreams.

'Yes, but it's only money, Josef.'

'It's money that will buy a little shop for my brothers back home in Latvia. We have everything we need here but they have so very little.'

For no reason at all, Father Flynn thought of his friend James O'Connor who had been ordained the same day as he had. James had left the priesthood, married Rosie, had two little sons. James worked in computer technology of some kind, he said it was great, easy work, and when you came home from the office you could put it all behind you.

Not at all like parish work. No more of this standing up for the indefensible, or staying silent on matters you cared about. Father Flynn thought he would have loved it. Just loved it.

Skunk Slattery looked up as Kitty Flynn came into his shop with a good-looking woman he hadn't seen before.

'How are you, Skunk?' asked Kitty. 'We're getting ourselves a few glossy magazines and going off to Fabian's for a makeover.'

'More power to you, Kitty. It's never too late, I say,' Skunk responded, not very gallantly.

'Always the man to flatter you,' Kitty said.

'Are you going to introduce me to your friend?' Skunk asked.

'That's not my friend, Skunk, that's my sister-in-law—don't you remember her?' Kitty said.

'Kitty is another person who'll always flatter you!' Judy said. 'I'm Judy Flynn, by the way. Brian and Eddie's sister.'

'Pleased to meet you, I am Sebastian Slattery,' said Skunk.

'You are not!' Kitty would argue with her shadow. 'You're Skunk—you always were and always will be.'

Skunk and Judy exchanged glances of despair as Kitty burrowed among the glossy magazines.

'I'm amazed I never met you before. Will you be around for long?' Skunk asked.

'For as long as it takes,' Judy Flynn said mysteriously.

Naomi approached Father Flynn. Normally she steered well clear of him. Naomi was used to steering clear of people, there were a fair few she had to avoid. Like Eddie's wife Kitty, like Eddie's children, like his mother, and most certainly his brother Brian, the local priest.

'Excuse me, Brian?' she began.

Father Flynn nearly dropped to the ground in shock. 'Yes . . . um . . . Naomi.' What on God's earth could the girl want?

'Brian, I was wondering if you could explain to me how Eddie could get an annulment of his marriage.'

'With great, great difficulty, Naomi,' Father Flynn said.

'No, I mean, it *can* be done obviously, it's a question of how.' Naomi turned her big nineteen-year-old eyes on him.

'Annulment is saying that no marriage existed,' Father Flynn said. 'And I have to tell you, Naomi, that a marriage did exist between Eddie and Kitty, and they have four children as a result of it.'

'It wasn't a real marriage,' she began.

'It was, Naomi. I was there. It happened, and you can't say it didn't. Now, have I said one word to you about your living with Eddie? No, I have not. It's your business, yours and his, but don't go dragging the principles of canon law and the Church into it. Please.'

'Eddie didn't know his mind then. What does a young fellow of twenty know about taking on a wife and having children?'

'What's brought all this on, Naomi?' Father Flynn's voice was level. It would be nice to know why after two years of living with the man, this girl wanted respectability and the approval of Church and State.

'It's just that I want things to be fair and open . . .' she began.

'Really?' Father Flynn was doubtful.

'And, you see, my parents have discovered that I'm not a student any more. They thought I was going to college and now they're being a bit troublesome . . .'

'Yes, I'm sure.'

'And so, you see, I told them that I was going to marry Eddie, and now they're all delighted again and getting ready for the wedding, so that's what we have to organise.'

Father Flynn looked at her wildly. On this occasion he could not summon up one single word of comfort.

Neddy Nolan brought his father in to see the canon once a week. The two old men used to play chess together and Josef would serve them coffee and biscuits.

'Tell me, Canon, shouldn't we all be voting against this road if we get a chance?' Marty Nolan asked.

'I don't think we do get a chance.' Canon Cassidy's grasp on the matter was tenuous.

'But you know what I mean, Canon. Going to the meeting in the square and having banners, maybe. Don't we owe it to St Ann?'

'Why don't you ask Father Flynn, he's the brains of this parish,' the old man said.

'I did ask him, Canon, but he just went on about doing what our consciences told us to do.' Marty Nolan shook his head in disappointment. 'That's no use at all, suppose everyone's conscience told them something different. Where would we be then? It's guidance we need.'

'Do you know, Mr Nolan, I think the days of guidance are long gone. I never thought I'd live to hear myself say this but it appears to be true.'

'It's a great worry for us,' Marty Nolan said. 'You see, people are making us offers for the land and I know it has Neddy awake at night wondering what to do.'

'But nothing has been agreed yet. Why would people be offering to buy your land?' The canon was bewildered.

'I'm not sure, Canon, maybe they know more than we know. But you see the problem for Neddy. I mean, his own mother was cured at that well. No amount of money could ever pay for that.'

'Where is Neddy at the moment?' the canon said, possibly trying to change the subject. It worked.

'Ah, you know Neddy, Canon, always the dreamer. He's wandering around Rossmore interested in everything, understanding nothing.'

'Well, we'd better get on with our game of chess then,' the canon said. 'Was it my move or yours?'

Neddy Nolan was in fact in Myles Barry's law office. 'I've always been a bit slow, Myles,' he began.

'I wouldn't say that at all. Haven't you done very well for yourself, married a grand girl? Aren't you a friend to everyone in Rossmore?'

'Yes, but I might not be for much longer. All kinds of people are coming to me and suggesting we sell our property to them.'

'Well, isn't that good?'

'Not really, Myles. They must have inside information or whatever it's called. They must know that the road really is coming and will go over our land.' He looked very troubled.

'I know, Neddy, but isn't that the luck of the draw? It couldn't happen to a better family.' Myles Barry couldn't see where the problem lay.

'But I can't sell our land to speculators, people who are buying up bits here and there so that they can hold the authorities to ransom by cornering all the available acres. Then when the time comes they can hold out and eventually sell it on again at a huge profit to the government and the builders. That's not the kind of thing we want to be involved in.'

'Well, no . . . no . . .' Myles Barry wondered where this was leading.

'It's just a few of them have told me they are approaching you about it,' Neddy said anxiously.

Myles Barry played for time. 'That's a fact, Neddy. But it's not illegal, you know, to make an offer for someone's land. You name a price and they pay it, and you put the money in the bank, and they sell the land on later for more money, because they'll have lots of little bits here and there to offer. Or you refuse it and take less from the government when the time comes and that's that. It's the system. Where's the problem?'

'The problem is that it's all just about making money,' Neddy said.

Myles Barry sighed and decided to be very direct. 'Yes, it's true some clients have asked me to put in an offer to you but I said you'd need to get a solicitor of your own, and maybe an estate agent to advise you and I couldn't be acting as a sort of an intermediary and twisting your arm.'

'Could you be our solicitor, Myles? I've known you for ever. You were at school with my brother Kit.' Neddy's face was without guile.

'I could indeed be your lawyer, Neddy, but I suggest you get someone more high-powered than me. A big firm from Dublin maybe. There's serious money tied up in this. You'd want a really professional team working for you.'

'Is it that you don't want to let the other people down, Myles, by changing horses and representing me?' Neddy wanted to know.

'No, there would be no conflict of interests. Nobody has mentioned any sums involved. I have seen no papers or proposals. I just said I wouldn't do anything until you got representation.'

'So you could do it if you wanted to?' Neddy was distressingly direct.

Of course Myles Barry could. But there would be much more money in it for him if he were to represent a consortium of local businessmen. He couldn't charge Neddy Nolan and his father proper fees. Especially if things were as they looked and the Nolans were going to hold out. The land would be bought eventually if the road went ahead, which it looked very likely to. Those particular businessmen who had approached him would not have sought out the Nolan farm unless they knew something from the council. Myles Barry had been given to understand that any reasonable demand from the Nolans would be met.

Of course it was speculation. But that's how an economy worked. People took risks; they won or they lost. Only Neddy Nolan would see anything dubious about the whole system.

Myles Barry was only too aware that the rumours were going to become a reality and the heat was about to be turned on. Cathal Chambers in the bank had told him about two local councillors who were coming into the bank these days with large wads of cash that they wanted lodged in savings accounts. It was so obviously vote-buying, yet what could he do except invoke the law about banks needing to know where any lodged money came from? They looked him in the eye and told him that it was from poker games. The vote about the road when it came would be first at local council level, and then nationally. And it looked like a foregone conclusion.

Myles Barry looked at Neddy. He needed someone to look after his interests, to frighten off anyone trying to cheat him. 'Sure, Neddy,' he sighed. 'I'd be honoured to be your solicitor.'

Judy Flynn walked up to Whitethorn Woods on her own. She wore her best outfit, a navy silk dress with a navy and white scarf. Her newly streaked hair was elegant and shiny. She wanted to show St Ann the raw material for her quest.

In the cave were half a dozen people muttering and praying near the statue. Judy knelt down and got straight to business.

'I'm going to be completely honest with you, St Ann. I don't really know whether you exist or not, and, if you do exist, whether you deal with cases like this or not. But it's worth a try. I am going to come here and pray for peace on earth, or whatever you yourself think may be needed, for nine mornings in a row. And in return you are going to guide my steps towards meeting a man I can marry and have children with. You see, I do drawings all the time for children's books and yet I have no children of my own. And because of doing these drawings I sort of believe in magic, well, a magical world where marvellous things happen. So why shouldn't I find a husband in this place?

'Oh, and you'll want to know why I didn't find one already. That's easy. I looked in the wrong place. I looked in publishing and advertising and the media, that kind of world. Not the right base. What I would like is someone maybe from this town. Then I could help my brother Brian to look after our mam, I could help Kitty—I'm sure she's been up here asking you to get my brother Eddie to go back to her. Don't do it, it wouldn't work.

'I don't think that marriage is all about appearances and dressing well, but it's only fair to tell you that this is the best I can look. I am inclined to be a bit impatient and short-tempered but I think that I am keeping it under control. And that's it now. I'll say a rosary for your intentions and I'll come again tomorrow. I can't say fairer than that.'

Eddie Flynn came out of the bar in the Rossmore Hotel. Times were very worrying. He had a good business deal possibly going ahead with a gang of people who knew what they were doing. It should bring him in some very badly needed money. And did he need money just now!

Young Naomi had been telling her parents a pack of lies, saying she was a second-year student in Dublin. Now she was telling them more lies, saying that Eddie's marriage was going to be annulled and that he was going to marry her. It would never happen, not in a million years. The girl was soft in the head.

In many ways it would be easier to have stayed with Kitty. At least there was always a meal on the table when he got home, and there were the children to entertain him. But now they seemed to think he was some kind of rat who had deserted them. Kitty would let him take them to the pictures in the middle of the week, but young Naomi wanted to go out at weekends. And everyone was on his case about not going to see his mam enough.

He was weary of it all. If he went home now, Naomi would be there with pictures of wedding dresses and lists of the people they would invite. Apparently she had had a highly unsatisfactory conversation with Brian about it all and now thought they should go straight through the canon who would surely have a more helpful attitude.

On the other side of the road he saw Kitty. Or was it Kitty? Her hair was totally different and she was wearing make-up. He pulled back into the shadows and watched. It *was* Kitty. But she had done something to herself. She looked years younger.

He saw her talking animatedly to that poor Lilly Ryan, the one whose baby had been stolen all those years ago and then her husband had turned violent. Eddie watched as Kitty moved along the street. Life would be a great deal easier if he were going home to Kitty for his tea.

The march against the new road was held right through the town and up to the Whitethorn Woods. Some people carried posters with 'Save Our Saint' on them, others had 'No to the New Road'. Television teams and journalists from national newspapers came to cover it.

Father Brian Flynn knew he would have to make some kind of statement to someone. He couldn't sit like a dummy looking on. But he hated the thought of himself on national television. 'I have such desperate hair, I look like a lavatory brush,' he confided to his sister.

'Go to that man Fabian, he's brilliant,' Judy advised.

'Are you mad—you'd feed a family for a week on what he charges.'

'You don't have a family to feed. Go on, Brian, it's my treat,' she said.

He went into the salon feeling more foolish than he had ever felt in his whole life. He couldn't see what the guy who called himself Fabian actually did to him but he did look a lot more normal afterwards.

So he was interviewed and said that St Ann's Well was a place of local piety and it was always sad to see parishioners upset and their sensibilities offended.

Then a week later he was interviewed again. This time Father Flynn told the interviewer that the authorities had a duty to do all in their power to make sure that a young life was never lost again because of heavy traffic in Rossmore.

'I'm sure that anyone who saw both of those interviews will think I am a complete clown,' he said to Judy.

'No, they'll think that when you're in a hole you're right to stop digging,' Judy said.

She was proving to be a much more restful companion than he had feared. She said she knew it was mad but she was getting a lot of comfort from visits to that old well. She had also painted her mother's kitchen and had found her a kitten, which had cheered the old woman up—but not yet to the extent of admitting that she recognised Judy.

The brother and sister would have a drink together each evening in the Rossmore Hotel. Once they saw Eddie there and waved him to join them. Nobody mentioned Naomi, Kitty or Mother.

It was a perfectly pleasant chat.

'I think we're all getting seriously grown up round here,' Judy Flynn said afterwards.

'Oh, if only,' said Father Flynn. He saw immense problems ahead once the council's vote was known, which would be any day now.

The voices for and against the road, the voices from the woods, were only gathering their strength—they had seen nothing yet.

CHAPTER 6

Talking to Mercedes
Part 1—Helen

AH, THERE YOU ARE, Mercedes. I was having a little sleep there. I dreamed I was back in Rossmore, walking down the crowded main street. I often dream that. But you wouldn't know where it is, it's over in Ireland across the sea from here. Ireland is only fifty minutes on a plane from London. You should go there some time. You'd like it there, you're religious and it's very Catholic. Well, it was anyway.

I've always liked you, Mercedes, much better than the day nurses—you have more time for people. You listen. They don't listen, it's sit up and wake up and get up and cheer up. You never say that.

You have a nice cool hand, you smell of lavender, not of some disinfectant. You are interested.

You say your name is Mercedes and that you would like to marry a doctor. You would like to send your mother more money. But it took me weeks to find even that out about you, Mercedes, because you only want to talk about me and how I feel.

I wish you would call me Helen rather than Madam. Please don't call me Mrs Harris. You are so friendly, so interested in my family who come to visit. My tall, handsome husband James, my gracious mother-in-law Natasha, my wonderful, beautiful daughter Grace.

You ask me all kinds of questions about them and I tell you, it's a pleasure to tell you things. You smile so much. And you aren't curious and act like the police, always asking questions. That's what David seems like to me. You know David, he is Grace's boyfriend. I think you sense that about him, you often move him gently on when he is here. You know that he distresses me.

But you I could talk to for ever.

You love the story about the night I met handsome James Harris twenty-seven years ago when I borrowed my flatmate's dress to go to a party. He said that it was the same colour as my eyes and that I must be very artistic. In fact it was the only dress we had between us that was smart enough for me to wear!

I told you the truth about that, and about how fearful I was about meeting his mother Natasha for the first time. Their home was so big and impressive, her questions so probing. I told you the truth about a lot of things, about how kind they always were to me in the orphanage where I grew up and how they insisted on making my wedding cake. Natasha had objected at first because she thought it would be amateurish, but even she was pleasantly surprised.

I went back to see them often at the orphanage. They told me I was the only child in the home who didn't ask about my parents. But I wanted to know nothing. This was my home. Someone had given me, Helen, away, no doubt for good reasons at the time. What more was there to ask? To know?

I haven't told the Sisters there that I am so ill, Mercedes. I told them that I'm going abroad with James and will be in touch later. I have left them something in my will and a letter of thanks. It's important that people be thanked for what they do. Really it is. Otherwise they might never know how much they are appreciated. Like you, for example. I thank you a lot because I am truly grateful to meet someone who will listen to me and be so interested in my story.

You who have worked so hard and saved so much would understand how hard I too worked when I did my secretarial course here in London. I used to read novels about people like James, but I didn't believe they really existed. He was such a gentleman in every sense. He never raised his voice, he was always courteous, he had a way of smiling that lit up his whole face. I was determined to marry him and I hid nothing about my past. I did not want his mother Natasha investigating and discovering things about little Helen from the orphanage, so I was totally up-front about everything. And it paid off. Natasha finally agreed to the wedding.

I was a beautiful bride. Did I show you the pictures? Of course I did. I just wanted to look at them once more.

All we were waiting for was a child, but after three years there was no sign of my becoming pregnant. We needed a child who would one day inherit the family estate. I was anxious, James was concerned, and Natasha was incensed.

I went to a doctor in a completely different part of London and had an examination. I wasn't ovulating, it turned out, so I would need fertility treatment. I knew only too well that James would object to this. If it were proven that he was well capable of fathering a child, but that his wife could not conceive, things would change between us. If Natasha were to find out, then the world as we knew it now would end.

So I realised there was no way James and I could go together like normal couples who had problems conceiving and could have *in vitro* treatment. Nor could I go on my own to have artificial insemination. It didn't work like that apparently.

James wouldn't consider surrogate parenting, so there was no point in discussing it. Nor adoption, even if there had been any children to adopt. No, Mercedes, you are very kind but I'm not upsetting myself, no, I'm just trying to explain it all to you. You see, I want to tell you this, I need to tell you.

Yes, I will have a sip of tea, thank you so much, my dear. You are always there when people need you.

So, as I was saying, I had to think what to do next.

Now this was twenty-three years ago, you were only a little toddler then, running around in the sunshine in the Philippines. But I was here in London, worried out of my mind.

I had always been good at finding solutions, though. One of the girls at work had been on a holiday in Dublin, over in Ireland, and when they were there they had gone to this place, Rossmore. It was a small but beautiful town, with an old castle and a forest called Whitethorn Woods, where there was a wishing well. St Ann's Well it was, actually. That's who it was, St Ann, the mother of Mary who was the mother of Jesus, but you'd know all about her, being Catholic, Mercedes. People went to pray to St Ann and they got their wishes answered. They left things there to thank her.

What did they wish for? I wondered.

Everything apparently, the saint had a big job on her hands. People prayed for husbands and for cures from illness, and for babies. There were lots of little baby bootees and things tied to the thorny bushes, put there by people wanting babies of their own. Imagine!

Well, I did imagine. These people wouldn't have gone on praying unless there had been results. That is where I would find our child. So next time James went away on a business trip, I took a couple of days off work and sneaked over to Ireland, where I took a bus to Rossmore.

It was extraordinary, the whole thing. Just a mile out of town there were dozens of people at the well, each person with their own story. There was this old woman asking that her son, who was a drug addict, would get cured, and then there was a young girl praying that her boyfriend would not hear that she'd had a stupid fling with another man, and a fourteen-year-old boy was asking that his father would go off the drink.

So I closed my eyes and I spoke to this saint and I said I'd go straight back to my religion, which I had sort of forgotten about since I met James and Natasha, if she would arrange for me to get pregnant. It was very peaceful there, and anything seemed possible. And I felt so sure she would arrange it.

Until the afternoon bus came, I spent the day looking around Rossmore. There wasn't much traffic back then, you could walk about easily. I believe it's changed now. Everyone seemed to know each other, greeting one another in Castle Street, which was the main street.

There were a lot of families, I noticed, and many of the parents left their children sort of parked outside shops, since the prams were too big and bulky to take in. Passers-by would pause to admire the chubby babies in prams. Dozens of them. Soon I would have our baby in a pram, James's and my baby. Natasha's grandchild. And when we did, we would never leave the child out of our sight.

I went back home and the months went on and on, with no sign of any intervention on St Ann's part. I looked back with rage at my useless trip over to her well. I kept thinking of that town where the parents just left their babies for all to see in the main street without anyone to mind them, while so many of the rest of us were aching for a child.

That's when I got the idea.

I would go to Ireland, find a pram and bring our baby home. It didn't matter if it was a boy or a girl. If we'd had our own child we couldn't have chosen anyway so this made it more natural somehow.

It needed a lot of planning. There was more chance of being spotted on a plane or at an airport than on a ferry. So I made my plans to go by sea. I told James that I was pregnant, and that I had gone to an all-women-doctors' clinic, and that I preferred it this way. He was totally understanding and, of course, delighted with my great news.

I begged him not to tell his mother yet. Said that I needed time. He agreed that it should be our secret until we were sure that everything was on course. After three months I said that I now preferred to sleep alone. He agreed reluctantly.

I read all the symptoms of pregnancy and acted accordingly. I went to a theatrical costumier and got a special mould made to simulate a pregnant stomach. I explained that it had to look good under a night-dress for my stage part.

Natasha was overjoyed. When she came to lunch on Sundays she even helped me clear the dishes instead of sitting there like a stone.

'Helen, my dear, dear girl, you have no idea how happy this makes me,' she said, laying her hand on my stomach. 'When will we feel the baby kick, do you think?'

I said I would ask them at the clinic.

I realised that I would have to go away around the time of the so-called birth. I told James and Natasha that there was something about approaching motherhood that made me nostalgic for the orphanage, the only home I remembered. James wanted to come with me but I said that this was a journey I needed to make on my own. I would be back in a week, long before the baby was due.

I had already begun my maternity leave from the office, but it took a lot of persuasion before James and Natasha let me go.

I drove to the orphanage where the sisters were delighted with my pregnancy. The next day I left them and drove to the ferry terminal. I parked my car there, put on a wig, then whipped off my false tummy and put it in the boot of the car. I had bought a cheap raincoat, a blanket and a lifelike doll. I was ready.

I wanted to make sure that if there was a hue and cry in Ireland, nobody would be alerted to a woman with a baby boarding a boat for the UK—someone else would be sure to mention having seen her arriving with a baby too. I sat out in the open air cuddling the doll.

One or two other mothers approached me to have a look at the baby, but I said apologetically that she didn't like strangers. You see, I had already begun to think of 'the baby' as my daughter.

I caught a bus from the ferry terminal to Rossmore, cuddling the doll very close to me. It was a busy Saturday in the town and I walked the length of Castle Street until my feet were sore. I did some shopping as well: talcum powder, nappies, soothing creams. As on my last visit, there were many prams sitting outside stores. Innocent, trusting people in a safe town, some might say. Criminally careless, neglectful parents who didn't deserve children, was what I said.

I had to be careful. The bus that I must catch would leave at three, arriving at the ferry two hours later. I must take the baby just before the bus left, no earlier, no point in giving the authorities time to search.

It's strange, I could almost draw a picture of the people in the crowded street that day. I remember an old priest, wearing a black soutane, shaking the hands of all who passed him. Half the population seemed to be out shopping.

I was standing on the steps of the Rossmore Hotel when I noticed a pram had been parked on the other side of the road. A small Yorkshire terrier was tied by his lead to the handle. I crossed over and saw that a baby was lying asleep inside. It was all over in seconds: the doll was in a litter bin and the baby was in my arms, wrapped in my blanket. Its eyes were tightly closed but I could hear a little heart beating close to mine. It all felt right, as if it were meant to happen. As if in some curious way St Ann had led me to this child.

I got on the bus and looked back for one last time at Rossmore. The bus bumped across-country to the ferry and then I moved with my baby onto the boat. I would have been well away long before the alarm was raised. And who would have thought to search the ferries immediately anyway? I must have been settled in my car and on my way back to London by the time the authorities realised that this was a full-blown child abduction.

I had done what I set out to do: I had found my child. A little girl who would be called Grace Natasha. She must be about two weeks old. It was despicable, leaving a child that age to fare for herself, I told myself. It was better by far that I had come along to claim her, to give her a better life. No one could find me now, I told myself, as I prepared her first formula bottle on a spirit stove at the back of the car.

And the wonderful thing, Mercedes, was that nobody ever did. I had it all very well sorted out, you see.

I reinstated my false tummy, and left the baby in the car while I checked into a shabby guest house. During the middle of the night I pretended to wake with labour pains and insisted on driving myself to the hospital. In fact I drove back to my orphanage. I told them that I had delivered the baby myself and needed them to look after me for a couple of days until I recovered from the shock.

One of the staff said that I couldn't possibly have had this baby since I'd been there a day or two before. This was a two-week-old baby.

Another wanted to get me a doctor. But these were women I had lived with for seventeen years of my life. And they loved me, don't forget.

They knew—of course they knew. Maybe they should have reported me; I suppose you could say that. But they must have thought that I'd bought the baby and I was hiding it from my rather grand husband and mother-in-law. Anyway, they went along with the fiction.

I burned the false stomach, the wig and the cheap raincoat in their incinerator. They called James to tell him he had a daughter, and he called Natasha to tell her she had a granddaughter.

James cried on the telephone. He told me that he loved me more than ever and he would look after us both for the rest of his life. And Grace slept on, delighted with herself and everyone, and never caused anyone any trouble for twenty-three years.

She is a strong girl with a forceful character. She is so like me in the way she behaves. She is my daughter in every sense of the word.

You've seen that for yourself, Mercedes. No, I did not enquire about the family who lost her in Ireland. They have different newspapers over there, so I didn't have to read about it either. No, of course I would never tell Grace, never in a million years.

She's got a boyfriend now. His name is David . . . but of course you know. James isn't crazy about the boy. He doesn't say it but I know. I don't like him very much, but he's Grace's choice and so I say nothing.

David is Irish, as it happens. Extraordinary, isn't it! Grace has never been over there . . . not yet anyway. But I had a real scare yesterday when out of the blue David started saying that there is this big drama going on in Ireland about a roadway that's going to bypass Rossmore. Huge protests about it, apparently.

'Rossmore?' I said, with my blood turning into ice.

'Yeah, a one-horse town back of beyond. Much better bypassed. No one would have any call to go there.'

I raked my eyes across his face. Suppose he was actually from Rossmore? Suppose that it was his sister who had disappeared from her pram? Could it possibly be that he and Grace were brother and sister?

I felt very faint. I asked myself, why would he mention that town of all towns unless there was some connection? Perhaps he had been tracking me down for years. I had to know.

'Have you ever been there yourself, David?' I asked.

But no, he said he'd probably passed through it on the way to the west of Ireland but he had never stopped. He and Grace had been talking about it, because of something there that might be of interest.

Grace looked at him adoringly. 'I'll tell you what we were talking about, Mother—David was telling me that there's a sort of shrine there, a wishing well or something. And, you know, people get cured there . . .' She looked at me hopefully.

'No, Grace, and David, thank you, but I'm fine,' I said. 'Those places don't really work, you know.'

'But they say that they work in some fashion, Mother. People who go there get strength and confidence, they often feel better.'

'I took what I could . . .' I began and then I saw all of them looking at me. 'I took what I could from everything and it made me very strong. I feel absolutely fine,' I said firmly.

And Grace lifted my thin hand and kissed it.

Her grandmother is settling all this money on her in two years' time when she's twenty-five. She will have the whole Harris estate. What would she have had if I had left her in that pram with the dog tied to the handle? I won't be here to see her inherit everything, of course, but that doesn't matter. I gave her a good start in life. I did everything a mother could do. For her, for her father, for her grandmother.

I have nothing to blame myself for. I never told James a lie in my life except this one, and I did it from love. We have had such a wonderful marriage, I know in my heart that he has never told me a lie. Not ever. But as I say, I have nothing to blame myself for.

Stop crying, Mercedes, please stop. You're meant to be helping me to feel strong. Things are hard enough without having the nurses getting all weepy.

That's better. That's the smile I like.

And maybe if there's a little more tea, do you think?

Part 2—James

MUMMY ALWAYS TELEPHONES me at 9 a.m. A lot of people think that's rather odd but I find it quite reassuring. It means that I don't have to remember to phone her and that I am kept up to date with all that's happening in her world, which is full of writers and lawyers, bankers and politicians, and always interesting.

We live a very quiet life, Helen and I, so it's entertaining to hear first-hand about the kind of people you might only read about in the newspapers. Helen never answers the phone at that time because we both know it's Mummy. Not that Helen doesn't like talking to her, they get on very well and Helen is utterly charming to her. From the beginning she was the one who decided that we must make Mummy part of our lives, invite her to Sunday lunch with us once a week.

Mummy came round to Helen very quickly—after some initial doubts, shall we say. She was genuinely admiring of someone so direct and unaffected as Helen.

She also knew that I had never loved anyone before and would never love anyone again. I had made it very clear that Helen would be my wife very soon after I first met her, wearing a dress exactly the same colour as her blue eyes.

When I was younger, the family had always wanted me to work in the City like Father had. But I hated the whole idea. Instead I insisted on serving my time with an antiques dealer. I did history of art courses and shortly after I married Helen my career took off like a rocket. Helen taught me to dress smartly, rather than in the slightly fuddy-duddy clothes I used to wear, and to present myself more forcefully. She encouraged me to give little talks on eighteenth-century furniture, and to let the press know when I had something interesting to sell. My antique shops are all over the country now, and I appear regularly on television as an expert.

I have made my own way and I am very proud of that. Just as I was proud of marrying Helen. We had our twenty-sixth wedding anniversary a few days ago and Mummy, Grace and I took some crystal champagne glasses into the hospital. Helen looked quite as beautiful as the day we were married. She even pretended to drink a little champagne.

After that we went out to dinner: Mummy, Grace and I. The three of us went to a small French restaurant that Helen and I used to go to a lot before she became ill. Fortunately Grace hadn't insisted that the loutish David come with us.

Mummy proposed a toast. 'To one of the happiest marriages I have ever known.' she said in one of her tinkly voices. I smiled a gentle, knowing smile. This was the same woman who had railed and wept at me over a quarter of a century ago, begging me not to marry a girl of whom we knew nothing, except that she'd been given to an orphanage.

I couldn't taste the food, it could have been chopped-up cardboard. The sense of unfairness welled up in me again. Why was this marriage drawing to a close? Next year, next month even, we would be talking about my late wife. What reason could there be that Helen who had never hurt a fly was dying, and others whose lives had been full of malevolence and greed were allowed to live on? Why was I here at this table when I wanted to be by Helen's bed holding her hand, telling her that our marriage had been a magical time?

But that Filipino woman—Mercedes, the one with the big, sad eyes—had kept assuring me that Helen would be happy tonight. Apparently, Helen had talked about her family a lot today and had taken out pictures of our wedding day, and snaps of Grace when she was a little girl. And I know that she had wanted me to go out and have a happy dinner with my mother and Grace. She had said it was the one thing I could do to help her, I must keep the show on the road.

My mother did not look her seventy-something years. She was a credit to her hairdresser, her beauty salon and her own good taste in clothes. She wore a lilac dress and jacket that suited her perfectly.

Grace with her blonde hair and dark eyes was always striking. But tonight in a scarlet dress with those little straps she looked dazzling. Much too good for that David fellow, too beautiful and too bright, but I would not go down that road . . .

She was still talking about David. When was she not? He worked in the City too. People said he was bright. Bright in the sense of having native cunning. Like a bookie at a race track, not like the accountants, bankers and financial experts with whom Grace moved with such ease.

No, indeed, young David was a different breed. But there was no doubt that Grace loved him. She had never brought anyone home before this.

'David was in to see Mother today.' Grace spoke his name as if she loved saying it. 'He said, wasn't it extraordinary that I looked so different from both of you. He's the image of his father, of course; they have the same nose and mouth, the same way of pushing hair out of their eyes.'

I restrained myself from saying that this must be unfortunate for both of them, and managed a weak little sign of interest.

'And what did your mother say?' I asked.

'Oh, you know Mother. She said she agreed with him, then she wasn't feeling so well so she called for Mercedes.'

'It wasn't the boy's fault, the pain comes and goes for Helen, we were told that,' my mother said. Astoundingly Natasha has always stood up for the young pup.

'And she was fine later, Dad, for the little anniversary ceremony, wasn't she?' Grace's big dark eyes looked at me questioningly.

'Yes, she was fine,' I managed to say.

I managed a lot of things in the next hour. Like smiling at my mother and my daughter, and telling them little stories about happier times. And then finally my mother was back in her tall town house, and my daughter was back in her flat, where undoubtedly that David, who looked so like his father, would come and sleep in her bed.

And I was free. Free at last to go and see Helen.

They let you in at any time. That was the great thing about having enough money for private medicine. I could just push through those big quiet doors into the lobby which looked more like a grand hotel than a hospital. The night receptionist greeted me pleasantly.

'If she's asleep I promise you that I won't disturb her,' I said with my practised smile.

Helen and I had often talked about how we have to pretend a lot of the time in life. We sighed over it and told each other that at least we never pretended with each other. But we did. The biggest pretence of all was between the two of us.

She never told me about Grace and I never told her that I knew. That I had always known.

I had known since the time I went into her room during the so-called pregnancy when she had said she preferred to sleep alone. She was tossing in her sleep, with the sheets cast aside, and I put my hand on her forehead to reassure her. And then I saw it. The white garment with the foam belly attached to it, which she was wearing under her nightdress.

The shock was overwhelming. Helen, my wife, was lying to me. But it was followed by an aftershock of sympathy and love. The poor, poor woman, how terrified she must be of my mother and, indeed, of me that she would go to such extremes. And what was she going to do when the time came, or rather when she told us that her time had come?

Possibly she had arranged to buy a child from somewhere. But why hadn't she told me? I would have shared anything, everything with her. Why could she not have told me?

I went back to my room that night full of alarm. What did she intend to do without me by her side? I knew I had to wait. I had to let her go ahead. Nothing would be worse than her humiliation if I were to let her know that I had discovered her deception.

As time went on, Helen looked pale and anxious. Mummy put it down to her pregnancy, but I knew that there was a greater reason. I was very relieved in the end when she said that she wanted to go back to visit her old orphanage, the place where she had been brought up. I guessed this was the place where she would find a baby and pretend that it was ours.

It surprised and shocked me that a respectable institution like that would go along with her in such a subterfuge. It was against the law, and it was against everything they stood for. Surely they would have found a legal way for Helen to adopt a child rather than be a party to all this deception? But I knew they would always look out for Helen. There were still women there who had been on the staff when she was a baby herself. They would have nothing but compassion and pity for her.

So when I heard the news that our baby had been born suddenly—a little girl, strong and lovely, and that everyone was being so helpful, I started to breathe again.

When Helen returned home, I realised that Grace had to be older than the tender age that Helen claimed her to be. But I reminded everyone that I too had been a very big child at birth and, amazingly, my mother agreed and said that I was quite mountainous.

Helen gave no descriptions of the delivery. It had all passed in a blur, she said, but now that she held her little Grace to her it didn't seem important, and wasn't she lucky that she had been with people who knew how to help her. I glossed over the whole birth registration business, easily filling in documents here and signing my name there.

Nobody thought it was unusual. Well, why would they? They had seen Helen over the last six months swelling gently, planning the birth of her child.

Only I knew and I would never tell.

I walked along the carpeted hospital corridors to Helen's room. I had only one more thing to tell her, which was that her secret would be safe with me. That it didn't matter one damn what that foolish, insensitive boyfriend David said, no one would ever know that Grace wasn't our daughter. But I couldn't tell her straight out. I would sit and look at her and it would come to me. I would know what to say.

The room was dark, just a small light and the big shape of the Filipino woman, Mercedes, sitting beside her. Mercedes was holding Helen's hand. Helen's eyes were closed.

'Mr Harris!' Mercedes was surprised to see me.

'Is she awake?' I asked.

She was asleep apparently; she had just had her cocktail of drugs. The palliative care nurse had been half an hour ago.

'I believe that David upset her today.'

'She didn't say, Mr Harris. She told me only of you bringing in champagne for her wedding anniversary.'

I asked, could I sit with her alone. Apparently not. She was to be watched all night. They were worried about her chest.

I sat by her bed for two hours, stroking her thin white hand. They must expect her to die today or tomorrow if there was a twenty-four-hour watch arranged.

At last Helen opened her eyes and smiled at me. Mercedes moved across the room to allow us some privacy.

'I thought you were at dinner.' Helen's words came with difficulty.

'I was, it was wonderful,' I said. I told her we talked about lots of things and I reported Grace telling us that David had said, wasn't it odd that Grace had dark eyes while we were both fair? And I told Grace that she must have got her dark eyes from my father, who'd had eyes as black as soot. And Mummy had agreed and even added that Grace could also have got the dark eyes from Helen's side of the family. It was just that we didn't know them.

Helen looked at me long and hard. 'You don't like him,' she croaked at me. 'You can't fool me, James, we never lied to each other, not once, remember?'

'I know.'

And then I told her the last lie.

'I don't really *dislike* him, my darling. It's just that I love my little girl so much nobody will ever be good enough for her. She's my daughter, my flesh and blood: nothing can make me think any other man will make her happy like we did.'

And Helen's smile was wonderful. I could have looked at it for ever but something changed in her face and Mercedes was about to go for the Sister.

Before she left the room she said to me: 'You are a wonderful man, Mr Harris. You made your wife very happy by what you said.'

And even though it's utterly ridiculous, I felt for a moment that she knew our secret. That she knew all about Grace. But, of course, that's not possible.

Helen would never have told her. Not in a million years.

CHAPTER 7

Going to the Pub
Part 1—Poppy

WHEN I WAS YOUNG our gran lived with us and we adored her. She was far more entertaining than our parents, having been around so long and having seen so much, and she understood things. She used to take Jane and myself on long rambles through Whitethorn Woods, always finding something interesting to show us. Like a treehouse built years ago by her brothers, or how to press flowers in a book, or best of all St Ann's

Well. She said we must never laugh at the people who prayed there because one day we would undoubtedly come here to pray ourselves.

When she was young she'd thought they were all mad to mumble and mutter and leave mementoes, but it became comforting once you got older. She taught us to listen to people. Well, she taught me anyway. That's probably where I got the idea of working with older people.

It wasn't met with much enthusiasm at home.

'You'll have to get some kind of qualification first,' my dad said.

'Old people can be very demanding,' my mum said.

'You'll never meet a fellow if you get stuck in geriatrics,' said my elder sister Jane.

Jane had turned out to be very different to me—she wore blusher and eye shadow and had a steam iron for her own clothes. She took great care of her shoes, always stuffing them with newspaper. My friends and I called her Elegant Jane.

Even though they were all against the idea at home I took no notice, because, to be honest, they were pretty negative about everything. I applied to train as a nurse at the hospital in Rossmore, and when I had qualified I asked to work on the wards with the elderly.

And there I met marvellous people and got huge advice about life from them all. One man taught me all about stocks and shares, another all about planting window boxes, one old lady who had had seven proposals of marriage told me how to attract men, and another taught me how to polish copper. So I was well advanced in the ways of the world by the time I saw the advertisement for a matron in a place called Ferns and Heathers five miles outside Rossmore.

The old house had once been owned by two marvellous dotty old dears who were obsessed with gardening. After their death, it had become a nursing home and the garden was now neglected.

I was thirty-seven and I had put all the advice I'd been given to good use. I had a small but satisfactory portfolio of shares. Men had certainly fallen in love with me, but unfortunately I had married a man called Oliver, who fell in love rather too easily and too often, so I had left him after a year of marriage.

I had copper saucepans that shone like jewels. I could make anything grow in a window box and had very successful year-round garden colour. None of these things were really qualifications for the job of matron at Ferns and Heathers, but I was a well-qualified nurse and enthusiastic so the four directors liked me at the interview and I got the job. A little cottage went with the post.

As soon as I was appointed I went to meet the staff and the people for whom Ferns and Heathers was home. The residents seemed a happy enough group. They had liked the previous matron, who had left to work in television apparently.

'I hope that you're not going to use this place as a jumping-off ground to a media career like she did,' grumbled Garry who, I could tell, was going to be the mouthpiece of any discontent.

'No. If I'd wanted to go that route I'd have done so,' I said cheerfully.

'Or go away and get married on us?' a frail woman called Eve asked fretfully. I put her down in my mind as a worrier.

'Married? Oh, no, I've been there and done that,' I said.

They looked at me open-mouthed. They had probably been used to a more genteel approach.

I asked, would everyone mind wearing name badges for the first three days and that if I didn't know everyone by then, well, it meant I wasn't up to the job. I told them my name was Poppy. I agreed it was a deeply silly name but there's a worse one on my birth certificate so, if they could get their heads round it, Poppy it would be. I said I loved to listen and learn and if any of them had any ideas I'd be thrilled.

They seemed to like that. I could hear them saying that I was unusual anyway, as they went off to their tea. I looked around the place that was going to be my new home with some pleasure. The home that I had grown up in was becoming ever more remote. I realised this when I didn't feel any need to ring my dad and mum about the new job. I didn't feel like listening to all the negative things they would say. They would tell me what a huge responsibility it all was and that if any of these people broke their hips, or something, it would be my fault.

I certainly didn't ring my sister Jane because she would tell me yet again that there was nothing wrong with Oliver, who was handsome and wealthy, and that I had been foolish to throw him out, and that all men wandered a little. It was in their nature.

I didn't ring Oliver because I never rang him.

I rang my best friend Grania, who was also my lawyer, and who had helped me deal with the contracts for Ferns and Heathers. I told her that the place was fine and she must come and see me.

'I might be coming over sooner than you think,' Grania said. 'My dad has been told he shouldn't be living on his own.'

Grania's father, Dan Green, was a marvellous man. I had always enjoyed going to their house. He was unfailingly cheerful, with a big red face and a loud laugh.

'I would love to have him in Ferns and Heathers,' I told Grania. I said I'd make a room ready for him as soon as she wanted.

'That's the problem,' she sighed. 'He says he hasn't a notion of going into any kind of home, he's staying put and going to the pub every night for a pint. The problem is that he can't do it any more, Poppy.' She sounded very upset.

'There's got to be a way round it,' I said. 'Invite him here for tea some day—I won't do the hard sell.'

'I'll try.' Grania didn't have much hope.

One of my first tasks at Ferns and Heathers was to reclaim the neglected gardens. 'A happy matron is a good matron,' I told the residents. 'And I am deeply unhappy with our garden. I'm going to need help with planting the beds.'

Garry said that they paid good money to be in this place and he had no intention of working with earth and dirtying his hands. So I said, fine, of course he must do as he pleased. But when he heard all the laughter and the reading aloud of seed packets, and saw the examination of bedding plants, not to mention the glasses of iced tea I prepared for the gardeners, he changed his tune.

As a reward I gave them all a window box each and supervised their planting. It became highly competitive and they all asked their visitors to bring them something exotic from the garden centre. By the time the board made its first visitation, we were seriously discussing a little water feature. It was all going very well.

Then Grania brought her father to visit.

Dan Green was still a jolly man, but he had been weakened by illness and he was no fool. He realised that he couldn't live alone for much longer, though he knew he couldn't live with Grania and her big family. We walked in the garden together and I showed him all the planting and told him that when the winter came we were going to have painting classes and maybe an exhibition of our work.

'You want me to come and live here, Poppy, don't you?' he said. 'I can read you like a book, you've been Grania's friend since you were ten. If I were to go anywhere it would be here, but I can't. I really am not able to give up what I like best: going to the pub for a drink every evening.'

'You can drink here, Dan. I do, believe me. You could come and have a glass of wine every evening.'

'No, it's not the same,' he said, really testily as if this was an argument he had fought many times before. 'Women never understand about going to the pub. It's the draught beer, the whole ritual of the thing.'

And he was right. I didn't understand it. Why not buy a few beers and go to a friend's house or invite them to yours? But it wasn't the time to argue this down to the bone with Dan Green.

I moved to safer waters. I told him about the new big flat-screen television we had and how we were going to make another room into a real old-fashioned cinema. I told him how we had set up the library with a huge notice saying SILENCE and the daily papers laid out for all to read.

I explained that every week a minibus came and took us up to Whitethorn Woods and how I told them my gran's tales, and those from round here shared their own memories, and we collected bark and leaves and flowers. I introduced him to Maturity, the marvellous shaggy dog that had been given to us by a local who had needed to find a home for the animal. Maturity was the perfect old people's home dog, allowing everyone to fondle him and pat his head.

I showed Dan the hens in the backyard, which were my pride and joy—seven White Leghorns, each with a name and a laying record, clucking about happily in a coop. He was quite interested in all this but still he assured me that no inducement would work—Ferns and Heathers was too far from a pub. Nothing wrong with the place apart from its location. It was five miles from Rossmore and civilisation.

I didn't think of Dan for a couple of weeks until Grania told me that he had had a bad fall and was in hospital. When he came out he would need looking after. 'Please, Poppy,' she begged me, 'would you take him? Just for a couple of weeks until I can see what can be done?'

There was only one big corner room available. I had been going to make it into a music room, but now I fixed it up for Dan. When he arrived, he was very down and showed no interest whatsoever in meeting any of his fellow residents. There was no sign of his loud laugh and his big red face seemed smaller and grey. But, as it happened, I couldn't give him much attention. There was too much else happening.

Garry, the voice of any dissident opinion, had led a protest against Dan getting a bigger room than anyone else. Eve, who worried about everything, said that some of the new books for the library included real hard-core pornography. The board of Ferns and Heathers announced that one of their number was going to cash in his shares and they needed to do a detailed examination of the home in order to establish its worth.

So I sent Garry in to talk to Dan face to face. I knew Dan would explain that he had no intention of staying permanently and that this would calm Garry down. I went with Eve to examine the hard-core pornography, which turned out to be a few innocent bodice rippers. I told the board that I would be very happy to bid for a quarter-share in Ferns and Heathers once they had done their valuation. I also said that they were free to come at any time so long as they didn't disturb the residents.

It all worked really well: Dan and Garry became fast friends; Eve started a feminist group in Ferns and Heathers to see whether anyone could understand the psyche of men since they were basically decent, just confused. And the board came on a secret inspection to see Ferns and Heathers one day, when we were out at the woods, and pronounced themselves very pleased and asked me for an enormous sum for twenty-five per cent of the business.

But I was ready for them. I explained that my buying into it would ensure my continued presence there. I listed the improvements I had made and hinted at further planned developments. I asked them to speak freely to the residents to enquire how they would view continuing to live here if I had moved on. Grimly they agreed that as I had contributed so much already to the whole project, my financial input would be considerably less than they had originally suggested.

'You are quite unorthodox, Poppy,' they said. 'Just make sure that Ferns and Heathers keeps its licence, that no one breaks the rules.'

I didn't think we had broken any rules to date, but there was something niggling at the back of my mind. It had to do with Grania's father. Dan was somehow too cheerful. I would have to keep an eye on him. There was no way that he could go out to a pub. The nearest one was four miles away and if he were to take a taxi I would have known in ten seconds. And yet he had returned to his previous good form and florid complexion.

When Dan had decided to stay on he had gone back to his own place for his possessions. We had offered to help him install them but he had said no. If he were to have any dignity he must be allowed to put his own few bits and pieces around the place himself. His new friend Garry would help him, he said.

We believe that our residents should indeed have as much independence and dignity as possible, so of course we agreed. There was a bit of hammering but nothing untoward. He had an old sideboard with a mirror at the back of it, some hunting prints, a notice board, a dartboard on the back of the door. There were some vague furniture shapes covered with rugs and velvet cloths. Cupboards, chests of drawers possibly?

But his room was so big there was plenty of space for them all. And Dan said he had brought a few folding chairs in case he invited people in, and two high stools which he used as stands for vases of flowers. I noticed that before lunch several people would drop in to Dan's room for half an hour, and again in the evening.

The women had started to dress slightly better. They had their hair done more regularly by our visiting stylist, even put on jewellery and perfume. The men wore cravats sometimes and slicked down their hair.

It took me longer than it should have done to work out that Dan had set up a pub in his room. He had optic measures fitted into his sideboard. The rug-covered furniture had been turned into a counter. The vases were taken off the high stools, and the chairs were assembled round occasional tables.

Eve would have a small dry martini, some of the other ladies had thimble-sized glasses of sherry, and the men mainly had beer taken from a metal barrel, well disguised during non-pub hours as a giant magazine stand.

How did I discover this?

By spying on them.

And what I discovered looked a very happy scene. They were never drunk and it was doing nobody any harm. But of course they were breaking the law. You are not actually allowed to sell intoxicating liquor without a licence. Anywhere. And certainly not at a nursing home where there are all kinds of rules and regulations and none of them include allowing the residents to have a cash bar.

But they were enjoying it so much. It would be a shame to end it. I resolved that I must never know about it. So whenever any member of the staff began to tell me that maybe I ought to know something, I managed to avoid hearing it. The board continued to visit and I always managed to let Dan know what day they were coming well in advance, since they sometimes called on residents to know how they were getting along and I didn't want them to arrive when the cocktail hour was at full throttle. In time, another board member sold out and I now owned half the nursing home.

One day, after our successful art exhibition, I went for a walk by myself in the woods, accompanied by Maturity, who found something interesting at every turn. As we arrived at the well, I saw notices around it about the intended road.

We won't let them take you away, St Ann, said one of them. Another had a pencil attached and asked people who opposed the huge highway to add their names to a list below. I was going to put my name on it. Most of my people back at the home were against the change. Then I wondered, might it in fact mean that some of my residents would get more visitors if all that traffic congestion was eased?

At that very moment my mobile phone rang. There was a bit of sighing around me, as if to say that nowhere was sacred these days.

It was the home. Three inspectors from the Health Board had arrived unannounced. I had to think quickly. I looked up at the statue for some advice. 'Come on, St Ann, you didn't do much for me in the husband stakes,' I said. 'Get me out of this one anyway.'

Then I asked to be put through to Dan's room. 'Mr Green?' I said with as much authority as I could muster. 'Mr Green, there's been a little change of plan. I won't be able to join you and discuss your artwork with you as arranged. I wonder if I could ask you all to go almost at once to the dining room. You see, some health inspectors have arrived and I'm not in the building. I'll be back shortly and I want to show them around. It would be a great ease to me if I could know that everyone was heading for lunch. Having of course cleared up all your artwork before you leave, if you know what I mean. Thank you so much for being cooperative, Mr Green.' I hung up.

Dan would do it. Maturity and I raced back to the car and I drove like the wind back to Ferns and Heathers. The inspectors were having coffee and shortbread in the hall. They were looking at the exhibition of local flora in glass cases and studying the notices on the wall about upcoming cookery demonstrations, a matinée showing of *Brief Encounter*, which was a regular favourite, and a debate on the new road.

I apologised for not being there and suggested a tour of the premises. As I was leading the inspectors along the ground floor I saw the little line of lunchtime drinkers full of giggles heading for the dining room. Not even the flappers who drank bathtub gin during Prohibition could have had as much fun as they were having.

All I had to do now was make sure that Dan never acknowledged what I had done: how I had saved his pub enterprise and my home.

'Afternoon, Poppy,' he said cheerfully. Then he nodded at the inspectors. 'Fantastic place this, but my God, she's a stickler for law and order. Every bylaw has to be observed: fire drill, hygiene, you name it. Still we all like it here and that's saying something, isn't it?'

The inspectors were impressed, the gigglers went to their lunch, and I knew that we could go on like this for ever.

Part 2—Elegant Jane

THEY USED TO SAY about me when I was young that I was a perfectionist. I liked the description, actually. It meant that I wanted things to be perfect, which I did. But as I got older they stopped using the phrase. Probably thought it meant finicky, picky, hard to please.

Nobody ever said Poppy was a perfectionist. Dear me, no. She always had cut knees or scabs on them. Her hair was constantly falling over her face, her clothes ripped or torn from climbing up in the Whitethorn Woods or sliding down things. And yet, amazingly, people always liked Poppy. Quite disproportionately in fact.

The house was full of her friends. That loud noisy Grania practically lived in our house, for heaven's sake. Oh, and crowds more. And it was the same with boys when the time came. She had dozens of them around the place too. When she left St Ita's school in Rossmore she could have gone to university as I did. I have a degree and became a librarian, but, no, Poppy, who always knew her own mind, had insisted on nursing.

Mother and Father were, I suppose, relieved that it didn't cost them anything, but still. When she was qualified, Poppy went into a ward for the elderly, most of them mad, poor dears, and confused. She found them fascinating and hilarious. You'd swear she was working with Einstein and Peter Ustinov, not a lot of elderly people who barely knew what day it was.

Among the seemingly endless series of young men who all wanted to be with Poppy there was one called Oliver. His people owned a lot of property all over Rossmore. Very good-looking, a bit of a philanderer, I suppose. He didn't really work because he didn't really need to. And his family were all torn between relief that he was settling down at last and concern that he had chosen as his bride a nurse called Poppy with no background. I warned Poppy that he might not be the entirely faithful type and she said that life was all about taking risks and marriage was just a giant optimistic step.

I didn't see marriage like that. I saw it as something you thought about a lot and made sure it was the right thing to do. Oddly, I had never really been close enough to consider seriously marrying anyone.

Oliver and Poppy's wedding was just what you'd expect. Haphazard, disorganised, everyone laughing. Lots of champagne and little chicken sandwiches. And a wedding cake. That was all. No proper banquet with place names or anything.

Mother and Father enjoyed it. I didn't. That loud Grania was braying all over the place, brought her dreadful red-faced father with her. Mother and Father said that Poppy had never been a day's trouble in her whole life.

I thought that was rich. Poppy? No trouble?

Poppy and Oliver had a marvellous house, well, compared to my small flat it was marvellous, but of course hopelessly neglected, what with Poppy still out slaving away in a geriatric ward.

I'll tell you, if I had married Oliver and all his money I would have stayed at home, done up that house and invited people in. Then he mightn't have wandered so much.

I knew about his wandering quite early on actually. I saw him nuzzling a girl in a wine bar. Naturally he saw me too and disengaged himself. He came over full of charm.

'We're adults, you and I, Jane,' he said. 'And adults don't run home with silly tales, do they?'

'Not unless they see other adults doing silly things in wine bars,' I said, proud of myself.

He looked at me for a while. 'I suppose in the end, it is your call, Jane,' he said and went back to the girl.

I paid my bill and left. As it happened I did not tell Poppy. I had tried to warn her before she married him and she had been shruggy and so dismissive—let her find out herself.

She found out about six months later when she came home unexpectedly and opened her bedroom door to find Oliver and an old flame having a nostalgic whatever. She asked him to leave. That very day. She wanted no explanations or excuses, no promises of a faultless life from then on. She said to him that she just wanted the house, no maintenance, that it was actually a good deal he would be getting, which he would realise when he came to talk it over with the legal briefs.

And then, as if that wasn't bad enough losing this great catch, Poppy threw up her dull but safe job in the hospital and went to work at a crazy retirement home called Ferns and Heathers.

I mean, what a name! But Poppy, being Poppy, said she liked it. It was better, she said, than calling it St Something as a lot of these places were called, and it made the people who lived there feel they were not being hurtled rather too swiftly towards the next world.

Against all the odds the nursing home took off and became very successful, and Mother told me that Poppy owned a great deal of it nowadays. She said they would both like to go and live there one day when they were old. And Poppy said they should go there while they still had all their energy for the marvellous things that the residents did.

I hated going there. I went out of solidarity from time to time, but really it was looking at the old people's crêpey skin that upset me.

Lots of the residents in the home had strong feelings about the bypass that was going to be built around Rossmore. Some of them welcomed it, saying it was progress. It would be easier for folk to cross the road because the traffic would be less. Others were against it and said that their relatives would now fly by and not come to see them at all. Poppy began to organise debates on it at the home and bring in representatives of both sides. Is that mad or what? But even Oliver, when he called to visit me from time to time, said she was a bloody marvel.

I took to keeping big juicy olives and little slices of salami in my fridge in case Oliver called. And I always dressed up anyway so he never found me looking like a slattern. Poor Poppy often looked as if she had been doing hard manual labour all day . . .

And of course we went to bed together. I mean, Oliver is that kind of person. There was nothing serious in it. I was his ex-sister-in-law, and I didn't really see him as husband material. No, if St Ann were going to answer my prayers, I don't think it was going to be with Poppy's ex.

Oliver talked rather a lot about Poppy, which was irritating. I said once that we had gone beyond Poppy as a topic of conversation but he looked puzzled. He always wanted to know if she was seeing anyone and I said, you know Poppy, seeing everyone, seeing no one. This puzzled him further and he asked, did she want to know about him? He seemed to think we were much closer than we were, asking me little titbits about when we were girls. As if I can remember!

I decided to go over to Ferns and Heathers to see Poppy, well, really so that I would have something to tell Oliver about her. I wanted him to think we were more loving and bonding than we actually were.

The first thing I saw when I arrived was Poppy's bottom up in the air as she dug at some hole in the ground. Beside her were assorted geriatrics including, of all people, that loud Grania's red-faced father, Dan. What was he doing here? They were all laughing hysterically at something. I felt that when my shadow fell on them they stopped laughing.

'Why, it's Elegant Jane!' cried the awful Dan. Poppy came up from the hole in the ground, her hands filthy and streaks of mud on her face.

'Oh, hello, Jane, what's wrong?' she asked. As if there would have to be something wrong for me to come and see my only sister.

'Why should there be anything wrong?' I snapped at her.

They all understood, the old folk, and Dan understood better than most. 'Fasten your seatbelts,' he said.

'Light the touchpaper and retire,' said another old man with hardly any teeth.

'Right, folks, I have to go away for a short while. Please stay well away from the hole, I don't want to be digging you all out with broken hips,' Poppy ordered them. Then she led me to her little house in the grounds. She washed her hands, poured me a sherry and sat down.

'You still have mud on your face,' I said.

She ignored me. 'Is there anything wrong with Dad?' she asked. 'His blood pressure was up last week.'

'How on earth would you know?' I asked.

'I take it every week when I go round on my half-day,' she said.

Poppy goes to Mother and Father every week on her half-day? How extraordinary!

'So what is it then?' Poppy asked, looking wistfully out at the garden where she wanted to be.

'I was talking to Oliver,' I began.

'Oliver?' She sounded bewildered.

'Yes, Oliver. Your husband, the man you were married to.'

'But, I'm not married to him now, Jane,' Poppy said as if she was talking to someone retarded. She talks to those old bats outside on much more equal terms than she talks to me.

'No, but he was making enquiries about you,' I said, wondering how this had got so out of control. 'Like were you good at games at school, like what we did on your birthday at home.'

'Oliver wants to know all that? Lord, he must be madder than we thought,' Poppy said cheerfully.

'I don't think he's mad at all, I think he is very sane. I really believe that he wanted it all to work, you know, when you were married.'

'Yes, of course he did, that's why he brought his old girlfriend back to my bed,' Poppy said in a matter-of-fact way.

'Well, it was his bed too,' I heard myself say idiotically.

'Oh, well, of course, that makes it all right then,' Poppy said.

There was a silence between us. Twice she looked as if she were about to confide in me and then stopped at the last moment.

'Go on. Say it,' I ordered her eventually.

'All right, I will. I don't fancy Oliver remotely, so go right ahead if you do. You won't be stepping on any toes. But he's really very boring, clinging and boring. You'll find that. So he's rich and good-looking, but actually that's not very important in the long run. The rich can often be tight with spending their money and the handsome are often vain. And Oliver hasn't the remotest notion of being faithful. But you told me that years back and I didn't believe you. So why should you listen to me?'

I looked at Poppy, so assured and mud-spattered, with a sherry in her hand. 'And all this is better?' I said, indicating the garden, the residents and the whole set-up with a nod of my head.

'Vastly,' she said.

I knew then that I had never understood her and never would.

As I was getting back into my car I heard them all cheer at the reappearance of Poppy. Well, it was what she wanted.

I got my hair done and bought some smoked salmon—in case Oliver came round. As it happened he didn't. But he came the next evening.

He came often after that, but he never brought a gift and he did look at himself in the mirror quite a lot. Sometimes he would stay the night, but he never suggested that we go out anywhere. And there *was* something a bit clinging about him.

There was very little laughter around at the library or at home. The days often seemed long. Compared to that madhouse at Ferns and Heathers where there was never a spare moment in the day and the inmates were laughing all the time.

Was it at all possible that Poppy could have been right? Poppy whose skin had never been cherished, whose hair had never been styled and whose wardrobe was a bad joke. Surely Poppy couldn't have discovered the secret of life? That would be too unfair for words.

CHAPTER 8

Your Eleven-O'Clock Lady
Part 1—Pandora

I HOPE IT'S GOING to be busy today at the salon. When you have to hang about between clients, time seems to drag a lot. I don't want any free time in which to think about the conversation at breakfast.

I was in at 8.45 a.m. as usual. Fabian, who is a legend not only in Rossmore but for four counties around, likes to have what he calls 'grooming control' before he opens the door to the clients. His salon sinks or swims, he says, by what the staff look like. No grubby fingernails, no down-at-heel shoes, and he expects us to have shining, well-conditioned hair every morning. Our uniforms are laundered on the premises so they always look bandbox fresh. That's a funny word, bandbox. I wonder what it means . . .

Fabian insists that we smile a lot and look pleased to see customers. He said the salon wasn't the place to be if you were going to look glum. He could only charge the top prices he does if people felt they were in a special place. Worries had to be left outside the salon. That was an absolute. No one with hangovers, headaches, difficult children or unhappy love lives had any place on the staff. There was to be no talk about the traffic, or illness, or being mugged. An expensive perfume was sprayed around the salon just before opening time and several times during the day. This was to set the tone of the place. Glamour, peace, elegance: a place with the power to transform all who came in and paid big money. The tips were good too.

You would find a job in any salon anywhere you wanted, if you had worked for a few years in Fabian's. But, usually, you'd leave to set up your own place. If you said that you were 'late of Fabian's' people would come to you from far and wide.

Not that I was going to be in a position to set up my own salon. Once I thought I might—and Ian had been behind me all the way, assuring me that I was management material.

But breakfast today had changed everything.

Stop it, Pandora. Smile. Teeth and eyes, Pandora, we are nearly on show. Pandora is my salon name, and that's what I think of myself as being while I'm here. At home, I'm Vi. Don't think of home. Smile, Pandora, the day is starting.

My nine-o'clock lady was in the door like a greyhound out of a trap. She came every Thursday without fail, attached almost surgically to her mobile phone. Fabian was very strict about this. He only allowed phones that vibrated to show there was someone looking for you. No ringing tones to disturb the other clients.

My smile was nailed to my face. Her conversation was quickfire and one way, she wanted agreement, nods of affirmation and acknowledgement, all in the right place. So no thoughts of Ian and his guilty, shifty account of where he had been last night were allowed room in my head.

The nine-o'clock lady was always in a lather about some aspect of her work. Some fool had done this, some idiot hadn't done that, some bloody courier had been late. Rossmore was the boondocks of the world. All that was needed was immense sympathy, a litany of soothing sounds—and speed. The nine-o'clock lady had to be out screaming at a taxi at nine forty-five.

My nine-thirty lady had been shampooed and was deep in a magazine story about Princess Diana. She was a regular also, currently trying out a different style every week until she found the perfect way to look at her daughter's wedding, which was going to be a huge affair. The nine-thirty lady had not been invited to get involved in the planning of it all. There was a wedding organiser. Nothing in her whole life had ever hurt her so much. Her only daughter had turned her back on her on this the most important day of her life. Mighty soothing was called for here also. Huge reassurance that it had been a kindness rather than a rejection on the daughter's part. Useless bleatings that it gave her much more time now to concentrate on her own hair, her own outfit, her own enjoyment of the day.

'Don't marry, Pandora,' the nine-thirty lady warned me as she left. 'It's never worth it, believe me, I know.'

I had told her many times in answer to her absent-minded questioning that I *was* married, to Ian. But she didn't remember, and as Fabian said, we mustn't expect them to remember anything about us. We are just a well-groomed, charming set of props. It was certainly not the occasion to tell her that she was spot on about marriage.

The ten-o'clock was an out-of-town person who had seen a write-up of Fabian's in a magazine. She had to come to the town to get fabric for soft furnishings and had decided to have a hairdo as well. No, nothing new, thank you, she knew what suited her, like she knew what fabrics she needed. The tedium and monotony of her life seeped all over me.

My ten-thirty was a model. Well, actually, Katerina was a glamour model for a photo catalogue for underwear. She was nice, and she came in every six weeks to have her roots done.

'You look a bit peaky today,' she said.

I suppose it was good that she even saw me, most of them didn't. But peaky wasn't a good thing to look. I hoped that Fabian hadn't heard. I smiled more brightly than ever, hoping to beat off whatever dull, dead sort of vibes I must be giving off.

'I know, I know. I have to smile like that every night,' Katerina said sympathetically. 'Sometimes I feel like a big bawling session and that's when I have to smile most.'

She was very kind and interested and made me think she cared. I looked around to see whether Fabian was in earshot.

'It's just my husband, I think he's seeing someone else.'

'Believe me, he is,' she said, applying her lip liner.

'What?' I cried.

'Sweetheart, I work for a place that is packed with people's husbands getting the lingerie catalogues just to ogle over the models. That's what husbands do. It's not a problem unless you make it into one.'

'What do you mean?'

'Listen to me—I know this—they like to look at pictures and chat up birds. They don't want to leave their wives. They're not sorry they married them, it's just that they hate to think that it's all over and they're missing out on whatever else is on offer. They sometimes feel that they've been filed away under "Married Man". Cross-reference, "Dull Man". A sensible wife would make nothing of it; the problem is that a lot of them make a great, useless fuss about it.'

I looked at her in amazement. How did she find such wisdom?

'You mean, put up with infidelity and cheating and pretend it isn't happening? You seriously mean that?' I asked her.

'Yes, I did mean that, for a bit anyway, until you know definitely it's true. And even then, is it going to be the end of the world if he has a bit of a whirl? Soon it could be nothing but a confused memory.'

'But suppose it's not just a bit of a whirl. Suppose he really does love her and not me. What happens then?'

'Well, then he walks,' said Katerina. 'And there's nothing any of us can do. I'm just saying that the very worst scenario is to make a fuss now. Right?' She looked as if she had finished with the subject so I went on to autopilot again, got her hair blow-dried to perfection.

As she left she gave me a big tip.

'You'll survive, Pandora, see you in six weeks,' she said and glided like a lithe panther out of the salon.

'Your eleven-o'clock lady not in yet, Pandora?' Fabian had a control of the salon that would have been envied by any military leader. He knew what was going on, or not going on, in every corner. Together we looked at the appointment book. New client. A Ms Desmond. It meant nothing to either of us.

'Find out how she heard of us, won't you, Pandora?' he said, on the ball about work twenty-four hours a day.

'Yes, of course, Fabian,' I said automatically.

Actually I would spend the time trying to work out how my five-year-old marriage to Ian was unravelling.

First, I had accidentally seen the bracelet in his drawer. *For my darling, to celebrate the new moon, all my love, Ian.* I had no idea what he meant. We hadn't seen any new moon together recently.

But it might be referring to something that was about to happen. I checked the diary: there would be a new moon on Saturday next. Possibly he was going to take me away somewhere to celebrate it. I wouldn't spoil the surprise. But there was no mention of an outing on Saturday, instead the rather depressing news that Ian would be away for the weekend on a conference. Still it didn't dawn on me.

But last night Ian was very late home from the office and I went to bed at eleven because I was exhausted. I woke at four and he still wasn't back. Now this was worrying. He has a mobile phone, he could have called me. I tried calling him but he had the phone on voicemail. At that very moment I heard his key in the door. I was so angry with him that I decided to pretend to be asleep and avoid a row. He took ages to come to bed, but I never opened my eyes. At one stage he went to his sock drawer and took out the bracelet. I opened my eyes just wide enough to see him smiling at the engraving and then he put it away. Deep in his briefcase.

Ian always left the house earlier than I did. It took him ages to get to work in his car but he needed it for work. And for who knew what else? He could only have had three hours' sleep. This morning he asked me what time I had gone to bed.

'Eleven o'clock, I'm afraid I was dropping. What time did you come back?' I asked.

'Oh, early hours of the morning, such a fuss in the office . . . You were sleeping so very peacefully I didn't want to wake you.'

'Well, think of all the overtime,' I reassured him, trying to force the suspicion out of my mind.

'Not sure they'll pay anyway. Listen, love, I have to go away for the weekend. There's a conference, bit of an honour really—I suppose I should be pleased but I know it's your weekend off so I'm so sorry.' He put on his little-boy face that I used to find endearing.

Until this morning when I found it sickening.

He was having an affair. Lots of things fitted into place now.

I had an hour before I needed to go out myself, but I put on my coat and headed out of the door as soon as I heard Ian's car leave. I got on the first bus that came to the stop. It wasn't going to the part of Rossmore where Fabian's was but I didn't care. I just wanted to get away from the house where I had once been so happy.

The bus stopped at the far edge of Whitethorn Woods and then was going to turn round and go back to wherever it had come from. Like a zombie I walked up through the woods. People said that they were going to be dug up to make a new road, but that might just be a rumour.

I walked on, fighting back the sick feeling of dread in my chest, the feeling that our marriage was all over and Ian loved someone else.

He had been taken in by whoever she was, had bought her a bracelet and was going to see the new moon with her.

I had followed the wooden signs and arrived at the well, where we used to come when we were kids. Even at this early hour there were people praying: an old woman with her eyes closed; two children with a picture of someone, their mother probably, asking for a cure. It was unreal and kind of sad.

Yet, I thought, now that I'm here, it can't do any harm. I told St Ann the situation. Quite simply. It was amazing what a short story it was really. Boy loves girl, boy finds other girl, first girl heartbroken. There must have been thousands of similar stories told here.

I didn't feel any sense of hope or anything. In fact I felt a bit foolish. I didn't know what I was asking her. To change Ian's mind, really, I suppose that's all I wanted.

Then I walked briskly to the gates of the woods and caught a bus to work. I travelled with a grim face into Rossmore and all morning I kept remembering more damning proof of the affair. The way he had refused to go bowling last week, normally he couldn't be kept away from it. How he had changed the subject twice when I asked him to do a business plan on buying that corner newsagent's which was for sale near us, and making it into a hair salon.

'Let's not be too hasty,' he had said. 'Who knows where we'll be in a year or two?'

Suddenly my thoughts were interrupted.

'Your eleven-o'clock lady is in,' one of the juniors called.

Ms Desmond was waiting at the desk. She had a nice smile and she asked me to call her Brenda.

'What a lovely name, Pandora!' she said wistfully. 'I'd love to have been called that.'

Fabian didn't encourage us to tell clients that these were made-up names, in fact he actively discouraged it.

'I think my mother was reading an over-fancy book at the time,' I said, taking the grandeur away from it to reassure her.

I liked this woman. Brenda Desmond handed her coat to the junior and sat down while we looked at her in the mirror.

'I want to look terrific for the weekend,' she said. 'I'm going off to a really gorgeous place in the country to look at the new moon with a new fellow.'

I looked at her reflection in the mirror and told myself that all over this town there were people going away for the weekend with new fellows. It didn't have to be Ian. My pleasant interested smile was still there.

'That's nice,' I heard myself say. 'And are you serious about him?'

'Well, as much as I can be. He's not entirely free, alas. He says that's no problem but, you know, it does throw a wrench in the works. Funny phrase, that, I wonder where it comes from.'

'Probably it's quite a literal thing, like, you know, if a wrench falls into the works of some machine or is thrown into it, it sort of wrecks the whole machine,' I said.

She listened, interested. 'You're right, it's probably quite straightforward. Are you interested in phrases and where they come from?'

She was treating me like a real person with views, not someone who would crimp her hair. But I had to be sure that she was the one before I pulled every tuft of her flat, greasy hair out by the roots.

'Yes, I am interested in words, I was just thinking about the word bandbox this morning. Do you know where that came from?'

'Well, oddly I do, I looked it up once: a bandbox was a light box that held bands, like hairbands, I suppose, millinery, that sort of thing.'

'Does it now?' I was actually interested. Imagine her knowing that! And why should a bandbox be so fresh and clean? But enough speculation. Back to work.

'What do you think you'd like done?'

'I don't really know, Pandora, I'm not much good about hair, I have to work so very hard, you see. I called in a sickie this morning, I can't go in tomorrow with a new hairdo or they'd suspect, and then on Saturday I'm off for my wicked weekend with a colleague.'

'Where do you work?' I asked her. I could hear the words booming, resounding, echoing in my head.

Please may she not say Ian's company.

She said Ian's company.

My hands were on her shoulders. I could have raised them and put them round her neck and choked her until she was dead.

Instead I talked about hair.

'You wear it fairly flattish,' I said, amazed that I could function at all. I thought of my Ian running his hands through this woman's horrible limp hair, telling Brenda she was beautiful as he so often told me I was beautiful. It was almost too much to bear.

'It's quite stylish the way it is,' I said thoughtfully. 'But let me ask Fabian, he always knows.'

I tottered on unsteady legs to Fabian.

'New lady, Ms Desmond, just loves her hair the way it is, think she could be a regular, can you come and tell her she looks fine.'

He peered across the salon, then glided over and touched her head in that way he does. 'Ms Desmond, Pandora, who is one of our most esteemed stylists here, asked me to give my opinion. I think the classic style you have chosen complements your features and I feel that all you need is a little, tiny trim.'

'You think it's nice?' she asked foolishly and the great Fabian closed his eyes as if to say it was almost too nice to describe. It also prevented him from having to lie to her face.

'Lucinda,' I called to a junior. 'Take my lady and give her a very good, thorough shampoo,' I called. I hissed to Lucinda—who in real life was called Brid—to beat her head on the basin and get lots of soap in her eyes. The girl, not unnaturally, wondered why.

'Because she's an evil tramp and is sleeping with my best friend's husband,' I hissed.

Brid-Lucinda obliged. Brenda Desmond was brought limping, near blinded and aching back to my station. Brid-Lucinda had kicked her for good measure, pretending to fall over her feet. I cut her hair so that it ended up wispy and uneven. Then I put the greasiest gel I could find into it and dried it until it looked like rats' tails on either side of her head. When any of the others looked over at it, I shrugged as if to ask, what could I do when these were the instructions I got?

When I had finished and made her look as awful as I could, she looked at herself doubtfully in the mirror.

'This is classical, you say?'

'Oh very, Brenda, he'll love it.'

'I do hope so, he's very stylish, you know. What with being French and everything.'

'He's *French*?'

'Yes, didn't I say? They sent him over from the Paris office! Imagine! And yet he does seem to fancy me . . .' She looked childishly delighted.

I looked at her in horror.

'Do you know Ian in your office?' I said suddenly.

'Ian? Ian Benson? Of course I do. He's a great guy, Ian. How do you know him?'

'I know him,' I said glumly.

'He's married to Vi, he's always talking about her.'

'What does he say about her?'

I was so wretched now that I nearly threw myself on the ground and held her around the knees, sobbing out my apologies for making her look like a madwoman.

'Oh, everything, he was hoping to take her away this weekend and then they sent him on a conference. It's an honour and everything but he said he'd have preferred to take Vi to this place with a lake and they could have watched the new moon. And made a wish.'

'What do you think he's wishing for?'

'He didn't say but I think he might have been thinking they'd have a baby soon. And that he would get Vi a salon much nearer home. He's been doing endless overtime recently. He's saving for something . . .'

And then she was gone, out there with her horrible hairstyle, about to make a mess of her weekend with the sophisticated Parisian man.

I think they told me that my eleven-thirty was in but I didn't hear. Like I haven't really been hearing much of anything lately.

You're meant to give something to charity if St Ann grants your request. But she didn't really, did she? I mean, Ian had never stopped loving me at all.

Part 2—Bruiser's Business

MY REAL NAME is George. Not that anyone would know it. I have been called Bruiser since I was two. And in the salon I'm called Fabian.

So when anyone calls out 'George Brewster', like at an airport if I am on standby and they are reading my passport, I take ages to answer. Then I leap up guiltily as if I am travelling on forged documents.

At our school, The Brothers in Rossmore, everyone had nicknames and sadly they heard my mum calling me Bruiser so that was that. I wasn't colossal or anything but I was a sturdy thick-set boy, I suppose, so they leaped on that name. In a way it wasn't a bad name to be called. New people I met thought that I had some terrific reputation with my fists and so they kept away from me, which was a relief.

I was ten when my mate Hobbit told me that my dad was going after the ladies. He said he had seen my dad in a car with this blonde one who was much, much younger and they were going at it like knives.

I didn't believe Hobbit and I hit him. Hobbit was annoyed.

'I only told you so that you'd be ready for it,' he complained, rubbing his shoulder where I had thumped him. 'I actually don't care if your dad runs from here to Timbuktu.'

So I gave him two KitKats from my lunchbox as a consolation and everything was all right.

I always had a terrific lunchbox because my mum knew I loved chocolate and peanut butter sandwiches. Poor Hobbit had awful things like apples and celery and cheese and bits of very dull chicken.

Shortly afterwards my mum discovered that Dad was going after the ladies and everything changed.

'It's all our fault, Bruiser,' she told me. 'We are not attractive people, we haven't been able to hold your father's attention and interest. Everything must change.' And everything did.

First she kept dragging me up to St Ann's Well to discuss the matter with a statue. Then I got horrible lunchboxes, worse than Hobbit's, then I had to jog four bus stops every morning before catching the bus. After school I went to the gym with my mum. It was very expensive so we both had to work there in order to be allowed to use the machinery. She used to man the reception desk for two hours and I went round picking up towels.

I liked it, actually. I liked talking to the people there, they told me their stories, and why they were there. There was a fellow who had hoped to meet birds but hadn't met many; there was a man who had had a heart scare; a woman who wanted to look well for a wedding; and a singer who had seen a video of herself and said that her backside was the size of a mountain, which it more or less was.

Because I really was interested in their stories they talked more and they told the people who ran the gym that I was a great asset. And though I wasn't really meant to be working there at all, what with being way under age, they gave me more hours. They were afraid to give me money because of the law, but they bought me nice things like a good brand-new school blazer and a camera, and it was great.

My mum lost a lot of weight and apparently Dad said that no one should ever underestimate the power of St Ann and a healthy diet. And everything was fine again at home.

It was fine at school too because I had got a lot fitter and when we were thirteen and I went to the disco, Hobbit said that most of the babes there thought I was a fine thing. Which was terrific for me but not for Hobbit.

Neither Hobbit nor I knew what to do as a job, a career, whatever. My dad was a sales executive for electric goods and I sure as hell didn't want to do that. Hobbit's dad and mum ran a corner shop and he hated even the thought of working in it. My mum worked full time in the gym now she had done a course and she taught aerobics there. But none of that made it any easier for Hobbit and myself to know what we would do.

Even Miss King, the careers teacher who came to the school as a consultant, seemed hard pushed to advise us. She said to me that I was interested in people, I should take that into account. I told her straight out I wouldn't be a social worker, I'd hate it. No, she didn't mean that, she said. Nor teaching. I couldn't *stand* teaching. She nodded sympathetically. She was always nice, Miss King was.

'Some job where you'd be talking to people and making them feel good?' she suggested.

'A gigolo?' I wondered. I just wanted to tell Hobbit that I'd said it.

'Yes, that sort of thing, certainly that's the area where we should be looking,' she said agreeably.

So I didn't tell Hobbit about it after all. Then, amazingly, Hobbit said that we might do hairdressing. There were loads of babes at the classes in college and we'd be stroking women's heads all day in the salon.

'*Hairdressing?*' I said.

'We've got to do something,' Hobbit said reasonably.

Nobody liked the idea except Hobbit and myself. My mum said I could have done something more intellectual, my dad said it wasn't for real men. Hobbit's parents said they wouldn't be able to hold their heads up again in the corner shop.

It wasn't bad at all, as it turned out. Hobbit got a job at a ritzy salon where he was called Merlin. I got a place in a family-style salon way out in the suburbs of Rossmore called the Milady Salon. I liked the owner, Mr Dixon. We all called him Mr Dixon, even people who had been there twenty years.

It was a very middle-aged, middle-class, once-weekly shampoo-and-blow-dry brigade, and a nervous request for a cut, which they called a trim, once every six weeks, discreet colour twice a year. Nothing innovative, no experiments, no chance to show off any style.

Their eyes seemed big with anxiety as they looked in the mirror. Every hairdo was some kind of dream. A lot of them were lacking in self-confidence, which was why they never tried anything new. Sometimes I noticed that they didn't really look all that much better when they left the salon, but they felt better and they walked straighter with more purpose and half smiled at their reflection in the shop window rather than scuttling past it as they had done on the way in.

It had been a bit like that with my own mum.

She didn't look hugely changed after her first weight loss at the gym. She just had more confidence, that was all. She felt better about herself and she didn't bite the head off Dad and ask him where he had been and accuse him of ignoring her. She was just a nicer person to live with and so he was nicer to her. It was as simple as that.

And that's just the way these women at the salon felt too.

I think they liked me, they gave me nice tips, they loved my name Bruiser. They asked about my family and if I had a girlfriend. A good fifty per cent of them said I should settle down and the other half said I should take my time. Some of them said I could do worse than visit St Ann's Well, because she was the last word on matters of the heart.

I was taking my time as it happened. Hobbit and I would go out clubbing but we only met awful screeching girls, not settling down material at all. Hobbit, now that he was called Merlin, was full of confidence and ambition. He said to me that I would end up an old man who only knew how to do tightly permed grey heads unless I moved.

We needed to branch out, go somewhere where there might be a bit of action, where we might win competitions.

So Merlin and I put our savings together and opened our own salon. Rossmore had certainly changed over the years. New affluence meant people had to have the best. There was a young and apparently endless line of clients with money. Girls with tigerish manes, girls with close-cropped, plum-coloured hair. They were leggy and languid and came to the salon twice a week. I marvelled at their wealth and their interest in their hair. It made Milady's seem light years away.

Naturally, my name was changed as well. I was Fabian now and, though Merlin laughed at me, I still went back to Milady's on the last Friday of every month to help Mr Dixon. They still called me Bruiser there and admired my own very different hairstyle and smart waistcoats. I told them that people were totally mad in the zany salon in Rossmore and liked us all to dress up. They loved hearing these stories and felt safe in their own place. I had more confidence nowadays and so I suggested a little adventure for some of them. Mr Dixon even accepted some of my ideas about slightly more up-to-date décor.

They all asked me about my love life and I told them truthfully that I had been working too hard to find anyone to love. Better not wait too long, they advised, and I nodded gravely.

What I didn't tell them in Milady's was that everyone in the zany place, everyone except Merlin, that is, thought I was gay. Now, I had no problems with this, for in very many ways it actually worked to my advantage. Women confide in gay men more, as if they were somehow the best of both worlds. Not predatory and about to pounce, not thick and male and wordless; like a girlfriend, really, but not in competition.

It didn't do me any harm; in fact it did me a lot of good. The clients seemed to like it; it helped them to confide in me. Boy, did they confide. Like that amazing girl Hazel who told me about all her one-night stands and how lonely and used she would feel afterwards.

And there was Mary Lou who couldn't get her fellow to commit. He was happy with her but he wouldn't let her move her things in. And, of course, no mention of a ring or anything. I said I thought she should be more independent and go on a holiday with girlfriends. She was doubtful but of course it paid off. He was very worried when she looked as if she could survive without him.

So there I was as happy as anything. I was beginning to fancy a beautiful girl called Lara, a designer who came to have her hair done regularly. All the time I still went back to Milady's. Sometimes I brought Mr Dixon a fancy mirror, a turbo hairdryer or a bale of new towels as a gift, but I always took my wages from him even though I didn't need them.

Mr Dixon was of the old school. You wouldn't want to offend him.

He had come to visit me in our salon once and he took in the whole scene. He said to me later that I was a good lad, the best he ever had, and that he didn't care about my personal habits; it was up to me. My personal life, so to speak.

And I just couldn't explain it all. It was too complicated. Mr Dixon died shortly afterwards and he left me the salon. I couldn't believe it. But he had no close relations and he didn't want his life's work wound up and sold off to someone who would open a fast-food outlet.

I had no idea what to do with the place. It was old-fashioned and losing money but I knew it had to be kept on as a salon. And I didn't want to dispossess all the old ladies who had been going there for years. Anyway I wasn't giving it much thought at that time. I had other things on my mind. By then I had fallen totally in love with Lara, but she thought I was gay and I couldn't convince her otherwise.

'Nonsense, Fabian, you can't fancy me, sweetheart, you're as gay as a carnival!' she would laugh. 'We're *friends*, you and me!'

'I am not a gay man, Lara,' I said in a level voice, 'I am one hundred per cent heterosexual.'

'And so are Gerry and Henri and Basil in the salon, I suppose,' she mocked.

'No, of course not. But I am.' I told her my name was Bruiser, and she laughed even more. Or George, I suggested in desperation, but it was no use.

Now, to top it all off, one of my best stylists was having some kind of hysterics in the staff room, bawling and incoherent about having ruined someone's hair and not having understood that her husband was desperate to have children.

It was all we needed on a busy morning.

Gerry and Basil, who were usually great with tantrums and nervous breakdowns and people howling, couldn't make head nor tail of it. Henri said we should call the paramedics. I went in and sat with her.

'Pandora,' I said gently.

'Vi, my name is Vi,' she cried. I had forgotten. She was always Pandora in the salon.

'I'm Bruiser. That's my real name,' I said. I thought it might help. It didn't.

'Bruiser?' she said in disbelief.

'I'm afraid so,' I confessed.

'Oh my God,' she said. 'That's all we need—you're called Bruiser.'

She started to sob again: there was Ian, her husband, there was poor Brenda Desmond and the Frenchman, and there was the new moon.

I wondered if Henri was right. Maybe she had just gone mad. I got her a drink of water and patted her hand.

I was told that Lara was in the salon. I said she'd have to wait.

'You don't want to annoy Lara,' Pandora-Vi blubbed at me.

'I don't care if we annoy Lara. Lara has annoyed me, she persists in thinking I'm gay, she makes fun of me and sends me up. Let her bloody hair extensions wait until I'm ready.'

Vi looked up. 'But that's idiotic, Fabian, just to look at you, anyone would know you swing both ways.' She was red-faced and earnest.

I wanted to give her a good slap, but this was not the moment to argue my sexuality down to the bone with her. 'I am not bisexual, Vi. I have sex with women, do you hear? Not enough of them, I have to say, not nearly enough. From now on I'm going to sleep with any woman who has a pulse. And that will show those know-all Laras out there.'

I saw Vi's mouth in a round O of horror. She was staring not at me but over my shoulder. I knew it before I turned. There was Lara, listening to every word and looking very disapproving indeed.

'How dare you make Pandora cry,' she began. 'Big bully.'

Pandora was of course in floods of tears again, triggered by this sympathy. Again I heard a few key words: babies, new moon, Ian, eleven-o'clock lady, Frenchman, bracelet. Totally disjointed, completely off the wall. Yet Lara understood at once. There was no problem, she said, we were all to pretend we knew nothing about anything.

Well, that would be easy for me. I did know nothing about anything.

The eleven-o'clock lady could be given a voucher, Vi was to stop taking the pill, Ian loved her, the bracelet was for Vi, not the eleven-o'clock lady: all was well, nothing to cry about. Main thing was to avoid stress.

It was complete gibberish, yet Vi was actually smiling. 'Hard to avoid stress in a salon like this,' she said ruefully to Lara.

'Go somewhere calmer, somewhere nearer home,' Lara suggested. 'I'm sure Tiger or Bruiser or whatever he's called here will have a master plan for you.' She was smiling at me. A different kind of smile, as if she saw me properly for the first time.

And I did have a plan there and then.

Vi, as it happened, lived fairly near Milady's, out in the farthest suburbs of Rossmore near the Whitethorn Woods. She could be manager there. She could have babies and bracelets, and new moons, whatever she wanted, and the eleven-o'clock lady would be kept away from her. Was that all right, could we all go back to work now? Please?

We all did, and I looked at Lara's eyes in the mirror and told her she didn't need hair extensions, her hair was beautiful as it was.

She said, she wondered was there something a bit unprofessional about the way I was stroking her neck. Was it rather like a doctor and a patient and maybe I could be struck off for unprofessional behaviour?

I said I thought not, I thought that different rules entirely apply in a salon and she laughed a warm enthusiastic laugh and said I was not to dream of sleeping with every woman who had a pulse.

She had been there for that bit too . . .

CHAPTER 9

The Road, the Woods and the Well—3

EDDIE FLYNN WAITED outside the church after Mass until he saw his brother leaving.

'Brian, can I have a word?' he began.

'Not if that word is "annulment",' the priest said without stopping in his progress back to his house.

'You know it isn't.' Eddie was almost running to keep up. 'Hang on a bit, this isn't the four-minute mile.'

'I'm going for my breakfast, I'm hungry, I have a lot to do today, talk away if you want to.' Father Flynn continued purposefully down the road, greeting parishioners along the way.

'Right. A cup of coffee?' he said when they got back to his kitchen.

'I thought you'd have someone to cook your breakfast. Haven't you got a Russian or something working for you?' Eddie seemed disappointed.

Father Flynn had put three pieces of bacon and a tomato in a frying pan and was now turning them expertly. 'Josef, who is Latvian, as it happens, looks after the canon, not me.'

'The canon should be in a home for the bewildered,' Eddie said.

'Naomi didn't have much luck with him either, is that right?' Father Flynn smiled.

'Leave it alone, Brian. I wanted to ask you about the well.'

'The well?'

'The well, man. It's in your territory, for heaven's sake—the holy well, the sacred well, whatever. I'm asking, will they let it go?'

'Will who let it go?' Father Flynn was confused.

'God, Brian. Will your lot let it go, the Church, the Pope, all that?'

'Oh, *my* lot, I see,' said Father Flynn. 'The Pope has never mentioned it to my certain knowledge, or if he has, the burden of what he said hasn't trickled down to us here. Don't you want a piece of bacon?'

'No, I don't want any bacon, and you shouldn't be having any either, clogging up your arteries.' Eddie Flynn was very disapproving.

'Yes, but then I don't have so many social demands on my life, I don't have to keep so many ladies happy.'

'I'm serious, Brian.'

'So am I, Eddie. The best part of my day is often sitting here peacefully at my breakfast reading the paper. And here you are in my kitchen picking on everything I say or do.'

'Some people asked me to join up with them in a syndicate,' Eddie said in a tone of great gravity. 'This is my chance to make real money, Brian. And boy, am I going to need real money. Do you know what this wedding is going to cost?' Eddie seemed agitated.

'A simple registry office wedding? Not much, surely?'

'Oh, no, we have some dissident priest or other, and somebody is lending him a church to give us a blessing. There are going to be bridesmaids, groomsmen, a huge reception, the whole works. God, I need this break, that's why I have to know about the well.'

'*What* do you have to know about the well, Eddie?'

'All right. I'll tell you but it's for your ears only. The new road is all ready to go bar the shouting, and the syndicate has bought up a lot of land in little bits here and there. Everyone will have to negotiate with us when the compulsory purchase order goes out so we are sitting on a fortune. There's only one snag: the well in the woods will have to go and some of the syndicate are afraid the bloody thing is going to balls things up. Is it going to be an issue? That's what we need to know.'

'I know nothing about the situation, but I certainly wouldn't use that kind of language about the well,' Father Flynn said disapprovingly. He started to do the washing up.

'Of course you know something about it, Brian.'

'No, I don't, I have managed to stay out of everything. Deliberately. I would not support either side in the issue.'

'But you're the one who *knows* whether we'll be taking on a crowd of religious nutters or if the fuss will just die down. You have the feel for these things and we have to know.'

'"We" being the syndicate who are investing money in land?'

'Don't sneer at it, *Father* Flynn. Plenty of money was spent educating you as a priest, wasn't it?'

Father Flynn was extremely annoyed but he tried hard not to show it. 'If that's everything, I have to go about my work.'

'*Work?* What work?' Eddie scoffed. 'Sure, nobody is bothered about God these days. You have nothing to do. You've never really done a proper day's work in your life.'

'Fine, Eddie, I'm sure you're right.' Father Flynn sighed wearily and packed his briefcase. He was going to visit his mother in her home with a series of old photographs that might jog her memory about the past.

After that he was going to take Lilly Ryan and one of her sons to visit Aidan in the jail. Aidan Ryan, apparently in a window of calm, had relented enough to agree to talk to his wife.

Then he was going to take Holy Communion to Marty Nolan and another old man out on that road; he was going to open a multicultural World Food Day in aid of world famine at St Ita's; he was going to Ferns and Heathers to admire their new prayer and meditation room. They didn't call it a chapel but he said Mass there on Sundays for the residents.

Maybe Eddie was right and it wasn't really a proper day's work. But it sure felt like it.

Judy Flynn had done eight days of praying at St Ann's Well. Just one more left.

She had enjoyed her visit far more than she had ever expected she would. It had been a pleasure getting to know Brian again, he was such a good-natured young fellow and the people here loved him. Her mother was lost in a strange, half-waking, half-sleeping world but had become less hostile. Poor Eddie was being well and truly punished for having strayed from home. Kitty said she wouldn't have him back if he crawled the whole way through Whitethorn Woods to ask her.

Judy had tried to assist St Ann in the search for a man by going to the local bridge club in the Rossmore Hotel. She'd met two handsome men called Franklin and Wilfred. Con men, both of them, talking dreamily about a mobile phone service they were going to set up. They lived with an older lady who seldom went out because of some scandal . . . anyway they were too shallow for her, so she left them to their plans.

She had managed to work out a satisfactory routine to her day. Visiting her mam, then spending three hours in her hotel room doing her drawings with no distractions. She would have a cup of coffee with Kitty and then dress herself up for her walk to the well. On the way there she would buy a newspaper from Slattery's newsagent's, and then later in the evening she would have a drink with Brian.

She had her hair shampooed at Fabian's again. The young man who seemed to own the place told her that he hoped to marry before the year was out. This surprised her. She had been certain he was gay.

'I'm hoping to get married too,' she confided to him. 'I've enlisted St Ann at the well in the woods to help me find a husband.'

'I'd say you'll have no problem there.' Fabian was flattering. 'Beating off the offers is what you'll be.'

She was smiling as she thought of beating off the offers.

On her way to the well, she picked up a newspaper in Slattery's and brought it to the counter.

'Just the usual, Sebastian,' she said.

'You're very beautiful when you smile, Judy.'

'Well, thank you,' she said, surprised.

The man they all called Skunk Slattery wasn't known for pleasantries.

'I mean it. I was wondering, would you be free perhaps any evening to have a . . . I mean, maybe we could have a meal together?'

'That would be very nice, Sebastian,' Judy said, trying to work out his matrimonial status. She hadn't heard Kitty saying anything about Mrs Skunk but then you never knew.

'If you're not sick of the food at the Rossmore Hotel, they do a very nice dinner,' Skunk said eagerly.

'What night would you suggest, Sebastian?' she asked. There couldn't be a Mrs Skunk if he were taking her somewhere as open as that.

'Should we strike while the iron is hot? Tonight at eight, maybe?'

Judy walked up to the shrine with a spring in her step.

Neddy Nolan said to Clare that he must get in touch with his brothers in England about the land and see that they get something from it.

'I don't see why. Kit's in jail, it can't matter one way or the other to him, and we don't even know where the others are.'

'But they have a right to share in whatever there is to share if we do have to sell,' Neddy said.

'What right, Neddy? Honestly now, what right? They never gave anything, never kept in touch, never knew or cared what happened to your father.' Clare was very firm on this.

'But things didn't work out well for them, like they did for me.'

Her face was full of loyalty to him and Neddy wondered again as he did so often how she could possibly love him so much.

'Anyway, it may all come to nothing, this business about the road,' he said, rather forlornly.

'I wouldn't rely on it, Neddy,' said Clare, who had heard a great deal in the staffroom at St Ita's, and when she'd left a big bag of laundry for a service wash at the Fresh as a Daisy. Nowadays nobody was saying *if* the road came, they were saying *when* the road came.

One of these days her Neddy was going to have to make up his mind. Would he sell his father's farm for a small fortune to that syndicate which had people like Eddie Flynn in their number? Or would he hold out in case he alone could stop the march of progress and save the woods and St Ann's Well, which in his big innocent heart he believed had cured his mother and given her so many more years of life?

'You're never going to dinner with Skunk?' Father Flynn was astounded.

'Are you going to tell me he has a wife and ten children?' Judy asked in a slightly brittle tone.

'Lord, no, who'd marry Skunk?' her brother said and then wished he hadn't said it. 'I mean, he's never been married so you think of him as always being single,' he said lamely.

Judy was crisp in her response. 'Why do you all call him Skunk?'

'I can't tell you,' he said truthfully. 'He was always Skunk as far back as I remember. I actually thought that was his name.'

Lilly Ryan couldn't believe the change in her husband Aidan over the last months. He was gaunt-looking, with dark circles under his eyes. Their son Donal, who hadn't wanted to come, seemed to shrink back.

'Please, Donal,' she begged in a whisper. So the boy stretched out his hand unwillingly.

'I hope you are looking after your mam properly.' Aidan sounded very stern.

'Yes, I'm trying,' Donal said.

He was eighteen and wanted to be a million miles from here. In the past, he had seen his dad beat his mam. He couldn't bear that his mam was so pathetically grateful that they had been allowed to come.

'You can't make a worse job of it than I did,' Aidan Ryan said. 'In front of Father Flynn and you, Donal, I want to apologise for the way I treated Lilly. I have no excuse so I am not going to struggle to find one. Alcohol and the grief over our lost baby is a sort of explanation but it's no excuse.' He looked from one face to another.

Father Flynn said nothing because this was family business.

Lilly was lost for words, so Donal answered. 'Thank you for saying all this publicly. It can't have been easy for you. If it were just myself and my forgiveness you were asking for, I would never give it to you. I have seen you take the leg off a chair to beat my innocent mother. But life goes on, and if my mother asks me to forgive you, I will consider it. We will go now, Mam and myself, and leave you with Father Flynn and we'll see do you still feel the same next week at visiting time.' He stood up.

Aidan Ryan pleaded with him. 'Of course I'll feel the same, son. I'm not going to change my mind.'

'You used to change your mind within half an hour before they locked you up here.' Donal spoke without emotion. He made to leave.

'Don't go!' Aidan Ryan cried. 'Don't leave me for a week not knowing if you'll forgive me.'

'You left my mam for years not knowing what she had done to make you so violent. You can wait a week.' He was propelling his mother out before she could speak. They were nearly at the door.

Father Flynn admired the boy so much he wanted to cheer aloud but he kept his face impassive.

'It was grief, Donal,' said Aidan Ryan. 'It takes everyone in different ways. I grieved so much for your sister who disappeared.'

Donal spoke calmly. 'Yes, it does take people in different ways. In my case I didn't ever know Teresa but I envied her because whoever took her had taken her far from you and your drunken rages.'

And then they were gone.

Outside in the corridor Lilly said, 'Why didn't you let me speak to him? He's so sorry . . .' Her eyes were full of pity.

'Speak to him next week, Mam, if he's still sorry.'

'But think of him sitting there all that time—'

'You sat there all that time, Mam,' Donal said.

In the visiting room, under the eyes of the warders, Father Flynn sat beside a weeping Aidan Ryan. He knew that Lilly Ryan would forgive her husband next Tuesday. Donal Ryan probably knew it too.

But let Aidan sweat a little.

Myles Barry, the lawyer, went out to the Nolans' farm. His face was grim. He'd had a communication from one of Her Majesty's prisons in England. A Mr Christopher Nolan (otherwise known as Kit) had read of the compensation about to be offered to farmers near Rossmore whose land might be acquired in the scheme for the new road. Mr Christopher Nolan wished it noted that his father Martin Nolan was elderly and unable to make any real decision on the matter. To add that his younger brother, Edward Nolan (otherwise known as Neddy), was in fact mentally handicapped. He had not ever been able to hold any position of responsibility or trust. It would therefore not be in the interests of justice if either of these men were to reach a decision that would affect the Nolan family. He, Christopher Nolan, would like his interest in the property recorded and acknowledged.

Myles Barry had never been so angry. It would seem that the worthless Kit, having read in some paper in jail that there was money to be made out of the home he had long abandoned, was coming in for the kill.

He had to show Marty and Neddy the letter, or tell them of its contents. It wasn't something he looked forward to.

He met Father Flynn, who was just leaving the Nolan farm.

'Nothing wrong, is there?' Myles Barry asked.

The priest laughed. 'No, it's not Last Rites or anything. Marty likes Communion brought to him now and then, he's not able to get into the church for Mass as well as he used to.'

'I suppose he should be in care?'

'Hasn't he the best care in the world here with Neddy and Clare?' the priest said, unaware that Neddy had come out of the house behind him. 'If I was an old person in Rossmore I'd much prefer to have that couple looking after me than anyone else. It would be desperate to be like my poor own mother and the poor old canon, determined to stay independent but really struggling . . ."

The priest got into his car and drove off and the lawyer shook hands with Neddy, who had come out to greet him. The pair of them walked into the kitchen. Myles Barry noted the gleaming surfaces, the scrubbed table, and the blue and yellow china arranged on the open shelves.

Neddy said his father was having a rest in his own room, poured the lawyer a big mug of coffee and offered a plate of homemade biscuits. He had seen a cookery expert do them on television last week, he said, and thought they looked easy enough.

He was an innocent, certainly, but he was not a foolish man.

Suddenly Myles Barry decided to show to Neddy the hurtful, greedy letter written by his brother Kit from an English jail.

Neddy read it slowly. 'He doesn't think much of us, does he?' he said.

'Wasn't I at school with Kit? He was always dismissive of people, you know the way he went on, it really meant nothing . . .'

'Was he ever in touch with you since he left school?' Neddy asked.

'No, but you know the way it is, people's lives are different. Maybe he has nothing to tell.' Myles Barry was wondering why he seemed to excuse Kit Nolan when really he wanted to punch him in the face.

'That's true. Every day must be like the day before in there.' Neddy shook his head sadly. 'He never writes to me either, but I send him a letter every month. I told him all about the road, of course.'

'And you heard from Eddie Flynn's syndicate, did you? I believe they were coming to see you.'

'Oh, yes, a confused sort of visit.'

'And what did you say to them, Neddy?' Myles Barry held his breath.

'I told them I couldn't possibly deal with them, and that we would never take that huge sum of money, it was just outrageous.'

'And what did they say to that?' Myles Barry's voice was only a whisper.

'You won't believe it, Myles, but they just offered me more money still! Like as if they hadn't been listening. But we'll get it sorted out when the time comes—when the compulsory purchase order comes.'

Myles Barry wiped his brow. 'You do understand, Neddy. I mean, I did explain to you, the government won't pay nearly what Eddie Flynn's pals will. You see, those syndicate people are operating from strength—they've bought up little bits of land everywhere.'

'Yes, I know all that, but if I sold it to them it would be theirs and I'd have no say in what happens.'

Myles Barry pondered over whether he should say that Neddy Nolan wouldn't ever have any say in what happened once he sold the land. But it hardly seemed worth it.

'So what will we say to Kit?' he asked despairingly.

'There's no need to say anything to Kit—he doesn't have any rights to anything from this place, only what I choose to give him.' Neddy looked around him proudly at the refurbished kitchen.

'Well, I agree it sounds as if it would be hard for him to prove any legal claim but of course as your father's son he might be able . . .'

'No, Myles.' Neddy was again very calm. 'No, when I bailed him the second time, I had to go across to England to do it. And I found a nice old English lawyer. He made Kit sign a document saying that in return for the bail money he would relinquish his claim on the family estate. I mean, I told this lawyer it was only a few acres of poor land, but still it was an estate technically.' He smiled, thinking of it all.

'And do you still have that document, Neddy?'

'Oh, I do. You see, Kit skipped bail that time, so I never got our money back, and when he was inside again they wouldn't give him bail.'

'Could I see this document, do you think?'

Neddy went to a small oak cabinet in the corner. Inside were neat files that would have done credit to any company. Within seconds he pulled out the right piece of paper. Myles Barry looked back into the filing drawer. He saw files marked 'Insurance', 'Pensions', 'St Ita's School', 'Medical', 'Household Expenses', 'Farm' . . . And all this from the man whose brother said he was not the full shilling.

Sebastian Slattery was proving to be an excellent companion. Judy found it very easy to talk to him and he was very interested in her work too. How she set about illustrating a children's story. Were there some stories that she didn't enjoy and did she find them harder to do?

He asked her, did she ever go to France on the Eurostar train? It was something he had always promised himself that he would do when he was next in London. He told her that he had hardly any family himself. He was an only child and his parents were dead. He did have cousins some miles out, in a small village called Doon—a nice place actually. He had been invited to the opening of a building out there called the Danny O'Neill Health Centre, in memory of some Irishman who went to America, and his grandson, who was half Polish, was doing it in his honour. Maybe Judy might like to come with him as his guest?

'Why do they call you Skunk?' she asked suddenly.

'I don't know, to be honest. They did at school and it stuck. Maybe I smelt awful then. I don't smell awful now, do I?'

'No, Sebastian, you do not, you smell fine to me,' she said.

At that moment Cathal Chambers, the bank manager, walked by.

'Evening, Skunk, evening, Judy,' he said affably.

'Oh, Cathal, we were just discussing this. Sebastian is going to be called by his real name from now on,' Judy said.

'Sure, I'm sorry, Skunk, I mean Sebastian, no offence ever meant.'

And Skunk Slattery, who had been called by that name for over thirty years, graciously forgave him.

Cathal Chambers was concerned because Neddy Nolan had borrowed so much money from the bank. Of course he had put the farm up as collateral; still it was a heavy sum. And this from a man who would think twice before buying a pair of shoes in the charity shop.

'Could you let me know what the money's for, Neddy?' Cathal asked.

'It's for my advisers,' Neddy explained.

'But what kind of advice are you getting that could cost all this?' Cathal was bewildered. 'You wouldn't want cowboy advisers who might bleed you dry or anything.' Cathal was sincere. He was as much out for Neddy Nolan's good as for the bank.

'No, indeed, Cathal,' Neddy said with a calm little smile. 'Experts in their field charge high fees.'

When Neddy had gone, Cathal went to see the lawyer, Myles Barry.

'Myles, I don't want to get into the lawyer–client relationship but who are all these advisers Neddy Nolan has?'

'Advisers?' Myles Barry was confused.

'Yes, some people he's paying huge fees to apparently.'

Myles Barry scratched his head. 'I don't know who they are. I haven't sent him even one bill, and he can hardly have retained another firm of lawyers without telling me. I don't know, Cathal. I really don't.'

Lilly Ryan and her son Donal went to the prison on visiting day. This time they wanted to go without the priest.

'I'll be there visiting someone else in case you need me,' he said.

Father Flynn had an entirely unsatisfactory conversation with poor Becca King, who had got a very long prison sentence for being involved in the murder of her rival in love. She showed no repentance at all. He hoped that she wouldn't ask him again to arrange a prison wedding with that young man she was obsessed with. A young man who wouldn't even come to visit her in jail. But no, today she had a petition for St Ann, a card that she wanted pinned on to the shrine for all to see.

She showed it to the priest. It was a photograph of Gabrielle King, her mother, and underneath was written: *Please, St Ann, punish this woman severely for having destroyed her daughter's life. And if any of your loyal followers should see her in the streets of Rossmore, they should spit at her in your name.*

Father Flynn felt very old and tired. He said he would go there this afternoon and do it, he would give it priority.

'It must be in a place where everyone can see it,' Becca called as he was leaving.

Outside, Kate, one of the warders, laid her hand on his arm. 'You are a kind man, Father, not to upset her.'

'You do know that I'm going to throw the petition away, don't you?' Father Flynn said.

'Of course I do, but you'll wait until you get home and burn it rather than leaving it round here for anyone to pick up,' Kate said.

Father Flynn put the photograph and petition in his wallet beside a cheque that had come from London that morning. It was money left by a lady who had died, a Helen Harris. She wanted to thank the shrine of St Ann for having answered her prayers for the safe delivery of a baby twenty-three long years ago. Perhaps the priest could spend it as he thought best to honour the saint.

As he sat on a wooden bench in the waiting room, in case Lilly Ryan might need him later, Father Flynn speculated to himself about the role of a priest in today's society. He hadn't come to any satisfactory conclusion when Lilly and Donal came up to him.

'All well?' he asked anxiously and felt annoyed with himself at the very question. How could all be well in a family where the father was in jail for domestic violence, a family that had lost a child nearly a quarter of a century ago?

But surprisingly Lilly nodded as if it were a normal thing to ask. 'Just fine, Father. I realise now he's a very weak man. I didn't know this, you see, what with him being so big and strong, and hurting me for being stupid. But he's actually weak and frightened, I see that now.'

'And my mam realises that just because she is understanding and forgiving to him, the State will not be forgiving and allow him to go home. He will have to finish his sentence,' her son said.

'Yes, and Donal was very good. It's not really in his heart, but to please me he shook hands with his dad and wished him courage.' Lilly's tired face looked less strained than before.

'So would you say we have a result then?' Father Flynn said.

'Best result in the circumstances,' Donal agreed.

'That's all any of us can hope for,' Father Flynn said.

Clare had taken some pupils from St Ita's to the Heartfelt Art Gallery to do a project. Emer, who was the director there, was a friend of hers. They had decided they would let the girls wander around the gallery while the two of them had a cup of coffee.

Emer was getting married shortly to a Canadian called Ken, and Father Flynn was going to take the service.

'I see your Neddy often these days, because he has business in an office near Ken's office up in the converted flour mills,' Emer said.

'Neddy? Business?'

'Well, I assume so. I saw him today when I was bringing Ken some lunch in his office. And yesterday . . .'

Clare was silent. Neddy had mentioned nothing about any business. She felt a cold lump of dread in her heart. But not Neddy. No, never.

Emer realised what was happening. 'I could have been mistaken,' she said lamely.

Clare said nothing.

'I mean, it's all offices there. It's not as if it was flats, apartments. No, Clare, not Neddy. He worships you, for heaven's sake.'

'I think these girls have had enough time, don't you?' Clare said in a very brittle voice quite unlike her own.

'Please, don't jump to conclusions . . . you know men,' Emer begged.

Clare knew men better than anyone in Rossmore.

'Come on, girls, don't take all day,' she said in a voice that was not going to be disobeyed.

Later, after school, she was getting into her car when she met Cathal Chambers from the bank. He greeted her warmly.

'You and Neddy must be making great plans up in that farm of yours,' he said. 'What are all these advisers for?'

'I don't know about any advisers.'

'Maybe I got it wrong. But you do know you have huge borrowings, don't you?' Cathal's round face was anxious.

'Huge borrowings? Oh, yes, yes indeed, I know . . .' Clare said in a voice that would be obvious to anyone that she had absolutely no idea.

There was a time she had thought that Neddy was just too good to be true. Maybe she had been right.

When she got back home, her father-in-law Marty was asleep in a big wicker chair on the porch that she and Neddy had built together. This place had meant peace and refuge to Clare, and now it was all over.

Neddy was sitting at the kitchen table surrounded by papers.

'I have something important to tell you, Neddy,' she began.

'And I have something very important to tell you, Clare,' he said.

Judy Flynn stood back to get the full effect of the new sign over Slattery's newsagent's. It looked very splendid.

'It may take time for them to stop calling me Skunk,' he said anxiously from the top of his ladder.

'Well, we have time,' Judy said.

'You don't have to go back home for a while yet, do you?'

'No, I'm my own boss, but I'm not made of money, I can't go on staying in the Rossmore Hotel for much longer.'

'Well, what about my place then? You could stay here over the shop for a while until . . . until . . .'

'Until what, Sebastian?'

'Until we get married and look for somewhere nicer for you and for me, for us, I mean.'

'Are we going to get married? We barely know each other,' Judy said.

'I do hope so,' Sebastian said, coming down the ladder.

'Right. I'll move in tonight,' she said.

'I'll have your brother after me, saying I am the wages of sin.'

'Don't be ridiculous, Sebastian. Brian will just be delighted to see us happy. He won't go on with all that kind of stuff.'

Father Brian Flynn was surprised to see Chester Kovac, the big American who had financed the Danny O'Neill Health Centre in Doon.

'I was wondering if I could prevail on you to marry Hannah Harty and myself quietly, you know, no big ceremony.'

'Well, of course I will, and my warmest congratulations. But why won't you be getting married out in Doon where you live?'

'No, we'd have to ask everyone if we had it in Doon. And anyway there's Dr Dermot there—we don't want to be sort of showing off in front of him. It's complicated.'

Father Flynn knew Dr Dermot—a mean, crabbing man. He could well believe that it was complicated.

'I just didn't want you to miss out on a big day, that's all,' he reassured Chester.

'Oh, don't worry about that, Father. There will be plenty of people at a big do when I go back to the States for a honeymoon. In fact we will be bringing my mom back here for a vacation. Her name is Ann, too, so she is very anxious to visit the well here.'

Father Flynn thought to himself that she had better come fairly quickly if she wanted to see the well, and he examined his diary to get a suitable early date for the wedding.

Eddie Flynn was nowhere to be found when the decision to build the new road was announced. The vote in the council had been in favour of building the bypass. Eddie's syndicate had bought every piece of property, except for the Nolans' farm, which was central to the plan. The road would go straight through the farm and up through the woods in a straight line, taking the well and the shrine with it.

Eddie had assured the others that buying land from Neddy Nolan was like taking candy from a baby. Yes, true, it was Neddy who was the loser. The compulsory purchase order would not pay anything like what he had been offered by the syndicate. But Neddy had always been soft in the head. The real problem was that Eddie Flynn had not delivered the whole deal, so he had disappeared.

Kitty and the children barely noticed that he was gone. Naomi, however, was very distressed. She had fabric for bridesmaids and flower girls, and she needed to talk to him about it. And he had left her no money to be getting on with . . .

Clare and Neddy sat one on either side of the table. Clare didn't even look at the papers spread out all over the place. She was about to have her first and last row with Neddy Nolan on the day she had been going to tell him that her period was three weeks late and they might possibly be looking at the pregnancy they both longed for. Now it was too late.

Neddy spoke very quietly.

'The permission for the road has been given today, Clare. As we thought, it's going straight through here and on up to the well.'

'We knew that would happen, but you refused to sell to Eddie Flynn just at a time when you might actually need money more than any other time of your life.' Clare's voice was cold.

'But I couldn't sell to them or we'd have had no control,' he said as if explaining it to a toddler.

'And what control do you have now? Less money, that's all . . .'

'No, Clare, that's not true, we have all this . . .' He waved at the papers and maps on the kitchen table.

'This?'

'I took advice, I got experts to draw up an alternative plan, another way the road would go so that it wouldn't take away St Ann's shrine and the well. It involved architects, engineers, quantity surveyors, and cost a fortune. Clare, I had to borrow from Cathal Chambers and he thinks I'm into heroin or gambling or something.'

Suddenly she knew that this was indeed what he was doing with the money, rather than feathering a little love nest for himself in the converted flour mills. Her relief was followed by a wave of resentment.

'And why didn't you tell him and tell me, for God's sake?'

'I had to keep it quiet, have meetings where no one would see me.'

'In the old flour mills?' she guessed.

Neddy laughed sheepishly. 'There's me thinking no one knew!'

The resentment had gone. Clare felt only relief that he still loved her.

'Will it work, Neddy?' she asked weakly.

'I think it will,' Neddy said calmly. 'You see, I hired a public relations expert as well to show us how to get public sympathy.'

'But, Neddy, couldn't we have done that without all these experts?'

'No, that's just the point,' Neddy cried. 'Now we have a perfectly possible alternative plan. A plan that you and I paid for with our own money.' He nodded over at the little oak cabinet. 'I have every detail of it recorded there. They'll know we are telling the truth and putting our money where our mouth is.'

'And where will the road go?'

She bent over the map with him and he stroked her hair with one hand as he pointed with the other. The new road would still go through the Nolan farm, but would then follow a route that would allow a sizeable part of the woods to remain, the part that held the shrine. There would be a big car park there and a side slip road from the new road to bring visitors directly to the shrine instead of going through Rossmore. Local people could walk there through what remained of the woods.

Clare looked at him with admiration. 'I wish you'd told me,' she said.

'Yes, I was going to, but you looked tired, and you have to go into a classroom every day. I just stay here. I have a much easier life.'

She looked around the house that he kept so well for the three of them. It was not such an easy life, but Neddy never complained.

'Hey, you said you had something to tell me . . . what was it?' he asked.

She told him that there was a chance she might be pregnant. Neddy got up and held her in his arms.

'I was up there at the shrine today and I know it's nonsense but I did say that it was something we both wanted badly,' he said into her hair.

'Well, she had to do something for the man who saved her well,' Clare said.

They were still standing there, arms around each other, when Marty Nolan came in. 'Father Flynn arrived and he couldn't get any answer so I came in to see were you two all right.'

As they had tea and homemade biscuits, the sun began to set over the woods that Neddy Nolan had almost certainly saved. And Father Flynn knew that his sister Judy was up there at the well, thanking St Ann and saying she hadn't expected that it would all work so quickly. He listened, as it grew dark, to Neddy's plans.

Neddy was going to buy a house much nearer Rossmore, and then maybe Father Flynn's mother and the canon could come to stay. He had seen a grand place with a garden that the canon would like.

Neddy would look after them all. And if they were to have a little baby he would look after the baby too. It would be nice for the older people to have a new young life around the place.

And for once Father Flynn could find nothing to say. He looked at the good honest man in front of him and for the first time for a long time he saw some purpose in a life that had so recently been confused and contradictory on every front.

He looked back up at the ever-darkening woods. And it wasn't fanciful to think of them as a very special place, where so many voices had been heard and so many dreams answered.

When Maeve Binchy announced her retirement from writing novels in 2000, at the age of sixty, she was more than ready to contemplate a traditional leisurely life in Dalkey, County Dublin, where she has lived since childhood. 'I started looking speculatively at our garden, planning waist-high flowerbeds where I could grow prize-winning things while sitting on a stool with a glass of wine in my hand!' She was also looking forward to a few decades of jam-making and embroidery, but says she found that she had

Maeve Binchy

failed to appreciate one important thing: 'As far as giving up my weekly newspaper column was concerned, retirement was fine. But as regards writing books, it didn't work at all. Writers are not meant to retire. Apparently we are meant to go on telling stories until we fall off the perch. I didn't know this at the time.'

A long-term sufferer from osteoarthritis, Maeve had begun to find the tours to promote her books increasingly difficult to cope with, which was the major reason behind her decision to retire. 'I was getting ever less fit, ever fatter and ever more lame. Worse, the shopping malls where the bookstores were had become more inaccessible, the railway platforms longer and the aircraft were always leaving from Gate 223 instead of Gate One. But then the publishers said that if I was too feeble for book signings and promotion, that was all right.'

As a result, *Whitethorn Woods* is Maeve's third book (after *Quentins* and *Nights of Rain and Stars*) written in retirement, and the author feels that she has found the perfect situation. 'I just went on writing stories—a book every second year, as always—except that now I feel retired and I love it. For one thing, all the guilt has gone. In the morning when I wake and hear on the radio about all the traffic on the roads I can snuggle back under the duvet again, knowing I don't have to face it. I can savour the newspapers at breakfast instead of thinking that it's a shameful indulgence. I write my stories gently, at my own speed, reply to fan letters slowly, and finish work at one thirty every day so that the afternoon belongs to me and my husband Gordon. Most of our friends are retired now, which means we can meet them for lunch.'

Gordon Snell, also a writer, and Maeve still live in the same cottage in Dalkey that they bought in 1980, three years after their marriage. They have been supremely happy together for thirty-three years, and still write side by side in a bright upstairs room. 'We sit at our laptops and work from eight thirty until lunchtime, when we usually go to the pub next door and have lunch, and maybe a game of chess. I am honestly happier now than I ever was. I don't feel beached or parked or on the sidelines, or any of those words that I once wrongly associated with retirement. I feel in the centre of our world without the stress and the competitive urge . . . If people overtake me in book sales, then so what? I overtook people in my time and with retirement comes a lovely, peaceful, weekend feeling where nothing matters as much as you once thought it did. I am lucky in that I have a wonderful companion to share this time with me and a great warm family and an unequalled circle of friends.'

Anne Jenkins

PROFILE

Birthplace: Dalkey, County Dublin.
Education: Holy Child Convent in Killiney and University College, Dublin.
Other jobs: Worked on a kibbutz, as a teacher, and as a journalist on the *Irish Times*.
Interesting fact: On a visit to a Jerusalem cave, she lost her Catholic faith and found her literary vocation.
Relaxation: Playing bad chess and spectacularly bad bridge.
Motto: We have to make our own happiness.
Most proud of: Being a storyteller and a good friend.

Novels: *Light a Penny Candle*
Echoes
London Transports
Dublin 4
The Lilac Bus
Firefly Summer
Silver Wedding
Circle of Friends
The Copper Beech
The Glass Lake
Evening Class
Tara Road
Scarlet Feather
Quentins
Nights of Rain and Stars
Whitethorn Woods
Non-fiction: *Aches and Pains*

Painting
Mona Lisa

Jeannie Kalogridis

For centuries, people have asked: 'Who was the Mona Lisa?' and 'Why did Leonardo da Vinci keep the "Mona Lisa" painting with him until his death?' Through meticulous research, Jeanne Kalogridis has conceived a bold and plausible answer, not only as to the identity of the woman in the painting, but also as to how the haunting image came into being.

PROLOGUE: LISA

June 1490

I

MY NAME IS Lisa di Antonio Gherardini Giocondo, though to acquaintances I am known simply as Madonna Lisa, and to those of the common class, Monna Lisa.

My likeness has been recorded on wood, with boiled linseed oil and pigments dug from the earth or crushed from semiprecious stones, and applied with brushes made from the feathers of birds and the silken fur of animals. I have seen the painting. It does not look like me. I stare at it and see instead the faces of my mother and father. I listen and hear their voices. I feel their love and their sorrow, and I witness again and again, the crime that bound them together; the crime that bound them to me.

For my story began not with my birth, but a murder, committed the year before I was born.

It was first revealed to me during an encounter with the astrologer, two weeks before my eleventh birthday, which was celebrated on the 15th of June. My mother announced that I would have my choice of a present. She assumed that I would request a new gown, for nowhere has sartorial ostentation been practised more avidly than my native Florence. My father was one of the city's wealthiest wool merchants, and his business connections afforded me my pick of sumptuous silks, brocades, velvets and furs. I spent those days studying the dress of each noblewoman I passed, and at night, I lay awake contemplating the design.

All this changed the day of Uncle Lauro's wedding.

I stood on the balcony of our house on the Via Maggio between my mother and grandmother, staring in the direction of the Ponte Santa Trinita, the bridge which the bride would cross on her ride to her groom.

My grandmother had come to live with us several months earlier. She was still a handsome woman, but faded and frail. She would not live out the year. My mother was dark-haired, dark-eyed, with skin so flawless it provoked my jealousy; she, however, seemed unaware of her amazing appearance. I was mature for my years, already larger and taller than she, with coarse dull brown waves and troubled skin.

Downstairs, my father and Uncle Lauro, attended by his two sons, waited in the loggia that opened onto the street.

My mother suddenly pointed. 'There she is!'

From our vantage, we could see a small figure on horseback headed towards us, followed by several people on foot. When they neared, I could make out the woman riding the white horse.

Her name was Giovanna Maria. I had met her often during her six-month courtship with my mother's brother. She was a friendly, plump fifteen-year-old with golden hair. Never again would she look as lovely as she did that day, in a pink overgown covered with seed pearls, her curls tamed into ringlets beneath a tiara of braided silver. When she arrived, my uncle helped her dismount. He was twice Giovanna's age, a widower whose eldest son was two years her junior.

Before we joined them downstairs, my grandmother eyed the pair sceptically. 'It cannot last happily. She is Sagittarius, with Taurus ascendant, and Lauro is Aries. The two of them will constantly butt heads.'

'Mother,' my own reproached gently.

'If you and Antonio had paid attention to such matters—' She broke off at my mother's glance and urged us downstairs to greet the bride.

I was intrigued. My grandmother was right; my parents had never been truly happy. I realised that we had never discussed my natal chart.

I decided to bring up the matter with my mother as soon as possible. Well-to-do families often consulted astrologers on important matters. Charts were routinely cast for newborns. In fact, an astrologer had chosen that very day in June as the most fortuitous for Lauro and Giovanna Maria to wed.

After the feast as the dancing commenced, I sat beside my grandmother and questioned her further about the futures of the bride and groom. I discovered that Lauro had been born with his moon residing in Scorpio. 'As a result, he has never been able to resist a Scorpio woman. It caused much heartache in his first marriage. Giovanna Maria's moon is in Sagittarius, so she would be happiest with a man of her own sign . . .' Grandmother sighed. 'I married twice. Once for love—and we were miserable. The second time, I made no such mistake. I went to the astrologer, and when I met your grandfather'—her expression and tone softened—'I knew the stars smiled on us. Our charts were perfectly matched. A gentler, finer man was never born.'

'My sign . . . and my moon . . . What are they?' I asked. 'Who would be a good match for me?'

She gave me an odd look. 'Born in June . . . You would be Gemini, then. As for the others, I cannot say.'

'But you were at my birth,' I persisted. 'Wasn't an astrologer hired?'

'I was too busy helping your mother—and you—to worry about such a trivial thing,' she said. Politely, I did not point out that she had only just finished telling me of its importance.

That night, I lay awake puzzling over why I did not know such important information. Certainly my parents had consulted an astrologer at my birth. I was, after all, a rare creature: an only child, the bearer of my family's hopes.

The next morning I went to my mother's room. She was abed, though it was late; her health was poor and the wedding festivities had exhausted her. I clasped her hand and settled on the edge of her bed.

'I have been thinking,' I began solemnly. 'I know I am Gemini, born mid-June. But I am now old enough to know the full details of my horoscope. What is my moon, and what sign is ascendant for me?'

My mother hesitated. Clearly, she had expected a discussion of fabrics and fashion, not this. 'I am not sure.'

'But you must have kept a copy of my birth chart?'

Her face flushed. 'You did not come easily into the world, Lisa. You were small and I was ill afterwards. We did not think to have it done.'

I was aghast. 'But I *must* know these things, to make a proper match. Grandmother has said so.'

My mother sighed and leaned back against her pillows. 'Lisa . . . people marry every day without worrying about their stars. Your father and I are such an example.'

I dared not respond to this. Instead I countered, 'A chart is less costly and involved than a gown. And it is what I want as my birthday gift.' Deliberately pitiful, I said, 'Please.'

If the astrologer was not a wealthy man, he certainly behaved as one. From a top-floor window in the corridor near my bedroom, I watched secretly as his gilded carriage arrived in the courtyard behind our house. Two elegantly appointed servants attended him as he stepped down, clad in a *farsetto*, the close-fitting garment which some men wore in place of a tunic. The fabric was a violet velvet quilt, covered by a sleeveless brocade cloak in a darker shade of the same hue.

Zalumma, my mother's slave, moved forward to meet him. She was devoted to my mother, whose gentleness inspired loyalty, and who treated her like a beloved companion. Zalumma was a Circassian, from the high mountains in the mysterious East; her people were highly prized for their physical beauty and Zalumma—tall as a man, with hair and eyebrows black as jet and a face whiter than marble—was no exception. Her tight ringlets were formed not by a hot poker but by God, and were the envy of every Florentine woman. She generally kept them hidden beneath a cap.

Zalumma curtsied, then led the man into the house to meet my mother. I was to remain out of view, for this first encounter was solely a business matter, and I would only be a distraction.

The initial meeting did not last long. I heard my mother open the door and call for Zalumma; I heard the slave's quick steps on the marble, then a man's voice.

As I watched from above, Zalumma escorted the astrologer from the house—then, after glancing about, handed him a small object, perhaps a purse. He refused it at first, but Zalumma drew close and addressed him earnestly, urgently. After a moment of indecision, he pocketed the object, then climbed into his carriage and was driven away.

I assumed that she had paid him for a reading, though I was surprised that a man of such stature would read for a slave. Or perhaps it was as simple a thing as my mother forgetting to pay him.

Three days later, the astrologer returned. Once again, I watched from the top-floor window as he climbed from the carriage to be greeted by Zalumma. I was excited; Mother had agreed to call for me when the time was right.

Before entering the house, the astrologer paused and spoke to Zalumma furtively; she put a hand to her mouth as if shocked by what he said. He seemed to ask her a question. She shook her head, then put a hand on his forearm, apparently demanding something from him. He handed her a scroll of papers, then pulled away, irritated, and strode into our palazzo. Agitated, she tucked the scroll into a pocket hidden in the folds of her skirt, then followed on his heels.

I left the window and stood listening at the top of the stairs, mystified by the encounter and impatient for my summons.

Less than a quarter-hour later, I started violently when downstairs, a door was flung open with such force it slammed against the wall. I ran to the window: the astrologer was walking, unescorted, back to his carriage.

I lifted my skirts and dashed down the stairs. Breathless, I arrived at the carriage just as the astrologer gave his driver the signal to leave.

I put my hand on the polished wooden door and looked up at the man sitting on the other side. 'Please stop,' I said.

He gestured for the driver to hold the horses back and scowled down at me, clearly in a foul mood, yet his gaze also held a curious compassion. 'You would be the daughter, then?'

'Yes.'

'I will not be party to deception. Do you understand?'

'No.'

'Hmm. I see that you do not.' He paused to choose his words carefully. 'Your mother, Madonna Lucrezia, said that you were the one who requested my services. Is that so?'

'It is.'

'Then you deserve to hear at least some of the truth, for you will never hear the full of it in this house.' His pompous irritation faded and his tone grew earnest and dark. 'Your chart is unusual—some would say it is distressing. I take my art very seriously, young lady, and employ my intuition well, and it tells me that you are caught in a cycle of violence, of blood and deceit. What others have begun, you must finish.'

I recoiled, startled into silence by such unexpected harshness. When I found my voice, I insisted, 'I want nothing to do with such things.'

'You are fire four times over,' he said. 'Your temper is hot: a furnace in which the sword of justice must be forged. In your stars, I saw an act of violence, one that is your past and your future.'

'But I would never do anything to hurt someone else!'

'God has ordained it. He has His reasons for your destiny.'

I wanted to ask more, but the astrologer called to his driver and a pair of fine black horses pulled them away.

Perplexed and troubled, I walked back towards the house. My mother still sat in the great chamber where she had received the astrologer. She smiled when I entered, apparently unaware of my encounter with him. In her hand she bore a sheaf of papers.

'Come, sit beside me,' she said brightly. 'I shall tell you all about your stars. They should have been charted long ago, so I have decided that you still deserve a new gown. Your father will take you today into the city, to choose the cloth; but you must say nothing to him about this.' She nodded at the papers. 'Otherwise, he will judge us as too extravagant.'

I sat stiffly, my back straight, my hands folded tightly in my lap.

'See here.' My mother set the papers in her lap and rested her fingertip on the astrologer's elegant script. 'You are Gemini, of course—air. And have Pisces rising, which is water. Your moon is in Aries—fire.

And you have many aspects of earth in your chart, which makes you exceedingly well-balanced, and this indicates a most fortunate future. You need not worry about which man you marry, for you are so well-aspected towards every sign that—'

As she spoke, my anger grew. I cut her off. 'No, I am fire four times over,' I said. 'My life will be marked by treachery and blood.'

My mother rose swiftly; the papers in her lap slipped to the floor and scattered. 'Zalumma!' she hissed, her eyes lit by a fury I had never seen in her before. 'Did she speak to you?'

'I spoke to the astrologer myself.'

This quietened her at once, and her expression grew unreadable. Carefully, she asked, 'What else did he tell you?'

'Only what I just said. Nothing more.'

Abruptly drained, she sank back into her chair.

Lost in my anger, I jumped to my feet. 'All that you have said is a lie! What others have you told me?'

It was a cruel thing to say. She glanced at me, stricken. Yet I turned and left her sitting there, with her hand pressed to her heart.

My mother never spoke to me again of my stars. I often thought of asking Zalumma to find the papers the astrologer had given my mother, so that I could read the truth for myself. But each time, a sense of dread held me back. I already knew more than I wished.

Almost two years would pass before I learned of the crime to which I was inextricably bound.

PART I

April 26, 1478

II

IN THE STARK, massive cathedral of Santa Maria del Fiore, Bernardo Bandini Baroncelli stood before the altar and fought to steady his shaking hands. He pressed palms and fingers together in a gesture of prayer, and held them to his lips. Voice unsteady, he whispered, pleading for the success of the dark venture in which he found himself entangled, pleading for forgiveness should it succeed.

'God forgive me, a most miserable sinner,' he murmured. His quiet prayer mingled with the hundreds of hushed voices inside the cavernous church of Saint Mary of the Flower—in this case a lily. The sanctuary was one of the largest in the world, and was built in the shape of a Latin cross. Atop the juncture of the arms rested the architect Brunelleschi's greatest achievement: *il Duomo*. Dazzling in its sheer expanse, the huge dome had no apparent means of support. Visible from any part of the city, the orange brick cupola majestically dominated the skyline, and had, like the lily, become a symbol of Florence.

As he prayed, Baroncelli was overwhelmed with foreboding and regret. The latter emotion had always marked his life: born into one of the city's wealthiest and most eminent families, he had squandered his fortune and fallen into debt at an advanced age. He had spent his life as a banker, and knew nothing else. His only choices were to move his wife and children down to Naples and beg for sponsorship from one of his rich cousins—an option his outspoken spouse, Giovanna, would never have tolerated—or to offer his services to one of the two largest and most prestigious banking families in Florence: the Medici, or the Pazzi.

He had gone first to the most powerful: the Medici. They had rejected him, a fact he still resented. But their rivals, the Pazzi, welcomed him into their fold, and it was for that reason, that today he stood in the front row of the throng of faithful beside his employer, Francesco de' Pazzi. With his uncle, the knight Messer Iacopo, Francesco ran his family's international business concerns. He was a small man, with a sharp nose and chin, and eyes that narrowed beneath large brows; beside the tall, dignified Baroncelli, he resembled an ugly dwarf.

In order to provide for his family, Baroncelli was forced to grin while the Pazzi treated him as an inferior. When the matter of the plot presented itself, Baroncelli was presented with a choice: risk his neck by confessing everything to the Medici, or let the Pazzi force him to be their accomplice, and win for himself a position in the new government.

Now, as he stood asking God for forgiveness, he felt the warm breath of a fellow conspirator upon his right shoulder. The man praying just behind him wore the burlap robes of a penitent.

Standing to Baroncelli's left, Francesco fidgeted and glanced right, past his employee. Baroncelli followed his gaze: it rested on Lorenzo de' Medici, who at twenty-nine years old was the de facto ruler of Florence. Technically, Florence was governed by the Signoria, a council of eight Lord Priors and the head of state, the gonfaloniere of justice; these men were chosen from among all the notable Florentine families. Supposedly the process was fair, but curiously, the majority of those chosen were always loyal to Lorenzo, and even the gonfaloniere was his to control.

Francesco de' Pazzi was ugly, but Lorenzo was uglier still. Taller than most, and muscular in build, his fine body was marred by one of Florence's plainest faces. His nose—long and pointed, ending in a pronounced upward slope that tilted to one side—had a flattened bridge, leaving Lorenzo with a peculiarly nasal voice. His lower jaw jutted out so severely that whenever he entered a room, his chin preceded him by a thumb's breadth. His disturbing profile was framed by a jaw-length hank of dark brown hair.

Lorenzo stood waiting for the start of the Mass, flanked on one side by his loyal friend and employee, Francesco Nori, and on the other by the Archbishop of Pisa, Francesco Salviati. Despite his physiognomic failings, he emanated profound dignity and poise. In his dark, slightly protruding eyes shone an uncommon shrewdness. Even surrounded by enemies, Lorenzo seemed at ease. Salviati was a Pazzi relative, and no friend, though he and Lorenzo greeted each other as such; the elder Medici brother had lobbied furiously against Salviati's appointment as Archbishop of Pisa, asking instead that Pope Sixtus appoint a Medici sympathiser. The Pope had turned a deaf ear to Lorenzo's request, and then—breaking with a tradition that had existed for generations—he fired the Medici as the papal bankers to replace them with the Pazzi.

Yet, despite the bitter insult, today, Lorenzo had received the Pope's nephew, the seventeen-year-old Cardinal Riario of San Giorgio, as an honoured guest. After Mass in the great Duomo, Lorenzo would lead the young cardinal to a feast at the Medici palace, followed by a tour of the famed Medici collection of art.

Like his fellow conspirators, Baroncelli knew that neither feast nor tour would ever take place. Events soon to occur would change the political face of Florence for ever.

Behind Baroncelli, the penitent whispered, 'Where is Giuliano?'

Giuliano de' Medici, the younger brother, was as fair of face as Lorenzo was ugly. He was called the darling of Florence—so handsome, it was said, that men and women alike sighed in his wake. It would not do to have only one brother present in the great cathedral. Both were required, or the entire operation would have to be called off.

On his other side, Francesco de' Pazzi hissed, 'What did he say?'

Baroncelli leaned down to whisper, '"Where is Giuliano?"'

He watched the weasel-faced Francesco struggle to suppress his stricken expression. Baroncelli shared his distress. Mass would commence soon now that Lorenzo and his guest, the cardinal, were in place; unless Giuliano arrived shortly, the entire plot would evaporate into disaster. It was unthinkable—there was too much danger, too much was at stake; too many souls were involved in the plot, leaving too many tongues free to wag. Even now, Messer Iacopo waited alongside a small army of fifty Perugian mercenaries for the signal from the church bell. When it tolled, he would seize control of the government palace and rally the people against Lorenzo.

The penitent pushed forward until he stood alongside Baroncelli; he then raised his face to stare upwards at the dizzyingly high cupola overhead, rising directly above the great altar. The man's burlap hood slipped back slightly, revealing his profile. For an instant, his lips parted, and brow and mouth contorted in a look of such hatred, such revulsion, that Baroncelli recoiled from him.

Francesco clutched Baroncelli's elbow and hissed, 'We must go to the Piazzo de Medici at once!'

Smiling, Francesco steered Baroncelli to the left, away from the distracted Lorenzo de' Medici. The pair moved down the outermost aisle that ran the intimidating length of the sanctuary—past brown stone columns the width of four men, which were connected by high, white arches framing long windows of stained glass. Francesco's expression was at first benign, as he nodded greetings along the way.

The first group of worshippers they passed consisted of Florence's wealthy: glittering women and men weighed down by ostentatious displays of gold and jewels, by fur-trimmed heavy brocades and velvets. The smell of the men's rosemary and lavender water mingled with the more volatile, feminine scent of attar of roses, all wafting above the base notes of smoke and frankincense from the altar.

The aroma of lavender increased as the two men walked past the rows of the richest merchants—the men and women dressed in silks and fine wool, embellished with a glint of gold here, and silver there. Unsmiling now, Francesco nodded once or twice, to lower-ranking business associates, as Baroncelli struggled to breathe; the onrush of faces—witnesses, all of them—triggered a profound panic within him.

But Francesco did not slow. As they passed the middle-class tradesmen—the smiths and bakers, the artists and their apprentices—the smell of fragrant herbs gave way to perspiration and the fine fabrics to the coarser weaves of wool and silk.

The poor stood in the rows at the back. The garments here consisted of tattered wool and rumpled linen, perfumed with sweat and filth. Both Francesco and Baroncelli involuntarily covered their mouths and noses.

At last, they made their way out of the huge open doors. Baroncelli took a great sobbing gasp of air.

'This is no time for cowardice,' Francesco snapped, and dragged him down the steps into the street, past the outstretched arms of beggars.

It took the two men barely four minutes to reach the Palazzo de Medici, which dominated the corner of the Vias Larga and Gori. The two conspirators stopped at the thick brass doors of the palazzo's main entrance. Francesco pounded on the metal; his efforts finally rewarded by the appearance of a servant, who led them into the magnificent courtyard.

Thus began the agony of waiting while Giuliano was summoned. Had Baroncelli not been in the grip of fear, he might have been able to enjoy his surroundings. At each corner of the courtyard stood a great stone column, connected by graceful arches. On top of those was a frieze, adorned with medallions depicting pagan scenes in-between the Medici crest. They had been sculpted by one of Donatello's students.

The famous seven *palle*—or balls—of the Medici crest were arranged in what looked suspiciously like a crown. To hear Lorenzo tell it, the *palle* represented the dents in the shield of one of Charlemagne's knights, the brave Averardo, who had fought a fearsome giant and won. So impressed was Charlemagne that he allowed Averardo to design his coat of arms from the battered shield. The Medici claimed descent from the brave knight, and the family had borne the crest for centuries.

The cry *'Palle! Palle! Palle!'* was used to rally the people on the Medici's behalf.

Beside Baroncelli, Francesco de' Pazzi was pacing the floor with hands clasped behind his back, and small eyes glaring downwards at polished marble. Giuliano had best come soon, Baroncelli reflected.

But Giuliano did not appear. The servant, as well-oiled as every part of the Medici machinery, returned with a look of practised sympathy. '*Signori*, forgive me. I am sorry to tell you that my master is indisposed.'

Francesco leapt forward, and barely managed to replace his fright with jovialness in time. 'Ah! Please explain to Ser Giuliano that the matter is most urgent.' He lowered his tone as if confiding a secret. 'Today's luncheon is in the young Cardinal Riario's honour, and he is at the Duomo now with Ser Lorenzo, asking after your master. Mass has been delayed, and I fear that, should Ser Giuliano fail to attend with us, the cardinal will take offence. We have come at the behest of Ser Lorenzo.'

The youth gave a quick lift of his chin, signalling his understanding of the urgency. 'Of course, I will relay all that you have said to my master.'

As the lad turned, Baroncelli gazed on his employer, and marvelled at his talent for duplicity.

In less time than either he or Francesco expected, Giuliano de' Medici stood before them, in a tunic of pale green velvet embroidered at the neck and sleeves with gold thread. Though his brother's features

were imperfect, Giuliano's were without flaw. His nose, though prominent, was straight and nicely rounded at the tip; his jaw was strong and
square; and his eyes were large and golden brown. Delicate, well-
formed lips rested atop even teeth, and his hair was full and curling. At
twenty-four, life was good to Giuliano; he was young, lively and fair of
face. Indeed, his jocular demeanour, sensitive character and generous
nature made him generally loved by Florence's citizens.

The faint morning light that had begun to paint the bottoms of the
columns, revealed that today Giuliano's glory was sorely dimmed. His
hair had not been combed, his clothes had obviously been hastily
donned—and his eyes were noticeably bloodshot, as though he had
not slept. For the first time in Baroncelli's memory, Giuliano did not
smile. His manner was sombre.

'Good day, gentlemen. I understand Cardinal Riario has taken
offence at my absence from Mass?'

'We are so sorry to disturb you,' Francesco de' Pazzi said, his hands
clasped in an apologetic gesture. 'We have come at the behest of Ser
Lorenzo . . .' Despite the business rivalry between the Medici and the
Pazzi, they were related by the marriage of Giuliano's elder sister to
Francesco's brother Guglielmo. This called for a public show of cordial-
ity, even affection—a fact Francesco was relying on now.

Giuliano released a short sigh. 'I understand. God knows, we must
take care to please the cardinal. Let us go, then.' He gestured for them
to move back towards the entryway, and as he lifted his arm, Baroncelli
noticed that Giuliano had dressed so hurriedly that he wore no sword.

Out they went, the three of them, into the bright morning.

As they walked, Baroncelli marvelled that, although he was terrified,
his hands no longer shook and his heart and breath no longer failed
him. Indeed, he and Francesco joked and laughed and played the role
of good friends trying to cheer another. Giuliano smiled faintly at their
efforts but lagged behind, so the two conspirators made a game of alter-
nately pulling and pushing him along.

'Pray tell, good Giuliano,' Francesco said, catching his young
brother-in-law by his sleeve. 'What has happened to make you sigh so?
Surely your heart has not been stolen by some worthless wench?'

Giuliano lowered his gaze and shook his head—not in reply, but to
indicate that he did not wish to broach such matters. Francesco
dropped the subject at once. Yet he never eased their rapid pace, and
within minutes, they arrived at the front entry of the Duomo.

Baroncelli paused. He was already doomed to Hell, so saw no point
in suppressing any further urge towards deceit . . . and the sight of

Giuliano moving so slowly, as though he were heavy laden, pricked at him. Feigning impulsiveness, he seized the young Medici and hugged him tightly. 'Dear friend,' he said. 'It troubles me to see you so unhappy. What must we do to cheer you?'

Giuliano gave another forced little smile and a slight shake of his head. 'Nothing, good Bernardo. Nothing.'

And he followed Francesco's lead into the cathedral.

Baroncelli, meanwhile, had laid one more concern to rest: Giuliano wore no breastplate beneath his tunic.

On that late April morning, Giuliano faced a terrible decision: he must choose to break the heart of one of the two people he loved most in the world. One belonged to his brother, Lorenzo; the other, to a woman.

Though a young man, Giuliano had known many lovers. Now, for the first time in his life, he desired only one: Anna. She was handsome, to be sure, but it was her intelligence that had entrapped him, her delight in life and the greatness of her heart. He wished to marry her, to father her children and none other's. And it seemed like a miracle when she had at last confided her feelings: that God had created them for each other, and that it was His cruellest joke that she was already given to another man.

Giuliano, accustomed to having whatever he wanted, tried to bargain his way round it. He pleaded with her to come to him in private—simply to hear him out. She wavered, but then agreed. They had met in the ground-floor *appartamento* at the Palazzo de Medici. She had indulged his embraces, his kiss, but would go no further. He had begged her to leave Florence, to go away with him, but she had refused.

'He knows.' Her voice had been anguished. 'Do you understand? He knows, and I cannot bear to hurt him any longer.'

Giuliano was a determined man. For Anna, he was willing to give up the prospect of a respectable marriage; for Anna, he was willing to endure the censure of the Church, even excommunication and the prospect of damnation. It seemed a small price in order to be with her.

And so he had made a forceful argument: she should go with him to Rome, to stay in a family villa. The Medici had papal connections; he would procure for her an annulment. He would marry her. He would give her children.

She had been torn, had put her hands to her lips. He looked in her eyes and saw the misery there, but he also saw a flicker of hope.

'I don't know, I don't know,' she had said, and he had let her return to her husband to make her decision.

The next day, Giuliano had gone to Lorenzo. He had woken in the middle of the night and was unable to return to sleep. It was still dark—two hours before sunrise—but he was not surprised to see the light emanating from his brother's antechamber. Lorenzo sat at his desk, with his cheek propped against his fist, scowling down at a letter he held close to the glowing lamp.

Normally Lorenzo would have glanced up, would have forced away the frown to smile, to utter a greeting; that day, however, no greeting came; Lorenzo gave him a cursory glance, then looked back at the letter. Its contents were apparently the cause of his bad humour.

It had been hard for Lorenzo, first to lose his father, then to be forced to assume power when so young. After nine years, the strain showed. Permanent creases had established themselves on his brow and shadows had settled beneath his eyes. Lorenzo fretted over Florence as a father would a wayward child. He spent every waking moment dedicated to furthering her prosperity and the Medici interests. But he was keenly aware that no one loved him, save for the favours he could bestow. Only Giuliano adored his brother for himself. Only Giuliano tried to make Lorenzo forget his responsibilities; only Giuliano could make him laugh. Lorenzo loved him fiercely.

And it was the repercussions of that love Giuliano feared.

Giuliano straightened and cleared his throat. 'I am going,' he said, rather loudly, 'to Rome.'

Lorenzo lifted his brows and his gaze, but the rest of him did not stir. 'On pleasure, or on some business I should acquaint myself with?'

'I am going with a woman.'

Lorenzo sighed; his frown eased. 'Enjoy yourself, then, and think of me suffering here.'

'I am going with Madonna Anna,' Giuliano said.

Lorenzo jerked his head sharply at the name. 'You're joking.' He said it lightly, but as he stared at Giuliano, his expression grew incredulous. 'You *must* be joking.' His voice fell to a whisper. 'This is foolishness . . Giuliano, she is from a good family. And she is *married*.'

Giuliano did not quail. 'I love her. I won't be without her I've asked her to go with me to Rome, to live.'

Lorenzo's eyes widened. 'Giuliano . . . Our hearts mislead us all, from time to time. You're enthralled by an emotion, but it will ease. Give yourself a fortnight to rethink this idea.'

Lorenzo's paternal, dismissive tone only strengthened Giuliano's resolve. 'I've already arranged the carriage and driver, and sent a message to the servants at the villa to prepare for us. We must seek an annulment,' he said. 'I want to marry Anna. I want her to bear my children.'

Lorenzo leaned back in his chair and let go a short, bitter laugh. 'An annulment? Courtesy of our good friend Pope Sixtus, I suppose? He would prefer to see us banished from Italy.' He pushed himself away from his desk, rose, and reached for his brother; his tone softened. 'This is a fantasy, Giuliano. I understand that she is a marvellous woman, but . . . She has been married for some years. Even if I *could* arrange for an annulment, it would create a scandal. Florence would never accept it.'

Lorenzo's hand was almost on his shoulder; Giuliano shifted it back, away from the conciliatory touch. 'We'll remain in Rome, if we have to.'

Lorenzo emitted a sharp sigh of frustration. 'You'll get no annulment from Sixtus. So give up your romantic ideas. If you can't live without her, have her—but for God's sake, do so discreetly.'

Giuliano flared. 'How can you speak of her like that? You know Anna, you know she would never consent to deception. And if I can't have her I won't have any other woman.'

'You'll do what? Refuse to marry anyone at all?' Lorenzo's voice grew louder. 'You have a duty, an obligation to your family. You think you can forget it, go to Rome on a whim, pass our blood on to a litter of bastards? You would stain us with excommunication? Because that's what would happen, you know—to both of you! Do you have any idea of what will happen to *Anna*? What people will call her? She's a decent woman, a good woman. Do you really want to ruin her? You'll take her to Rome and grow tired of her. And what will she have left?'

Angry words scalded Giuliano's tongue. He wanted to say that though Lorenzo had married a harridan in the form of Clarice Orsini, from the powerful, princely Orisini clan, he, Giuliano, would rather die than live in such loveless misery. But he remained silent.

'You'll never do it. You'll come to your senses.'

Giuliano looked at him a long moment. 'I love you, Lorenzo,' he said quietly. 'But I am going.' He turned and moved to the door.

'Leave with her,' his brother threatened, 'and you can forget that I am your brother. Leave with her, and you'll never see me again.'

Giuliano looked back over his shoulder at Lorenzo, and was suddenly afraid. 'Please don't make me choose.'

Lorenzo's jaw was set, his gaze cold. 'You'll have to.'

The following evening, Giuliano had waited in one of Lorenzo's ground-floor apartments until it was time to meet Anna. He had spent the entire day thinking on Lorenzo's comment about how she would be ruined if she went to Rome. For the first time, he considered what Anna's life would be like if the Pope refused to grant an annulment.

She would know disgrace, and censure; she would be forced to give up her family, her friends, her native city. Her children would be called bastards, and be denied their inheritance as Medici heirs.

He had been selfish. He had spoken too easily of the annulment, in hopes that it would sway Anna to go with him. And he had not, until that moment, considered that she might reject his offer. Now he realised that it would save him from making an agonising choice.

But when he went to meet her at the door and saw her face in the dying light, he saw that his choice had been made long ago, at the moment when he gave his heart to Anna. Her eyes, her skin, her face and limbs exuded joy; even in the shadowy dusk, she shone. The swift grace with which she lifted her skirts and rushed to him relayed her answer more clearly than words.

Her presence breathed such hope into him that he moved quickly to her and held her. In that instant, Giuliano realised that neither of them could escape the events now set in motion. And the tears that threatened him did not spring from joy; they were tears of grief, for Lorenzo.

He and Anna remained together less than an hour; they spoke little, only enough for Giuliano to convey a time, and a place. No other exchange was needed.

And when she was gone again—taking the light and Giuliano's confidence with her—he went back to his own chamber, and called for wine. He drank it sitting on his bed, and thinking of Lorenzo.

He sat for hours, watching the darkness of night deepen, then slowly fade to grey with the coming of dawn and the day he was to leave for Rome. He sat until the arrival of his insistent visitors, Francesco de' Pazzi and Bernardo Baroncelli. He could not imagine why the visiting cardinal should care so passionately about his presence at Mass; but if Lorenzo had asked him to come, then that was good enough reason to do so.

He hoped, with sudden optimism, that Lorenzo might have changed his mind; that his anger had faded, and left him more receptive to discussion. Thus Giuliano rallied himself and came as he was bidden.

Inside the Duomo, the air was redolent with frankincense and heavy with sweat. The sanctuary's massive interior was dim, save for the area surrounding the altar, which was dazzling from the late-morning light streaming in from the long arched windows of the cupola.

After the interminable walk down the aisle, Baroncelli and his companions arrived at the front row of men. They murmured apologies as they sidled back to their original places. Baroncelli craned his neck to look further down the row, to see if Lorenzo had noticed Giuliano's arrival; fortunately, the elder Medici brother was busy bending an ear to a comment from the manager of the family bank, Francesco Nori.

Miraculously, all the elements were now in place. Baroncelli had nothing to do save wait—and pretend to listen to the sermon while keeping his hand from wandering to the hilt at his hip.

The sermon ended.

The elements of the Mass proceeded with almost comical swiftness: the Creed was sung. The priest chanted the *Dominus vobiscum* and *Oremus*. The Host was consecrated with the prayer *Suscipe sancte Pater.*

Baroncelli drew in a breath and thought he would never be able to release it. He could feel the desperate thrum of his heart.

The priest's assistant approached the altar to fill the golden chalice with wine; a second assistant added a small amount of water from a crystal decanter. At last, the priest took the chalice and lifted it heavenwards, proffering it to the large wooden carving of a crucified Christ suspended above the altar. He chanted, '*Offerimus tibi Domine . . .*'

Francesco de' Pazzi jabbed Baroncelli fiercely in the ribs, relating the unspoken message perfectly: *The signal has been given!*

Baroncelli released an inaudible sigh and drew his great knife from its hilt. Hefting it overhead, he remembered all the dozens of phrases he had rehearsed for this instant; none of them came to his lips, and what he finally shouted sounded ridiculous to his own ears.

'Here, traitor!'

The church bells had just begun clanging when Giuliano looked up. At the sight of the knife, his eyes widened with mild surprise.

Baroncelli did not hesitate. He brought the blade down.

A moment earlier, Lorenzo de' Medici had been engaged in courteous but muted conversation with Cardinal Raffaele Riario. Although the priest was finishing up his sermon, the wealthy power brokers of Florence thought nothing of discussing matters of pleasure or business—*sotto voce*—during Mass. The social opportunity was simply too great to ignore, and the priests had long ago become inured to it.

A scrawny lad, dressed in scarlet robes, Riario looked younger than his seventeen years. Nephew, Sixtus called him. It was the euphemism by which popes and cardinals sometimes referred to their bastard children.

Even so, Lorenzo was obliged to show the young cardinal a fine time while he was visiting Florence. Riario had asked to meet the Medici brothers and to be given a tour of their property and collection of art; Lorenzo could not refuse. He had called for a magnificent feast to be served after Mass in honour of the young cardinal. And if it happened that young Raffaele had come only out of a desire to enjoy the Medici art, he could at least report to his uncle that Lorenzo had treated him lavishly and well. It could serve as a diplomatic opening, one that Lorenzo would use to full advantage, for he was determined to reclaim the papal coffers from the clutches of the Pazzi bank.

At the start of the sermon, the boy cardinal gave a strange, sickly smile and whispered, 'Where is your brother? I thought surely he would come to Mass. I had so hoped to meet him.'

The question took Lorenzo by surprise. Although Giuliano had made polite noises about coming to the Mass in order to meet Cardinal Riario, Lorenzo felt certain no one, least of all Giuliano, had taken the promise seriously. Besides, Giuliano had already proclaimed himself unable to attend the luncheon.

Lorenzo had been thoroughly taken aback the previous day when Giuliano had announced his intention to run off to Rome with a married woman. Up to that point, Giuliano had never taken his lovers very seriously. It had always been understood that, when the time came, Lorenzo would choose a bride for him and his brother would submit.

But Giuliano had been adamant about getting the woman an annulment—an achievement that, if Cardinal Riario had *not* come as a papal overture, was well beyond Lorenzo's grasp.

Lorenzo was frightened for his younger brother. Giuliano was too trusting, too willing to see the good in others, too good-natured to realise he had many enemies—enemies who hated him solely for the fact he had been born a Medici. He could not see, as Lorenzo did, that they would use this affair with Anna to tear him down.

Lorenzo had not relished being cruel to him. But he could not blame Giuliano for his weakness when it came to women. He himself was a passionate worshipper of the fairer sex, but, though he had loved many women, he had kept them secret from his wife Clarice. Most wives were tolerant, even forgiving, of their husband's desire to keep a mistress. But Clarice tolerated nothing. Lorenzo treated her kindly, though the favour was not returned. He reminded himself that Clarice had presented him with three of his greatest joys in life: his sons, four-year-old Piero, Giovanni, a toddler, and little Giuliano, who was still an infant.

At times, Lorenzo yearned for the freedom his brother Giuliano enjoyed. This morning, he particularly envied him as the Pope's nephew still gazed at him, waiting to hear the whereabouts of his brother. It would be impolite to tell the cardinal the truth—that Giuliano had never intended to come to Mass, or to meet Riario—and so Lorenzo indulged in a polite lie. 'My brother must have been detained.

Surely he will be here soon; I know he is eager to meet Your Holiness.'

'*Maestro* . . . your brother has just arrived,' Francesco Nori whispered.

'Alone?'

Nori glanced briefly to his left, at the north side of the sacristy. 'He has come with Francesco de' Pazzi and Bernardo Baroncelli. I do not like the look of it.'

Lorenzo frowned; he did not care for it, either. He had already greeted Francesco and Baroncelli when he had first entered the cathedral. His diplomatic instincts took hold of him, however; he inclined his head towards Raffaele Riario and said softly, 'You see, Holiness? My brother has indeed come.'

Beside him, Cardinal Riario looked to his left and caught sight of Giuliano. He gave Lorenzo an odd, tremulous grin, then forced his gaze back to the altar, where the priest was blessing the sacred Host.

The lad's movement was so peculiar, so nervous, that Lorenzo felt a faint stirring of anxiety. Beneath the cover of his mantle, he fingered the hilt of his short sword, then gripped it tightly.

Only seconds later, a shout came from the direction Riario had glanced—a man's voice, the words unintelligible, impassioned. Immediately after, the bells of Giotto's campanile began to toll.

At that moment the front two rows of men broke rank and the scene became a clumsy dance of moving bodies. In the near distance, a woman screamed. Salviati disappeared; the young cardinal flung himself at the altar and knelt, sobbing uncontrollably. Guglielmo de' Pazzi, Lorenzo's brother-in-law, clearly terrified, began wringing his hands and wailing, 'I am no traitor! I knew nothing of this! Nothing! Before God, Lorenzo, I am completely innocent!'

Lorenzo did not see the hand that reached from behind him to settle lightly on his left shoulder—but he felt it as though it were a lightning bolt. He pushed forward out of the unseen enemy's grasp, drew his sword, and whirled about. During the sudden movement, a keen blade grazed him just below the right ear; involuntarily, he gasped as warm liquid flowed down his neck.

Lorenzo faced two priests, one clutching a sword and trembling behind a shield as he glanced at the crowd scrambling for the cathedral doors. He was obliged to face up to Lorenzo's attendant, Marco, who, no expert with a sword, made up for it with brute strength.

The second priest—wild-eyed and intent on Lorenzo—raised his weapon for a second attempt.

Lorenzo parried once, twice. Haggard, pale-skinned, unshaven, this priest had the fiery eyes, the open, contorted mouth of a madman. He also had the strength of one, and Lorenzo came close to buckling beneath his blows. Steel clashed against steel, ringing off the high ceilings of the now mostly deserted cathedral.

As the two fighters locked blades, pressing hilt against hilt, neither willing to give way, Lorenzo half shouted, 'Why should you hate me so?'

He meant the question sincerely. He had always wished the best for Florence and her citizens. He did not understand the resentment others felt at the utterance of the name 'Medici'.

'For God,' the priest said. And he drew back his weapon so forcefully that Lorenzo staggered forward, perilously close to the blade.

Before the priest could shed more blood, Francesco Nori stepped in front of Lorenzo with his sword drawn. Other friends and supporters began to close in round the would-be assassins, sealing Lorenzo off from his attacker and pressing him towards the altar.

Lorenzo resisted. 'Giuliano!' he cried. 'Brother, where are you?'

'We will find and protect him. Now, go!' Nori ordered, gesturing with his chin towards the altar, where the priest, in alarm, had dropped the full chalice, staining the altar cloth with wine.

Lorenzo hesitated.

'*Go!*' Nori shouted again. 'They are headed here! Go past them, to the north sacristy!'

Lorenzo had no idea who *they* were, but he acted. Still clutching his sword, he hurdled over the low railing and leapt into the carved wooden structure that housed the choir. Cherubic boys shrieked as they scattered, their white robes flapping like the wings of startled birds.

Followed by his protectors, Lorenzo pushed his way through the flailing choir and staggered towards the great altar.

At the moment that Lorenzo ran north across the altar, Francesco de' Pazzi and Bernardo Baroncelli were in the sanctuary, pushing their way south, clearly unaware that they were missing their intended target.

Lorenzo stopped mid-stride, straining to see past those surrounding him, to look beyond the moving bodies below to the place where his brother had been standing, but his view was obstructed.

'Giuliano!' he screamed, praying he would be heard above the pandemonium. 'Giuliano . . .! Where are you? Brother, speak to me!'

'He is not there,' a muffled voice replied. Thinking this meant that his brother had moved south to find him, Lorenzo turned back in that direction, where his friends still fought the assassins. A glint of swift-moving steel caught his eye.

The blade belonged to Bernardo Baroncelli. With a viciousness Lorenzo would never have dreamt him capable of, Baroncelli ran his long knife deep into the pit of Francesco Nori's stomach. Nori's eyes bulged as he stared down at the intrusion, and his lips formed a small, perfect *o* as he fell backwards, sliding off Baroncelli's sword.

Lorenzo let go a sob, as his supporters took his shoulders and pushed him away, across the altar and towards the infinitely tall doors of the sacristy. 'Get Francesco!' he begged them. 'Someone bring Francesco. He is still alive, I know it!'

He tried again to turn, to call out for his brother, but this time his people would not let him slow their relentless march to the sacristy. Lorenzo felt a physical pain in his chest, a pressure so brutal he thought his heart would burst.

He had hurt Giuliano in his most vulnerable moment, and when Giuliano had said, *I love you, Lorenzo . . . Please don't make me choose*, he had been cruel. Had turned him away.

Inside the airless, windowless sacristy, Lorenzo grabbed each man who had pushed him to safety; he studied each face, and was each time disappointed. Giuliano was not here.

'My brother!' Lorenzo cried. 'Where is my brother . . .?'

III
December 28, 1479

BERNARDO BARONCELLI RODE kneeling in a horse-drawn cart to his doom. Before him, in the vast Piazza della Signoria, loomed the great, implacable Palazzo della Signoria, the seat of Florence's government and the heart of her justice. Before the building, rising out of a colourful assembly of Florence's rich and poor, stood a hastily built scaffold and the gallows.

The weather had turned bitterly cold. Baroncelli's cloak gaped open, but he could not pull it closed for his hands were bound behind his back. In this manner, unsteady and lurching each time the wheels encountered a stone, Baroncelli arrived in the piazza. No fewer than a thousand had gathered to witness his end.

At the crowd's edge, a small boy caught sight of the approaching cart and sang out the rallying cry of the Medici: '*Palle! Palle! Palle!*'

Hysteria rippled through the throng. Soon its collective shout thundered in Baroncelli's ears. '*Palle! Palle! Palle!*'

Baroncelli had heard the tales of his fellow conspirators' gruesome fates: how the Perugian mercenaries hired by the Pazzi had been pushed from the tower of the palazzo, how they had fallen into the crowd below, who had hacked them to pieces with knives and shovels.

Even old Iacopo de' Pazzi, who during his life had been respected, had not escaped Florence's wrath. Upon the sound of Giotto's chiming campanile, he had climbed upon his horse and tried to rally the citizens with the cry, *Popolo e libertà!* The phrase was a rallying cry to overthrow the current government—in this case, the Medici.

But the populace had answered with the cry: *Palle! Palle! Palle!*

Despite his sin, he had been granted a proper burial after his execution. But the city had been so filled with hatred in those wild days, he had not been at rest long before his cadaver was dragged through the streets and reburied outside the city walls, in unhallowed ground.

Francesco de' Pazzi and the rest had swiftly met justice; only Guglielmo de' Pazzi had been spared, because of Bianca de' Medici's desperate pleading with her brother Lorenzo.

Of the true conspirators, Baroncelli alone had managed to escape. He had fled on horseback—without a word to his family—due east, to Senigallia on the coast. From there, he had sailed to Constantinople.

Baroncelli had had more than a year before Lorenzo's agents had located him, during which time he had immersed himself in pleasure. Then Lorenzo had sent an emissary laden with gold and jewels to the Sultan. Thus was Baroncelli's fate sealed.

The cart rolled to a stop in front of the gallows. Baroncelli was helped to the ground and staggered up the wooden steps.

On the scaffold, the executioner, hidden beneath a mask, stood between Baroncelli and the noose. 'Before God,' the executioner said to Baroncelli, 'I beg your forgiveness for the act I am sworn to commit.'

'I forgive you.'

The executioner guided Baroncelli to a particular spot on the platform, near the noose. 'Here.' He produced from within his cloak a white linen scarf, which he tied over Baroncelli's eyes before guiding the noose over his chin and tightening it round his neck.

In the instant before the platform beneath him dropped, Baroncelli whispered two words, directed at himself: 'Here, traitor.'

The instant that Baroncelli's body ceased its twitching, a young artist near the front of the crowd set to work. The corpse would hang in the piazza for days, but the artist could not wait; he wanted to capture the image while it still possessed an echo of life.

He sketched on paper pressed against a board of poplar, to give him a firm surface to work against. He had carved the nib of his quill pen himself to a fine, sharp point, and he dipped it regularly into a vial of brown ink securely fastened to his belt. His bare hands ached from the cold, but he dismissed the observation as unworthy of his time.

Baroncelli's regret was blatant. Even in death, his eyes were downcast, as if contemplating Hell. His head was bowed, and the corners of his thin lips were pulled downwards by guilt.

The artist struggled not to yield to his hatred, though he had very personal reasons for despising Baroncelli. But hate was against his principles, so—like his aching fingers and heart—he ignored it.

As was his habit, he jotted notes on the page to remind himself of the colours and textures involved, for there was an excellent chance the sketch might become a painting.

Small tan cap. The quill scratched against the paper. *Black serge jerkin, lined woollen singlet, blue cloak lined with fox fur, velvet collar stippled red and black, black leggings.*

The artist was still struggling to overcome his rustic Vinci dialect, and spelling bedevilled him. No matter. Lorenzo de' Medici, *il Magnifico*, was interested in the image, not the words.

He did a quick, small rendering at the bottom of the page, showing Baroncelli's head at an angle that revealed more of the gloom-stricken features. Satisfied with his work, he then set to his real task of scanning the faces in the crowd. He watched as many men as possible as they left the piazza. There were two reasons for this. The ostensible one was that he was a student of faces. The darker reason was the result of an encounter between himself and Lorenzo de' Medici. He was looking for a particular face: one he had seen twenty months earlier, but for only the briefest of instants. Even with his talent for recalling physiognomies, his memory was clouded—yet his heart was equally determined to succeed.

'Leonardo!'

The sound of his own name startled the artist; he jerked involuntarily and, out of reflex, capped the vial of ink lest it spill.

An old friend from when he had been a student in Andrea del Verrocchio's workshop now moved towards him.

'Sandro,' Leonardo said. 'You look like a lord prior.'

Sandro Botticelli grinned. At the age of thirty-four, he was several years Leonardo's senior, in the prime of his life and career. He was indeed dressed grandly, in a scarlet fur-trimmed cloak; a black velvet cap covered most of his golden hair, cut chin-length, shorter than the current fashion. Like Leonardo, he was clean-shaven.

Sandro eyed Leonardo's sketch with sly humour. 'So. Trying to steal my job, I see.'

He was referring to the recently painted mural on a façade near the Palazzo della Signoria, partially visible behind the scaffolding now that the crowd was beginning to thin. He had received a commission from Lorenzo in those terrible days following Giuliano's death: to depict each of the executed Pazzi conspirators as they dangled from the rope. One murderer had been altogether missing: Baroncelli. Botticelli had probably taken notes himself this morning, intending to finish the mural. But at the sight of Leonardo's sketch, he shrugged.

'No matter,' he said breezily. 'Being rich enough to dress like a lord prior, I can certainly let a pauper like yourself finish up the task. I have far greater things to accomplish.'

Leonardo, dressed in a knee-length artisan's tunic of cheap, used linen, and a dull grey wool mantle, slipped his sketch under one arm and bowed, low and sweeping, in an exaggerated show of gratitude.

He and Sandro parted with smiles and a brief embrace, and Leonardo returned at once to studying the crowd. He reached absently into the pouch on his belt and fingered a gold medallion the size of a large florin. On the front, in bas-relief, was the title '*Public Mourning*'. Beneath, Baroncelli raised his long knife above his head while Giuliano looked up at the blade with surprise. Behind Baroncelli stood Francesco de' Pazzi, his dagger at the ready. Leonardo had provided the sketch, rendering the scene with as much accuracy as possible, although for the viewer's sake, Giuliano was depicted as facing Baroncelli.

Two days after the murder, Leonardo had dispatched a letter to Lorenzo de' Medici:

My lord Lorenzo, I need to speak privately to you concerning a matter of the utmost importance.

No reply was forthcoming. Lorenzo, overcome with grief, hid in the Medici palace, surrounded by scores of armed men.

After a week without a reply, Leonardo borrowed a gold florin and went to the door of the Medici stronghold. He bribed one of the guards there to deliver a second letter straight away, while he waited.

My lord Lorenzo, I have critical information concerning the death of your brother, for your ears alone.

Several minutes later he was admitted after being thoroughly checked for weapons—ridiculous, since he had never owned one.

Pale and lifeless in an unadorned black tunic, Lorenzo, his neck still bandaged, received Leonardo in his study, surrounded by artwork of astonishing beauty. He gazed up at Leonardo with eyes clouded by grief—yet could not hide his interest in hearing what the artist had to say.

On the morning of the 26th of April, Leonardo had stood several rows from the altar in the cathedral of Santa Maria del Fiore. He'd had questions for Lorenzo about a joint commission he and his former teacher Andrea del Verrocchio had received to sculpt a bust of Giuliano, and hoped to catch il *Magnifico* after the service. Leonardo was on very good terms with the Medici. Over the past few years, he had stayed for months at a time in Lorenzo's house as one of the many artists in the family's employ. To Leonardo's surprise that morning, Giuliano had arrived, late, dishevelled, and escorted by Francesco de' Pazzi and his employee.

Leonardo found men and women equally beautiful, equally worthy of his love, but he lived an unrequited life by choice. An artist could not allow the storms of love to interrupt his work. He avoided women most of all, for the demands of a wife and children would make his studies—of art, of the world and its inhabitants—impossible.

But when Leonardo became a protégé of the Medici and a member of their inner circle, he had been drawn, physically and emotionally, to Lorenzo's younger brother. Giuliano was infinitely lovable. It was not simply the man's striking appearance—Leonardo was himself often called 'beautiful' by his friends—but rather the goodness of his spirit. This fact Leonardo kept to himself. He did not wish to make Giuliano, a lover of women, uncomfortable; nor did he care to scandalise Lorenzo, his host and patron.

When Giuliano had appeared in the Duomo, Leonardo—only two rows behind him—could not help but stare steadily at him. He noted Giuliano's downcast demeanour, and was filled with neither sympathy nor attraction, but a welling of bitter jealousy.

The previous evening, the artist had set out with the intention of speaking to Lorenzo about the commission.

It was dusk as he had made his way onto the Via de' Gori, past the church of San Lorenzo. The Palazzo de Medici lay just ahead, to his left.

Given the hour, traffic was light, and Leonardo paused in the street, lost in the beauty of his surroundings. He watched as a carriage rolled towards him, and enjoyed the crisp silhouettes of the horses, their bodies impenetrably black, set against the backdrop of the brilliant sky.

He became lost in the play of shadow on the horses' bodies, so much so that as the carriage came rumbling down upon him, he had to collect himself and move swiftly out of their way.

A short distance in front of him, the driver of the carriage jerked the horses to a stop and the door opened. Leonardo hung back and watched as a young woman stepped out. The drabness of her gown and veil marked her as the servant of a wealthy family. There was furtiveness in her posture as her gaze swept from side to side. She hurried to the palazzo's side entrance and knocked insistently.

A pause, and the door opened with a sustained creak. The servant moved back to the carriage and gestured urgently to someone inside.

A second woman emerged from the carriage and moved gracefully, swiftly, towards the open doorway.

Leonardo spoke her name aloud without intending to. She was a friend of the Medici, a frequent visitor to the palazzo; they had spoken on several occasions. Even before he saw her clearly, he recognised her movements, the way her head swivelled as she turned to look at him.

He took a step closer. She had always been beautiful, but now the dimness gave her features a haunting quality. Her luminous face, her décolletage, her hands, seemed to float suspended against the dark forest of her gown and hair. Her expression was one of covert joy; her eyes held sublime secrets, her lips the hint of a complicitous smile.

He murmured her name again, this time a question, but her gaze had already turned towards the open doorway. Leonardo followed it, and caught a glimpse of another familiar face: Giuliano's. He did not see Leonardo, only the woman.

And she saw Giuliano and bloomed.

In that instant, Leonardo understood and turned away, overwhelmed by bitterness, as the door closed behind them. He did not go to see Lorenzo that night. He went home to his little apartment.

The following morning, gazing on Giuliano in the Duomo, Leonardo dwelled on his own unhappy passion. He recalled the painful instant when he had seen the look pass between Giuliano and the woman, when he had realised Giuliano's heart belonged to her, and hers to him; and he cursed himself for being vulnerable to jealousy.

He had been so ensnared by his reverie that he had been startled by the sudden movement in front of him. A robed figure stepped forward a fraction of a second before Giuliano turned to look behind him, then released a sharp gasp.

There followed Baroncelli's hoarse shout. Leonardo had stared up, stricken, at the glint of the raised blade. In the space of a breath, the frightened worshippers scattered, pulling the artist backwards with the tide of bodies. In the wild scramble, Leonardo's view of Baroncelli's knife entering Giuliano's flesh had been blocked. But Leonardo had seen an unspeakably brutal attack from Francesco de' Pazzi—the dagger biting, again and again, into Giuliano's flesh.

The instant he realised what was happening, Leonardo let go of a loud shout—inarticulate, threatening, horrified—at the attackers. At last the crowd cleared; at last no one stood between him and the assassins. He had run towards them as Baroncelli and Francesco moved on.

Leonardo dropped to his knees beside Giuliano. He lay half-curled on his side, blood foaming at his lips and spilling from his wounds.

'Giuliano,' Leonardo had gasped, tears pouring down his cheeks at the sight of such suffering, at the sight of beauty so marred.

Giuliano did not hear him. He was beyond hearing, beyond sight: his half-open eyes already stared into the next world. As Leonardo hovered over him, his limbs twitched briefly, then his eyes widened. Thus he died.

Now, standing in front of Lorenzo, Leonardo said nothing of Giuliano's final suffering, he spoke not of Baroncelli, nor of Francesco de' Pazzi. Instead, he spoke of a third man, one who had yet to be found.

The artist recounted that he had seen, in the periphery of his vision, a robed figure step forward on Giuliano's right, and that he believed it was this man who had delivered the first blow. As Giuliano tried to back away from Baroncelli, the figure had stood fast—pressed hard against the victim and trapped him. The unknown man did not even recoil when Francesco struck out wildly with the dagger.

Once Giuliano had died, Leonardo had glanced up and noticed the man moving quickly towards the door that led to the piazza.

'Assassin!' the artist had shouted. 'Stop!'

There was such outraged authority, such pure force in his voice that the conspirator had stopped and glanced swiftly over his shoulder.

Leonardo captured his image with a trained artist's eye. The man wore the robes of a penitent—crude burlap—and his clean-shaven face was half-shadowed by a cowl. Only the lower half of his lip and his chin were visible. Held close to his side, his hand gripped a bloodied stiletto.

After he had fled, Leonardo had gently rolled Giuliano's body onto its side, and discovered the puncture—small but deep—in his midback.

This he relayed to Lorenzo.

'I am certain this man was disguised, My Lord.'

Lorenzo was intrigued. 'How can you possibly know that?'

'His posture. Penitents indulge in self-flagellation, they wear hair shirts beneath their robes. They slump, cringe and move gingerly, because of the pain each time their shirt touches their skin. This man moved freely, but his muscles were tensed. I believe, as well, that he was from the upper classes, given the dignity and gentility of his aspect.'

Lorenzo's gaze was penetrating. 'All this you have ascertained from a man's movements, a man who was draped in a simple robe?'

Leonardo stared back. 'I would not have come if I had not.'

'Then you shall be my agent.' Lorenzo's eyes narrowed with hatred and determination. 'You shall help me find this man.'

So, over the past year, Leonardo had been summoned several times to the prison in the Bargello, to carefully examine the lips and chins and postures of several unfortunate men. None of them had matched those of the penitent he had seen in the cathedral.

The night before Baroncelli's execution, Lorenzo had sent two guards to bring Leonardo to the palazzo on the Via Larga.

'Perhaps you have already deduced why I have called for you,' he said.

'Yes. I am to go to the piazza tomorrow to look for the third man. And if I fail tomorrow, I will not stop searching until he is found.'

Lorenzo nodded, then turned his head away. 'You should know that this man . . .' He stopped himself, then started again. 'This goes deeper than the murder of my brother, Leonardo. They mean to destroy us.'

'To destroy you and your family?'

Lorenzo faced him again. 'You. Me. Botticelli. Verrocchio. All that Florence represents.' Leonardo opened his mouth to ask *Who? Who means to do this?*, but Lorenzo lifted a hand to silence him. 'Go to the piazza tomorrow. Find the third man. I mean to question him personally.'

As he stood in the square on the cold December morning of Baroncelli's death, staring intently at the face of each man who passed, he puzzled over *il Magnifico*'s words: *They mean to destroy us . . .*

PART II: LISA

IV

I WILL ALWAYS REMEMBER the day my mother told me the story of Giuliano de' Medici's murder. It was a December day more than thirteen and a half years after the event; I was twelve. For the first time in my life, I stood inside the great Duomo, my head thrown back as I marvelled at the magnificence of Brunelleschi's cupola while my mother, her hands folded in prayer, whispered the gruesome tale to me.

Midweek after morning Mass, the cathedral was nearly deserted, save for a priest replacing the tapers on the altar's candelabra. We had stopped directly in front of the high altar, where the events of the assassination had taken place. I loved tales of adventure, and tried to picture a young Lorenzo de' Medici, his sword drawn, leaping into the choir.

I turned to look at my mother, Lucrezia, and tugged at her embroidered brocade sleeve. 'What happened after Lorenzo escaped?' I hissed. 'What became of Giuliano?'

My mother's eyes had filled with tears. 'He died of his terrible wounds,' she said, and sighed. 'And the executions of the conspirators were horribly brutal . . . It was a terrible time for Florence.'

'Didn't anyone try to help Giuliano?' I asked.

'Hush,' Zalumma warned me. 'Can't you see she is becoming upset?'

This was indeed cause for concern. My mother was not well, and agitation worsened her condition.

'She was the one who told the story,' I countered. 'I did not ask for it.'

'Quiet!' Zalumma ordered. I was stubborn, but she was more so. She took my mother's elbow and in a sweeter tone, said, 'Madonna, it's time to leave. We must get home before your absence is discovered.'

She referred to my father, who had spent that day, like most others, tending his business. He would be aghast if he returned to find his wife gone; this was the first time in years she had dared venture out so far.

We had secretly planned this outing for some time. I had never seen the Duomo, even though I had grown up looking at its great brick cupola from the opposite side of the Arno, from our house on the Via Maggio. All my life, I had attended our local church of Santo Spirito. Our main altar · was also centred beneath a cupola designed by the great Brunelleschi, his final achievement; I had thought Santo Spirito impossibly grand, impossibly large—until I stood inside the Duomo. The great cupola challenged the imagination. Gazing on it, I understood why, when it was first constructed, people were reluctant to stand beneath it.

My mother had brought me to the Piazza del Duomo not just to marvel at the cupola, but to slake my yearning for art—and hers. She was well-born and well-educated and had acquired a wealth of knowledge about the city's cultural treasures. She had long been troubled by the fact that her illness had prevented her from sharing them with me. So, on that bright December day, we took a carriage east and headed across the Ponte Vecchio, into the heart of Florence.

On our way to the Duomo, our carriage paused in the vast piazza, in front of the imposing fortress known as the Palazzo della Signoria, where the Lord Priors of Florence met. On the wall of an adjacent building was a grotesque mural: paintings of hanged men. I knew nothing of them save that they were known as the Pazzi conspirators, and that they were evil. One of the conspirators, a small naked man, stared wide-eyed and sightless back at me, but what intrigued me most was the portrait of the last hanging body. His form differed from the others, was more delicately portrayed; its subtle shadings poignantly evoked the grief and remorse of a troubled soul. I felt as though I could reach into the wall and touch his cooling flesh.

I turned to my mother. She was watching me carefully. 'The last man was done by a different artist,' I said.

'Yes. The artist has an amazing refinement, doesn't he? He is like God, breathing life into stone.' She nodded, pleased by my discernment, and waved for the driver to move on.

We made our way north to the Piazza del Duomo.

Before entering the cathedral, I had examined Ghiberti's bas-relief panels on the doors of the nearby octagonal Baptistery. Here, near the public entry at the southern end, scenes of Florence's patron saint, John the Baptist, covered the walls, but what truly tantalised me was the Door of Paradise on the eastern side. There, in fine gilded bronze, the Old Testament came to life in vivid detail.

One item caught my attention: Donatello's dark wooden carving of Mary Magdalen, larger than life. Her features were worn down by decades of guilt and regret. Something about the resignation in her aspect reminded me of my mother.

We three made our way into the Duomo proper then, and once we arrived in front of the altar, my mother began speaking of the murder that had taken place there. I had only moments to draw in the astonishing vastness of the cupola before Zalumma grew worried and told my mother it was time to leave.

'I suppose so,' my mother reluctantly agreed. 'But first, I must speak to my daughter alone.'

This frustrated the slave. She scowled until her brows merged into one great black line, but her social status compelled her to reply calmly, 'Of course, Madonna.' She retreated a short distance away.

Once my mother satisfied herself that Zalumma was not watching, she retrieved from her bosom a small, shining object. A coin, I thought, but after she had pressed it into my palm, I saw it was a gold medallion, stamped with the words '*Public Mourning*'. Beneath the letters, two men with knives readied themselves to attack a startled victim. Despite its small size, the image was detailed and lifelike.

'Keep it,' my mother said. 'But let it be our secret.'

I eyed her gift greedily, curiously. 'Was he really so handsome?'

'He was. It is quite accurate. And quite rare.'

I tucked it at once into my belt. My mother and I both shared a love of such trinkets, and of art, though my father disapproved. As a merchant, he had worked hard for his wealth, and hated to see it squandered on anything useless. But I was thrilled; I hungered for such things.

'Zalumma,' my mother called. 'I am ready to leave.'

Zalumma came to fetch us at once, and took hold of my mother's arm again. But when my mother began to turn away from the altar—she paused. 'The candles . . .' she murmured. 'Something is burning . . .'

Zalumma's expression went slack with panic, but she recovered and said calmly, 'Lie down, Madonna. Here, on the floor. All will be well.'

'It all repeats,' my mother said, with the odd catch in her voice I had come to dread.

'Lie down!' Zalumma ordered. My mother seemed not to hear her, and when Zalumma tried to force her to the ground, she resisted.

'It all repeats,' my mother said swiftly, frantically. 'Don't you see it happening again? Here, in this sacred place.'

I lent my weight to Zalumma's; together we fought to bring my mother down, but her arms moved involuntarily from her sides and shot straight out, rigid, and her legs locked beneath her. 'There is murder here, and thoughts of murder!' she shrieked. 'Plots within plots once more!'

Her cries grew unintelligible as she went down, and Zalumma and I clung to her so that she did not land too harshly.

My mother writhed on the cold floor of the cathedral, her blue cloak gaping open, her silver skirts pooling around her. Zalumma lay across her body; I put my kerchief between her upper teeth and tongue, then held on to her head.

I was barely in time. My mother's dark eyes rolled back until only the veined whites were visible—then the rigors began. I focused on the linen kerchief in my mother's mouth—on her champing teeth, and the small specks of blood there—and on her jerking head, which I now held fast in my lap, so I was startled into fright when a stranger beside us began praying loudly, in Latin.

I looked up to see the black-frocked priest who had been tending the altar. He alternated between sprinkling my mother with liquid from a small vial and making the sign of the cross over her while he prayed.

At last the time came when my mother gave her final wrenching groan, then fell limp; her eyelids fluttered shut.

Beside me, the priest—a young red-haired man with florid, pock-marked skin—rose. 'She is like the woman from whom Jesus cast out nine devils,' he said with authority. 'She is possessed.'

Sore and halting from the struggle, Zalumma nonetheless rose to her full height—a hand's breadth taller than the priest—and glared at him. 'It is a sickness,' she said, 'of which you know nothing.'

The young priest shrank. 'It is the Devil.'

I glanced from the priest's face to Zalumma's stern expression. I was mature for my age and knew responsibility: my mother's delicate health had forced me to act as mistress of the household many times, playing hostess to guests, accompanying my father in her place on social occasions. But I was young in terms of my knowledge of the world and of God. I was still undecided as to whether He was punishing her for some early sin, and whether her fits were indeed of sinister origin. I knew only that I loved her, pitied her, and disliked the priest's condescension.

Zalumma's cheeks turned pink. I knew her well: a scathing reply had formed in her mind, but she checked it. She had need of the priest.

Her manner turned abruptly unctuous. 'I am a poor slave, with no right to contradict a learned man, Father. Here, we must get my mistress to the carriage. Will you help us?'

The priest could not refuse. I ran to find our driver, who brought the carriage round to the front of the cathedral, then he and the priest carried my mother to it. Exhausted, she slept with her head in Zalumma's lap.

Our unadorned palazzo on the Via Maggio had been built by my father's great-great-grandfather from *pietra serena*, an expensive but subtle grey stone. We rode inside the gate, then Zalumma and the driver lifted my mother from the carriage.

To our horror, my father Antonio stood watching in the loggia.

My father had returned early. Dressed in his usual dark *farsetto*, a crimson mantle and black leggings, he stood with his arms crossed at the entry to the loggia. He was a sharp-featured man, with golden brown hair, a narrow hooked nose, and thunderous eyebrows above pale amber eyes. His disregard for fashion showed in his face; he wore a full beard and moustache at a time when it was common for men to be clean-shaven or wear a neat goatee.

Yet, ironically, no one knew more about Florence's current styles and cravings. My father owned a *bottega* in the Santa Croce district, near the ancient Wool Guild, the *Arte della Lana*. He specialised in supplying the very finest wools to the city's wealthiest families. He often went to the Pallazzo de Medici on the Via Larga, his carriage heavy with plush fabrics coloured with *chermisi*, the most expensive of dyes made from the dried carcasses of lice, which produced the most exquisite crimson, and *alessandrino*, a costly and beautiful deep blue.

Sometimes I rode with my father and waited in the carriage while he met his most important clients at their palazzi.

My father was, for the most part, a self-possessed man. But certain things goaded him—my mother's condition was one of them—and it could induce an uncontrollable rage. As I crawled from the carriage to walk behind Zalumma and the driver, I saw the danger in his eyes.

For the moment, love of my mother took precedence over my father's anger. He ran to us and took Zalumma's place, catching hold of my mother tenderly. Together, he and the driver carried her into the house; as they did, he glanced over his shoulder at Zalumma and me. He kept his tone low so it would not distress my semiconscious mother, but I could hear the anger coiled in it, waiting to lash out.

'You women will see her to bed, then I will have words with you.'

My father carried Mother up to her bed. I closed the shutters to block out the sun, then helped Zalumma undress her down to her *camicia*, made of embroidered white silk. Once that was done, and Zalumma was certain my mother was sleeping comfortably, we stepped quietly out into her antechamber and closed the door behind us.

My father was waiting for us. His tone was low but faintly atremble. 'You knew of the danger to her. You knew, and yet you let her leave the house. What kind of loyalty is this? What shall we do if she dies?'

Zalumma's tone was perfectly calm, her manner respectful. 'She will not die, Ser Antonio; the fit has passed and she is sleeping. But you are right; I am at fault. Without my help, she could not have gone.'

'I shall sell you!' My father's tone slowly rose. 'Sell you, and buy a more responsible slave!'

Zalumma lowered her eyelids; I saw the muscles in her jaw clench with the effort of holding words back. I could imagine what they were. *I am the lady's slave, from her father's household; I was hers before we ever set eyes on you, and hers alone to sell.* But she said nothing.

'Go,' my father said. 'Get downstairs.'

Zalumma hesitated an instant; she did not want to leave my mother alone, but the master had spoken. She passed by us, her skirts sweeping against the stone floor. My father and I were alone.

I lifted my chin, instinctively defiant.

'*You* were behind this,' he said. His cheeks grew crimson. 'You, with your notions. Your mother did this to please you.'

'Yes, I was behind it.' My own voice trembled and I fought to steady it. 'Mother did this just to please me. Do you think I am happy that she had a spell? She has gone out before without incident.'

He shook his head. 'Do you not *know* how terrified I was, to come home and find her gone? Do you not feel at all ashamed that your self-ishness has hurt your mother so? Or do you care nothing for her life?'

His tone steadily rose throughout his discourse, so that by its end, he was shouting at me.

'Of *course*—' I began, but broke off as my mother's door opened and she appeared in the doorway.

Both my father and I were startled and turned to look at her. She looked like a wraith, clutching the doorjamb to keep her balance. Zalumma had taken down her hair, and it spilled darkly over her shoulders, her bosom and down to her waist.

She spoke in nothing more than a whisper, but the emotion in it could be clearly heard. 'Leave her be. This was my idea, all of it. If you must shout, shout at me.'

'You mustn't be up,' I said, but my words were drowned out by my father's angry voice.

'How could you do such a thing when you know it is dangerous? Why must you frighten me so, Lucrezia? You might have died!'

My mother gazed on him with haggard eyes. 'I am tired of this house, of this life. I don't care if I die. I want to live as any normal woman does.'

She would have said more, but my father interrupted. 'God forgive you for speaking so lightly of death. It is His will that you live so, His judgment. You should accept it meekly.'

I had never heard venom in my gentle mother's tone, had never seen her sneer. But that day, I heard and saw both.

Her lip tugged at one corner. 'Do not mock God, Antonio, when we both know the truth of it.'

He moved swiftly, blindingly, to strike her; she shrank backwards.

I moved just as quickly to intervene. I pummelled my father's shoulders, forcing him away from her. 'How dare you!' I cried. 'How *dare* you! She is kind and good—everything you are not!'

His pale amber eyes were bright with rage. He struck out with the back of his hand; I fell back, startled to find myself sitting on the floor.

He swept from the room. As he did, I got up and ran to my mother and helped her back into bed. I held her hand while she wept softly.

'Hush,' I told her. 'We didn't mean it. And we will make amends.'

'It all repeats,' she moaned, and her eyes at last closed. 'It all repeats.'

'Hush now,' I said, 'and sleep.'

I sat at my mother's bedside for the rest of the day. When the sun began to set, I lit a taper and remained. As I sat watching my mother's profile in the candleglow, I felt a stirring of regret. Out of love and a desire to protect her, I had permitted my rage to overtake me. My eyes filled; I knew my father and I added to my mother's suffering every time we fought. As the first tear spilled onto my cheek, my mother stirred.

I put a gentle hand on her arm. 'It's all right. I am here.'

The instant I uttered the words, the door opened softly. I glanced up to see Zalumma, a goblet in her hand.

'I brought a draught,' she said quietly. 'When your mother wakes, this will let her sleep through the night.' She set the goblet beside the bed. 'You mustn't cry.'

'But it's my fault.'

Zalumma flared. 'It's not your fault. It's never been your fault.' She sighed bitterly as she looked down on her sleeping mistress. 'What the priest in the Duomo said—'

I leaned forward, eager to hear her opinion. 'Yes?'

'It is vileness. It is ignorance, you understand? Your mother is the truest Christian I know.' She paused. 'When I was a very young girl . . .'

'When you lived in the mountains?'

'Yes, when I lived in the mountains. I had a brother, a twin.' She smiled with affection at the memory. 'Headstrong and full of mischief he was.' Her smile faded. 'One day he climbed a very tall tree. He wanted to reach the sky, he said. He crawled out onto a limb . . .' There was a catch in her voice. 'Too far. And he fell.'

I straightened in my chair, aghast. 'Did he die?'

'We thought he would; he had cracked his head and it bled terribly, all over my apron. When he was better and could walk, we went outside to play. But before we went too far, he fell, and began to shake, just as your mother does. Afterwards, he could not speak for a while, and slept. Then he was better again until the next time.'

'Just like Mother.' I paused. 'Did the fits . . . did he . . .?'

'Did the fits kill him? No. I don't know what became of him after we were separated.' Zalumma eyed me, trying to judge whether I had grasped the point of her tale. 'My brother never had fits before he hurt his head. His fits came because of his injury.'

'So . . . Mother has struck her head?'

Zalumma nodded. 'I believe so. Now . . . Do you think God pushed a little boy from a tree to punish him for his sins?'

'No, of course not.'

'I knew my brother's heart, and I know your mother's; and I know that God would never be so cruel, nor allow the Devil to rest in such sweet souls.'

The instant Zalumma said it, my doubts about the matter vanished.

Despite what the priest said, my mother was not a host to demons.

But one thing still troubled me. *There is murder here, and thoughts of murder. Plots within plots once more.*

I could not forget what the astrologer had told me almost two years earlier: that I was surrounded by deceit, doomed to finish a bloody deed others had begun. *It all repeats.*

'The strange things Mother cries out,' I said. 'Did your brother do that, too?'

Zalumma's fine porcelain features reflected hesitation; at last she yielded to the truth. 'No. She spoke of those things before the fits came, since she was a girl. Many of the things she has said have come to pass. I think God has touched her, given her a gift.'

Murder and thoughts of murder . . . This time I did not want to believe what Zalumma said. 'Thank you,' I told her. 'I will remember what you have told me.'

She smiled and leaned down to put an arm round my shoulder. 'No more vigil; it's my turn now. Go and get something to eat.'

So I rose and left them—but I did not go in search of the cook. Instead, I went downstairs with the intent of going to pray. I wandered outside into the rear courtyard and garden. Just beyond them, in a small separate structure, lay our chapel. The sky was clouded and moonless, but I carried a lamp so that I would not stumble.

I opened the chapel's heavy wooden door and slipped inside. The interior was dark and gloomy, lit only by flickering candles, and as I lifted my lamp towards the noise, I saw a dark figure kneeling at the altar railing. My father was praying earnestly.

I knelt beside him. He turned towards me; the lamplight glittered off the unshed tears in his amber eyes, eyes full of misery and remorse.

'Daughter, forgive me,' he said.

'No,' I countered. 'It is you who must forgive me. I hit you.'

'And I struck you, without cause. You were only thinking to protect your mother. And that was my intent, yet I find myself doing the opposite.' He looked up at the image of the suffering Christ and groaned. 'After all these years, I should have learned to control myself . . .'

I wished to coax him from his self-reproach, so I rested a hand on his arm and said lightly, 'So. I inherited my ill temper from you, then.'

He sighed and ran the pad of his thumb tenderly over the contours of my cheek. 'Poor child. This is no fault of yours.'

Still kneeling, we embraced. At that instant, the forgotten medallion chose to slip from my belt. It struck the inlaid marble flooring, rolled in a perfect circle, then fell flat on its side.

Curious, my father reached for the coin, lifted it, and examined it. He narrowed his eyes and drew back his head slightly, as if threatened by a slap. After a long pause, he spoke.

'You see,' he said, 'what comes of anger. Dreadful acts of violence.'

'Yes. Mother told me about the killing in the Duomo.'

'It was a terrible thing. There is no excuse for murder, regardless of the provocation. Such violence is heinous, an abomination before God.' The piece of gold, still held aloft, caught the feeble light and glinted. 'Did she tell you the other side of it?'

I tried and failed to understand; I thought at first he referred to the coin. 'The other side?'

'Lorenzo. His love for his murdered brother drove him to madness in the days after.' He closed his eyes, remembering. 'Eighty men in five days. A few of them were guilty, most simply unfortunate enough to have the wrong relatives. They were tortured mercilessly, drawn and quartered, their hacked, bloodied bodies heaved out of the windows of the Palazzo della Signoria. And what they did to poor Messer Iacopo's corpse . . .' He shuddered, too horrified by the thought to pursue it further. 'All in vain, for even a river of blood could not revive Giuliano.' He opened his eyes and stared hard at me. 'Mark my words: no good can come of revenge.' He pressed the cold coin into my palm and rose; I followed suit.

'Have you eaten?' I asked.

He shook his head.

'Then let us find Cook.'

V

THE NEW YEAR BROUGHT ice-covered streets and bitter cold. Despite the weather, my father abandoned our parish of Santo Spirito and began crossing the Arno to attend Mass daily at the cathedral of San Marco, known as the church of the Medici.

The new prior, one Fra Girolamo Savonarola, had taken to preaching there. Fra Girolamo, as the people called him, had come to Florence less than two years earlier. An intimate of Lorenzo de' Medici, Count Giovanni Pico, had been much impressed by Savonarola's teachings, and so had begged Lorenzo to send for the friar. Lorenzo complied.

But once Fra Girolamo gained control of the Dominican monastery, he turned on his host. No matter that Medici money had rescued San Marco from oblivion; Fra Girolamo railed against Lorenzo—not by name, but by implication. The parades organised by the Medici were pronounced sinful; the pagan antiquities assiduously collected by Lorenzo—blasphemous; the wealth and political control enjoyed by him and his family—an affront to God.

Such behaviour appealed to the enemies of the Medici and to the envious poor. But my father, who strove to understand and appease God, was entranced by Savonarola's prophesies of the soon-to-come Apocalypse. The friar believed that an astrological event had augured the arrival of the Antichrist (widely believed to be the Turkish sultan Mehmet, who had stolen Constantinople and now threatened all Christendom), and that it predicted a spiritual cleansing in the Church.

My father returned one morning breathless after Mass; Fra Girolamo had admitted during the sermon that God had spoken to him. 'He said that the Church would first be scourged, then purified and revived,' my father said, his face aglow. 'We are living at the end of time.'

He was determined to take me with him the following Sunday to hear the friar speak. And he begged my mother to accompany us. 'He is touched by God, Lucrezia. I swear to you, if only you would listen with your own ears, your life would be for ever changed. He is a holy man, and if we convinced him to pray for you . . .'

Normally my mother would never have refused her husband, but in this case, she held firm. It was too cold for her to venture out.

The following day, a visitor came to our palazzo: Count Giovanni Pico, the very man who had convinced Lorenzo de' Medici to bring Savonarola to Florence.

Count Pico was an intelligent, sensitive man, a scholar of the classics. He was handsome, with golden hair and clear grey eyes. My parents received him cordially—he was, after all, part of the Medici's inner circle . . . and knew Savonarola. We gathered in the great chamber; Pico sat beside my father, directly across from my mother and me.

The conversation began with a discussion of il Magnifico's health. It had been poor of late. Lorenzo suffered terribly from gout and recently his pain had become so extreme that he had been unable to leave his bed.

'I pray for him.' Ser Giovanni sighed. 'It is hard to witness his agony. But I believe he will rally. He takes strength from his three sons, especially the youngest, Giuliano, who spends what time he can spare away from his studies at his father's side.'

'I hear Lorenzo is still determined to win a cardinal's hat for Giovanni,' my father said, with the faintest hint of disapproval.

I had seen both boys. Giuliano was fair of face and form, but Giovanni looked like an overstuffed sausage with spindly legs. The eldest brother, Piero, took after his mother, and was being groomed as Lorenzo's successor—though rumour said he was a dullard, entirely unfit.

Pico hesitated before continuing; his mien was that of a man being pulled in two directions. 'Yes, Lorenzo is quite attached to the idea . . . though, of course, it would require a . . . bending of canon law.'

'Lorenzo is quite talented at bending things,' my father said offhandedly. Even I had overheard enough of this particular topic to know of the outrage it had incited in most Florentines; Lorenzo had lobbied to raise taxes in order to pay for Giovanni's cardinalship. My father's mood grew abruptly jocular. 'Tell Madonna Lucrezia what he said about his boys.'

'Ah.' Pico lowered his face slightly as his lips curved gently upwards. 'You must understand that he does not say it to them directly, of course. He dotes on them too much to show them any unkindness. Just as you so obviously do on your daughter, Madonna.'

I did not understand why my mother flushed. She had been uncharacteristically quiet up to this point, though she was clearly taken, as we all were, with the charming Count.

Pico appeared to take no note of her discomfort. 'Lorenzo always says: "My eldest is foolish, the next clever, and the youngest, good".'

My mother's smile was taut; she then said, 'I am glad young Giuliano is a comfort to his father. I am sorry to hear of Ser Lorenzo's illness.'

Pico sighed again, this time in mild frustration. 'It is hard to witness, Madonna. Especially since—I am sure your husband has spoken of this—I am a follower of the teachings of Fra Girolamo.'

'Savonarola,' my mother said softly, her posture stiffening at the mention of the name. Suddenly, I understood her reticence.

'I have begged Lorenzo to send for Fra Girolamo. I truly believe, Madonna Lucrezia, that, were Fra Girolamo permitted to lay hands upon Lorenzo and pray for him, he would be healed at once.'

My mother averted her face; Pico's tone grew more impassioned.

'Oh, sweet Madonna, do not turn from the truth. I have seen Fra Girolamo work miracles. In my life, I have met no man more devoted to God. He lives in poverty; he fasts. When he is not preaching or ministering to the poor, he is on his knees in prayer. And God speaks to him, Madonna. God gives him visions.' As he spoke, Ser Giovanni's eyes seemed brighter than the fire. 'Forgive my boldness, but your husband has told me of your suffering, Madonna Lucrezia, and I know, with infinite certainty, that Fra Girolamo's prayers can cure you.'

My mother was mortified, furious; she could not meet Pico's gaze. Yet despite the intensity of her emotions, her tone was controlled as she replied, 'Other holy men have prayed to God on my behalf. If you are so convinced of the efficacy of Fra Girolamo's prayers, why do you not ask him to pray for me from afar?'

In his urgency, Messer Giovanni vacated his chair to bend on one knee before my mother in a posture of outright supplication.

'Madonna . . . you have heard of the prophecy of the *papa angelico*?'

Everyone knew of the prophecy of the angelic pope—one elected not by a committee of cardinals but by God, who would come to cleanse the Church of its corruption and unite it shortly before Christ's return.

My mother gave the most cursory of nods.

'He is Fra Girolamo; in my heart, I am convinced. He is no ordinary man. Madonna, what harm can it do for you to come hear him once? I will arrange for him to meet you privately after Mass, this very Sunday if you are willing. Think of it: through Fra Girolamo's hands, God will heal you. You need be a prisoner in this house no longer. Only come once, Madonna . . .'

She glanced over at my father. There was reproach in her gaze at first, for he had put her in the most awkward possible situation; yet that reproach melted away as she caught sight of his face.

There was nothing conniving in my father's expression—his face was aglow with the purest, most desperate love I had ever seen.

It was that, more than Pico's persuasive charm, which made her yield; and when at last she answered the count, she was gazing upon my father, with all the pain and love that had been hidden in her heart now visible in her expression.

'Only once,' she said—to my father, not to Pico. 'Only once.'

That Sunday the sky was blue, lit by a sun too feeble to soften the gripping cold. My thickest cloak, of scarlet wool lined with rabbit fur, was not enough to warm me. In the carriage, my mother sat rigid and expressionless between me and Zalumma, her black hair and eyes a striking contrast to the white ermine cape wrapped about her emerald velvet gown. Across from us, my father glanced solicitously at his wife, eager to obtain a sign of affection, but she gazed past him, as if he were not present.

Count Pico rode with us and did his best to distract my father and me with pleasant comments, but there was no ignoring my mother's humiliation, icy and bitter as the weather. Arrangements had been made for us to meet Fra Girolamo privately, directly after the service, so that he could lay hands upon my mother and pray for her.

I gasped as we rolled up to the entrance of the church at San Marco. My awe was not generated by the building—a plain structure of unadorned stone, of the same style as our parish at Santo Spirito—but rather by the number of people who, being unable to find room inside the sanctuary, pressed tightly against each other in the doorway, on the steps, and all the way out into the piazza.

Had Count Pico not been with us, we would never have gained entry. He called out as he stepped from the carriage, and at once, three generously sized Dominican monks appeared and escorted us inside. In a moment, I found myself standing between my mother and father not far from the pulpit and the main altar.

Compared to the grand Duomo, San Marco's interior was sedate and unremarkable, with its pale stone colonnades and simple altar. Yet the mood inside the sanctuary was one of breathless feverishness.

The choir began to sing, and the processional began.

With rapt expressions, worshippers turned eagerly towards the parade. First came the young acolytes, one holding the great cross, another swinging a thurible which perfumed the air with smoky frankincense. Next came the deacon, and then the priest himself.

Last of all came Fra Girolamo, in the place of highest honour. At the sight of him, people cried out: 'Fra Girolamo! Pray for me!' 'God bless you, Brother!' Loudest of all was the cry, 'Babbo! Babbo!', that sweet term only the youngest children use to address their fathers.

I caught only the impression of a frayed brown friar's robe poorly filled by a thin figure; the hood was up, and his head was bowed. Pride was not among his sins, I decided. He sat huddled and intimidated with the acolytes; only then did the people grow calmer. Yet as the Mass progressed, their restlessness again increased. When the choir sang the *Gloria in excelsis*, the crowd began to fidget. The Epistle was chanted, the Gradual sung; when the priest read the Gospel, people were murmuring continuously—to themselves, to each other, to God.

The instant Fra Girolamo ascended the pulpit, the sanctuary fell profoundly silent. Above us stood a small gaunt man with sunken cheeks and great, protruding dark eyes; his hood was pushed back, revealing a head crowned by coarse black curls.

No messiah was ever more unseemly. Yet the timid man I had seen in the procession and the one who ascended the pulpit could not have differed more. This new Savonarola, this touted *papa angelico*, had increased magically in stature; his eyes blazed with certainty, and his bony hands gripped the sides of the pulpit with divine authority. This was a man transformed by a power greater than himself, a power that radiated from his frail body and permeated the chill air surrounding us. Even my mother, silent throughout the ritual, let go a soft sound of amazement.

On the other side of my father, Count Pico lifted his hands, clasped in prayer, in a gesture of supplication. 'Fra Girolamo,' he cried, 'give us your blessing and we will be healed!' I glanced at his upturned face, radiant with devotion, at the sudden tears filling his eyes. At once I understood why Zalumma had derided Savonarola and his followers as *piagnoni*—'wailers'.

But the emotion swirling about us was infinite, wild, genuine. Men and women stretched forth their arms, palms open, pleading.

And Fra Girolamo responded. His gaze swept over us; he seemed to see us, each one, and to acknowledge the love directed at him with eyes shining with compassion and humility. He made the sign of the cross over the crowd with hands that trembled faintly from contained emotion—and when he did, at last the sanctuary again was still.

Savonarola closed his eyes, summoning an internal force, and then he spoke. 'People of Florence! I can no longer hold back the word of the Lord. He has spoken unto me, and it burns in me so bright I must speak or be consumed by its flame.'

He gazed down at us, his eyes and voice becoming tender. 'I weep for Florence, and the scourge that awaits her. Yet how long do we offend God, before He is compelled to unleash His righteous wrath? Like a loving father, He has stayed His hand. But when His children continue to err grievously, when they mock Him, He must, for *their* good, mete out harsh punishment.

'Look at you women: you, with sparkling jewels hanging heavy round your necks, from your ears. If one of you—only *one* of you— repented of the sin of vanity, how many of the poor might be fed? Look at the swaths of silk, of brocade, of velvet, of priceless gold thread that adorn your earthly bodies. If but *one* of you dressed plainly to please God, how many would be saved from starvation?

'And you men, with your whoring, your sodomy, your gluttony and drunkenness, were you to turn instead to the arms of your wife alone, the Kingdom of God would have more children. Were you to give half your plate to the poor, none in Florence would go hungry; were you to forswear wine, there would be no brawling, no bloodshed in the city.

'You wealthy, you lovers of art, you collectors of vain things: cast off your earthly riches, and look instead for that treasure which is eternal.

'Almighty God! Turn our hearts from sin towards you. Spare us the torment that is surely coming to those who flout your laws.'

I started as a woman close behind us let out an anguished howl; the sanctuary walls echoed with wracking sobs. Overwhelmed by remorse, my own father buried his face in his hands and wept.

But my mother stiffened; she seized my arm protectively, and, blinking rapidly from anger, tilted her chin defiantly at Fra Girolamo. 'How dare he say such horrid things?' she said.

Just as my mother had clutched my arm protectively, so Zalumma took my mother's. 'Hush, Madonna. You must calm yourself . . .'

'This is not right,' my mother whispered hoarsely. She was staring with a furious gaze, not at Savonarola but at a point far beyond him.

'Mother,' I said, but she could not hear me. She had turned stone rigid, with me caught in her grasp. Zalumma recognised the signs at once and was speaking gently, rapidly to her, urging her to free me, to lie down here, to know that all would be well.

'*This* is the judgment from God!' my mother shouted, with such force that I struggled in vain to lift my hands to my ears.

Fra Girolamo heard. The congregation looked to my mother and me. My father and Pico regarded us with pure horror.

Zalumma put her arms about my mother's shoulders and tried to bring her down, but she was firm as rock. Her voice deepened and changed timbre until I no longer knew it.

'Hear me!' Her words rang with such authority that it silenced the whimpering. 'Flames shall consume him until his limbs drop, one by one, into Hell! Five headless men shall cast him down!'

My mother fell heavily against me. I crumpled beneath her, landing on the unforgiving marble, striking my head, my shoulder and my hip.

My mother lay atop me. Her limbs thrashed; her elbow spasmed and dug into my ribs. At the same time, my mother's teeth champed; the air released each time she opened her mouth whistled in my ear. The sound terrified me: I should have been holding her head, making sure she did not bite her tongue.

Suddenly I heard Zalumma's loud command. 'Pull her out!'

My father at once came to himself. With uncanny force, he clasped my upraised arms and dragged me out from under my mother's writhing body. The movement caused an excruciating surge of pain in my ribs.

But the instant I was free, it was forgotten. I did not acknowledge my father's aid; instead, I clambered to my knees and turned to my struggling mother. Zalumma had already crawled forwards and used her body to weigh down her mistress's kicking legs.

I found the furred edge of my mother's cape and jammed it between her gnashing teeth. My intervention came late: she had bitten through her tongue, with frightening result. Blood stained her lips and teeth, cheeks and chin; the white ermine round her face was spattered with crimson. Though I held her head fast, it jerked violently in my hands.

'It is the Devil!' A priest stepped forward—young, red-haired, with pockmarked skin. 'I saw her do this in the Duomo. She is possessed; the evil inside her cannot bear to stand upright in the house of God.'

Murmurs surrounded us, and increased to a rumble, until, above us, Savonarola cried out, 'Silence!'

All looked to him. His eyebrows were knit in a thunderous scowl of indignation at such an offensive display. 'The Evil One desires nothing more than to interrupt the word of the Lord,' Fra Girolamo intoned. 'We must not let ourselves be distracted. God will prevail.'

He would have said more, but my father moved towards the pulpit. He gestured with his arm towards his afflicted wife and called desperately, plaintively, 'Fra Girolamo, help her! Heal her now!'

I still held my mother's head, but like the others, I watched San Marco's prior closely, breathlessly.

His frown eased; his eyes flickered briefly with uncertainty before his sense of complete authority returned. 'God will help her, not I. The sermon will continue; Mass will be celebrated.' As my father bowed his head, downcast, Fra Girolamo signalled to Count Pico and two Dominican monks in the congregation. 'Attend to her,' he told them softly. 'Take her to the sacristy to await me.'

Then in a loud voice, he began again to preach. 'Children of God! Such evil portents will only increase, until all in our city repent and turn their hearts to the Lord; otherwise, a scourge will come . . .'

From that moment, I heard the cadence and pitch of his sermon, but not the sense of it, for two brown-robed monks had appeared at my mother's side. Pico took charge.

'Fra Domenico,' he said to the larger one, who possessed a great square head and a dullard's eyes. 'I will have the women move away. Then you lift Madonna Lucrezia'—he gestured at my mother, still in the throes of her fit. 'Fra Marciano, help him if he needs it.'

Neither Zalumma nor I budged. 'My mother cannot be moved—it might injure her,' I insisted, indignant.

Fra Domenico listened silently. Then, with movements calm and deliberate, he grasped my mother's waist and lifted her with ease, forcing Zalumma to fall back. I reached vainly for my mother as her head rose from my lap. Flinching only slightly at her flailing limbs,

Domenico slung her over one shoulder, as a baker might a sack of flour.

'Stop!' Zalumma cried out at the monk.

'Leave her be!' I shouted at Fra Domenico. I struggled to stand, but bystanders stood on my skirts, and I fell again.

'Let her rise!' a male voice commanded above me. A strong arm reached down and pulled me to my feet. I rose, gasping, to stare up into the eyes of a stranger—a tall, thin man with a sharp chin, wearing the distinguished dress of a *Buonomo,* a Goodman, one of the twelve elected every two months to counsel the eight Lord Priors. He encountered my gaze with an odd, intense recognition, though we had never met before.

I pulled away from him immediately and followed the implacable Domenico, who was already making his way through the crowd. I walked beside Fra Marciano and behind Fra Domenico and his burden until we arrived at the sacristy. The monk carried my mother to a narrow wooden table and set her down, in the most cursory fashion. My father pushed him away with a vehemence that startled me.

Domenico turned and lumbered off. Fra Marciano remained with us, apparently hoping to lend what comfort or aid he could.

At some point during her journey, my mother's fit had passed. Now, as she lay stuporous and limp, my father removed his crimson mantle and covered her with it. Count Pico laid a hand upon his shoulder.

'How could God permit such a thing?' My father's tone was bitter. 'And why did Fra Girolamo permit her to be handled by that beast?'

Pico spoke softly. 'Fra Domenico is always by Fra Girolamo's side; you know that, Antonio. Perhaps God has let Madonna Lucrezia suffer this indignity just so that her healing will be a marvellous testament to all. Have faith, Antonio. He has not brought us this far to disappoint us.'

'I pray not,' my father said, then surrendered to tears. He cupped his hands over his eyes. 'I cannot bear to see her so. When she learns what has happened . . . the shame will be more than she can bear.'

He parted his hands and gazed down at my sleeping mother. Gently, he brushed a dishevelled lock of hair from her brow.

For a quarter-hour, we waited in the unheated sacristy. I wrapped my mantle tightly about me to no avail. My poor mother, in her stupor, shivered despite my father's mantle and the fur cloak in which she lay.

At last, the heavy door opened with a creak. We turned. Savonarola stood in the doorway, flanked by the burly Fra Domenico.

My father stared at Fra Domenico even as he spoke to Savonarola. 'We have no need of *him*.' He inclined his chin at Domenico.

'If he does not enter, *I* do not enter,' Fra Girolamo said.

My father blinked and lowered his gaze, defeated. The two monks stepped inside. Just behind them in the open doorway, the red-haired, pockmarked priest from the Duomo appeared.

'Surely God has sent you to Florence, Fra Girolamo!' he exclaimed, his face florid with adulation. 'You bring countless sinners to repentance each day. You are this city's salvation!'

Fra Girolamo struggled not to be swayed by such flattery. 'It is the Lord who shall save Florence, not I. Keep your devotion focused on God, not on any man. I have other business now.'

The priest sidled inside the sacristy. 'Ah! This is the woman possessed of many devils! Fra Girolamo, you said it yourself: the Evil One tried to stop the people from hearing the message God has given you. No one would ever have uttered such words as she did if the Devil himself had not authored them.'

'It's true, Babbo,' Domenico said to his master. 'Your presence would provoke devils. How angry you must make them! How frightened! Here is a chance to show the true power of the Lord.'

Uncomfortable with the direction of the conversation, yet unable to ignore it, Savonarola moved to my mother's head, and gently laid his hands upon her shoulders. 'Let us pray silently.'

We all obeyed, bowing our heads.

After a long pause, Savonarola proclaimed, 'God has spoken to me. Unexpiated sin has led to this woman's malady—a sin too long secret and buried; it has tainted her soul. I shall pray for God to open her heart and remove her burden, that she may be freed from any influence of the Evil One.' He lifted his face, and in a lower tone asked my father, 'Do you know, sir, of a grievous sin she may have been unwilling to confess?'

My father glanced up at him with unalloyed surprise; sudden emotion so overwhelmed him that he let go an anguished sob.

'I shall pray with you!' said the red-haired priest, excited.

Savonarola gave him a look of warning. 'Those who wish may lay hands upon her with me and follow silently with my prayer.'

The priest and Fra Domenico quickly laid their palms upon my mother's upper arms and waist; my father put a hand upon her right arm, along with Pico. Zalumma and I could do no more than rest our hands upon my mother's ankles.

The little monk lifted his hands, pressed them more firmly against my mother's shoulders, then squeezed his eyes shut. 'O Lord!' he exclaimed thunderously, 'You see before you a miserable sinner . . .'

Beneath his hands, my mother stirred. Her eyelids fluttered. Hoarsely, she whispered: 'Antonio?'

He took her hand and spoke softly. 'Lucrezia, I am here. All will be well. Fra Girolamo is praying for your healing. Rest, and have faith.'

During their gentle exchange, the friar continued his prayer. 'There is darkness buried here, an opening for the Evil One.'

My mother's eyes widened from fright. 'Antonio! What is he saying?'

At that very moment, the priest—who had begun to tremble with righteous fervour, cried out: 'Devils possess her, O Lord!'

'Yes!' Domenico rumbled, in a great, deep voice. 'Devils, Lord!'

'Stop—' my mother whispered.

Zalumma interrupted. 'You are frightening her! She must stay calm!'

'All will be well, Lucrezia,' my father said.

Savonarola paid no heed; his earnest conversation was between himself and God. 'O Lord! None can save her but you. Heal her . . .'

The pockmarked priest, lost in his own frenzy, continued the prayer as if it were his own. 'Free her from Satan's grip! Hear me, Devil! In the name of Christ Jesus, leave her body and set her free!'

Fra Domenico, prompted to righteous zeal by the priest's words, leaned down and seized both my mother's arms with undue force, saying directly into her face, 'Go, Devil, in the name of Christ!'

'Help me,' my mother called out weakly. 'Antonio . . .'

At the same time, my father gripped Fra Domenico's thick wrists, shouting, 'Unhand her! Let her go!'

'Stop this!' Zalumma commanded, over the cacophony of prayer. 'Can't you see what you are doing to her?'

My mother's body went rigid. Her jaw began to work, her limbs to pound against the wooden table. Her head jerked from side to side.

'You see, Babbo, the Devil shows Himself!' Domenico crowed in triumph, and laughed. 'Begone! You have no power here!'

'Let us pray to God,' Fra Girolamo thundered. 'O Lord, we beg you for this woman's freedom from sin, from the influence of the Evil One!'

Fra Domenico cried out, 'Leave, Satan, in the name of the Son!'

As he uttered the words, my mother's body heaved upwards in spasm, so violently that the men lost their hold upon her. An odd silence ensued; startled, the priest and Savonarola ceased praying. In response, Domenico brought the heels of his massive hands down, with full force, upon my mother's heart.

'Leave, in the name of the Spirit!'

In the unexpected quiet, I heard a soft but horrible noise: a snap dulled by the cover of flesh, the sound of my mother's breastbone breaking. I screamed, scarcely aware of Zalumma's own shrieks, or of my father's furious roar.

My mother's eyes bulged. Blood welled up from deep within her and spilled from the corners of her mouth down the sides of her cheeks, into her ears. She tried to cough, and instead inhaled blood; there followed the wretched sound of gurgling, of one desperately seeking air and finding only liquid. She was drowning.

My father wrested Domenico away from my mother, then returned to her side. I, too, moved to my mother's side. There I bent low, my elbows resting on the table, my face close to my mother's, near my father's. Zalumma was beside me, her shoulder pressed against mine.

'Lucrezia!' my father cried. 'Oh God, Lucrezia, speak!'

But my mother could not. The movement of her limbs grew weaker and weaker until at last they stilled. Her face had taken on the colour of a dove's breast; blood bubbled from her lips as she fought to draw air. I tried to help in the only way I knew: I pressed my face close to hers and said that I loved her, and all would be well.

My mother and I gazed upon each other. I don't think she was truly able to see me. I watched as the terror faded from her eyes along with life itself, and I saw the instant her stare grew dull and fixed.

Unmindful of the blood, I lay my head upon her breast. Zalumma took my mother's hand and pressed it to her lips; my father pressed his cheek against hers. We three mourned over her a time; and then rage swept over me. I raised my face, wet with my mother's blood, and turned to Domenico, who drew back timidly. I opened my mouth to accuse him, but before I could speak, my father screamed, his voice raw, wrenching.

'You have murdered her!' He flung himself at Domenico, his hands like claws, reaching for the big man's throat. 'I will see you hang for it!'

The monk lifted an arm to protect himself. Pico and the red-haired priest threw themselves on my father and managed to hold him back.

Savonarola stayed well clear of the fray. Once Pico and the priest had subdued my father, Fra Girolamo stepped in front of Domenico, who cringed. 'God forgive me,' he whimpered. 'This was a dreadful accident.'

There came my father's voice behind me, soft and deadly. 'This was no accident. You meant to kill her . . .'

'Here now,' Pico stated firmly. 'This *was* an accident. Fra Girolamo and Fra Domenico both came here with the godly intent of healing her.'

Savonarola stepped forward. 'These are the words the Lord has given me: Madonna Lucrezia is free of her affliction. In the hour of her death, she repented of her sin and is now in purgatory; in time, she will be with God. Be joyful in the knowledge that her soul will soon be at peace.'

Tears spilled onto my father's cheeks. 'That is true,' he whispered. 'But it is no less true that Domenico murdered her.'

Fra Girolamo was unrelenting. 'What happened here was an act of God. Fra Domenico was merely an instrument. Women!' He turned to exhort the two of us. 'Rejoice that your mistress shall soon be in Heaven.'

With a baleful glance, Zalumma spat in his direction, then turned back to her grieving.

I looked up at him. 'God sees the guilty,' I said viciously, 'God knows the crime that was committed here. He will see justice done to you and to Fra Domenico, *signore*, in His own time.' Then, with an abrupt practicality that amazed me, I said, 'If you wish to make any effort towards recompense, you can see her brought to our carriage.'

'That can be done,' Savonarola said. 'Afterwards, I will pray for you, that God might forgive your bitterness and hateful words. But first, we shall pray for Madonna Lucrezia, that her time in purgatory might be short.' He spoke to all of us, but his gaze was directed at my father, who still stood defiant. 'Kneel, and pray for your wife's soul to enter Paradise.'

My father let go of a sob that was also a roar. He stayed on his feet and stared at Domenico with Hell in his eyes.

Fra Domenico knelt behind his master. He opened his eyes and met my father's gaze. It was a gloating expression, with nothing of God or righteousness in it; in his eyes came a flash of calculating intelligence— so infinitely wicked and cold I could not find my breath. Then Domenico inclined his head ever so slightly at the table, where my mother lay, and slowly, deliberately, inclined his head at me.

My father saw it and recoiled.

'Kneel,' Domenico echoed softly.

My father's chest rose and fell so hard, I thought it might burst. And then, covering his face with his hands, he sank to his knees beside Pico.

Domenico smiled and closed his eyes.

But I would not bow. Zalumma would not bow. I did not understand what had transpired between the big monk and my father; I only knew that my father had let himself be broken.

After she received Last Rites, my mother was taken to our carriage. Most of the crowd had dispersed by then, but even in my grief, I noticed that the sharp-featured stranger who had helped me to my feet stood on the church steps, watching.

We rode back over the Ponte Santa Trinita. Swaddled in bloodied ermine and emerald velvet, my mother lay limp in my father's arms. He would let no one else touch her. Pico insisted on accompanying us. The count's presence offended me, but Ser Giovanni's distress was unfeigned. The turn of events had sincerely devastated him.

But my father would not look at Pico, and sat rigidly beside him so that their legs, their elbows, did not accidentally touch. Oddly, I sensed no anger in my father's behaviour, but rather shame.

I felt both pity and anger towards my father. At the same time, I was overcome by a sense of responsibility, and it was that which directed my actions when the carriage rolled to a stop behind our house.

'Ser Giovanni,' I addressed Count Pico, as if we were both adults and I his peer. 'Arrangements must be made for a gravedigger today, and a priest for the morrow; she would want to be buried at Santo Spirito.'

Before I could finish, Pico answered solemnly. 'It would be my honour, Madonna Lisa. In the meantime'—he turned to my father, who still cradled my mother's body—'let us carry her inside.'

'Up to her chambers,' I said. 'Zalumma, go before them and cover her bed so that it is not soiled, and have servants fetch towels and water.'

'I will carry her myself,' my father said.

'Come now,' Pico soothed. 'You will need help, at least, getting out of the carriage.'

My father remained distant, refusing to meet Pico's eyes, but he nodded. The men lifted my mother from the carriage; but the instant she was free, my father seized her from Pico. 'I have her now.' He would not be cajoled, so Pico left for Santo Spirito.

I walked a few steps ahead of my father, who muttered, '*Ave Maria, gratia plena, Dominus tecum, benedicta tu* . . . Almighty God, let her soul rise swiftly to you. Such hell, and all my doing, from the start . . .'

At my mother's chambers, Zalumma, red-eyed but tentatively composed, waited at the open door. 'The water to bathe her is coming,' she said, 'but I have readied the bed.'

With infinite care, my father laid my mother down.

'Here,' I said. 'Let us take this away.' I reached for the white ermine cape, now stiff with darkening blood. Zalumma helped me pull it from beneath my mother. When we were done, my father dropped to his knees, clasped his wife's hand and kissed it.

Wails emanated from downstairs as the driver began to tell the other servants. The water and towels soon arrived. 'You must go now,' I told my kneeling father. 'We must wash her. We will not be long.' I led him to the door and shut it firmly behind him.

Then I turned back to face the bed. As I did so, I caught sight of Zalumma, looking down at her mistress with a grief mixed with the purest love. In an instant we were both clinging to each other, sobbing.

'How can this be?' I gasped. My chin pressed into her shoulder. 'How could God author such a terrible thing?'

'God gives the power of choice to men, to do good or ill.' Zalumma murmured, 'All too often, they accomplish the latter.'

I had loved my mother more than anything in all the world; as for my father, whatever love I possessed for him was now tainted. There was only Zalumma now, only Zalumma. My mother and her need for care had always united us; now we would have to find a new purpose.

Zalumma patted my back as gently as she might an infant's. 'Enough, enough,' she sighed. 'We must hurry.' Her expression darkened as she fought tears. 'She will grow stiff quickly now.'

We moved to opposite sides of the bed and set to work. The unlacing of the extravagant brocade sleeves, with their gold embroidery, came first; then my mother's heavy overgown, also of green velvet with a cut pattern. The close-fitting dress, the *gamurra*, was next, and last was the spattered, stained *camicia,* the undergown of ivory silk. We removed it all from her, until she lay naked, then Zalumma removed her emerald ring and presented it solemnly to me. Earrings and necklace, all had to be removed; no adornment was permitted.

I took my mother's best white woollen *camicia* from the cupboard, and a white linen veil—the laws were such that she could wear only a simple white garment, and only plain wool and linen were permitted. Then I found her comb and did the best I could to unfasten her hair. It was tangled, but I drew the comb gently through the ends, then carefully worked up towards the scalp. As I proceeded, I felt the teeth of the comb dip, then rise slightly as they ran over her scalp.

The sensation was odd enough that I stopped, set down the comb, and with unsteady fingers, found the indentation in my mother's skull, between her temple and left ear. I parted the hair there, and found the depression and the scar.

My mother had always insisted that only Zalumma should arrange her hair. 'There is a wound on my mother's head,' I said, my tone rising with emotion. 'A wound and a scar.'

I followed Zalumma with my gaze as she deliberately wrung one of the towels out in the basin of water. 'You knew,' I said. 'Why didn't you tell me? You only hinted at it—but you knew it for a fact.'

The towel hung limp in her hands; she lowered her face, overwhelmed. When she raised it at last, she wore a look of bitter resolve. She opened her mouth to speak, but before she could utter the first word, a pounding came at the door.

My father opened it without being bidden. 'Please,' he said, 'let me be with her now, before she is gone for ever.'

Zalumma turned on him, her fists balled as if ready to strike. 'How dare you!' she seethed. 'When you are the one responsible for this!'

'Zalumma,' I warned.

'It's true!' she hissed. 'You have finally finished what you started so long ago. So leave—leave now, and let us care for her!'

My father withdrew, closing the door behind him without a word.

I put a hand on Zalumma's shoulder, but she shrugged it away, then wheeled on me. Years of repressed loathing tumbled from her:

'He struck her! Do you understand? He struck her, and I was bound so long as she lived not to tell!'

I could not respond. Instead, I moved heavily, silently, as Zalumma and I finished cleaning my mother's body, then dressed her in the woollen *camicia*, and affixed to her loose, unplaited hair the linen veil.

The following day, during her burial, my father proclaimed loudly that Savonarola had been right, the end of the world was coming; a good thing, for that meant he and his Lucrezia would soon be reunited.

Afterwards, when evening had fallen, he came to call on me.

I was alone in my mother's chamber—prompted by an odd determination to sleep in her bed—when a knock came on the door. 'Enter,' I said. I expected Zalumma to entreat me again to have something to eat.

Instead, my father stood in the doorway. 'Zalumma,' he said, his tone unsure. 'Did she say anything more to you? About me and your mother?'

I stared at him with contempt. 'She said enough.'

'Enough?' The anxiety in his eyes made me hate him all the more.

'Enough,' I said, 'to make me wish I had never been born your child.'

He lifted his chin and blinked swiftly. 'You are all I have now,' he said, his voice soft, hoarse. 'The only reason I draw breath.'

VI

OURS WAS AN UNHAPPY home. While Zalumma and I became inseparable, our time was taken up with domestic chores, empty of meaning. I continued my routine: going to market on grey winter days in my mother's stead, buying meat from the butcher, and doing other errands necessary to maintain the smooth running of the household, accompanied always by Zalumma and the driver.

I avoided my father as much as possible. We ate uncomfortably when we supped together; many nights, he lingered late in the city under the pretence of work, and so I dined alone. In his misery, he clutched at the teachings of Savonarola: twice a day, like a good Christian, he attended Mass at San Marco with Giovanni Pico always at his side.

Pico became a frequent visitor to our home. My father and he began to dress alike—in simple black clothes, which could have been taken for priestly garbs were it not for the fine tailoring and the exquisiteness of the cloth. Although my father treated the count with the greatest hospitality, there was a reticence in him, a coolness towards Pico that had not been there before my mother's death.

I walked with Zalumma twice a day, in sun or rain, to our nearby church of Santo Spirito. I did so, not because I wished to be pious—I possessed a good deal of rancour towards God—but because I wanted to be close to my mother. Santo Spirito had been her favourite refuge. I knelt in the cold church and stared at Michelangelo's graceful wooden carving of Christ, expired upon the cross. On His face was a look not of suffering, but of deep repose. I hoped my mother shared a similar peace.

Three miserable weeks passed in this fashion. Then, one evening, after I had supped alone, a knock came at my chamber door.

Zalumma was with me. She had grieved in private as best she could, hiding her tears, but she had known my mother far longer than I had.

'I am your slave now,' she had told me, after my mother's burial, and at night slept on the mattress on the floor beside my bed, just as she had always slept beside my mother.

When the knock came that evening, she was squinting next to the oil lamp we shared, decorating one of the handkerchiefs for my *cassone*, my wedding chest, with fine embroidery.

'Come,' I said reluctantly. I recognised the knock and had no desire for conversation.

My father opened the door halfway. He still wore his heavy black mantle and his cap. He slumped against the jamb and said, in a tired voice, 'There is cloth downstairs, in the great chamber. I had the servants spread it out for you. Choose what you wish, and I will bring a tailor for you. You are to have a new gown. Have no concern regarding the expense: it must be as becoming as possible.'

'Why?' I could not imagine what had prompted this in him, other than a sudden desire to win back my affections. But such behaviour was at total odds with the teachings of Savonarola: the friar frowned on sartorial display.

He sighed. 'You are to attend a function at the Palazzo de Medici.'

The palace of *Il Magnifico*—the very target of Savonarola's preaching against wealth and excess. I was too stunned for an instant to reply.

He turned and left then, heading quickly down the stairs.

Zalumma and I went down that night, but in order to better see my father's gift, we returned in the morning so that we had the light.

In the reception chamber, measures of Florence's most breathtaking fabrics had been arranged in a dazzling display. There were peacock blues, turquoise, blue-violets and bright saffron, vivid greens and roses; there were delicate shades known as 'peach blossom', 'Apollo's hair', and 'pink sapphire'. For the *camicia*, there were fine white silks, as light as air and embroidered in silver thread, others in gold. There were shiny damasks, rich brocades, multiple-pile velvets, and thinner silk velvets. What caught my eye was the *cangiante*, shot silk with a stiff taffeta weave: when held to the light, it reflected at first a deep scarlet; yet when the fabric was slowly moved, the colour changed to emerald.

Zalumma and I indulged ourselves, unwinding the fabrics, placing some together to better imagine the finished product. I draped them over my shoulder, across my body, then stared into my mother's hand mirror to see which colour most suited me; Zalumma gave her blunt opinion on each. For the first time in weeks, we laughed softly.

And then a thought struck me, abruptly darkening my mood. I had not been able to fathom why my pious father would permit me to attend a party at the Medici palazzo. First, it was too soon after my mother's death for me to be seen dressed in a party gown; second, he was, by virtue of his devotion to Savonarola, an enemy of the Medici now (business matters, of course, had nothing to do with those of the soul, and so he continued to sell his wares to them). There was only one explanation for his desire to send his daughter in magnificent attire to see *il Magnifico*: Lorenzo was the unofficial marriage broker for all of moneyed Florence. No child of the upper classes dared to wed without his approval, and most families preferred that Lorenzo choose the spouse. But almost every bride had seen fifteen summers.

'I am not quite thirteen,' I said, carelessly dropping the bewitching *cangiante* into a pile on my lap. 'Yet he cannot wait to be rid of me.'

Zalumma set down a fine measure of voided velvet and smoothed it with her hand, then gazed steadily at me. 'You *are* too young,' she said. 'But Ser Lorenzo has been very ill. Perhaps your father merely wishes to have his counsel while he is still among us.'

'Why would my father consult him at all, unless he saw a way to marry me off quickly now?' I countered.

Zalumma moved to a sumptuous piece of celery-coloured damask and lifted it. Sunlight reflected off its shiny, polished surface, revealing a pattern of garlands woven into the cloth. 'You could refuse,' she said. 'And, as you say, wait a few more years and then be married off to one of Savonarola's wailers. Or . . .' She tilted her head. 'You could let *il Magnifico* make the choice. Were I the bride, I would prefer the latter.'

I considered this, then set the *cangiante* aside. I rose, took the damask from Zalumma's hand and set it beside a deep blue-green voided velvet, a pattern of satin vines running through the thick plush. 'This,' I said, resting a finger on the velvet, 'for the bodice and skirts, edged with the damask. And the brocade with greens and violets for the sleeves.'

The dress was assembled in a week, after which I was called upon to wait. A second week passed; then, at supper, my father was uncharacteristically silent. When I excused myself from table, he interrupted.

'*Il Magnifico* has summoned you.' His tone was curt. 'Tomorrow, in the late afternoon, I am to take you to the palazzo on the Via Larga.'

The next day found me overcome by anxiety. I was to be on display, my good attributes and bad noted and used to determine my future. I would be studied and critiqued by Lorenzo and, I expected, a group of carefully chosen high-born women in Florence.

The gown, cunningly fitted to suggest a woman's shape where there was none, was far grander than anything I had worn. The full skirts, with a short train, were of the deep blue-green velvet with its pattern of satin vines; the bodice was of the same velvet with insets of Zalumma's pale green damask. At the high waist was a belt of delicately wrought silver. The sleeves were slashed and fitted, made from brocade woven from turquoise, green and purple threads interlaced with those of pure silver. Zalumma pulled my *camicia* through the slits, and puffed it according to the fashion; I had chosen the gossamer white silk, shot through with silver thread.

With my hair there was nothing but frustration. I wore a cap made from the brocade, trimmed with seed pearls, and since I was an unmarried girl, my hair was allowed to fall free onto my shoulders.

As it was late February, I put on the sleeveless overdress—the brocade trimmed with a thick stripe of the damask, then by white ermine. It lay open at the centre to reveal the full glory of the gown. Round my neck I wore my mother's necklace of seed pearls, with a large pendant of aquamarine.

At the last, Zalumma took me to stand before a full-length mirror. I drew in a breath. I had never looked so much like my mother.

I sat beside my father in the carriage, as I often had when I used to accompany him on business. I wore a dark blue wool cape to hide my finery, in compliance with the sumptuary laws.

As he drove, my father was gloomy and reticent; he stared at the late winter landscape, his eyes haggard. He wore his usual attire of plain black wool tunic and worn leggings with a black mantle—not at all appropriate for the function we were about to attend.

When we crossed the bridge onto the broad Via Larga, I realised that, if I wanted to voice the question that had been gnawing at me, I should do so quickly, as we would soon be at our destination.

'Fra Girolamo does not approve of the Medici,' I said. 'Why do you take me to Lorenzo?'

My father gazed out at the landscape and rubbed his beard. 'Because of a promise. One that I made long ago.'

Perhaps my mother had asked that her daughter's husband be chosen by the wisest marriage broker in town and my father, when he was still besotted with his wife instead of Savonarola, had agreed. And knowing that Lorenzo's health was failing, my father was simply being cautious and choosing the groom well ahead of time.

Shortly thereafter, my father pulled the carriage up to the gated entry of Lorenzo's palazzo. An armed man opened the iron gate and we rolled inside, near the stables. I waited for my father to rise and help me down, then escort me into the palazzo. But he surprised me.

'Wait,' he said, extending a warning arm when I moved to rise.

I sat in a torment of anticipation until, minutes later, the side doors to the palazzo swung open, and a man, followed by a pair of guards, walked out slowly, gingerly, with the help of a wood-and-gold cane.

Lorenzo was only a few years past forty, but his skin was sagging, jaundiced, and he looked decades older. Only one thing pointed to his relative youth: his hair, pure black without a single lock of grey.

Even so, despite leaning on the cane, he walked with grace and dignity. He glanced over his shoulder at one of the guards, and gave a nod; the summoned man hurried forward and offered me his arm. I took it and let him help me down.

My father followed, and bowed to our approaching host.

'God be with you, Ser Antonio,' *il Magnifico* said as he stepped up to us.

'And with you, Ser Lorenzo,' my father replied.

'So this is our Lisa?'

'This is she.'

'Madonna Lisa.' Lorenzo bowed stiffly. 'Forgive me if I cannot make proper genuflection to such a beautiful young woman.'

'Ser Lorenzo.' I made a full proper curtsy.

'Lisa.' My father spoke softly, swiftly. 'I leave you to Ser Lorenzo's care. I will be in the chapel. When you are ready, I will fetch you.'

'But, Father—' I began; before I could say more, he had bowed again to Ser Lorenzo, then followed one of the guards into the palazzo.

I was abandoned. I understood my father's intention then: no one but the parties directly involved would ever know he had brought me here. Even those who saw us come in the gate would think that he was simply conducting business, with his daughter to accompany him.

Panicked, I looked back at il Magnifico.

He was smiling sympathetically. His eyes were amazing; kind now, and reassuring for my sake, but beneath that was brilliance, breathtakingly shrewd and sensitive. 'Don't be afraid, young Madonna,' he said, in a weak, nasal voice. 'Your father has personal and religious reasons for being uncomfortable at our gathering; it is kinder to release him from such an obligation, don't you think?'

He held out his free arm to me and I took it, winding mine round his so that my hand lightly clasped his wrist. His own hands were gnarled, the fingers so misshapen he could scarcely grip his cane.

'I am afraid that you are burdened with me for an escort this evening,' he said, as we made our way to the entry. 'And I am sorry for it. Other marriageable young women who have entered my household have been nervous enough, but at least they have been comforted by the presence of family. I hope, dear Lisa, that you are not too uncomfortable.'

'I am terrified,' I answered, then blushed at my unintentional candour.

He lifted his face to the waning sun and laughed. 'I like that you are given to frank speech, Madonna. You will fare better than most.'

We made our way into a wide hallway with polished marble flooring and displays of centuries-old armour and weapons; from there, we passed into a corridor, its walls adorned with oil paintings.

'I gave my condolences regarding your mother's death to your father,' Ser Lorenzo said. 'I should like now to give them to you. Madonna Lucrezia was a fine woman, of great beauty and intelligence.'

I studied him askance. 'You knew her?'

He smiled wanly. 'When she was younger, and well.' He said no more, for we had arrived at a pair of tall arching doors. Servants, one on either side, threw them open.

I expected a chamber of moderate size, filled with at most a dozen Florentine noblewomen. I encountered something quite different.

The room could easily have held more than a hundred people; it was high-ceilinged and torches and candelabra of every description blazed.

Banquet tables—laden with roast lamb and pig and every type of fowl imaginable, as well as nuts, fruits, bread, cheese and sweets—had been pushed against the walls. But there was to be no formal dining. The guests helped themselves to refreshment, then stood talking, or seated themselves upon convenient groupings of chairs. My impression was that there were at least thirty persons in the room.

And I the only female.

As was the custom for girls being considered for marriage, I expected all talking to cease; I expected each man to turn round, and for Lorenzo to make an announcement that I had arrived.

But Lorenzo said nothing, and as we entered the room, the men—divided into several small groups, some laughing, some arguing, some telling tales—did not so much as look up at us.

I did not refuse when he summoned a servant, who brought a single goblet of exquisite gold, adorned with the darkest blue lapis lazuli I had ever seen. It contained watered wine, the most delicious I had ever tasted. The goblet was embarrassingly full.

'This is quite a lot of wine,' I remarked, then silently cursed myself. 'Will you not have some?'

He shook his head, his smile grown sheepish. 'My time for indulgence is long past, I fear. Here'—he glanced up, and with his jutting chin indicated a small group of men sitting in the centre of the room—'I should like to introduce you to some of my dearest friends.'

I took another swift sip of wine. So, I was to be judged after all.

Il Magnifico steered us towards a group of four men, three sitting and one standing beside a table, where plates of food and goblets of wine rested. The man on his feet was approaching the half-century mark in age. In one hand was a small plate, heaped with food; in the other, the tiny leg of a roasted quail, which he addressed as if it could hear him.

'Alas, sweet bird,' he intoned mockingly, 'how tragic for you that you were never rescued by our friend here—and how fortuitous for me that you have instead made my acquaintance first!'

Off to the side sat a dark-haired, dark-eyed lad of perhaps eighteen, whose great high brow seemed precariously balanced atop a jaw so foreshortened it looked as though he had lost all his teeth; his appearance was not helped by the fact that his eyes bulged. He clutched his wine, sipping it while the others enjoyed amicable conversation. The second was an old man, wizened and almost bald. And the third . . .

Ah, the third. The third, the 'friend' to whom the speaker referred, I judged was between the ages of thirty and forty—or perhaps ageless, for his dress and grooming were quite out of fashion. He wore a tunic so long it reached his knees, of rose-coloured, unadorned fabric and untailored construction. His hair, pale brown streaked with gold and silver, fell in perfect waves past his shoulders, almost to his waist, and his beard, also waving, matched it in length. Despite the oddity of his attire, he was, quite simply, the most beautiful thing in the room. His teeth white and even, his nose straight and narrow, and his eyes . . . In his eyes was a remarkable sensitivity, a razor-keen perceptiveness.

I prayed silently: *Dear God, if I must have one man in Florence—one man out of thousands—let it be he.*

Lorenzo lingered just far enough back so that the four need not interrupt their conversation to acknowledge him. Just as the first man finished speaking, the old one, sitting in the chair next to my beautiful philosopher, frowned at him and asked, 'Is it true, then, what they say? That you go to market to buy caged birds, then set them free?'

My philosopher grinned; the standing man with the quail answered for him. 'I have accompanied him several times on such missions.'

The old man stared in disbelief at the philosopher. 'You eat *no* meat?'

'I do not, sir. Have not, for the course of my adulthood.'

The old man recoiled. 'How is it, then, that you have survived?'

'Through wit alone, and barely then, dear Marsilo. That, and soup, bread, cheese, fruits, and fine wine.' He raised his goblet and took a sip.

There came a pause; Lorenzo stepped into it, with me on his arm. 'Gentlemen. Here is a young lady you must meet.' Lorenzo took a step back from me, and gestured at me as though I were a prize. 'This is Madonna Lisa di Antonio Gherardini, daughter of the wool merchant.'

The consumer of quail set down his plate, put a hand to his breast, and bowed grandly. 'Sandro Botticelli, a humble painter. I am pleased to make your acquaintance, Madonna.'

'And this is my dear friend, Marsilo Ficino,' Lorenzo said, gesturing at the elderly gentleman, who by virtue of his age and infirmity did not rise; Ficino greeted me with a disinterested nod.

'An honour, sirs,' I said to both men, and curtsied, hoping that the great Botticelli would not detect the quaver in my voice. He had created his greatest masterpieces by then: *Primavera*, of course, and *The Birth of Venus*, both of which graced the walls of Lorenzo's villa at Castello.

'This young lad'—Lorenzo smiled at the youth—'is the talented Michelangelo, who resides with us. Perhaps you have heard of him?'

'I have,' I said, emboldened perhaps by the young man's extreme shyness. 'I attend the church of Santo Spirito, where his handsome wooden crucifix is displayed. I have always admired it.'

Michelangelo lowered his face and blinked.

My philosopher rose. He was slender and tall—his body, like his face, was perfectly proportioned. At first sight of me, he had recoiled slightly, as if troubled; as his unease faded, it was replaced by an odd, tender melancholy. 'I am called Leonardo,' he said softly, 'from the little town of Vinci.'

I stifled a surprised gasp. I remembered my mother staring at the last portrait on the wall in the Piazza della Signoria, that of the murderer Bernardo Baroncelli. Here, then, was its creator.

'Sir,' I said, 'I am honoured to meet so great an artist.'

He took my hand and studied me so intently that I flushed. I saw deep appreciation, mixed with an affection I had not earned. 'And I am honoured, Madonna, to meet a living work of art.' He bent down and brushed the back of my hand with his lips.

Please, I repeated silently. *Let him be the one.*

'I thought you were bound to Milan now,' I said, wondering why he was present.

'It is true, the Duke of Milan is my patron,' he replied amiably as he let go my hand. 'Though I owe my career entirely to *il Magnifico*.'

'Quite the genius, our Leonardo,' Botticelli interjected drily. 'In Milan, he paints, he sculpts, he sketches plans for magnificent *palazzi*, he directs the construction of dams, he plays the lute and sings . . .' He faced his old friend. 'Tell me, is there anything you do *not* do?'

'That is the extent of it,' Leonardo responded mildly. 'Although I do have plans for altering the course of the sun.'

Laughter followed—issuing from all save Michelangelo, who huddled more closely to his goblet, as though frightened by the noise.

'Good Leonardo,' Lorenzo said, with an abrupt switch to seriousness. 'It is my wish to give Madonna Lisa a tour of the courtyard—but I require a moment of rest, and the time has come for me to partake of one of the noxious potions my physician has prescribed. Would you be so kind?'

'I can think of nothing more delightful.' The artist proffered his arm.

I took it, unnerved but not about to show it. Was this a sign that *il Magnifico* considered him a likely candidate for my husband? The prospect of life with this charming, talented, famed stranger—even in faraway Milan—seemed agreeable, even if I were too young.

'I shall retire for a moment, then.' Lorenzo took his leave with a short, stiff bow.

Leonardo directed me towards a pair of doors; servants on either side opened them as we approached.

As we passed over the threshold, Leonardo said, 'You must not be nervous, Lisa. I perceive you are a woman of intelligence and sensitivity; you are among your peers, not your betters.'

'You are kind to say so, sir, but I have no talent. I can only admire the beauty others create.'

'An eye for beauty is itself a gift. Ser Lorenzo possesses such talent.'

The air outside was chill, but there were several large torches and a small bonfire, contained by a circle of heaped stones. Beside it, on a high pedestal, was the bronze statue of a naked young man, his hair long and curling beneath a straw shepherd's hat, his body soft and rounded as a woman's. He stood with a fist braced coquettishly against one hip; the other hand grasped the hilt of a sword, its sharp tip resting on the ground. At his feet lay the grotesque, severed head of a giant.

I walked up to it; the firelight glinted off the dark metal. 'Is this David?' I asked. 'He looks like a girl!' I put my hand to my mouth, immediately embarrassed by my thoughtless remark.

'Yes,' my guide murmured, a bit distracted. I glanced at him to find he had been scrutinising me the entire while, as if he had never before set eyes upon a woman. 'David, by the great Donatello.' After a long and unselfconscious pause, he came to himself and said, 'He has guarded this courtyard since Lorenzo was a boy. But other things have been brought here for your enjoyment.'

For *my* enjoyment? I pondered this, then decided Leonardo was indulging in flattery.

We moved next to a pair of busts, each set upon its own pedestal, and each so worn that I could not determine the stone. 'These look old.'

'They are indeed, Madonna. These are the heads of Caesar Augustus and the general Agrippa, created in the times of ancient Rome. Lorenzo is fond of antiquities. This house contains the greatest collection of art, both modern and ancient, in the world.'

I moved to another bust, this one of white stone, of an older man with a round, bulbous nose and a full beard, though not so impressive as Leonardo's. 'And who is this?'

'Plato.'

There was another statue as well—a contemporary one—of Hercules, muscular and robust, the purported founder of Florence. At some point, I was so distracted I set down my goblet and forgot it altogether.

Despite my excitement, I was growing chilled and on the verge of asking that we go back inside, when my gaze lit upon another bust—life-sized, of terracotta—in a corner of the courtyard. This was a modern man, handsome and strong-featured, in the prime of life. His eyes were large, and the hint of a smile played on his lips. I liked him immediately.

'He looks familiar.' I frowned with the effort to recall precisely where I had seen him.

'You have never met,' Leonardo countered; though he tried to keep his tone light, I detected a hint of emotion. 'He died before you were born. This is Giuliano de' Medici, Lorenzo's murdered brother.'

'He looks so alive.'

'He was,' my guide answered, and at last I heard grief.

'You knew him, then.'

'I did. I came to know him well during the time I was a familiar of the Medici household. A more good-hearted soul was never born.'

'I can see it, in the statue.' I turned to Leonardo. 'Who was the artist?'

'My master Verrocchio began the piece when Giuliano was still alive. I completed it—after his death.' He paused to reflect on a distant sorrow, then forced it away. With practised movements, he reached for a pad and quill, both attached to the belt hidden beneath his mantle; his tone became animated. 'Madonna, will you do me a kindness? Will you permit me to do a quick sketch of you, here, looking at the bust?'

I was taken aback, overwhelmed by the notion that the great artist from Vinci would deign to sketch *me*, the insignificant daughter of a wool merchant; I could find no words. Leonardo did not notice.

'Stand there, Lisa. Could you move to your right? There. Yes. Now, look up at me, and relax your face. Close your eyes, take a breath and let it go slowly. Now, don't see me at all. See, instead, Giuliano, and remember how you felt when you first laid eyes on him.'

It was difficult, but I found the strength to relax, to soften, and to let go of the fear. I thought of Giuliano's smile and how he had no doubt looked kindly upon the artist who had asked him to sit.

And when I had at last forgotten myself, my gaze wandered beyond Leonardo's shoulder, to the window of the great chamber where the festivities awaited us. The heavy tapestry covering it had been pulled aside, and a man stood staring out at us, backlit by the room's brilliance. Though his face was in shadow, I recognised the figure from his stooped posture and pained demeanour: it was Lorenzo de' Medici.

The artist and I returned shortly afterwards to the party. Leonardo only had time to create what he called a cartoon—a quick rendering in ink of my basic features. It unquestionably resembled me.

Il Magnifico now approached us, accompanied by a boy perhaps a year or two my senior, and a young man of perhaps twenty. Lorenzo took my hand in his and squeezed it with a warmth that startled me.

'Lisa, my dear,' he said. 'I trust you enjoyed our few displays out in the courtyard?'

'Very much, yes.'

'They are nothing compared to what you shall now see.' He turned to the youths beside him. 'But first, let me introduce you to my sons. This is my eldest, Piero.'

With an insolent boredom, Piero sighed as he bowed. Tall and broad-shouldered, he had inherited his mother's arrogance and ill temper.

'And this is my youngest, Giuliano.' His tone warmed subtly.

The lad was well named. He favoured his father little, for he had even features and the same wide eyes as his deceased uncle. Yet like his father, he had a gracious poise. 'Madonna Lisa,' he said. 'An uncommon pleasure.' He bowed low and kissed my hand. When he straightened, he held my gaze so long that I looked away, embarrassed.

'My middle boy, Giovanni, was unable to leave Rome for the celebration. He takes his duties as cardinal most seriously.' He paused. 'Boys, go and see that Leonardo is well fed and cared for, after his long journey. As for you, young Madonna . . .' He waited until the others had wandered away before continuing. 'I should be most honoured if you would consent to an examination of the art in my personal chambers.'

There was no suggestion of lechery; it was a chivalrous offer. Yet I was perplexed. I was not well-bred enough to be considered marriageable to his youngest son (Piero was already married to Madonna Alfonsina, an Orsini), and so did not understand the purpose of the introduction. And if I were here to be sized up by potential grooms—especially, as I hoped, Leonardo—why was I to be separated from the group?

Perhaps the shrewd il Magnifico wished to examine my faults and assets more closely. Despite my confusion, I was also ecstatic. I had never dreamed that I would live to see the famed Medici collection.

'Sir, I should be thrilled,' I answered honestly.

I took his arm again and we walked back through the corridors lined with paintings and sculptures, to a great wooden door—guarded, as always, by a servant who opened it when we approached.

'This is my study,' he said as we entered.

How shall I describe such a room? It was of modest size, yet no matter where my focus settled, on a wall, on the inlaid marble floor, on shelves and pedestals, it found a gem, a glittering antiquity, an exquisite creation by one of the world's great artists.

I was dizzy at the sight of so much beauty gathered in a single place. We moved past a pair of earthenware vases the height of my shoulders, painted with beautiful eastern designs. Lorenzo acknowledged them with a casual nod. 'And there, a painting by Uccello, and del Pollaiuolo, one of my favourites.' These were names known to every educated Florentine, though few had the good fortune to set eyes upon their works.

Before I could begin to absorb such wonders, Lorenzo called for my attention again. He led me to a long table that contained a collection of coins and stones. A wall lamp had been hung just above it, so that the light glinted off the shining metal and gems.

'These are from the times of the Caesars.' He gestured at a row of dull, worn coins, irregular in shape. 'Others come from the Orient. We have many medallions, too, designed by our best artists. Here is one made many years ago by our own Leonardo. It is quite rare; few were cast.' He reached with great reverence for a gold coin.

I took the medallion and read the inscription: 'Public Mourning'. There was Giuliano, vainly lifting his hands against the blades wielded by his soon-to-be assassins.

'Please,' he said. 'Take it, as a gift.'

'I have one,' I said—and was immediately embarrassed by my thoughtless response to such a generous offer. 'My mother gave it to me.'

At my words, his gaze sharpened, then gradually softened. 'Of course,' he said. 'I had forgotten that I presented some of these to friends.'

Instead, he gave me a different medallion, featuring the image of his grandfather Cosimo and the Medici crest. I was perplexed by il Magnifico's generosity.

He seemed to grow tired after that, but he persisted in showing me other collections—cameos of chalcedony, goblets carved from precious stones—but he was near the end of his strength by then, and so singled nothing out from among them. Instead, he led me to a pedestal where a single shallow dish was displayed.

'This also is chalcedony,' he said. On top of the darker background was a milky cameo of several figures from ancient times. 'It is my single greatest treasure. This was used by the kings and queens of Egypt in their rituals. Cleopatra herself drank from it.' He read my poorly restrained eagerness and smiled. 'Go ahead. Touch it.'

I did so, marvelling at its perfection. Its edges were perfectly smooth. I glanced back at Ser Lorenzo with a smile, and realised that he was studying, with great fondness and enjoyment, not the dish, but me.

My rapture was interrupted by the sound of footfall. I turned and saw Giovanni Pico, bearing in his hand a goblet filled with dark liquid. He was as surprised to see me as I him. Caught off guard, I recoiled.

'Why, it is Antonio Gherardini's daughter,' he remarked. I doubt he remembered my name. 'How are you, my dear?'

Lorenzo faced him with great weariness. 'So, Giovanni, you know our Madonna Lisa.'

'I am a close friend of Antonio's.' Pico acknowledged me with a nod.

It was impolite, but I said nothing; I had not seen Count Pico since the day of my mother's funeral. While he had come often to visit my father, I had refused to receive him and stayed in my room.

Pico's expression was studied, but he could not entirely hide his curiosity as to my presence; although he was part of the Medici household, he was apparently neither a part of this evening's celebration nor privy to its cause. 'I have been looking for you, Lorenzo,' he scolded amiably. 'You are late in taking the physician's draught.'

Lorenzo grimaced mildly. 'Ser Giovanni has been one of our most cherished household guests for many years. We do not agree on certain subjects . . . but we remain friends.'

'I shall convert you yet,' Pico replied with good humour, yet there was a sense of unease in the air. 'Forgive me for interrupting your conversation. I shall wait patiently until you are finished. But mind, dear Lorenzo, that you do not forget your health.'

Lorenzo noted my curious glance regarding the draught; after all, he had left Leonardo and me alone in the courtyard with the comment that he was going inside to take it. 'I was . . . detained by other business,' he murmured, for my ears alone.

'You have been most gracious, Ser Lorenzo,' I said, thinking only of escape, for the proximity of Pico left me unnerved. You would benefit from a time of rest. With your permission, I should like to take my leave.'

Perhaps he heard the distress in my voice, for he did not protest. 'Leave the draught,' he told Pico. 'Go and see that Ser Antonio's carriage is ready, and tell him his daughter will meet him there. You will find him in the chapel. Then go and find Piero and send him to me.'

I felt great relief the instant Pico left. Once he did, *il Magnifico* said, 'The presence of Ser Giovanni upsets you.'

'He was present when my mother died.'

'Yes; I recall him mentioning it.' He gathered his thoughts. 'There is nothing more bitter than losing those we most love. An early death, a wrongful one, provokes the worst sort of grief. It turns the heart easily towards hatred.' He lowered his gaze. 'I lashed out vengefully when my brother died. It has come to haunt me now.' He paused. 'Ser Giovanni is a man given to great extremes. A more educated man does not exist, yet his heart belongs to the friar Girolamo. The world has lost one of its greatest philosophers. Have you heard of his theory of syncretism?'

I shook my head.

'It proposes that all philosophies and religions hold a kernel of truth—and all contain errors. Our Giovanni thought that each should be examined, to determine common truths and dismiss the fallacies.'

He smiled wryly. 'For that, the Pope suggested he be burnt. He came here two years ago, to enjoy my protection. And now he supports a man who would see me brought down.'

His face clouded suddenly. 'Child, I must be discourteous and ask to sit in your presence. This evening has drained me more than I expected.'

I helped him to a chair. 'Shall I bring you the draught?'

He smiled thinly, then gazed on me with affection. 'No. But will you hold an old man's hand, my dear, to comfort me until Piero comes?'

'Of course.' I bent down to clasp his hand; it was cold and so thin I could easily feel his twisted bones.

We remained this way in easy silence until *il Magnifico* said softly, 'Our Leonardo was quite taken with you. I confess, I saw him sketch you in the courtyard. I shall commission him to paint your portrait when he is able to leave his duties in Milan. Would that be agreeable to you?'

I was stunned. When I could speak, I said, 'It would be more than agreeable, *maestro*. I am thrilled by the thought.'

'Good,' he replied, and gave a short, determined nod. 'It is done.'

The door opened again, and Lorenzo's son entered.

'Giuliano,' he said. His tone betrayed his irritation. 'I sent for your brother. Where is Piero?'

'Indisposed,' Giuliano answered swiftly. His face was flushed, as though he had run in response to the summons; at the sight of me, his expression brightened.

'My youngest,' Lorenzo said to me with unmistakable fondness, 'is as quick to indulge my wishes as my eldest is to ignore them.' He paused. 'I regret that I cannot accompany you back to your father,' Lorenzo continued, 'but Giuliano is a responsible young man. I give you my guarantee that he will see you safely there. God be with you, my dear.'

'And with you, sir. Thank you for your kindness and for the commission of the portrait.' I felt a sadness as I took young Giuliano's arm and left his father, a frail and ugly man surrounded by the wealth and beauty of the centuries.

In the corridor, Giuliano and I walked past more sculptures and portraits in awkward silence; I rested my hand stiffly upon his forearm, he stared straight ahead and moved with a natural dignity.

'I am sorry, Madonna Lisa, that my father's illness interrupted your visit. He has been so sick the past few months that we all thought he would die. He is still very weak; the doctors told him not to invite any guests, but he was determined to see his friends again. He especially wanted to see Leonardo. And—he did not tell me, but I assume that he wished to meet you for the purpose of a future marriage arrangement?'

'Yes,' I answered. 'But please don't apologise. I'm sorry that Ser Lorenzo is still unwell. What ails him?'

Giuliano gave a frustrated shrug. 'Lately, he has been plagued by a dozen different complaints, none of which his physician seems able to relieve.' He shook his head. 'I have been so worried.'

'I am so sorry.' I had just lost my mother; I understood well his fear.

He came to himself suddenly. 'Forgive me, Madonna! You are our guest, and I should not trouble you with such concerns . . .'

'But I wish to know such things. Ser Lorenzo was so kind to me; he was showing me his collection, even though he was so tired.'

Giuliano smiled wistfully. 'That is just like my father. He loves to collect beautiful things, but they bring him no real pleasure unless he can share them with others. Did you enjoy the tour, Madonna?'

'Very much.'

'Perhaps we could arrange for you to visit our villa at Castello; there are many amazing paintings there, and beautiful gardens.'

'I would like that.' Though I reeled happily at the thought, my answer was hesitant. I doubted my father would ever allow me a second chance to visit the Medici. I was still worrying whether he would consider letting an artist—even one as renowned as Leonardo—enter our home.

Giuliano smiled at my response. 'That would be wonderful, Madonna Lisa! Perhaps my father will permit me to serve as your guide.'

I was suddenly unsettled by the realisation that he was taken with me. Surely Lorenzo had not invited me here as a potential bride for his son? Giuliano was still a few years away from the marriageable age for men. And when he did wed, his bride would certainly not be the daughter of a wool merchant.

A proper reply escaped me. Fortunately, by that time we had arrived at the side entry to the palazzo. I remembered dimly that guards stood on the other side of the door. Giuliano halted.

'I leave you here only an instant, Madonna, to make sure your father is waiting for you. I shall return to escort you to him.'

He leaned forward impulsively, unexpectedly, and kissed my cheek. Just as swiftly, he was gone.

I was glad for his disappearance and the absence of witnesses. Judging from the heat on my face and neck, I must have blushed deep crimson. This was a kind, likable lad, and handsome—a catch certainly beyond my hopes, and I could not help but respond to his kiss with a rush of giddiness. At the same time I reminded myself that I was smitten with Leonardo da Vinci. And he came from a good family, of roughly the same wealth and prestige as my father's.

By the time Giuliano returned, I was still too abashed to meet his gaze. He led me out into the chill night, past the guards, and helped me into the carriage without any acknowledgment of the illicit kiss. And when I settled beside my father, he said simply, 'Good night, Madonna. Good night, Ser Antonio. May God be with you both.'

'And with you,' I replied.

As we rode out onto the Via Larga my father asked, 'How was it? Did they put you on display for the women?'

'There were no women there. Only men.'

'Men?' He turned his head to glance at me.

'Friends of *il Magnifico*.' I did not want to reveal too much, but my curiosity would not let me rest. 'Many artists. Leonardo da Vinci was there.' I knew better than to mention Lorenzo's commission of my portrait. I paused, suddenly timid. 'Does he have a wife?'

'Leonardo?' Distracted, my father frowned in the failing light at the road ahead. 'No. He is one of our most famous sodomites. Years ago, he was brought up on charges; they were dropped, but he has lived for years with his "apprentice", young Salai, who is surely his lover.'

With apparently great effort, he asked me the appropriate questions. Who else had been there? Had Ser Lorenzo given any indication as to what man he thought might be suitable? I answered with fewer and fewer words and at last he fell quiet.

We rode without speaking through the cold dark city towards home.

VII

I SPENT THE NEXT week newly eager to meet my father for supper, in case he had received word from Lorenzo. I still ached over the news about Leonardo's preference for men. A part of me hoped my father was wrong, or perhaps lying in order to dissuade me from marrying an artist, since such men were generally judged to make unreliable husbands. I knew I had seen the light of attraction in the artist's eye.

During this time, I received a brief letter from the so-called sodomite, smuggled to me without my father's knowledge.

Greetings, Madonna Lisa, from Milan.

Our good Lorenzo has commissioned me to paint your portrait. I can think of nothing more agreeable; your beauty begs to be recorded for all time. As soon as I fulfil certain obligations for the venerable Duke Ludovico, I will come to Florence for an extended stay.

I enclose a more careful rendering, based on the cartoon I made that evening in the Palazzo de Medici. I am eager to begin work on the painting, and look forward to seeing you more than I can say.

Your good friend,
Leonardo

I studied the the drawing with reverence. I understood completely now why Leonardo had been called upon to finish the sculpture of Giuliano de' Medici after his death: his recollection of my features was astonishing. From the sparsely rendered ink drawing made in the courtyard, he had produced, in crisp and delicate silverpoint on cream paper, a remarkable rendering of my face—neck, shoulders, lips curled ever so slightly; not a smile, but the promise of one—truer, it seemed, and more profound than any image reflected by my mirror.

Dazzled, I stared at the drawing for some time before I finally directed my attention to the letter itself. *I look forward to seeing you more than I can say* . . . Was this an allusion to love? But he had signed the letter, *Your good friend.* Friend, and nothing more. At the same time, his words thrilled me: Lorenzo's commission, then, was a reality.

So I waited each night for my father, desperate for word of the portrait or, more importantly, mention of an invitation to visit Castello.

Each night I was disappointed. Yet after one such discouraging supper, as I retired to my bedroom, Zalumma met me, lamp in hand, and closed the door behind us.

'Do not ask how I acquired this; the less you know, the better,' she said, and withdrew from her bodice a sealed letter. I seized it immediately, thinking it would be from Lorenzo. The wax bore the imprint of the *palle* crest, but the content was far from expected:

My esteemed Madonna Lisa,

Forgive the liberty I took when you came to my father's palazzo recently; and forgive the one I take now by writing you this letter. I am too bold, I know, but my courage springs from a desire to see you again.

Father is very ill. Even so, he has given leave for me to take you, with an escort of his choosing and one chosen by your father, to our villa at Castello, for the tour I promised. My brother Piero is writing this very day a letter to Ser Antonio asking him to grant permission for you to accompany us.

I am filled with anticipation at the prospect of meeting you once more. Until then, I remain

Your humble servant,
Giuliano de' Medici

For the next few days, I forced all thoughts of Leonardo da Vinci away. Foolish girl that I was, I focused instead on that moment Giuliano had leaned forward to place a soft kiss upon my cheek.

Recently, my father's business had increased, requiring him to return even later than usual; I waited steadfastly, sitting for hours at the supper table until he at last came. I asked no questions of him; I merely sat and ate, certain each night that he would at last mention Lorenzo's invitation. This I did for four nights, until I could suffer my impatience no longer. When Cook had brought the soup and set it before us, I let a moment pass while my father addressed his supper, then asked, 'Have you received a letter of late on my behalf?'

Slowly he set down his spoon and gazed across the table at me.

'From Lorenzo de' Medici?' I pressed. 'Or perhaps Piero?'

'Yes, I received a letter,' he said, then picked up his spoon again.

Did he enjoy tormenting me? I was forced to ask, 'And your reply?'

He paused over his bowl, then slammed his spoon down against the table. 'There will be no reply,' he said. 'I kept my promise to your mother: I will let Lorenzo serve as your marriage broker. But he had best choose a godly man—if he lives long enough to make a decision.'

His anger aroused my own. 'Why can I not go? What harm is there in it? I have been so unhappy! This is the only thing that can ease it.'

'You will never again set foot in the house of the Medici.' His eyes were lit with fury. 'Their time is about to end. God will cast them down; their fall shall be great. Relish the memory of all the beautiful treasures you were shown, for they will all soon be gone, reduced to ash.'

I judged him to be parroting the words of his new saviour, and so ignored this. But I demanded hotly, 'How do you know I was shown treasures? How do you know?' I knew the answer: Count Giovanni Pico, but I wanted to hear him say it.

He ignored the question. 'I have been patient with you, out of respect for your sorrow. But I fear for your soul. You will come with me tomorrow to hear Savonarola preach. And you will ask God to turn your thoughts away from worldly things and towards the heavenly. And you will pray, too, for forgiveness for your anger at Fra Girolamo.'

My fists clenched; I set them upon the table, bitter at the realisation that a bright and beautiful world—one filled with art and the Medici, with Leonardo and the rendering of my own image—was going to be denied me. 'It is *you* who should pray to God for forgiveness, Father. You are the one who caused your wife's malady; you are the one who led her to her death. You are the one who camps now with her murderers, and remains blind to their guilt in order to suppress your own.'

He stood so rapidly the chair behind him screeched against the stone. His eyes filled with angry tears; his right hand trembled as he struggled to keep it from striking me. 'You know nothing . . . I ask you this only because I love you! May God forgive you.'

'May God forgive *you*,' I retorted. I abandoned my chair and turned, skirts whirling; it gave me some small satisfaction that I left the room before he could.

Later that night, lying in bed listening to Zalumma's breath, soft and regular, I revelled in my disappointment. The inability to see Giuliano made me yearn all the more to set eyes upon him again.

The following morning, as Zalumma helped me dress, a knock came at my door. 'Lisa,' my father called. 'Hurry and finish. The driver is ready to take us to Mass.' So; he intended to make good on the previous evening's threat. My heart began to pound.

'He intends to take me to hear Savonarola,' I hissed at Zalumma. 'Before God, I will not go!'

Zalumma, unshakably on my side, ceased lacing my sleeves and called out, 'She was slow to wake, Signore Antonio. Can you return?'

'I cannot,' my father answered, his tone unyielding, determined. 'I will stand here until she comes out. Tell her to hurry.'

Zalumma looked at me and lifted a finger to her lips, then she crept to the door and silently slid the bolt to lock us in. I stood while she returned to lacing my sleeves.

After a long pause, my father again pummelled the wood. 'Lisa? I can't wait longer. The time has come to go. Zalumma, send her out.'

Zalumma and I faced each other, our eyes wide and solemn. The long silence that followed was interrupted by the sound of the door being tried, then muttering, then renewed pounding.

'Do you dare defy me? Child, I do this for love of you. Is it so horrible going to listen to Fra Girolamo, knowing that it will please me?'

His tone was so pitiful that I was almost moved, but I held my silence. Zalumma remained motionless.

'It is the End of Days, child,' my father said mournfully. 'God comes to pass judgment. Lisa, please, I cannot lose you, too.'

I bowed my head and held my breath. At last I heard him move away; there followed the sound of his tread upon the stairs.

That evening, I did not go down for supper. Zalumma smuggled me a plate, but I had little appetite and ate sparingly.

The knock came later, as I expected; once again, my father tested the door, which I had bolted. This continued for more than two weeks. I began to take all my meals in my chamber and ventured out only when I knew my father was absent. When he was at Mass, I slipped to Santo Spirito, arriving late and worshipping briefly, then leaving before the service had ended.

I began to despair. My only escape was marriage, yet I had given up hope of the artist from Vinci, and Giuliano, given his high position, was unattainable. In the meantime, Lorenzo—who alone was capable of uttering the name of an appropriate groom—was too ill to speak.

Yet my spirits were lifted when Zalumma, smiling, returned from market one day and slipped another letter, stamped with the Medici seal, into my hands.

My dearest Madonna Lisa,

I am truly disappointed that your father has yet to respond to our letter requesting that you be permitted to visit Castello with us. I can only assume that this is no oversight, but a tacit refusal.

Forgive me for not writing to you sooner. Because of Father's poor health, I have not troubled him; however, I have spoken to my eldest brother, Piero, who has agreed to write a second letter on my behalf to Ser Antonio. He will suggest to your father whether, should he deem a visit to Castello inappropriate, he might entertain the possibility of my visiting you at your palazzo—with your father and my brother present, of course.

Should that be refused as well, I must ask: is there a public place, perhaps, and a time, where we might accidentally encounter one another?

I apologise for my brazenness. It is desperation to see you again that makes me so. I remain

Your humble servant,
Giuliano de' Medici

The letter remained in my lap for some time as I sat, thinking.

The marketplace was the obvious choice. I went there often, so no one would think it strange. Yet it was likely that I would also encounter a neighbour there, or a family friend. If I went anywhere out of the ordinary, the driver would certainly report it to my father.

Zalumma stood beside me, consumed by curiosity. Courtesy, however, kept her silent.

'How long,' I finally asked her, 'would it take for Ser Giuliano to receive a reply?'

'It would be in his hands by the morrow.' She favoured me with a collusive smile. I had told her everything of the tour in the Medici palazzo: of Ser Lorenzo's kindness and frailty, of young Giuliano's boldness, of Leonardo's graciousness and beauty. She knew, as I did, the impossibility of a match with Giuliano, yet I think a part of her revelled in flouting convention.

'Bring me quill and paper,' I said, and when they came, I scratched out a reply. Once it was folded and sealed, I handed it to her.

Then I unbolted my door, and went downstairs to seek my father.

My father embraced me when I told him I would attend Mass with him. 'Two days,' I told him. 'Give me but two days to pray and ready my heart, then I will go with you.' He granted it happily.

The next day, as Zalumma had promised, the letter was delivered into Giuliano's hands; Giuliano made my unknown messenger wait and penned a reply that very hour.

The evening of the second day was as beautiful as one could hope for in early April. As we rode up to the church of San Lorenzo—so great were the crowds who now came to listen to Savonarola that he had moved from the smaller church of San Marco to the massive sanctuary at San Lorenzo—the sun hung low in the sky.

The crowd covered the church steps and spilled out into the piazza, yet there was no sense of excitement, no liveliness or joy here. It was as hushed as a funeral, every form draped in sombre colours.

As my father helped me climb from the carriage, Giovanni Pico appeared. Setting my eyes upon him still made me flinch. My father embraced Pico, but I knew him well enough to notice his enthusiasm was feigned. His arm upon my father's shoulder, the count turned and led us towards the church. The crowd parted for him; most recognised him and bowed, acknowledging his close tie to Fra Girolamo. He sidled easily into the sanctuary, guiding my father as he held my arm and pulled me along; Zalumma followed closely as Pico led us to the front of the church.

The stolid, bulky monk Fra Domenico held our place. I turned my face away, lest he or the others see my hatred. He lumbered past us, speaking briefly only to Pico, and disappeared into the throng. Only then did I notice the distinctive and familiar face of a gangly, taciturn youth. It took me a moment to recall where I had seen him: in the Palazzo de Medici, sitting silently with Botticelli and Leonardo da Vinci. It was the sculptor, Michelangelo.

The ritual of Mass was brief, pared to its bones in acknowledgment that the people had not come to partake of the Eucharist; they had come to hear Savonarola speak.

And so he did. The sight of the little monk gripping the edges of the pulpit pierced me far more painfully than the presence of Pico, or even the murderer Domenico. I could focus little on Savonarola's words, given my anxiety about my plan. Instead, I heard only snatches of the sermon:

The Holy Mother Herself appeared unto me and spoke . . .

The scourge of the Lord approaches . . . Cling you unto the love of riches, of jewels and vain treasures while the poor cry out for want of bread, and the Lord will strike you down. Cling you unto art and adornment which celebrates the pagan and fails to glorify Christ, and the Lord will strike you down. Cling you unto earthly power, and the Lord will strike you down.

Disaster shall befall you, Florence; retribution is at hand.

The time is here. The time is here.

I turned and whispered to Zalumma. I put my hand to my forehead and swayed as if dizzied. My actions were not entirely feigned.

She reacted with concern. She leaned past me, towards my father and said, 'Ser Antonio. She is ill; I fear she will faint. It is the crowd. With your leave, I will take her outside briefly for some air.'

My father made an impatient gesture for us to go; his face was radiant, his eyes wide and shining, directed at the man in the pulpit.

Pico, too, was so captivated by the words of Fra Girolamo that he paid us no mind. I turned—to find standing behind me a man, tall and thin, whose face, with its long, narrow nose and sharp chin, provoked an elusive and unpleasant recognition. He nodded in acknowledgment; startled, I nodded in return, though I could not place him.

Zalumma and I forced our way through the sea of contrite flesh out into the piazza, then hurried to the church garden, walled in and hidden behind a gate. Inside, two cloaked men—one tall and one of average height—stood beneath a budding tree. The light was fading, but when the shorter pulled back his hood, I recognised him at once.

'Giuliano!' I half ran to him, and he to me. Our escorts—his scowling and sporting a long sword—remained two paces behind us.

He took my hand—this time with some awkwardness—and bent to kiss it. His fingers were long and slender, as his father's must have been before they grew twisted from age and disease. We stared at each other and lost our tongues. His cheeks were flushed and streaked with tears.

After a struggle to regain composure, he said, 'Father is so sick he can barely speak. The doctors are worried. I was afraid to leave him.'

I squeezed his hand. 'I am sorry. So sorry . . . I will pray for him.'

He gestured with his chin at the sanctuary. 'Is it true, what they say? That Savonarola preaches against him? That he says unkind things?'

I answered reluctantly. 'He has not spoken of him by name. But he condemns those with wealth and art and power.'

Giuliano lowered his face; his curling brown hair spilled forward. 'Why does he hate Father? Why would anyone want to destroy everything my family has done to help Florence? All the beauty, the paintings and sculptures . . . My father is a kind man. He has always given freely to the poor . . .' He lifted his face again and eyed me. 'You don't believe such things, do you, Madonna? Are you one of the *piagnoni* now?'

'Of course not!' I was so offended by the statement that my ire convinced him at once. 'I would not be here at all, were it not for the chance of seeing you. I despise Fra Girolamo.'

His shoulders slumped slightly, relaxed by my words. 'For that I am glad . . . Lisa—may I address you so?' At my nod, he continued. 'Lisa, I regret that my sorrow intrudes on our meeting. For I have come to speak of a matter you might find preposterous . . .'

I drew in a breath and held it.

'The evening you came to visit us—I have thought of nothing else. I think of nothing but you, Lisa. And though I am too young, and though my father might have objections, I want . . .' He grew embarrassed and dropped his gaze as he fumbled for words. For my part, I could scarce believe what I was hearing, though I had dreamt of it.

He still held my hand; his grip tightened. At last he looked up at me and said, his words rushing together, 'I love you—it is awful, I cannot sleep at night. I want no life without you. I wish to marry you. I am young, but mature enough to know my own mind. Father would want a more strategic match, I am sure, but when he is better, I have no doubt that I could make my case to him. We would have to wait a year, perhaps two, but . . .' At last he ran out of breath, then took in a great gulp of air and said, his eyes shining not with tears now, but pure fear, 'Well, first I must know how you feel.'

I answered without pause. 'I want nothing more fervently.'

His smile dazzled. 'And your feelings . . .?'

'Are the same as yours. But,' I added softly, 'my father would never permit it. He *is* one of the *piagnoni*.'

His enthusiasm was limitless. 'We could negotiate with him. If we required no dowry . . . I have met Ser Antonio. He seems to be a reasonable man.' He fell silent, reflecting. 'Father is too ill to consider this now . . . but I will take it up with my elder brother, Piero. He has always indulged me, and this time will be no different. By the time Father recovers, the engagement will have been announced.'

He spoke with such wild optimism that I found myself convinced. 'Is it possible?'

'More than possible,' he said. 'It is done: I shall see to it. I will speak to Piero tonight. And I will bring a report of my sure success to you tomorrow. Where shall we meet, and when?'

'Here.' I could think of no better place. 'And at the same time.'

'Tomorrow evening, then.' Abruptly, he leaned forward and kissed me full on the lips.

That was, of course, the impetus for our respective escorts to pounce and separate us. Giuliano was herded towards a waiting carriage, while Zalumma led me back to the church.

I whispered to Zalumma, 'Am I foolish, or is it possible?'

'Nothing is impossible,' she said.

I slept not at all that night—knowing that Giuliano, too, probably lay awake in his bed on the other side of the Arno. I surrendered all heartbreak over learning that Leonardo favoured men; I told myself that his admiring gaze had been that of an artist assessing a potential subject, and nothing more.

But Giuliano . . . handsome, intelligent, appreciative of the arts, and young, like me. I could dream of no better husband. And the love he bore for me provoked my own. Yet I could imagine no earthly bribe that would convince my father to give me to a Medici.

Just before dawn, when the darkness was beginning to ease, I was seized by an unpleasant revelation: the stranger who had nodded at me in the sanctuary was the same man who had helped me to my feet in the church of San Marco the day my mother had died.

The morning had been clear, but sunset found the sky eclipsed by heavy, blackening clouds. Had I not been so desperate to see Giuliano, or my father so desperate to hear the teachings of the prophet, we might well have stayed at home to avoid the imminent deluge.

Once again, I was forced to set eyes upon Count Pico, who greeted us with his usual unctuous courtesy, and upon Fra Domenico, who held our place near the pulpit, then disappeared. Given my nerves, I remember little of the ceremony or the sermon; but Fra Girolamo's opening words were delivered so forcefully I will never forget them.

'*Ecco gladius Domine super terram cito et velociter!*' he shouted, with such vehemence that many of his listeners gasped. 'Behold the sword of the Lord, sure and swift over the earth!'

God had spoken to him, Fra Girolamo claimed. God's patience had been tried; no more would He hold back His hand. Judgment was coming and nothing could stop it. Only the faithful would be spared.

The air was warm and close. I closed my eyes and swayed, then felt the sudden conviction that I had to break free of the crowd or else be violently sick, there in the sanctuary. I caught Zalumma's arm with fierce desperation. She had been waiting for my signal, but at the sight of my honest distress grew alarmed.

'She is sick,' she told my father, but he was once again utterly beguiled by the prophet and did not hear. And so Zalumma pushed me through the barricade of bodies outside, into the cool air.

The black, roiling clouds made early evening as dark as night as we made our way to the church garden. Inside, there was darkness, and against it the blacker shapes of trees whose branches writhed with each fresh gust of wind. But Giuliano was not there.

Not *yet* there, I told myself firmly, and raising my voice above the wind, said to Zalumma, 'We will wait.' I stood, my gaze fixed on the open gate as I tried to conjure Giuliano and his guard from the shadows.

We waited for as long as we dared. I would have stayed longer, but Zalumma patted my shoulder. 'It's time. Mass is almost over. If he had been able to come, he would have been waiting for you.'

The next morning, I was distracted, downcast over the possibility that Giuliano had experienced a change of heart, that his father or Piero had finally convinced him of the foolishness of marrying beneath his station.

I took to my bed and told my father that I was ill and could not attend the evening Mass with him. I spent that day and the next waiting for a letter from Giuliano that never came.

It was the evening of the 8th of April. I lay in bed, but my eyes would not close; I tossed until I annoyed Zalumma, who murmured a complaint. When I heard the sound of a carriage rumbling to a stop behind our palazzo, I pulled on my *camicia* and hurried out to the corridor to peer out of the window. The driver was climbing down by that time. I could make out the outline of horses and a man moving beneath the glow of the torch he held aloft. The cant of the driver's shoulders, his rapid pace, spoke of unhappy urgency.

He was headed for the loggia. I turned and moved swiftly to the top of the stairs, listening carefully. He pounded the door and cried out my father's name. Some confusion ensued, with the scuffling sounds of sleepy servants, until at last the driver was admitted.

After a time, I heard my father's stern voice, and the driver's unintelligibly soft reply.

By the time my father's footfall—the hurried steps of a man startled into wakefulness—rang on the stairs, I had already wrapped myself in my *mantello*. I held no candle, and so he started at the sight of me. His face, ghoulishly illuminated by the candle in his hand.

'Get dressed, and quickly. Bring your cloak, the one with the hood.'

Utterly confused, I returned to my chamber and roused Zalumma. She was sleepy, and could make no sense of my strange explanation, but she helped me tug on a gown.

I went downstairs, where my father waited with his lamp. 'No matter what he says to you,' he began, then was seized by an unidentifiable emotion. When he recovered, he repeated, 'No matter what he says to you, you are my daughter and I love you.'

I did not reply, for I had no idea how to respond. He led me outside, through the loggia, to the waiting carriage and driver. I stopped mid-stride at the sight of the *palle* crest upon the door. Giuliano? But that was impossible—my father would never happily surrender me to him.

My father helped me inside, then closed the door and reached through the window for my hand. At last, he said, 'Be careful.' And with that, he stepped back and motioned the driver to move on.

The hour had dulled my ability to think clearly—but by the time the carriage rattled over the flagstones on the Ponte Vecchio, I realised I had been summoned. We headed not to the Palazzo de Medici, but out of the city into the countryside. At last we rolled past the black shapes of trees and onto a gravel driveway. Though the hour was late, every window was golden with light; here was a house where no one slept.

Inside, a servant girl, dressed in black, was waiting in the grand hall. 'How is he?' I asked, as she led me at a swift pace down the corridor. 'Dying, Madonna. The doctors do not expect him to survive this night.' I felt pierced by this news, heartsick for Giuliano and his family.

We arrived at Lorenzo's bedchamber door to find it shut. The antechamber, like the one in the Via Larga palazzo, was filled with carefully arranged jewels, goblets and gold *intagli*. Piero's wife, Madonna Alfonsina, sat in the small room, slumped, pregnant and ungainly. She wore a simple *camicia* with a shawl thrown over her shoulders. Beside her sat Michelangelo, who held his great head in his hands.

Alfonsina shot me a baleful glance when I introduced myself.

The old philosopher Marsilo Ficino stood at the door. 'Lisa,' he said kindly, though he struggled to contain his tears. 'I am glad to see you again, and sad that it must be under such circumstances.' He reached for my arm to take me inside the inner sanctum, but halted as shouts came echoing down the corridor, moving towards us with the sound of rapid footsteps. I turned to see Giovanni Pico leading Savonarola in our direction; behind them, Piero and Giovanni de' Medici followed.

Piero's face was red and streaked with tears. 'You have betrayed us, bringing him here!' he shouted.

At the same time, his brother Giovanni thundered, 'Do not disregard us! Come away from him, or I shall fetch the guards!'

As Pico and Savonarola neared Ser Marsilo and the closed door, Alfonsina rose, unmindful that her shawl slipped from her shoulders, and slapped Pico with such force that he took a faltering step back.

'Traitor!' she screeched. 'Get out! Get out, both of you!'

Pico was stymied in the face of such hostile resistance. 'Madonna Alfonsina, I wish to cause no pain—but I must do as God directs me.'

Savonarola remained silent, his stiff posture betraying his discomfort.

The door to the inner chamber opened; and my Giuliano stood in the doorway. 'Hush, all of you! What is this?'

Even as he asked the question, his gaze set upon Savonarola. There was a swift, subtle flash of contempt in his eyes, immediately replaced by careful poise. His tone turned gentle and concerned.

'Please, all of you. Remember that Father can still hear us. We have a responsibility to make his last moments as serene as possible.'

Alfonsina, still glaring at Pico and his companion, picked up her shawl and flung it over her shoulders.

Giuliano took note. 'Piero,' he called to his brother in a lighter tone. 'Your wife has not eaten all day. Could you see that she gets some food?'

Piero visibly surrendered his anger. He nodded and put his arm round Alfonsina's shoulders. She looked up at her husband with affection; clearly, she loved him, and he her.

Giuliano then addressed his brother, the cardinal: 'Dear brother, have you finished the arrangements?'

Giovanni shook his head. 'Not all the details of the service.' A slight exasperation entered his tone. 'Father did a poor job, choosing only the Gospel and one hymn. Such things need to be given a great deal of forethought, as they will make a lasting impression on the crowd.'

Giuliano's speech was sincere. 'Of any person, we trust you to choose rightly, even though the time is short.' He sighed. 'Brothers, go and do what you can. You know we will send for you the very instant Father worsens. Now let me deal with our unexpected guest.'

Alfonsina and the two brothers swept past Pico and Savonarola with disdain. When they were out of earshot, Giuliano turned and with uncanny graciousness addressed Pico and the friar: 'Gentlemen, please seat yourselves. I will ask my father as to whether he is strong enough to receive you. But first, I must speak to a friend.'

At last, he took my arm and led me over the threshold, then closed the door behind us. We looked at each other and Giuliano's eyes were filled with strain. 'It was kind of you to come when Father called for you,' he said softly, flatly, as though kindly addressing a stranger. 'I must apologise for not being able to come to the garden—'

'Do not even speak of that,' I said. 'I am so sorry, so sorry. Your father is a good man, and you are too.' I moved to take his hand.

He drew back; emotion welled up within him. 'I can't . . .' His voice broke. 'Nothing has changed for us, Lisa. But I must be strong, and any show of gentleness makes it difficult. It's for Father, do you understand?'

'I understand. But why did he send for *me*?'

Giuliano seemed perplexed by the question. 'He likes you. It's his way. And . . . you know that he has raised Michelangelo as his son, yes? He saw him one day on our property, sketching a fawn. He saw his talent. And he must see something in you worth nurturing.'

He led me to where Lorenzo sat propped up by several pillows on a large bed covered with throws of fur and velvet. His eyes, once so sharp and bright, were glazed, distant.

'The others . . .' Lorenzo rasped.

I realised then that he could not see well enough to know me.

'They are all well cared for, Father,' Giuliano said, in a clear, cheerful voice. 'Piero has taken Alfonsina to get something to eat, Giovanni is preoccupied with arrangements for your service.'

Blindly, with great effort, Lorenzo lifted a hand a few inches into the air; his son caught it and leaned down. 'My good boy.'

'You have a visitor. It is Lisa di Antonio Gherardini. You sent for her.'

I moved closer until my hip pressed against the edge of the bed.

'The dowry,' the older man whispered.

'Yes, Father.' Giuliano's face was barely a finger's breadth from his father's. He smiled, and Lorenzo, just able to discern the sight, smiled faintly back.

'The only one,' he breathed. 'Like my brother. So good.'

'Not so much as you, Father. Not ever so much as you.' Giuliano paused, then turned his face towards me and said, again very clearly so that Lorenzo might understand, 'My father wishes to let you know that he has made arrangements for your dowry. Enough money so that you might marry a prince, if you so wish.'

I smiled in case Lorenzo could see, but my gaze was on Giuliano. 'Then you have not chosen the man?'

Lorenzo did not hear, but his son already had the answer. 'He has not chosen the man. He has bequeathed that task to me.'

I pressed against the bed, and leaned closer to the dying man. Boldly, I reached for his hand. It was a talon, yet I pressed it to my lips.

'You have been so kind to me, a wool merchant's daughter; you have been so generous to so many people. The beauty, the art, that you have given us all, Ser Lorenzo—it is a debt we can never repay.'

His eyes filled with tears; a small moan escaped him. 'Pray . . .'

'I will. I will pray for you each day I live.' I paused, and squeezed Lorenzo's hand before letting go of it. 'Only tell me why you have shown me such favour.'

He struggled hard to enunciate the words clearly. 'I love you, child.'

The words startled me; at the same time, I acknowledged their truth. I had been drawn to Ser Lorenzo from the moment I saw him; I had recognised a dear friend. So I answered, most honestly, 'And I love you.'

At that, Giuliano turned his head, that his father might not see his struggle to contain himself. Lorenzo, a look of the purest adoration on his face, moved feebly to pat his arm. 'Comfort him.'

'I will,' I said loudly.

Then he uttered something that made no sense. 'Ask Leonardo . . . The third man. I failed you . . . Leonardo now, he and the girl . . .'

The ravings of a dying man, I thought, but Giuliano turned back towards his father at once. He understood Lorenzo's meaning very well, and it troubled him. He put a comforting hand on his father's shoulder.

'Don't worry about that, Father. I'll take care of everything.' He looked up at me. 'It is best he rest for a moment now.'

'Goodbye, Ser Lorenzo,' I said loudly.

He seemed not to hear. His eyes were still fixed on the past.

I straightened and stepped back from the bed. Giuliano accompanied me as we went together towards the door, and the small lobby outside that gave us a measure of privacy.

I did not know how to rightly take my leave of him. I wanted to tell him that until that moment, I had been a silly girl with a foolish infatuation based upon his social charms and letters, a girl who had thought she was in love because she yearned for a life filled with beauty and art, and to be free of the miserable life beneath her father's roof.

I wanted to tell him how he now truly had my love—a love as real as if he were my brother, my kin. And I was amazed and humbled that one so compassionate and strong should have chosen me.

I did not tell him these things for fear of making him cry. But I could not resist the impulse to embrace him before leaving; with honest affection and grief, we pressed against each other without saying a word.

He opened the door, and handed me to Marsilo Ficino, then closed it again. I was escorted to the carriage. It was a clear night, and I leaned out of the window and stared up at the stars, too saddened to weep.

When I returned home, my father was sitting in the great chamber staring into the hearth, the tormented expression on his face painted coral by the fire. As I passed by, he leapt to his feet, his face a question.

'He has bequeathed me a large dowry,' I said shortly.

He looked at me, his gaze keen, searching. 'What else did he say?'

I hesitated. 'That he loved me. And that Giuliano was good. His mind was failing him, and he said a few things that made no sense.'

He bowed his head. 'Did anyone see you?'

'Lorenzo, of course. Giuliano. Piero, his wife, and Giovanni . . . and Michelangelo.' I took a step away from him. I was in no mood to recount the events of that evening. As an afterthought, I added, 'Pico brought Savonarola. The family was very upset.'

'Pico!' he said, and before he could stop himself, added, 'Was Domenico with him?'

'No. I'll talk about it another time, please.' I was profoundly exhausted. I lifted my skirts and went up the stairs.

VIII

LORENZO LAY IN STATE in the church where his brother was buried. All of Florence turned out to mourn him, even those who had so recently agreed with Savonarola that il Magnifico was a pagan and a sinner, and that God would strike him down.

Giovanni Pico came to our house to discuss the loss. 'On his deathbed, Ser Lorenzo received Savonarola and was greatly comforted by him,' Pico reported, dabbing his eyes. 'I believe that he indeed repented of his sins and prayed with Fra Girolano.'

Savonarola did not preach that day. Instead, the citizens who had so recently swarmed upon the steps of San Lorenzo to listen to Florence's prophet now waited to catch a final glimpse of her greatest patron.

We entered the church sometime after noon. Near the altar lay Lorenzo, in a simple wooden box atop a pedestal. He had been dressed in a plain white linen robe, and his hands—the fingers pulled and carefully arranged so they no longer appeared so contorted—had been folded over his heart.

I glanced up from his body to see Giuliano, standing a short distance from the coffin between his brother Piero and a bodyguard. Behind them stood a haggard Michelangelo, and the artist from Vinci.

The sight of Leonardo brought me no hope, no joy. My thought was only of Giuliano, and I stared steadily at him until our gazes met. His expression was composed, but his misery showed in his stance.

At the sight of me, a light flickered in his eyes. It was inappropriate for us to speak, even to acknowledge each other, but I learned, in that instant, all I wanted to know. I had only to be patient.

Over the next few months, as spring turned to summer, my life became an agony of waiting. I heard nothing from Giuliano.

His elder brother, however, fuelled much gossip all over the city. It had long been said that his father had often despaired over Piero's lack of acumen and mourned over his arrogance, and Lorenzo was proved right. Only months after il Magnifico's death, Piero managed to alienate most of the Lord Priors. It did not help matters that his mother Clarice had been from the noble and powerful Orsini clan, who considered themselves princes; nor did it help that Piero had married Alfonsina Orsini from Naples. For this reason he was considered an outsider— only one-third Florentine, and two-thirds self-proclaimed royalty.

Savonarola astutely used this in his sermons, rallying the poor against their oppressors, though he took care not to mention Piero by name. Anti-Medici sentiment began to grow.

I, in my misery, no longer had excuses to avoid Fra Girolamo's sermons. I tolerated them, hoping that my obedience would soften my father's heart and keep him from rejecting Giuliano as a suitor. So I found myself twice daily in San Lorenzo, listening to the Dominican.

In late July, when Pope Innocent died, Savonarola proclaimed it a sign of God's wrath; in mid-August, when a new pope ascended St Peter's throne, he grew red-faced with rage. Cardinal Rodrigo Borgia, now Pope

Alexander VI, dared to take up residence in the Vatican with his four illegitimate children: Giovanni, Cesare, Lucrezia and Jofre. And he did not, as most cardinals and popes had in the past, refer to them as niece and nephews; he blatantly insisted that his children be recognised as his own.

Autumn came, then winter and the new year. At last, Zalumma smuggled me a letter bearing the Medici seal; I tore it open with a mixture of desperation and wild joy.

Madonna Lisa, it began, and with those two distant words, my hope was crushed.

> *I am at wits' end. Piero has steadfastly denied me permission to wed you; he seeks for me a bride who increases the family's standing and better secures his position as Father's successor. He thinks only of politics, not of love.*
>
> *I tell you such things not to discourage you, but rather to explain my long silence and assure you of my frustration and my determination. I will be matched to no one else. I think day and night of nothing but you, and of a way for us to be together. I am committed to designing that way.*
>
> *I will be with you soon, my love. Have faith in that.*
> *Giuliano*

I let the letter fall to my lap and wept inconsolably. I wanted to feed the letter to the lamp, to shred it into a thousand pieces.

Fool that I was, I folded it carefully and put it away with other keepsakes: Giuliano's medallion, and that of Cosimo and the Medici crest; the drawing of me by Leonardo, and his letter; and Giuliano's letters.

The year after Lorenzo's death—the first full year of Piero's reign—passed grimly for me. I began my monthly bloods and did everything possible to hide the fact from my father, bribing the laundress not to mention the stained linens. Even so, Father began to speak of potential husbands. He had kept his promise to my mother, he said; it was not his fault that Lorenzo had died before giving his opinion on a match.

That same year, the legend of the *papa angelico*—that unworldly pope who would be chosen by God, not man—merged with a second old story, that of the coming of a second Charlemagne, who would cleanse the Church. This Charlemagne would then unite Christendom under the spiritual rule of the *papa angelico*.

It did not help matters that the French king was named Charles, or that he listened to such legends and took them to heart. Nor did it help that he set his sights on Naples, deciding that the southern principality by the sea rightly belonged to him. After all, it had been wrested from French control only a generation earlier.

Savonarola seized on these ideas, merging them with his holy vision. He was shrewd enough never to suggest directly that he was that angelic pope, but he began to preach that Charles would wield the Lord's avenging sword. Charles would scourge Italy and bring her to penitent knees, and the faithful should welcome him with open arms.

But with the passing of another year, the spring of 1494 brought— for me, at least—new hope. Long after I had surrendered my dream of seeing Giuliano again, Zalumma dropped another letter bearing the waxen Medici seal into my lap.

My most beloved Lisa,

Perhaps now you will believe that I am a man of my word. I did not give up, and here is the result: my brother Piero has at last given me permission to ask for your hand.

I hope that my long silence did not make you doubt the depth of my feelings for you, and I pray God that your own feelings have not changed towards me. I must in good faith warn you: public sentiment has turned against the Medici and if your father and you accept my proposal, be aware that you might well be marrying into a family whose influence is waning. Piero remains confident that all will be well, but I fear a different outcome. He has received a letter from Charles's ambassadors demanding that the French army be given free passage through Tuscany, as well as arms and soldiers. Piero feels he can give no clear answer; he is bound by family ties to support Naples, and Pope Alexander has threatened to withhold our brother Giovanni's benefices as cardinal should Piero fail to protect Naples from Charles's advance.

Yet every member of the Signoria is required by law to take an oath never to raise arms against France, and Florence has always relied heavily on her trade. And so my eldest brother finds himself in an impossible situation.

I cannot help but think that he is the victim of a concerted effort to discredit and bring down our house.

Ponder this before you write to me, love, and give me your answer. If you give me word, I shall call on your father. My happiness resides in your hands.

Whether yea or nay, I remain,

Yours for ever,

Giuliano

I raised my hands to my burning cheeks. Zalumma was, of course, standing over me, eager to learn what the letter contained.

'He is coming here to ask for my hand,' I said.

I responded immediately to Giuliano. So great was my hope that I refused to remember my father's railing against the Medici. Instead, I clung to Giuliano's promise that he would find a way to strike an agreement. He was, after all, *Il Magnifico*'s son, skilled at diplomacy and the art of compromise. I trusted him to achieve the impossible.

A few weeks before Easter, on an overcast morning, Zalumma and I arrived home early from market. As our carriage pulled round to the back of our palazzo, I spied a second vehicle—one bearing the Medici coat of arms on its door. It had not been there long; the handsome white horses were still breathing heavily from their trip across the Arno.

'God have mercy on us!' Zalumma muttered.

I seized her hand. 'You must find a way to hear their conversation! Go!'

She set off immediately, while I approached the house. The door to the great chamber stood open, and I heard my father's calm and earnest tone, which relieved me at once; I had expected it to be hostile. As I passed the open door, he glanced up.

Had I been gifted with more self-control, I might have continued on, but I stopped to gaze at Giuliano. I had not seen him since the morning of his father's funeral. He was taller, his face leaner and more angular, his shoulders and back broader. I was relieved to see that my father had received him properly, summoning wine and food for his guest.

Giuliano, in turn, studied me, and his radiance stole my breath.

'Lisa,' my father called. 'Go to your chambers.'

I moved numbly up the stairs. Behind me, Zalumma's voice enquired whether Ser Antonio wanted more wine. She would serve as my eyes and ears, but this comforted me little. I went to my room where, helpless, I stared out of the window at the driver and the fine horses.

At last I saw Giuliano emerge from our loggia and cross the courtyard to his carriage. I flung open the window and cried out his name.

He turned and looked up at me. The distance was enough to hinder speech, but I learned all I needed in a glimpse. He was downcast. Yet he raised a hand in the air as if reaching for me; and he took that hand and pressed the palm against his heart.

I did an outrageous thing, an unspeakable thing: I lifted my skirts high and ran down the stairs at speed, determined to stop Giuliano in his carriage, to join him, to ride away from the house where I was born.

I might have made it, but my father had just walked out of the chamber where he had entertained his guest and, realising where I was headed, stepped in front of the door and barred my path.

I raised both hands to strike him, but he seized my wrists.

'Lisa, are you mad?' He was honestly amazed.

'Let me go!' I shouted, my tone anguished, for I could hear Giuliano's carriage already rumbling towards the gate.

'How do you know why he came?' His tone had turned from one of amazement to one of accusation. 'What made you think this was anything other than business? And how did you come to be so infatuated with him? You have been lying to me, hiding things from me!'

'How could you turn him away? You care nothing for my happiness!'

Instead of raising his voice to match mine, he lowered his. 'On the contrary,' he said. 'I care everything for your happiness, which is why I turned him away.' Then in an impatient burst, he demanded, 'Do you not hear the discontent in the streets? The Medici have attracted God's wrath, and that of the people. For me to give my daughter over to them would be to put her directly in harm's way. It is only a matter of time before the French King comes, bearing the scourge of God in his hand; then what will become of Piero and his brothers? You attend Mass twice daily with me. How is it you have not heard all that Savonarola has said?'

'Fra Girolamo knows nothing,' I replied heatedly. 'Giuliano is a good man, from a family of good men, and I will marry him someday!'

He reached forth to slap me so swiftly that I never saw his intent; in the next instant, I was holding my hand to my stinging cheek.

'God forgive me,' he said, as surprised as I by his action. 'God forgive me, but you provoke me.' He turned away, helpless, confused and angered. 'I am frightened for your sake, Lisa. You are following a dangerous path. Safety lies only with Fra Girolamo and the Church.' He drew in a shuddering sigh, then faced me, his expression tortured. 'I will pray for you, child. What else can I do?'

'Pray for us both,' I countered, as unkindly as possible, then turned imperiously and ran up the stairs to my chamber.

Zalumma had not managed to hear all the conversation between my father and Giuliano, but she heard enough to know that an offer of land and ten thousand florins had been refused. When Giuliano finally asked what offer would be acceptable, and what he could possibly do to prove the sincerity of his intent, my father had finally replied, 'You know, Ser Giuliano, that I am a disciple of Fra Girolamo.'

'Yes,' admitted Giuliano.

'Then you understand my reasons for refusing you, and why I will never yield on this subject.' Then my father had risen, and proclaimed the discussion at an end.

'But,' Zalumma confided in me, 'I saw Ser Giuliano's eyes, and the set of his jaw. He is just like his uncle; he will never give up. Never.'

During that spring and summer, I refused to abandon hope. I was convinced I would hear from Giuliano again.

With my father and Count Pico—who was growing sickly—I listened to Savonarola's Easter sermon. He had delivered the Lord's message, he said, and this sermon was the last he would deliver until God summoned him again. It took all my resolve not to smile with relief.

I needed no God to provide torment; my own heart provided it easily enough. One evening after supper, in the privacy of my chamber, I penned a single line with my quill. After signing it, I carefully folded the paper twice, and sealed it with red wax.

I proffered it then to Zalumma.

'It is no longer so easy,' she said. 'Your father watches me closely.'

'Then someone else can go to the Palazzo de Medici. I don't care how you do it; just get it done.'

'First you must tell me what it says.'

Had it been anyone other than Zalumma, I would have reminded her at once that she was exhibiting dangerous impertinence for a slave. But I sighed, then uttered the words, *'Give me a sign and an opportunity, and I will come to you.'*

This was monstrous, beyond scandal; a proper marriage could never be obtained without parental consent. I risked disapproval not only from society but from Giuliano himself.

I sat and waited wearily for Zalumma's tirade.

It did not come. She studied me for a long, silent moment. And then she said, softly, 'When you leave, I will go with you, of course.'

Near October's end, Piero rode north for three days, accompanied by only a few friends. His destination was the fortress of Sarzana, where the French king, Charles, camped with his army. Inspired by the late Lorenzo, who had once gone alone to King Ferrante and averted war with Naples, Piero hoped his gesture would similarly save Florence.

By the 4th of November, every citizen knew that Piero had, without coaxing, handed over the fortresses of Sarzana, Pietrasanta and Sarzanella to Charles. My father was furious. 'A hundred years it took us to conquer those lands, and he has lost them in a day!' he stormed.

The Signoria was just as angry. The priors had decided to send a small group of envoys to Pisa, to meet Charles there. Piero would not be among them—but Fra Girolamo Savonarola would.

Such news left me dizzy with anxiety, but my determination never wavered, nor did my plans change.

On the 8th of November, I set off alone in the carriage, leaving Zalumma behind on the agreed-upon pretext that she was unwell. My father had gone to the public baths.

The driver took me over the Arno on the ancient Ponte Vecchio. I was dressed in my plain dark gown. Hidden in my bodice, for luck, were the gold medallions. I bore the basket Zalumma always carried over her arm—although on this day, I had lined it with a cloth.

Before departing, I had told the driver that I would be visiting the butcher's today. Now, when I told him to wait for me by the greengrocers' stalls, he pulled the horses to a stop and did not even watch as I climbed out and headed for the butcher's, which was out of his line of sight.

The butcher was a good man, but times were hard and uncertain. He had his price, even if he suspected the source of the bag of gold florins.

As I neared, he was laughing with a young woman. At the sight of me, the butcher's smile faded; he quickly wrapped a thick oxtail in a cloth. 'Buon appetito, Monna Beatrice. God keep you!' He turned to the other woman waiting. 'Monna Cecelia, forgive me, I have urgent business, but Raffaele will attend to you.' As his son stepped forward to wait on their next customer, the butcher said, far more loudly than needed, 'Monna Lisa. I have in the back some excellent roasts. Come with me.'

He led me behind a makeshift curtain to the back of the stall. It was a short walk to the exit. The warm flagstones were slick with blood draining from the stall and the hem of my skirts was soaked. But my dismay was short-lived, for only steps away waited another carriage—this one black and carefully devoid of any family crest announcing its owner.

Those few strides—given the gravity and significance they bore—seemed impossible, interminable. Yet I made it to the carriage. The door opened and through magic, through miracle, I found myself sitting next to Giuliano, the basket by my feet on the floor.

The driver called out to the horses. The wheels creaked and we began to rumble along at a good pace, away from the butcher, away from the waiting driver, away from my father and my home.

Giuliano was glorious, as unreal and perfect as a painting. He wore a bridegroom's *farsetto* of crimson voided velvet embroidered with gold thread, with a large ruby pinned to his throat. He stared at me with wide-eyed amazement—me, with my plain hair and translucent black veil, with my drab brown dress, as if I were exotic and startling.

I spoke in a swift, breathless rush; my voice shook uncontrollably. 'I have the dress, of course. I will send for my slave when the thing is done. She is packing my belongings now . . .' All the while I was thinking: *Lisa, you are mad. Your father will come and put a stop to all this. Piero will return and throw you from the palazzo.*

I might have prattled on out of sheer nerves, but he seized my hands and kissed me.

I returned his kiss with equal fervour, and by the time we arrived at the palazzo, our hair and clothing were in disarray.

Had my life been like that of other girls, my marriage would have been arranged by a *sensale*, an intermediary, most likely Lorenzo himself. My father would have paid at least five thousand florins, and had the amount recorded in the city ledger.

On my wedding day, I would have worn a dazzling gown designed, as custom demanded, by Giuliano himself. Followed by my kinswomen on foot, I would have ridden a white horse across the Ponte Santa Trinita to the home of the Medici. A garland of flowers would have stretched across the street in front of my new home, which I would dare not cross until my future husband broke the chain.

From there, we would have gone to the church. After the ceremony, I would have returned on foot to my father's house and slept alone. Only the next day, after a great feast, would the marriage be consummated.

But for me, there was no *sensale*. There was only Giuliano's determination and yearning, and mine.

As for the dowry, Lorenzo, not my father, had paid it long ago—although Giuliano, through his government connections, had the amount recorded as coming from Antonio di Gherardini. I had no doubt that when my father learned of the deception, he would have the amount stricken from the ledger.

My dress was of my own design, worn by me more than two years earlier to the Palazzo de Medici: a gown with skirts of deep blue-green voided velvet, with a pattern of satin vines, and a bodice of the same with insets of pale green damask. I had grown since then, and Zalumma and I had made alterations in secret, lengthening the skirt and sleeves, letting out the bodice to accommodate a woman's body, not a girl's.

I rode no white horse, was accompanied by no kinswomen—not even Zalumma, who would have known how to soothe my nerves. A house servant of Giuliano's named Laura helped me dress in an unoccupied bedchamber—beneath a portrait of Clarice de' Medici.

As the servant was pulling my *camicia* through my sleeves, I stared up at Clarice's intimidating image. 'Were these her rooms?'

'Yes, Madonna. They belong to Madonna Alfonsina now. She has been at Poggio a Caiano for several days. I suspect Ser Giuliano will not share news of you with her until she returns.'

My stomach fluttered; I could imagine her reaction. 'And the others?'

'You know that Ser Piero has gone to Sarzana . . .' When I nodded, she continued. 'You need have no worry there, he is sympathetic. But there is His Holiness, Ser Giovanni, the cardinal. He has gone to Mass and business meetings. He is not privy to anything; I do not think Ser Giuliano intends to tell him unless it is necessary.'

She lifted a fine hairbrush—one that I assumed belonged to my soon-to-be sister-in-law. 'Shall we just brush it out, then?'

I nodded. Had I attempted any elaborate style that morning, my father or the servants would have noticed—and so I wore it falling loose onto my shoulders, as befitted an unmarried girl. She then fastened in place the brocade cap I had brought. For a final touch, I donned my mother's necklace of seed pearls, with the large aquamarine pendant.

It was difficult, touching it, not to think of my mother, of how she had married foolishly, how unhappily she had lived and died.

'Ah!' Laura put a gentle hand upon my elbow. 'You should not be sad at such a time! Madonna, you are marrying a man with the noblest heart and the best brain in all Tuscany.'

Thinking we were finished, I made a move for the door. At once Laura said, 'But you are not complete!' And she went to a wardrobe and drew forth a long white veil, embroidered with unicorns and mythical gardens in thread of gold. She placed it upon my head, covering my face.

'Madonna Clarice wore it when she married Ser Lorenzo,' she said, 'and Alfonsina when she married Piero. Giuliano made sure that the priest blessed it again, just for you.' She smiled. 'Now you are ready.'

She led me down to the ground floor, to the Medici's chapel. I had expected Zalumma to be waiting there, but the corridor was empty.

Panicked, I turned to Laura. 'My slave . . . She should have arrived by now with my things. Giuliano was to have sent a carriage for her.'

'Shall I enquire after her for you, Madonna?'

'Please,' I said. I had made my decision, and would follow through. But Zalumma's absence troubled me deeply.

Laura left to investigate the matter. When she returned a few moments later, I knew from her expression that the news was not what I wanted to hear. 'The carriage has not returned, Madonna.'

I put fingertips to my temple, bracing it. 'I cannot wait for her.'

'Then let me serve as your attendant,' Laura said.

I drew a breath and nodded. The situation demanded that the wedding take place as swiftly as possible, before we were discovered.

Laura opened the door to the chapel to reveal Giuliano, waiting with the priest in front of the altar. Next to them both stood the sculptor Michelangelo—a surprise, since rumour had it that he had fallen out with Piero and had left for Venice. His presence filled me with trepidation. Bad enough that Pico should be accepted by the Medici. Now there was yet another of Savonarola's chosen, here at my own wedding.

My unease disappeared with a single glance at my waiting bride-groom. Giuliano glanced up at me with joy, longing and fright. Even the priest's hands, which bore a small book, trembled; as for Michelangelo, he looked even more uncomfortable than usual. Faced by their terror, my own faded. I walked towards the three men, with Laura holding my train.

'Madonna, stop!' The servant Laura paused. I glanced about, con-fused. Not until the priest gestured did I look down at my feet and see the garland of dried roses and wild flowers strewn across the floor.

Giuliano knelt and broke the garland in two.

I could not have been more thoroughly won. He rose, took my hand, and drew me to stand beside him at the altar.

Despite his nerves, and despite his youth, Giuliano turned to Michelangelo with the assuredness of a man who has borne much responsibility in his life. 'The ring,' he said. He might not have been able to provide the gown, a great cathedral filled with people, or my father's blessing, but he had endeavoured to give me those things he could.

Michelangelo—as usual unable to meet the gaze of anyone else in the room—handed the item to Giuliano.

Giuliano took my hand and slipped the ring onto my finger. It adhered to the city ordinance concerning wedding rings, being of unadorned gold. He nodded to the priest, and the ceremony com-menced. I remember nothing of the words, save that Giuliano gave the priest his answer in a strong voice, while I had to repeat myself in order to be heard. We knelt at the dark wooden altar where I prayed, not just for happiness with my new husband, but for his safety.

Then it was over, and I was wed. Married in the eyes of God, at least, if not in those of my father or Florence.

Our small wedding party moved to the antechamber of Lorenzo's former apartments where, three years earlier, il Magnifico had encour-aged me to touch Cleopatra's cup. That jewel of antiquity was gone now, as were almost all of the displays of coins and gems. Only one case of cameos and intagli remained; paintings still covered the walls, and wine had been poured for us into goblets carved from glittering semi-precious stones inlaid with gold.

In a corner of the room, two musicians played lutes; a table, fes-tooned with flowers, held platters of figs and cheeses, almonds and pretty pastries. Though Laura prepared me a plate, I could not eat, but I drank wine undiluted for the first time in my life.

I asked Laura again to find out whether Zalumma had come. She left me at a most subdued celebration, which consisted of my husband, Michelangelo, and me; the priest had already left.

Awkwardly, after a prompting elbow administered by Giuliano, Michelangelo raised his goblet—from which he had not yet drunk— and said, 'To the bride and groom; may God grant you a hundred healthy sons.'

For a fleeting moment, the sculptor smiled shyly at me. He drank then, a small sip, and set his goblet down. 'I must now take my leave of the happy couple,' he said, then bowed and made his exit, clearly eager to be free of his social obligation.

The instant he was gone, I turned to Giuliano. 'I am fearful of him.'

'Of Micheletto? You are joking? We were raised as brothers!'

'That is precisely why I am worried,' I said. 'It increases the danger to you. He is one of the *piagnoni.*'

'One of the *piagnoni,*' he said. 'If you were threatened by the *piagnoni,* how could you best protect yourself from them?'

'With guards,' I answered.

The corner of Giuliano's mouth quirked. 'Well, yes, there are always guards. But isn't it better to know what your enemies are planning?'

'So, then,' I began, with the intention of saying, *Michelangelo is your spy.* But a knock came at the door before I could utter the careless words.

I had hoped it was Laura, with news that Zalumma had come—but instead it was a manservant, his brow furrowed. 'Forgive the intrusion, Ser Giuliano. There is a visitor. Your presence is required at once . . .'

My husband frowned. 'Who? I gave instructions that we—'

'The lady's father, sir.'

'My father?'

Giuliano gave the servant a nod and put a comforting arm round my shoulder. 'It's all right, Lisa. I expected this, and am ready to speak with him. Please, don't worry. I will reassure him and, when he is calm, I will send for you.' And he quietly ordered the servant to stay with me until Laura reappeared, and to inform her to wait with me. Then he kissed me gently upon the cheek and left.

Fear gripped my heart, but there was nothing to do but pace nervously inside the strange yet familiar chamber. I walked back and forth, my hem whispering against the inlaid marble floor. I cannot say how many times I crossed the long room by the time the door opened again.

Laura stepped over the threshold. Her expression was guarded—and after the manservant relayed Giuliano's command to her, it became even more so. The manservant left, and Laura stayed; the instant we were alone, I demanded of her, 'Zalumma has not come, has she?'

'No. Our driver was sent back without her.'

I had expected as much; even so, the news struck me with force. I loved Giuliano and would not leave him—but I could not imagine what life would be like if my father forbade Zalumma to come to me.

The better part of an hour passed. I sat on a chair, addressing myself sternly. For Giuliano's sake, I would be poised and calm, no matter what followed. My determined thoughts were interrupted by a loud clattering sound; something had struck the window's wooden shutters, which were closed. Laura rushed over and opened them.

I rose and sidled next to her in order to peer down.

My father bent down in the middle of the Via Larga, ready to grasp another stone. He had climbed out of his wagon and dropped the reins. The horse, confused, took a few paces forward, then a few back; the driver of the carriage behind his cursed loudly.

'Here, you! Make way! Make way! You can't leave your wagon there!'

My father seemed neither to see nor hear him. As he reached for the stone, one of the palazzo guards shouted, 'Move on! Move on, or I shall have to arrest you!'

'Then arrest me,' my father cried, 'and let the world know that the Medici think they can steal anything they want—even a poor man's daughter!' He clutched the stone and rose, ready to hurl it. The guard advanced and menacingly raised his sword.

Two floors above, I leaned out of the window. 'Stop, both of you!'

The guard and my father both froze, and stared up at me; so, too, did the gathering crowd. My father lowered his arm; the guard, his weapon.

'I am well,' I shouted. It was horrible, having to communicate such private matters in this way. 'If you love me, Father, grant me this.'

'They have taken everything, don't you see?' His voice was ragged, a madman's. 'I will not—I cannot!—let them have you.'

'Please.' I leaned out of the window, so far that Laura caught me by my waist. 'Please . . . can you not let me be happy?'

'Stay with *him*,' my father cried, 'and it will be only the beginning of sorrow for you!' This was no threat; his tone held only grief. He stretched out a hand towards me. 'Lisa,' he called. 'My Lisa! I can't protect you here!' He let go a wrenching sob. 'Please, come home with me.'

'I can't,' I replied. Tears dripped from my eyes onto the street below. 'You know that I can't. Give me your blessing; then we can receive you and you can rejoice with us. Come inside and speak to my husband.'

He dropped his arm, beaten. 'Child . . . come home.'

'I can't,' I repeated, my voice so hoarse, so faint that this time he could not hear me clearly. But he understood from my tone what had been said. He stood for a moment, silent and downcast, then climbed back onto his wagon. His teeth bared from the pain of raw emotion, he urged the horses on and drove furiously away.

Laura closed the shutters as I wiped my eyes on my brocade sleeve.

I sat down, overwhelmed. I had focused so thoroughly on my joy at going to see Giuliano, on my fear as to whether my escape would succeed, that I had forgotten I loved my father. And he loved me.

Laura appeared at my elbow with a goblet of wine; I waved it away, and rose. Poor Giuliano would be coming from a thoroughly upsetting encounter with my outraged father. It had been hard enough for him to get Piero's permission to marry me, and he still did not have his brother Giovanni's approval. But the deed had been done and now I could think of only one way to cheer my new husband.

I looked at Laura's worried face. 'Where is the bridal chamber?'

She seemed slightly taken aback. It was still daylight, after all. 'Here, Madonna.' She gestured at the door that led to the inner chamber.

'Lorenzo's bedroom?' I was somewhat aghast.

'Ser Piero was too uneasy to sleep there. Your husband was his father's favourite, you know, and I think it gave him comfort to take over his father's rooms. He has slept here ever since Ser Lorenzo died.'

I let Laura lead me into the chamber. The room was spacious, with a floor of pale, exquisite marble and walls covered with brilliant paintings. Dried rose petals had been strewn over the bed. On a desk nearby was a flagon of garnet-coloured wine, and two goblets fashioned of pure gold, intricately engraved, as well as a plate of candied fruit.

'Help me undress,' I told Laura. She removed my cap and sleeves, then unfastened my gown; I stepped out of the heavy garment. I wore nothing now except my *camicia*, delicate and sheer as spider's silk. Zalumma had prepared me for my wedding night, but I still struggled not to let my nerves get the better of me. 'I would like to be alone now,' I said. 'Will you tell my husband that I am waiting for him?'

She closed the door quietly behind her as she left.

I moved to the desk and poured some of the wine into a goblet, then took a small sip. As I stood in front of the desk, I could not help noticing that one item upon it was out of place, as if the reader had been called suddenly away. The green wax seal had been broken so that the letter lay half unfolded.

I might have ignored it, but the merest glimpse of a familiar script caught my eye, and I could not resist setting down my goblet and picking the letter up. It bore neither a signature nor any indication of its intended recipient.

I appreciate your willingness to release me from any formal obligation to locate the penitent—the one your father referred to as the third man. But I am morally bound to continue the search, despite the dwindling possibility that this man still lives.

All my efforts to sway Milan to your side have failed. Milan is no longer your friend. The Duke has turned the minds of Charles and his ambassadors against you, and now prepares to betray you. His distrust of Florence is the result of years of patient work by his advisers and certain associates. This, along with my investigation, has led me to the irrefutable conclusion that our Ludovico is influenced by those in league with the piagnoni.

I was startled by the last sentence. The *piagnoni* were sincere, if overly zealous, Christians. It was true that Savonarola believed King Charles had been chosen by God to punish Italy for her wickedness, but why would they want to influence the Duke of Milan? And how could an adviser influencing Ludovico *against* Florence possibly bring the author to the conclusion that the *piagnoni* were responsible?

But I was even more intrigued by the handwriting—distinctive, strikingly vertical and slantless, the *f*'s and *l*'s long and flourished, the *n*'s squat and fat. The spelling was uncertain. A moment passed before I at last recalled where I had seen it.

Greetings, Madonna Lisa, from Milan. Our good Lorenzo has commissioned me to paint your portrait . . .

I glanced up at the sound of the door opening, and did not quite manage to set the letter back down before Giuliano entered.

In one guilty glimpse, I noticed three things about him: first, that he came in wearing a forced smile; second, that the forced smile faded as his eyes widened at the sight of me in my sheer gown; and third, that he noticed the letter in my hand, and his sharp concern and irritation with himself took precedence over the other two emotions.

He took the letter from me at once. His voice filled not with accusation, but with worry. 'Did you read it?'

'Why would the *piagnoni* want to influence the Duke of Milan? I thought they were more interested in God than politics.'

A frown tugged at the corners of his mouth as he folded the letter and put it in the desk. 'I was a fool not to have concealed this.'

'I know Leonardo's hand.' I did not believe in hiding anything from him. 'I am your wife now, and you mustn't worry about what I know or don't know. I can hold my tongue.'

'It's not that,' he began. 'The Duke of Milan was always a help to our family, always our greatest ally. And now . . .' He looked away. 'Now that support has been taken from us, at a time when we need it most.' He sighed. 'And I have brought you into the midst of all this.'

'You didn't bring me. I would have come whether you had said yes or not.' I nodded at the letter on the desk. 'If I'm in danger, it's because of who I am now, not what facts are stored in my head.'

'I know,' he admitted, with faint misery. 'I came to realise that, if I truly wanted you safe, I might as well put you under my protection.' He managed a smile. 'You're even more headstrong than I am. You do realise we might have to leave Florence . . . I've sent a number of price-less objects out of the city, to protect them, and I've even packed away my things, just in case.' He drew back to gaze at me. 'We would go to Rome, where Giovanni has good friends, and where we would have the protection of the Pope. Rome is very different from Florence . . .'

'It doesn't matter,' I said, my voice soft. I took a step closer to him. He stood half a head taller than I, and his chest was broader than I was from shoulder to shoulder. He was still dressed in the fitted red velvet *farsetto*, and wore it with the casual poise of a prince. When he smiled, a dimple formed in his left cheek. I touched it with my fingertip.

'You are incredibly beautiful,' he said, and let out a long sigh.

I put my hands on his shoulders. 'We have everything to worry about: your family, my father, King Charles, the Signoria, the Duke of Milan, Florence herself. But there's nothing we can do about it right now. We can only rejoice that you and I are standing here to face it together.'

He had no choice but to lean down and kiss me. This time, we did not writhe, panting, in each other's arms, as we had in the carriage. He settled me carefully on the bed, and lay beside me to reach beneath my silk gown and run his palms slowly over my collarbone, my breasts, my abdomen. I trembled, and not entirely from nerves.

Brazenly, I reached up and ran my hands over his velvet-covered shoulders, his muscular chest, and the hollow in its centre. And then, wanting more, I fumbled, looking to free him from the *farsetto*.

He half sat. 'Here,' he said, and proffered me the neck of his garment.

Without thinking, I clicked my tongue. 'What makes you think I know how to unfasten a man's garment?'

'You have a father . . .'

'And his servant dresses him, not I.'

He looked suddenly, charmingly, sheepish. 'As mine does me.'

We both burst out laughing. It was a hard-fought battle, but in the end the farsetto yielded. And so did Giuliano.

'Is Leonardo still going to paint my portrait?' I asked drowsily. We were lying naked beneath fine linens and a crimson throw. By then, it was late afternoon and the light from the waning sun poured bittersweet through the shutters.

The naturalness of the deed had surprised me. I had expected to need careful instruction, had expected to fumble, but Giuliano's confidence and my own instincts had guided me surely.

'Your portrait?' Giuliano let go a long, relaxed sigh. 'Yes, of course. Father had asked for it. Leonardo is terrible about such things, you know. Most of the commissions Father paid him for, he never finished. But . . .' He directed a wicked little smile at me. 'I shall demand it. I shall chain him in his studio, and never let him free until it is done!'

I giggled.

Giuliano lit a pair of candles using the fire in the hearth, then returned to the bed and settled beside me.

'Why would the *piagnoni* want to work with the Duke of Milan to oust Piero from power?' I asked softly.

He propped himself on his elbow and rolled towards me, his face in shadow. 'I'm not sure exactly,' he said. 'But I know they want our family's downfall. Father did many unwise—even illegal—things. He stole from the city's dowry fund to buy Giovanni's cardinalship. And, in his younger years, he treated his enemies without mercy. There are many people, many families and groups, who have reason to hate him.

'But he had an uncanny knack for protecting himself, for making allies, for knowing—especially in his later years—when to yield, and ignore those who threatened him or spoke ill of him.' He paused. 'Piero and Giovanni . . . They're intelligent in their own ways, but they aren't Father. They don't understand the importance of how the public perceives them. They don't know how to be humble about their position.

'I told Piero to go to Sarzana—the way Father went to King Ferrante in the hope of preventing a war. But I wanted to go with him. "Don't listen to your advisers," I told him. "Let me guide you." But he wanted to prove he could do it himself.' He shook his head. 'It was a mistake, handing over Sarzana and the other two citadels. So now the Signoria is furious, and they're sending Fra Girolamo to talk to the French king. I just hope Piero will listen to me about how best to straighten it out.'

His frustration was clear; he had Lorenzo's quick mind, combined with his namesake's sweetness. 'So the *piagnoni*,' I said, trying to lead him back. 'Does Savonarola have political aims?'

He frowned at me. 'It's more complicated than that. I have agents working on it . . .'

Of which Leonardo was one. 'How complicated?'

We were interrupted by a knock at the bedchamber door, and a male voice. 'Ser Giuliano?'

'Yes?'

'Your brother has returned from Sarzana. He is waiting for you in the dining hall.'

'Tell him I'll be there shortly.'

I had already leapt from the bed and was pulling on my *camicia*. Giuliano looked at me, then at his leggings and *farsetto*, lying in a heap near the hearth, then at me again. 'Send Laura and my valet,' he called. 'We need help dressing.'

Once we were decent, Giuliano led me downstairs through the vast, quiet palazzo; our steps echoed against the shining marble.

'Perhaps I shouldn't go,' I hissed, my arm linked with his. 'Piero will want to discuss political matters.' In fact, I was nervous about meeting him. Despite Giuliano's reassurances, I was not at all certain that the eldest Medici brother had agreed to our marriage with enthusiasm.

Giuliano seemed to read my thoughts. 'It's true, my brother would not hear of my marrying you—at first. But I convinced him it made great political sense. I told him, "You've already made a strong alliance with the noble Orsinis—and Giovanni is a cardinal, which makes the Pope and Church our allies. It's time for us now to tie ourselves to the people, to show that we don't consider ourselves royalty, as they say." He finally listened. And while Alfonsina and Giovanni disagree—well, I have no doubt your charm will win them over.'

We stopped at last in front of a tall door of carved and polished dark wood. Giuliano pushed it open, then gestured for me to enter.

Warmth and light greeted me. Two men occupied the room. The first paced in front of a blazing fire, arms gesticulating wildly. He was dressed like a prince, in a tunic of sapphire velvet with purple satin trim. A great amethyst hung from his thick gold necklace and the diamonds on his fingers glittered.

'How dare they insult me so!' he raved bitterly. 'How dare they, when I have just saved the city! I deserve a hero's welcome, and instead—' He glanced up, scowling, at our interruption.

The second man sat at a long dining table. His manner was impassive as he meticulously carved the meat from the bones of a roasted pheasant. He wore a cardinal's gown of scarlet, a red silk cap, and a ruby ring; as we entered, he set down his fork and knife and rose. 'Giuliano! Who is this?' He was surprised but not entirely impolite.

'Who is this?' Piero demanded, echoing his brother.

'This is my wife, Madonna Lisa di Antonio Gherardini. Lisa, this is my brother Piero di Lorenzo de' Medici.'

My husband's answer left Giovanni aghast. 'Antonio the wool merchant? Is this your idea of a joke?'

'Do not insult my wife,' Giuliano replied, menacingly. 'The Gherardini are a good family. Piero gave us permission to marry some time ago.'

Piero dismissively waved a hand. 'I gave you permission. But now is hardly the time to meet the young lady, when we are set upon from all sides . . .' He bowed cursorily to me. 'Forgive us, Madonna, we have urgent and private matters to discuss.'

'She's not going anywhere, brother, she is family. The priest married us this morning.'

Piero let go a faint gasp. Giovanni dropped back into his seat and put a hand upon his barrel of a chest. The latter was first to speak. 'You'll have to get it annulled. You can't waste Medici seed on a commoner.'

I flushed, angry enough to forget my nervousness.

Giuliano spoke, his tone heated. 'She is my wife and she is staying here, under her husband's roof. The marriage has been consummated, and I will not tolerate talk of an annulment again.' He turned to Piero. 'As for our conversation—she already knows everything, so she will stay. You are both going to give her a kiss and welcome her into the family.'

Giovanni rose and with abrupt offhanded charm, smiled and said, 'I will give you a kiss because you are so beautiful.' Then, with resigned diplomacy, continued, 'Sit beside me, Madonna Lisa. You sit, too, Giuliano. This is your wedding feast then, is it? Let me ring for the servants.' He rose and pulled a nearby chain that hung from an opening in the wall, then returned to his chair and gestured for us to take ours.

Piero was too agitated to offer a kiss. He remained on the opposite side of the table as Giuliano and I sat beside the cardinal.

'Greetings will have to wait. I've just come from the Signoria.' Piero spread his hands in exasperation, as if to say, *I have given them everything . . . what more do they want?* 'I have saved Florence—saved her at the small cost of a few fortresses and some ducats—'

'How many?' Giovanni demanded.

Piero's voice lowered abruptly. 'Two hundred thousand.'

Giuliano did not react but merely gazed steadily at his eldest brother.

Giovanni set down his goblet with such force that wine spilled over the rim. 'Christ in Heaven!' he swore. 'What were you thinking? No wonder the Signoria won't talk to you! No wonder they've sent this fellow full of Doomsday nonsense—this Savonarola—to Pisa.'

Piero turned on him defensively. 'Savonarola? To Pisa? Now they mock me openly!'

Giuliano sounded weary. 'Didn't you read the letter I sent you?'

Piero's eyes darted to the side. 'You have no idea how busy I was, how beset . . . I can't be blamed for missing a detail.'

'You never read it at all,' Giuliano said calmly. 'If you had, you would have known that the Signoria was upset about the fortresses and the money. The French are laughing at us, brother. They hardly expected to gain Sarzana, much less Sarzanella and Pietrasanta and a mountain of gold. The Signoria is rightly furious. My letter asked you to come here directly so that we might plan a strategy to approach them.'

Piero sagged, deflated; the nuances of diplomacy and negotiation were beyond him, yet he maintained a weak defiance. 'Little brother,' he said, in a low tone, 'I had to go by myself. I have to do this by myself; otherwise, who would respect me? I am not Father . . .'

'None of us are,' Giuliano answered gently. 'But the three of us together can equal him.'

The speakers paused then as a servant entered. Giovanni directed him to bring wine, and 'food for the two lovers'. Once the man departed, the conversation resumed.

By that time, Piero had reclaimed his indignation. 'I'm not a complete fool. I know about the people's grumbling. I've taken no chances. I made arrangements with Paolo Orsini. Eight hundred Orsini soldiers—five hundred on horseback, three on foot—are camped at the San Gallo gate right now awaiting my signal, in case there's trouble.'

Giuliano pressed his hands to his face in disbelief and aggravation, then just as swiftly removed them. 'The Signoria and the people are already angry that you acted without approval. What's to keep them from assuming that you intend to seize complete power?'

'I would never do such a thing!'

'*They* don't know that. Our enemies take every opportunity to fuel rumour. We have to be extremely cautious, to think of every repercussion our actions might have. Savonarola is preaching that he had predicted Charles's coming two years ago. Don't you see that he is playing to the people's fears, making them worry that Florence and France will go to war? And that's precisely what they'll think, when they see the Orsini camped at the gate. Why didn't you consult me?'

Piero bowed his head then looked towards the fire; his face relaxed and drained of arrogance and outrage. 'I've tried to be what Father wanted me to be. But no matter how hard I try, I fail. What must I do?'

'Control your temper, for one thing,' Giuliano said. 'No more gestures.

Let's talk tonight about a plan for approaching the Lord Priors on the morrow, and then we'll go together to the Palazzo della Signoria.'

By then a maidservant had appeared with wine and goblets, leading a parade of servants with platters of fowl, hare and venison, cheeses and sweetbreads and every delicacy imaginable. Piero finally sat and ate with us, but he remained troubled, and made no attempt to join our more light-hearted conversation. I ate, too, but like Piero, I was filled with worry, and my gaze remained fastened on Giuliano.

That night, I waited alone in Lorenzo's bedchamber while my husband conferred with his brothers on how to approach the Signoria. I was exhausted beyond words, having also lain awake the previous night, but I still could not sleep. Added to my sorrow over my father was the fact that I missed Zalumma terribly, and was half mad trying to figure out what punishment he would inflict on her for conspiring with me. I was worried, too, about what would happen when Giuliano went with his brother to the Signoria.

Giuliano came to me in the hours before dawn. The candles still burned, and the light revealed the lines about his eyes—eyes that might have belonged to a man ten years his senior. I did not speak to him then of politics, or his plans for the Signoria, or my desire that he not go. Instead, I took him in my arms and made love to him.

It was the 9th of November. Morning brought with it such gloom that Giuliano and I slept quite late. I woke with the voice of the dying Lorenzo echoing in my mind: *Ask Leonardo . . . The third man . . . I failed you . . . Leonardo now, he and the girl . . .*

And then I experienced a spasm of fear, remembering what had passed with my father; and worse, remembering that Giuliano had promised to accompany his brother to meet with the Signoria that day.

The day passed too swiftly. Giuliano had business matters to attend to, and a meeting with a bank agent—although I suspected the agent informed him more of political matters than financial. Laura brushed out my hair, then coiled it at the nape of my neck and tucked it in one of Madonna Alfonsina's fine gold hairnets. 'You are a married woman, and it would not do to let your hair hang down like a maiden's.'

She then led me on a tour of the kitchens and the interior of the house, including the living quarters of Giovanni, Piero and Piero's wife Alfonsina, and their children. Afterwards, she showed me the library, which held countless leather-bound tomes and parchment scrolls.

I chose a copy of Petrarch's sonnets, and took the book back to Lorenzo's bedchamber, where I settled in a chair beside the fire.

I had thought Petrarch's love poetry would remind me of my reason for joy: Giuliano. Yet as I carefully turned the pages, I found nothing but torment, which left me troubled:

> But then my spirits are chilled, when at your departure
> I see my fatal stars turn their sweet aspect from me.

My fatal stars. I remembered something I hadn't thought about for a long time: my encounter with the astrologer. In my mind, I could hear the astrologer's voice: *In your stars, I saw an act of violence, one that is your past and your future.*

I thought of my mother dying at Savonarola's hands, and was seized by the abrupt, unreasoning fear that Giuliano—my future—was to be his next victim. They were all connected somehow: Leonardo, the third man, Lorenzo's death, the *piagnoni* . . . And me.

Giuliano did not return until late afternoon. He brought with him a valet who dressed him in a severe tunic of dark grey, untrimmed.

When the valet was gone, I said lightly, 'You look like a *piagnone*.'

He did not smile. 'I have to leave soon. Did Laura show you where Giovanni's suite is?'

'Yes.'

'Good.' He paused. 'If for any reason Piero and I are detained . . . if we're late, or if anything happens to worry you, go to Giovanni at once. Our things are packed. Giovanni knows where they are, and he knows where to take you. So, if we're detained—'

'I want to go with you. I can't stay here.'

He gave a soft laugh devoid of humour. My suggestion was outrageous, of course: I was a woman, and women were not welcome at the Palazzo della Signoria.

'Lisa.' He took my face in his hands. 'I love you.' He gave me a small, sweet kiss. 'And I'll be back soon, I promise you. Don't worry.'

'All right,' I said. Somehow, I managed to speak and behave calmly. 'I'll let you go without me on one condition.'

'What?' He tried to sound playful.

The connection between Leonardo's letter and Lorenzo's dying words still gnawed at me, and I feared that my opportunity to learn the truth was fast escaping. 'Who was the third man? The penitent?'

His hands dropped to his sides. 'He was the one man who escaped,' he said, and at that instant the bells began to ring.

We both started, but I persisted. 'Escaped what?'

'They caught everyone involved in the conspiracy to kill my uncle. But one man escaped. Leonardo saw him; my uncle died in his arms.' He shook his head, visibly anxious. 'Lisa, I have to go. Kiss me again.'

I wanted to cry from sheer worry, but instead I kissed him.

'The guards are just outside,' he said quickly, 'and they will tell you if you need to go to Giovanni. Stay here. Laura will bring you something to eat.' He opened the door, then turned his head to look at me one last time. His eyes were shining and anxious. 'I love you.'

'I love you,' I said.

He closed the door. I went over to the window and watched as Piero and Giuliano set out on horseback, accompanied by some thirty men.

'Leonardo,' I whispered. Somehow, I was connected to it all: the third man, the *piagnoni*, and the trouble that approached us now.

IX

I LISTENED TO the cascading harmony of the church bells until the very last note faded into the vibrating air. I was dressed in my wedding gown, since Zalumma had never arrived with my other clothes; because it was chilly, I put on the brocade overdress with its fur lining. Something made me retrieve my two gold medallions from the desk, where Laura had put them when she had undressed me the night before. I slipped them into the inside pocket of the overdress and sat down by the fire. How long I sat there I don't know, but I was suddenly brought from my reverie by a sound outside my window—the low, melancholy tolling of a bell. It was the bell that summoned all Florentine citizens to the Piazza della Signoria.

I ran to the window and flung open the shutters. Beneath me, a small army of men hurried out of the main and side entrances of our building, shields held at chest level, unsheathed swords clenched in their fists.

I clung fiercely to reason. The citizens had been summoned—I could not assume it was to cheer Piero's downfall.

I leaned out of my window for an eternity, awaiting a sign. Painful moments passed before it came: a distant, unintelligible rumble at first. Then a single man's voice, high and clear, rode upon the wind:

Popolo e libertà! Popolo e libertà!

I thought at once of Messer Iacopo astride his horse in the great piazza, trying in vain to rally the people to his cause. Only now it was my husband and his brother in that same piazza—

Beyond my window, servants ran back into the palazzi, slamming doors; pedestrians scattered, running towards the sound or fleeing it.

Go to Giovanni, my husband had said.

I rushed out into the antechamber to find the guard had gone, then ran into the corridor and there saw Michelangelo running towards me. We stopped just short of colliding; his breath came ragged, like mine.

'Where is Giuliano? Has he returned?' I asked.

He spoke at the same instant. 'Madonna, you must flee! Go quickly to Giovanni! I know Giuliano would want you to go with his brother.'

He took my elbow and steered me down the stairs. When we reached our destination, Michelangelo flung open the door. Giovanni, his movements deliberate and calm, was instructing a pair of servants on where his packed trunks should be taken.

'What is it?' He seemed irritated, almost hostile, at the interruption.

'You must take care of Madonna Lisa,' Michelangelo answered brusquely, with clear dislike. 'You promised your brother.'

'Oh. Yes.' With a flick of his fingers, Giovanni dismissed the servants, red-faced beneath the weight of their burdens. 'Of course.'

Michelangelo turned to me. 'I pray God we meet again, under better circumstances.' Then he was gone.

Giovanni studied me, then said, 'This is nothing more than a few Lord Priors trying to incite a riot. With luck, my brothers will be able to calm everyone down. In the meantime, go back to your quarters.'

I crossed the palazzo and returned to Lorenzo's bedchamber. I could not resist staring out of the window. Outside, dusk had fallen; in the failing light, torches flickered in the distance. Those holding them aloft cried out, again and again: '*Palle! Palle! Palle!*'

I stared at the shadowy forms. Most were on horseback, a few on foot; these were the wealthy, with their servants, probably friends and family from the palazzi lining the Via Larga, a Medici enclave. They took their places alongside the men guarding the Medici palace.

From the opposite direction, the sharp tines of pitchforks, the points of dented, crooked lances, the smoothed tips of wooden clubs, reared against a deepening sky.

Then a new contingent emerged from the ranks of Medici supporters. From my high perch, I recognised the scarlet cape, the broadness of his shoulders, his dignified carriage.

'*Palle!*' Giovanni cried at the approaching force, in a beautiful, thunderous voice. 'Good citizens of Florence, hear me out!'

But the good citizens of Florence would not listen. A stone flew through the air, striking the shoulder of Giovanni's black mount, causing it to rear. Giovanni managed to calm it, but a decision was made: rather than tackle their opponents head-on, the cardinal and his group galloped north, down an alleyway.

As Giovanni and his men receded from my view, the angry citizens advanced. Now realising they were overwhelmed, many Medici supporters rode off, abandoning the palazzo guards.

I left the window, lifted my skirts and ran down the stairs, through the corridors, into the courtyard, through the loggia and out to the stables. They smelt of dung and hay and hot, lathered horses. Perhaps thirty or forty mounts, reined in by their riders, stamped nervously.

'Giuliano!' I demanded. 'Where is Giuliano?'

Most of the men, caught up in the turmoil of war, ignored me; a few eyed me curiously, but did not reply.

A firm hand clamped onto my shoulder. I whirled about to see Piero. 'Where is Giuliano?' I repeated.

'He is still at the piazza, trying to quieten the crowd.' At the fury on my face, he added in a rush, 'I didn't want to leave him, he knows if things get bad to meet me at the San Gallo gate . . .'

I turned away, disgusted.

'Leave with us!' Piero called after me. 'Are you packed?'

I ignored him. There was a long line of stalls, almost every one of them empty. An elderly man was arguing with a pair of soldiers; I shouted louder than any of them. 'A horse! I need a horse, at once!'

'Here now,' said the older man, clearly master of the stables. His tone started out imperious, but a second glance at my dress changed his demeanour. 'Forgive me, Madonna—you are Giuliano's new wife, yes?' He had no doubt arranged the carriage that had brought me to this palazzo. 'Does Ser Piero know you have need of a mount?'

'Yes,' I said, 'He said I must have a horse *now*.'

A group of six armed men entered. 'Are the wagons filled?' one of them asked the stable master. 'Ser Piero wants plenty of hay and water.'

The old man lifted a hand at them, then turned to me. 'See, Madonna, I have only so many horses . . .' He turned to the soldiers. 'And only so much hay and water . . .'

Furious and shaking, I turned my back on him and walked away, past stall after empty stall. But one, at the far end, contained a mare, perhaps the mount the stable master was saving for his own escape.

She was already saddled, with the bit in her mouth.

'Here now,' I said, unintentionally echoing the stable master. I set a tentative hand upon her soft, twitching muzzle; her quick breath was warm on my skin. 'Can I mount you?' I asked. My long skirt, with its train, made the venture even more difficult, and once up, I tucked my gown round my legs as best I could.

The mare was used to a firmer hand than mine, but I gave her her head, knowing she would take the shortest way out of the stables; luckily, her preferred route did not lead us past the stable master.

Once we were out in the yard, I continued to let her lead, since she knew the way out to the Via Larga. Armed guards milled about in front of the bolted gate, topped with deadly sharp spikes and lined with iron bars thick as my arm. A soldier stood directly next to the bolt.

I rode up to him and leaned down. 'You there. Open the gate.'

He looked up at me; even the dim light could not hide the fact that he thought me mad. 'Madonna, they'll tear you to pieces.'

'Everyone's confused out there. No one will notice where I've come from; no one knows who I am. I'm not armed; who will attack me?'

He shook his head. 'It isn't safe for a lady.'

I felt around in the pocket of my overdress and pulled out one of the medallions without looking to see which it was. 'Here. It's worth more than a florin. Perhaps a lot more.'

He took it, frowned at it, then realised what it was. He glanced guiltily about him, then quietly slid the bolt and pushed the gate open—only a crack, since the press of bodies outside kept it from swinging very far. The mare and I sidled out, barely squeezing through.

The instant I cleared it, the gate clanged shut behind me and I found myself amidst a group of perhaps forty men who were guarding the gate. They stood shoulder to shoulder; as the mare picked past them.

'Mother of God!' one swore.

Another cried, 'Where in Hell's name did she come from?'

I ducked my head and goaded the mare into a gallop. We tore through the crowd, making our way east down the Via Larga, passing the palazzo's front entrance. Medici guards still fought in small, scattered groups, but the great entry doors had been deserted, and a group of rioters were attempting to batter their way in with a heavy wooden beam. I rode past the Church of San Lorenzo down to the Baptistery of Saint John and the Piazza del Duomo.

Only when I reached the Duomo did the growing crowds force me to slow. Abruptly, I was encircled by men, two of them holding flaming branches. They lifted them higher, to get a better look at me.

They were *giovani*, street ruffians.

'Pretty lady,' one called snidely. 'Pretty lady, to be out riding with her skirts pulled up! Look, such delicate ankles!'

'Let me pass,' I snarled.

The *giovani* laughed scornfully; they sounded like barking dogs.

'Look here!' one cried. 'Why, Lisa di Antonio Gherardini has teeth!'

He was sharp-chinned and scrawny, with wispy blond curls.

'Raffaele!' I cried, relieved. It was the butcher's son. 'Raffaele, thank God, I need to pass . . .'

'I need to pass,' Raffaele echoed, in a mocking singsong. One of his mates giggled. 'Look on her, boys. She's one of *them*. Married Giuliano de' Medici not two days ago.'

'A merchant's daughter?' someone asked. 'You lie!'

'God's own truth,' Raffaele said firmly. 'What happened, Monna Lisa? Has your Giuli already forsaken you?'

Something whizzed past me in the darkness; my mare shrieked and reared. I held on desperately, but a second pebble stung my wrist. The world heaved. I lost my reins, my sense of orientation, and went tumbling—against horseflesh, against cold air, against hard flagstone.

I lay on my side, sickened from pain, terrified because I could not draw a breath. Firelight flared overhead; I squinted as it spun slowly, along with the rest of my surroundings. A dagger appeared before my eyes, blade turned so that I felt the tip rest against my throat. I could see Raffaele's hand, and the black leather hilt.

Then hand and dagger disappeared, as light faded to darkness.

Have I died? I wondered. But no—my pain resolved into a fierce headache and agony in my shoulder. All at once, my chest gave a lurching heave, and I sucked in air as frantically as a drowning man.

Thus preoccupied, I noticed little more than blurry shadows, caught only an occasional word above the clatter of horses' hoofs, the tolling of the bell and the noise of the crowd.

Above me, men on horseback bore torches. One of the riders spoke clearly; his voice bore the dignity of high office. 'What are you doing with that lady?'

Beside me, Raffaele replied, 'She is the enemy of the people . . . bride of Giuliano . . . a spy.'

The mounted man made a brief reply. I caught only 'della Signoria', then I was lifted. The stabbing pain from my injuries made me cry out.

'Hush, Madonna. We don't mean to harm you.'

I was slung over a horse, my head and legs dangled against the horse's flank. A man nestled into the saddle behind me, pushing against my waist and hip; the reins brushed against my back.

We rode. The weight of my hair caused it to work its way free of Alfonsina's golden net, which fell, a treasure for some lucky soul to find. My face was jolted against hot, lathered horseflesh until my lip cracked; I tasted salt and blood.

'Giuliano,' I whispered, and began to weep.

They put me in a cell in the Bargello. Mine was a small, dirty room, windowless, with stained floors and walls. Some straw had been scattered on the floor and in the centre of the room rested a large wooden bucket that served as a communal privy.

There were three of us there: me, Laura, and a lady thrice my age, stunningly dressed in aubergine silks and velvets. I believe she was one of the Tornabuoni—the family to which Lorenzo's mother had belonged.

When the guard brought me in—groaning with pain—I pretended not to recognise Laura. Even for hours after the man had left, we did not look at each other.

After a time, the bell—deafeningly close, in the campanile next door—finally ceased ringing. I was grateful for only a short time. Afterwards, hour upon hour, we heard the crowd outside suddenly hush . . . and then, after a brief silence, cheer raucously.

I imagined I could hear the sound of the rope as it snapped taut.

The Tornabuoni woman, white and delicate as a pearl, twisted a kerchief in her hands and wept. Ignoring the spiders, I lay propped in a corner. Laura sat beside me, one arm coiled about her knees. When the crowd had briefly fallen silent, I asked, in a low voice, 'Giuliano?'

Her answer was anguished. 'I don't know, Madonna,'

Another shout went up, and we both cringed.

In the morning they took Laura and never brought her back.

I told myself they never executed women in enlightened Florence. Surely they had let Laura go, or at worst banished her?

I drew comfort from the fact that the crowds no longer roared outside. The quiet had to mean that the killing had stopped.

Rising unsteadily to my feet I sucked in my breath at the pain in my shoulder, but I was far more distraught by the fact that I had lost my wedding ring and the remaining gold medallion.

I passed the Tornabuoni woman to stand at the iron door and listened for the guard. While Laura had been with me, I had not wanted to utter Giuliano's name, lest I incriminate her, but now, when the jailer finally appeared, I called out softly, 'What news of Giuliano de' Medici?'

He did not answer at once, but came and stood in front of the door. He fingered through the jangling keys, muttering to himself, until the door swung open with a lingering screech.

'Giuliano de' Medici.' He sneered. 'If you have any news of that scoundrel, you'd best sing out when your time comes.'

He took no more notice of me. 'Madonna Carlotta,' he said, not unkindly. 'Will you accompany me? The Lord Priors want to ask you a few questions. They mean you no harm.'

Her gaze, her tone was pure viciousness. 'No harm? They have already caused me the greatest possible harm!' The old woman walked out and stood beside him. The door was slammed behind them and locked.

If you have any news of that scoundrel, you'd best sing out . . .

I hugged myself. Such things were said only of the living. Giuliano was gone, and they did not know where. I returned to my corner and settled into it as comfortably as I could. I heard church bells, but I dozed a bit, and could not remember how many chimes had sounded.

When I woke, I made a decision: I would admit to having married Giuliano. Such a crime would not necessarily mean my death, but more likely my exile, which would free me to find my husband. I thought of how I would point out that he had married me, a merchant's daughter, proof of his sense of commonality with less wealthy citizens.

At last I heard the jailer's step, and the jangle of keys, and forced myself awkwardly to my feet. Beside the nearing jailer walked Zalumma. When her gaze found me, her mouth opened with of gasp of relief, of joy—of horror. The jailer led her up to the bars of my cell, then took a step back. I reached for her, but the space between the bars was wide enough only to admit my fingers.

'No touching!' the jailer growled.

I dropped my hand. The sight of her made me sob so loud it startled even me. Once I began, I found I could not stop.

'Ah, no, no. This can't help matters. You must be brave.'

I stiffened.

'He's in the jail here, with the men. They set fire to the house last night, but the servants managed to put it out, finally—a lot was saved. But . . .' She ducked her head; I saw her swallow tears.

'My God! Giuliano—only tell me—is he unhurt?'

She looked up at me, her expression odd. 'I know nothing of Giuliano. The gonfaloniere came last night and arrested your father.'

'No.' I took a step back.

'They searched the palazzo. They found your letters from Giuliano.'
'*No.*'

'—and because Lorenzo was your father's best customer for so many years—they have charged him with being a spy for the Medici.' Her voice shook. 'They have tortured him.'

In my selfishness, I had thought only of myself and Giuliano. I had known my marriage would break my father's heart, but I had deemed it worth the price. Now my stubbornness had cost him far more.

'Oh God,' I groaned. 'Tell them to question *me*. Tell them he knows nothing of the Medici and I know everything.' I lurched at the bars in an effort to catch the jailer's jaded gaze. 'The crowd in the Via Larga, on Saturday after I was married! They saw my father shout at me from the street. He begged me to come home, he disapproved of my marriage, of the Medici—ask Giovanni Pico! My father is loyal to Savonarola.'

'I will tell them,' Zalumma promised, but her tone was sorrowful; the jailer had moved between us and nodded for her to leave. 'I will tell them!' she called, as she made her way down the corridor.

I spent the next few hours alone in my cell, without even the jailer's presence to distract me from the fact that I was the most monstrous of daughters. How could I have protected my father?

At last they came, and I rushed to the door of my cell.

The jailer accompanied a man dressed in rich, sombre blue to mark his importance; a Lord Prior or perhaps a *Buonomo,* one of twelve elected to advise the Signoria. He was tall and thin, perhaps forty; his hair showed quite a bit of grey, but his brows were thick, very black and drawn tightly together. His nose was long and narrow, and his chin sharp. As I stared at him. I realised I had seen him before, in church, when Savonarola was preaching; when my mother's fit had knocked me to the floor, he had lifted me to my feet and cleared the way for us.

'Madonna Lisa?' he enquired politely. 'Di Antonio Gherardini?'

I nodded, cautious.

'I am Francesco del Giocondo.' He gave a small bow. 'We have not been introduced, but perhaps you will remember me.'

I had heard the name. His family were silk merchants and, like my father, quite wealthy. 'I remember you,' I said. 'Why have you come?'

His eyes were pale blue, each with a dark circle at the outer edge. 'To speak to you about Ser Antonio,' he said.

'He is innocent of all charges,' I said swiftly. 'He did not know I was planning to go to Giuliano, he only delivered wool to the Medici, every-one knows how devoted he is to Fra Girolamo's teachings . . .'

He raised a hand for silence. 'Madonna Lisa. You need not convince me. I am quite certain of Ser Antonio's innocence.'

I sagged against the bars. 'Then has he been freed?'

'Not yet.' He let go a contrived sigh. 'His situation is quite serious: certain Lord Priors believe he is overly connected to the Medici. A sort of madness has seized everyone . . .' He gave another sigh.

'My father is close to Giovanni Pico,' I said, angry that my voice shook. 'He can verify that my father is no friend of the Medici.'

'Pico?' he murmured. His gaze flickered before returning to me. 'He was an associate of Lorenzo's, was he not? Alas, he suffers desperately from a wasting ailment. He is not expected to survive much longer.'

'What must I do? What *can* I do? My father is entirely innocent.'

'I have some influence,' he said, with maddening calm. 'I could speak to the Lord Priors on your father's behalf.'

'Will you?' I grasped the bars, eager, even as a distant, quiet thought puzzled me: *Why has he not done so already?*

He cleared his throat delicately. 'That depends entirely on you.'

I let go of the iron bars and took a step back. I stared at him until the long silence obliged him to speak.

Only a cold man could have said what he did without blushing.

'I am a widower,' he said. 'I have been too long without a wife. I have been waiting for God to direct me to the right woman, one from a good family. A young, strong woman who can bear me sons.'

Aghast, I stared at him. He gave no sign of discomfort.

'I have watched you. All those times you went to listen to Fra Girolamo. You are very beautiful, and I know you are a woman capable of great passion, Madonna. I have in my possession your letters to your prospective husband. No one connected to the Signoria has any knowledge of them . . . yet. No one need know that *you* had anything to do with the Medici. I can destroy the letters; I can protect you and your father from any reprisals.'

He paused, apparently waiting for a sign from me to continue, but I was struck dumb.

'I want to marry you. I have feelings for you, and I had hoped—'

'I can't,' I interrupted; surely he understood why.

His expression hardened. 'It would be a terrible thing, for your father to undergo any more suffering. A terrible thing, if he were to die.'

Had the bars not separated us, I would have put my hands upon his throat. 'I would do anything to save my father! But I cannot marry you. I am already married, to Giuliano de' Medici.'

'Giuliano de' Medici,' he said, his tone flat, 'is dead. Thrown off his horse while crossing the Ponte Santa Trinita, and drowned in the Arno.'

Ser Francesco told me that a patrolling guard had fished his body from the river. It had been taken immediately to the Lord Priors, who had identified it and buried it outside the city walls before anyone had a chance to desecrate the corpse. The grave's location was secret.

I cannot tell you what I did then. I cannot tell you because I cannot remember. They say that God, in His wisdom, causes mothers to forget the pain of childbirth so that they will not fear bearing more young. Perhaps that is what He did for me, so that I would not fear loving again.

The one thing I do remember of that night is greeting my father. It was dusk and the Piazza della Signoria was empty save for a solitary coach and soldiers hired by the Signoria—patrolling on foot and horseback.

Someone had splattered dark paint across the morbid portraits of the conspirators Francesco de' Pazzi, Salviati and Baroncelli. As their marred, life-sized images looked on, I clutched Ser Francesco's arm and staggered down the steps of the palazzo into a horrific new world.

At the end of those steps, the coach—ordered by Ser Francesco and occupied by my father—yawned open. My father sat, one shoulder pressed hard against the inner wall. The skin over his cheekbone was tight, violet, so puffed up that I could not see his eye. And his hand . . .

They had used the screws on him. His right thumb, protruding from the hand at a full right angle, had swelled to the size of a sausage; the nail was gone, and in its place was an open red-black sore. The same had been done to the forefinger.

When I saw him, I began to cry.

'Daughter,' he whispered. 'Thank God.' I sat beside him and wrapped my arms about him, careful not to brush against the injured hand. 'I am sorry.' His voice broke. 'Forgive me. Oh, I am sorry . . .'

When he uttered those words, all my resistance towards him, all my anger, melted. I understood. He did not just regret our current situation, or the promise I had been forced to make Ser Francesco in order to win his freedom. He was sorry for everything; for striking my mother, for taking her to San Lorenzo, sorry that Fra Domenico had murdered her. He was sorry for my sorrowful wedding day, and for the pity I was feeling for him now.

Most of all, he was sorry about Giuliano.

Order was restored fairly quickly throughout the city, though by then, every statue of Lorenzo de' Medici had been toppled, every stone crest of the Medici *palle* chiselled away. Four days after Piero's flight, the Signoria overturned the law exiling the Pazzi and encouraged all the offspring of Giuliano's assassins to return. A bill was passed stating that Francesco and Iacopo de' Pazzi had acted on behalf of 'the people's freedom'.

A week after my wedding to Giuliano, King Charles marched triumphantly into Florence, where he was welcomed as a hero. Ser Francesco wanted me to go with him, for the Lord Priors ordered the presence of all those in Florence who were able to attend, and that they wear their best finery.

I did not go. All my fine clothes had been burnt the night of the riots, and my wedding dress was ruined. More importantly, I was needed at home. My father's hand was red and putrid, and he shook from fevers. I sat at his bedside day and night, pressing damp cloths to his head and applying poultices to the sores. I did not let myself think of anyone else. He was all I had left now, besides Zalumma.

When it became clear that my father would survive, Ser Francesco came to pay his respects. I admit, when my father greeted him with wan cordiality, I was inwardly seething.

But, I reminded myself that my father smiled at the man who had saved his life. Ser Francesco, too, supported us: my father's *bottega* had been incinerated, and all his wools stolen or consumed in the blaze; and our palazzo had been vandalised. All the furniture on the ground floor and most of our clothing, drapes, tapestries and linens had been burnt. Ser Francesco had the best food delivered to our kitchen, had the apothecary deliver unguents and ingredients for poultices, and had sent his own physician to apply leeches. All this he did without asking for time alone with me—indeed, without referring once to our bargain. The one time he managed a private word with me, as I led him to the door of my father's chamber, he said, in a low voice so my father could not hear:

'I have left funds in Zalumma's care, for the replacement of furniture and other things that your father lost during the rioting. I did not want to be presumptuous and choose them myself; you know your father's taste better than I.' He paused. 'I am sorry to relay that Count Giovanni Pico died recently. I know such news will be difficult for your father. Perhaps it would be best to wait to tell him until he is well.'

I nodded, and looked into his face—into those eyes of icy blue—and saw something almost like affection, like the desire to please. But they were not Giuliano's eyes, and the difference left me bitter.

A fortnight passed. Charles and his soldiers grew increasingly demanding and abusive; Florentines no longer welcomed them as heroes, but came to see them as a great nuisance.

On the 27th of November—nineteen days after I became Giuliano's wife—Savonarola went to King Charles. He told the monarch that God demanded the French army move on, or risk divine wrath. And Charles, stupid Charles, believed him.

The next day, the French were gone.

December came. My father grew hale enough to leave his bed, though he became morose and silent when told of Giovanni Pico's death. Even Ser Francesco's visits, with their attendant discussions of preparations for our June wedding, failed to cheer him.

I, on the other hand, grew ill.

I thought it was grief at first: it made sense that the ache in my heart should spread outwards. One evening I eschewed supper and instead took to my bed, wrapping myself in furs because the cold seemed to pierce me with especial vengeance that winter. Zalumma brought me one of my favourite dishes: quail roasted with onions and leaves of sage.

She presented it to me as I sat up on my bed, and held the tray under my nose. I looked down at the little bird, gleaming and crisp, with juices visible swirling beneath its skin. The pungent scent of sage rose up with the steam . . . and I rose up from my bed, quite desperate, overwhelmed by nausea.

Zalumma moved out of the way quickly, but I never made it to the basin; I fell to my knees and retched violently. Then, while I sat on my haunches against the wall, eyes closed, gasping and trembling, she took the tray out of the room. In an instant, she returned, cleaned the floor, and pressed a cool cloth to my forehead.

'When was your last monthly course?' she demanded.

I blinked at her, not understanding. 'Two weeks,' I began, then broke into tears. 'Two weeks . . . before my wedding.'

'Oh.' As tears streamed down my cheeks, I watched her do a quick calculation. It was almost mid-December; I had consummated my marriage to Giuliano on the 8th of November. It had been five weeks.

'You are pregnant,' she said implacably.

We stared at each other for a very long, very silent moment.

I let go a sudden laugh, and she caught my hand and smiled.

Just as abruptly, I turned my face and stared into the fire.

'I want to see my mother,' I said.

Two days later, Zalumma swaddled me against the chill. With my father's leave, she and I took the carriage to the churchyard at Santo Spirito. The driver waited inside the narthex while we went outside to the churchyard. The cold air stung my eyes and made them water.

My mother was buried in a tomb of pink and white marble that gleamed like pearl where the feeble sunlight struck it.

ANNA LUCREZIA DI PAOLO STROZZI

Had the weather not been bitter, I think I would simply have sat down next to her, on the ground, and rested in her presence. As it was, I stood none too steadily and thought, *Mother, I am going to have a child.*

Aloud, I spoke to Zalumma. 'Three years ago,' I said. 'Three years ago this very day, she took me to the Duomo.'

'On your birthday,' Zalumma said. Her voice was taut; I thought she would cry. 'She wanted to do something special for you that day; something no one else would notice. But I knew.'

I turned my face towards her. 'That's impossible,' I said slowly. 'Everyone knows my birthday falls on the 15th of June.'

Zalumma bowed her head. 'You were born at your grandmother's country estate. Your father sent Madonna Lucrezia there when she began to show. And she stayed there for almost a year after you were born.' Her face was flushed. 'She and your father were agreed on this. And she swore me to secrecy.'

I had entirely forgotten the cold. 'What you're saying makes no sense, Zalumma. No sense. Why would so many people—'

'Your father had a wife, before your mother,' she said swiftly. 'He was married to her four years before she died of fever. And she never conceived. They blamed it on her, of course. They never question the man.

'But then he married your mother. Three years passed, and again, no child. No child, until . . .' She turned to me, suddenly filled with exasperation. 'Oh, child! Go look in a mirror! You look nothing like Antonio! But everyone else could see it—'

'See what?' I did not want to understand what she was saying. 'I know I don't look like my father, but . . . what does everyone *see*?'

She put her hands upon my shoulders at last, in a gesture of comfort, as if she had finally realised that what she was saying would hurt me. 'Madonna, forgive me. Your mother loved Giuliano de' Medici.'

'Giuliano—' I began, then stopped. My mind returned to that point in time when I had stood in Lorenzo's courtyard with Leonardo from the hamlet of Vinci, and the artist had asked me to pose in front of Giuliano's statue, with its oddly familiar features.

I thought of Leonardo's skilful, trained eye, and how he had so faithfully reproduced my image in a sketch after meeting me only once. I thought too of Lorenzo, staring through the window, waiting. I knew then he had been watching the artist for a sign.

My mother had to have known I was Giuliano's child from the start. My father, in his jealousy, had shunned her for months before I was conceived, and continued to do so long after I was born. That same jealousy caused him to strike her when she confessed she was pregnant.

Once Giuliano died, my mother and Antonio agreed upon a deception, to spare my father shame: she would deliver me in secret, in her mother's house in the country. I was baptised late; my false birth date was recorded in the city ledger.

That way, no one would suspect me of being Giuliano de' Medici's daughter. No one, except perhaps for the astrologer, paid by Zalumma in secret so that she and my desperately curious mother could learn the truth about my destiny.

No one, except Leonardo and Lorenzo, who had recognised their loved one's features from afar.

Zalumma and I rode home in silence.

Why, I had demanded of her in the churchyard, *did you not tell me this earlier? Why did you wait until now?*

Because your mother made me promise to keep this secret from you, she had replied. *And then—you were so miserable living with your father, there seemed no point in making you more miserable, until you were free of him. I had planned to tell you the day you married Giuliano. I speak now because you deserve to know the truth about the child you carry.*

I wanted to weep, for many reasons, but the tears remained trapped in my tightening throat. I remembered Lorenzo, whispering, *I love you, child*; I remembered my mother, giving me the medallion as a keepsake. And now it was gone, and I had nothing to remember my real father or my husband—my cousin—by.

Perhaps I should have felt angry with my father—with Antonio—for striking my mother. But I could remember only his crushed hands, his bleeding fingers where the nails had been torn away. I could only remember my father's words, as I left to attend the dying Lorenzo:

No matter what he says to you, you are my daughter and I love you.

He must have been terrified that I would learn the truth that night; yet he had let me go.

My heartbeat quickened. I thought of Leonardo. And I remembered some of the last words I had heard my husband speak.

Leonardo. Leonardo saw him, my uncle died in his arms.

Leonardo saw him: the man who killed my real father, Giuliano. The man the dying Lorenzo had called 'the third man'.

For my mother's sake, for my own, I wanted revenge.

To Leonardo da Vinci, at the Court of the Duke of Milan:

> *Ser Leonardo,*
>
> *I am writing to you because I have recently learned a certain fact—about myself, specifically in terms of my mother's relationship with Lorenzo de' Medici's murdered brother, Giuliano the elder. I believe, because of your actions the evening we were in the Medici courtyard, that you have long been aware of said fact.*
>
> *Forgive my boldness, but I believe I can trust you as a friend. Giuliano had told me that you were present in the Duomo the day of the assassination, and that you are privy to information—specifically, regarding the identity of a particular man who was also in the cathedral that day. It is my understanding that this man has never been found.*
>
> *He is now of especial interest to me. Please, Ser Leonardo, could you tell me all that you know about him? If you are able to describe him—or even to sketch him from your recollection—I would be very grateful.*
>
> *If he still breathes, I am determined to find him.*
>
> *May God keep you well,*
>
> *Lisa di Antonio Gherardini*
>
> *Via Maggio, Santo Spirito, Florence*

I wrote the letter at dawn. And from the instant I handed it to Zalumma, I impatiently awaited a reply.

That same morning, I forced myself to consider a very unpleasant fact: my husband-to-be insisted that I should have a proper wedding dress of his design, and wanted to give me a full, traditional wedding, as if I were a virgin bride—as if Giuliano had never existed. But by the time I sat upon the white horse in June, I would be more than six months' pregnant. Francesco would know the baby was Giuliano's.

I knew of only one solution: to convince Francesco the child belonged to him. And there was only one way to accomplish that.

A day passed before my opportunity came.

A traditional family gathering was held at my father's house to discuss the details of my wedding gown. Francesco's aged father, Ser Massimo—a grim, quiet man—and his widowed sister, a colourless ghost named Caterina, attended. My groom's three brothers all lived in the countryside, too far to travel at such short notice, though they assured Francesco they would come to the city in June. There were even fewer members of my family, for my father's siblings all lived in Chianti and could not attend, and my mother had lost two sisters at birth, and two older sisters to plague. That left only my uncle Lauro, and his young wife Giovanna Maria. They brought with them Lauro's two older boys, a nursemaid and three howling little children, the result of their four years of marriage.

I had requested the event take place later in the day—at supper, since most of my retching occurred around morning and midday. By evening, I rallied somewhat, but I was no less likely to cry. The thought of preparing for another wedding barely a month after losing Giuliano ravaged me. When my new relatives arrived at dusk, I graced them with an empty smile and red, swollen eyes.

My father understood. He had entirely recovered by that time and, thanks to Francesco's intervention, had revived his business by, ironically, selling woollen goods to members of the returned Pazzi family.

Stalwart and serious, he wound his arm round mine and stood beside me as we greeted our guests. At the supper table, he sat next to me, as my mother would have, and answered questions directed at me when I was too overwhelmed to think of replies. The meal ended and the discussion about the gown began. Francesco presented a sketch of his idea: a high-waisted gown with a square bodice. The sleeves were narrow, closely fitted, with the emphasis on the *camicia* being pulled through several slits and ostentatiously puffed. The neckline was quite low, so that a great deal of the *camicia* showed there as well.

This surprised me. My husband-to-be was supposedly a staunch *piagnone*, yet he had just presented me with a design of the latest Spanish fashion, fresh from the decadent Borgia papal court.

My father took my hand beneath the table and squeezed it. He behaved now towards Francesco with the same odd reserve he had shown Pico after my mother had died. 'The design is lovely,' he said. 'I know that Lisa likes it, too. Over the years, I have noticed that the colours that flatter her most are blues and greens and purples, the more vibrant, the better. And sapphires . . .' His voice faltered. 'Sapphires were her mother's favourite. They suit Lisa, too. And diamonds.'

'Thank you,' Francesco said. 'Thank you, Ser Antonio. Then Lisa must have sapphires and diamonds. And deep, rich blues to go with them, with perhaps a touch of purple. Any woman so lovely must *feel* lovely in her wedding dress. I owe her no less.'

I stared down at the table.

'You are so lucky, Lisa!' Giovanna Maria exclaimed, with a pointed look at her husband Lauro.

The event was agonising, but at last it ended, and only my father and Francesco remained at the table, which now held just the candelabrum, our goblets and a silver plate of chestnuts. The time to begin my deception was fast arriving.

My father and Francesco were speaking quietly, leaning forward on either side of me. Francesco had his sketch spread before him and was pointing to the gown's skirt. 'Not so heavy a fabric, I think now,' he said. The general consensus had been velvet for the skirt—but on reflection, Francesco decided the choice had been prompted by the fact that this particular December night was exceptionally cold. 'June can be warm. Lisa, what do you think?'

My voice sounded astonishingly cool to my ears. 'I think,' I said, 'that my father is tired and should retire for the evening.'

'Lisa,' my father admonished mildly. 'Ser Francesco is still discussing the gown. And he has a right to enjoy his wine.'

'Yes. He should continue to enjoy his wine. And you should retire.'

Francesco turned his face sharply towards me.

My father blinked and drew in a soft breath. For a moment he studied me intently. 'I . . . am tired,' he said at last.

He stood up and put a hand on Francesco's shoulder. 'God be with you.' Then he leaned down and kissed my cheek sadly.

I gripped the stem of my goblet and listened to his steps as he left the room, crossed the great chamber, ascended the stairs.

The sound had not yet faded when Francesco spoke. 'I brought a gift for you.' From beneath the pile of fabrics, he drew out a small square of red satin, tied with ribbon. 'Would you like to see it?'

I nodded, trying to slow my rapid breath. I expected him to pass it to me, to let me open it, but instead he pulled the ribbon and pulled something bright from the shining satin.

Francesco's eyes were shining, too, with a light intense and strange. He held my gift up to the glowing candles: a pendant, an emerald set in gold filigree. The chain rested over the fingers of his upturned hand as the gem revolved slowly. 'You were so eager to have your father leave. Was there a reason you wanted to be alone with me?'

'Perhaps there was.' I kept my voice soft.

'Were you ever with him?' Francesco asked. His gaze pierced me. 'Your father said you were there less than a day.'

I stared down at the table, at the goblet before me and shook my head. It was the first of many bold lies.

My answer pleased and excited him. 'Look up at me,' he said; he dangled the jewel in front of me. 'Do you want it?'

'What?'

'The necklace.' He leaned forward, his breath upon my face; his voice grew hard, flat, dangerous. 'Tell me you want it.'

My mouth fell open. I stammered, disbelieving. 'I . . . I want it.'

'What will you do for it?' The words lashed like a whip.

'Anything you wish,' I whispered.

He rose quickly, went to the doors and pulled them shut. In another few strides he stood next to me. He was on fire, his chest heaving, his eyes bright and feral. 'On your knees,' he said. 'Beg for it.'

I burned with hate. I looked down at the floor, and considered what I was willing to do to protect Giuliano's child. Our child. What I was willing to do to protect my father. I slid from the chair onto my knees.

'Give it to me. Please.'

'So.' He was flushed, trembling, exhilarated. 'This is your price, then. This is your price.' He tossed the necklace aside carelessly; it landed on the carpet in front of the hearth.

He came to me then, and yanked me up to my feet. I expected him to kiss me, but he wanted nothing to do with my face. He set me upon the dining table and swept away the goblets. One fell and shattered on the stone floor.

He pushed me down against the hard oak; my legs hung down, the toes of my slippers brushed against the floor. Instinctively, I pressed my palms to my thighs, holding down my skirts, but he moved between my legs and pulled the fabric up with such force that my *camicia*, of fine French lawn, ripped with a stark sound.

Frenzied, he pulled down his black leggings with one hand and pushed his undershirt away. My struggling only fuelled his ardour; at this realisation, I forced myself to lie back, limp, submissive.

His manner was loveless, animal. He entered me so roughly that I cried out in pain. I left myself then. I was no longer in my body, but in the light and shadows that played upon the ceiling. I became a fortress. He was a beam trying to shatter me. In the end, I held. Giuliano and our child remained safe on the other side.

I came to myself with the sensation of hot liquid flowing into me, out of me. I gasped as he pulled away as quickly as he had entered.

Slowly, I righted myself, settled unsteadily onto my feet. Still breathing hard, he stood efficiently tucking his undershirt back into his leggings, adjusting his tunic, his belt. He saw me staring at him and smiled. He was cheerful, brisk, his tone playful.

'Lisa, Lisa. What a fine Jezebel you make. Go and fetch your payment.'

I turned from him, walked slowly to the necklace and picked it up from the floor. I had never seen anything so ugly.

He walked over and clasped it round my neck. Once the transaction was accomplished, he transformed. He was gentle, solicitous.

'Here, then,' he said kindly. 'Before you call for the servants'—he nodded at the shards of glass on the floor—'let me help. It is my fault that your hair and gown are in disarray.'

He tucked errant locks back into my silk hairnet, smoothed my skirts. 'I am so sorry your lovely *camicia* is torn. I shall have it replaced.'

I called for the kitchen maid in a voice that shook. As she swept up the glass, Francesco joked about his own clumsiness. I said nothing.

I did not respond when he bowed and wished me a good night.

Francesco called again two days later, ostensibly to discuss progress on the gown and to arrange a fitting. This time it was he who hinted that my father should leave us alone.

I did not protest; I had known it would happen. I had already discussed this with Zalumma, who had agreed that, for the child's sake, I had no choice but to comply. The more I offered myself to Francesco, the more convinced he would be that the child was indeed his.

The gifts stopped. Now Francesco demanded I beg for the sexual act itself, since I had proved myself to have wanton cravings. He called me terrible names: whore, harlot, slut.

After two weeks, immediately following another brutal encounter with Francesco, I mentioned casually that I had missed my monthly course.

He snorted like a man who had a great deal of experience with such things. 'You shouldn't worry. Nerves are no doubt the cause. You'll see.'

I let another week pass. And then I had Cook prepare me quail with sage and onions. I sat beside Francesco at dinner and when my plate arrived, I leaned over the little bird and inhaled deeply.

The result was gratifying. I dashed from the table but I didn't make it out of the room in time. There, before my father and Francesco, I leaned against the wall and retched violently.

Even in my desperate state, I could hear the screech of a chair being pushed back quickly from the table. When, gasping, I was finally able to turn my swimming head to look, I saw my father standing, fists clenched, staring across the table at my future husband.

A servant came to clean the mess and wash my face. Once we were all reseated and I felt well enough, I said, 'I don't want to be married in June. I would prefer March.'

'The 5th of March,' my father said, his tone so ominous that neither my betrothed nor I had anything further to say about it.

The 5th of March came all too soon, on a day that was damp and cool, and uncommonly warm. I could easily have ridden a white horse over the bridge to Francesco's palazzo, but we had anticipated a cold day and so I, my father, and Zalumma rode in a carriage, with Uncle Lauro, his wife and children all riding in a wagon behind us.

I wore vivid blue velvet, with a necklace of gold and sapphire and a headdress of small diamonds woven into the finest gold thread. Every time I turned my head, the sun caught the gems and in the corner of my eye I saw flashes of rainbow light.

My husband's palazzo was in a side street behind black iron gates; it had been built expressly for him and his first bride. Rectangular, and starkly elegant, it rose four storeys into the air.

As we approached the gates, I heard a shout. Francesco stood there with one palm thrust forward, fingers spread out, indicating that we should stop. Beside him, draped in dark *mantellos*, stood his stooped father and three middle-aged dark-haired men: his brothers.

I peered out of the window at the road. A garland of braided satin ribbons, gleaming white and dark blue, lay upon the flagstones, stretching all the way from one edge of the street to the other.

There were no flowers to be had in March.

As his brothers cheered and catcalled, Francesco—smiling abashedly—went out and pulled a single strand. The garland was suddenly undone in the centre, and as the men clapped, he hurried to pull the two halves far enough apart to permit our carriage to pass through.

The iron gates swung open. Francesco and his brothers emerged on horseback, followed by two wagons holding his family. My nuptial carriage headed east, towards the great Piazza del Duomo.

When we stopped, my intended and the guests took their places inside the Baptistery of San Giovanni and I waited until the signal was given. Zalumma held my train as I stepped out. My father took my arm.

I walked with him past Ghiberti's amazing doors. I had lived all my life in the city, yet had only once set foot inside this octagon of stone. I walked across marble floors adorned with images of griffins and spirals, beheld golden walls, and stared up at the gilded cupola and the blazing candelabra. The walk was a blur of sensations: the pull of the long velvet train behind me, the sparkle and flash of diamonds, the intense blue of my sleeve, the shimmering white of puffed gossamer silk.

My father held on to me tightly until the time came for him to give me away. As he handed me to Francesco then stepped back, he wept.

An interminable Mass followed. I fumbled over prayers I had known since childhood, listened to the priest's sermon without comprehension. Each time I knelt, I felt I would never again be able to stand.

Will you? the priest asked at last.

Francesco smelt of rosemary. I looked at him, at his deceptively gentle expression, and saw my bleak future. I saw my child being born, my father growing old. I saw Giuliano's memory fading.

I will, I said. My voice surprised me with its strength, its steadiness. I will, until my father dies. Until my father dies, and we can escape.

A ring appeared—another plain and slender ring of gold—and caught the candles' glow. Francesco forced it on my finger.

With my husband beside me, I stepped outside into the great piazza and drew in a breath. The afternoon was grey; mist hung in the air. Soft as steam rising from water, it settled on my face, but its touch was cold.

Afterwards, our party returned to my new home. The carriage stopped, and Francesco helped me out. Crouched upon high pedestals, a pair of majestic stone lions guarded the threshold. We walked between them and the doors opened for us as if by magic.

A servant led us to the room on our left: a vast hall, the walls pristine white, the floor gleaming pale marble with black inlay of classical design. Beyond, past an archway, was a dining chamber, the surface of its long table entirely obscured by platters heaped with food. The size of the rooms startled me: they were better suited for a prince and his court than our small gathering. None of my father's relatives had chosen to come from the country, but Francesco's brothers had brought their wives and children with them. Once his family had followed us inside, along with Uncle Lauro's brood, the building seemed less empty.

I greeted more guests, Lord Priors and *Buonomini,* Francesco's peers. A wedding meal soon followed, one that Savonarola would have frowned on for its excesses: whole roast mutton, two whole roast pigs, three geese and a swan, countless pheasants, several rabbits and dozens of fish; six different types of pasta in broth, cheeses, nuts, dried fruits.

After the food came dancing, with music from a quartet of players Francesco had hired. With the ritual and the meal both behind me, I felt a temporary relief. I laughed and danced with my new nephews and nieces, and looked on them with new-found wistfulness.

I turned once to find my father watching me with the same emotion.

But when the sun began to set, the revellers departed, and my father went home to his house, empty of family—even Zalumma had left him. And my bravado waned with the light.

I was numb as Francesco introduced me to some of his servants: his chambermaids, Isabella and Elena, his valet Giorgio, the cook, Agrippina, a kitchen maid, Silvestra, and the driver, Claudio. I repeated the names aloud, but my heart was beating too loudly for me to hear even myself clearly. Elena, a sweet-faced woman, led Zalumma and me up the stairs to the third floor, past Francesco's rooms on the second, to the vast chambers that now belonged to me. Holding a lamp aloft, she showed me my sitting room, which had chairs, a table bearing a lamp, a desk, and a shelf with books suited to a lady's taste. Then we crossed the corridor and Elena opened the door to the bridal chamber.

The room was unabashedly feminine. The walls were white, the floor of variegated cream, pink and green marble, the mantel and hearth made from white granite that glittered in the light of a generous fire. Two delicate lady's chairs, their padded seats covered in pale green brocade, faced the hearth. The bed, large enough to accommodate four people, was covered by dried rose petals, and an embroidered tasselled throw sewn from the same blue velvet as my gown. Matching curtains, trimmed with gold, hung from an ebony canopy.

On either side of the bed stood tables; one held a white basin, painted with flowers and filled with fragrant rosewater. Above it hung an oval mirror. The other table held a lamp, a silver plate of raisins, a flagon of wine, and a silver goblet whose solitude struck me as ominous.

Elena showed me the iron chain hanging from the ceiling near the bed, which, if pulled, would sound a bell in the servants' quarters across the hall.

'Thank you,' I said, by way of dismissing her. 'I have everything I need. I will undress now.'

She curtsied then left, closing the door behind her.

Zalumma unlaced my sleeves and my bodice. The cumbersome gown with its heavy train dropped to the floor and, clad only in the shimmering *camicia*, I stepped out of it with a low groan, then took my place in front of the mirror and let her unloose my hair. I stared at my reflection and saw my mother, young and terrified and pregnant.

Zalumma tenderly lifted the brush and brought it down, then smoothed the hair with her free hand. Each stroke of the brush was immediately followed by another stroke of her hand; she wanted to comfort me, and this was the only way she had.

At last, the brushing stopped. I turned to face Zalumma.

'If you need anything—' she began.

'I will be fine. Will you come afterwards?' I asked. 'This room is too large, and this bed; I cannot bear to sleep alone.'

'I will come,' she said softly.

Francesco arrived a quarter of an hour later. I was sitting by the hearth staring into the fire, my arms wound round my legs, my cheek resting on my bent knees, my bare feet pressed against the warm granite.

I rose and walked towards him. Still dressed in his wine-coloured wedding clothes, he smiled sweetly. 'The festivities went quite well. I think our guests were pleased, don't you?' he said.

'Yes,' I replied.

'Do you find your rooms satisfactory?'

'They are beyond my expectations.'

'Good.' He paused. 'I have a gift for you.' He drew a silk pouch from his pocket and loosened the drawstring for me; the contents spilled into my hand. It was a lady's brooch. A large one, made of an acorn-sized garnet surrounded by seed pearls and set in silver.

'It's . . . a family tradition,' Francesco said, suddenly uncomfortable. 'It was my mother's, and my grandmother's.'

The stone was clouded, dull, the piece unremarkable.

'Thank you,' I said stiffly, bracing myself for the cruelty that would certainly follow. But Francesco's expression remained mild, almost bored. He stifled a yawn.

'You're certainly welcome,' he said, his manner diffident. 'Well, then.' He glanced around awkwardly, then smiled again at me. 'It has been an exhausting day for you. I'll see you come morning. Good night.'

I stared up at him in disbelief. 'Good night,' I said.

He left. I quickly set the brooch down, put my ear to my closed door and listened to him move down the hall and descend the steps. Once I was sure he had gone, I opened my door to call Zalumma—and started to find her already there.

'Is he coming back?' she whispered.

'No.' I pulled her into the room.

Her jaw went slack. 'What happened?'

'Nothing.' The realisation that my performance was finished overwhelmed me. I barely made it to the bed before my legs gave out.

'What did he say?' Zalumma demanded.

'He gave me a gift.' I nodded at the garnet brooch on the bedside table. 'He said I must be tired, and then he excused himself.'

She stared at the brooch. 'He's mad.'

'Perhaps he's ill,' I said. I looked at the plate of dried grapes beside me and frowned. The servants had left these as sweet morsels to be enjoyed with the wine; they did not yet know I disliked raisins.

Zalumma noticed. 'Are you hungry? You've eaten nothing today.'

'I would love some bread and cheese.'

'I'll find some.'

I paused. 'Bring another goblet—for yourself. And whatever else you wish.' Francesco would think it improper, but I didn't care. I was giddy with relief and suddenly in the mood for a small celebration.

While she was gone, I sat with my eyes closed. I was grateful beyond words to be left alone on my second wedding night; I had not wanted to profane the memory of the first. Aloud, I promised Giuliano: 'I will tell your child everything I know of you, of your goodness, and of your father's. I will tell him of your uncle—my father. And I will teach him everything I know of love and kindness.'

I closed my eyes, and saw Giuliano kneeling on the floor of the chapel after parting the garland of flowers, smiling up at me.

I smiled, too. And when Zalumma appeared at the door with a tray balanced on one hand, my lips were still curving. On the tray were three different cheeses and half a round loaf of bread. I was pleased to see she had brought a second goblet.

'Here.' I lifted the flagon of wine. 'Drink with me and have some food. I've survived my first night here.'

When we grew tired, I insisted Zalumma lie down beside me. I dozed for a while, too, dreaming that I was in the wrong house, with the wrong man; the grief of it woke me.

It came to me clearly, then, that I was truly married to Francesco, that Giuliano was dead, that these facts could never be undone. I realised that I was going to cry, and I did not want to be seen or heard.

I slipped from the bed and hurried quickly, quietly, out of the room. I closed the door behind me and ran halfway down the stairs, then sat upon a step. Before I could release the first sob, a sound stopped me: clumsy footsteps coming in my direction.

I knew before he appeared that it was my husband. Lamp in hand, he paused to orientate himself on the second-floor landing below.

'Francesco,' I said softly. I meant only to think it; I did not want to be noticed, least of all by him.

But he heard and looked up at me, startled.

'Lisa,' he said. His tongue slurred the 's' of my name. He was very drunk. He held up the lamp and squinted at me. The hem of his tunic was bunched up and the white wool of his undershirt protruded.

I let go an amused snort at the sight, and when I breathed in again, I noticed the sharp smell of cheap lavender. I had detected it before a few times at market on bawdily dressed, brightly rouged women.

I heard Francesco's voice in my mind, saw his lecherous, glittering gaze. *Whore. Harlot. Slut.*

'I wasn't able to sleep,' I said. 'But I think I can now. Good night.'

'Good night,' Francesco said drowsily, and as I ran up the stairs, I heard him groan.

X

SPRING CAME, THE WEATHER warmed, and the child in my belly grew.

My husband never touched me. We behaved towards each other like distant but cordial acquaintances; he gave me whatever I asked for. He did not protest when I ordered that a cot for Zalumma be put at the foot of my bed. But to a great extent, I was his prisoner: I was no longer to go to market. I could attend Savonarola's sermons, and if I wished, go to our family chapel at Santissima Annunziata. All other outings required my husband's express permission.

Francesco and I usually saw each other once daily, at supper. My father joined us. He seemed to take special joy in my company, and brightened at any mention of the coming child. But he had lost weight, so much so that I worried for his health. I detected a silent misery gnawing at him. I doubted he would ever be happy again.

Nor would I, though my life had not become as hellish as I had feared. Francesco heard Savonarola preach in the mornings and visited his whores at night; if he worried over the discrepancy between his public and private life, he did not show it.

Fra Girolamo had made many changes to our city. He had decided that God should be deeply involved in the workings of the Signoria. Laws were passed: sodomy brought a fiery death at the stake, poetry and gambling were outlawed. Adulterers quaked in fear of death by stoning, men and women who dared sport jewels risked losing them, for the streets were now patrolled by young boys loyal to the friar and determined to seize any unnecessary wealth as a donation to the Church.

We all grew afraid.

Francesco taught me a new term: *Arrabbiati*, the mad dogs. These were the men who snarled at Savonarola, who said that a friar had no business meddling in politics.

My father, who had once been an outspoken proponent of the friar, said little on the matter; the fire had left him, though he went with Francesco—just as he had gone with Pico—to hear Savonarola preach.

Talk of the prophet annoyed me, but I told myself I did not care. His sermons now excluded women except for each Saturday, when he preached directly to members of the gentler sex. I was obliged to attend. Zalumma and I sat and listened in rigid silence.

During this time, King Charles of France made his way to Naples, only to be ultimately defeated there. His army retraced its steps northwards, passing unimpeded again through Rome, until at last it arrived barely two days' ride from Florence.

In May, a flood drowned all the tender young corn growing on the banks of the Arno. A sign of God's displeasure, the prophet said. If we did not repent, He would send Charles next.

August was sultry and I could not sleep because of the heat, because of the restless child, because of the ache in my back. Zalumma and I expected the baby to arrive the first or second week of the month. By the last week, Zalumma was pleased—the child's tardiness would only serve to convince Francesco it was his—but I was too desperate to appreciate my good fortune.

By the 1st of September, I was unpleasant to everyone, including Zalumma. That week, on one particularly hot night, I woke abruptly, filled with a strange alertness. I rose awkwardly and pulled on my gown. I was thirsty and thought to go downstairs to get some fresh water to drink. I took no candle.

As I began to descend the stairs, I saw light advancing from the opposite direction—Francesco, I assumed. I turned, intending to go back up discreetly; but a feminine giggle made me stop and look down.

On the landing below stood young, pretty Isabella in a white linen *camicia*, with a key in one upraised hand and a candle in the other. She leaned backwards into the grasp of a man who had wound his arms beneath her breasts. As he kissed her neck, she fought to repress her laughter—and when she failed, he shushed her, and she pulled away from him to open the door to my husband's chambers. A lamp burned there in anticipation of his return.

Francesco, I thought, *and Isabella*. He had returned early.

But the man who raised his face was not my husband. He was darkhaired, perhaps my age, around sixteen. I had never seen him before. Had Isabella admitted a thief?

The maid left him to go back downstairs, taking the candle with her. He went alone into Francesco's rooms, guided by the lamp shining there.

With all the awkward grace I could summon, I moved downstairs, past the intruder, who had paused in my husband's study.

I went to the kitchen hearth and took the large iron poker, then moved quietly back up the stairs, to Francesco's study.

Draped in shadow, I watched as the stranger stood in front of

Francesco's desk. The drawer was open and the key placed beside it; the stranger had unfolded a piece of paper and was frowning at it. He was a pretty young man, with a large, strong nose and sharp eyes; brown-black curls framed his oval face. He wore an artisan's clothes: a grey tunic that fell almost to his knees, covering patched black leggings.

He didn't see me until I stepped out of the darkness and demanded, 'What are you doing?'

He stopped, his chin lifting in surprise, and when he turned to look at me, the paper fell from his fingers. Miraculously, I reached out and caught it before it reached the ground. He moved to take it from me, but I raised the poker threateningly. He saw my weapon and his lips curved in a crescent smile. There was lechery in it, and good humour.

'Monna Lisa.' His tone was that of someone mildly startled to find a friend they knew well, but not in the place they had expected.

'Who are you?' I demanded.

'The Devil Himself.'

'How do you know my name?'

'Your husband will be coming home soon. I should leave, don't you think? Or else we both will be in a good deal of trouble.' He eyed the poker, decided I wouldn't use it, and reached for the paper in my hand. 'If I could only have another moment with that letter, please—nothing more—then I shall happily return it to you and be on my way.'

His fingers grazed the paper and I made a decision.

'Help!' I cried. 'Thief! Thief!'

His smile broadened to show white teeth.

'I will say goodbye then,' he said, and dashed downstairs. I followed him as swiftly as my bulk allowed and watched him fling open the doors to the front entrance. He left them open behind him and I stared after his dark form as he raced across the flagstone drive into the night.

When Claudio and Agrippina called out to me, I refolded the paper and slipped it in my nightgown. They arrived, breathless, frightened, I said, 'I must have been dreaming. I thought someone was here . . .'

They shook their heads as I sent them back to their rooms; Claudio muttered something about pregnant women.

Once they were gone, I went back upstairs to Francesco's study, and held the paper to the lamplight.

Your worries about retribution from Pope Alexander are unfounded; the excommunication is mere rumour. When it becomes more than that, we shall use it to our advantage.

In the meantime, continue to encourage him to preach against Rome and the Arrabbiati. And send me the names of all Bigi—

The *Bigi*. The grey ones, generally older and established nobles, who supported the Medici.

—but do nothing more; a strike now would be premature. I am investigating Piero's plans for invasion. He has settled in Rome, and I have found agents there willing to deal with him as you did with Pico. If we accomplish that, the Bigi *will pose little threat. As always, your help will be rewarded.*

I refolded the letter and set it back in the desk, in the place Francesco kept his correspondence, then locked the desk. I paused a moment to study the key. Isabella had given it to the intruder; was it the one belonging to my husband, or a copy?

I kept it in my hand. If Francesco missed its presence, Isabella would have to do the explaining, not I.

Then I returned to my bedchamber and went out onto the balcony to think. The air was oppressively warm; I breathed it in, and felt it settling heavy inside me, against my lungs, my heart.

. . . *continue to encourage him to preach against Rome and the Arrabbiati.*

I thought of Francesco faithfully attending Savonarola's every sermon. Listening carefully to every word.

. . . *willing to deal with him as you did with Pico.*

I thought of Pico with the goblet in his hands, smiling at Lorenzo; of Pico, hollow-eyed and gaunt. Of Francesco saying softly, *Pico? He was an associate of Lorenzo's, was he not? He is not expected to survive much longer.*

I had thought the greatest danger to myself, my father, was for Francesco to reveal my connection to the Medici.

I thought I had understood my husband. I understood nothing.

The world was hot and heavy and stifling. I put my head upon my knees, but couldn't catch my breath to cry.

My body opened up; I heard the splash of liquid and realised that I was the source. My chair, my legs, my gown were all soaked, and when I stood, startled, a cramp seized me so violently I thought I was turning inside out. I cried out and seized the balcony's edge, and when Zalumma, wide-eyed and gasping, appeared, I told her to bring the midwife.

Francesco named the boy Matteo Massimo: Massimo, after Francesco's father, and Matteo, after his grandfather. I accepted the patriarchal naming dutifully; I had always known I could not name him Giuliano. And I was pleased to learn that Matteo meant *gift of God*.

Matteo was amazing and beautiful, and gave me back my heart. Without him, I could not have borne what I had learned in my husband's study; without him, I had no reason to be courageous. But for his sake, I kept my counsel, and told only Zalumma of the letter.

Matteo was baptised the day after his birth, at San Giovanni, where I had been married for the second time. The formal christening was held two weeks after, at Santissima Annunziata, some distance to the north. For generations, Francesco's family had kept a private chapel there.

Since my son's birth, I kept my distance from Francesco; my hatred, my disgust, my fear were so great I could scarcely bring myself to look at him. His manner remained unchanged—solicitous and mild—but now, when I studied him, I saw a man capable of Pico's murder and perhaps Lorenzo's. I saw a man who had helped to oust Piero, and thus brought about my Giuliano's death. As I sat in the chapel and beamed at my child, the knowledge that Francesco sat beside me sickened me.

Uncle Lauro and Giovanna Maria served as godparents. Matteo slept through most of the ceremony, and when he woke, he smiled. I sat, still weary after a long labour, and watched with joy as my father held the baby and Lauro answered for him. Afterwards, as my father proudly bore his grandchild down the aisle and the others followed, I paused to take Matteo's certificate from the priest. He was young and nervous; his voice had cracked several times during the ceremony.

When I took hold of the certificate, he did not let go, but hissed at me, 'At night. Read this only at night—tonight, when you are alone.'

He had given me more than the single piece of parchment; beneath it he had tucked a piece of paper, neatly folded. Thinking he was mad, I walked swiftly away from him and hurried after the others.

Outside, in the piazza, I had almost caught up with them when a young monk stepped into my path. He wore the black robes of the Servants of Mary, the monastic order whose convent was housed at Santissima Annunziata. As I swept by him, he said, in a low voice, 'A beautiful child, Monna.'

I turned my head and found myself looking at the Devil Himself.

'*You,*' I whispered.

The recognition pleased him. 'Tonight,' he said softly. 'Alone.' Then he turned and walked briskly on.

As I joined the others, my husband looked up from his presumed son, his gaze gentle, absent. 'Who was that?' he asked.

'No one,' I said, moving to join him. I held the certificate tightly in my hand, making sure it entirely covered the smuggled note.

I told no one about the note—not even Zalumma. When she was asleep, I rose. In the darkness, I lit a candle, opened the drawer beside my bed, very slowly, and retrieved the paper given to me by the priest.

Feeling both foolish and frightened, I held it up to the flame.

I stared into the white blankness and frowned—until inspiration struck. I brought the paper closer to the heat, so close that the flame flared towards it and began to darkly smoke.

Before my eyes, letters began to appear, transparent and watery.

Greetings.

  I regret I could not respond to your earlier letter.

  Tomorrow at sext, *go unaccompanied to ask God for the answer.*

For centuries, the faithful had divided the day into hours of prayer: the most familiar were matins, at dawn, and vespers, in the evening. After dawn, there came the third hour of the morning, *terce,* and the sixth hour, *sext,* at midday.

I stared at the writing, at the perfectly vertical letters, with the long, flourished *f*'s and *l*'s, the squat *n*'s, the careless spelling. I recognised it at once. *Greetings, Madonna Lisa, from Milan . . .*

In the morning, I rose without saying anything to Zalumma, but she sensed my agitation and asked me what was troubling me. When I told her of my intention to pray—alone—she scowled.

'This has to do with the letter,' she said. Her words gave me a start, until I realised she was referring to the letter the devilish young intruder had dropped, the one I had told her about. 'I would not like to think you are becoming involved in dangerous matters.'

'I would never be so foolish,' I said, but even I heard the uncertainty in my tone.

'Go alone, then,' she said darkly, pressing against the limits of what a slave might say to a mistress. 'Just remember that you have a child.'

My answer held a trace of heat. 'I would never forget.'

The driver took me to Santissima Annunziata. I directed him to wait in the square in front of the church. Just as the bells began to call the faithful, I stepped into the sanctuary and made my way to our little chapel.

The room was empty, which both disappointed and relieved me. No priest awaited; the candles were unlit. Uncertain, I went to the altar and knelt. For the next few minutes, I calmed myself by reciting the rosary. When I at last heard light, quick footsteps behind me, I turned.

The Devil stood smiling, in his guise as Servite monk. 'Monna Lisa,' he said. 'Will you come with me?'

In answer, I rose. As I approached him, he proffered a black cloak.

'This is silly,' I said, more to myself than to him.

'Not at all,' he replied. 'It will all make sense shortly.'

I let him drape the cloak over me, let him raise the cowl and pull it forward so that my cap and veil were covered, my face obscured. The black cotton hung low, trailing on the floor so that it hid my skirts.

'Come,' he said.

He led me back out onto the street, a safe distance from where my carriage waited, and steered me to a rickety wagon tied to a post and harnessed to an ageing horse.

'Let me help you up.' He did so, then untied the reins and climbed up beside me. 'A few precautions first.' He reached for a bit of cloth on the seat between us. Quickly, deftly, he shook out the folds and reached inside my raised hood. His fingers, so fast and nimble, teased the fabric round my eyes, round the back of my head, and tied it before I grasped what he was doing. I was blindfolded. Panicked, I raised my hands.

'Hush. No harm will come. This is for your safety, not mine.' I shuddered as something soft was stuffed into my ears. All sound was dulled.

The cart jerked and began to move; I swayed and held the edge of the seat to keep my balance. Several minutes later the wagon rolled to a stop. I climbed blindly down. The young Devil took my elbow and urged me to move quickly I lifted my skirts, fearful of tripping.

Fingers gripped my arm, forced me to stop; my guide gave a low whistle. A pause, then we walked a short way and climbed a flight of stairs. I was made again to stop, and listened to the groan of heavy wood sliding against stone. A faint breeze stirred as a door opened.

I was led over a floor gritty from a dusting of sand. I had passed by enough artists' *botteghe* to recognise the pungent smells of boiling linseed oil and caustic lime. I was pressed to sit upon a low-backed chair. In a smug, cheery tone, the Devil addressed a third party, loud enough so that I could clearly distinguish each word.

'Ask and you shall receive.'

'Will you bring what I asked for?'

'If I must. After that, how long do I have to myself?'

'Give us no more than half an hour, to be safe.' The voice was masculine, soft. 'Make sure we don't run over the time.'

At the sound of the voice, I reached for the blindfold and pulled it up and off my head.

The Devil was already gone, his steps sounding in the corridor. The man standing over me was clean-shaven, with softly waving shoulder-length hair streaked brown and iron, parted in the middle. He, too, wore the habit of a Servant of Mary.

For an instant, I failed to recognise him. Without the beard, his chin appeared sharply pointed, his cheekbones and jaw more angular, his stubble now mostly silver. Leonardo smiled gently at my confusion, which made the creases in the corners of his grey eyes more prominent.

I pulled the wool from my ears and said his name. Instinctively, I rose. The sight of him evoked memories of my Giuliano, of Lorenzo. I remembered his letter to Giuliano, advising him of the Duke of Milan's intentions, and felt grateful. I wanted to embrace him as a dear friend, as a family member.

He felt the same. I saw it in his brilliant if uncertain smile, in his arms, which hung determinedly by his sides, but tensed with the desire to rise, touch, enfold. He loved me, and I did not understand why.

'Please sit,' he said, then gestured to a stool. 'May I?' When I nodded, he pulled it across the stone and sat down in front of me.

Behind him stood an easel bearing a large wooden slate. To the left of the easel, a lamp burned on a small table bearing scattered pieces of charcoal and a small pile of downy chicken feathers.

'Madonna Lisa,' he said warmly. 'It has been a long time.' Abruptly, an odd reserve overtook him. 'Please forgive the secrecy. It protects you as well as us. I hope Salai did not frighten you.'

Salai: Little devil. The perfect nickname. I let go the briefest of laughs. 'No. Not much.'

He brightened at my amused expression. 'You look well, Madonna. Motherhood suits you. Salai says you have a fine son.'

'Matteo, yes.' I bloomed.

'A good name. Does he take after you?'

'I think so. His eyes are blue now, but they'll darken soon enough, I'm sure. And he has so much hair, so soft, with little curls . . .' I faltered as I caught myself. Francesco's eyes were icy blue, his hair quite straight. I had been on the verge of describing the sweet dimple in his cheek—Giuliano's dimple.

My tone cooled. 'Are you back in Florence? I thought you were at the Duke's court in Milan.'

His expression was indecipherable. 'I am. But I have come to Florence for a little while, on holiday.'

'And why have you brought me here, with all this secrecy?'

He did not answer because Salai arrived with a bronze tray bearing wine, cheese and nuts. Leonardo rose and took it, then banished his assistant. He took the tray over to a long, narrow table that covered almost the entire expanse of the wall behind us. He had a good deal of difficulty making enough space to set it down.

I rose and went over to investigate. On the table were levels and wooden slices with long, sharp edges; heaps of grey-white miniver pelts, with holes where the hairs had been plucked and arranged in heaps next to a pair of scissors. There were piles, too, of feathers—the largest, darkest ones from vultures, the paler ones from geese, the most delicate from doves—and of translucent, wiry pig bristles. On the far end was a wooden bucket, streaked with lime and covered with a cloth. Near it, in neat, careful rows, small, rolled pellets of colour—white, black, yellow-tan, warm pink—lay drying on a cloth beside a large bronze pestle and mortar. A large slab of red stone held a pile of dark yellow-brown powder, a palm-sized grinding stone, and a thin wooden spatula with a sharp edge. A number of brushes were in various stages of construction.

'This is a painter's studio,' I said to myself, delighted.

Leonardo had set the tray down and studied me, amused, as he poured wine into a goblet and handed it to me. 'After a fashion. It's only temporary. The one in Milan is much nicer.'

I was too nervous to want the wine, but I sipped a little so that he felt free to drink from his own glass. He took a token swallow and set it down. 'I had hoped we might relax a bit before launching into difficult subjects. And I had hoped you might consent to sit for me again.'

'Sit for you?'

'For your portrait.'

I let go a laugh of disbelief. 'What would be the point?' I challenged. 'Lorenzo is dead. And Giuliano . . .' I didn't finish.

'I would still like to complete the work.'

'Surely you are doing this for some other reason than a sense of obligation to dead men.'

He did not answer at once. When he did, he spoke so softly I was not sure I had heard aright. 'I saw your mother,' he said.

I jerked up my head. 'You knew my mother?'

'I was acquainted with her. She and your . . . her husband, Ser Antonio, were often guests at the Medici palace in those days. Before she became infirm. Like you, she had a good eye for art.'

'Yes.' I could not speak beyond a whisper. 'So she was often at the Palazzo de Medici?'

He gave two slow nods. 'Lorenzo was quite taken with her—as a friend. He showed her his collection, of course. He respected her opinion greatly. Through Lorenzo, of course, she met Giuliano.'

'Was she . . . Did everyone know she was having an affair with him?'

His eyelids lowered. 'No, Madonna. Your mother was a woman of great virtue. I don't believe that she and Giuliano . . .' He broke off.

'You don't believe they were together until . . .?' I prompted. I did not want to embarrass him, but I had waited for years to learn the truth.

He lifted his gaze, but would not look directly at me. 'The last night before Giuliano was murdered, I saw her outside the palazzo. She was going to see him; she was radiant with joy. It was dusk, and she stepped from the shadows. I . . .' His voice trailed. 'There was no clear delineation between her skin and the air that surrounded it. She emerged from the darkness, yet she was not separate from it. She looked to be more than a woman. She was a Madonna, an angel. The light was . . . remarkable.' He stopped himself. 'You must forgive me for such foolish ravings.'

'They're not ravings. They sound like poetry.'

'You know how beautiful she was. Imagine her a hundred times more beautiful. Lit from within. I wanted very badly to paint her, but Giuliano was murdered, of course. And then Anna Lucrezia fell ill.'

'She wasn't ill,' I said. 'Her husband couldn't father children. He struck her when he learned she was pregnant.'

Leonardo's eyes flickered with anger and pain. 'So. He always knew.'

'He always knew.'

It took him a long moment to gather himself. 'I am sorry for it. That night, I had resolved to paint your mother. She possessed a natural radiance—and you have it too, Madonna Lisa. And if I could be permitted to record it . . .' He broke off. 'I know it is awkward for you to sit now, but I have learned the capriciousness of life. She was with Giuliano that night; she was happy. And the next day, he was gone. Who knows where you or I will be tomorrow?'

He might have said more in an effort to make his argument, but I silenced him by laying a hand upon his forearm. 'Where,' I asked, 'would you like me to sit?'

He let me look at the charcoal sketch upon the easel first. It was made from the drawing done in the Palazzo de Medici. I sat with my full face shown directly to the viewer, with my shoulders and body turning only slightly away. I had a décolleté that would bring down the wrath of Savonarola's militant cherubs.

As I stood beside Leonardo, gazing at the drawing on the easel, he glanced at me, made a small sound of disgust, and at once retrieved a chicken feather from the table and very lightly swept it over the paper. The feather's edge darkened; the charcoal beneath it disappeared.

'Sit,' he said, utterly distracted. 'Your chin, I must get it right.'

I sat in silence as he finished erasing his crime, then he took up the charcoal fastened to a wooden stick and corrected the chin. He stared at me and checked my nose against the drawing; my right eye, my left, each eyebrow and my nose. I grew restless, and let my gaze wander to a small panel of wood that had been coated with plaster and was drying.

'Is that what you will use—for the painting?' I asked.

He frowned, faintly annoyed at the interruption. 'Yes. It needs to dry for a few days. Then I'll transfer this sketch to it. We will start the painting the next time we meet, if fate permits.' He gave a small sigh. 'Please take some more wine, Madonna.'

'You are trying to get me drunk,' I said. I meant it as a joke, but, when I caught his eye, he did not smile.

'We have enough difficult things to talk about, don't you agree?'

In answer, I took a gulp of my wine. 'Why don't we talk about them, then? I'm tired of appearing content and angelic. You didn't bring me here just to paint my portrait or speak of happier times.'

His tone grew dark. 'Very well, tell me the truth, Madonna. I saw you with Francesco del Giocondo at your child's baptism.'

So. He had been watching when Salai arranged for me to get the note.

He continued. 'Am I mistaken, or are relations between you strained—at least, on your part?'

My cheeks burnt. 'How do you know that?'

My answer seemed to please him. 'It is very difficult to completely conceal one's emotions. I did not detect much affection in your gestures.'

'I . . .' Guilt surged through me. I remembered those horrible days when I had sacrificed myself to Francesco for Matteo's sake. 'My father had been arrested. Francesco offered to save him, if . . .'

I could not finish. He nodded to indicate I did not need to. 'Then I must ask you whether you are still loyal to Giuliano. To the Medici.'

I suddenly understood. He had had no way to know that I had been forced into marriage with Francesco; he had no way of knowing whether I approved of Francesco's political schemes.

'I would never betray Giuliano! I loved him.'

'Do you not love him still?'

'Yes,' I said. Tears welled in my eyes and overflowed. 'Of course, yes. When he died, I wanted to die. I would have, by my own hand, had I not carried his child . . .' I panicked at my unintended admission. 'You must tell no one—not even Salai! If Francesco ever knew—!'

'Giuliano . . . dead.' Very slowly, he set the charcoal down on the little table. 'Few people have heard this. Most believe he is still alive.'

'No, Francesco told me. His body was found in the Arno . . . The Lord Priors took it and secretly buried it outside the city walls. They were afraid, because of what happened to Ser Iacopo.'

He digested this. 'I see. This explains a great deal.' Then he said, very carefully, 'So you are still loyal to the Medici. You would not shrink from helping Piero to recapture Florence? And you can guard your tongue?'

'Yes, to both questions. I would do anything—so long as it brings Matteo no harm.' I wiped away my tears and looked up at him.

'I would never ask you to do anything that directly endangered your child.' He paused. 'I was rather surprised when I received your letter,' he said, his tone soft in deference to my weeping. 'I . . . had reason to think you had perished the night the Medici brothers fled Florence. Later, I learned you had married Francesco del Giocondo . . .'

'I read the letter Salai dropped. The one written to my husband. I . . . had no idea he was somehow involved with Savonarola until that night. I don't even know who sent him the letter.'

'It is true,' he said, more to himself than me. 'When you saw Salai at the christening, you could have told your husband that Salai took the letter from his desk. But it seems you have not.'

'Of course not. Why would you not trust me?'

'Because you are married to an enemy of the Medici. And because, though I have known you for a long time, I do not know you well. And there is also the fact that I am not . . . a disinterested party.'

I made a sound of disgust. 'Don't think you can fool me by pretending you have feelings for me. I know you can never love me . . . that way. I know what you were charged with.'

His eyes widened abruptly, then narrowed again, bright with fury. '*You know*—' He caught himself. 'You are speaking of Saltarelli.'

'Who?'

'Iacopo Saltarelli. When I was twenty-four, I was accused of sodomy. I was arrested by the Officers of the Night and taken to the Bargello, where I learned that it was alleged that I and two other men had engaged in various sexual activities with Iacopo Saltarelli. My *denuncia* was written by one Paolo Sogliano. He happened to be a painter for, and assistant to, a goldsmith on the Via Vaccarechia who I also worked for. The charges were dropped for lack of evidence.'

'There was no truth to it, then.' I looked down at my hands.

'There was no truth to it. I ask you to consider how you would have felt being taken from your bed at night to the jail for questioning. How you would have felt, having to rely on your connections with Lorenzo de' Medici . . . asking him for help.' The next words came out hesitant. 'That does not mean I have never fallen in love with a man. Nor does it mean I have not fallen in love with a woman.'

I kept looking down at my hands. 'I know what the Bargello is like. They took me there the night Giuliano died. My father was there, too. We were freed only because of Francesco.'

His face softened at once.

'Before today, I had only my son. Now I have this, too. Do you understand? So don't deny me usefulness.'

'I won't,' he said softly. 'You can be of great use to us. Tell me what you remember of the letter Salai was reading when you encountered him in Ser Francesco's study.'

I told him that my husband had been ordered to collect the names of all the *Bigi* and to encourage Fra Girolamo to preach against Rome. Salai, it seemed, was a poor reader with a poorer memory. I would make a far better informant.

I was to search Francesco's desk on a nightly basis, if possible, and, if I discovered anything of import, was to signal my discovery by setting a certain book from my library on my night table. I did not ask why: it was obvious to me. Isabella, who had provided Salai with entry into the study, also cleaned my bedchamber each morning and lit the fire each night.

The day after I gave the signal with the book, I was to go at *sext* to Santissima Annunziata, ostensibly to pray.

I was relieved at last to be able to work towards the removal of Savonarola, the fall of Francesco from power, the second advent of Piero.

I sat no longer than half an hour lest Claudio become suspicious. As Leonardo painted, he became intense; his full attention was focused on the work in front of him. He stared at my face, seeing each curve, each line, each shadow, but he did not see *me.* I frowned at that. At once he chided softly, 'No, no . . . Only smiles. Think only of happy things.'

'What happy things? I have none in my life.'

He looked up from his drawing with a look of faint surprise in his pale eyes. 'You have your son. Is that not enough?'

I gave a short, embarrassed laugh. 'More than enough.'

'Good. And you have memories of your Giuliano, yes?'

I nodded.

'Then imagine . . .' His voice grew sad. 'Imagine you are with Giuliano again,' he said. 'Imagine that you are introducing him to his child.'

I let go of my sadness. I imagined. But I could not quite smile.

I left eager to do whatever I could to facilitate Piero's advent, but for days after my meeting with Leonardo, my surreptitious nocturnal searches were in vain: the old letter had disappeared from Francesco's desk, but no new one appeared in its place.

On the seventh night, however, I found a letter folded into thirds, with a broken seal of black wax. I opened it and read:

Piero has been in touch with Virgines Orsini, his soldier-cousin from Naples. He appears to be gathering troops—ostensibly, in response to Pope Alexander's request for an army to protect the Pisans from King Charles's return. But who is to say that, once gathered, such a force might not well make its way to Florence, with a different aim?

Cardinal Giovanni is of course arguing his brother's case. He has the Pope's ear—but so do I. His Holiness has written a brief, by the way, which shall soon be delivered to the Signoria. He has threatened King Charles with excommunication if he and his army do not leave Italy, and threatened Florence herself with the same if she continues to support Charles. He has also ordered the prophet to cease preaching.

Ignore this last, and trust in me. Our prophet should now redouble his fervour, specifically against the Medici. As for Charles—it would be best for the friar to begin to distance himself.

I appreciate your invitation, but my coming to Florence would be premature. Let us see first what Piero plans.

Send my cousins my regards—how sweet it is to see them home again after so many years, and Messer Iacopo avenged. Florence has always been, and will ever remain, our home.

My cousins . . . Messer Iacopo avenged.

My memory travelled back through the years, to my mother standing in the Duomo, weeping as she spoke of her beloved Giuliano's death. To the moment I stood staring up at the astrologer, as he sat in his carriage. *In your stars, I saw an act of violence, one that is your past and your future . . . What others have begun, you must finish . . .*

XI

'THE CORRESPONDENT IS one of the Pazzi,' I said.

Leonardo was a master of his emotions. Yet, as I spoke on that rainy autumnal day, two days after finding the letter, I could see his unease.

Carefully posed, I sat on the chair while he bent over the easel. I had insisted on seeing the beginnings of the portrait before I settled down to sit for him: my features were outlined in black, the edges softened by pools of shadow beneath my right jaw, in the hollow of my right cheek and beneath my right nostril. I stared out at the viewer with unsettlingly blank white eyes. My hair had been filled in with flat black. I was surprised to see that Leonardo had apparently remembered exactly how it appeared, years ago, when I wore it loose and flowing to the Palazzo de Medici. It hung with just the right amount of waviness.

Leonardo lifted his gaze and stroked his chin thoughtfully. 'It is dangerous,' he said at last, 'for you to interpret what you have read.'

'I don't care,' I responded. 'Piero is coming. He's gathering an army. And when he is here, everything will change.'

'Perhaps he is coming. Perhaps not . . . Do you really think he would let the Pazzi become aware of his movements?' He lowered the brush.

'This all began long ago, didn't it? With Lorenzo?'

He blinked, and I saw the disapproval in that tiny gesture. 'Lorenzo made a grave mistake, giving full vent to his hatred when his brother was murdered. It came to haunt him. Even after his death, it haunts his sons. The question is whether the cycle of violence can be halted.'

'You know who I am,' I said. 'You told Lorenzo. You gave him a sign, that night at the palazzo, when you showed me Giuliano's sculpture.'

He lifted a brow at that. 'You are far too perceptive, Madonna.'

'Did . . . did *my* Giuliano know?'

'Not when you married him, but—' He caught himself. 'You should take care that your emotions don't reveal themselves to others. Sometimes I wish you had never discovered Salai that night.'

'I won't be caught.'

'Perhaps not. Again, I urge you not to meditate on your discoveries. Doing so may well lead to your detection and cost you your life.'

'I can hold my tongue,' I answered, sharply. 'I won't be discovered. After all, I live with a man I despise—and he doesn't know how I feel.'

'But I do. Others may. I saw it on your face, in your every gesture.'

I fell silent.

His tone eased. 'Here. I am not helping matters by speaking glumly. And worse, I have caused you to lose your smile. Let us speak about something more cheerful. Your son? I'm sure he must resemble you.'

His words had the intended effect; I remembered Matteo and softened at once. 'He's getting so big. He crawls,' I said proudly. 'Faster, sometimes, than I can walk. And he looks like me. Dark-eyed, with great long lashes. And when I look at him I see his father's hair, of course.'

He looked up from his easel, smiling faintly.

'When you look at me, do you see my father?' I asked suddenly. 'My *real* father?'

His expression grew unreadable. Then he replied, 'I see him. But most of all, I see your mother. You have the same sadness I saw in her when—'

'When? Did you ever see her outside of the Palazzo de Medici?'

His gaze lowered. He looked at the portrait, not at me, as he replied. 'I saw her, some time after he died. At Santo Spirito.'

'Was she praying? At Mass?'

'Leaving Mass. Her husband was not with her, but her maid—'

'Zalumma.'

'The one with the wild hair? I so wanted to draw it . . . Yes, her maid was with her. Your mother was pregnant with you.'

I was entranced. 'How did she look?'

'Beautiful. And broken,' he said softly. 'Broken, yet somehow hopeful. You gave her reason to continue, I think.'

I turned my face away, towards the window.

'I am sorry,' Leonardo said, looking up at me again. 'I did not mean to make you sad.'

I shrugged. 'I can't help wondering whether he let her go to Giuliano's funeral.'

'He could not stop her,' he answered, with sudden vehemence.

I turned to stare at him. 'You saw her there?'

'Yes.' His stubbled cheeks flushed.

I thought of the two of them there—two people in love with the same man—and wondered whether my mother had known, whether they had ever spoken of the fact.

Leonardo set his brush down carefully into a little dish of oil and stepped from behind the easel. 'Madonna, nearly an hour has passed; you dare not stay longer,' he said firmly. 'I will be returning to Milan for a time. I have a commission to paint a Last Supper scene for a refectory.'

'You are leaving?' I could not keep the disappointment from my voice; I rose.

'I'll be returning, of course, though I cannot say when. In the meantime, Salai will remain here. You will continue just as you have before, except that you will now tell him the content of any letters you discover. And he will relay that content to me. You may well learn many things that disturb you, or even anger you. Please understand that there are many things I don't tell you now because it would increase the danger.'

'If you are to return to Milan,' I said, 'and we may not meet again for a long time . . . I must ask you your response to the letter I sent you so long ago. The first man to attack Giuliano in Santa Maria del Fiore, the man who escaped. My Giuliano, my husband, told me that you told Lorenzo about this man. That you had been in the cathedral when Giuliano the elder was murdered.'

'He was wearing a penitent's robes,' Leonardo answered shortly. 'With a hood. I couldn't see his face clearly.'

'But you must have seen part of it. My Giuliano said that you saw him. That his uncle died in your arms.'

'I saw him only for an instant. You can't expect me to remember.'

'But I can,' I said. 'You remembered my face when you saw me only once, at the Palazzo de Medici. You sketched it perfectly, from memory. You *have* sketched the penitent, haven't you? You must have been looking for him for years. I have the right to see the face of the man who killed my father. Why won't you show it to me?'

'Has it occurred to you, Madonna, that it might be better for you *not* to know certain things? Giuliano was murdered a long time ago,' Leonardo said. 'The assassin—if he still breathes—will certainly not live much longer. What good will it do to distract ourselves looking for one man? No noble cause can be served by revenge. We would only stir up old pain, old hatred. We must hope not to repeat our mistakes.'

'I still deserve to know,' I countered. 'And I don't want to be lied to.'

He raised his chin. 'I will never lie to you. But I *will*, if I deem it best for you, hide the truth. I do not do so lightly. Do not forget, you are the mother of a Medici heir. You and the boy must be protected. And I am sworn to do so, even if my heart did not already demand it.'

I stared at him. I was angry, frustrated; yet I trusted him.

'You need to leave,' he said softly.

I stepped forward and took his hand; his grip was warm, with the perfect degree of firmness. 'Be safe. And well.'

'And you, Madonna Lisa. I know that these are difficult times. I can only promise that great happiness awaits you at their end.'

His tone carried conviction, but I took no comfort in it. My Giuliano was gone; happiness was, for me, buried in the past.

One year faded into the next. On the very first day of 1496, Ludovico Sforza, Duke of Milan, betrayed Florence.

One of the treasures that King Charles of France had stolen from Florence, on his march south, was the fortress of Pisa. Pisa had always been ruled by Florence, but had long yearned to be free. Since the invasion, the city had been controlled by the French.

But Ludovico bribed the keeper of Pisa's fortress to hand over the keys to the Pisans themselves. And with that single move, Pisa gained her freedom—from Charles, and from Florence.

Ludovico, the crafty man, worked to keep his involvement secret. The result was that the Florentines believed King Charles had given the

Pisans self-rule. Charles, hailed by Savonarola as God's champion, who would bring Florence great glory, had instead betrayed her.

And the people blamed Savonarola. For the first time, their praise turned to discontent.

Winter yielded to spring, which brought relentless rains. The Arno flooded, washing away all the young crops. By the time the sky dried up in summer, the city suffered from an outbreak of fever. For Matteo's sake, I permitted no visitors to the nursery, nor did I allow him to leave the palazzo.

I left the house rarely. Once the fever became widespread, I forbade Zalumma to go with Agrippina to the market, and I went to Santissima Annunziata only irregularly, owing to the fact that I found no new letter in Francesco's desk.

Wishing to appear a good wife and allay suspicion, I continued to attend Savonarola's Saturday sermons for the women. His ranting against the Medici was combined with another obsession: Pope Alexander's cohabitation, in the Vatican, with his young mistress, Giulia Farnese, and his penchant for inviting prostitutes to his parties.

'You leader of the Church!' he railed. 'Each night you take your concubine, each morning you take the Sacraments; you have provoked God's anger.' And when the cardinals grumbled that Savonarola ought not speak so of the Pope, he proclaimed, 'It is not I who threaten Rome, but God!'

Several nights later, after my husband had gone to visit his own concubines and the servants had all retired, I made my way to Francesco's study. The letter hidden in the desk was plaintive.

> *Let him rail against the Medici, I said. But I did not encourage him to attack Alexander—far from it! He is undoing all my careful work here in Rome. Make it exceedingly clear to those involved: if they do not stop this foolishness at once, they will pay dearly!*
>
> *In the interim: the people's hunger could lead to grumbling. Rally them. Focus their attention not on their bellies, but on Heaven, and Fra Girolamo.*

I silently repeated the words to myself, emblazoning each one in my mind, so that I could summon them again easily.

The next morning, I left the book for Isabella to see. The following day, I rode to Santissima Annunziata just as the bells announced *sext*.

Salai took me to the room where I had met with Leonardo.

The portrait of me still rested on the easel. I studied it. I looked like a half-materialised ghost.

I smiled at the painting. And I smiled at Salai as I recited the contents of the letter to him. He wrote the words down slowly, laboriously, stopping several times to ask me to repeat what I had said.

I left feeling light-hearted. Leonardo's efforts were bearing fruit. The Pope would surely silence Savonarola. The Medici's enemies were flailing, and it was only a matter of time before I would greet Piero.

I smiled because I was ignorant. I smiled because I did not realise that the letter in fact threatened all that I held dear.

In the autumn, plague came. Savonarola still preached, but Francesco allowed me to remain at home. No letters arrived for him from Rome.

The loss of the spring crops devastated Tuscany. Farmers and peasants left the barren countryside and swarmed into the city seeking food. Men and women lined the streets, begging for scraps and alms. They slept on the steps of churches and in doorways. As the nights grew colder, some froze to death, but most died from starvation and plague. The streets of Florence began to stink.

Despite Francesco's wealth and connections, we felt the lack. The cook, Agrippina ran out of bread first, then flour, so we went without our customary pasta in broth. By winter, even we rich had grown desperate.

At last, word came that the Signoria had elected to allow stores of government grain to be sold at a fair price to the people at the Piazza del Grano on the morning of Tuesday the 6th of February, the last day of Carnival; Lent began on the morrow.

Agrippina had lost a nephew to plague only a few days before. For fear of bringing *la moria* back to the house, she had not attended his funeral—but she opined, loudly, that she would find comfort if only she could go to the Duomo to pray for his soul.

Of course, it was her duty to go and buy grain and bread for us. It made sense that she should visit the Duomo and offer her prayers, then walk the short distance to the Piazza del Grano and make her purchases.

And I, restless as I was, presented to Francesco my argument for accompanying Agrippina to the Duomo. It was not far; there would be few crowds; I was anxious to pray. To my delight, he relented.

And so, on the appointed Tuesday, I climbed into the carriage with Agrippina and Zalumma, and Claudio drove us east, towards the orange brick dome.

The sky was clear and fiercely blue. I stared outside the carriage, at the people moving slowly through the streets. Before Savonarola had seized the heart of Florence, Carnival had been a beautiful time; as a child, I had gaped at the façades of the grey buildings transformed by bright banners, gold-shot tapestries and garlands of paper flowers. Revellers had danced through the streets wearing painted masks.

Now the streets were quiet and dull, for under Savonarola's guidance, the new Signoria had outlawed such pagan displays.

We had agreed that it would be best to pray later and buy the food first, before supplies ran scarce. In the Piazza del Grano, a modest-sized square, stood large bins of wheat and corn behind sturdy wooden fences; in front of those stood makeshift stalls, with scales for the transactions. In front of the stalls was a low gate, which remained locked until there was business to be done.

Claudio pulled the carriage up to the outer perimeter of the square; we could go no farther. The place was crammed with bodies, so many that not a speck of ground was visible. There were hundreds of bareheaded peasants with dirt-smudged faces and blackened hands, all crying out for mercy, for alms, for a handful of grain.

Claudio swung down from the driver's seat, scowling.

'Perhaps I should go,' he said. 'Agrippina is small; she'll never be able to fight her way to the gate.'

'I've fed this family for forty years. No crowd can stop me.'

'Both of you go,' I said. 'That way, your chances are better. Zalumma and I will wait in the carriage.'

Claudio gave a curt nod, and opened the door for Agrippina. I watched them disappear into the throng—until a face appeared abruptly in the carriage window, startling me.

The woman was young, her uncovered hair was matted, her blue eyes wild. A silent infant was slung in a scarf at her breast.

'Pity, Madonna,' she said. 'A coin, a bit of food for my baby . . .'

Had it not been for the baby, I might have been more wary. As it was, I fumbled for the purse at my waist and pulled out a *soldo*. I meant to put it in her filthy hand, but the thought of Matteo and the plague made me instead toss it in her direction. It fell just outside the window, and she dived to find it. She was not alone. Another nearby peasant had seen, and fell on her. She started shrieking, and soon others were attracted to the row.

'She had one coin—there are more!' someone said. Our horses shrieked and lunged forward; the carriage jerked and began to rock.

'Death to the wealthy!' a man shouted. 'They take our food and leave us nothing!'

Dirty faces filled the window; arms reached through. Someone pulled open the door.

Beside me, Zalumma sprang to her feet and, from her bodice, unsheathed a slender, two-edged knife. She slashed out at the flailing arms; a man yelped and cursed.

And then, from the direction of the crowd came shouts, the lightning crack of wood splitting, and the beggars assaulting our carriage turned like flowers to sunlight; in an instant they were running towards the sound, leaving us quickly abandoned.

I clung to the frame of the open carriage door and stared out.

The crowd had broken through the locked gate and, as I watched, they swarmed the fence that guarded the bins of grain and tore it down. Two men scrambled up the sides of the bins and scattered handfuls of grain onto the desperate crowd below.

It was then that I heard a low, rhythmic chant, soft at first, then growing louder and louder, spreading swift as fire through the frenzied crowd: '*Palle! Palle! Palle!*'

Dozens were killed that day—trampled or suffocated—in the rush for food. Agrippina's chest and legs were crushed; Claudio came limping back to the carriage with her in his arms. Amazingly, he had managed to collect some of the pilfered grain in a pouch. I half expected Francesco to demand that he return it—it was, after all, stolen—but my husband said nothing.

News of the crowd's call for the Medici was everywhere, and when Francesco returned from his shop that afternoon, he was stone-faced and uncharacteristically silent. Upon learning of Agrippina's injuries, he sent for his physician, but I had never seen him in such foul temper.

Zalumma and I spoke little. But when we had retired for the night in the bedchamber—when she lay on her cot, and I on my bed—I said softly, in the darkness, 'You had a knife. I would like one, too.'

'I will give you mine,' she said.

And in the morning, she made good on her promise.

Inside the hidden studio, I recited the letter to Salai. He wrote it down as I dictated— clumsily, with maddening slowness.

> *An attack from Piero is imminent. The word is that he plans to approach from Siena. Prepare for this—but do not be too alarmed. He has only the Orsini and mercenaries, perhaps thirteen hundred men all told. Not enough.*
>
> *When he does fail, use the opportunity to make the new council public. The Arrabbiati have grown too noisy, as have Bernardo del Nero and his Bigi. The council must bring them down.*

When he had at last finished and rose to escort me out, I stood my ground. 'Do you know how to use a knife?' I asked, and he grinned.

'I was born with one in my hand.'

Awkwardly—taking care I did not cut myself—I drew Zalumma's double-bladed knife from the sheath tucked into my bodice.

Salai made a face. 'So like a girl. If you don't cut yourself to ribbons first, your opponent will be doubled over laughing by the time you get your weapon out.'

'Don't make fun of me. Show me how to use it.'

Piero never came. A fortnight after I delivered the message to Salai, Zalumma came to my chambers wearing an expression of abject defeat. I dreaded the instant she drew breath and opened her mouth.

The news was spreading all over the city, she told me. Piero and his men had set out from Siena and headed down as far as San Gaggio. But the sky had opened up en route, and a violent rain had forced the army to seek shelter and wait out the storm, with the result that they lost the cover of night. The delay allowed word of them to reach the Florentine troops stationed at Pisa, to the north. Piero was forced to retreat in order to avoid being overpowered.

Savonarola's followers said, of course, that God had spoken. The rest of us were downcast, and afraid to speak.

Given the failure of the Medici invasion, I had expected Francesco to be in good spirits—indeed, I expected him to gloat. But the following evening at supper, he was in a noticeably preoccupied mood, and said nothing whatsoever about Piero's disastrous attempt on the city.

'I hear,' my father said neutrally, 'that the newly elected Signoria is all *Arrabbiati*. Fra Girolamo must be sorely frustrated.'

Francesco murmured, 'You know better than I,' then, more loudly, 'It doesn't matter. The Signoria always ebbs and flows. For two months, we suffer with the *Arrabbiati*. Who knows? The next group might all be *piagnoni*. At any rate, the new Signoria won't be able to cause too much trouble. We succeeded just recently in creating a Council of Eight, thanks to our recent threat.'

My gaze flickered down to my plate. I knew he meant Piero.

'Eight?' my father asked conversationally.

'Eight men, elected to police the city against the threat. They will keep a special eye on Bernardo del Nero and his *Bigi* party. And they will take stern measures to stop all espionage. All letters going to and from Florence will be intercepted, and read. The Medici supporters will find familiar avenues closed to them.'

'What does Fra Girolamo say of this?' my father ventured.

Francesco's tone was terse. 'Actually, it was his suggestion.'

We finished the meal in silence.

That night, I left Zalumma to go down to Francesco's study. I unlocked his desk quickly, expecting to find nothing and to return quietly to my own bed.

But there, in the drawer, was a letter, with a freshly broken seal.

> *It seems our prophet still vehemently denounces Rome from the pulpit. His Holiness is displeased, and there is little more I can do at this point to assuage him. Our entire operation falters! At whose feet shall I lay this monstrous failure? Giving the prophet free rein against the Medici alone was my intent— how could you misunderstand? You know I have worked for years to gain papal access, papal trust . . . And now you would see it all undone? Or shall I give you the benefit of the doubt and credit Antonio with this? If he truly has the prophet's ear, he must be forceful. Exhort him to use all his powers of persuasion. If he fails, it is your decision as to whether to dispose of his services altogether, or make use of the daughter and grandchild. I defer to your preference in this matter, as you are hardly a disinterested party. If Antonio quails, rely again, as you did so long ago, on Domenico, who has proven he can do whatever needs to be done.*
>
> *If Pope Alexander does act against the friar, we have little choice but to resort to extreme measures. Perhaps Bernardo del Nero and his Bigi shall need to serve as examples to the people.*

'Antonio,' I whispered. I reached out and steadied myself against the night table. I stared at the letter, read it again and again.

I had thought Francesco had married me because I was beautiful.

If Antonio quails, rely again, as you did so long ago, on Domenico—

I remembered that terrible moment so long ago in San Marco's sacristy, when Fra Domenico had stood over my mother's body. When he had caught my father's eye, then looked pointedly at me.

A threat.

And my father had knelt. Choking on his fury, but he had knelt.

I remembered him begging later for me to go with him, to listen to Savonarola preach. When I had refused, he had wept. Just as he had wept the day of my marriage to Giuliano, when he had told me frantically that he could not keep me safe.

I remembered my father's cooling friendship with Pico after my mother died. I thought of Pico's death, and my father's current unhappy friendship with my husband.

—make use of the daughter and grandchild—

I could not cry. I was too horrified, too hurt, too frightened.

I stared at each separate word, emblazoning it on my memory. When I was done, I replaced the letter in the desk, and locked it.

XII

THE NEXT MORNING, I sent Zalumma on foot to visit my father at his workshop and let him know that I wanted to see him alone. She returned less than two hours later to say that my father felt unwell, that he was going home directly, and hoped I would call upon him there.

My father was waiting for me in the great chamber where he had greeted Giuliano the day he came to ask for my hand, the same room where my mother had met the astrologer. He rose when I entered.

I did not bother with a greeting. 'I know that you and Francesco are involved in manipulating Savonarola.' I sounded amazingly calm. 'I know about Pico.'

His face went slack. He had been moving forward to embrace me; now he took a step back and sat down again on his chair. 'Dear Jesus,' he whispered. He ran a hand over his face and peered up at me, stricken.

'I know you go to Savonarola. I know you're supposed to tell him to preach against the Medici, but not against Pope Alexander. But you are not doing a very good job.'

'Who? Who tells you this?' And when I remained silent, his expression became one of bald panic. 'You're a spy. My daughter, a spy for the Medici . . .' He put his head in his hands, terrified by the thought.

'I'm no one's spy,' I lied. 'I came by the information accidentally.'

He groaned; I thought he would weep.

'I know . . . I know you have done this only to protect me,' I said. 'I'm not here to accuse you. I'm here because I want to help.'

He reached for my hand and squeezed it. 'I am so sorry,' he said. 'So sorry you had to learn about this. I still . . . Fra Girolamo is a sincere man. He wants to do God's work. I once had his confidence, his trust.'

I held on to his hand tightly. 'It doesn't matter. What matters is that you've displeased your masters. You're in danger. We have to leave Florence. You and Matteo and I—there's no reason to stay any longer.'

'You've never been safe.' My father looked up, hollow-eyed.

'I know. But now you aren't safe, either.' I sank to my knees beside him, still holding his hand.

'Don't you think I thought of leaving? Years ago—after your mother died, I thought I would take you to my brother Giovanni in the country, that you and I would be safe there. They found out. They watch us. Even now, when I take you out to the carriage, Claudio will study your face. If you are upset, he'll tell Francesco.' He drew in a sharp, pained breath. 'There are things I can't tell you, do you understand? Things you can't know, because Claudio, because Francesco, will see it in your eyes. Because knowing, you'll endanger us all. Endanger Matteo.'

I hesitated. 'I don't think Francesco would truly permit anyone to harm Matteo.' My husband showed genuine fondness for the boy.

'Look at him,' my father said, and at first I did not know of whom he spoke. 'He is still a baby, but even I can see his true father in his face!'

The words pierced me; I grew very still. 'And when you look at me, whose face do you see?'

He looked on me with pain and love. 'I see a face far more handsome than mine.' He drew my hand to his lips and kissed it; then he stood, and drew me to him. 'I don't care if they threaten me, but you and the baby—I will find a way. I will find us a safe place, somewhere. You can say nothing of this, you can speak to no one. We will talk again.'

He gave me a sudden, fierce hug. I held him tightly. I was not his blood, but he was my father more than any man.

I had no choice but to leave a book on my night table that day. What I had learned was too important to ignore: our enemies were losing their influence over the Pope and the friar—and, more importantly, they were considering taking action against the *Bigi*.

I lay awake that night, silently reciting the letter to myself, omitting all reference to Antonio, to the daughter, to the grandchild. Leonardo and Piero would still learn everything of import.

I had determined to make my recitation quickly, to spend no time in conversation, but Salai broke with our custom, which was for him to sit immediately at Leonardo's little table and serve as scribe, while I dictated what I had learned.

Instead, he gestured at my low-backed chair, smiling and excited. 'If you would, Monna Lisa . . . He will come to you right away.'

He. I drew in a startled breath and looked about me. My portrait was still on the easel; beside it stood the little table, covered now with new brushes, small dishes of tin, a crushed pellet of *cinabrese* for painting faces, a dish of *terre verte*, and a dish of a warm brown.

I lifted a hand to my collarbone. *Nothing is different*, I told myself. *Nothing is changed. Leonardo is here, and you will recite exactly what you planned. And then you will sit for him.*

In less than a minute, Leonardo stood smiling in front of me. His hair was longer, sweeping his shoulders, and he had regrown his beard; it was short, carefully trimmed, and almost entirely silver.

'Madonna Lisa,' he said, standing over me, and took my hands. 'It is wonderful to see you again! How is your family? Matteo?'

'Everyone is fine. Matteo is running now. He wears us all out.' I gave a little laugh, hoping that Leonardo would assume the exhaustion I would soon plead was the result of motherhood.

He let go of my hands and took a step back, assessing me. 'Good. All good. Salai says you have something to report today. Shall we get it over with quickly, then?' He folded his arms. Unlike Salai, who wrote everything down, Leonardo simply listened to my recitations.

'All right, then.' I drew in a determined breath and began. The first six sentences of the letter came easily. And then, without intending to, I began: '*And now you would see it all undone? Or shall I give you the benefit of the doubt—*'

I broke off, panicked. I knew how the phrase should be finished: *and credit Antonio with this.* But I dared not say my father's name; yet I was obliged to complete the thought. '*—and credit our friend with this.*' At that point, in order to make the letter seem all of a piece, I recited all the lines that referred to my father, taking care to replace his name with the phrase 'our friend'. And I exerted my full concentration so that I would not stumble when I omitted: *or make use of the daughter and grandchild.*

When I was finished, I looked at Leonardo. He stood gazing at me, his eyes intense.

At last, he spoke. 'You are a poorer spy than I gave you credit for, Lisa. I think you know who "our friend" is. Perhaps I should ask you to recite that particular line for me again and again, until you finally tell it to me as it was written.'

I was furious with myself, ashamed. 'I've told you what you need to know. You can't—you think you know everything, but you don't.'

He remained calm, sad. 'Madonna . . . You won't be telling me something I don't already know. I understand that you want to protect him, but it's too late for that.'

I closed my eyes. When I opened them again, I said, 'You must promise me that no harm will come to him . . . If I thought that you—that Piero—was a danger to him, I—'

'Lisa,' he said. His tone was sharp. 'You are trying to protect someone who isn't worthy of your protection.' He left the room and I could hear him shuffling about in the next room, searching for something.

When he returned, he held a portfolio in his hand. 'I had hoped this moment would never arrive; that you would be spared. I see now, of course, that it was only a matter of time.'

'If you hurt him, I won't help you.' My voice shook.

Leonardo picked up a folio and took it over to the long table against the far wall, and opened it, and began going through the drawings until he found the one he sought.

I moved to stand beside him; I looked down at the drawing.

'You were right,' he said. 'I made a sketch immediately after the event, and kept it for a very long time. This is one I made recently, in Milan. After you asked me, I realised the time might come for you to see it.'

It was a fully rendered drawing of a man's head, with a hint of the neck and shoulders. He was turning to look over his shoulder. He was draped in a cowl, which hid his hair, his ears, and left most of his face in shadow. Only the tip of his nose, his chin and mouth were visible.

The man's lips were parted, one corner drawn lower as his face turned; in my mind, I could hear his gasp. Although the eyes were hidden in blackness, his terror, his spent anger, his dawning regret were conveyed surely in the one brilliant, horrified downward turn of a lower lip, and in the straining muscles of his neck.

I looked at the man. I felt I knew him, but I had never seen him before. 'This is the penitent?' I asked. 'The man you saw in the Duomo?'

'Yes. Do you recognise him?'

I hesitated, and at last said, 'No.'

He cleared a space upon the table, took the drawing from the portfolio, and set it down. 'I did not learn what I am about to show you until recently.' He took up a piece of crumbling red chalk and began to draw. He made light, staccato strokes over the jaw first, and the chin; it took me a moment to realise he was drawing hair, a beard. As he did, the penitent's jaw softened; the upper lip disappeared beneath a full moustache. The corners of the man's mouth were suddenly braced by age.

Slowly, beneath his hand, appeared a man I knew, a man I had seen every day of my life.

'You recognise him now.'

I nodded, blind.

'His involvement was not born of innocence, Lisa. He was part of the conspiracy from the beginning. He joined not out of piety, but out of jealousy, out of hate. He destroyed Anna Lucrezia. Destroyed her.'

I turned my back on him, on the drawing. I took a step away.

'Did you go to him, Lisa? Did you speak to him of me, of Piero?'

I went to my chair and sat. I wanted to be sick.

Leonardo remained next to the table, but he faced me. 'Please answer. We are dealing with men who do not shrink from murder. Did you go to him? Did you say anything to him, to anyone?'

'No,' I said.

I had told Leonardo half the truth—that I had said nothing about him, about Francesco's letters. Perhaps it was the half-truth that showed on my face, in my aspect, for Leonardo asked me no further questions.

But even he, for all his charm, could not convince me to sit for him that day. I returned home early.

Francesco was late returning from his *bottega*. He went straight into his chambers and did not venture out until summoned to supper.

My father was also late in arriving for the meal, and he, too, did not come to the nursery first, as was his custom. I arrived at the table to find Francesco stone-faced, defeated, gripped by a cold, powerless rage. He uttered my name and gave a curt nod in greeting.

My father did his best to smile—but given what I had learned from Leonardo, I found it difficult to meet his eyes. Once the food was served, he enquired after Matteo's health, after mine; I answered with awkward reserve. After those pleasantries were dispensed with, he began to speak a bit about politics, as he and Francesco so often did.

'Fra Girolamo is working on an apologia, *The Triumph of the Cross*. There are those who claim that he is a heretic, a rebel against the Church, but this work will show just how orthodox his beliefs are.'

I glanced sideways at Francesco. 'Well,' I said tentatively, 'he has certainly preached strenuously against Rome.'

'He preaches against sin,' my father countered gently. 'Not against the Papacy. His writings will show his absolute respect for the latter.'

After a moment's silence, Francesco surprised me by speaking—suddenly, with cool bitterness. 'Let the prophet write what he will. There are some who believe he has little chance of placating His Holiness.'

My father looked up sharply from his food; in the face of Francesco's icy gaze, he soon looked down again.

Supper ended without another word; my father took his leave immediately—a fact for which I was glad—as I was far too troubled by my new knowledge to be comfortable with him. Francesco returned to his room. I went up to the nursery and played with Matteo in an effort to blot out the image of my father plunging his blade into Giuliano's back.

It was not until I had put my son to bed and returned to my chamber that I understood Francesco's anger. Before I could reach for the door, it opened before me, and Zalumma seized my arm and pulled me inside. She closed the door quickly behind us, then leaned against it.

'Did you hear? Did you hear, Madonna? Isabella just told me—'
'Hear what?'
'Savonarola. The Pope has excommunicated him!'

Summer brought a second fiercer outbreak of *la moria*, the Death. My visits to Santissima Annunziata came to a halt. Even if I had wanted to venture out onto the plague-ridden streets, I had no news to share with Leonardo, since I no longer had access to my husband's letters. Fearful of contagion, Francesco had given up his nightly prowling and stayed in his chambers. He went out only to his *bottega* and, more rarely, when the most important business called, to the Palazzo della Signoria. Yet, despite *la moria*, he received more visitors than ever: members of the Signoria, *Buonomini*, and other men who were never introduced to me. Savonarola was in political danger, and Francesco was desperate to save him.

To avoid the danger of travelling back and forth over the Arno, my father came to stay with us for a time.

One morning I was at the breakfast table, with Matteo squirming in my lap; I had never before brought him downstairs to eat, but he was almost two years old, and I dreamed of teaching him to eat with a spoon. When Francesco and my father arrived, Matteo was happily pounding the utensil against the surface of Francesco's fine, polished table: I expected my husband to speak sharply, since he had been in foul temper of late. But Francesco, for the first time in days, smiled.

'Wonderful news!' he exclaimed, raising his voice to be heard over Matteo's drumming. 'We have captured a Medici spy!'

I tried to draw a breath and failed; I sat up straight, barely averting my head in time to avoid Matteo's wildly flailing arm. 'A spy?'

My father seemed to sense my sudden fear; he pulled out a chair and sat beside me. 'Lamberto dell'Antello. He was one of Piero's friends,' he said quietly, next to my ear. 'He even went with Piero to Rome. He was discovered trying to get into Florence with a letter . . .'

Francesco stood smiling across from us; I put a restraining hand on Matteo's wrist, and ignored him when he complained. 'Yes, Lamberto dell'Antello. He was captured yesterday, and is now being interrogated. This will be the end of the *Bigi*. Lamberto is talking, giving names.' He moved towards the kitchen. 'Where is Cook? I need some food, and quickly. I must leave for the Palazzo della Signoria this morning.'

Once Francesco had eaten and left in the carriage, my father and I took Matteo out to run in the gardens behind the palazzo. I strolled beside my father, letting my son run slightly ahead of us.

I was still angry with my father. I knew he would never cause me harm, but each time I looked on him, I saw the penitent. Even so, I worried for his sake. 'I am afraid,' I told him. 'The excommunication—Francesco will say that you've failed him.'

He gave a little shrug to make light of it. 'Don't worry about me. I have spoken with Fra Girolamo—I, and others. He knows he has been foolish—that he has failed to control his tongue. He will write his apologia. And he has already sent private letters to His Holiness, begging for forgiveness. Alexander will be soothed.'

'And if he isn't?'

My father stared ahead at his sturdy grandson. 'Then Florence will be placed under papal interdict. No Christian city will be allowed to do business with us unless we turn over Savonarola for punishment. But that won't happen.' He reached for my hand, to comfort me.

I did not mean to pull away, but could not stop myself.

His eyes filled with hurt. 'You have been angry with me. I don't blame you, for all I've done. Terrible things I pray God will forgive.'

'I'm not angry,' I said. 'I want only one thing: for us to leave Florence with Matteo. I can't bear it here any longer. It's growing too dangerous.'

'It's true,' he admitted sadly. 'But, right now, it's impossible. When they found Lamberto dell'Antello, the Lord Priors closed all nine gates of the city: no one can come in, no one can go out; every letter is intercepted and read by the Council of Eight. They are questioning everyone, looking for Medici spies. Were it not for my usefulness to Francesco, they would question us.' His voice grew hoarse. 'They will destroy the *Bigi*—every man who looked kindly on Lorenzo or his sons. And they will have Bernardo del Nero's head.'

'No,' I whispered. Bernardo del Nero was one of Florence's most revered citizens, a long-time intimate of Lorenzo de' Medici. He was a strong, clear-headed man of seventy-five years of age, childless and widowed, and so he had devoted his life to the government of the city. 'They wouldn't dare hurt him! No citizen would stand for it.'

My father was shaking his head. 'They will have to stand for it. The appearance of Lamberto dell'Antello has filled every *piagnone*'s heart with fear. After the food riots in the Piazza del Grano, the Signoria is desperate to stifle any more cries of *palle! palle!*' He looked out across the garden at his grandson and his eyes grew haunted.

'There will be no mercy now,' he said. 'There will only be blood.'

I wanted desperately to go to Santissima Annunziata, to warn Leonardo of the imminent peril of Bernardo del Nero and his political party, but Francesco would not hear of me leaving the house.

Arrests were made; people were tortured. In the end, five men were held and brought before the Signoria and the Great Council for sentencing: the august Bernardo del Nero; Lorenzo Tornabuoni, Piero's young cousin, who, though titular head of the *Bigi*, was nonetheless a much-loved citizen and a pious *piagnone*; Niccolo Ridolfi, an older man whose son had married Lorenzo's daughter Contessina; Giannozzo Pucci, a young friend of Piero's; and Giovanni Cambi, who had previously had many business dealings with the Medici.

Pity! supporters cried, certain that the sentences would be light, and in the case of Bernardo del Nero, commuted. The accused were all admired, upright citizens; their confessions—that they were actively involved in arranging for Piero de' Medici's return as the city's self-proclaimed ruler—had been elicited under the most brutal torture.

The people looked to Savonarola for guidance. Surely the friar would call for forgiveness, forbearance.

But Fra Girolamo was too distracted by his efforts to placate an angry Pope. He could no longer be bothered, he said publicly, with political matters. 'Let them all die or be expelled. It makes no difference to me.'

On the morning of the 27th of August, Francesco summoned me to accompany him, but would not tell me where we were going.

The carriage rumbled to a stop in front of the Bargello prison where I had been held, where Leonardo had been taken by the Officers of the Night. Great torches burned on either side of the massive entrance.

As Claudio opened the door, my heart quailed. *They have captured Leonardo*, I thought. *Francesco knows everything. He has brought me here to be questioned* . . . But I showed no outward sign of my turmoil. My face was set as I took Claudio's arm and stepped onto the flagstone.

Francesco stepped from the carriage after me and gripped my elbow. As he directed me towards the doors, I expected to be led to a cell, or to a room filled with accusatory priors. Armed guards scrutinised us as we passed through the entry hall, then outside into a large courtyard lit by the wavering orange light of many torches.

Against the far wall was a steep staircase leading down from a balcony above, and at the foot of those stairs stood a recently constructed platform. Mounds of straw had been scattered atop its surface.

Francesco and I were not alone. There were other high-standing *piagnoni* present; several sweating Lord Priors in their *chermisi* scarlet tunics, a handful of *Buonomini*, and members of the Council of Eight. We nodded silent greetings, then joined the crowd waiting in front of the low platform. I let go a shuddering breath; I was here as a witness, not a prisoner—at least for now.

People had been murmuring to each other, but they fell silent as a man mounted the scaffold: an executioner bearing a heavy single-edged axe. With him came another man, who set down a scarred wooden chopping block upon the straw.

'*No*,' I whispered to myself. I remembered my father's words about the *Bigi*; I had not wanted to believe them.

Bernardo del Nero was first. He had been a dignified white-haired man, with large, solemn eyes. Those eyes were now puffed almost entirely shut. He could no longer stand straight, but leaned heavily on his captor as he took each halting step down.

I did not recognise young Lorenzo Tornabuoni; his face was so bruised and swollen he could not see at all, but had to be led down the stairs. Three other prisoners followed: Niccolo Ridolfi, Giannozzo Pucci, Giovanni Cambi, all of them broken, resigned.

When they at last stood upon the scaffold, the gonfaloniere read the charges and the sentence: espionage and treason, death by beheading.

Bernardo del Nero was granted the mercy of dying first. The executioner asked his forgiveness, and was told, in a frail, thick-tongued voice that he was forgiven. And then Bernardo squinted out at our small assembly and said, 'May God forgive you, too.'

I closed my eyes as the executioner lifted the axe. And suddenly I remembered a day years before, in the church at San Marco, when my mother, her gaze fixed and terrible, had stared up at Savonarola in the pulpit. And I had heard her cry out: *Flames shall consume him until his limbs drop, one by one, into Hell! Five headless men shall cast him down!*

Five headless men.

I opened my eyes as guards came and took Bernardo's headless body away; Tornabuoni was pushed forward, forced to murmur words of forgiveness, to kneel, to die. Two more followed. Giovanni Cambi was last.

Francesco and I rode home in silence until my husband spoke abruptly. 'This is what becomes of Medici supporters.' He was watching me curiously. 'This is what becomes of spies.'

Perhaps he spoke out of a desire to relish his political victory. In any case, I did not answer. I was thinking of my father, and what would happen to him when the prophet was cast down.

As the weather cooled, the plague's grip on the city eased. My father returned to his house, Francesco took up with his prostitutes again, and I went to church as often as I could. One morning I placed the book on my night table, even though I had found no new letter in Francesco's desk, and the next day I went to Santissima Annunziata.

Leonardo was well, to my relief. He had even worked on the painting. The bold outlines and shadows of my features had been softened to produce a translucent curtain of flesh. I was beginning to look human.

But when I told him of my father's warning that the *Bigi* would pay with their blood—of my anguish that I had not been able to come and warn him—he said, 'You bear no guilt. We knew of the danger, well before your father spoke of it to you. The horror of it was, even had we been able to arrange a rescue . . .' He could not bring himself to continue.

'Even if they could have been rescued—they should not have been,' I finished.

'Yes,' he murmured. 'That is the horror of it. It is better that they have died.' It was true; the executions had outraged everyone in Florence, even most of the *piagnoni*, who felt that the friar should have extended his forgiveness.

'Years ago, my mother told me . . . that Savonarola would be brought down. By five headless men.'

'Your mother? Your mother spoke to you of Savonarola?'

'I know it sounds very strange. But . . . I believe what she said was true. I think that this will cause Savonarola to be defeated. I think that he might even die.'

'Did she ever say anything else about Fra Girolamo?'

'I believe she was speaking about him when she said, "Flames shall consume him until his limbs drop, one by one, into Hell. Five headless men shall cast him down."'

What he said next astounded me. 'He will die by fire, then. And these executions shall be his undoing. We will expect it, prepare for it.'

'You believe me,' I said.

'I believe your mother.'

I stared at him for so long that he lowered his gaze and said, with unexpected tenderness, 'I told you that I had seen your mother once when she was pregnant with you.'

'Yes.'

'She told me she was carrying a daughter. She told me I would paint your portrait.'

I wanted suddenly to cry. I reached for his hand.

I have tried to deal with His Holiness as with Pico, but Alexander is too canny, too well guarded. There is no hope we can replace him with one more sympathetic to our aims. The prophet's time is waning too quickly, and my own *has not yet come. I have not enough friends in the Signoria. But there is still a way. If Savonarola is cast in the role of devil, then I must be presented as a saviour. Consider this, and give me your thoughts.*

In the studio, I stared at the portrait on the easel. The paint was still drying—a coating of the palest shell pink, which brought a gentle bloom to my cheeks and lips—so I dared not touch it, though my finger hovered, yearning, over a spot in the hollow of my neck.

'There is a bit of blue there,' I said. And green; the slightest hint of a vein lurking beneath the skin. I followed the line with my finger; I felt, if I could set it down on the panel, I would feel my own pulse. 'It looks as though I'm alive.'

Leonardo smiled. 'Have you not noticed it before? At times, I think I can see it beating. Your skin is quite translucent there.'

'Of course not. I have never stared in the mirror that long.'

'A pity,' he said, without a trace of mockery. 'It seems that those who possess the greatest beauty appreciate it the least.'

He spoke so honestly that I was embarrassed; I changed the subject at once. 'I will sit now.'

And, as always, before I sat for him, I recited the letter. He listened, frowning slightly, and when I finished, he said, 'He is growing desperate.'

'And he—whoever he is—wants to seize control of Florence.' I paused. 'Who *is* he? I already know that he is one of the Pazzi, but I want to understand why he craves power.'

Leonardo studied me a moment, then let go a small sigh. 'His name is Salvatore. He is the illegitimate son of Francesco de' Pazzi. He was perhaps ten years old at the time of Giuliano's murder. Many of his family were executed by Lorenzo and the rest were exiled. They lost everything: their possessions, lands . . . He and his mother fled to Rome.

'Most of the Pazzi are good, honourable people; they had been horribly wronged by Lorenzo, and there was a good deal of bitterness. But they simply wanted to return to Florence, to their ancestral home.

'In the case of Salvatore, though—his mother instilled him with intense hatred from an early age. He was very precocious and ambitious; he decided, early on, to take Florence for the Pazzi, out of revenge.'

'It all repeats,' I said. 'Lorenzo took his revenge, and now the Pazzi want theirs.'

'Not all of the Pazzi. Just Salvatore. He took advantage of the family's position as papal bankers in order to ingratiate himself with the Pope.'

I leaned forward, perplexed. 'Then why . . . Why would he get involved with Savonarola?'

'That,' he said, 'is a very long story. It began with Giovanni Pico. As a young man, he was a womaniser and a fair philosopher. Pope Sixtus was eager to excommunicate him—and was even considering him for the stake—for his rather unchristian syncretism.

'It was Lorenzo de' Medici who used his diplomacy to save him in 1490, well before the Medici's relationship with the papacy soured. Pico, however, possessed a short memory. He took a Pazzi mistress, who turned him against Lorenzo. When Giuliano died and Lorenzo took his horrible vengeance on the Pazzi, Pico began looking for ways to influence the people against the Medici, to bring the Pazzi back.

'When Pico went to hear Savonarola speak in Ferrara, he saw a very charismatic man who disapproved of the wealthy and corrupt. He saw an opportunity for swaying the people against Lorenzo.'

'Does Savonarola know about the Pazzi? About this Salvatore?'

He shook his head. 'Not at all. Savonarola listens to your father, and to Fra Domenico. But that is another part of the story.

'As for Pico . . . Through his mistress, he knew of Francesco de' Pazzi's son Salvatore. And when the Pazzi were expelled from Florence, Pico exchanged letters with Salvatore. Pico suggested the use of Savonarola to sway public opinion—and came up with the notion of using a slow-acting poison on Lorenzo. Pico was intimate enough with the Medici to know that Piero had never nurtured his father's political connections, and so would be weak and easily removed. The original plan was to kill Lorenzo, oust Piero, and install Salvatore as the new ruler of Florence.

'Unfortunately—or fortunately, as you prefer—Lorenzo died before Salvatore was able to muster enough support in the Signoria.

'But Salvatore managed to find one stalwart supporter in the government: a Pazzi advocate, one Francesco del Giocondo. And he put Francesco in touch with Giovanni Pico. Together, they concocted a plan to turn Florence against the Medici. I'm sure it worked far better than they ever dreamed it would.

'After a time, though, Pico's guilt over Lorenzo's murder overcame him. He actually began to take Savonarola's words to heart, to repent. This made him dangerous and liable to confess. For that, he was killed.'

'By my father,' I said miserably.

'By Antonio di Gherardini,' he corrected, not unkindly. 'Antonio had his own reasons for supporting the Pazzi. He never meant to become entrapped in a political scheme.'

I looked down at my hands—out of habit they rested one on top of the other, the way Leonardo preferred to paint them. 'And Francesco married me so that he could control my father.'

Leonardo's reply was quick in coming. 'Don't underestimate your-self, Lisa. You are a beautiful woman.'

I shrugged off the flattery. 'If they have no choice but to let Savonarola be ruined—if they murder him, or arrange for him to die—then they'll have no use for my father. For Antonio . . .'

His expression softened. But I could see, too, his reserve.

'What can I do?' I believed whole-heartedly in my mother's prophecy that death was coming for the prophet. 'You must help us. Take us out of Florence. Take us with you to Milan.'

'Lisa . . .' I heard pity in his tone. 'If I could have, I would have done so long ago. But it is not so easy. There are you, your father, and your child . . . and your slave, I assume. Four people. And you realise, of course, that your comings and goings are watched. You will never make it past the city gates, so long as your husband retains any influence.'

'So I am to stay? Until it is too late, and my father dies?'

My words hurt him, but his voice remained gentle. 'Antonio is not a helpless man. He has survived this long. And the time will come soon enough for you to leave. I promise you that. It will come.'

'It will never come soon enough,' I said.

I wish now I had been wrong.

XIII

ON PALM SUNDAY, Francesco did not attend church, but chose to remain at home and forbade the rest of us to leave. On Monday morning, my husband told me to have the servants prepare the house for a presti-gious guest, who would be coming to stay with us for a few weeks; then he left for the Signoria. Florence was in turmoil after the deaths of the *Bigi*, and many had taken to the streets calling for Savonarola's arrest. The *piagnoni* had lost their leader, Francesco Valori, who had been mur-dered and still lay in the gutter. Although the streets were calmer now, Francesco requested that Claudio drive him, and had two armed men accompany him in the carriage.

I was stranded at home, without a driver. Zalumma and I fetched Matteo from the nursery and took him down to the garden, since the day was pleasant. Later, when Matteo was asleep and the servants were all downstairs eating in the kitchen, I went to Francesco's study.

It was foolish, going in the middle of the day, but I was consumed by restlessness and a mounting sense of worry. And I had not even considered how I would get to Leonardo if I found a new letter.

It is time to join the Arrabbiati *and sacrifice the prophet. We have already translated into action your suggestion of luring Piero to Florence and making public example of him. The people are angry; we will give them a second scapegoat. Otherwise, with Savonarola gone, they might soften too much towards the Medici. We are taking Messer Iacopo's plan as our model: I shall expose the traitor in the midst of his crime, take him to the piazza for public spectacle, and rely on mercenary troops as reinforcement.*

Let us not confine our public spectacle to Piero. We must dispense with all Medici brothers—for if even one survives, we are not free of the threat. Cardinal Giovanni presents the least danger, and my agents will try to deal with him in Rome, where he will surely stay.

But the youngest—he is the most dangerous, having all the intelligence and political acumen his eldest brother lacks. And in your house sleeps the perfect lure to bring him to Florence.

I carefully refolded the letter and slipped it back into the envelope; I went upstairs to my room. Slowly, I took a book from the trunk and set it on my night table. I could not let myself think or feel.

Rapid footsteps sounded on the stairs, in the corridor; as I went to open the door, Zalumma pulled it open first.

She did not notice that I was stunned, wild-eyed and pale. Her black brows, her lips, were stark, broad strokes of grief.

'Loretta,' she said. 'From your father's house. She is here. Come.'

He was dying, Loretta said. Three days earlier, his bowels had turned to blood, and he had not been able to eat or drink. Fever left him delirious. Not plague, she insisted. For two days, he had been asking for me.

And each time Loretta had come, Claudio or Francesco or one of the armed men had sent her away.

Loretta had driven herself in the wagon. I did not stop or think or question; I said nothing to the other servants, nothing to anyone. I went immediately to the wagon and climbed in. Zalumma came with me. Loretta took the driver's seat, and together we left.

It was a terrible ride over the Arno, over the Ponte Santa Trinita, over the murky waters where Giuliano might have drowned. I tried to stop the words repeating in my mind, to no success.

But the youngest—he is the most dangerous . . .
And in your house sleeps the perfect lure.

The letter had to be a trap; Francesco must have discovered me rifling through his desk, or else Isabella had lost her nerve and told all. It was impossible, of course. The world could not have known he was alive and not told me.

I drew a deep breath and remembered that my father was dying.

For the first time in my life, I entered my father Antonio's bedchamber.

It was midday; a cool breeze blew outside. In my father's room it was dark and hot from the fire. Antonio lay naked beneath a blanket. His eyes were closed; in the light filtering through the half-closed shutters, he looked greyish white. I had not realised how thin he had become.

I stepped up to the bed and he opened his eyes. 'Lisa,' he whispered.

'Father,' I answered. Loretta brought a chair. I thanked her and asked her to leave, but asked Zalumma to stay. Then I sat down and took my father's hand; he was too weak to return my grip.

His breath came quick and shallow. 'How like your mother you look . . . but even more beautiful.' I opened my mouth to contradict him, but he frowned. 'Yes, more beautiful . . .' His gaze rolled about the room. 'Is Matteo here?'

Guilt pierced me; how could I have denied him his one joy, his grandson? 'I am sorry,' I said. 'He is sleeping.'

'Good. This is a terrible place for a child.'

I did not look at Zalumma. I kept my gaze on my father, and said, 'They have poisoned you, then.'

'Yes. It happened faster than I thought . . .' He grimaced at a spasm of pain, then gave me an apologetic look once he had recovered. 'I tried to get us out of Florence. I had a contact I thought could help us . . . They gave him more money than I did. I'm sorry. Can't even give you that . . .' All the speaking had wearied him; gasping, he closed his eyes.

'There is one thing you can give me,' I said. 'The truth.'

He opened his eyes a slit and gave me a sideways glance.

'I know you killed the elder Giuliano,' I said. Behind me, Zalumma released a sound of surprise and rage; my father began to mouth words of apology. 'I'm not asking you to explain yourself. And I know you killed Pico. I know that you did whatever Francesco told you, to keep me safe. But we are not done with secrets. You have more to tell me. About my first husband. About my only husband.'

His face contorted; he made a low, terrible noise that might have been a sob. 'Ah, daughter,' he said. 'It broke my heart to lie so cruelly.'

'It's true, then.' I wanted to rail, to give vent to my fury and joy and grief, but I could not make a sound.

'If I had told you,' he whispered, 'you would have tried to go to him. And they would have killed you. They would have killed the baby.'

I could not keep the pain from my voice. 'Why did he not come to me?'

'He did. He sent a man; Francesco killed him. He sent a letter; Francesco made me write one, saying you had died. I don't think even then he believed it; Francesco said someone had gone to the Baptistery, and found the marriage records.'

Salai. Leonardo. Perhaps Giuliano had heard of my marriage, and had it confirmed; perhaps he thought I wanted him to think me dead.

Imagine you are with Giuliano again, Leonardo said. *Imagine that you are introducing him to his child . . .*

'You want the truth . . .' Antonio whispered. 'There is one thing more. The reason I was so angry with your mother . . .'

His voice was fading; I leaned closer to hear.

'Look at your face, child. Your face. You will not see mine there. And I have looked at you a thousand times, and never seen Giuliano de' Medici's. There was another man . . .'

I dismissed the last statement as the product of delirium; I did not consider it long, for my father began to cough. Blood foamed on his lips.

Zalumma was already beside me. 'Sit him up!'

I reached beneath his arm and lifted him up and forwards; the movement caused a fountain of dark blood to spill from his mouth into his lap. Zalumma went to call for Loretta while I held my father's shoulders with one arm and his head with the other. I wanted to ask him whose face he saw in mine, but I knew there was no time.

'I love you,' I said into his ear. 'And I know you love me. God will forgive your sins.'

He heard. He groaned and tried to reach up to pat my hand.

'I will leave soon with Matteo,' I whispered. 'I will find a way to go to Giuliano, because Francesco has little use for me now. You mustn't worry about us. We will be safe, and we will always love you.'

Loretta came in with towels, then, and we cleaned him as best we could, then let him lie down. Soon after, he closed his eyes and slept.

I stayed beside my father until the hour past midnight, when I realised he had not been breathing for some time. I called Loretta and Zalumma, and then I went downstairs to the dining room, where Francesco sat drinking wine.

'Is he dead?' he asked, his indignation over my escape from the palazzo constrained.

I nodded. My eyes were dry.

'I shall pray for his soul. What did he die of, do you know?'

'Fever,' I said. 'Brought on by an ailment of the bowels.'

Francesco studied my face carefully, and seemed satisfied by what he saw there. Perhaps I was not such a bad spy after all. 'I am so sorry. Will you be staying with him?'

'Yes. Until after the funeral.'

'I need to return home. I am awaiting word on our guest's arrival, and there are still matters to take care of in regard to the Signoria.'

'Yes.' I had heard from Zalumma that Savonarola had been arrested. 'Will I see you, then, at the funeral?'

'Of course. May God give us all strength.'

'Yes,' I said. I wanted strength. I would need it, to kill Francesco.

I stayed at my father's house that night and slept in my mother's bed. Zalumma went back to Francesco's palazzo and fetched me personal items and a mourning gown and veil for the funeral. She also brought, at my request, the large emerald Francesco had given me the first night I had sullied myself with him, and some earrings of diamond and opal. Matteo remained at home, with the nursemaid.

I did not watch Loretta wash my father's body as I waited for Zalumma to return. Instead, I went to his study and found a sheet of writing parchment, and a quill and ink.

Giuliano di Lorenzo de' Medici, Rome

My love, my love,

I was lied to, told you were dead. But my heart never changed towards you.

A warning: Salvatore de' Pazzi and Francesco del Giocondo, plan to draw you and Piero here, to kill you. They are amassing an army in Florence. They want to repeat—this time, with success—Messer Iacopo de' Pazzi's plan, to rally the people in the Piazza della Signoria against the Medici.

You must not come. Give me a place, in some other city, and I will come to you. You dare not communicate it by regular correspondence, though—your letter would be confiscated and read, and I and our son endangered.

I have been separated from you because of a monstrous falsehood. I cannot tolerate the distance between us an instant longer than I must.

Your loving wife,

Lisa di Antonio Gherardini

When Zalumma arrived, I handed her the folded parchment.

'I cannot send this as correspondence,' I said. 'The Council of Eight would intercept it and have my head. I will have to bribe someone willing to hide the correspondence on his person and ride all the way to Rome with it, and see it personally delivered.' I showed her the emerald and the earrings, and handed them to her.

'You are the only one I can trust,' I told her. I had thought I could trust Leonardo; now, I could not speak his name without venom. He had knowingly kept from me the one truth that would have healed my heart.

Giuliano dead? Few people have heard this. Most believe he is still alive.

Do you not love him still?

He had been reticent at our first meeting because he thought I had married another man while my first husband still lived. He had thought me capable of complete betrayal—because he was capable of it himself.

Zalumma took the jewels and nestled them carefully in the pocket hidden in her gown. 'If it is at all possible,' she said, 'I will see it done.'

The Mass said for my father was short and sad. Francesco came and sat impatiently through the service, then left abruptly, saying there was an emergency at the Signoria. I was relieved.

Few stood at my father's graveside, only Uncle Lauro, his wife and children; Loretta, and my father's stable hand, his cook and me. Matteo remained at home with the nursemaid. As I cast the first handful of earth onto my father's coffin, I shed no tears. Perhaps fear stole them from me: Zalumma had left and not yet returned.

The time came to return to my father's home for a funeral supper. Uncle Lauro and the others tried to coax me into walking back with them to my parents' house, but I refused.

When the others left, I was alone only briefly. One of Santo Spirito's Augustinian monks approached, in his order's traditional habit. I wanted no conversation. But he came to stand directly beside me and said, softly, 'Madonna Lisa. I am so terribly sorry.'

The sound of his voice disgusted me. I turned my face away.

'I am saddened to learn of Antonio's passing.'

My voice was ragged. 'Go away and never come back again.'

In the periphery of my vision, Leonardo bowed his head. 'You are right to be angry: I could not save him, though you begged me to. But I could find no way. No way short of endangering you and Matteo. Perhaps when your grief eases, you will understand—'

'I understand that you are a liar, that you have been one from the beginning. You *knew*—' I tried to utter the words and choked; I wheeled on him. 'Giuliano is alive. And you let me live in grief, in agony, all this time. Like a good spy, you used me without heart!'

He lifted his chin; he straightened. 'I told you long ago that I could not tell you everything because it would endanger you. I have not used you. I care more for you than you know.'

'Liar! You look at me so you can moon over your dear lost Giuliano.'

He coloured at that, and had to compose himself. 'How did you learn he was alive? From the letter?'

'And from my father, before he died.'

'Does Francesco have any idea that you know Giuliano is alive?'

'No,' I said. 'I'm not that big a fool. *Why* didn't you tell me?'

'Look at you,' he said, with a coldness I had never heard in him. 'You're answering your own question. People kill and die because they cannot control their emotions. If I had told you Giuliano was alive, you would have written to him. Or you would have tried to go to Rome to find him. Nothing I might have said could have stopped you. And you, or he, or both of you, would have died as a result. If I ever told him that you married Giocondo because you thought he was dead, he'd—'

'He'd have come to me, wouldn't he? So you've lied to him, too. Why should I ever trust you now?' My face contorted; the tears that had been so long suppressed suddenly streamed unchecked down my cheeks. 'Why should I tell *you* the contents of the letter? I'm warning him myself of the danger—'

'*God,*' he whispered, his face so slack with fear that I fell silent. 'Lisa—swear to me you have not tried to contact him!'

'I'll swear nothing.' My voice was ugly. 'They mean to entice him here, and Piero, then kill them. They want to make it all repeat—rally the people against the Medici, as Messer Iacopo meant to do, and this time succeed. Do you think I am such a child that I would let Giuliano endanger himself? I told him not to come. I told him to stay away.'

'Lisa . . . They will discover this. They will kill you.'

'They won't find out. I've seen to it.'

In the distance, someone called my name. I turned, and saw Loretta in the distance, half running towards us.

'Lisa, *please.*' I had never heard such desperation in his voice. 'You cannot go back with her—they will trap you, try to kill you, or use you against Giuliano. What must I do to convince you . . .? Everything I have ever done has been for your safety, and your child's.' His eyes glittered; I realised, to my surprise, that they were filling with tears.

A brilliant performance, I told myself. 'I am going home.' And I turned my back to him and took a step towards Loretta.

'Lisa, I love you,' he said quickly.

I glanced at him over my shoulder. 'Not so much as you loved Giuliano,' I said nastily.

'More,' he said. 'More, even, than I loved your mother.'

I slowed. I stopped. I turned to look up at him.

'Giuliano de' Medici was not your father,' he said. 'I am.'

'Madonna Lisa!' Loretta called. 'Matteo is sick! He is sick, they think it is *la moria*! Claudio is here, waiting to drive you home!'

'Matteo is sick,' I said to him. He opened his mouth and reached for me, but before he could touch me, before he could speak, I lifted my skirts and ran to meet Loretta.

I rushed into the front entry of our palazzo and would have run up the stairs, but my husband called out from the dining hall.

'Lisa! Come and meet our guest!'

Francesco emerged, wearing his typical benign smile, and took my arm. 'Come,' he said, and drew me with him before I had time to protest.

A man sat at the middle of our long dining table; at the sight of me, he rose and bowed. He was a good head shorter than Francesco and twenty years younger. His short tunic, sharp goatee and accent smacked of Rome. 'Madonna Lisa, is it?'

'Sir,' I said, 'you must forgive me. My son is ill. I must go to him.'

Francesco smiled. 'There is no hurry. Come and sit with us.'

His placid expression was entirely out of place. I panicked. Had my child died, and was Francesco now going to attempt to soothe me? Was this stranger a physician, here to comfort me? 'Where is Matteo?' I demanded.

'Safe,' he said, and that single, sharp word was double-edged.

He did not try to stop me as I fled up the stairs, stumbling over my skirts, frantic. When I threw the door to the nursery open, I saw the room was empty—neatly cleaned of Matteo's things; the nursemaid's room was empty as well. There were no linens on his little bed.

I went back downstairs, a madwoman. Francesco stopped me on the second level, on the landing in front of his chambers.

'Where is he?' I demanded, seething, trembling. 'Where have you taken him?'

'We are all in the study,' he said calmly, and took my arm the instant before I reached for the knife.

I scanned the study: my baby was not there. Instead, our guest was sitting at the little round table in the centre of the room, in front of the fireplace. Two men flanked him: Claudio, and one of the soldiers who guarded our palazzo.

The soldier held a knife to Zalumma's throat.

'How can you do this?' I hissed at Francesco.

He made a soft sound of disgust. 'I have eyes. Matteo is like his mother: of questionable heritage.' My cold Francesco.

He guided me to a chair across from our guest; I sank into it, my gaze fastened on Zalumma. Her face was stony, her stance unrepentant. I looked down. On the table in front of me was the letter to Giuliano, unfolded and open so that it could be easily read. Beside it rested a quill and inkpot, and a fresh piece of parchment.

Francesco stood beside me and rested his hand on my shoulder. 'There is a problem with this letter. It needs to be rewritten.'

I baulked. I looked at Zalumma's eyes: they were unfathomable black mirrors. Our esteemed guest nodded faintly at the soldier, and he pressed the tip of the knife against her white throat until she gasped. A dark trickle escaped the flesh there and collected in the hollow at the base of her neck. She looked away; she did not want me to see her face and how frightened she was, to see that she knew she was going to die.

'*Don't*,' I said. 'I will write whatever you want.' I sized up the soldiers, Claudio and the goateed man, all on the other side of the table. I glanced at Francesco, standing beside me. If I reached for the stiletto hidden in my belt, I would be stopped before I ever got round the table, and Zalumma would be killed.

Francesco made a gracious gesture to the goateed man. 'Ser Salvatore,' he said. 'Please.'

Salvatore put his elbows on the table and leaned forward on them, towards me. 'Copy the first two lines,' he said. 'The letter must sound as if you wrote it.'

I dipped the quill in the inkpot and scratched out the words:

My love, my love,
> *I was lied to, told you were dead. But my heart never changed towards you.*

'Very good,' Salvatore said, then dictated the next lines.

> *Your son and I are in mortal danger; we are captured by your enemies. If you and your brother Piero do not appear at Santa Maria del Fiore for High Mass on the 24th of May, they will kill us. Send troops, send anyone else in your place, and we will die.*
> *Your loving wife,*
> *Lisa di Antonio Gherardini*

Francesco folded the letter and handed it to Claudio, who pocketed it. 'Now,' Francesco said, turning to me, 'let's talk about your spying.'

'I was curious,' I said. 'I read just the one letter . . .'

'Curious. That's not what Isabella says. She says that you leave a book on your night table as a signal, for her to tell a certain Salai that you will be going to pray the next day.'

Salvatore spoke, in a tone that was casual, almost friendly. 'Who do you meet, Lisa?'

'Just Salai,' I answered quickly.

'She's lying.' Francesco's tone was brutal.

Salvatore was very, very still. 'I think your husband is right, Madonna Lisa. And I think that he is right when he says that you are very fond of your slave. She was your mother's, yes?'

I stared down at the table. 'I go to meet a spy,' I said. 'An older man, with grey hair. I don't know his name. I found Salai in your study one night, with the letter, and I was curious. I read it.'

'How long ago?' Salvatore asked.

'I don't know—a year, perhaps two. He said he worked for the Medici. I decided to do what he told me—to go to Santissima Annunziata, and tell the old man about the letters.'

Salvatore glanced back at the soldier who held Zalumma—glanced, and lifted a finger.

I followed his gaze. The soldier's knife made a quick, small movement beneath Zalumma's jaw. Quick and simple; I heard the sound of fluid spilling. She would have fallen straight down but he caught and lowered her. She went to the floor languid and graceful as a swan.

'Call a servant,' Salvatore told the soldier, 'to clean this up.'

I screamed and reared up; Francesco pushed me straight back down.

Salvatore faced me. 'You are lying, Madonna Lisa. You know the old man's name.'

I sobbed, unable to speak. Zalumma was dead and I wanted to die.

Francesco had to speak very loudly to be heard over my weeping. 'Come, now, Lisa, shall I send for little Matteo? We can bring him in here as well. Or will you tell us the name of your old man?'

'Bring him,' I gasped. 'Bring him, and show me he is alive.'

Salvatore nodded to Francesco to leave the room. He returned moments later, followed by the frightened nursemaid, leading Matteo by the hand. He laughed and wanted to come to me; he held out his arms for me. But when he saw Zalumma on the floor and his mother sobbing, he began to cry himself. I reached for him as Francesco lifted him up and handed him back to the nursemaid.

'All right,' Francesco said, and closed the door after them.

He and Salvatore turned to me. 'The name, Lisa,' Francesco said.

I bowed my head and looked down at my hands, and said very softly, 'Leonardo da Vinci.'

XIV

FOR THE NEXT FEW WEEKS, I was confined to my chamber. Different men stood guard in the corridor outside my door. Francesco told the servants that I had been discovered spying for the Medici, and that the Signoria had not yet decided whether to bring charges.

On the first day they locked me in my room, I was alone for an hour and despite crippling grief, I realised that I should hide Zalumma's knife. I slid it deep into the feather layer of my mattress, on the far side by the wall; and when, that night, Elena came with a tray of food and the intention of unlacing my gown, I faced her without concern.

'I want to wash Zalumma's body. She was very dear to me. And'—my voice began to break—'I want to see her properly buried. Please . . . if you would ask Francesco?'

Saddened, she bowed her head. 'I will ask him, Madonna. He has no heart and will refuse, but I will ask.'

I sat in a chair in front of the cold hearth, closed my eyes. 'And Matteo,' I said, anguished. 'If I could know whether—'

'Your child is well. They haven't hurt him. They are keeping him near the servants.'

The ache in my chest eased. Emboldened, I asked, 'And Isabella?'

'Gone. Escaped—' She broke off and said no more, realising that she might be endangering herself.

She unlaced my gown and put it in the closet, and I was left alone.

Francesco, of course, would not hear of my assisting with Zalumma's burial or attending the service; he let the disposition of her corpse remain a cruel mystery.

Until my father and Zalumma died, until Matteo was taken from me, I had not realised how thoroughly hatred could usurp a heart. As my father Antonio had been at the thought of losing his wife to another, I was consumed. I dreamt of murder; I knew I could never rest until I saw Zalumma's dagger buried in Francesco's chest, up to the hilt.

Your temper is hot, the astrologer had said, *a furnace in which the sword of justice must be forged.*

I cared nothing for justice. I wanted revenge.

You are caught in a cycle of violence, of blood and deceit. What others have begun, you must finish.

What was to repeat? How was I meant to finish it?

I recalled, as best I could, what my mother had told me of Giuliano's death; I contemplated each separate step.

In the Duomo, the priest had lifted the wine-filled chalice, offering it to God for blessing; this had been the signal for the assassins to strike.

In the adjacent campanile, the bells had begun to chime; this had been the signal for Messer Iacopo to ride to the Piazza della Signoria, where he would proclaim the end of the Medici's reign, and be joined by mercenary soldiers who would help him seize the Palazzo della Signoria—in effect, the government.

Messer Iacopo's plan was foiled because his hired soldiers had failed to join him, and because of the people's loyalty to the Medici.

In the Duomo, however, the plan was partially successful.

In the instant before the signal was given, my father Antonio struck, wounding Giuliano in the back. Baroncelli's blow followed; third came Francesco de' Pazzi's frenzied, brutal attack. But Lorenzo—on the other side of the church—proved too swift for his aspiring assassins. He suffered only a minor wound, and fought off his attackers until he was able to escape to the north sacristy.

If Piero and Giuliano came, they would play the role of the two brothers. And I had no doubt that Francesco and Ser Salvatore would ensure that there were numerous assassins waiting for them in the cathedral. Salvatore clearly dreamt of re-enacting Messer Iacopo's role, and riding, this time victorious, into the Piazza della Signoria, to tell the crowd that he had just rescued Florence from the Medici.

But what was my role to be? I would not sit passively and wait to be killed; I knew my life was forfeit regardless of the plan's outcome. And so was my son's, unless I took measures to prevent it.

And then I realised: I would be the penitent, the one fuelled by personal, not political rage. The one to strike the first blow.

I thought often of Leonardo. My tears in those days sprang from many wells; guilt over my betrayal of him was one of them. I hoped Isabella had warned Salai and his master. I could only pray that he had left Santissima Annunziata long before Salvatore's men arrived.

I thought of his last words to me. *Giuliano de' Medici was not your father. I am.*

Lisa, I love you, he had said. His tone had reminded me of someone else's, someone who had spoken long ago, but it was not until I pondered for some time that I remembered whose it was.

Lorenzo de' Medici had lain dying, and I had asked him why he had been so kind to me. *I love you, child.*

Had he believed himself to be my uncle? Or had Leonardo told him the truth?

I lifted my hand mirror and peered into it. I had lied to Leonardo when I once said that I did not often look at my reflection. When I had learned of my mother's affair with Giuliano, I had diligently searched my face for hints of the smiling young man who had posed for Leonardo's terracotta bust. And I had never seen him there.

Now, as I looked into the mirror, Leonardo gazed back at me, haggard and owlish.

I woke late on the 23rd of May, the day before Giuliano was to meet me in the Duomo. I had slept poorly the night before, woken by the muffled sounds of Matteo wailing downstairs; I cried, too, until well after dawn, then fell into a heavy, sodden sleep.

When I rose, I went out to my balcony. The sky was exceptionally blue and cloudless, save for a long finger of dark smoke rising up in the east.

I stared at it, entranced, until Elena entered. I went back into the room just as she set a tray of bread and fruit on the table. She glanced up as she straightened, her expression grave. 'You saw the smoke, then.'

'Yes,' I said slowly, still dazed from sleep. 'Is it—?'

'Savonarola,' she said.

'They burned him, then.' I had heard no news for the past few weeks, since learning Savonarola had been arrested. But I had known at once, when I saw the smoke.

'Hung him first,' she replied unhappily. 'In the piazza, then they lit the fire. Some fool had put firecrackers in the tinder, terrifying everyone at first. They put chains round the monks, so that when the nooses burned away the bodies wouldn't drop into the fire, but would roast slowly. The Signoria wanted a spectacle.'

'Yes,' I said. 'Yes, of course.' I looked at Elena. 'You said "the monks". He wasn't the only one executed?'

'No. Fra Domenico chose to die with him.'

The next morning, when Elena came to dress me, she carried a small velvet purse. When she opened it on the table, out spilled the sapphire necklace and the diamond-studded headdress I had worn the day I married Francesco.

Elena went to my wardrobe and brought out the vivid blue velvet wedding gown and my finest chemise. 'Ser Francesco says you are to look especially lovely today.' So; I was to be a fine lure.

I said nothing as she laced me into the gown; this time, I wore the brocade belt low, so that I could reach it with a swift move of my hand.

I was silent, too, as Elena brushed my hair. When she was finished and I was ready, she moved to open the door.

'Stop,' I said. 'I need a moment alone, to compose myself.'

Reluctantly, she faced me. 'I am not to leave you alone, Madonna.'

'Then don't leave me alone,' I said swiftly. 'I left my shawl out on the balcony. Would you fetch it for me, please?'

She knew. She gave a little sigh and nodded, yielding, and walked slowly to the balcony, keeping her back to me the entire while.

I moved faster than I had ever thought I could. I pulled Zalumma's dagger from the feather mattress and slipped it into my belt.

Elena returned slowly from the balcony. 'Your shawl is not there.'

'Thank you for looking,' I said.

The soldier who had killed Zalumma led me to the carriage, where Francesco and Salvatore de' Pazzi sat waiting. Francesco was dressed in his best prior's gown; for the first time since I had known him, he wore a long knife on his belt. Salvatore wore an elegant muted green tunic. He, too, was armed, with a fine sword at his hip.

'Beautiful, beautiful,' Salvatore murmured at the sight of me.

'She makes a pretty picture, doesn't she?' Francesco remarked.

'Indeed.' Salvatore graced us with a haughty smile.

It was a warm day—too warm for a heavy velvet gown—yet I felt cold. The air still carried a hint of smoke from the previous day's fire.

In the Piazza del Duomo, the crowds were few; I suspected they were even more sparse at San Marco that morning. Flanked by Francesco and Salvatore, and followed by my soldier, I walked past the octagonal Baptistery of St John, where I had been married and my son baptised. Francesco took my arm and steered me straight ahead.

The Duomo's interior was dim and cool. As I passed over its threshold, the edges of the present blurred and melted, like shadows, into the past. I could not judge where one ended and the other began.

We moved together down a side aisle: Salvatore on my far left, Francesco to my immediate left. On my right was the murderous young soldier. Our pace was brisk; I tried to see past my false husband, past Salvatore. I searched desperately for a beloved face—praying that I would see it, and that I would not.

But I saw little as we swept relentlessly towards the altar. I gleaned only impressions: a sanctuary less than a third full. Beggars, black-wimpled nuns, merchants; a pair of monks hushing a group of restless urchins of varying ages. As we walked past other nobles to take our place—second row from the altar, on the side by the wooden choir—Francesco smiled and nodded to acquaintances.

At last we came to rest beneath the massive cupola. I stood between my husband and the soldier, and turned my head to my right at the sight of bodies moving towards us.

Matteo. Matteo walking on strong little legs, clinging to the hand of his nursemaid. Stubborn boy; he would not let her carry him. As he neared, I let go a soft cry. Francesco gripped my arm, but with the other, I reached out to my son. He saw me, and with a shattering smile, he called to me, and I to him.

The nursemaid seized him, pulled him off his feet and carried him until she stood beside the soldier, our barrier. Matteo writhed, trying to worm his way to me, but she held him fast, and the soldier took a slight step forward so that I could not touch my child. I strained to see him, but failed, and turned away, anguished.

'We thought it best,' Francesco said softly, 'for a mother to be able to see her son, so that she is always reminded to act in his best interest.'

I had come to the Duomo with one aim: to kill Francesco before the signal was given. Now I faltered. How could I save my child *and* still see my tormentor dead? I had only one blow. If I struck at the soldier, Francesco would surely strike at me—and Salvatore de' Pazzi was within sword's reach of Giuliano's heir.

Your child is already dead, I told myself, *just as you are.* We had no salvation; I had only one chance—not for rescue, but revenge.

I put my hand—the one that had reached for Matteo—lightly on my waist, where the dagger lay hidden. And I marvelled that I was willing to abandon my son in the interest of hate; how like my father Antonio I had become. But he had only faced one loss, I had suffered many.

Mass began. The priest and acolytes processed to the altar crowned with a carving of Christ upon the cross. The swinging thurible bled frankincense-laden smoke into the shadowy dimness, and the choir sang the *Introit* and *Kyrie*. Behind us, a scattering of giggling orphans pushed their way towards the front of the church, mixing with the offended nobility. One of the monks followed, hissing reprimands. The smell of filthy children wafted our way; Francesco lifted a kerchief to his nose.

As the priest's assistant chanted the Epistle, I detected motion in the periphery of my vision. Someone dark and cowled had sidled through the assembly to stand behind me. I knew that he had come for me.

He will not strike yet, I told myself, though the urge to reach for my weapon was strong. *He will not kill me until the signal.*

The choir sang the *Gradual*.

Far to my left, a ripple passed through the row of priors and nobles and flowed to Salvatore de' Pazzi. He turned to my husband and whispered. I strained to hear him. '. . . have spotted Piero. But not . . .'

Francesco recoiled and unintentionally strained his neck, peering to his left at the crowd. 'Where is Giuliano?'

I tensed, agonisingly aware of the assassin at my back, at the soldier standing beside my child. If Giuliano had failed to come, they might kill us immediately.

I did not hear the Gospel. I heard the priest droning during the sermon but could not interpret his words. The fingers of my right hand hovered at the edge of my belt.

Salvatore murmured to Francesco and gestured with his chin at a distant point to his left. 'He is here . . .'

He is here.

Here, somewhere near me, beyond my sight or voice, I did not cry at the knowledge, but I swayed beneath its weight.

The priest chanted the *Oremus*, took the Host and lifted it towards the crucified Christ in offering. *Offerimus tibi Domine . . .*

Salvatore rested his hand upon the hilt of his sword and leaned towards Francesco. His lips formed a word: *Soon.*

As he did so, my assassin leaned in instantly, smoothly, stepping upon my train so that I could not bolt, and pressed his lips to my ear.

'Monna Lisa,' he whispered. Had he not uttered those two words, I would have taken up the dagger. 'When I signal, fall.'

I could not breathe. I parted my lips and took in air through my mouth, and watched as the priest's assistant moved to the altar and began to fill the chalice with wine. Francesco's hand hovered at his hip.

The second assistant stepped forward with a decanter of water.

'*Now*,' Salai whispered, and pressed something hard and blunt against my back, beneath the ribs, to make it appear as though he were delivering a fatal thrust.

Wordless, I sank to the cool marble.

Beside me, Francesco cried out and dropped to his knees just as he drew his knife; it clattered beside him on the floor. I pushed myself up to sit. Salai's army of street urchins streamed forward, surrounding the soldier. One knifed him in the back and pulled him down so that a second could slash his throat.

The world erupted. I clawed my way to my feet, screaming Matteo's name, cursing my tangled skirts. The orphans had swarmed him and his nursemaid, too; I pulled Zalumma's knife free and lurched towards them. My son was nestled in the arms of a monk.

'Lisa!' the monk cried. 'Lisa, come with us.'

The bells in the campanile began to ring. 'Leonardo, take him!' I shouted. 'I will follow, I will follow—only *go!*'

He turned reluctantly and ran. I held my ground despite the fleeing crowd, and turned back to Francesco.

He had fallen onto his side and hip; Salai had wounded him, and kicked his knife away. He was helpless.

'Lisa,' he said. His eyes were feral, terrified. 'What good will it serve?'

What good, indeed? I crouched down and approached him with the dagger raised overhand—the wrong way. Salai would not have approved. But I wanted to bring it down the way Francesco de' Pazzi had brought his weapon down on Lorenzo's brother.

'You aren't my husband,' I said bitterly. 'You never were. For the sake of my true husband, I will kill you.' I leaned down.

And he struck first. With a small blade, hidden in his fist. It bit into my flesh just beneath my left ear and would have sliced quickly to my right. But before it reached centre I pulled away, astonished.

'Bitch,' he croaked. 'Did you think I would let you ruin it all?' He sagged to the floor, still alive, and glared at me with hatred.

I put a hand to my throat and drew it away. It was the colour of garnet—a dark necklace, Francesco's final gift.

I heard a roaring in my ears like the sound of the tide. I did not worry for Matteo. I knew he was safe in his grandfather's arms. I did not worry about Francesco or my hatred of him. I would let God and the authorities deal with him; it was not my place. I knew my place now.

Dear God, I prayed. *Let me rescue Giuliano.*

Through a miracle, I rose. I moved in the direction Salvatore de' Pazzi had gone, I went in search of my beloved. The stiletto was heavy, and my hand trembled with the effort to hold it.

I heard his voice.

Lisa! Lisa, where are you?

Husband, I am coming. I opened my mouth to cry out, but my voice was no more than an anguished wheeze. I felt as if I were drowning. The waters inside the cathedral were murky; I could scarcely see the wavering images of fighters against the dizzying backdrop of innocents in flight. I could make no sense of it.

Sunlight streamed in from the open door leading to the Via de' Servi, and in its shaft, I saw him. He wore a monk's robes. His cowl was thrown back, revealing his dark curling hair, and a beard I had never seen. In his hand he carried a long sword, the point tilted towards the ground as he rushed forward. He was entirely a man; in my absence, he had aged. He looked amazing, and beautiful, and gave me back my heart.

But I was no longer there to surrender to emotion: I was there to redeem the transgressions of others. And then I saw him, Salvatore, Francesco de' Pazzi's son, moving towards Giuliano.

But Giuliano did not see him. Giuliano only saw me. His eyes were lights from a distant shore; his face a beacon. He mouthed my name.

I yearned to go to him, but I could not make the mistakes Anna Lucrezia, Leonardo, the elder Giuliano, made. I could not yield to my passion. I forced my gaze from Giuliano's face and kept it fastened on Salvatore. It was impossible to walk, yet I staggered behind him. God granted a miracle: I did not fall. I did not faint, or die. I half ran.

As I neared both men, Giuliano's joyous brilliance faded to concern, then alarm. He could now see the blood spilling from my throat, soaking my bodice. He did not see Salvatore approaching from the side; only me, following. He did not see Salvatore, only an arm's length away, raising his sword, ready to kill Lorenzo's most loved son.

But I saw. And in the instant that Salvatore raised his blade, in the instant before he brought it down upon Giuliano, I reached farther than was possible. With the dagger, I found the soft spot beneath Salvatore's ribs and buried it there.

I remembered the painting of Bernardo Baroncelli on the wall of the Bargello. And I whispered, 'Here, traitor.'

EPILOGUE: LISA

July 1498

XV

I DID NOT DIE, nor did Francesco. The blow I dealt Salvatore de' Pazzi downed him, and, as he lay bleeding, he was killed by another.

His mercenaries, who rode into the Piazza della Signoria at the chiming of the bells, were met by formidable opposition. Upon encountering Piero's men—and upon realising that Salvatore would not arrive to incite the crowd against the Medici, and lead the storming of the palazzo and the overthrow of the Signoria—the mercenaries disbanded and fled.

Messer Iacopo never was avenged.

It was not time, my husband explained, for the Medici to return to power in Florence; there was insufficient support in the Signoria. Piero had learned the wisdom of patience. But the time will come.

I have learned, to my amusement, that Francesco has told everyone in Florence that I am still his wife, that I have merely gone to stay in the country with my child because of nerves caused by the fright I experienced in the Duomo. He used his wits and connections to escape the noose, but he is disgraced. He will never serve in the government again.

At last, I am in Rome with Giuliano and Matteo. It is hotter here, with fewer clouds and less rain. Mists and fog are less common than in Florence; the sun reveals everything in sharp, crisp relief.

Leonardo has come to visit us now that I have regained some of my strength. I am sitting for him again—despite the bandage on my neck—and I am beginning to think he will never be satisfied with the painting. He alters it constantly, saying that my reunion with Giuliano will be reflected in my expression. He promises that he will not stay in Milan for ever; when he fulfils his obligations to the Duke, he will come to Rome, with Giuliano as his patron.

Shortly after Leonardo's arrival, when I first sat for him in Giuliano's Roman palazzo, I asked him about my mother. He had told me that I was his child and I knew it was true. Because I had always looked for another man's face in my reflection, I had never seen his. Yet I looked on his features every time I smiled down at my image on the panel.

He had indeed been smitten with Giuliano—until, through Lorenzo, he met Anna Lucrezia. He never expressed his feelings to her because he had sworn never to take a wife, lest it interfere with his art or his studies. But the emotion became quite uncontrollable, and when he first realised my mother and Giuliano were lovers—that evening on the shadowy Via de' Gori, when he had first yearned to paint her—he was overtaken by jealousy. He could, he confessed, have killed Giuliano himself at that moment.

And the following morning in the Duomo, that jealousy had distracted him from reading the tragedy about to occur.

That was why he had never told anyone about his discovery. Shortly after coming to Santissima Annunziata as the Medici's agent, he had realised that my father was the penitent in the Duomo. How could he arrest a man, for yielding to jealousy when he himself had been so tormented by it? It had made no sense; nor did it make sense to pain me unnecessarily with such news.

When the murder occurred, Leonardo had been devastated. And on the day of Giuliano's funeral he had gone out to the churchyard to silently vent his sorrow. There, he found my weeping mother and confessed his guilt and his love to her. Shared grief bound them together, and beneath its sway they lost themselves.

'And see what misery my passion caused for your mother, and for you,' he said. 'I could not let you make the same error. I would not risk telling you Giuliano was alive, for fear you would try to contact him and endanger him and yourself.'

'Why didn't you tell me this, from the beginning?' I pressed gently. 'Why did you let me think I was Giuliano's child?'

'Because I wanted you to have full rights as a Medici; they could care far better for you than a poor artist. It harmed no one and gave Lorenzo joy on his deathbed.' His expression grew sadly tender. 'Most of all, I did not want to tarnish the memory of your mother. She was a woman of great virtue. She confessed to me that, in all the time she was with Giuliano, she would not bed him—though all the world believed she had. Such was her loyalty to her husband; and so her shame, when she lay with me, was all the greater.

'Why should I confess that she and I—a sodomite, no less—were lovers, and risk damaging the respect due her?'

'I respect her no less,' I said. 'I love you both.'

He smiled brilliantly.

I will send the portrait back to Milan with Leonardo when he leaves. And when he finishes it—if he ever does—neither I nor Giuliano will accept it. I want him to keep it.

For he has only Salai. But if he takes the painting, my mother and I will always be with him.

I, on the other hand, have Giuliano and Matteo. And each time I gaze into the looking-glass, I will see my mother and father.

And I will smile.

Jeanne Kalogridis

Could you tell me a little bit about yourself?

OK, here are the bare facts. I was born in Florida on December 17, 1954, and I've been interested in books ever since. My interest in language led me to earn a BA in Russian in 1976, although my major was Microbiology until my senior year. This was soon followed by a two-year stint as a legal secretary. The good part about that was, I learned how to type, which comes in useful these days. Then I wound up in grad school, and earned an MA in Linguistics from the University of South Florida, after which I taught English as a second language.

Where do you live now?

I live in a beautiful little town in southern California, far away from freeways and crowds. We have gorgeous mountains here, and most days the dogs and I manage to go hiking and enjoy the views.

What sort of writing regime do you have and where do you write?

I get up at five a.m. and, while I'm sitting in bed with my first two cups of tea, I begin writing by hand. After two hours, it's time for a break—a nice long walk. After I get back, the dogs and I move into my office. I find it impossible to work without at least one labrador retriever in the room.

Did you live in Florence while researching Painting Mona Lisa_?_

Ahhh, I only wish I could have! My research is limited to books and the Internet. The lovely thing about the Internet is that I can stop what I'm writing and say, 'What did this minor historical character that I need for this scene look like?' I Google the name, and boom! There's a face to go with the name. The Internet spoils me—and helps enormously with accuracy.

The Medici family were lavish patrons of art. Was this why they feature at the heart of the novel?

I knew very little about the Medici when I began writing *Painting Mona Lisa*—I think I write historicals so that I can remedy my gross ignorance about world history. When I was researching them, I came across the compelling murder of young Giuliano de' Medici in Florence's famous cathedral. The event fascinated me; I knew it had to be featured centrally in the novel. The fact that they were great patrons of art was icing on the cake.

Do you think you might have enjoyed the life of an aristocrat in fifteenth-century Florence?

Not in the least! I'm addicted to modern plumbing and health care—and I like no more than one extra person (my husband) and two dogs in my bed, thank you. In the Renaissance, they used to pile them in—four, five people to a bed. And those corsets . . . no way!

How long did it take you to write Painting Mona Lisa?

The novel took about eighteen months to write. It was delayed because my husband (who's now fine) was undergoing chemotherapy for cancer, and I was his sole carer. I usually produce a novel in a year.

What fascinated you primarily: Leonardo da Vinci or the 'Mona Lisa' painting?

Ooh, a tough chicken-and-egg question. It started with wondering about the living, breathing woman behind the portrait. And I challenge anyone in the world not to be fascinated by Leonardo; what an amazing human being.

Is there one piece of art you would love to own?

This one's easy. Leonardo did a sketch, in silverpoint, called 'head of a girl'. It's a three-quarter profile of a young woman peering over her shoulder. She looks like an angel, and she looks so lifelike that I half expect her to speak.

If you could put one question to Leonardo da Vinci, what would it be?

'Why didn't you finish all those works?'

What are your hobbies when not writing?

My hobbies are hand quilting and dog training. Can I brag here about my chocolate labrador, Hershey, and mention that he's trained to fetch the newspaper and carry the mail? I can even trust him to carry a bag of scones.

What do you enjoy most about being an author?

Hmm. The day I finish a book—the very hour, in fact, when I realise it's done. I like to print out the manuscript and pat the nice big fat pile of pages, so I can feel like I've accomplished something. But I have to say that the solitude can be dreadful; I just know I'm going to become one of those weird little old ladies who chatters to her dogs all day long.

Jane Eastgate

Catherine Alliott

Ever since she got married, Imogen has been jealous of wealthy Eleanor Latimer, an old family friend with whom her husband, Alex, once had an affair.

So when a financial crisis forces her and Alex to leave London and rent Shepherd's Cottage on the Latimer estate, Imogen is far from happy. Throw into the mix a bunch of psychotic chickens, unruly cows and an infuriatingly bossy vet and the result is bound to be explosive.

Chapter One

BY THE TIME the suicide victim had been cleared from the Piccadilly Line, I was, inevitably and irrevocably, half an hour late. As the train lurched out of the tunnel I glanced feverishly at my watch. Half past one! I went hot. I mean, naturally my heart went out to the deceased man—or woman even—but why did the severely depressed have to pick my line—for the second time this year? It was almost as if they saw me coming. Saw me putting on my good suede jacket for a foray into the West End and thought, Yikes, if *she's* getting out and about, if *she's* having a good time, that's it. I'm out of here. I'm toast. And hurled themselves into the path of an oncoming train.

Which is an extremely selfish and uncharitable reaction to a truly tragic event, Imogen Cameron, I told myself severely as I got off at the next stop and hurried up the escalator. Sorry, God.

I raced out of the tube entrance and down Piccadilly in the direction of Albemarle Street. Late, for my first meeting with anyone who'd ever shown even the remotest interest in my work: a gallery owner, no less, who'd offered to buy me lunch, discuss terms, but who—I glanced at my watch again—had probably got bored of waiting.

I'd met him at Kate's last week, at a seriously smart drinks party surrounded by her fearfully social friends. There'd been buckets of pink champagne sloshing around, and since Alex and I were on an economy drive and only knocked back the cheapest plonk these days, I'd got stuck in. By the time Kate sashayed up with the gallery owner, introducing me as 'my artist friend across the street who does the most *fabulous* paintings', I was practically seeing double. She'd then proceeded to lure him into her study—simultaneously tugging me along with her—to admire a rather hectic oil she had hanging above her desk.

'Yes . . .' He'd peered closely, then flicked back his floppy chestnut waves and nodded contemplatively. 'Yes, it's charming. It has a certain naive simplicity—'or was it a simple naiveté?—'that one doesn't always come across these days, but which, personally, I embrace.'

He'd turned from the picture to look me up and down in a practised manner, taking in my wild blonde hair and flushed cheeks. I was delighted to hear he embraced simplicity as there was plenty more where that came from, and I beamed back drunkenly.

'Tell me, do you exhibit a lot?'

I didn't, not ever. Well, not unless you counted that time in a pub in Parsons Green where me and three other painter friends had paid for the upstairs room ourselves and only our mothers had turned up. I was about to tell him as much when Kate chipped in, 'Yes, quite a lot, don't you, Imo? But not so much recently. Not since that carping critic in *The Times* burbled on about the possibility of overexposure.'

I regarded her in abject amazement. That she could *tell* such flagrant lies, standing there in her Chanel dress, but then Kate hadn't been named Most Promising Newcomer at the Chelsea Players Theatre, her very up-market am-dram group, for nothing.

'Yes, well, critics are a loathsome bunch,' he growled. 'Don't know talent when it hits them in the face. I should know,' he added bitterly. He drew himself up importantly. 'Casper Villiers,' he purred, pressing a card into my hand. 'Let's do lunch. I'm planning a mixed media exhibition in the summer, and I need an abstract artist. Say Tuesday, one o'clock at the Markham? Bring your portfolio.'

And off he sauntered. I hadn't liked to tell him that the 'abstract' art before him was in fact an extremely figurative hay cart in an extremely figurative barley field and that I didn't even possess a portfolio, I'd just felt my knees buckle.

'Seriously influential,' Kate hissed in my ear. 'Knows literally everyone in the art world and can pull all sorts of strings. Rather cute too.'

'Very!' I gasped back as, at that moment, my husband sauntered up.

'Pulled?' Alex enquired.

'Hope so,' I gushed back happily. 'He's a gallery owner, in Cork Street. He wants to look at my portfolio.'

'Terrific!' He had the good grace not to question the existence of that particular work of fiction. 'About time too. I was wondering when my artist wife was going to be discovered and I could plump for early retirement. I'm looking forward to adopting Kept Man status.'

I laughed, but could tell he was pleased, which thrilled me. Recently I'd started to get rather despondent about my so-called work and its lack of remuneration, and wondered if I shouldn't retrain as an illustrator or something. Something to get a few much-needed pennies into the Cameron coffers, something to make me feel like a useful working mother now Rufus was at school full time. It had begun to seem grossly self-indulgent to shut myself away in the attic with my oils. Casper Villiers's invitation, then, was the lifeline I needed.

I'd spent the whole of last week feverishly photographing my paintings and arranging the prints in a leather portfolio, which I now clasped in my hot little hand, along with a couple of small oils, which I was sure he'd like, in a carrier bag. If only he was still there! Here we are, the Markham. I gave a cursory glance to the rather grand pillars that heralded the entrance and hastened on in, emerging into a sort of panelled lobby. Luckily there was a girl behind a desk directing traffic. 'I'm meeting a Mr Villiers,' I breathed, peering anxiously through the door to the restaurant. 'But I'm terribly late and he might well have— oh! Oh no, he hasn't, there he is.' And I was off.

'I *do* apologise—' I began breathlessly as he got up to greet me, looking much younger than I remembered and much better-looking.

'Couldn't matter less,' he interrupted smoothly. 'I was late myself. Drink?' He gestured to a bottle in an ice bucket. 'I took the liberty of ordering some champagne, but if you'd prefer something else?'

'Oh! No, how marvellous.'

I sat down and reached for my glass eagerly, taking a greedy sip. Steady, Imogen. Take it easy. But champagne was a good sign surely? You didn't expend that sort of outlay unless you were interested?

I was horribly nervous, I realised. 'Obviously I've brought along my Portaloo.' I glanced down at it, propped up by my chair. No . . .

'Portfolio?'

'That's it.' I flushed. *Shit.*

'Only I'm pretty sure this place is fully equipped on the sanitary front,' he laughed.

'Yes, bound to be, ha-*ha*! Oh, and plus, I've brought along a couple of small oils, but I don't know if you want to eat first or . . .?'

'Oh, eat first, definitely. Plenty of time for all that.' He grinned, and twinkled at me as he flicked out his napkin.

Ah, right. A bit of chatting and flirting were in order first. Well, fine, I could do that. I managed to twinkle back, then, taking the quickest route to any man's heart, asked him all about himself.

Casper rolled over like a dream: he leaned back in his chair and launched expansively into 'My Glittering yet Thwarted Career', while I leaned in, eyes wide, murmuring, 'Really?' or, 'Gosh, how marvellous,' then later, 'How dreadful!' when we got to the thwarted bit. It transpired that Casper had been the most promising student at St Martin's but his ideas had been cruelly stolen by jealous, inferior rivals. He'd reluctantly given up his dream of becoming an artist and opened a gallery instead, and he now enjoyed great acclaim as a talent spotter.

'Benji Riley-Smith, Peter De Cazzolet—you name them, I've discovered them,' he murmured.

'Really?' I hadn't heard of either of them and tried to sneak a look at my watch under the table. I had to pick Rufus up from school at three thirty and Casper still hadn't looked at my work.

'So. You're a friend of Kate's,' he said, suddenly. 'She's kept you quiet.'

'Has she? Oh, well, I haven't known her that long. Only since she moved to Putney a few years ago. We've been there a while.'

'We?'

'My husband and I. And my son, Rufus. He's nine.'

'Ah.' I could feel his attention wandering.

'How do you know them?' Nice one. Back to him.

'Oh, Kate knows everyone,' he said airily. To an extent, this was true. Or to be more precise, everyone knew Kate.

Married to an eminent surgeon and with her very own designer label and boutique in the Fulham Road, Kate was one who attracted others. If I hadn't liked her so much I'd have envied her horribly—beautiful, fun, but kind too, and terribly self-effacing. I'd heard about her long before I'd met her. 'Oh, you *must* know the Barringtons,' people said when Kate and Sebastian moved to Hastoe Avenue. 'They live across the road from you. Everyone knows Kate.' Well, I certainly knew their house. Huge, red brick and imposing and on the right side of the Avenue (south-facing gardens and off-street parking), it was as hard to miss as our modest little semi opposite (north-facing pocket handkerchiefs and parking in the street if you were lucky) was easy to. And I knew the girl they meant too. Had seen her sailing off to work, blonde hair flying, and then returning from the school run later, hordes of gorgeous blonde children in the back of a gleaming four-wheel drive. I'd seen her in the evening too, going out to dinner, swathed in cashmere, but I hadn't met her, and might not have done either, had she not knocked on my door one Monday morning looking wild-eyed and desperate.

'Have you got a hacksaw?' she'd blurted urgently. 'Orlando's got his head stuck in the banisters, and I remember seeing you sawing up some boards in your front garden.'

'Oh!' My painting boards. Cheaper than canvas, but sometimes too big and unwieldy to fit in my easel, so requiring surgery. 'Hang on!'

I ran up two flights of stairs and seized it from my studio, then together, we'd dashed across the road.

The Barringtons' hall was about the size of a hockey pitch and had a grand sweeping staircase, up which marched hundreds of very expensive-looking balusters. Orlando's face was going a nasty shade of purple between the top two so I hastened up with my saw and hacked away close to his left ear with Kate shouting, 'It's either that or his neck!' Orlando emerged unscathed, but causing wilful damage to a listed house left me in serious need of a sharpener. Since it was only ten in the morning Kate had produced a box of Lindor chocolates and we'd bonded.

Yes, everyone liked Kate, and it seemed my young gallery owner was no exception. He'd long been an admirer, meeting her first at St Martin's where she'd designed shirts and he'd painted landscapes and . . . oh, he still painted landscapes, did he? . . . Really? . . . still dabbled in oils, and—oh Lord, we were back to him again. I really *did* have to collect Rufus soon. Oh, *please*, perhaps over a coffee, could we look at my work? Find out when this wretched exhibition was?

'So . . . coffee?'

I beamed. Finally. 'Please!'

'And shall we take it upstairs? Where it's more comfortable?'

Oh, even better. Clearly there was a lounge or something where we could spread the pictures out. 'Good idea.' I was on my feet.

In retrospect I suppose I did notice a flicker of surprise pass over his eyes, but he soon recovered. I let him guide me, his hand perhaps a touch too solicitous on my back, through the restaurant and back to the front desk. He was talking nineteen to the dozen now, rather nervously in fact, about the new Turner Whistler exhibition. I smiled and nodded indulgently at his prattle, although I did pause to wonder why we were getting in a lift. Up it glided and on he chattered, and then, as the doors slid open, he ushered me out into a long corridor, with lots of oak-panelled doors on either side. He walked me down it, rummaging in his trouser pocket, jingling loose change, but it was only when we passed a girl with a mop and bucket that it struck me . . . that this was a hotel. And that the jingling in his pocket was not coins, but keys, which he was bringing out even now, and fitting into a door.

I gave a jolt of horror. Blood surged up my neck and face and to other extremities I didn't even know could flush. I stood there, aghast. Casper gently pushed open the door to reveal an enormous double bed with a bright red quilt in the middle of a dimly lit room. The curtains were drawn, and there was another bottle of champagne in the corner in an ice bucket. As I gazed in disbelief, the saliva dried in my mouth.

'Shall we?' Casper murmured, indicating we should move on in. 'We can spread your paintings out on the bed.'

I panicked. And for one awful moment, was tempted to believe the fiction—but in the very next moment it came to me with absolute clarity that if I set foot in that room, I had also to be sure I could survive a leap from a third-floor window. I turned. Took a deep breath.

'There's . . . been a misunderstanding.'

His smile wavered for a second. 'I'm sorry?'

'Yes, you see, I had no idea this was a hotel. When you said coffee upstairs, I assumed you meant in a bar or something. I had no idea you meant . . .' I trailed off, gesturing helplessly at the bed.

'Oh! Right,' he said shortly.

For a moment, I thought he was going to hit me. Then he did something far worse. His face buckled and he ran a despairing hand through his hair. 'This is so not the sort of thing I do,' he said softly.

Oh Lord. 'Look,' I began, 'it's fine. You don't have to explain.'

'My wife, Charlotte, and I—well, we've split up. Recently, if you must know.'

Must I? I hadn't asked, had I?

'We—we're having a trial separation.'

'Right.' I looked longingly down the corridor to freedom.

'And I loathe it, *loathe* it. Seeing the kids only at weekends, not living at home, all that crap. But—I get so lonely, and I'm staying here, at this hotel, and I thought—well, we were getting on so well downstairs—'

'It's an easy mistake to make,' I said quickly. 'And my fault too. I expect I missed the signs. Forget it. And now I really must be—'

'And when you said something like, "Let's go and look at my etchings,"' he looked at me accusingly, 'I thought—well, I assumed . . .'

Did I? God, *stupid* Imo. 'Yes, yes, I do see.' I blushed hotly.

'And the thing is, she's seeing someone else.' His eyes, to my horror, filled with tears. 'Someone younger than me,' he blurted out, 'her personal trainer.'

Younger? Younger than Casper? How young could they get?

'He's Spanish, called Jesus, would you believe, probably performs miracles, probably takes her to heaven and back,' he said bitterly. 'The children call him Jeez. They ride on his back at the local swimming pool.' At this his voice broke and his shoulders gave a mighty shudder.

I stared at him aghast. He was struggling for composure but seemed to be losing the battle. I hesitated, but only for a moment, then plunged my hand into my bag for my mobile. I quickly punched out a number.

Casper leapt back in fear, his eyes wide with terror. 'What are you doing?' he squeaked. 'Are you ringing the police?'

'No.' I sighed resignedly. 'I'm ringing my son's school. I'm going to ask them to put him into after-school club and then I'm going to ask Kate to collect him for me. You, meanwhile, will come with me. You will have a brandy and I will have a coffee, and you can tell me all about your wife and her faithless ways. On second thoughts,' I muttered as I marched him off down the corridor, 'I think I'll have a brandy too.'

'**O**h God, I'm so sorry!' Kate wailed, hurrying through from the kitchen to put a mug of tea on the coffee table in front of me.

'Why should you be sorry?'

'Because it's all my fault! I thought he was going to sign you up for the Cork Street equivalent of the Summer Exhibition, not try to molest you, then weep all over you.'

'I suppose I should be flattered,' I mused, sipping my tea in a dazed fashion. 'I can't remember the last time a man other than my husband even tried to hold my hand, let alone have sex with me. Unless you count the deputy head at the school carol concert last year.'

'The deputy head tried to have sex with you?'

'No, tried to hold my hand. I was miles away and hadn't realised we'd been urged to greet our neighbours with the sign of peace. Nearly slapped him.'

Kate snorted. 'Very Christian. But I'm surprised at young Casper,' she said thoughtfully, sinking into the squashy pink sofa beside me. 'He's always had an eye for the girls, but I wouldn't have thought he'd try it on with you as blatantly as that. I shall have words with him.'

'No, don't,' I said quickly. 'It was a complete misunderstanding and, actually, probably my fault too. And anyway, he's miserable and lonely.'

'I suppose.' She eyed me wickedly. 'And you weren't tempted?'

'Not remotely. Too wet behind the ears for my tastes. Anyway,' I added, 'I hadn't shaved my legs.'

'Ah. Now we get to the nub of it.'

We giggled.

'Thank you for collecting Rufus for me,' I said, watching my son assemble a Playmobil fort with Orlando, while Tabitha and Laura, Kate's daughters, who were enjoying an exeat from boarding school, painted each other's toenails. Not for the first time I reflected that daughters would have been nice. Would still be nice.

I gathered up my son's belongings—book bag, lunch box, PE kit—

and attempted to prise him away from the joys of Orlando's toy box with its mountains of Lego and remote-control cars, and back to his own, less exciting quarters. 'Come on, Rufus.'

'We're going?' The eyes he turned on me now were anguished. 'Aren't we staying for tea?' My son had yet to enter polite society.

'No, darling,' I said quickly before Kate could offer, 'because Daddy's coming home early tonight so we can all have supper together.'

'Alex is coming home early for a change?' Kate got up to show us out.

'Well, relatively,' I said. 'Nine o'clock rather than ten o'clock, probably.'

She grimaced. 'Tell him from me to break the habit of a lifetime and make it back for bath time for once. Really bust a gut.'

I laughed, but was aware of a whiff of disapproval in Kate's tone. A suggestion that Alex's after-work socialising—even though it was client-orientated and he loathed it—was excessive and at odds with family life. But then as Alex had pointed out as he'd flopped down exhausted on the sofa the other night, his handsome face racked with tiredness, fresh from yet another City cocktail party, it went with the territory. As a mergers and acquisitions specialist at Weinberg and Parsons, his job was to drum up new business and schmooze clients.

Rufus and I said our goodbyes to Kate and walked across the road. I let us into the little semi with the Queen Anne door and followed Rufus to the kitchen, where he'd hopped up onto the counter and had got the bread out of the bin. He was hacking away fairly adeptly with a knife.

'Hey, what about having supper with Daddy?'

'Oh.' He paused, mid-slice. 'I thought you were just making that up to be like the Barringtons. I didn't know we really were.'

I laughed and dumped his book bag on the table. 'You're too shrewd for your own good, Rufus Cameron. Come here, I'll do it.'

I cut the bread, spread it with peanut butter and folded it into a sandwich for him. It was true, I thought, this was a very shrewd child. One who tuned into my moods very acutely: who knew when his mother was happy or sad, pensive or nervous. My beautiful boy, with his auburn curls and deep chocolate-brown eyes: edible, clever. Sometimes I wondered if our bond was too strong. Alex said I molly-coddled him, but then Rufus and his father . . . To be fair, Rufus wasn't altogether the son Alex had expected.

'Throw a ball at him and he ducks!' Alex had complained after a disastrous trip to the park. 'He needs to be more of a lad.'

'He's nine! You want him sinking pints and singing rugby songs?'

'No, but I don't think he should be doing this, either.' He'd plucked a piece of tapestry Mum had given Rufus from behind a sofa cushion.

'It's just a bit of sewing,' I'd said, snatching it angrily. 'What's wrong with that?' Though I myself had wondered guiltily about Rufus taking it into school. 'Are you sure you want to take that, darling?' I'd said, eyeing him nervously one morning as he packed the sewing in his bag. 'I mean, when will you have time to do it?'

'Oh, I do it at break,' he'd said calmly. 'When the other boys are playing football.'

'Right,' I'd breathed. 'But don't they think that's . . . odd?'

He'd shrugged. 'I don't know. Is it?'

'No! No, of course not.' I'm ashamed to say, though, that the following morning, when he couldn't find it, it was at the bottom of my underwear drawer.

'A sensitive, musical child,' his teacher had smiled at Alex and me one parents' evening, 'but not a shrinking violet. He's got it up here.' She'd tapped her head and I'd glowed proudly. 'Why, only the other day on our nature walk he was telling us the difference between a buttercup and a celandine. He's definitely our wild flower expert!' I couldn't look at Alex.

Now, though, Rufus was settling down in front of *The Simpsons*, which surely was what any other nine-year-old boy would be doing?

I hovered in the doorway. 'No homework, Rufus?'

'Only reading, and I've already done it.' He kept his eyes on Bart and Marge.

'Right.' Probably finished the book, if I knew Rufus.

'I've finished the book.'

I smiled. 'Well done, darling.'

He turned. 'Mum, go. We don't need quality time every night and I've had a play with friends so I've done the interactive bit, and there's protein in the peanuts and fibre in the bread, and I promise I'll have an apple for pudding, so go.'

Spooky, this child.

'Well, I might just pop up for half an hour, if you're sure.'

'Course.' He turned back to the television. 'And if the phone goes I'll say you're in the middle of turning out the treacle tart, OK?'

I grinned. This was a reference to being accosted at the school gates one morning by Ursula Moncrief, all-round terrifying professional mother, who had said accusingly, 'I rang last night about your contribution to the Harvest Festival, and Rufus said you were upstairs painting!' From her tone Rufus might just as well have said I was upstairs flaying a couple of naked rent boys.

'Um, well, yes, I do occasionally,' I'd stammered.

'So where's Rufus?'

'Well, he's . . . downstairs. Doing his homework,' I added quickly.

More teeth sucking at this, because of course I should be down there with him, strapped into my pinny, ready to help him.

'Tell them to fuck off!' Alex had roared when I'd reported back.

I didn't, but was grateful for his support. Alex had little truck with the mummy mafia, having seen it all before with Lucy and Miranda, his daughters from his first marriage, now sixteen and fourteen respectively. His views on school-gate mothers—'a load of frustrated, overqualified women channelling their thwarted careers into overstimulated children'—were trenchant, and possibly true. Nevertheless, I was easily cowed, and these days Rufus and I were more circumspect about my whereabouts. The treacle tart ruse seemed to work.

Yes, the girls. It was probably time they came to visit again, I thought nervously as I mounted the stairs. Lucy and Miranda lived with their mother, a stunningly beautiful woman called Tilly, who, after the divorce, had gone to America. When we were first married and the girls were younger, I'd hardly seen them at all because Alex often had business in the States and visited them when he was there. Last year, however, now that they were teenagers, they'd crossed the pond alone, to stay with us in London. It hadn't been the most auspicious visit. They were the most self-possessed, scary creatures I'd ever encountered. I remember coming back from Tesco one afternoon to find both of them draped across Alex on the sofa as they watched a movie. Instinctively, I'd said, 'Oh—sorry.'

Lucy had mocked me with her eyes. 'Why are you sorry?'

I blushed. 'Well, I just meant . . . . I felt like I'd intruded!'

'Bit late for that, isn't it?'

I remember my face burning as I went through to the kitchen to unpack my shopping. It wasn't even a justified remark. Their parents' marriage had been over long before I came along.

Alex had come up behind me and put his arms round me as I unpacked. 'She doesn't mean it,' he whispered. 'She's just a kid.'

I turned round in his arms. 'I know, but . . . Alex, doesn't she know about Eleanor?' I searched his face.

He shrugged and looked away. 'Eleanor's her godmother, Imo. She adores her. I can't tell her that.'

'But surely Tilly's told her? Told her what happened?'

He shook his head.. 'I doubt it. Tilly's far too proud.'

So I took the rap. I was The Other Woman who'd broken up the happy home. And he was right, why dig up the past? That would hurt them even more, and they'd been through enough. And I'd try harder with them next time, I thought, going on up the next flight of stairs and opening the studio door, although the very idea brought me out in a muck sweat. I scuttled across to my paints in panic. My paints. This tiny, north-facing, and therefore perfect, room, was my sanctuary, my retreat. Here I could unwind. Be me.

Under the slanting dormer window that looked onto the street, an old pine table was covered in paint tubes, rags, drawing pads, books, pencils and my palette. The heady, oily aroma hit me as I stood over it, making me beautifully woozy for a second. Stacked on the floor around the walls were my canvases, or, more recently, boards, painted in my swirling, free style, lots of them—I was nothing if not prolific—and in the middle of the room, my easel, with a half-finished painting in it. It was a stubble field in winter, and since Putney didn't throw up many stubble fields, I had a photo of one propped up behind it.

'Isn't that cheating?' Kate had asked in astonishment.

'Why? I'm painting from a photograph, not another work of art. How is that cheating?'

She'd made a 'suppose so' face, but I was aware people still felt it wasn't quite right. A bit rum. I wasn't actually *in* that field, feeling that light, those shadows. But then again, punters liked country landscapes on their Fulham walls. Needs must.

As I took a brush from a jar of turps and wiped it on a rag, I spotted Kate emerging from her house. She came down the path, looking supremely elegant, and slid into a taxi at the kerb. Meanwhile Sandra, the nanny, would be bathing the children. I smiled. Other people's lives.

I was just getting to grips with the sky, adding a touch of Prussian Blue among the swirling clouds to darken it, when a head came round the door. 'Oh! Rufus. You startled me.'

'There's nothing on, so I'm going to bed.'

'Already? But you haven't had a bath or anything yet.'

'It's ten o'clock, Mum. When are we going to get Sky?'

'Is it?' I glanced at my watch, horrified. 'God, so it is. You should have been in bed ages ago. Come on, chop chop.'

Guilt making me brisk. I put my brush down and hustled him off to his room and into his pyjamas, muttering darkly as if it was *his* fault, for heaven's sake. How would this child turn out with such a distracted mother? As I kissed him good night I decided my painting had got out of hand. Instead of heading back to my studio where I knew I could stay until midnight, I went determinedly downstairs, did the washing-up, turned off all the lights, then headed to bed. An early night for once, I decided. And then when Alex came home, maybe . . .

I got into bed. I tried to stay awake for Alex but was aware of my eyelids growing heavier. At some point I stirred as a taxi drew up and rumbled outside. I listened for Alex's tread, but it was Kate, paying the driver, and then Kate's voice as Sandra came to the door, asking her how the children had been, then silence.

Sometime later, Alex crept in beside me.

'Sorry, darling,' he whispered. 'Did I wake you?'

'No, it's fine,' I murmured sleepily. 'How was your evening?'

He groaned. 'Averagely ghastly, thanks. I suggested a light supper in a wine bar, but the Cronin brothers were over from the States and wanted some traditional English fare. We ended up in Simpson's having roast beef and Yorkshire pudding. I'm about a stone heavier.'

I smiled and rolled over to hug him from behind, my cheek on his back. 'Well, you don't feel it.' I ran my hand up his bare thigh. 'Perhaps you need to wind down?'

He sighed. 'If I wasn't so exhausted, that's exactly what I'd like to do. But I'm shattered tonight, Imo.'

Ten minutes later I was aware of my husband's rhythmic breathing beside me. The Land of Nod had claimed him. It took me a while longer, though. My eyes were wide in the dark for quite some time.

In the morning Alex put his lips to my ear. 'Guess who's downstairs.'

'Hmm? What? Who is it?' I opened my eyes blearily. He was standing over me in his dressing gown, cup of tea in hand.

'Your mo-ther!' he sang.

'Oh God,' I groaned. 'You're kidding.'

'Nope. Apparently we're all going to this match of Rufus's this afternoon, a nice big family outing. I for one can hardly wait. Please tell me your sister's coming too?' His eyes widened in mock appeal.

'Of course she's not,' I snapped, 'and the match isn't till three, so what the hell's Mum doing here at seven? Where's Rufus?'

'Downstairs having a passive cigarette with her.'

I giggled. 'Probably in heaven.' I pulled on my dressing gown. 'How are you, anyway?' I eyed my husband. 'After your night on the tiles?'

'God, hardly.' He sat down heavily on the end of the bed. 'Americans are very clean-cut these days. No, it was a club soda apiece and then they bustled back to the Waldorf.'

'But you got the deal?'

'Who knows, Imo, who knows.' He nonchalantly swept back his blond hair from his high forehead, but his blue eyes were troubled and I knew better than to ask more. Alex had been specifically employed to drum up new business and, so far, the only business being done was old.

'It'll get better, you'll see,' I soothed 'These things go in waves.'

'In my case with a wave bye-bye.'

'Oh, don't be ridiculous,' I said staunchly.

'You're right, things go in cycles. Meanwhile you'd better get downstairs before your mother cleans Rufus out of pocket money.'

I picked up my mug and hastened downstairs to the kitchen, where . . . oh, I see.

The air was heavy with cigarette smoke, but through the fug, perched on stools either side of the breakfast bar, I could make out Mum and Rufus, three cards apiece, re-enacting a scene from *The Sting*.

'Twist,' said Mum tersely. 'Twist again . . . Twist . . . Stick.'

'You can't stick,' pointed out Rufus. 'You're bust.'

'No, I'm not.'

'Yes, you are, look—ten, nine and three is twenty-two. It's pay twenty-ones.' He reached across and took her coins.

'Morning, Mum.' I eyed her beadily. 'You're early.'

'Not really, darling,' she said in her gravelly voice, dealing out the cards again. 'When you get to my age you only need a few hours' sleep—ask Margaret Thatcher. I've been up since five. Dealer takes all.'

'You were dealer last time,' Rufus reminded her.

Mum eyed him defiantly, opened her mouth to object, then shut it again and handed him the pack.

'She cheats,' Rufus observed to me, without rancour, as he dealt.

'I know, I grew up with her,' I said, reaching in the cupboard for the cereal packets. 'Rufus, what have you had to eat?'

'Granny bought me a *pain au chocolat*. I don't want any cereal.'

'Oh, fair enough. Mum? Cup of tea?'

'Please. Twist . . . twist . . . damn!'

She really minded about winning, I thought, watching her with a smile. And, of course, that was why Rufus enjoyed it so much. She wasn't indulging or patronising him—oh, no, she was after his pocket money. I watched as she scrutinised Rufus's shuffle, perched straight-backed on her stool, slim and elegant in a cream jacket over khaki cargo trousers, her fading red hair piled loosely on her head. Always stylish, her clothes now had a French flavour as she'd spent much of the last ten years at her house in the South of France. Her story was she'd moved there for the weather, but my sister, Hannah, and I privately thought she'd gone abroad to get over losing Dad to Marjorie Ryan. Why she was back now, swapping the glorious colours of a Provençal spring for the rainy streets of Belgravia was a mystery to us, but she seemed happy in the flat she'd rented and she loved spending time with Rufus.

'The match isn't until three o'clock, you know,' I told her.

'I know, but I thought I'd have a go at your garden. Pay twenty-ones.'

'Oh, Mum, would you?' I swung round gratefully. 'It's such a mess and I just haven't had a chance to get out there.'

'Of course you haven't, you're far too busy,' she said loyally.

I glowed. My mother, unlike my sister, was one of the few people who didn't think that because my art was unremunerated, it was a waste of time. 'I sold one last week, you know,' I said.

'I know. Alex told me. But I don't think you charged nearly enough.'

'She didn't,' said Alex, coming in and doing up his cuff links. 'And it was one of the big jobbies; should have gone for twice the price.'

'I don't actually charge for the amount of paint used or the size of the canvas,' I countered. 'It's not like selling tomatoes.'

'Well, make sure you get some decent prices out of that gallery chappie Kate recommended. When are you meeting him?' Alex went to collect his overcoat and briefcase from the hall. 'Shit, I'm late.'

'I have met him,' I said, following him so Rufus couldn't hear. 'Turned out he was only after my body after all.'

He swung round at the front door in astonishment. 'You're kidding.'

'Is that so extraordinary?'

'Well, no, of course not, but blimey,' he boggled. 'Bloody cheek!' he spluttered. 'No dice on the paintings then?'

'No dice,' I agreed, amused that it hadn't occurred to him to ask if I was still intact. Unraped as it were. I opened the door for him. 'We'll see you this afternoon.' He looked blank as he stepped outside. 'At the match.'

'Oh, the match! God, wouldn't miss that for the world.' He popped his head back and yelled down to the kitchen. 'What position are you playing, Rufus?'

There was a pause. 'I'm playing rugby.'

'Yes, but what position?'

'I dunno.'

Alex and I exchanged smiles. 'See you on the touchline.'

As I shut the door and made to go up and get changed, noting that, as ever, Rufus was already in his uniform ready to go, I reflected on what it had taken to get us to this touchline position. Being in a team—any sort of team—had not remotely flickered on Rufus's radar until the day when the lists had gone up for the nine and under A and B squads, with Rufus's name on neither. I'd felt my blood pressure rise, felt fury mounting.

'Never mind, darling,' I'd muttered.

'What?' He looked blank.

'Not getting in the team.'

'Oh. That.'

'Don't you mind?'

He shrugged. 'Not really.'

The following morning I strode into school and ran the games master to ground. 'Mr O'Callaghan, Rufus seems to be the only boy in his year not in a rugby team—is that fair?' As I said it, I nearly cried.

Mr O'Callaghan turned and frowned. 'He's not the only one, Mrs Cameron. There's Magnus Pritchard.'

'Magnus Pritchard has a broken leg!' I yelped.

Mr O'Callaghan fiddled nervously with his whistle. 'Well, the list stands for Wednesday's match, I'm afraid, but I'll see what I can do for next week, OK? It obviously has to be entirely on merit, though.'

'Oh, obviously,' I'd purred obsequiously, and I'd scurried away, hugging my precious secret. Next week. Next week he'd be in.

The following Monday Rufus and I hastened into the school together. By now even Rufus had caught my excitement and had admitted the night before that he'd actually quite like to be in the team. His disappointment was all the more acute, therefore, when he realised he wasn't.

'I'm not there,' he said, his eyes quicker than mine.

I couldn't speak I was so angry.

'I'm in again!' came a voice. Orlando, his face wreathed in smiles.

'Oh, well done, darling.' Kate scanned the list. I wanted to hit her. 'Not you, Rufus?' she frowned. 'That can't be right, surely?'

'Of course it's not right!' I said in a shrill, unnatural voice.

Kate looked startled. 'Oh, well, maybe next week,' she murmured.

'No,' I said breathing hard through clenched teeth. 'No, this week.'

I'm not very proud of what happened next. Kate, to this day, swears I pushed Mr O'Callaghan into the PE cupboard, locked the door and threatened to take all my clothes off, but of course that's nonsense. What really happened was that I saw Mr O'Callaghan already *inside* the PE equipment room—cupboard, Kate insists, snorting—followed him in, shut the door, and rationally asked him to reconsider. I do remember seeing the naked fear in his eyes as he backed into a pile of clattering hockey sticks whimpering something like, 'Help me!'—I expect I misheard—but I have no idea why the top button of my shirt came undone nor why he was seen running, wild-eyed from the cupboard, grabbing a pen from a passing child and writing, 'Rufus Cameron' in large, shaky letters at the bottom of the B team list.

I sighed as I mounted the stairs to my bedroom now and peeled off my dressing gown. Hell certainly hath no fury like a woman whose child has been scorned, but I wondered, if Rufus wasn't an only child, if I'd feel everything so keenly. If I could share my emotions out between some siblings, would they dilute, or would I just emote even more until I became one gigantic emotion? I didn't know, because as yet it hadn't happened and however much I hollered, 'Come in, Cameron minor, your time is up,' nobody showed. Obviously I knew I had to do more than holler, but sometimes I wondered if Alex did.

I had a shower and dried myself slowly, keeping an eye on my reflection in the long mirror. My figure still wasn't bad—at least I hadn't completely gone to pot—but those thighs could definitely be slimmer. I really ought to lose a few pounds but I worried that dieting affected fertility and I couldn't help thinking that if I ate well, a big fat baby would follow. And it suited my face too, I thought.

'Are you going to paint today?' Mum called up.

'Yes, why?' I reached quickly for my bra and pants.

'I'll take Rufus to school if you like, then get out in the garden.'

'Oh, Mum, would you?' How lovely to lock myself away in my studio all day while she revamped my garden. What a treat! Of course, I should have known better. After all, I've known her thirty-four years.

Later that day, as we stood together on a windy school playing field among other shivering parents, waiting for Rufus and his team to materialise and for Alex to appear from work, we exchanged furious whispers. At least, mine were furious. 'I'm not being a bore,' I hissed, 'I just think it defeats the object of a garden.'

'Nonsense, darling, it's terribly low maintenance. Economical too.'

'Yes, but it's not real!'

'But you wouldn't have known that, would you? When you came out, you thought it was marvellous.'

I gazed at her helplessly. It was true, I'd emerged from my studio at midday feeling woozy and sated—my usual euphoric state after four blissful hours at the canvas—and had fairly marvelled at the sight that met my eyes. Gone was the tired strip of pale brown lawn surrounded by depressing darker brown beds, and instead, a gloriously tasteful green and white garden frothed around a patch of soft emerald lawn. Well, I say soft. It was only when I bent to stroke my new grass that it hit me: it was all fake. Not one petal, leaf, or blade of grass was real.

'You never have to water or prune, and it never dies—what more could you ask for? It works beautifully in my little roof terrace.'

'But you can't even smell it!'

'Oh, you can, darling, you can get scented sprays. Just blast it on first thing in the morning. I've got lavender and fresh pine.'

'What, like a lavatory?'

'No, I bought them in Harrods; they're the real thing. I'll get you one if you like. Honestly, you are ungrateful, Imogen, after all my hard work. Ooh, look, here they come. Come on, Rufus!'

Twenty-two little boys came running onto the pitch in white shorts and red and blue rugger shirts, looking fit to burst with pride.

Where was Alex? He was cutting it very fine. I looked around anxiously, but saw only Mr O'Callaghan running onto the pitch. A palpable frisson rippled around the assembled mothers. Mr O'Callaghan was tall, blond and rugged, wearing very short shorts.

Kate came up behind me wrapped in scarves. She found my ear. 'I think Mr O'Callaghan's shorts could go up an inch, don't you?'

I giggled. 'You know my mum, don't you?'

She did, and they kissed and exclaimed delightedly, and before long were admiring each other's cashmere. I had absolutely nothing to contribute to this conversation so I kept my eyes firmly on the game.

It set off at a breakneck pace and I waited excitedly for Rufus to get the ball. It didn't take long to realise that wasn't going to happen. The pack raged up and down the field, but Rufus seemed to regard it as more of a spectator sport. If the action came down his end he dodged the ball neatly. If the action was up the other end, he stood staring into space with his hands behind his back like Prince Charles.

'He's skipping,' Mum muttered to me.

'I know,' I groaned, watching as he skipped happily after the pack when it came towards him. 'Rufus, run!' I hollered.

He smiled, waved at me, and skipped even faster.

I pulled my hat down over my eyes. 'I can't watch.'

'You don't have to,' Mum informed me. 'He's off the pitch now.'

'What!' I squeaked indignantly. 'Where?'

'Over there. Stroking a dog.'

The match finally ended at 22–14 to us, no thanks at all to my son, who didn't touch the ball once.

As the boys shouted their three cheers for each side, I decided perhaps it was just as well Alex hadn't made it. Inwardly, though, I was fuming. Where the hell was he? I'd tried his mobile all through the game and it had been switched off. I finally managed to get through to Judith, his secretary, who said in a rather strained voice that someone had rung, and he'd taken the call and gone home.

'What, not to the school? He was supposed to meet us here. Hang on, Judith, who called?'

'I'm not sure, because it went straight through to his private line.'

'Yes, but I'm the only one who rings on that line, aren't I?'

'Um, I'm not sure.'

She sounded uncomfortable. Suddenly I went cold. I switched off my phone and turned to Mum. 'Mum, Rufus has to have a shower and then a quick match tea. Could you possibly wait and bring him back?'

'Yes, of course. Why, darling, where are you going?'

'I just want to go and find Alex.'

Mum looked surprised at being charged with so important a duty and I could sense Kate's eyes on me too, but in a moment I'd gone. Seconds later I was reversing out of the playground and racing down the backstreets of Putney. As I turned the corner into our road, my eyes scanned the line of parked cars. I couldn't see it; couldn't see the horribly familiar dark green Range Rover, so I told myself I was being stupid.

As I let myself in the house, I saw the coat immediately. It was thrown casually over the back of the sofa, and a handbag and some keys were on the hall table. As I went through the sitting room to the kitchen, willing myself to be calm, I saw them through the French windows in the garden together. They each had a glass of champagne in hand, and Alex was laughing at something she'd said. He turned as he saw me approach and I saw the light in his eyes.

'Oh, hello, darling, look who's here. Isn't it marvellous? It's Eleanor!'

Chapter Two

WHEN I FIRST MET ALEX he was married to Tilly. The fact that the marriage came unstuck, though, was nothing to do with me. It was 1995, and I'd just returned from Florence where I'd spent a happy year as a postgraduate studying portraiture and sculpture. I was going out with a sweet Italian boy called Paolo, and now I was back in London conducting a rather complicated long-distance relationship with him. Life, in the main, was rosy; money, however, was tight, and in order to pay my rent in Clapham where I shared a house with three fellow painters, I took a job as a secretary in the City. Just for a few months, I reasoned, then I'd have enough to set myself up properly as an artist. The offices were in Ludgate Circus, and Alex Cameron was my boss.

From day one, when he swept down the corridor, coat flying, pushing his blond hair out of his blue eyes and calling, 'Morning, Maria!' as he passed my desk, I had a feeling my plans were scuppered.

He stopped, just a few paces away, swung round, and did a double take. 'You're not Maria.'

'No, I'm Imogen Townshend. I'm a temp.'

'Of course you are! It's all coming back to me. And actually, you're nothing like Maria. You're not . . .' he made a bump over his stomach with his hand, 'pregnant.'

I grinned. 'Hope not.'

He laughed. 'Coffee-making skills in order?'

'Perfectly.'

'Good, because I've got a meeting in ten minutes and I could badly do with something strong and black before I face the Powers That Be.'

And off he went. And off I scurried, thinking that if I was going to be skivvying for someone, he might as well be as decorative as this.

Two months passed and Maria had her baby and then decided she couldn't possibly leave it and I promised to stay for as long as it took Alex to find a permanent secretary. And so the interviewing process began. Alex would chat to the prospective secretaries first, then hand them over to me, the idea being that I'd explain the job in more detail. One particularly foxy blonde came out of his office with her eyes shining.

'He's heaven,' she breathed as I showed her the photocopier.

I showed her to the lift.

'I thought she was fine,' remarked Alex later, as he signed some letters I'd put in front of him.

I smiled thinly. 'Lazy.'

He looked up surprised. 'Oh? How can you tell?'

'Trust me, it's the eyes.'

It was the same with the next one. 'Too timid.'

The next one was too simpering, the next too tidy, and it was at that point, when I was running out of insults, that I realised I had to make a decision. I couldn't possibly stay on as a temporary secretary for ever. I had to become a permanent one. Alex was delighted.

My friends back in Clapham, however, threw up their hands in horror. What about my art? My mother was aghast—a *secretary*, after all that studying, with all that talent! My father, not a man to get involved, even put in his two pennyworth—'You're barking mad, girl!'—but by now I was beyond reason. I'd already written a long letter to Paolo explaining that I'd met someone else. I didn't mention that the man in question had no idea, and that he was in fact married. Details.

I was in love. Painfully and properly, and it was the first time it had ever happened. I couldn't keep it a secret either. I had terrible mentionitis, and hardly a day went by when his name wasn't dropped. My family were onto it like vultures.

'A banker!' My mother hooted when I went out to see her in France. 'You'll be telling me he's got a Porsche next.'

He had, but I couldn't tell her that. My family were arty, bohemian—my sister, Hannah, was a potter, my father an actor—bankers and their Porsches were anathema to them. They'd expected me to rock up with a floppy-haired poet one day, not a thrusting young executive who got his thrills from playing the money markets. And the worst of it was, I knew it was hopeless. Alex was married to Tilly—a gorgeous, languid ex-model of a creature—had two young daughters, and lived happily with his perfect family in a dear little house in Flood Street, Chelsea.

I knew I should leave—my painting was suffering—but every time I tried, I couldn't go through with it. The thought of not seeing him every day, his blue eyes glancing up as I came through the door, his face creasing into a smile—or what was worse, imagining it creasing up for someone *else*—brought me out in a muck sweat and sent me scurrying back to my desk again.

And then, a little over a year down the line, something changed. Alex seemed distracted and upset, and Tilly, when she rang, sounded tense. Curt, even. She rang less and less, and one day, came in solely, it seemed, to have a blazing row with him. When she'd gone I turned to Jenny, a fellow secretary. She'd looked at me in amazement.

'Oh, yes, didn't you know? He's been having an affair. Tilly caught him out and she's livid. I think they might be splitting up.'

I sat there staring at her, speechless. Alex? My Alex? Having an *affair*? I felt sick. How? It was outrageous. Why, I knew his every move, I'd have *noticed*. Surely no one at work?

'No, no one here,' Jenny assured me. 'And I only know because I know someone who knows her. It's an old family friend. Eleanor Latimer.'

'Eleanor Latimer!' I shrieked.

Eleanor Latimer was indeed a good friend, a *great* friend, who'd grown up with Alex in the country, and whose husband was a friend of Alex's, and whom they went skiing with every Easter, and to Tuscany in the summer. I knew. I booked the tickets. Why, I'd even met her when she'd come in with her husband once, some frightfully grand titled chap, tall, lean and consumptive-looking, and again when she'd popped in on her own to have lunch with Alex . . . Lunch with Alex. Why didn't I think? But I hadn't, because, well, why shouldn't they have lunch together? And she was so jolly and nice, with her curly brown hair and merry eyes and laughing mouth. Eleanor *Latimer*!

That he could have an affair with another woman, and for it not to be me! The sense of betrayal was almost too much to bear. I'd leave, I thought, I'd hand in my notice in the morning.

And I'd really meant to do it, but the following morning, Alex called me into his office and shut the door behind him. He was distraught. He wanted to talk to me as a friend, he said, as someone he knew wouldn't blab to the senior partners, who, it being an American bank, took a very dim view of anything immoral. He wanted my counsel. Tilly had thrown him out. He was staying in a hotel in Bayswater. It was all over between him and Tilly, had been for a long time. After the second baby was born, she'd . . . well, you know. Lost interest. Become so wrapped up in the children, he'd felt excluded. And Eleanor—well, of course he loved Eleanor. Should have married her really, but she'd married Piers, with his title, and his inheritance, Stockley. But he, Alex, had *always* loved her, and when Tilly had been so cold and remote and they, he and Eleanor, were together so often on holidays, well, they just couldn't help themselves, do you see? His blue eyes had appealed to me.

'And will she leave Piers for you? Is that what's going to happen?' I asked, half of me hating him for loving her and not me, and half ridiculously thrilled to be sitting here listening to his confidences.

'No,' he said in despair. 'She's too devoted to her children, her family. She won't break up the home. She won't leave Piers.'

'But, you and Tilly . . .?'

'I can't go back to Tilly now.' He raised anguished eyes to me. 'I don't love her, Imogen. I can't pretend to patch something up if there's nothing there any more. Can't live a lie.'

'Not even for the girls?'

He shook his head sadly. 'Not even for the girls.'

'But what will you do?' I'd asked.

'Me? Oh, I'll be fine. I've said I'll let Tilly stay on in the house for as long as she wants. I'll find a flat somewhere. Putney, maybe, near the Common. I've always liked it round there.'

From then on, Alex and I shared the odd wine-bar supper together. Well, he was lonely and he seemed to enjoy my company. Time passed, and eventually, of course, the inevitable happened. It was after one of those suppers, I'd gone back to advise him on the decor of his flat in Putney, which, I'd assured him, didn't have to be all white and minimalist just because it was a bachelor pad—books always warmed a room up— and in the bedroom, why, that magnolia just cried out for a set of

Beardsley prints. Here, I demonstrated, with a sweep of my hand: over the bed . . .

Did I think about getting pregnant? Did I deliberately neglect to ask him to use a condom? No. Not deliberately, but it was the last thing on my mind. The only thing on my mind was that finally, *finally*, this heavenly man was here in my arms. I was indescribably, heart-soaringly, ecstatic. And so was he. If a little surprised. It felt so natural, so right, he told me afterwards. He'd been so blind, he hadn't seen what was so manifestly right in front of him all along, and was amazed that I had.

'You knew? You knew this might happen one day?'

'I've loved you pretty much from the word go,' I admitted in an extremely uncool manner. But why not. I reasoned: this was me; upfront, honest. Take it or leave it.

And he took it. He was flabbergasted, staggered, but also, I think, incredibly touched and flattered, and humbled that I'd kept it so quiet.

'So you never knew?' I asked him, lying there in the dark, looking up at his face, stroking the crook of his arm. 'Never suspected?'

'Had no idea,' he admitted. 'And why would I? I mean, it occurred to me often to wonder why you were working for me, this beautiful girl with her flowing blonde hair, who everyone assures me paints like a dream and speaks fluent Italian, but it never occurred to me that . . . well, I'm fifteen years older than you, and you're so . . .' He hesitated. 'I always thought I was out of your league.'

'And I thought I was way out of yours.'

We'd gazed at each other in the darkness, the realisation of what might have been, creeping up on us.

'And Eleanor?' I asked eventually.

He sighed, stroked my hair. 'Eleanor was there at the time. She filled a gap. I'll always be very fond of her, but . . . well, we're just friends.'

I smiled into the handsome open face beside me and conveniently forgot how he'd said, not so long ago, how much he loved her.

'Stay with me, Imogen?' he said softly. And I did. I moved into his flat and brought all my ramshackle worldly goods with me; but when I discovered I was pregnant, I moved out again.

I'd done the test with shaking hands, watching in horror as the blue line appeared. I did it again in disbelief, but it came back stronger than ever. I'd taken the day off work, pleading sickness, so I left Alex a note on the table saying that the age gap *was* too great, and I went to Clapham, where my friends welcomed me back with open arms. At ten o'clock that evening, however, he appeared on the doorstep.

'What's going on?' he whispered brokenly.

I almost managed to go through with it. Then I said, 'I'm pregnant.'
He didn't flinch for a second. 'And your point is?'

'M-my point is,' I stammered, 'that I'm going to keep it. But I don't
want to trap you—' Whatever other selfless utterances were going to
gush from my lips were halted, however, as he crossed the room, took
me in his arms, and stopped my mouth with his kisses.

'Marry me,' he whispered urgently, his eyes scanning my face. 'Marry
me, Imo, and have the baby and let's be together for ever.'

I'd like to tell you I gave it some thought, but who am I trying to kid?
'Yes,' I whispered, equally urgently. 'Yes, let's do that.'

And so my happiness was complete. Mum, Dad, and even Hannah
came round to the fact once they'd realised it was a fait accompli, and
Alex and I moved from the tiny flat—stretching our finances to the
limit now that half went to his other family—to the semi round the
corner in Hastoe Avenue, where we live now. I had a heavenly time
doing it up, and positively breezed through my pregnancy.

One Monday morning, when I'd returned from visiting my mother
in France, Alex took me up to the attic. Gone was the dusty, cavernous
loft space filled with piles of suitcases and cobwebby old furniture, and
instead, I found myself walking into an empty white room, with a sheet
shrouding what appeared to be a cross in the middle of it.

'It's a studio,' Alex told me. He whipped the sheet off the cross with a
flourish like a magician, and revealed my easel. His eyes burned into
mine, full of love. 'Paint,' he urged me. 'Paint.'

And I did. All through my pregnancy: joyful, instinctive paintings,
which seemed to flow out of me. I'd never been so happy.

And then, one day, about two weeks before I was due, I was strolling
around Peter Jones and walked straight into Tilly.

She looked at my huge stomach, then up at my eyes. If she knew,
which she probably did, it was still, clearly, a terrible shock. She managed
a faint smile. 'Imogen.'

'Tilly!' I gasped. I felt my face burn, my whole body flush.

She put a hand on my arm. 'Good luck. You'll need it.'

I looked up, startled, and saw, not bitterness in her eyes, but pity,
almost. 'What d'you mean?'

She seemed about to shrug and move on, but then gave an odd little
smile. 'In all my married life, Imogen, only one person made me want
to behave like a victim. Only one person made me want to outline my
eyes in black, raise them theatrically to camera and whisper, "There are
three of us in this marriage." I think you know who I mean. So good
luck. As I say, you'll need it.'

'Eleanor.' I forced a smile and made my way out through the French windows to the garden. 'How lovely, but what on earth—'

'I came up for lunch with a girlfriend and called Alex just on the off chance.' She came towards me, smiling broadly. 'I have to practically drive past your front door to get back to Stockley and I thought, oh God, let's give it a go, they might just be in—and here you both are! Wasn't that lucky?'

'Terribly,' I agreed, as her proffered cheek brushed mine. 'But, Alex,' I turned, my voice unsteady, 'you were supposed to be at the match—'

'My fault entirely.' Eleanor held up her palms. 'Alex said he was going to watch Rufus and I promised faithfully to meet him here in time for us to go together—but the bloody traffic!'

'Sorry, darling,' Alex looked sheepish. 'How did he do?'

'Brilliantly.'

Alex passed me a glass of champagne. I was so angry I nearly knocked it back in one. I took a gulp and regarded Eleanor, standing before me. Her brown curls were discreetly highlighted these days and swept back from her face, tucked behind her ears, showing off her fine cheekbones and startling, slanting hazel eyes. The passage of time had been kind to Eleanor; she was still very beautiful.

'Well, good for Rufus,' she was saying in her husky voice. 'I didn't think he was the sporty type!'

'Oh, he's pretty much an all-rounder,' I lied.

'Just like my Theo. I went to watch him play at Ludgrove last week, and he got four tries!'

'Four!' Alex spluttered with wide, overimpressed eyes. Pillock. I wanted to hit him. He turned back to me. 'Did Rufus get any?'

'Yes, he got five.'

'Five!' He looked astonished, as well he might.

'More champagne, Eleanor?' I calmly filled her glass. 'Although,' I went on, 'what on earth we're doing standing in a chilly garden on a Wednesday afternoon drinking champagne, Lord only knows!'

'I'll tell you why we're drinking this,' Alex began portentously, looking remarkably pleased with himself. 'Eleanor's offered us a cottage.'

'A cottage?' I was momentarily nonplussed.

'Yes, at Stockley. She's got one vacant at the moment, and she says we can use it. Isn't that wonderful?'

'Well, it's . . . terribly kind . . .' My mind was whirring. A cottage. At Stockley. Jesus. 'You mean . . .' I stalled for time, 'for the summer?'

'Oh, no, not just for the summer, for as long as you like. And to be honest, you'd be doing me a favour by taking it,' Eleanor was saying.

'The place is empty and has been for some time, so it needs quite a bit of work. Alex said he wouldn't mind doing that—nothing structural, only decorating—but I'd much rather have it inhabited than be constantly worried about the Gypsies getting hold of it.'

'Yes, but,' I licked my lips, 'couldn't you let it out to tenants? I don't know if Alex has misled you, but we couldn't possibly afford to—'

'Oh, no, I don't want any money for it. If I let it out properly I'd have to do it up, and I can't be fagged with that.'

'Isn't that marvellous?' said Alex. 'A place in the country, where Rufus can run wild and play in the woods and dam streams, and you can grow vegetables and paint—just like you've always wanted!'

It was true, I had always wanted it, and if it had been anywhere else I'd have leapt at it. 'Where exactly is it?' My voice was tight. Eleanor looked anxious now, sensing perhaps that I felt boxed in.

'It's on the edge of the home farm, a tiny little detached cottage called Shepherd's Cottage. And years ago that's exactly what it was: the shepherd's place. I promise you it's minute, Imogen, absolutely tiny, nothing flashy at all. I think we've even still got a few animals down there. Piers will probably task you off to keep an eye on them. That's how much you'd be doing us a favour.'

'No trouble at all,' gushed my husband.

I straightened my shoulders and cranked up a smile. 'How lovely, Eleanor, and of course we'll think about it. We'll discuss it later.'

'Oh, but what is there to dis—'

'Yes, of course,' broke in Eleanor hastily. 'You'll need to talk about it. But the offer's there if you want it. So!' she said with some finality. 'I was just admiring your garden, Imogen. What a triumph!'

I clenched my teeth. 'Yes, well, I'm afraid my mother's a bit of a loose cannon these days. She gets carried away.'

'Oh, but I think it's terrific,' she enthused, bending down to finger a rose. 'So realistic, and just think, you never have to water it! I really think it's a must for Stockley,' she mused. 'Just one little patch—terribly amusing. Imagine all the old dears' faces when we're open for the public: "Oh, look, a *Maximus pergalitor* Mabel—oh heavens, it's plastic!" With any luck they'll be so appalled we'll be boycotted and Piers will never make me open the gardens again!'

They enjoyed this hugely and laughed gustily. Why couldn't I join in? Why did I always force myself to adopt this sour position, like some lemon-sucking killjoy, someone I didn't recognise, didn't like?

'Oh, and here she is!' she cried, glancing through the house as the front door opened. 'The creator—the *artist*! How marvellous!'

My mother came down the hall with Rufus beside her. He ran through the kitchen and jumped into Alex's arms. 'Daddy, I was in the team and you were supposed to come and watch!'

'I'm sorry, but you obviously didn't need me, Rufus. Five tries!'

Rufus drew back in his arms, perplexed. 'What?'

'Bath time now, darling,' I broke in hurriedly, prising him from his father's arms. 'Quickly, say hello to Eleanor, and then straight upstairs.'

'But I had a shower,' he was saying as I seized his hand and hastened him away, giving Eleanor only a millisecond to congratulate him. We were up those stairs with a bath running in moments.

'I *did* have a shower, Mummy,' he said as I shut the bathroom door.

'I know, Rufus, but humour me and have a bath too.'

Something in my voice made him catch my eye. He looked alarmed, but didn't question my logic as he began to peel his clothes off. The tiny bathroom window overlooked the garden, and I could hear Eleanor greeting my mother like a long-lost buddy.

'Celia, this is inspired!' Eleanor was enthusing gustily.

Mum bent down beside Eleanor to show off the faux foliage, while Alex looked on indulgently. I bet he wouldn't have done that if I'd shown him, I thought savagely. I bet he'd say, 'Don't be absurd, Imogen. This garden's ridiculous. Your mother's a perfect menace!' But because Eleanor admired it—oh, no, all at once it was delightful.

When I came down, Mum and Eleanor had gone. Alex was in the kitchen, putting the champagne glasses in the sink and throwing the bottle in the bin. It was chilly now.

'Eleanor's gone?' I said casually, as I shut the French doors.

'She had to dash off. Wanted to miss the traffic.'

'We must think about her offer,' I said lightly. 'It's very kind of her, but I can't quite see what's in it for her!' Except to have my husband on her doorstep morning, noon and night, I thought feverishly.

'Well, in return, we do the place up. That's the idea. And it's more than kind, actually,' he said in a strained voice. 'It's a lifesaver.'

'What d'you mean?'

'I've . . . actually had quite a lot of time to think about this, Imo. She rang me a week ago and offered it.'

I turned round to face him properly. This. *This* was what I hated. *So* much. The secret collaboration, the two of them whispering away together, without Piers and me involved. Ooh!

'Right,' I said lightly. 'Why didn't you say?'

'Because I needed to think it through. But, the thing is, Imo, I really think we ought to move down there. Permanently.'

I stared at him incredulously. 'Leave London? For some crummy country cottage on the Latimers' estate? Oh, don't be ridiculous!'

'Imogen, we have no choice.'

'What d'you mean, we have no choice?' My voice was shrill, fearful.

He made a helpless gesture. 'Imo, we're so overdrawn the bank won't let me have any more. And if we moved down there, we could let this place out. Think of the money we'd save. I could commute.'

I stared at him in horror. He meant it. He really meant it. 'Alex, things can't be that bad. You're exaggerating.'

'I'm not exaggerating. Things are—' he flicked a quick, nervous tongue over his lips—'well, they're pretty fucking hopeless, actually.'

I went cold. 'Have you lost your job?'

'No. But . . .' he hesitated, 'well, I've had a warning.'

'Oh God.' My hand went to my mouth.

'No bonuses will be given to anyone in my department this year, and apparently, if we don't "shift our asses and get some new business in"— well . . .' He shrugged his shoulders despairingly. 'Who knows?' He looked shaken. Responsible. For his family. For their plummeting fortunes. Suddenly I felt ashamed. How long had he been living with this? Worrying he was going to get fired, not telling me?

'Everything's going to be fine, you'll see. Things will pick up.'

He shrugged. 'Maybe. And meanwhile?'

'Meanwhile, well, meanwhile we'll think about it. Golly, there are all sorts of things to consider. What about Rufus? His school—'

'There's a little local school he could go to in Stockley. It's a church school—free. And he'd probably get a place. I've checked.'

'You've already . . .' I stared. My mouth dried. He was serious. Deadly serious. 'But . . . he loves Carrington House. All his friends . . .'

'We can't afford Carrington House any more. Even if we decide to stay in London, he'll have to go to a state school.'

'A state school!' My blood froze. What—where they sniffed glue and beat up the teachers? Over my dead body. Not my precious Rufus.

'And move somewhere smaller. We could still stay in Putney, but it would have to be a flat. A maisonette, maybe.'

I clutched the tops of my arms, my heart pounding. What, in the area where everyone would know we'd gone down, not up? With Rufus at a state school where he'd be picked on?

Alex moved to the far end of the kitchen, his back to me, his shoulders sagging in his blue jumper. It struck me, for the first time, that he looked older. I took a deep breath and went across to him. I put my arms round him and rested my head on his back.

I sometimes wondered if Alex ever missed the life he'd had. The house in Flood Street, the glamorous social life. As I held him, I felt his disappointment at the way things had turned out permeate through him. It cut me like a knife. He didn't want to be bailed out by old friends. He didn't want to be shamed into accepting charity, and Eleanor had done it in such a way that it didn't seem like that. We'd be doing *her* a favour. As usual, she came out of this shiny and bright, a far, far nicer person than I was, who just wanted to hold on to the trappings of my life, to be like Kate across the road, when we were out of our depth. Alex had clearly known it for some time, and I . . . well, I'd known too, but I suppose I'd been fooling myself. I swallowed hard. 'We'll sleep on it, darling, hmm?' I whispered. 'We'll see.'

Kate dropped the frozen packet and a million petits pois shot, like tiny green missiles, to every corner of her kitchen. She turned, her face shocked. 'You're not.'

I nodded miserably. 'We have to, Kate. We've been through it so many times now. Unearthed every unpaid bill, every final reminder, every threatening letter. I tell you, it's not a pretty sight.'

It wasn't. Alex and I both suffered from brown envelope syndrome, my policy being to ignore them, but I was horrified to discover he'd gone one step further and popped them under cushions. We'd decorated the kitchen table with them last night and forced ourselves to face reality.

'Yes, but this is so drastic. Moving out! Things will improve, surely?'

'Apparently not. This is the second year running he hasn't had a bonus. And as far as the house is concerned, if we don't jump now, we might be pushed,' I said, echoing the master's voice.

Kate looked stricken. I hoped she wasn't going to cry, because if she did, I surely would too. Recently, Kate and I had become very close. What had started as a convenient friendship had blossomed into something rare and precious. 'Bloody peas,' she muttered, brushing them rather ineptly into a dustpan. She threw them in the bin.

'You've thrown the dustpan in too,' I commented.

'What? Oh.' She retrieved it absently and slung it back in the cupboard. Then she turned and folded her arms. 'I can't help feeling you're panicking. That this is crisis management.'

'Oh, we are,' I agreed. 'We're going under here, Kate, sinking well below the surface. Eleanor's offer is a lifeline.'

'Eleanor,' she spat, opening the fridge door to get some salad out for lunch. 'I thought you reckoned she still had her claws into Alex and was just waiting for her chance to pounce. Well, now you're offering it to her on a plate!' She tossed a cucumber and a pepper on a chopping board. 'She'll be all over him like a rash!'

'I think I've overreacted,' I mumbled, chewing a fingernail. 'In fact, I'm sure I have. Eleanor, is, in actual fact, a very sweet person.'

'Bollocks,' Kate scoffed, chopping up the cucumber with alarming zeal. 'Last week you told me she was a conniving hussy who'd married for money and was regretting it on a daily basis. You told me she was looking for some extracurricular action with your husband!'

'I did not,' I spluttered. 'I remember saying that if you marry money you pay for it, but I'm pretty sure I was generalising.'

Kate turned and waved her knife dangerously at me. 'You said the last time you went to stay with them, you walked into the billiards room after coffee and she was bending over the table with Alex bending over behind her showing her how to pot the red. You reckoned he'd have been potting something else if you'd come in two minutes later.'

'Yes, but I misinterpreted that,' I said quickly. 'Alex explained to me in the car on the way home, it's a bit of a running joke with them. He's always tried to teach her billiards, ever since they were little.'

'Ever since they were little,' Kate scoffed. 'He plays on that as if that excuses their overfamiliarity.' She stopped suddenly. Saw my face. Went a bit pink. 'Sorry. That was out of order. I didn't mean . . . well, I'm sure you're right. You misinterpreted it. And I'm just upset.'

I got up and we hugged each other tight. 'I'm upset too, Kate; can't *bear* the thought of going. Or of being beholden to her.'

She drew back sharply. 'Oh, I wouldn't take it rent free.'

'We're not going to,' I said quickly. 'Alex has written to Piers saying it's a terribly generous offer, blah blah blah, but we'll only accept if they let us pay rent. I do have some pride.'

'Quite right,' she said. She went back to butchering the cucumber. 'And what about your house?'

'We're not going to sell it, we're going to rent it out. In a year or so, when we're back on our feet, maybe we can move back?'

Kate smiled down knowingly at her red pepper and chopped away. 'You won't,' she said eventually. 'No one ever comes back. Once they've gone, they realise how much better life is out there. And aside from the fact that I'll miss you like hell, I think that's what's upsetting me so much. The fact that I'll still be in sodding London and you'll be in a little cottage in the country with roses round the door.' She brought the knife down with such force that half the red pepper leaped off her board in alarm. I picked it up and she gouged away at the seeds inside it like a Shakespearean henchman going for Gloucester's eyes. I gulped.

'Well, you'll come down and see us, of course. Spend weekends, and we'll come up here. You know, to dinner, the theatre . . .'

Even as I said it, though, I knew it wouldn't happen. Knew that, while Kate would be blissfully happy mucking in with the steam stripper and the Polyfilla, Sebastian, after a hard week at the operating table, could probably think of better things to do. Likewise, theatre trips would be unlikely to feature for obvious financial reasons. The truth was that our lives, which up to now had been so intricately stitched together, were going to be pulled apart with alarming ease.

That evening I told Rufus, who was much more stoic and phlegmatic than I'd imagined. He mulled it over for an hour or two, then came to find me in my bedroom. 'Where will I go to school?' he demanded. He was sitting at my kidney-shaped dressing table, playing with old lipsticks in my drawer, while I changed the sheets behind him.

'Oh, Rufus, you'll love it. It's a dear little church school in the village, much smaller and cosier than Carrington House.'

I'd steeled myself to ring Eleanor a couple of days ago and she'd instantly raved about it and given me the headmaster's number.

'Everyone says it's a brilliant school,' she'd gushed down the phone. 'All the local children go. And the head's great, apparently. He's new, really dynamic. Terribly charming too, I gather.'

He must have been having an off day when I rang.

'This term? No, I'm not convinced I can. We're full to bursting.'

I'd explained that my husband had already telephoned and secured, I'd been led to believe, a place for Rufus.

'Oh, yes, I remember now. I certainly didn't promise anything.'

Oh, splendid.

'Um, I'm a friend of Eleanor Latimer's,' I breathed shamelessly.

'Are you indeed?' he'd barked back. 'Yes, well, you can tell her from me that the next time her dogs crap all over my playground I'll bloody shoot them.'

'Right, will do,' I'd quaked. 'But in the meantime . . .?'

'Leave it with me. I'll see what I can do.' And the line had gone dead.

A week later I'd received a curt missive via email informing me that since a child's father in year two had tragically been killed in a combine-harvesting accident, the family were moving away and there was now a place for my son. Dead man's shoes, I thought, reading it in horror. Heavens, was this the sort of place we were going to? Did people fall into combines as a matter of course?

'A church school?' Rufus turned to face me from the dressing table. 'What—you mean it's in a church?'

'No, sausage, it's run by the Church. Which makes it, well . . .' I shook a pillow into its case, smiling, 'Christian. Caring. Nice.'

In my mind's eye I imagined a chubby vicar beaming kindly down at the rows of rosy-cheeked children sitting crosslegged before him.

'Do they have Dib Dabs in the country?'

'Of course they do. You'll buy them at the village shop.'

Now Rufus and a couple of the aforementioned apple-cheeked boys were stretching up over a counter, conkers hanging from their pockets, to hand their pennies over to a dear little currant bun of a lady.

'But you know, Rufus,' I regarded him kindly, 'the pace is slightly slower in the country. You might find it's all humbugs and catapults rather than Dib Dabs and Game Boys.'

'Oh.' He looked disappointed. 'What's a humbug?'

'A humbug is a slimy bastard who says one thing and then does something entirely different,' snarled Alex, sweeping into the bedroom and flinging his briefcase on a chair. 'See my boss on this subject.'

'Golly, you're early. Good day?' I hazarded nervously.

'Reasonably diabolical, thanks. Roger Bartwell has taken over my Hedges and Butler account. I hope the brakes on his new BMW fail and he dies in a heap of twisted metal. Put Mummy's lipstick down, Rufus.'

'She said I could.' Rufus dabbed experimentally at his lip.

'I don't mind,' I said indulgently.

'YES, WELL I DO!' Alex roared. Rufus dropped the lipstick and glared at his father. A silence ensued as Alex changed out of his suit. He took off his jacket and tie while I smoothed down the bottom sheet and plumped the pillows.

'We'll be near Aunt Hannah, won't we?' Rufus hazarded at length. If this comment was designed to get back at his father, it worked.

'Yes, that's the downside of this little venture,' Alex snapped, sitting on the bed and taking his shoes off. He hurled one across the room. 'Your bloody sister!'

'And Uncle Eddie,' Rufus reminded him brightly. 'I like him.'

Hannah, my elder and much more forthright sister, had married Eddie Sidebottom many years ago when they'd met at a commune in Istanbul. Hannah, in those days, was a right-on lefty with a heart that bled all over the place. She traipsed round the world looking for causes, desperate to revolt against the bourgeois, middle-class upbringing she'd never had. That we lived in bohemian Highgate, my father was an actor and my mother wafted round in beads, not knowing what day it was, was a source of constant annoyance to Hannah. It irked her that no one noticed her rebellion. In fact, when she came back from the commune,

Mum asked if she'd had a nice time in Cornwall.

'Cornwall? I've been to Istanbul!'

'Oh, I thought you said Cornwall. And who's this?' She smiled.

'This is Eddie. We're getting married.' Hannah squared her shoulders defiantly.

'That's nice,' said Mum. 'Is he a taxi driver?'

'No, why?'

'You get a lot of taxi drivers in Istanbul.'

Eddie was in fact a teacher from Wigan, and was as different in his laid-back, laissez-faire way from Hannah—who could be chippy and bossy—as was possible to be. He was tall and shy, with long grey hair—even at twenty-three—and delightfully charming. They duly got married and settled down in East Sheen. They both taught at the local poly—Hannah, art, and Eddie, English—and Hannah got fatter and Eddie's hair got shorter and whiter. The move to the country came some years later when they decided to get away from the rat race, buy a cottage, teach locally and, of course, have loads of children. They achieved all of the above effortlessly, but sadly, no children. After years of trying, it was discovered that they were both culpable and they decided to give up. They were surprisingly philosophical about their infertility, discussing it at length with all-comers.

'My vagina's too acidic,' Hannah informed the entire family over a pub lunch one Sunday when we'd gathered to meet Dad's latest girl-friend—Mum included. 'And even if I douche it with yoghurt on a regular basis, which, frankly, defies gravity and makes a terrible mess, it's still not going to create a conducive enough environment. Eddie's sperm are terribly lazy.'

There was a short silence as our little group digested this.

At length Dad sighed, patted Eddie sympathetically on the shoulder, and tottered off to the bar. 'Bad luck, laddie,' he muttered. But Eddie didn't mind. As a self-confessed hypochondriac, he viewed his lack of fecundity with resigned fatalism.

Neurotic about his health he might be, but to Rufus, Eddie was simply a joyous uncle who always had time for him, who played chess with him endlessly and took him birdwatching.

'Will we be quite close to Hannah and Eddie?' asked Rufus, swivelling on the stool now.

'Too close,' muttered Alex as he headed for the shower.

'Yes, nice and close, darling,' I said quickly as Alex disappeared.

After a moment, though, his head popped back round the door. 'You're changing the sheets again? I thought you'd only just done that!'

'I dropped some tea on them this morning,' I lied. For some reason my husband found clean sheets incredibly provocative and, in the old days, couldn't resist ravaging me on them.

'Oh. Right. What's for supper?'

'I bought a couple of fillet steaks. And *Four Weddings* is on again later. I thought we might watch that when Rufus has gone to bed.'

Alex yawned widely. 'I'm a bit knackered actually, Imo. I'll probably just watch a bit of footy in the kitchen and then turn in, but you watch your film.' And off he padded to the shower.

Chapter Three

'BYE, THEN.' I looked damply at Kate and walked into her arms. Out of the corner of my eye I saw Rufus and Orlando sheepishly kicking gravel, unsure how to handle this.

'Bye,' muttered Orlando eventually, thrusting his hands in his pockets.

'Bye,' agreed Rufus, throwing a stone at a tree for composure.

'We'll speak soon,' I sniffed, fishing a hanky out of my pocket.

Kate nodded mutely, her face stoical, but tears were spilling down my cheeks now. Alex came over to extract me before we were awash.

'Bye, Kate.' He squeezed her shoulders affectionately and gave her a kiss, before disentangling me and leading me away. 'Come on, darling.'

With a last buckled smile at Kate, who had her arms tightly folded, lips compressed, I got in the car beside Alex. He let out the handbrake, and in another moment we were away. I was ambushed by tears, and sensibly, Alex didn't attempt to console me.

At length, though, we hit the M4 motorway and I dried up. Rufus was listening to *Harry Potter* on his headphones, oblivious to his mother's snivelling, and Alex slipped in a CD, a frisky little Mozart number, which was cheering. And actually, the further we drove, the better I felt. By exit 8 I was tapping my foot and humming merrily, and it was only when we hit the B roads that I remembered what we were doing here and felt sick. 'I'd forgotten how rural it was,' I commented as lush spring meadows flashed by in a haze of emerald green. 'Are you sure this is only Buckinghamshire? Not Herefordshire?'

'Quite sure.'

'And it's still commutable?'

'An hour and a quarter door to door, Piers assures me.'

We purred through the Latimers' village. My village, I thought, looking around with interest, Little Harrington. It wasn't exactly picturesque, no duck pond or village green or creeper-covered pub, just a ribbon of featureless houses running alongside the roadside, but it had . . . well, it had integrity, I decided staunchly. Oh, and look, a village shop! Well, OK, a Spar. It flashed past in lurid green and orange. There didn't seem to be anyone about, though. Didn't Eleanor get lonely? I wondered nervously as the car plunged into semidarkness and we began our ascent through some woods, climbing to the top of the hill to where Stockley sat.

When the trees parted and Stockley came into view, I decided solitude had its compensations. I'd forgotten how beautiful it was. It was large, but not overly high and mighty. Its pretty Queen Anne windows looked out like benign eyes, and the sun glanced off its mellow stone façade. I could quite see why Eleanor had fallen in love with it. The fact that Piers came with it was just a minor inconvenience, I imagined. We swept on past the gates with its little lodge house, and my head swivelled back in surprise.

'We're not going in?'

'Not yet. I thought we'd go to our place first, don't you think? She's left a key out for us. Under a pot.'

'Oh. Fine.' Alex, as usual, was party to more arrangements than I was but I was determined not to be piqued. 'And you know where the cottage is?' I asked pleasantly.

'Just down this lane, apparently. Then left down a track.'

'There's a track!' cried Rufus, and Alex obediently swung the wheel and we lurched through a gap in the hedgerow. 'And there's the house, look!' He pointed as, sure enough, after we'd rattled over a couple of cattle grids and snaked down a chalky zigzag track, it came into view. A tiny whitewashed cottage flanked by a small square yard, a barn full of hay, and acres and acres of wide open space.

'Looks like a farm,' Rufus commented excitedly, undoing his seatbelt.

'Perhaps it once was. It's tiny, though, isn't it?' I said nervously.

It could have been pretty, I decided, as we waded through knee-high grass to get to it, but it had a forlorn, decrepit look: the green paint on the front door was peeling; the small front garden was just a jumble of nettles and ragwort. The back garden, as I've said, was a yard. With a stinking manure heap parked centrally. I swallowed and glanced at

Alex, who was standing and nodding appreciatively, hands on hips, eyes narrowed, like a man who's Come Home.

Next to the front garden was a field, which appeared to be inhabited.

'Cows!' yelled Rufus excitedly, running to the fence to see.

'Bulls, actually,.' I said, looking at their huge horns with horror. 'Fancy putting them all together in one field? Surely they'll fight?'

'Oh, I'm sure they're friendly,' said Alex jovially.

'And sheep! Look at all the sheep!' Rufus was running to an adjacent field and jumping on the fence in excitement.

'You can get a terrible disease from sheep,' Alex said as we followed at a distance. 'Eddie told me.'

'Eddie,' I scoffed. 'What does he know about sheep? And as Hannah pointed out, you do actually have to fondle them to get it—RUFUS, DON'T TOUCH THEM!' I rather bravely scaled the fence to rescue my son from the jaws of a tiny white lamb. 'Let's go and see the cottage.'

Alex had already deserted the bucolic scene for the relative safety of the front doorstep. 'I've found the pot, but there's no key.'

'Perhaps she meant round the back.'

We traipsed round to another peeling green door, but there wasn't even a pot by this one. Just that manure heap. Alex frowned.

'Right. Well, I suppose we'll have to go up to the house. She must have forgotten.' As we made for the car a cry went up behind us.

'Mum, I'm in! The window was open.'

'Oh, well *done*, darling!'

We hastened back, full of renewed optimism as Rufus ran to open the door. The optimism was short-lived, though. The cottage was even smaller than it looked from the outside. There was a tiny sitting room, an even smaller everything-else-room, a cupboard-sized kitchen, and upstairs, two bedrooms and a bathroom you surely wouldn't want to linger in on account of the distressed sanitary ware. Everything was covered in a thick layer of dust. I set my mouth firmly and came back downstairs. I flashed my husband a look that went beyond hatred and hissed, 'Marvellous. Absolutely marvellous.'

'Well, it's certainly got potential,' he said foolishly.

I swept past him to the kitchen. 'I know we're not parting with much money here, Alex, but common courtesy dictates that you at least sweep the kitchen floor or put some milk in the fridge. Look at the dirt!' But even as I stormed around, I knew I couldn't really give a monkey's about the size of the rooms or the dust. What was *really* depressing me was that it was glaringly apparent that there was nowhere to paint.

'Let's go and find Eleanor,' said Alex. 'I think perhaps you're right,' he added cleverly. 'We should have gone to find her in the first place. Shouldn't have arrived unannounced.'

I nodded wordlessly, following him out to the car. And of course, he'd be in London most of the time, I thought. He wouldn't be back before dark, and then at the weekends he'd no doubt find any excuse to be up at the big house, fishing for trout with Piers, flirting in the kitchen with Eleanor. That was where he'd seen himself all along, I thought with a sudden flash of realisation. Not in Shepherd's Cottage at all. Up there in the pale yellow drawing room, leaning against the marble mantel, looking gorgeous, being terribly charming, an asset to any house party. Eleanor would introduce him as her oldest friend and everyone would purr and coo and say how lucky she was to have him close by, and then the phone would go and Eleanor would carefully put her hand over the mouthpiece. 'Alex, darling,' she'd make a face, 'it's Imogen. She wants to know if you're coming back for lunch.'

Alex would sigh and roll his eyes and . . . oooh! My blood came to a rolling boil as I slammed the car door shut.

'Where's Rufus?' said Alex as he got in beside me.

At that moment, a shriek went up. 'MUMMY!'

Together we raced round the side of the house to find Rufus, by the back door, surrounded by a huge posse of aggressive-looking chickens. There must have been at least forty of them. He gazed at us, wide-eyed.

'Every time I move, they move with me!' he shrieked.

'Right,' I breathed, heart pounding. 'Don't panic—*oh!*' In another moment they'd left Rufus and rushed to surround me, attaching themselves firmly to my legs, pushing and clucking menacingly. I clutched a drainpipe and nearly fainted with fear.

'Move slowly,' commanded my husband from behind the safety of the dustbin lid he'd commandeered as a shield.

I gingerly took a step, but they swarmed with me, cackling horribly. 'H-e-lp!' I whimpered, feeling like Tippi Hedren in *The Birds*.

'Wait there,' cried Alex. 'We'll get the car.' Alex and Rufus raced off, while I, petrified, stood rooted to the spot, glancing down at the sea of feathers. Oh dear God, there were *hundreds* of them.

Moments later the car roared round the side of the cottage. The door flew open like something out of *The Sweeney*.

'Come on!' yelled Alex in seventies cop mode. 'Run for it!'

I shut my eyes, summoned up every ounce of courage—and legged it, half expecting to hear brittle bones and webbed feet snapping beneath my kitten heels. I threw myself in the car, heart pounding; Alex performed a dizzy-making handbrake turn and we flew off.

'This isn't going to work,' I gasped.

Alex patted my knee. 'Nonsense,' he soothed, 'it'll be fine. It'll all work out. Come on, we'll go up to the house the back way.'

The back way? I swung round, confused as we went past the cottage and plunged further down the track. His local knowledge was clearly more intimate than mine, which only added to my irritation.

'How come you know this way?' I snapped, still trying to get my breath. 'I thought you hadn't been to the cottage before?'

'Oh, I remember now, we came down here when I was shooting with Piers in the autumn. The second drive was down this way. It's where I shot that partridge. You couldn't come, remember?'

Oh, yes, that weekend. The shooting party. The one I'd dreaded, but had been absolutely determined to go to. Rufus had got chickenpox the day before, so after weeks of quizzing Kate on shooting etiquette and raiding her country wardrobe and spending a small fortune on a hat in Lock's, I'd had to watch Alex drive off on his own, a vision in lovat green. Well, there'd be plenty more opportunities to wear the bloody hat, I thought grimly as we drew up at Stockley's back door.

'Hi there!' sang out Alex, walking straight in. I followed him down the flagstoned back passage and the dogs came wagging, but other than that, there were precious few signs of life.

'He-lloo!' yelled Alex again, sticking his head round the kitchen door. It was the sort of kitchen I'd dreamed about in my shallower moments. Huge, high-ceilinged and baronial, with the ubiquitous Aga at one end and an open fireplace at the other.

'No one about,' commented Alex needlessly. 'Tell you what, I'll head down to the front hall and you check out the playroom.'

The playroom was about three rooms further back on the left, deep in the bowels of the intimate family side. Rufus had already zoomed off, sniffing for toys. I sighed and made to follow him, as Alex walked towards the green baize door and the more formal side of the house. Before he reached the door, however, we heard shouts coming from that direction, but from upstairs. Voices raised in anger. I turned back in surprise, as Alex's step quickened and he disappeared. I made to follow him, pushing through the baize door, from where I was afforded a view of the main front hall, dark, echoing and oak panelled with a sweeping Jacobean staircase. As my eyes adjusted to the gloom, I was just in time to see Eleanor run lightly down the stairs, her face stained with tears, and fly into Alex's arms. 'Oh, Alex darling,' she cried in a choked little voice, 'thank God you've come. Thank God!'

Don't ask me what possessed me to stand there in the gloom and watch as his arms encircled her waist and his fair head bent over her dark one. I think the answer is that I just froze. They perceived themselves to be entirely and exquisitely alone. As she lifted her face to his, though, I felt scared. I didn't want to know what came next. I turned and exited quietly through the green baize door, then barged back in again noisily, giving a loud cough. The two of them sprang apart.

'Imogen!' Eleanor regarded me in horror. 'Oh—I thought . . .' she glanced up at Alex in confusion. 'I thought you'd come alone.'

This struck me as a remarkably obtuse thing to say. 'Why?' I didn't recognise my voice. It was harsh, rasping.

'Well, you're not due till tomorrow so I assumed Alex had just popped down to look at the cottage.' She'd recovered her composure now. 'But if you've both come to look, that's marvellous. It's just I haven't had a chance to get in there yet, and it's filthy—'

'Tomorrow?' Alex interrupted. 'That's when you expected us?'

'Yes, the 25th.'

'That's right—Sunday. Look, it's in my diary.' I rummaged in my bag and drew it out. 'Here, Sunday, to Stockley.'

'But *Monday* is the 25th,' said Alex, peering over my shoulder as it simultaneously dawned on me. I flushed to my roots.

'Oh, darling, you idiot!' Alex laughed.

'Oh, well, never mind,' Eleanor said quickly. 'It doesn't matter at all. It's lovely that you're here. I'm afraid the cottage is uninhabitable tonight, though, I've got Vera and her girls going in tomorrow to scrub it from top to bottom. Don't go and look at it yet. I'll die!'

'We've already seen it,' laughed Alex.

'*No!*' she shrieked. 'How *embarrassing*. You must think I'm dreadful!'

'Not at all,' I muttered, still horrified that we were a day early. Shit.

'But that's perfect,' Eleanor was saying. 'You can stay here tonight, in much more comfort. Oh, Piers, look who's here! Isn't it marvellous?'

Piers, in a flat cap, Viyella shirt and corduroy trousers, came through from the back passage, holding two bottles of wine in each hand. I was surprised. Somehow I'd assumed he'd been upstairs with Eleanor, involved in that shouting match. Who had she been shouting at, then?

'Marvellous,' agreed Piers, coming forward with impeccable manners, sweeping off his cap and stooping to kiss me and pump Alex's hand. 'I'll get Vera to lay another couple of places at dinner then, shall I?' he went on lightly. 'I was just off to decant the port.'

'Oh—yes, of course.' Eleanor looked flustered suddenly. 'I'm so sorry, we're going to submit you to a ghastly black-tie dinner tonight.'

She grimaced. 'That's your penance, I'm afraid. You can meet all our—or all *your*—neighbours in one fell swoop.'

'Oh God—you're having a party. No, we couldn't possibly—'

'Of course you can. The more the merrier,' Piers boomed.

'Particularly with the motley crew we've got coming this evening,' Eleanor said with feeling. 'It's a bit of a duty party.'

'But—I haven't got anything to wear,' I stammered. 'I left a case of evening clothes with my neighbour. I was going to pick them up later. Why don't Alex and I just go to the pub?' I said desperately.

'Nonsense, I won't hear of it,' said Piers. 'I've got a spare dinner jacket Alex can wear and I'm sure Eleanor can find you something.'

I could feel everyone wondering how the fuller-figured Imogen, without the assistance of a crowbar and a jar of Swarfega, would ever fit into one of Eleanor's teeny-weeny dresses.

'Of course I can. In fact—I have the very thing. Come with me, Imogen.' Eleanor seized my hand and, in a moment, was bounding up the stairs with me in tow.

'Oh, but I'd better check on Rufus, I haven't seen him since—'

'He's in the playroom,' Piers informed me. 'I saw him as I came through, happy as a sandboy with Theo. You girls go and play. Alex, come and help me decant this port, would you?'

And so it was that I found myself in Eleanor's bedroom being squeezed, like a fat sausage, into a red velvet dress the size of a napkin.

'It's not actually velvet, you see, it's velour, so it stretches,' Eleanor assured me, panting with the exertion of doing up the side zip as I held my arm aloft. 'It's one size, and it fits anyone. My sister wore it last Christmas, and she's the size of a house.' Oh, marvellous. 'There!' She stood back in triumph as I regarded myself in the long mirror.

My hands instantly went to cover my cleavage. The dress was very low cut, and as I spilled voluptuously over the top, my hips splayed out even more voluptuously at the bottom. My hand scrambled in horror for the zip. 'Oh, no, I couldn't possibly wear this.'

'Nonsense, it's perfect. Honestly, Imogen, you look terrific. And look, I've got these amazing bra cups that you just slip in and attach with glue so you don't have any straps.' She was producing a couple of black triangles but I'd already scrambled out.

'No, no, honestly. Um, maybe some trousers . . .'

'Well . . .' She crossed doubtfully to her wardrobe. 'These Joseph ones are Lycra, so maybe . . .' I snatched them gratefully but of course it was wildly optimistic: I could hardly get them over my thighs.

'The red,' Eleanor said decisively, whipping out the velour number again. 'With these fantastic M&S grippy pants that hold all your bits in. Hang on, they're around somewhere . . .' She was rummaging again.

'*I have . . . the pants!*' I squeaked with feeling. Christ.

She sensed the defiance in my voice and turned quickly. 'Look, I'm sorry you've been landed with this wretched party,' she said anxiously, 'and I'm sorry you saw the cottage in such a dreadful state, but I just know everything's going to be fine. You'll love it here, really you will.'

Her eyes were wide and appealing, and actually this should have been my moment to say, yes, OK, I'm sure I will love it, but why did you fall on my husband's neck and gaze adoringly into his eyes, and why do I always get the feeling you're after him, and why should I believe you're not when you wrecked his marriage to Tilly? But I didn't. Perhaps because I didn't want to know the answers.

By the time I was ready and had settled a highly overexcited Rufus into Theo's room amidst much giggling and boyish chat, it was getting late and Alex had already gone down. The red dress, ably assisted by my very own grippy knickers and the two bra cups—a feat of engineering that relied worryingly on something called body-glue—actually didn't look too bad. I caught a glimpse of myself in a long mirror halfway down the stairs. Rather obvious, of course, a voluptuous blonde in a skimpy red dress, but as long as I ate *nothing*, I'd be fine.

Quite a few guests had arrived and gathered in the beautiful yellow drawing room. They were mostly middle-aged, these neighbours—and by neighbours I knew we were talking people who lived in the same county and not next door—the women formidable, statuesque, with lots of powder and jewellery, and the husbands, mainly ruddy-faced with paunches. They were standing in little clutches, braying loudly. One much younger man, with dark Gypsy looks and black curls that hung over his collar, was standing apart on his own, sipping a whisky. His head was cocked contemplatively as he regarded the spines of the books in the shelves. His head didn't move, but his eyes tracked right to look at me as I came in; they roved up and down as he mentally undressed me, which, since I was only wearing a napkin, didn't take long. His face lit up as if to say—ooh, good, a trollop. I flushed hotly.

My eyes darted to—ah, yes, there they were. By the fireplace. Eleanor was leaning on one end of the ornate Adam mantel in a simple black sheath dress and pearls, while Alex propped up the other. He looked so absolutely as if he belonged here, it almost took my breath away.

I fumbled in my bag for an uncharacteristic cigarette. Would Piers even notice if Alex moved in here? I wondered. It occurred to me that there might even be some grand plan going on. Maybe he was glad to have another man around; maybe it took the heat off him, or maybe, I thought wildly, he was secretly gay? Maybe he'd fathered his children and now wanted to be let off the leash? My mind whirled with possibilities and it took me a moment to realise Piers was at my elbow, offering me a glass of champagne.

'Oh. Thank you.'

'That's quite a dress, Imogen,' he murmured appreciatively.

'Thanks. It's Eleanor's.'

'Is it? Well, it doesn't look like that on her. I'd have remembered.'

Right. Perhaps not gay.

'Sorry to be boring, Imogen, but we're a bit of a non-smoking house. It's Mummy, I'm afraid.'

'Oh. Sorry.' I looked around wildly for somewhere to put it out.

'Oh, finish it now you've lit it. She's not here tonight. No, I just meant for future reference. Tell you what, come and meet Robert and Pamela Ferrers. They're terribly nice. Farmers.'

Farmers, right. By that I knew he meant landowners. Gentry.

'This is Imogen, Alex's wife. They're taking Shepherd's Cottage.'

Alex's wife. Always Alex's wife, never Imogen Cameron, she's a wonderful artist, you must see her paintings. Oh, stop it, Imogen.

Pamela was imperious-looking with a hawklike nose down which she peered from her great height. I instantly warmed to her though when she affected a mock cockney accent. ''Ello, luv, I'm Pamela.'

'Ooh, 'ello, pet, I'm Imogen!' I grinned.

'You settlin' in nicely, then?'

I gulped. Flushed. Shit. She spoke like that. Except it wasn't a cockney accent, it was a strong West Country accent. Piers looked aghast.

'Y-yeah. We are.'

'Tha's nice. Tha's a grand little cottage you got there.'

'Ooh, it's that orright,' I faltered. If I wasn't to offend her, I had to continue in this bucolic vein. All night, if need be.

'Tha's lovely soil you got down there,' Pamela was saying sagely, tapping my arm. 'Drains well an' all. Lovely an' loamy.'

'Mmm . . . ooh, it is. Loamy!'

She looked rather quizzical, hopefully puzzled by my lack of small talk and not my peculiar accent. Piers, happily, was alive to the pitfalls, and was steering me away, saving my bacon. 'And you haven't met the Middletons either,' he said loudly, walking me across the room.

'Thank you,' I whispered. 'So much.'

'My pleasure,' he growled. 'Now this is Tom and Sandra Middleton. More tenant farmers.'

'Got it,' I breathed as the Middletons broke off their conversation to smile interestedly. *Tenant* farmers. The real McCoy. Sandra Middleton, petite and pretty, smiled and extended her hand. 'Hi.'

My fingers still clenched my cigarette, which had gone out ages ago and was now a dead butt. I looked around wildly for an ashtray but there wasn't one, so I popped it in my open handbag.

'Hi,' I grinned, and took her hand.

Sandra, clearly delighted to have first crack at some new blood, was busily filling me in on her role as helper at the local playgroup. Anxious not to make any more blunders, I found myself blithely agreeing that I might well come in to help, until Sandra was practically hyperventilating with excitement. Suddenly she rested a cool hand on my arm.

'God, your bag.'

I glanced down, and saw to my horror that the little straw bag on my arm was on fire. Smoke and flames were pouring from it. 'Oh!' Instinctively I shook it off. It smouldered brightly on the carpet.

In one swift movement, a man's arm reached across, picked up the handle, and flicked it deftly into the fire, between Eleanor and Alex's legs. 'What the hell . . .?' Alex looked aghast.

'Oh God, I'm so sorry!'

'Anything precious in there?' Tom Middleton was jabbing at the burning bag with a poker. A bit of a crowd had gathered.

'No, just a lipstick, but—oh God, Eleanor, your carpet!'

All heads swivelled like a Wimbledon crowd to look at the nasty dark patch on the Persian rug.

'Oh, I wouldn't worry about that. It's ancient.' She deftly pulled a smaller fireside rug to cover the burn. 'There. It'll be our secret,' she giggled. 'Anyway, I've never really liked it.'

Alex was by my side now. 'What the hell are you up to?' he hissed.

'I put a cigarette butt in my bag. It obviously hadn't quite gone out. I would have thrown it in the fire,' I snarled suddenly, 'but you and Eleanor were hogging it!'

'Don't be so childish,' he snapped. 'Come on, we're going in to dinner.'

Seething quietly we walked silently together into the dining room. It was a beautiful room, the walls hung with dark red silk and ancestral portraits, and tonight, lit entirely by candles, which shimmered in a sea of polished mahogany and silver and white roses.

It looked as if I had Piers on my right and an old man on my left, but suddenly I saw Eleanor dart across to the twinkly-eyed Gypsy, nod and whisper conspiratorially in my direction. In a moment the old boy had been spirited away, and in his place was Heathcliff. Eleanor nipped back and directed Alex to sit next to her. She winked at me and I gave her a tight smile back. Oh, you think it's that easy, don't you? I thought. Put the local stud on Imogen's left and she'll be happy. Meanwhile you can flirt your little socks off with my husband.

As I sat down I realised the pants were a big mistake. They were clearly made of cast iron and, as such, wouldn't bend. I caught my breath. Damn. I'd only ever worn them to a drinks party before.

'Pat Flaherty,' said my neighbour with a flashing smile.

'Imogen Cameron,' I murmured, briefly taking his fingers before turning smartly to Piers, but not before I'd caught the surprise in his dark eyes and then a snort of laughter as I turned my back on him.

'So good of you to have us here,' I smiled ingratiatingly at my host, realising with horror, as I crossed my legs, that this ghastly dress was split to the thigh. It gave Pat whatever-his-name-was a bird's-eye view. I spread my napkin over my leg and leaned forward.

'Well, terribly good of you to look after all the animals,' Piers brayed.

'Not at all,' I murmured, aware that a pair of eyes was roving down my bare back now. 'What?' I came to, suddenly. 'What animals?'

'Well, only the ones down at your place, obviously. The main herd is taken care of by Ron, my farm manager, but we've always kept a few down at the cottage.'

It came to me in a flash that this was what Alex had cannily glossed over when he'd mentioned 'keeping an eye on the animals'. What he'd agreed with Piers and Eleanor—as no doubt part of our rent—and why he'd gone a bit pale when he'd seen the bulls. We were looking after them. 'You want us to feed the bulls?' I breathed.

Piers threw back his head and roared with laughter. I heard my other neighbour stifle a laugh too. Didn't he have anyone else to talk to?

'They're not bulls, they're Longhorns,' Piers explained. 'Terribly tame and very sweet-natured. We've always bred them here.'

'Oh. Right. And what do they eat, these Longhorns?'

'Four bales of hay a day as a rule,' he said airily, 'which you just pop in the roundels for them. It's all in the barn. Butter?'

'Oh. Thanks.' I took a knob. Well, that didn't sound too taxing. 'And the sheep?' I enquired nonchalantly.

'The sheep are just on grass, which is where the cows will be soon. You don't have to bother with them. The ewes are lambing, of course, but we've never had a problem with Jacobs. Won't be asking you to stick your hand up any twats, ha-ha!'

'Ha-ha, no, quite.' My eyes bulged in horror.

'Obviously the silkies need corn in the morning and then Layers

Pellets at night, but nothing more than that.'

He was talking a foreign language now. What *was* he on about?

'I'm not much of a fan myself, but Mummy's always liked them. Frightfully good sitters. Prolific layers too.'

'Oh—the chickens!'

'That's it. Silkies. Exotic breed.' He looked at me doubtfully. 'I say, are you sure you can manage? Only I can ask Ron to give a hand if not.'

'No, no.' I straightened my back. If Alex had said we could do it then we bloody well could. 'I'll be fine. My, um, aunt farms, actually.'

'Really?' He looked surprised.

'Yes. Aunt . . .' I looked around wildly. A portrait of a woman who looked a bit like the Queen hung opposite me. 'Elizabeth.'

'Right. Whereabouts?'

I paused. Gave this some thought. 'America.' Somewhere far away.

'Ah. What does she farm?'

Yes, what *did* she farm, Imogen, this mythical American aunt of yours? Fields of billowing corn sprang to mind, but I couldn't think what animals she might have. Then I remembered a chap called Bill, who I was pretty sure dabbled in farming.

'Buffalo.'

Piers looked astonished, as well he might. 'Buffalo! Oh well, you'll be fine with our little herd then,' he mused, as our starters arrived. Happily his attention was attracted at that moment by his other neighbour, a toothy woman in maroon.

'Sounds like a plucky little woman, your aunt,' said a low voice in my ear with an Irish lilt.

I turned to find a pair of dark eyes twinkling at me. 'I'm sorry?'

'Your aunt Lizzie. With the buffalo herd.'

'Yes,' I said, reaching for my glass.

God, these pants were tight. I'd only had a glass of champagne and picked at my starter and they were killing me. Was I going to pass out? I slid down in my seat, trying to straighten my body out a bit.

'Are you all right?'

'Yes, why?'

'You look rather uncomfortable. And you seem to be coming adrift.' He gestured vaguely at my chest with his fork. I glanced down to see one of my black bra cups poking cheekily out of my cleavage.

'Shit!' I dived under the table and tried to poke it back in, but the body-glue seemed to have lost its stick. In the end, in desperation, I had to pull it out, and then of course the other cup had to come out too. No handbag to stuff them in, so I sat on them. Face flaming, I turned back to Piers. Luckily he was offering to refill my glass.

'After all, you're not driving.'

'No, quite!'

I was, though, nearly passing out with the pain in my nether regions, and it occurred to me that I might faint. I slowly levered myself upright.

'Everything all right?' Piers looked up, surprised.

'Yes, thanks. Might just nip to the loo, though.'

The downstairs loo was occupied. I glanced up the huge staircase. Could I face tottering up there? No. Instead I limped through the green baize door and down the back passage to the other loo.

'Won't be a mo!' sang out a fruity male voice as I rattled the handle.

Damn. Unable to bear it any longer, I went out of the heavy back door by the boot room. In a trice, I'd hitched up my dress and peeled the wretched things off. Ooh, the relief. I rolled the pants in a ball and glanced around furtively. No handbag, so—

'I should pop them in the azaleas,' came a voice out of the night.

I froze, horrified. 'Who's there?'

A wisp of smoke drifted up my nostrils, and at the same moment, I made out a dark figure in the shadows by the woodpile: my neighbour from dinner, grinning delightedly. 'I like a girl who takes her bra off at the table then nips out to take her knickers off too,' he drawled. 'Hadn't realised it was that sort of party. Things *are* looking up.'

'How dare you spy on me!' I gasped, horrified.

'Hardly spying. I was here first. Having a mid-course ciggie. What's next, the dress? Or are you going to set fire to yourself again?'

Suddenly I realised who had flicked my bag in the fire.

'Although I have to tell you, if it *is* the dress, I'm not sure I can retain my sang-froid at the table, but I'm willing to give it a go.'

He roared with laughter as I stalked back inside. Clutching my pants, face flaming, I walked, everything jiggling about a fair bit, back into the dining room. As I neared the table I realised, with horror, my bra cups were still on my chair, for all the world to see. Oh, this was a *horrible* dinner party, I thought miserably as I added my pants to the sorry little pile and sat on them. *Horrible.*

Somehow I managed to get through the rest of the evening. I monopolised Piers during pudding, and only when politeness dictated that he turn to address a few comments to his other neighbour did I steel myself to turn to mine. His chair was empty.

'He's pissed orf,' the woman on his left informed me loudly. 'Knowing Pat, he's got some gel in the next parish keeping his bed warm.' She chuckled, showing very yellow teeth.

'Ah.' I smiled thinly. 'Yes, I might have known.' I glanced down the table to where Alex and Eleanor, heads close together, almost touching, were deep in conversation. Suddenly I felt very empty. Very alone.

A while later, during coffee in the drawing room, I slipped away. I stole upstairs and crawled into bed. As I lay there, staring at the ceiling, listening to the sound of the chatter and laughter drifting up from below, tears fell silently, sideways down my cheeks, soaking my pillow.

Sometime later, Alex crawled in beside me, smelling faintly of port. I could smell her perfume too. 'Why are you crying?' he whispered.

'I . . . don't know,' I whispered back. 'I think I'm just tired.'

'Don't cry, Imo.' He kissed me full on the mouth. 'Don't cry. It'll all be fine. I'll make it fine. You'll see.' And then he made love to me: beautifully, gently and tenderly. And when, later, he rolled over with a deep sigh and went to sleep holding my hand, I realised my cheeks were wet again. This time, though, they were tears of relief.

Chapter Four

THE FOLLOWING MORNING at breakfast, Eleanor apologised for the ghastliness of the evening. 'We do have to do these things periodically.'

'I rather enjoyed it, actually,' I lied.

I hadn't, on any level, but was still on air after last night. I felt ridiculously smug sitting here in her kitchen, knowing that, after all her efforts, my husband had come up those stairs and made love to me.

'Pat's amusing, isn't he?' she said lightly, packing Theo's book bag for school as he sat tapping his empty, upside-down eggshell and chanting a rhyme with Rufus. He was the youngest of her brood and, as such, had not yet been sent away to school.

'Mm, very,' I agreed.

'He's from Ireland, as you probably gathered. Single too. Split up with his wife last year. He's set a few hearts afluttering in the village!'

She waited, and I knew she was hoping I'd want more, but instead I nodded out of the window at her garden. 'Fabulous daffodils, Eleanor. You must have a terrific gardener.'

She looked momentarily disappointed, then rallied. 'Dick? Yes, he's very good. He's Vera's husband, you know. Ah, talk of the devil.'

At that moment, Vera and her army of helpers, three very solid-looking women in housecoats, bustled past the window up to the back door with buckets. They came down the passage, then Vera stuck her head round. 'Morning, all!'

'Morning, Vera!' Eleanor sang.

'You want us to start down at Shepherd's Cottage then?'

'Please. It's in a bit of a state, I'm afraid.'

'Right you are.' Vera grinned at me. 'Must 'ave got the shock of your life when you saw it. But don't worry, luv, I'll have it gleaming like a new pin in no time.'

I drained my coffee and got to my feet. 'I'll give you a hand. Alex has gone off with Piers, but Rufus and I could help out.'

'Ooh Lord, no, I wouldn't hear of it. You come down 'bout teatime when we've finished, eh?' She disappeared with her cronies, still talking.

'Do that, Imogen,' Eleanor advised me. 'Let Vera crack on, she'd much rather, and then you can spend the day with me,' she said happily. 'I thought we could go shopping and have lunch somewhere. There's a terrific new bistro in town I haven't tried yet.'

I smiled. 'I'd love to, but actually, I promised Hannah I'd have lunch with her today. She rang this morning, and they haven't seen Rufus for ages and he starts school the day after tomorrow. Mum's there too.'

Eleanor looked disappointed. 'I forgot your sister lives round here.' She knew everyone in the county but my sister and Eddie would not register on her social radar. 'Oh, well, maybe some other time?' She regarded me anxiously. 'I would so love us to be friends.' It was said with candour, and her hazel eyes were wide and hopeful.

'That would be lovely,' I said pleasantly. 'But right now, if Vera's sure she's all right, I might get off and do a quick food shop. I gather there's a Tesco in town?'

'There's a Waitrose too. I'm going that way myself, maybe I—'

'No, no, don't worry, I'll find it.' I waved away her offer and, taking Rufus's hand, practically dragged him off his chair. 'I like to explore.'

When Rufus had stroked every horse's nose in the stable yard, we got in our car and purred down the front drive, through the woods and into the village.

'Is that where I'll get my humbugs?' asked Rufus, pointing.

'Er, possibly.' I looked doubtfully at the Spar.

'Can we go in?'

'Yes, why not? I'll get the newspaper.'

We parked on the forecourt and went inside.

'You'll 'ave to move that,' a voice came from behind a copy of the *Daily Mirror*. 'I don't allow vehicles up against the window like that.' A woman behind the counter lowered her newspaper.

'OK, I'll move it. Choose some sweets, Rufus, and I'll be back.'

'And I don't allow unaccompanied children, neither.'

I regarded this charmless individual in her pink jogging suit. 'Right,' I muttered. 'Come on, Rufus.'

Silently we withdrew, reparked, then came back. Rufus chose some Polos—humbugs not appearing to be an option—and I picked up my *Daily Mail*. I flashed a wide smile as she took our things.

'I'm Imogen Cameron, by the way. We've just moved into the village.'

A couple of old ladies by the freezer turned and stared. Pink Jogging Suit carried on ringing up her till.

'Rufus is going to the village school, so I'll probably pop in for my paper when I drop him off. And you are . . .?'

She regarded me a long moment. 'I am what?'

'I mean, your name is . . .?'

There was a weighty silence. I could feel myself going red.

'Mrs Mitchell,' she said eventually.

As we left the shop I heard one of the old ladies say, '. . . and a packet of Rennies, please, Linda luv.'

'Linda. Her name's Linda,' Rufus said as we got back in the car. We drove off. 'Not particularly friendly,' he observed at length.

'No,' I agreed.

Having located Tesco and filled the boot of the car with groceries, we set off for Hannah's. 'Is Daddy meeting us there?' asked Rufus.

'No, Daddy's going into work today.'

'Is he? I thought he went out walking with Piers.'

'Yes, but he's going in after that,' I said shortly. I too had assumed that he'd taken the day off, but apparently an urgent piece of work on his desk required his attention. I couldn't help thinking this work had only materialised when I'd told him where we were going today.

We drew into their drive. 'Hi-ya!' I called through the letterbox, knowing the bell had long since given up the ghost.

No response and the radio was blaring, so I pushed the door, which was on the latch, and went through to the narrow hallway. It was as cluttered as ever. Hannah used to run a very tight ship, but these days it suited her to bustle around a chaotic house complaining she was far too busy to tidy up. I think a tidy house with nothing for her to do would have left her profoundly depressed. A pile of jumble blocked my way to the sitting room, but I skirted round it to the kitchen, where Hannah was making fairy cakes in her Sea Scouts uniform, complete with scarf and toggle. The bright blue shirt and skirt were stretched tightly over her ample bosom and bottom, and it occurred to me she'd put on even more weight. She must be nudging fifteen stone, I thought, quietly shocked.

'Ah,' I smiled. 'Scouts today?'

'No, Eddie likes it,' she replied drily.

I giggled and gave her a kiss. She was still quick on the draw, even if she'd let herself go in other respects.

'Yes, quite right, Scouts today. We had a meeting this morning.' She bent down to embrace Rufus. 'Hello, angel,' she beamed. 'How are you?'

'Fine, thanks. Where's Eddie?' My son cut ruthlessly to the chase.

She laughed. 'Out in the garden with Granny. Your uncle has decided to dig a pond, and your grandmother is advising him.'

'Cool. Can I go and see?' But he'd already gone.

'Where's Alex? I assumed you'd all be coming.'

I watched as Rufus flew into Eddie's arms. 'Oh, he's gone into work. Giving the commute a trial run, but he was a bit late this morning because he went for a wander with Piers first.'

'Strolling round his new estate, eh?' she said with a wry smile. 'How's it going?'

I stuck my finger in the cake mixture. 'Well, stupidly we got here a day early, so we saw the cottage at its very worst, and then had to go to a rather stuffy dinner party last night.'

'Oh Lord. Nightmare. What's it like?'

'The cottage? It's OK. It'll be fine for a bit.'

'A bit?' She eyed me knowingly. 'Cold feet already. How is Lady Muck?'

Hannah wanted no part of Eleanor's smart county set, who organised charity balls and played tennis and hunted, but I think it rankled that she couldn't even turn the invitations down.

'She's fine,' I said lightly. 'She's been very sweet, actually.'

'Sweet,' she snorted. 'I've heard that before, and then I've heard that she turns very sour.'

'What d'you mean?'

'Sue Fountain told me. Eleanor was all over her when she wanted Theo to be in some gymkhana team that Sue organises, and then when she saw her at a party, she cut her dead. And Val Harper said the same. Said she couldn't have been nicer when she wanted her to make some curtains right before Christmas, but then once she'd done them, she completely ignored her at the Carol Concert. She's not to be trusted.'

'That's a bit harsh. Just because someone's a bit fickle, doesn't mean they're not to be trusted.'

'Does in my book. Come on, let's go and find the others.'

I followed her slowly down the garden path, biting my thumbnail. If Hannah was deliberately trying to feed my neurosis she was doing a very good job of it. Mum and Eddie were standing by a rather muddy crater, showing Rufus the fish as he crouched down at the water's edge. 'Look, Mum.' He turned as I approached. 'They're enormous!'

I bent to look. 'Oh, yes, huge. And what fantastic water lilies!'

'Plastic,' beamed Mum proudly. 'All the greenery—everything.'

'Yes, and the thing is,' Eddie was hopping uncomfortably from foot to foot in the mud, 'the fact that they're not real means the fish aren't getting the oxygen they need from them.'

I made a sympathetic face. 'She'll be gone soon, Eddie, and then you can ship in as much oxygen-giving greenery as you like.'

'Perhaps I'll have a mixture,' said Eddie diplomatically. 'Shall we go to the pub?'

'Ooh, yes.' Mum quickly stubbed her cigarette out.

'Why so keen?' I asked, eyeing her suspiciously. Mum liked a drink or six but much preferred a smart wine bar to a country pub.

'Your father's going to be there,' she confided, 'and he's bringing Dawn. You haven't met Dawn, have you?'

'Er, no.'

'Oh, she's marvellous, Imogen,' she breathed. 'Your father met her in Currys—she was senior sales assistant on washing machines—but he's taken her away from all that, and now she wants to be a doctor.'

'Oh, right. Is she bright?'

'Breathtakingly stupid,' she chortled. 'Isn't it priceless? And her mother—ooh, you must meet her mother.' Her eyes sparkled.

'Must I?' I said nervously.

'Yes. Dawn never goes anywhere without her mother, a huge woman in a purple coat, who just sits, solidly, without saying a word. No one can remember her name, not even your father, and he's known her for three months so now it's too late to ask. Oh, they're terrific, darling.'

'Great,' I said uncomfortably as Hannah caught my eye.

It was marvellous that Mum could be so relaxed about Dad's girl-friends, but the delight Mum took in her ex-husband making a fool of himself was sometimes discomforting. She hadn't always been so phlegmatic about his love life. When Dad had first gone off with Marjorie Ryan, a great family friend whom Mum had modelled Dior gowns with in the sixties, she was devastated. I think she'd been relieved when he'd moved on to Audrey, a rather dumpy marketing executive; had perked up tremendously when Audrey had been traded in for Michelle, a peroxide-blonde hygienist, and was positively enchanted by Dawn.

As we all trooped off to the pub at the end of the road we passed Hannah's local, an attractive whitewashed pub with lots of hanging baskets, and went on to a rather forbidding red-brick place called the Royal Oak.

'Why are we going here?'

Hannah shrugged. 'Dad suggested it. God knows why. It's a dive.'

Happily it had a garden, albeit practically in the car park. Dad was already *in situ*, beside him was a girl decidedly younger than me and, sure enough, opposite her, a woman in a purple coat.

'Imogen darling,' boomed my father in his best John Gielgud voice, which is nothing like his native Welsh one, as he stood up to greet us. 'How simply wonderful.' He kissed us all, including Mum, and pumped Eddie's hand. 'Now, I don't think you've met Dawn yet, have you?'

'No, I haven't,' I agreed, smiling as I shook hands with the pasty-faced girl with too much eye make-up. 'Hello.'

'Hi,' she muttered, avoiding my eyes.

'And her mother . . .' went on Dad, 'er . . .' He gestured hopelessly. I put out my hand but Dawn's mother clutched her handbag grimly and gazed past me.

Dad rubbed his hands. 'Er, right. Now. Drinks, everyone?'

'I'll do it,' Eddie offered.

'Right you are, lad.' Dad beamed and sat down smartly, notoriously tight. My father had been considered rather good-looking in his day: his piercing blue eyes and high cheekbones were quite startling, but he was only about five foot eight and as such, suffered rather from small-man syndrome. He never walked, always strutted importantly, very much the actor, making grandiose, theatrical gestures with his hands. His acting career when we were young had mostly revolved around the theatre, but now it was more television-orientated he was becoming slightly better known. Recently he'd carved something of a niche for himself as the Attractive Older Man, and appeared regularly in a hospital soap opera. Sometimes he simply forgot he wasn't on screen.

'How about some crisps, laddie?' he boomed now, striding ostentatiously to the bar. When Eddie had sat down with the drinks and Dad was out of earshot, Mum turned innocent eyes on Dawn. 'I gather you're going to be a doctor?'

Dawn stared opaquely at Mum. 'Yeah, well, I was, only I can't now 'cos I haven't got biology GCSE, and the fing is they say you need that to go on to the next bit.'

Mum's brow puckered. 'Oh, what a shame. So what are you going to do instead?'

'I'm gonna be a beautician. Gonna go to college an' that. And the fing is, I'm still helping people, aren't I? I reckon it's still health care?'

'Oh, very definitely,' Mum purred. 'In fact the girl who does my nails wears a white coat, which says a lot, doesn't it?'

'Yeah,' Dawn brightened. 'Yeah, it does.'

Mum winked at me but I ignored her, uncomfortable. Dawn was a bit of a soft target. I turned to the mother. 'That'll be handy then,' I smiled. 'Having a beautician in the family.'

Even as I said it, I knew it was a mistake. She retreated back into her many chins and regarded me blankly. Luckily Dad came back.

'That's what I like to see,' he said, 'all my family round the same table together—marvellous. Cheers! God bless us all.' He raised his pint and beamed around, and actually, you couldn't help but smile back.

'Have you seen Dad's shoes?' Hannah murmured in my ear.

I nodded. The white Gucci loafers with elaborate tassels hadn't escaped me. 'And the black leather jacket,' I muttered back.

'Well, what do you expect from a middle-aged man with a twenty-six-year-old girlfriend . . . Oh God, he's not.'

'Not what?'

Hannah swung round. I followed her eyes. Dawn, her arm linked through Dad's, was leading him away conspiratorially.

'They have karaoke hour at lunchtime sometimes in this pub, and I've got an awful feeling that's why they wanted to—'

'Oi, listen, you lot.' Dawn turned back importantly. 'Martin's gonna sing "Love Me Tender" in the saloon bar if you wanna watch!'

Mum's face was a picture. 'Wouldn't miss it for the world,' she breathed, getting hastily to her feet. 'Come on, Rufus, quick.'

'Mum, d'you really think Rufus should—' But he'd gone.

'Consider it part of his education,' said Hannah, drily. 'The first time he saw his grandfather on stage. A defining moment.' She got up.

'You're not going too?' I said, appalled.

'No, I'm all through with being defined by Dad. I need a pee.'

She made her way heavily up the garden path. Eddie and I watched her go. 'Eddie . . .'

'Yes, I know,' he said quickly. 'She's put on weight.'

'*Lots* of weight, Eddie.' I turned to face him. 'Why?'

He shrugged miserably. 'I don't know. She just doesn't seem to be able to stop eating. She's touchy about it, Imogen. I can't talk to her.'

'What—about anything?'

He hesitated. 'This weight thing *is* everything, as far as she's concerned. And I know she's eating for a reason, but . . .'

'But the two of you are fine? I mean, as a couple?'

'Oh, yes, couldn't be happier. It's just,' he hesitated. 'Well, I know she feels there's something missing.'

'Eddie . . .' I licked my lips. 'Have you thought of adopting?'

He looked at me. 'We went down that route a year ago.'

'Did you?' I was astonished.

He shrugged. 'She didn't want to tell anyone at the time in case people got their hopes up for us. And then—well, then when we got turned down, she didn't really want to talk about it.'

I swallowed. 'Why did they . . .?'

'Turn us down? Oh, you know. Our combined ages, the state of the house, Hannah apparently being medically obese, that kind of thing.' He sighed. 'No matter how much love you've got inside to give, it's the outside that counts.'

I was silent. I couldn't even begin to imagine how that must hurt.

Eddie shifted in his seat, a regrouping gesture. 'But as I say, that was a year ago. The baby business is over as far as we're concerned. We'll never have them. Or she'll never have them. And that's the problem, Imo, she feels unfulfilled.'

'But having children isn't everything. I mean—she has such a full life! She's a wonderful teacher, all her kids adore her, and all that Sea Scouts and Brownies and youth club and everything—she never stops.'

'But that's just it. She never stops to pause for thought, because the sadness would overwhelm her. She's got to be busy.'

I swallowed. 'She's grieving, Eddie. It'll pass.'

'I know.' He nodded sadly.

'Come on.' I got to my feet and pulled him up with me. 'We're missing the cabaret.'

Inside, the pub was heaving. As I walked down the passage towards the saloon bar I recognised my father's tones booming out 'You're the One that I Want!' at full volume. It was still something of a shock, however, when I pushed through the smoky glass door.

Up on a makeshift stage at the far end of the room, my father, a.k.a. John Travolta, was on his knees and leaning back, as Dawn, a.k.a. Olivia Newton-John, stood astride him, hands on hips as she ooh, ooh, ooh, honeyed, down. The room was full of people urging them on with my mother and Rufus at the front, convulsed with laughter. Hannah appeared at my elbow from the Ladies, looking horrified.

'This is practically my local,' she yelled. 'What is he *thinking* of?'

'Well, it's my local too now, so let's get him off after this.'

The song ended on a rousing note and Dawn leapt into Dad's arms with a flourish as they took their applause. Dawn was helped off the stage by admiring hands, but as Dad was about to step down too, the opening chords of 'Brown Sugar' struck up. His face registered a flash of recognition and in another moment he'd morphed into Mick Jagger, strutting about and punching the air aggressively.

Hannah moaned. 'Tell me it's a bad dream. Someone pull the plug!'

But Dad was unstoppable. The crowd loved him and wouldn't let him go. As the opening chords of 'Satisfaction' struck up Hannah and I looked at each other determinedly. As one, we hustled to the front. We saw 'Satisfaction' through to the bitter end, but before the mournful opening chords of 'Angie' had even struck up we'd formed a pincer movement and hustled him bodily off the stage.

'But I was going to do "Don't Go Breaking My Heart" next,' Dad complained. He sulked all the way back to the table in the garden.

Mum and Rufus followed us, Rufus still giggling uncontrollably. 'You were awesome, Grandpa,' Rufus assured him.

Dad beamed. 'It's all in the timing, lad, you see. All in the timing. Now, another drink? Do the honours, Eddie, there's a good chap.'

'No, thanks, Dad,' said Hannah. 'I think we'll get off home.' We glanced around, keen to go, but there was no sign of Dawn's mother.

'Perhaps she went back inside and we missed her? I'll go in and take a look,' suggested Mum. When she reappeared two minutes later, her eyes were like dinner plates. 'Come and look at this!' she urged.

There, on stage, in a red spangly dress that had clearly been under the coat the whole time, was Dawn's mum, singing Barbra Streisand's 'Evergreen'. Our jaws dropped as we listened to the tones of pure gold that rang out. When she'd finished there was a moment's silence—then everyone broke into enthusiastic applause. 'She used to be an opera singer,' Dawn shouted over the din. 'Good, i'nt she?'

We all agreed that she certainly was, and as I said to Rufus on the way home later that afternoon, it just went to show that you should never judge a book by its cover.

'Or even,' he added sagely, 'by its purple coat.'

When Rufus and I got back to the cottage, the chickens rushed up in an enthusiastic gang. Rufus and I peered from the car windows in alarm. 'Can I have a piggyback?' Rufus whispered.

I swallowed, looking at the squawking, clucking squad that had surrounded the car. I'd quite like a piggyback myself.

'Right. Climb on my back then.' Gingerly I put one foot out of the driver's door. 'Off we . . . go!' With Rufus bouncing around on my back I sprinted across the yard and up the front path. As I ferreted feverishly in my bag for my key, they swarmed around my legs, pushing and shoving. Feathers and—ugh—*beaks*—brushed my legs. I was all for free range, but they'd be in the house soon if—'Oi!' One large mother-clucker steamed through the gap before I could stop her.

'No! Out!' I grabbed a cushion from a chair and shooed her out as Rufus hid behind the door.

'I don't like that, Mummy. I don't like that they want to come in.'

'No. I'm not wild about it either,' I admitted. I dropped the cushion and gazed around. 'Oh, but, Rufus, look at *this*!'

'Cool,' he agreed.

Vera and her team had worked wonders. The wooden floorboards shone like a ship's deck, and bright, jewel-coloured rugs had been put down to cover the knotty bits. The windows gleamed, and through them, the fields, green and pleasant, shone back. The furniture had been replaced with basic, but much more comfortable sofas and chairs in a cheerful floral pattern. Upstairs, the beds had been made and our clothes hung up in wardrobes.

'Golly.' I spun around in wonder as I came back down. 'Mary Poppins has been in.' A huge bunch of flowers sat in a jug on the kitchen table, and next to it, a bowl of fruit with a note. I picked it up.

Dear Imogen,

There's milk and eggs in the fridge and a pile of logs outside should you need a fire. The chimney's been swept so it should work! Hope everything is OK. So sorry you saw it in such a state yesterday.

Love, Eleanor

'How kind,' I murmured. 'She must have brought the fruit and flowers down herself.'

'It does look amazing, doesn't it, Mummy?' said Rufus anxiously. I could tell he wanted me to be pleased, not the complaining, carping mother of yesterday. 'It's very kind of Eleanor and Piers, isn't it?'

'Very,' I smiled. 'And it looks fantastic. And actually, Rufus, I think we're going to have a lovely time here.'

'But where will you paint?' His brow puckered up.

'Well, I can paint in here.' I sat down at the little table under the window. 'Not oils—too smelly and messy—but I can do watercolours. You know, try some book illustrations, like I've always meant to do.'

'Yes, and draw the lambs! You can see them from the window.'

I smiled. So I could. And I liked the sheep. They dotted the green hillside attractively, like bits of cotton wool; all sort of pastoral and calming. They kept their distance too. If only the cows could be encouraged to do the same, but they were lining up even now in a rather alarming manner at the gate, mooing horribly. They'd been doing it when we'd left this morning—surely they'd need to do some grazing now and again?

I moved around the cottage, familiarising myself with it, wondering, rather guiltily, if I'd got it all wrong. If Eleanor really did just want to help, and for us to be happy? I remembered her worried face and twisting hands this morning—'I would so love us to be friends'—and how I'd snubbed her. On an impulse, I picked up the phone. Eleanor had thoughtfully put a list of numbers by it—her own private line, the doctor, farm manager, vet—and I dialled her number.

'Hello?'

'Eleanor, it's Imogen. Listen, thank you so much. We've just got back here and I can't tell you how pretty the cottage looks. Vera and her girls have done a brilliant job.'

'You like it?' I could almost feel her flush with pleasure at the other end. 'Oh, Imogen, I'm *so* pleased. I was a bit worried you'd think they'd gone too far, unpacking all your stuff, but—'

'It's perfect,' I said, cutting her short. 'Honestly, Eleanor. And thank you for the fruit and flowers.'

'My pleasure,' she said happily. 'I was wondering if you'd like a kitchen supper with us tonight? We hardly got to speak to you yesterday.'

I hesitated. I quite wanted a quiet supper down here on our first night, but didn't want to appear rude.

'That's really kind. Can I ask Alex when he comes in?'

'Oh, but he's here now. I'll ask him, shall I? ALEX!' she called.

My heart began to pound. He'd gone straight to her house on returning from work? Was this to be a pattern?

'Hello, darling, had a good day?'

'Alex, what are you doing there?'

'What d'you mean, what am I doing here?'

'Well, why didn't you come back here from work?'

'Oh, I didn't go in the end, because by the time Piers and I got back from walking round the farm, it was nearly midday. Simply wasn't worth it. Piers had a meeting to go to, but Eleanor and I went to a really nice bistro in town. Apparently you were invited.'

I couldn't speak I was so angry. 'Why didn't you come and have lunch with Hannah and Eddie?' I hissed eventually. 'With us!'

'I tried,' he said patiently, 'but there was no answer from their house, and your phone was switched off.'

'You could have tried the pub!'

'I did, actually. Eleanor and I stopped at that pretty whitewashed one with the hanging baskets, but there was no sign. I'm sorry, darling.'

I had to sit down I was so furious. 'Right,' I said quietly. 'Right. OK. Fine. You're coming home now, I take it?'

'Well, Eleanor's asked us for kitchen supps. They've got a brace of pheasants from the freezer so—'

'COME HOME NOW AND FUCK THE PHEASANT!'

There was a long silence. 'Right,' he said eventually. 'I won't do the latter, if it's all the same to you, but I'll be back shortly.'

The line went dead. I sank back in the kitchen chair and imagined the scene unfolding now in the Latimers' kitchen: Eleanor, wide-eyed, while Alex explained that I was a bit tired from the move. Eleanor would be making sympathetic noises about how stressful moving was, or—or maybe, I thought suddenly, they'd just smile secretly at each other, before falling into each other's arms. My hands flew to my mouth. Was I going mad? Were they deliberately sending me mad, were they having a steaming, torrid affair, or was it all in my mind? Oh God. Had I overreacted? Yes, of course I had. She was an old family friend, who was simply trying to help, and here I was, behaving like a . . .

I was aware of a rustle behind me. I turned. A little white face was watching me through the banisters. 'Are you all right, Mummy?'

'Yes, love. I'm fine.'

'Is . . . Daddy coming home?'

'Yes. Yes, he is. Very soon.'

Rufus nodded and crept back upstairs.

This was not good. Not good for Rufus. And anyway, I thought, what if I did ask him if there was anything going on and he said—yes? Would I leave him? Would I walk out? My breathing became shallower. The awful truth was, I knew I wouldn't. I loved him too much.

Ten minutes later the front door slammed. Alex strode in, his face suffused with barely controlled rage. A muscle was going in his cheek.

'This is how you repay them.' He swept his hand round the room. 'For all this. This cottage, this hospitality, this—this *kindness*—this, this rudeness! This jealousy! *This* is how you thank them!'

I hung my head. 'I'm sorry,' I whispered.

'I had to tell them you were ill. They both heard you screaming—thought you were barking!'

'Piers was there too?'

'Yes, of course he was, jointing the bloody pheasants!'

Right. So he hadn't been exchanging secret smiles with Eleanor.

'I'll apologise,' I promised. 'Tomorrow. I'll go and see them.'

'Yes, well, don't make a meal of it,' he snapped. 'Just . . . get a grip, Imo, OK?' He looked at me pleadingly. Desperately, almost.

'OK.' I nodded, knowing I was about to cry.

After a moment, his face changed. His anger seemed to dissipate and he just looked tired. Defeated. His shoulders sagged. I took a step, uncertainly. He opened his arms and I walked into them. Clung on.

'I love you, Imo, you know that, don't you?' he whispered.

I nodded, tears streaming down my face. 'I love you too.'

The following morning, when Alex had gone to work, I rang Kate.

'Oh, hello, stranger!'

I laughed. 'Don't be ridiculous, I've only been gone a day. Anyway, I rang you yesterday and you weren't there.'

'Out at a rehearsal, probably. So how's it going?' she asked.

'Oh, Kate, it's great,' I enthused, determined to be upbeat; to support Alex in this decision, as we'd agreed last night.

'I know it's difficult, Imo,' he'd said, stroking my hair, 'but let's at least put a brave face on it, eh?'

I'd felt so ashamed. But I'd glowed inside too. For the second time in two days we'd made love. That was unheard of in London. Perhaps getting away from it all was making a difference.

'Really? You're enjoying it?' said Kate in surprise.

'Well, the countryside is glorious. Right now, for instance, just from my kitchen window I can see—'

'No, no, don't describe it,' she moaned. 'I beg you. What—baby lambs gambolling in clover? Go on then, make me puke.'

'Something like that,' I admitted, 'although I have to say, it's a lot noisier than I imagined. The lambs bleat all night—and the cows! They bellow, Kate, really bellow. Not to mention the chickens.'

'Probably hungry,' she observed. 'Animals tend to make themselves heard if they want something. And what about wicked Queen Eleanor in her castle on the hill? Still casting spells from her ivory tower?'

'Actually she's been terribly kind,' I said. 'She's provided us with a heavenly cottage, and left flowers and a basket of fruit for us.'

'Nice rosy apples?'

'Yes, why?'

'Don't touch them, Imogen. Think of poor Sleeping Beauty.'

I laughed. 'I've decided I've got that all out of proportion. How's the play going?' I deliberately changed the subject. 'Don't the Chelsea Players usually do a Shakespeare thingy at this time of year?'

She groaned. 'They do. *As You Like It*. And the answer is—slowly. The director has got some idiotic notion that we should play it in modern dress. I think I'm pretty dire too,' she said gloomily. 'Still,' she brightened, 'it's only am-dram. How's Rufus?'

'Fine.' I lowered my voice. 'Well, no, a bit nervous actually, Kate. He starts school tomorrow. We went to look at it yesterday.'

We'd cruised past it on the way back from Hannah's, and in a fit of enthusiasm, I'd stopped the car. 'Isn't it pretty?' I'd gushed as we'd drawn up outside a little brick schoolhouse with a clock tower.

'I don't think that's the school, Mummy. All the children are coming out of that building over there.' He'd pointed to some modern Portakabins beyond, where, sure enough, hordes of noisy children in red and grey uniform were running into a playground.

'Oh. Right. Well, let's wander over there, shall we?'

We got out and I walked breezily up to the railings, Rufus trailing behind. We watched as various games of skipping and football unfurled. The football came towards us and bounced over the low railings. As a shaven-headed boy ran to get it, I picked it up and smiled.

'Oi! Gimme that!'

I threw it back over. 'I was about to!' I said chummily. 'Catch!'

He caught it and glared at me. 'Tosser.'

We walked back to the car and got in silently. My hands felt rather clammy as I fumbled for the ignition and I wondered, nervously, if all the boys were like that. It was just a bit more . . . rough and tumble than Rufus was used to. Terribly good for him, actually. Less precious.

'And did he like it?' demanded Kate down the phone, now.

'Quite,' I said cagily. 'It—you know—gave him a flavour, anyway.'

'Well, let me know how it goes. Orlando's going to start fencing next term, isn't that adorable?'

'Lovely,' I said faintly, thinking that the only fencing Rufus would be doing at that school would be buying and selling stolen goods. I put the phone down and rang Hannah in a panic.

'No, no, it's a lovely school,' she chided. 'You've obviously just got a bad glimpse of it. It does very well in the league tables. OK, the children are quite noisy and boisterous, but they're little boys, Imo. They're hardly going to be sitting in huddles doing tapestry, are they?' She laughed and I tinkled along merrily; felt sick inside.

'And the headmaster's a real honey.'

'Is he?' I said eagerly, grasping at this like a drowning man to a float.

'Yes, the children love him. Quite strict, but very approachable. You always see them hanging round his legs. The mothers too.'

'Oh!'

'Well, Daniel Hunter is rather gorgeous. I'm surprised you haven't heard. Quite the local heart-throb, and unattached too. You'll meet him tomorrow. Apparently he always makes a point of greeting the new children. Has a little chat.'

'Right.'

Well, that sounded promising, anyway. Hannah was clearly rather taken with Mr Hunter and my sister was not easily charmed. Maybe he'd turn out to be Rufus's defender and champion, and all would be well. I reached into the fruit bowl for an apple and took a bite out of it. It was sourer than one would have hoped.

Chapter Five

THE FOLLOWING DAY when I tried to take Rufus to school, we could scarcely get out of the house. 'Oh, this is ridiculous,' I spluttered as we opened the door to twenty, tight-beaked, beady-eyed hens. 'Come on, darling, let's make a run for it.' We legged it to the car and roared off, scattering feathers, no doubt, in our wake.

'But where do they live, Mum?' asked Rufus, gazing out of the back window. 'I mean, where do they go at night?'

'Well, most chickens live in a pen but these are free range, so—God knows. Up in the trees, I expect.'

'Oh. Can they fly?'

'Of course they can fly. They've got wings, haven't they?'

I glanced at the clock. Christ, we were going to be late. First day, and we were going to be late. Alex had left early and forgotten to reset the alarm for us, so I'd woken about twenty minutes ago. Rufus was still swallowing his toast and Marmite beside me now in the car.

'Oh, look, another lamb's been born!' Rufus leaned out of his window as, sure enough, just as we'd witnessed yesterday, a tiny long-legged lamb was suckling, its tail whisking the air.

'Just two minutes, Mummy—please! I want to see!'

'You'll see it this afternoon, Rufus,' I said, accelerating brutally up the track. 'When you get home.'

'But I won't know which one it is!' He swung back.

'I'll remember,' I promised. 'The mother had a black face.'

'They've all got black faces,' he pointed out sulkily, twisting forward in his seat. 'We spotted that last night.'

Yes, last night, when Alex had finally returned from work after a bloody commute—'Two hours door to door,' he'd announced bitterly. 'So much for an hour and a quarter!'—we'd gone out into the fields, the three of us, to try to remember what the hell we were doing here. The crab apple blossom was heavy on the boughs over our heads, and beneath it, the new lambs skipped around bleating in the lush spring grass. It would have taken a heart of stone not to succumb.

'Worth it?' I'd hazarded at length, looking up at my husband's profile.

'Worth it,' he agreed, his face relaxing as he squeezed my hand.

We stopped to lean on a low, mossy stone wall and gazed into the misty blue yonder. Alex narrowed his eyes to the vista; a couple of fields away in the dip of the valley, a stream, clear and glistening, rushed on its way fringed by nodding buttercups, and beyond that, the hills rose up in a comforting swell, green and wholesome. He nodded. 'This is exactly what I wanted for us, Imo. What could be better?' He'd bent his head to kiss me.

Rufus had turned at that moment and wolf-whistled, and we'd laughed and strolled on. As we'd walked, the three of us, back to the cottage, I'd felt like we were a family in a cereal commercial. That was yesterday, though, and right now, we had to get to school pronto.

The children were all pouring in through the gates as we parked by the Spar—not too close—and made our way across the road. Even though I'd been short of time I'd made a bit of an effort for Rufus's first day, throwing on a little Armani jacket: a mistake, I now realised, as most of the other mothers looked like they'd just crawled out of bed. The bare legs, trainers and anorak look abounded, and I felt horribly self-conscious. I was also uncomfortably aware that Rufus appeared to be the only one wearing a blazer.

To achieve the school gates we had to negotiate a clutch of mothers who'd gathered for a gossip. They stared at me with hostile eyes as I approached, jaws rotating as they masticated gum, looking rather like the cattle I'd just left behind. They made no effort to move.

'Excuse me, please,' I said pleasantly.

An overweight, pasty-faced girl nudged her companion and they parted for me grudgingly. They all had identical stripy blonde hair with black roots and were pierced liberally. They looked about eighteen.

'Do I go straight to my class?' asked Rufus nervously as we pushed through a swing door to a noisy corridor, thronging with children.

'No, we go and see the headmaster first. He's down the end on the right, apparently, but that must be your class,' I said, as we passed a glass door marked Year Two. 'Doesn't it look nice?'

It didn't, in fact. All hell was breaking loose as two boys at the back of the room stood on desks; others were banging desk lids and shouting at each other. There wasn't a teacher in sight.

Rufus went pale. I swallowed and hurried him down the corridor to the office at the bottom. I knocked, and a voice barked back, 'Yep?'

Mr Hunter's head was buried in some papers, but he raised it when he saw us. Smiled. 'Mrs Cameron?'

I nearly fainted with relief. Someone was expecting us. 'That's it.'

'And you must be Rufus.' He came round the side of his desk, proferred his hand, and Rufus shook it. I relaxed. This was more like it.

'It's lovely to have you here with us,' he told Rufus. 'You're going to be in Year Two and I hope you'll be very happy at St John's.'

'Thank you,' whispered Rufus shyly.

'We, um, passed his classroom, actually.' I pointed tentatively back over my shoulder. 'But there didn't appear to be anyone . . .?'

'Ah, no, Mrs Harding's on her way. She got stuck in traffic, just called in. Sit down, sit down.' He waved us into seats. 'No doubt you saw it in uproar then,' he grinned. 'But don't worry, in no time at all you won't hear a pin drop. Ah, look, here she is now.'

I glanced out of the window. I half expected to see a grey-haired battle-axe emerge from her battered Escort, but instead, a red Mini performed an emergency stop and a ravishing blonde in a short skirt and long black boots got out. She grinned up at the window.

'Mrs Harding doesn't take any nonsense,' he said. 'Did you think I was running more of a zoo than a school, Mrs Cameron?'

'Oh, no,' I said, embarrassed. 'It's just—'

'It's not quite what you and Rufus are used to?'

'Sort of.'

He nodded. 'I understand. I used to teach at a very similar school to Rufus's. Not far from you actually, the Falcon, in Barnes.'

'Oh!' The Falcon was a very sweet school. 'So . . . how come—'

'I ended up head of a rural state school when I could still be in the cushy private sector?'

I blushed. Hannah was quite right. This man was devastatingly good-looking and had a very direct, engaging manner. Despite the slightly old-fogey corduroy jacket and the horn-rimmed spectacles, he had a head of springy tawny curls and a pair of bright blue eyes.

'I needed a change,' he said simply. 'Teaching well-behaved boys like Rufus,' he nodded at him sitting quietly in his chair, 'was not terribly testing. Running a school where discipline was a dirty word was a little more challenging. It's been an uphill struggle but the battle's been won. Ofsted have recommended us for commendation, this year.'

I smiled. 'I'm impressed.'

He grinned. 'Sorry. Blowing my own trumpet. But it's the kids I'm proud of, not me. Anyway, let's show Rufus to his class.'

He led the way; Rufus and I hurried after him. Sure enough, the room we'd passed earlier was now in silence.

I glanced at Rufus. 'Good luck, darling,' I whispered, feeling sick.

Daniel Hunter guided Rufus through the door with one hand on his shoulder. For a moment there I nearly scuttled in after them, but a surprised look from the headmaster stopped me. I waited in the corridor.

'This is Rufus Cameron,' I heard him say. 'He's just moved to the village and he's starting here today. Er . . . yes. Damien Phillips, you'll be in charge of looking after Rufus for the rest of the week, showing him the ropes et cetera. Thank you, Mrs Harding.'

He nodded to the teacher and came out, closing the door behind him, and made to move off down the corridor. I was still watching Rufus nervously. 'He's allergic to tomatoes,' I whispered.

Daniel Hunter came back. 'Well, he can help himself at lunchtime, so I'm sure he can avoid them. Shall we . . .?'

'And if there's any cross-country running, could he not participate? Only the one time he did it, he was sick. Terribly sick.'

'We don't make them go cross-country running aged nine. Rufus will be fine. Give him a couple of days and he'll be right in the thick of it.'

'Yes. Absolutely.'

I hurried away, knowing full well that he wouldn't. If Rufus wasn't in the thick of it at Carrington House, what chance did he stand here?

As I arrived back at the cottage, the usual bestial reception was waiting for me. I ran the chicken gauntlet to the front door, then slammed it shut behind me, irritated. Suddenly a thought occurred. What was it Kate had said about them being hungry? I wondered when Piers wanted us to take over the feeding from his farm manager. I glanced at the list Eleanor had left by the telephone and rang him on his mobile.

'Is there a problem?' Piers barked immediately.

'Er, no. No problem. I just wondered when you wanted me to start feeding the animals.'

There was a silence. 'I assumed you started two days ago when you moved in. I ran you through it at dinner the other night, remember?'

Out of the window, a posse of tight-beaked hens, and behind them, a row of wide-eyed, reproachful cows, waited with bated breath for my response. 'No, no,' I croaked. 'I meant . . . feeding them—you know—vitamins. Extra nutrients, that type of thing.'

'Oh, I don't hold with any of that nonsense,' he said impatiently. 'Supplements are a big con on the part of the manufacturers. The cows get enough nutrients from the hay, and there's everything but the kitchen sink in the chicken feed. I don't mollycoddle my animals.'

'Right,' I whispered. 'Just checking. I'll . . . pass, on the vitamins.'

I put down the phone. Oh God, I was starving them. How *awful*!

I tore outside—the chickens hot on my heels—and ran to the large covered barn. Right, now think, Imogen, think. I spun round wildly, looking at the various bins and sacks. What was it he'd said? Hay for the cows, and corn for the chickens? Or was it the other way round? I opened a dustbin full of yellow popcorn stuff. The chickens gathered eagerly, goading me on. Ah yes, this must be it—with a handy scoop too. I dug deep, took the brimming scoop out to the yard, threw it up into the air and, as the grain rained to the ground, the hens fell on it, famished.

'Sorry, sorry,' I whispered, as they pecked away furiously. One huge brown head waddled out from under a bush with a row of yellow chicks behind her. My eyes popped. Chicks! I didn't even know they existed! Oh, how divine! But the cows: their heads were over the yard gate and they were bellowing balefully.

'I'm coming, my darlings. I'm coming—oh, you poor things!'

I tore back to the barn. Hay, that was what I needed. Four bales, apparently. Oh, *so stupid*, Imogen. Never mind, you're doing it now. I seized a bale from the top of a stack by its binder twine, but—Jesus. I buckled under its weight. Literally, collapsed in a heap. It was nearly as heavy as me. Nearly as *big* as me. There was no way I could carry this. I wriggled free and, covered in hay, dragged it backwards out of the barn, across the yard to the gate, panting with exertion as the cows bellowed louder, pushing and jostling excitedly at the sight of it.

Somehow, I managed to open the gate, drag the bale through, and shut it just in time behind me. The cows were on top of me now, snatching at the hay with their teeth, and frankly, I was bloody terrified, but I wasn't going to just leave it in the mud to be trampled underfoot. Oh, no, I was jolly well going to put it in one of those jolly old roundel things like Piers had told me. Except—no. I tottered precariously as they jostled me. These were big beasts.

'Steady, Homer . . . easy now, Bart . . .' Rufus had had a hand in the naming, 'that's my foot . . . don't push, don't—oh!'

The next minute, Santa's Little Helper had given me an enthusiastic head butt in the backside and I nose-dived into the mud. And not just mud, mind, but . . . oh . . . Lordy. By measuring my length, though, I had made it to the roundel, and keen to complete the task—but knowing I didn't stand a chance of tossing the bale over as Piers had teasingly suggested—I began laboriously to work the hay free of its binder twine and chuck it over in handfuls.

Each bale, I worked out over a soothing cup of coffee some time later, would take precisely fifteen minutes to get out of the barn, drag to the field, break into sections, and throw over into the roundels. Ergo, each day, it would take me precisely one hour to feed the cows. Well, that was fine, I reflected. After all, I had nothing else to do, did I? My heart lurched with fear. What I'd generally do now, of course, I thought, was pop upstairs to my studio. I should go and buy that sketch pad, get some watercolours too. My heart wasn't in it, though. I gripped my mug, feeling panic rising. Well, I didn't *always* paint in London, did I? Sometimes I'd force myself to have an admin day. And then pop over the road for a coffee with Kate. Well, I couldn't do that; didn't *know* anyone. A lump rose in my throat. Apart from Eleanor, and I knew she'd be keen to introduce me to her friends, but . . . I sort of knew what they'd be like. Riding to hounds with one hand and juggling charity committees with the other. Hannah's friends, then? No, equally scary. I'd probably have to save the rain forests while simultaneously singing 'Ging Gang Goolie'. What about the mothers at school? I took a quick gulp of scalding coffee as my eyes bulged with terror. Right. Looked like I was going to be friendless. As well as occupationless. But . . . I narrowed my eyes out of the window. It was a beautiful day and the sun was dappling the grass in the orchard, throwing the distant hills into hazy relief. The wind rustled the leaves, seeming almost to beckon me on. Yes, of course. Of *course*.

In a trice I'd abandoned my coffee and opened the cupboard under the stairs. I'd carefully, and rather ruefully, stashed my easel and paints in here. I dragged them out. Why not set my easel up in the garden—or even the field? My heart raced with excitement. Also in the cupboard were about a dozen of my paintings, brought on the pretext that I might want to fiddle with them, but actually what I'd really wondered was whether some little country restaurant might like to hang them on their walls with a price tag on them. One of these days . . .

I set up my easel in the orchard, threw my old smock over my head, seized my palette, and squeezed out Prussian Blue and Cameron Yellow in thick swirls, savouring the heady smell I'd missed. God, those colours! Look at the way the sun was glancing off that field of rape in the distance. I needed more yellow. I squirted it out excitedly. I raised my brush again. I never sketched before painting, finding it too restrictive. I set off with a flourish.

I worked fast, my brush moving swiftly as it darted from palette to board, palette to board. Colours were rapidly filling the white space as I layered the paint on thickly. I didn't notice the passage of time, only that the sun, as it moved slowly overhead, began to cast different shadows: sharper, shorter ones. The sun went behind a cloud, throwing a ploughed field on the horizon into relief, and I was about to capture it when I became aware of a familiar noise behind me.

'Mooooooo . . . Mooooooo.'

I ignored it and painted on.

'Mooooooo . . . MOOOOOOOOOO!!' More insistent, this time.

I turned, exasperated. The cows were in a row again, staring at me with huge brown eyes, their heads over the fence.

'What?' I snapped. 'You've been fed, now jolly well shut up.'

They stared balefully back. I resumed my contemplation of the ploughed field. There was silence for a moment, then it started again. Loudly. I turned. They stopped. I turned back to paint—they started. Finally I flung my brush down with an angry flourish and stalked across. 'What?' I demanded. 'What is it?' They gazed mournfully back. The hay, I noticed, hadn't been touched. 'What's wrong? Why aren't you eating it?' I reached through the fence rails, picked up a handful and offered it to Marge. She turned her head away. Suddenly, I realised there was one missing. Where was the fifth cow? The little brown one called—don't ask—Princess Consuela Banana Hammock?

I picked my way fearfully through the mud until I got to grass, then ran towards the copse of trees where I'd noticed they sometimes sheltered from the rain. I had the most awful feeling. The most *awful* feeling. Inside the copse was a clearing. I pushed my way through to it, and there, in the middle of it, in a shallow ditch, lay Princess Consuela Banana Hammock. She was stretched out on her side, eyes shut, mouth gaping, surrounded by flies. Oh God—she was dead!

I backed away from her, but as I did, I saw a great glob of green slime flood from the corner of her mouth. There were bubbles in it. Foam. She was foaming. My eyes shot to her feet. They were stiff, and her cloven hoofs were sticking out straight, peculiar in their rigidity. I crept forward and bent down for a closer look. On the bottom of her hoofs were white lumps. Like giant clumps of acne. My eyes went back to her mouth, then to her feet again; from foot . . . to mouth . . . And then I turned and fled. I raced back to the cottage. With trembling hands I riffled through a pile of papers on the table by the phone. Oh, where was it, that handy list of numbers Eleanor had so thoughtfully—ah, there.

I pounced on it and punched out the vet's number.

'Marshbank Veterinary Practice,' purred the receptionist.

'Um, yes, hello.' I could barely speak. 'One of my cows has died and I think it might be foot-and-mouth,' I said in a rush.

'Where are you?'

'My name's Imogen Cameron,' I rattled on, 'and I'm just looking after the cows, they're not actually mine, but her feet look extraordinary and there's this like, green foamy stuff coming out of her—oh!'

She'd cut me off. A blast of music filled my eardrum for a brief moment, then a curt male voice cut in. 'Where exactly is this cow?'

'She's at Shepherd's Cottage. It's a little house on the Latimers' estate. You go past their main gates and—'

'Stay where you are and don't go near any other stock.'

'No, I won't, but—oh!' Now *he'd* cut me off. Rude man. Should I ring Piers? I wondered feverishly, standing in the open front doorway. No, let the vet do that. Leave it to the professionals.

Minutes later, a dark blue Land Rover sped down the zigzag track towards me, followed by a white van. The Land Rover screeched to a halt and out leapt a man in a white plastic boiler suit and a space mask. Two similarly dressed men jumped out of the van behind. They ran round the back to open the double doors and seemed to be dragging some sort of tarpaulin tent out between them. It looked like some kind of isolation unit. I went a bit hot; made to go towards them.

'*No, stay there!*' one of them shouted thickly through his mask.

'*This way?*' shouted another, pointing towards the cows' field.

'Um, yes. But listen, when I said I thought it was foot-and-mouth—'

'IS SHE SEPARATED FROM THE REST OF THE HERD?'

This was boomed at me from a loudspeaker, making me leap in the air. One of the masked men was directing his foghorn at me. A second seemed to be spraying stuff all over the wheels, all over the track, and all over my car too, from a long thin hose. Good Lord.

'Yes, she's in that copse over there,' I yelled back. 'But look—'

'STAY . . . IN . . . THE HOUSE!!'

This was blasted at a million decibels. I froze. The three of them were off at the double, running across the field towards the copse, looking for all the world like some sort of antiterrorist squad. Heavens. Was this really necessary? It seemed a bit over the top to me, I thought, going to the kitchen to put the kettle on.

A few minutes later the front door burst open.

'In here!' I sang, pouring boiling water in the pot.

A white-suited man strode through, still in his mask. 'Do you mean the Murray Grey?' he demanded thickly.

'Sorry?'

'Are we talking about the same cow? The Murray Grey?'

'Well, it's the little dark brown one, without the horns,' I said patiently. Golly, there were only five of them and only one was flat on her back with her legs in the air. Perhaps he was newly qualified? I went to the window. 'The others are all paler, see? With horns.' I pointed at them lined up at the fence. 'She's more—oh!'

'That one?' He jabbed his finger. My hand shot to my mouth. Princess Consuela Banana Hammock had mysteriously joined her friends, and was lined up alongside them, gazing over the fence at me.

'Oh. My. God.' I clutched the windowsill. 'That's *amazing*!' I turned to him. 'How did you do that?'

'I nudged her with my foot, Mrs Cameron. That cow has a dust cough. She does not have foot-and-mouth.'

'Oh!' I clutched my heart. 'But . . . the green slime—'

'Grass. Cud, regurgitated from her stomach as she slept.'

'But—what about all that white stuff on her feet?'

'Chalk. Which adheres to hoofs in clumps in the wet.'

'Gracious. Oh, *what* a relief.' I beamed delightedly at him. 'Rufus, my son, will be *so* pleased. She's his favourite. Tea?'

The eyes behind the mesh stared fixedly at me. 'Have you *no* concept, at all, of the mayhem you've caused? The chaos?'

I paused as I tipped the pot to pour. Righted it. 'Sorry?'

'On the way over here I put a restriction order on all neighbouring farms within a twenty-mile radius, stating that no livestock should be moved. On farms within a five-mile radius, I placed an order instructing that all cattle should be prepared for slaughter and incinerated.'

I stared at him. A vision of mountains of burning cows swam horrifically before my eyes . . . 'Oh Christ.'

'Happily I was able to reverse the order on my mobile just now.'

'Oh, thank God!' I clutched his plastic hand.

He snatched it away. 'And thankfully, no lives have been needlessly lost. But, Mrs Cameron, your reckless and alarmist behaviour would most certainly have spelt the end for this local farming community, and probably for the whole of the South of England.'

'I'm so sorry,' I whispered. 'I had no idea. I just knew cattle got that disease and—and I looked at her mouth and then at her feet, and I—'

'You applied the same impulsive, cavalier attitude that you do to your underwear?' He took off his white hat and mask. I stared. Oh my God. It was the Gypsy with the curls. Heathcliff. 'Clearly whipping your pants off and causing a national disaster are all in a day's work to you, Mrs Cameron. I'm not suggesting, incidentally, that the one could in any way lead to the other.'

'Oh!' I said, furious. 'How dare you?'

'I dare,' he said in level tones, taking a step towards me, 'because in one blasé knee-jerk reaction you almost brought down an entire community. And then you attempted to brush it off brazenly.'

I swallowed, caught in the barely controlled fury of his flinty dark eyes. 'I—I'm sorry,' I muttered as he made for the door.

I watched him go, rooted to the spot for a moment. Then I ran after him. He went down the path and stashed his suit away in the open boot of the Land Rover. The white van had disappeared.

'I'm sorry,' I said humbly, twisting my hands agitatedly. 'And will Princess Cons—the Murray Grey recover? I mean, from her cough?'

'She will if you stop giving her straw to eat and give her hay instead. The straw's full of dust. It's getting in her throat.'

'Oh Lord, you mean—'

'Don't you know the difference?' he said irritably. 'Come with me.'

In another moment he was striding off towards the barn. 'This is straw,' he said, plucking a handful of the stuff I'd given them, 'and this is hay.' He snatched an identical handful from another bale.

I blinked. 'Er . . .'

'Feel it,' he said impatiently. 'It's much finer.'

'Yes, it is, isn't it?' I marvelled as I fondled it. 'Gosh, how awful. I've been giving them the wrong stuff!'

'They'll live,' he said crisply. 'Cows eat straw *in extremis*. But if they're not getting hay they're not getting essential minerals so they're more prone to magnesium deficiency. Then you really will get them keeling over with their feet in the air, frothing at the mouth.'

'Heavens. But can't they just go in that lovely green field over there, behind the orchard?' I pointed. 'They keep looking at it longingly. I nearly let them in the other day.'

'It's too rich, got too much clover, and clover's got a hollow stem, full of air. If they eat too much they blow up like barrage balloons.' He looked at me. 'Cows can't burp. Didn't you know that?'

'No, I didn't.' *Why would I?* 'So . . . what happens?'

'They explode.'

I stared. 'Don't be ridiculous.'

He shrugged and made off towards his car. 'OK, give it a whirl. Put them in the clover field. I'd stand well back though, if I were you.'

I gazed after him. I wasn't at all sure I liked this man's attitude: half hectoring and half, I felt, poking fun at me. All the same, I wasn't sure I wanted bits of exploding cow all over the place.

'No—no, I'll give them hay,' I said decisively. 'And I'll take the straw out of the roundels.'

'And why isn't your husband feeding the cows for you?' His dark eyes flashed. 'That's hard work, heaving those bales.' He sat down in the open boot of his Land Rover and took his boots off.

'Oh, because he's not here during the day. He works in London. And actually,' I lied, as he stashed the boots and changed into deck shoes, 'he gets terrible hay fever.'

'Does he now.'

It was said in a slightly mocking way that made me bristle. And all in that lilting Irish accent. Why hadn't I recognised it in the first place? But his mask had muffled it. I felt stupid. He'd made a fool of me.

'Right. Well, if that'll be all . . .' I said crisply.

He stood up slowly and regarded me a moment. 'Yes. That'll be all. Good day, Mrs Cameron.'

'Good day,' I snapped back. Rude man, I thought.

At three o'clock, I went to get Rufus: I'd dressed down a bit this time. I got there deliberately early, hoping for a bit of a chat, but the only mothers that were there collecting their offspring—most children appeared to walk or cycle home—steadfastly refused to look at me.

At last the bell rang, the doors opened and the children spewed from all orifices like a bean bag that's burst its seams, with an awful lot of noise and dragging of coats and bags. I glanced around anxiously, trying to spot Rufus in the scrum. Finally I saw him, right at the back on his own, looking pale and tired. My heart lurched.

'Hi,' he muttered as I took his bags.

'Rufus, what happened?' He had a nasty cut above his right eye.

'I fell over.' He walked past me towards the car.

As we reached the car, a group of children turned and nudged one another. 'Woof!' one of them said to Rufus and giggled.

I smiled, thinking perhaps they were new chums, but they guffawed and turned away. 'They looked nice,' I said brightly as we drove off.

'They're not,' he said bitterly. 'No one is.'

I swallowed. Felt my throat tighten. 'Did you have a good day?'

'No.' He stared out of the window.

I licked my lips. 'Oh, well. First day is always tricky.'

He didn't reply. When we got home he went straight up to his bedroom and shut the door. I made to follow, then thought—no, food, that's what he needs. With trembling hands I made sausage and mash, then called from the bottom of the stairs. Finally, the door opened and he came down slowly. I could tell he'd been crying. I wanted to wrap him in my arms, but Rufus wasn't always amenable to that sort of behaviour. He ate his tea slowly and I washed up the pans behind him, prattling away about the cows, and my stupidity.

'Why did you give me a dog's name, Mummy?' he asked eventually.

I turned. 'I . . . didn't, darling. I gave you a lovely name.'

'Everyone says it's a dog's name.'

'Right,' I said faintly.

That night, as I put him to bed, though, he broke down.

'It's too different,' he sobbed into my neck. 'It's all too different, and I don't feel right. I'm *not* right!'

'Nonsense,' I said, my heart pounding. 'Who says you're not?'

'There's this boy,' he hiccupped, drawing back from me, face drenched in tears, 'called Carl. He's in the year below me. He started the woofing and everything, and then everyone joined in and started saying "walkies", and then I got pushed over by him on the way out of lunch. Accidentally, I think,' he said, seeing my horrified face.

'Right.'

'Mum, you won't say anything, will you?' he pleaded.

'Of course not, darling. Of course not.' I swallowed.

When I got downstairs, Alex was at the table eating a pork pie straight from the wrapper. He'd clearly just walked through the door.

'He's being bullied,' I said, my voice catching as I said it.

Alex swallowed the last mouthful. 'Is he?'

'Yes, by a boy called Carl in the year below. He pushed him over.'

'Well, tell him to push him back.'

'And they're making fun of his name.'

'Kids will, Imo. They'll get bored though.' Alex sighed. 'Good day at the office, darling? No, lousy, thank you. And good journey home? Well, if you can call two hours in a steel box full of human lasagne good, then yes, it was delightful.'

I noticed him properly for the first time. 'How was your day?'

'Oh, for God's sake!'

And then, for the second time that evening, another member of my family mysteriously flounced from my presence and stomped upstairs.

The next day, when I'd dropped Rufus off at the school gates, I went back to the car. I got in, but didn't drive away. Five minutes later, when the playground had cleared, I quietly entered the building via a side door and hurried furtively down the corridor to Daniel Hunter's office.

He waved me in. 'What can I do for you?'

'I'm afraid Rufus is being bullied.'

He frowned. 'I'm sorry to hear that,' he said. 'Anyone in particular?'

'Yes, he's called Carl. He got everyone to bark at him, and then he pushed him over on the way out of lunch.'

'Right.' He looked thoughtful. 'Mrs Cameron, it was only day one, and you know, things do have a habit of shaking down. I could wade in now and have a word with Carl but sometimes that exacerbates the problem. Since he's not in his class and Rufus won't come across him that much, my advice would be to let things be. Carl Greenway has a short attention span and he'll probably get bored with baiting Rufus.'

'You mean . . . you're not going to get him in here? Suspend him?'

He suppressed a smile. 'Not immediately. I'll certainly have a quiet word with Mrs Harding and ask her to keep an eye on the situation. Sometimes, in my experience, it's best not to meet these situations head-on. Sometimes it's better to go round the houses.'

'What d'you mean?' God, he was handsome. His eyes were blue, but flecked with gold, like a tiger's.

'Well, maybe have a go at charming Carl. Make a friend of him.'

I gazed at him. 'Oh!' A light bulb went on in my head. 'Oh—you mean like—invite him for tea or something? A sleepover!'

'Well, I wouldn't necessarily go that far but—'

'Oh, you're a genius, Mr Hunter. Thank you so much!' I stood up, eyes shining. He stood up too and our eyes met and d'you know, I damn nearly kissed him. Golly.

'Er, right.' He glanced away, shuffling some papers on his desk, breaking the moment. 'And now I really must get on.'

'Yes. Yes, I must too.' I hastened to the door. 'And thank you *so* much.'

The rest of the day couldn't pass quickly enough. First I fed the cows. I was an expert now. Then off to the chickens to give them some grain; feeding the baby chicks and the proud mother, before zooming off to Waitrose for provisions, my heart soaring. I had a plan, you see, a project, and armed with that, I could go from despair to elation in nought to sixty. At three o'clock exactly, I raced off to the school.

Outside the gates, as I assiduously chewed my gum, I scanned the mothers a little more carefully. Which one was Carl's? I did hope that wasn't his mother, I thought, nervously eyeing a woman I'd spotted yesterday. She was an unbelievably scary-looking specimen, massively overweight, with greasy jet-black hair and rings in every orifice. Hordes of small children—well, five at least—were grouped around a fully occupied double buggy, and a muddy Alsatian strained from the handle on a string. Even the other mothers seemed in awe as she cuffed her brood and tugged at the dog. She glared at me and I glanced hurriedly away.

A bell went, and children began to pour out. Rufus was well at the back, but he didn't look quite as despondent as yesterday.

'Good day, darling?' I took his bag.

He shrugged. 'All right.'

'Rufus, which one's Carl?'

'There.' He pointed to a tall, tough-looking boy with a shaved head.

'Right. Come on, we're going to ask him to tea.'

'What?' Rufus looked horrified.

'Clever tactics, you see, Rufus. Reverse psychology.'

'But, Mum, he left me alone today. I didn't really see him.'

'Nevertheless, it'll stand us in good stead for the future.' I marched towards him. 'Hello, Carl,' I smiled chummily. 'I'm Rufus's mummy. Rufus and I wondered if you'd like to come to tea today.'

'Wha'?' He screwed his freckled face up to me.

'Yes, we thought you might like to come and play, with your mummy, perhaps. Is she here?'

'Nah, she's inside.'

'Is she? Well, perhaps we could ring her.' I whipped out my mobile.

'Nah, I mean she's in prison.'

I swallowed. Put my phone away. 'Right. Well, um, maybe—maybe whoever looks after you, can come?'

'Me nan looks after me, but I don't wanna come to tea.'

Every mother and child at the gates was listening to this exchange, agog. Rufus tugged at my arm, puce with shame. 'Come on, Mum.'

'Oh, well, that's a pity. I've got some lovely Viennetta ice cream.'

'Nah, you're orright.' The boy looked embarrassed and turned away.

'And Rufus has got a PlayStation,' I wheedled desperately.

'I'll come,' said a voice behind me. I glanced round to see a skinny little girl with pigtails and a pinched face.

I laughed nervously. 'Well, I'm not sure—And you are?'

'Tanya. I'm in 'is class, ent I? And this is my mum.' She turned to the enormous black-haired woman with the zillions of children.

'Yeah, we'll come,' the mother agreed.

A profound silence fell. All eyes were on the new mum, Mrs Cameron, with the bright white legs and the posh voice.

'Right,' I gulped. 'Okey-doke.' I cranked up a smile. 'Marvellous.' *We'll* come—Christ, there were about twenty of them now that she'd collected what looked like half the school. I couldn't look at Rufus.

'D'you want to follow me?' I asked brightly as I opened the car door.

'Oh, we ain't got a car,' said the mother.

I licked my lips. 'Well, I'm not sure I've got enough seat belts to—'

'Nah, we don't want seat belts. They'll just pile in the back.'

And they did just that. Piled in. All twelve of them—I counted—squashed in any old how, on laps, in the boot, faces squashed against windows, looking like a family of illegal immigrants.

'Well, I hope we don't meet a policeman,' I twittered nervously. 'And I haven't a clue where you're going to sit because Rufus absolutely *has* to have a—'

''Ere, come on, little 'un. On my lap.' She'd plonked herself down in the front seat and scooped a startled Rufus effortlessly into her vast lap. His nose was about six inches from the windscreen. 'Anyway, our Frankie's the local bobby. He'll turn a blind eye. Come on, you, get in.'

Thinking she was talking to me I hastily obeyed, but she was addressing the Alsatian, somehow getting him past her legs to lodge him between us. He stood with his front paws on my handbrake, jaws wide, tongue lolling, saliva dripping.

Nervously, I burrowed around among the furry feet, found the handbrake, and let it out. I drove at a snail's pace, my eyes glued to the road, only leaving it to monitor the progress of my son's nose, which periodically jerked alarmingly towards the windscreen as she swung round to clout her recalcitrant brood. 'Shauna! Pack it in!' Or: 'Ryan! Shut it!'

Finally we reached the cottage and they all piled out, in an eclectic jumble, onto the grass. As they picked themselves up I opened the door. After only a moment's hesitation, the ones that were mobile ran through the front door and on up the stairs to check out Rufus's bedroom. Happily, he did have a PlayStation, and a football table.

I ran around getting the tea as my new friend—Sheila, she informed me—proceeded to change a brace of filthy nappies on the kitchen floor, pausing only to extract a toddler from inside a cupboard, and all the time punctuating proceedings with, 'Leave it, Darren,' or, 'Touch that and I'll knock your block off, Lorraine!'

As I arranged the tea things on the table, she sat up on her haunches and looked up at it doubtfully. 'It's a hot cheese sauce,' I said brightly. 'You dip bits of carrot and celery and bread in. Rufus loves it.'

She got to her feet and picked up a bit of cauliflower in wonder. 'They won't eat this. Got any chips?'

I had, as it happened, in a bag in the freezer, which I produced nervously. 'Yes, but I'm not convinced these will go with the—'

'Give it here.' She took it from me, waddled across to the oven, found a tray, then shook the entire bag onto it, and shut the door.

'Right,' I gulped. 'Good idea.'

All hell appeared to be breaking loose upstairs judging by the noise, and it occurred to me to wonder if Rufus was still alive. With shaking hands, I lit the fondue.

'Teatime!' I warbled up the stairs, and moments later, a stampede engulfed me. When I'd peeled myself off the stairwell wall, I tottered to the kitchen to find that, somehow, they'd all got round my tiny table. They fell on their chips greedily, then gazed in wonder as Rufus dunked cherry tomatoes and chunks of bread into the bubbling sauce.

In time it became hard to resist, and the oldest boy, Ryan, a disreputably handsome lad of about twelve, plonked a chip in with a giggle. The others watched in awe-struck silence as he chewed.

''S orright,' he declared grudgingly.

There was no stopping them then. Chips were dunked in by the fistful, then Ryan picked up a bit of celery. 'Whas this then?'

'Celery.' I eyed him. 'I dare you.'

'Yeah? What ya gonna give me?'

'A pound.'

He looked taken aback, but gamely dunked his celery in.

'Yeah, 's orright too.' He crunched away. 'Where's my pound?'

I reached in my bag and handed it over.

'Can I have some?' asked Tanya.

'Of course.' Feeling rather flushed and elated, I cut up some more for the others, who naturally also wanted to try.

'You won't like that,' Ryan advised them all. 'It's too s'phisticated. You might like the carrot, though.'

Well, of course they all wanted to be sophisticated, and after that, tea disappeared in a flash. Out of the corner of my eye I caught Sheila, giving a baby a bottle on a stool in the corner, looking impressed. She jerked her head outside. 'Who looks after the stock, then?'

'The stock? Oh, you mean the cows. I do.'

'Yeah?' She went to the open back door, jiggling the baby across her arm. 'And all them Jacobs. They're 'is majesty's, are they?' She nodded.

Jacobs. This girl knew her stuff. 'Yes, that's right,' I said, picking up a tray of tea and biscuits. I set it on the little table in the garden. 'They belong to Piers.' I sat down to pour. 'D'you know the Latimers then?'

She followed me out, sat down heavily opposite me and made a face.

'Everyone round here knows the Latimers. Me mum cleans for them, don't she?'

'Oh, so you're *Vera's* daughter. Does she enjoy working for them?'

''S all right, I s'pose. She's bin there twenty years so what's the difference? Mum says *she's* all right, but he's a funny one.'

'Piers?'

'Yeah, Piers. I wouldn't want to be married to him for all 'is money. Can't say I blame her neither, though there are some round 'ere say she should know better.'

'Who, Eleanor?'

'Yeah.'

'Blame her for what? Know better than—'

But Sheila's tantalising observations on the Latimer ménage were cut short as she got to her feet, pink with fury, and pointed at the bushes. 'CINDY! GET THAT COCK OUT OF YOUR MOUTH!'

My eyes bulged in horror, my teacup rattled. Lordy. What on earth was going on? Who was Cindy in the bushes with? *Where was Rufus?*

Sheila bustled away at the double and it was with some relief that I saw her emerge moments later from the undergrowth, wrestling the cockerel from the jaws of the Alsatian. The bird gave an angry squawk and bustled away indignantly, but intact. Sheila, though, was distraught. She dragged the dog back to the chair to tie her up.

'She ain't used to chickens,' she panted, 'not free range like that.'

'Don't worry,' I soothed, 'he'll live. So, um, Eleanor. I mean, Mrs Latimer. She can't be blamed for—'

'She's used to chasing birds, see. It's best we go,' she said nervously. 'Don't want Mr Latimer counting his chickens. I'll be shot. I'll get the kids rounded up.'

'Honestly, there's no need—'

But she was yelling like a sergeant major, calling the children to heel, and I realised it wasn't going to be possible to steer the conversation back to Eleanor again. I got to my feet with a resigned sigh and followed her. Most of the children were in the orchard with the lambs, where Rufus was proudly showing Tanya how to pick one up.

'You've got yer 'ands full,' Sheila observed, glancing at all the animals.

'Not as full as yours,' I jerked my head at her brood.

She laughed. 'Yeah, but only five are mine. We foster the rest.'

'Foster? Really?'

'Yeah, an' we don't do it for the money.' She looked at me sharply. 'We get sweet FA from Social.'

'I wouldn't dream of suggesting you did.'

'Well, there's some round here would, and they want to try cutting a hundred fingernails at bath time an' getting all them teeth brushed. They'd soon realise a few measly quid ain't worth it.'

'I agree,' I said. 'I find it hard coping with one.'

'And they're good kids, anyhow,' she reflected. 'Just 'aven't much of a chance, you know? Up to now.'

I nodded. Yes, I did know. And she was giving them one. Twelve children in all, and all in a tiny house, no doubt full to the brim with baskets of washing and socks drying on every radiator. Sheila working her butt off. I felt humbled as she gathered them all together now with what I realised was a lot of good-natured shouting, which the children took in their stride, getting as many as possible to come up and say goodbye and thank you. Sheila declined a lift back to the village, saying she only lived across the valley. Then, with two in the double buggy, another two riding pillion on the back and Ryan pushing all four, she scooped two little ones up in her arms and herded the rest down into the valley, and up the other side. When they got to the top of the hill, Sheila got them all to wave. We waved back frantically.

After a moment, I lowered my hand. 'Sorry, darling,' I murmured, 'for being such an embarrassing mother. For asking half the school over and getting it wrong as usual.'

'You didn't, actually,' he said slowly. 'I like Tanya.'

And flashing me a quick grin, he ran off to see the chickens.

Chapter Six

THE FOLLOWING DAY Rufus came running out of school beaming.

'How was it?' I hazarded nervously.

'Cool. Tanya and I played on the apparatus both breaks and I sat next to her at lunch. She showed me her goody spot.'

'Her *what*?'

'Her goody spot. A camp in the bushes where her gang hangs out.'

'Oh! Well, that's a relief. And Carl?'

He shrugged. 'Didn't see him. He doesn't hang out with us. He's with the losers, mostly. He tried to join in, but Damien told him to piss off.'

I blessed Damien from the bottom of my heart. But could it go on, I wondered. I slightly held my breath, but all the following week it was a similar story. 'I've cracked it,' I told Hannah proudly when she popped round a few weeks later in her lunch hour. 'It's quite extraordinary. Rufus has got more friends than he ever had in London and he's in with the real dudes. Not practising the oboe with the geeks, but really in the thick of it with the footballers and the conker boys.'

'The drug dealers of tomorrow, you mean,' she said, helping herself to salad at my little kitchen table. 'So how did you manage that?'

I told her about Sheila.

Hannah put the salad tongs down, astounded. 'Sheila Banks? Wife of Frankie "Fingers" Banks? Blimey, Imogen, you've tapped right into the local mafia. She and her old man rule the roost round here. No one farts without consulting Sheila and Frankie first.'

'They're not too dodgy, though, are they? I rather liked her.'

'Not *too* dodgy, but they do sail fairly close to the wind. They run the local pawnbrokers in Rushbrough, and rule it with a rod of iron. Put it this way: in ten years' time you wouldn't want Rufus getting Tanya up the spout and leaving her in the lurch. You might wake up to find a horse's head in your bed.'

'Thanks. I'll bear that in mind,' I said nervously.

She grinned. 'This is delicious, by the way. Any more?'

'There is,' I said doubtfully, getting up to reach for the bowl of coronation chicken on the side but privately thinking my sister had had enough. She'd eaten most of it already. And half a loaf of bread.

'How's Lady Many-Acres,' she said, through a mouthful of chicken. 'D'you see much of her?'

'Surprisingly little. Not since dinner that first night, which pleases me. She certainly doesn't feel compelled to "pop in", either. Although she did come past with her dogs the other day and admired the painting I was doing in the orchard.'

'Yes, I saw your easel out there as I came in. Rather idyllic, isn't it? Must be more inspiring than an attic in Putney?'

I shrugged. I didn't want to be disloyal to my lovely studio, but these last few days, I'd felt something profoundly moving as I'd painted out there in the long grass.

'Yeah, it's OK. I mean, obviously, it's not ideal not having a studio, but—oh, Hannah, you *can't* want more, surely!'

She glanced up at me, spoon frozen above the bowl of coronation chicken as she went to help herself. 'Why not?'

'Well, no, quite. Why not?' I said flustered.

'Imogen, is there something you want to say?' she said icily.

This was serious Siberia from my sister. I found some steel.

'No, absolutely nothing, Hannah. If you want to eat for England and end up with heart disease and respiratory problems and possibly diabetes, who am I to stop you? You go right ahead. It's your body.'

She regarded me stonily but I held her eye, and my nerve. She put the spoon back in the dish. Her face crumpled.

'I'm sorry,' I said quickly. 'I didn't mean that.'

She struggled for composure. 'No, you're right. And it's about time someone had the guts to tell me. Eddie certainly hasn't.'

'Because he's too scared to,' I said, hastening round and pulling my chair up beside hers. 'Hannah, what's wrong? You're so strict about everything else in your life, so disciplined—why not this?'

She shrugged miserably. 'I can't help myself. It feels nice, and so much of my life doesn't feel nice. It's sort of, the only bit I look forward to. But I hate myself afterwards. So much so that the other day I thought I'd make myself sick, to get rid of it.'

'You didn't!'

'No. I didn't. But it made me realise I had to do something about it. I've joined Weight Watchers, for a start. I'm going tomorrow.'

'*Are* you?' I clasped my hands delightedly.

'Anyone would think I've just told you I've won the lottery. Yes, and I'm going to see a counsellor. Correction, have *been* to see a counsellor.'

'Oh!' I was stunned into silence.

'Who rather predictably told me I'm eating for comfort, yawn, yawn, but she also said comfort eating is very common in women of my age. Apparently a lot of peri-menopausal women—'

'Peri-menopausal? Don't be ridiculous, you're only thirty-eight!'

'And Mum got hers at forty. It's hereditary, you know. Oh, I'm definitely going through the change.'

'I had no idea. I thought fifty, fifty-one . . .' Golly. Alex and I had better get a wiggle on, I thought. If we wanted to . . . you know.

'So. Tomorrow I stand up in front of a roomful of lardy women and say, "Hi, I'm Hannah, and I weigh fourteen stone." But right now . . .' she rolled her eyes lasciviously, 'what's for pudding?'

'Seeing as it's your last day of freedom, a cup of coffee and a piece of chocolate cake. Good for you. I'm proud of you.' I put an arm round her shoulders and gave her a squeeze before I got to my feet. I could see she was moved by this; we weren't demonstrative as sisters.

'How's Alex?' she asked brightly, changing the subject as I came back with the coffee, with only a little tremor in her voice.

'Fine,' I said, putting a mug down in front of her. 'Although . . .'

'What?' Hannah pounced, sensing my hesitation.

'Well, he loathes the commute. It's much worse than he was led to believe. He has to get up at six and doesn't get back till gone nine. He's thinking of getting a flat or something, actually.'

'What?' Hannah's jaw dropped theatrically.

'Well, not a flat, exactly,' I said quickly, although my reaction had been much the same as hers last night, when he'd told me. 'Charlie Cadbury's got a two-bedroom flat in Chiswick he says he can share with. Terribly cheaply, actually.'

'Charlie Cadbury! That old dog, the one who left his wife because he was having a fling with his secretary while still maintaining a girlfriend called Trisha and finding three women just a *little* too much to handle?'

'He's a reformed character now,' I said staunchly.

She snorted. 'A leopard doesn't change his spots just like that, you know, Imo. You're happy about Alex spending the week with him?'

'Of course,' I snapped, although I hadn't been so happy last night after Alex had come home at nine thirty yet again and suggested it.

'What—spend the whole week in London?'

'Only four nights, Imo. Only half the week, really. It's just that, to be honest, by the time I get to work I'm so knackered I can hardly think straight some days. It took me two hours to get in this morning.'

'But Charlie Cadbury. I mean, he's quite a lad, isn't he?'

'Not any more,' he said with his mouth full, one eye on the football. 'He and Trisha are blissfully happy, although word has it she's keen to have children.' He grinned. 'I'm not sure how old Charlie feels about that. He's already got two, and when I had lunch with him today he was bemoaning the fact that however hard you try, you always end up with the trouble and strife and 2.4 into the bargain.'

'Like you. Two kids first time round, and now Rufus. How dreadful.'

He put down his fork. Looked at me, surprised.

'How much more entertaining would it be if you and Charlie could just—just shag around to your hearts' content, with as many women as you liked, and have absolutely no ties or responsibilities at the end of it.' And with that, predictably, I burst into tears, and rushed upstairs.

A bit later, as I sobbed piteously, face down in my pillow, Alex came up and sat beside me. 'I won't take it, Imo. Won't take the flat.'

'No!' I sobbed, flipping over, my face wet. 'Of course you must. You're exhausted. It's just, I wish—'

'That I didn't have to. I know.' He sighed. 'Imo, I don't want to live with an overgrown schoolboy who still grades his farts for potency.

Believe it or not, it was not part of my plan.' His voice broke slightly at this. 'But needs must,' he went on firmly.

'I know,' I said quickly, 'you must take it. I'm just being . . .well . . .'

Insecure, was the word I couldn't say. I mustn't let him think I was a clinging wife who couldn't let her husband out of her sight for fear of him chatting up a pretty girl. 'I'll pop up occasionally, shall I? Leave Rufus with Hannah, and maybe spend one night a week in the flat.'

He hugged me delightedly, and with that we'd slipped under the covers and made love: seamlessly, beautifully, wonderfully.

I turned to Hannah now as I put the milk away in the fridge. 'We don't have a choice, I'm afraid. We don't *want* to have flatmates at our time of life, believe me,' I said, shamelessly parodying Alex, 'any more than we want to live in a crappy little grace-and-favour cottage in the sodding countryside, thanks to Lady fucking Muck!'

Hannah stared at me, frozen. Her head jerked slightly to the left. I swung round. Eleanor was hovering, embarrassed, on the back step.

'Sorry, but the door was wide open so I—'

'Oh God, yes, come in!' Golly, had she heard? She must have. How *awful*. 'How lovely to see you. You know my sister, don't you?'

'Yes, we have met, haven't we?' smiled Eleanor. 'It's Hannah, isn't it?'

'That's it,' said Hannah, getting to her feet to clasp her hand.

Despite my confusion, I couldn't help noticing the startling disparity between Hannah, huge and lumpen, and Eleanor, slim figure encased in skintight jodhpurs. 'Been riding?' I hazarded stupidly.

'Well, it's such a glorious day I thought I'd take Cracker for a gallop. I just came to see if you were around this weekend. Only the weather's supposed to be wonderful on Sunday and we thought we'd have a barbecue. Do say you'll come.'

Well, if she had heard me, she'd obviously forgiven me pretty swiftly.

'That's very kind, but actually, Hannah and Eddie are coming for lunch here on Sunday. They're bringing Mum with them.'

'But that's marvellous—come too!' She turned to Hannah. 'Do, it would be great to see you both. I've heard so much about you from friends. You're a potter, aren't you?'

'Oh, well,' Hannah demurred, 'I dabble.'

'More than dabble. I've seen your pots—they're beautiful.'

'How kind,' Hannah murmured pinkly. 'We'd love to come to lunch, only as Imogen says, we have got Mum . . .'

'Oh, but I adore your mother! And she can give me advice on my formal garden with her marvellous plastic flowers.' She giggled. 'We'll see you all on Sunday. About one o'clock? Dead casual.'

'As long as Alex hasn't got too much work,' I said firmly.

'Oh, don't worry, I've already spoken to him. I couldn't get hold of you so I rang, and he said he'd leave Sunday free.'

I stared. 'Right.'

'And isn't it marvellous about the flat?'

'The . . . flat?'

'Well, it'll ease the commute. Honestly, I don't know how these men do it. I get exhausted whenever I pop up to London for the day. Right, well, I must go,' said Eleanor. 'It was lovely to meet you properly.' She shot Hannah a smile. 'See you on Sunday. I'm *so* pleased you're all coming.' And with that she gave us a cheery wave and sashayed off across the grass, back to her mount. I watched her spring effortlessly into the saddle and then gallop off over the horizon in a cloud of dust.

I was so furious I could hardly speak. I slammed around the kitchen, throwing plates in the dishwasher. 'I can't believe you said yes to lunch,' I fumed, my voice shaking with emotion. 'I thought you didn't like her, couldn't bear her and Piers and their stuck-up ways! And how dare she have spoken to Alex already? Christ, I only knew about the flat last night. What is she—phoning him every day?'

'Do calm down, Imogen. You're sounding like a jealous schoolgirl. And anyway, if she *was* after him, she'd hardly be mentioning the fact that she'd rung him, would she? She'd be keeping that very quiet.'

'That's where she's so clever!' I hissed. 'It was the same with Tilly, the same pally friendship, and then—*wham!*—in she goes, under the wire. It's a cover—what, me and Alex?' I opened my eyes innocently, aping Eleanor. 'Lord, no, we're just good friends. Oh, she is *so* smart, Hannah, *so* smart. She manipulates people; it's her forte. I mean, Christ, look at you! A short time ago you thought she was scheming and untrustworthy. Remember the gymkhana lady, and the one she got to make curtains right before Christmas and then snubbed at church? Blimey, didn't take long to get round *you!*'

Hannah shot me a pitying look as she got to her feet. 'She didn't get round me, she simply asked me and Eddie to lunch and I accepted. Now grow up.' And she swept past me out of the cottage.

When she'd gone, I stood at the window, trembling slightly. What was happening to me? Why was I behaving like this?

Later, as I stood at my easel in the orchard, knowing this was the only way to clear my head, I calmed down. There was something about capturing the movement of nature—those beech trees, for example— about responding immediately to light and colour that was so exhilarating it almost took my breath away. It left no space in my head for gnawing doubts. I worked quickly, my brush moving in swift, confident strokes across the board, until I reached the point when I entered that heavenly phase where I almost lost consciousness and painted from instinct. Occasionally, during one of these moments of oblivion, the inevitable happened: a splash would fall on my nose, and by the time I'd come to my senses the skies would be opening.

Today, it was the wind that was against me. I impatiently brushed hair from my eyes. Occasionally a leaf stuck to the canvas, sometimes even a feather. A feather? I picked it off and carried on, but then another one landed on my palette, and another. I surfaced sufficiently from my creative reverie to wonder where they were coming from. I glanced around. A horrific scene met my eyes. A large hen—Cynthia, one of my precious silkies—lay about twenty feet away, decapitated.

I fled across. Omigod, Omigod! Had he killed them all—for he, I was sure, was the fox? Heart pounding, I tore round to the compost heap where I knew they liked to hang out, and saw, to my intense relief, that a fair-sized squad was perched on top. Most of them were there, surely? I counted feverishly. Ten, eleven, twelve . . . no. There should be fourteen. Cynthia was one, but another was missing. The big brown hen, Mother Theresa, and—oh sweet Jesus—the chicks!

I rushed to the barn where Mother Theresa often retreated and saw her, at the foot of the hay bales, keeping watch over a dead chick, all the others missing. Oh Christ, they'd all been taken, eaten, except this one little scrap, this chick, which . . . was still alive! To the hen's consternation, I picked it up, took one last tortured look around—no, all gone, all of them—and ran with it to the house. What would Rufus say? I had to save one! I barged through the back door and lunged across the table for the phone. 'Marshbank Veterinary Practice?' said a familiar voice as Mother Theresa skidded round the table after me.

'I need the vet,' I whispered. 'Fast.'

'He's on a call at the moment. Can I give him a message?'

'Yes, tell him it's an emergency. Tell him to get over to Shepherd's Cottage on the Latimer estate right away, please.'

I put down the phone. The chick was getting weaker. Maybe I should have left it in the stable where the mother had been keeping an eye on it? 'Sorry—sorry,' I whispered, scuttling back outside again.

Across the yard we hastened, Mother Theresa and I, and into the barn where I laid the chick down on the same patch of hay. Maybe she would sit on it; cover it with her feathery warmth. She wandered off to peck in the dirt. No! No, come back! I watched her go, impotently. 'You've got to keep it warm,' I begged, brokenly. 'It'll die!'

She shot me a sharp look and went back to her mates.

Desperate now, I knelt over the chick in the hay. I breathed hard on its little yellow body. I couldn't actually bring myself to give it the kiss of life, couldn't, you know, go beak to beak, but I was convinced I was getting somewhere when I became aware of footsteps behind me. Pat Flaherty was marching through the open barn door.

'What is it? What's happened?'

'Oh, thank goodness you've come!' I pointed a quivering finger at the body in the straw. 'The chick! It's dying, you must save it!'

He stooped, picked the chick up, gave it a cursory glance and tossed it in the straw. 'It's dead. What's the emergency?'

'Oh!' I picked it up tenderly. 'Oh, how ghastly!' I started to cry.

'Mrs Cameron, what exactly did you call me out for?'

'The chicks,' I sobbed, 'they're all dead. And Cynthia—the silkie. That bloody fox, he's killed the lot of them!'

'Well, that's bad luck,' he said impatiently, 'but what d'you want me to do about it?'

I turned my wet face up. 'Well, I thought you could save this one!'

He looked at me aghast. 'You called me out for a chick? I assumed, at the very least, a rabid dog had got among the sheep!'

'What'll I tell Rufus?' I trembled.

'That it's country life!' he snapped. 'Mrs Cameron, when I got your urgent message I was delivering breeched calf twins!'

'Oh, so my chickens aren't as important as someone else's cow?'

'Of course they're bloody not! Ted Parker's prize heifers are worth a damn sight more than your Easter chicks, I can assure you. This is the second time you've called me out on a wild-goose chase. Don't let it happen again. Good day to you.' He turned on his heel.

I got up and hastened after him. 'Aren't you even going to look at Cynthia? She's been decapitated, for God's sake!'

'Then there's not much I can do for her, is there? I suggest you shut them up for the night earlier. The fox is around at about five o'clock.'

'Shut them up? Oh!' I stopped.

He fixed me with a steely gaze. 'You don't shut them up?'

'Well, I . . . I sort of assumed they put themselves to bed.'

He gazed at me in wonder. 'Where?'

'Well, I don't know.' I looked around desperately. 'In the trees?'

'Have you ever seen chickens flying around your garden?'

'No, but—'

'Oh, perhaps they *climb* into the trees, hmm? To get to their nests?'

'Well, I've seen them roost!' I spluttered. 'In the barn.'

'Yes, *in extremis*, they will flutter up to roost, but their wings have been clipped so they don't fly into trees. Where's your chicken house?'

I stared at him. 'I . . . don't know.'

'You don't know? Well, where do they lay their eggs?'

I rubbed my forehead with my fingertips. Eggs. Yes, I had wondered about that. I cleared my throat. 'I had noticed they didn't lay, actually, but I assumed it was the wrong time of the month, or something.'

'Wrong time of the month?' He boggled, turned sharply and made off round the back of the cottage. I hurried after him. He was heading off along the long cinder path that led to the Wendy . . . oh.

'What the hell d'you think this is?' he said, lifting the wooden door.

I swallowed. 'Yes, well, I can see now . . . It's just that Rufus and I . . .' No. Don't tell him you thought they'd stupidly made the door too small for even children to get in.

'Jesus wept.' Pat lifted a flap at the back of the house. A little flap I hadn't noticed. In a row of small, straw-lined boxes, dozens, literally dozens, of eggs twinkled up at us.

'Oh Lord.' I crept across and stared.

He lifted another lid. 'Ah yes. You've got a broody one here. She's sitting, so if you don't disturb her, these eggs could hatch.'

'Oh! You mean, more chicks?'

'That tends to be the usual pattern,' he said drily. 'The cycle of life.'

'Oh, and this is the hen that went missing ages ago. And she looks just like Cynthia, identical! I could tell Rufus it *was* her.'

'Could do,' he eyed me. 'Or you could tell him the truth.' He let the lid go with a bang and started off back up the cinder path. I seemed to be forever running after this man.

'And what time should I put them to bed?'

He stopped in his tracks, a few feet short of his Land Rover. Turned. I saw his mouth twitch. 'What time? Well, the moment they've had their cocoa and you've read them a story, of course.'

I flushed. 'No, I just meant—'

'Jesus, when it gets dark. But if you're worried about the fox, a bit earlier for the next couple of days, OK?'

I nodded.

He got in his Land Rover, twisted round in his seat to face me. 'One more thing. If you anthropomorphise your animals and give them all names, it's very hard when they die. Particularly for children.'

'Thank you,' I nodded again, stiffly. His dark eyes on mine were softer than they were wont to be. 'I'll bear that in mind.'

'Do.' He reversed a smart circle in the yard. 'And now if you'll excuse me I'll get back to Ted Parker's place and stick my hand up that cow's arse.' And with that he sped off up the zigzag track.

He had to go and ruin it, didn't he? I thought, watching him go.

The following day, I rang Kate and told her the whole sorry tale.

'Oh dear. But you know, he's right. They're not pets, Imogen. You can't get too attached to farm animals. Where d'you think your M&S Chicken Kiev comes from?'

'I suppose,' I agreed humbly.

She sounded a bit sharp today. I'd forgotten to return a call last week and I wondered, guiltily, if she was feeling peeved.

'Rufus must have been upset, though,' she went on.

'Yes, he was, but actually he was more furious than anything else. He and Tanya spent the whole of last night setting traps for the fox.'

'Sounds like Rufus has a new best friend,' she observed.

'Oh, no, he really misses Orlando,' I said quickly.

'And he's in all the teams?' Kate probed. 'At school?'

'They don't exactly have teams, Kate. Dan—Mr Hunter favours ball skills at this stage, which Rufus loves because he's not always last, or left out. Mr Hunter thinks there's plenty of time for competitive sport.'

'Mr Hunter will be sprouting wings and a halo soon. Have you got a thing about him? Bugger. That's the doorbell. Can you hang on?'

''Course,' I agreed, relieved she'd been deflected, particularly since I was aware that I did have a tiny crush on Mr Hunter. It was only because he'd given us such marvellous advice about the bullying, for which I was so grateful. So grateful that I gathered a huge bunch of bluebells from the woods behind the cottage, leaving them on his desk one morning when I knew everyone was in assembly. Unfortunately, he'd forgotten his assembly notes and popped back in the room just as I was going.

'Oh!' I coloured up, horribly aware that through the glass partition, Mrs Harris, the school secretary, had eyes like saucers. 'I was—just leaving these. To say thank you.'

His eyes widened as he saw the flowers. 'For what?'

'Well, you know, for your advice. Rufus is really happy now.'

'Oh, well, good. I'm delighted. But you really shouldn't . . .' he gestured, embarrassed, at the flowers.

'It's nothing, only a few bits from the garden,' I said quickly.

'Well, I must be getting on,' he'd said. 'Er, thank you, Mrs Cameron.'

It would be good to see Mr Hunter in a more social setting, I mused as I waited for Kate. Maybe he'd like to come to supper? Meet Alex properly? Although, of course, as from Monday, Alex was away all week. My heart lurched at the thought. Away at that flat in town.

'Imo? Are you still there?'

'What? Oh, yes, still here. Who was at the door?'

'Someone with a leaflet. Listen, I'd better go. I'll ring you later.'

'Um, Kate, before you go, I've got a favour to ask. Quite a big one.'

'Fire away,' she said cautiously.

'It's just . . . well, Alex is going to stay in town during the week now.'

'Is he?' she said, surprised.

'Yes, he is, because the travelling's getting him down.'

'Oh, right. Where?'

'Well, that's the thing, Kate. He's been offered a room by this friend of his, Charlie Cadbury, but Charlie's a real rogue, and I was just wondering—it's a huge imposition—but now that Sandra's gone and you've got the nanny flat downstairs, I was thinking—well, if you haven't already rented it out—if you'd think about renting it to Alex?'

I held my breath. There. I'd said it. Ever since Kate had let slip that she was sick of having a nanny about the place now that most of her children were at boarding school and had been dithering over whether to keep the flat for guests or rent it out, I'd wondered if I'd dare suggest it. There was a pause on the other end. Suddenly I went hot. 'I shouldn't have asked. Kate, I'm sorry. It's just, I've been so worried recently, and I don't know why because I'm quite sure he *wouldn't* be led astray by Charlie—but, well, I don't know what I thought,' I finished lamely.

'I'll talk to Sebastian and let you know, OK?' she said slowly.

'Yes, and thank you, Kate. I feel awful asking . . .'

But would feel even more awful, I thought, putting the phone down, if I hadn't. I sat there a moment, a mixture of guilt and relief making me feel a bit heady, and watched as Paul, the postman, drove through the gate. I waved and went out to meet him, pleased to have a distraction.

'Morning, Paul. Anything exciting for me?' I said cheerily.

'Not unless you count a garden hose catalogue.'

'I might. Got to take your thrills where you can these days!'

As soon as I'd said it, I wished I hadn't. Paul looked startled, then reddened and hopped back smartly in his van. As he roared off up the chalky track, I scurried inside, smarting.

I went to the kitchen to chuck the junk mail in the bin, simultaneously opening a brown envelope. My eyes shot to the headed paper, Marshbank Veterinary Practice, and then, itemised:

March 27 . . . Home visit and consultancy £75

May 18 . . . Home visit and consultancy £75

My eyes bulged in disbelief. A hundred and fifty pounds? For a couple of visits? Oh, for heaven's sake. I reached for the phone.

'Marshbank Veterinary Practice?' purred my friend on the other end.

'Can I speak to Pat Flaherty, please?'

'Mr Flaherty is on a call at the moment,' she said icily.

'Well, it's Imogen Cameron here. Perhaps you can ask him from me why I've been charged a hundred and fifty pounds for nothing! All he did was prod a cow and show me where my chicken house is.'

'We have a basic call-out charge, Mrs Cameron.'

'Well, I could hardly bring the cow into the surgery, could I! Although I might just, next time.'

'You do that, Mrs Cameron. It might be worth watching.'

And she put the phone down. I seethed. *Bloody* woman. Well, it would be the last time I'd be calling on Marshbank's services. Meanwhile, though, there was the vexing little problem of this bill to pay. Alex had gone ballistic the other day because he'd seen a carrier bag with some new shoes—only flip-flops—what was he going to say about this?

Half an hour later saw me driving very fast down the country lanes into town. Fast, because if I slowed down and thought about what I was doing, I might turn round and go home. My heart was full of fluttering and trepidation, and not only that, I had a very full car too.

I parked squarely outside the wine bar that Sheila had assured me the other day was just the place—'Just opened, luv, and right poncey'— and regarded it nervously. It did look poncey, with its smart, bottle-green livery and 'Moulin Rouge' sign written in loopy gold scroll.

Inside it was dimly lit, and a long mahogany bar ran the entire length of the left-hand side; behind it a pretty girl with a shiny dark bob and a cupid's-bow mouth was polishing glasses. Aside from that, the place was empty. She smiled. 'Can I help?'

'Yes, I . . . is the manager in, please?'

'I am the manager. I'm also the washer-upper, glass polisher and general dogsbody.' She grinned and offered her hand. 'Molly.'

I grinned back, relaxing slightly. 'I know the feeling. I mean, the dogsbody one. My name's Imogen Cameron. I'm an artist. Someone said you occasionally have local artists' work hanging in here, and I wondered if you'd consider taking mine?' There. It was out.

'Oh, right. Who said that?'

'Sheila Banks.'

She threw back her head and laughed. 'Sheila Banks! Well, you've been misinformed. I've never had art here—haven't been open long enough—but if Sheila sent you, I'd better take a look. Don't want my legs chopped off, do I? What are they, watercolours?'

'No, oils actually. Rather large ones. They're in the car, I'll get them.'

I waited an agonising few minutes as she walked around them all, really looking at them properly. Finally she turned and smiled. 'I'll take them,' she said. 'What the hell, they're huge, but they look great. What shall we say—sixty forty on the price tag if they sell? To you, of course.'

I gaped. I hadn't got as far as that. 'Perfect,' I said, dazed. We then spent the next ten minutes writing prices on sticky labels and putting them on the frames, and then we set about hanging the pictures there and then. 'No time like the present,' Molly declared, halfway up a ladder. 'And it's not as if I've got any bloody customers!'

We hung eleven in all, and one, my largest and favourite, a Parisian street scene, we put right behind the bar. As I stood back and surveyed it, I felt such a rush of pleasure I was nearly sick.

'They look great,' said Molly in surprise, turning about. 'And they transform the place. Looks like a proper French café now.' It did. What had been a dark, gloomy bar now looked cheerful and atmospheric, like a nineteenth-century Impressionists' retreat.

Molly went to the fridge and took out a bottle. She popped the cork expertly. 'Come on, we need a drink.'

As we sipped companionably she told me about her dream of bringing a little bit of Paris, where she'd worked for some years, to this small market town, and about her despair as the clientele walked resolutely by to the Dog and Duck. To console her I told her about my own gnawing guilt that I wasn't a real artist at all, just a dilettante fake—unwise perhaps, since she'd just taken eleven of my pictures. We were on the point of going beyond work to our more personal lives when we were saved by the bell. A young couple stuck their heads round. 'We didn't know if you were open yet, or—'

'Yes! Oh, yes, we are.' Molly nearly fell off her stool, just managing to save herself, as she slipped behind the bar. 'What can I get you?'

I drained my glass, shooting her a wink, then I went out into the street. The air was still and calm, and a soft rain was falling. I stood there for a moment, letting it cool my cheeks, flushed with wine and success. I'd found a home for my pictures. I'd found a new friend— who, if I was honest, would probably turn out to be more of a soul mate than Sheila. I'd had a good day. Thank you, Mr Pat Flaherty, I thought. You've given me the very kick up the backside I needed.

The barbecue at the Latimers' started badly. I was getting ready upstairs when the phone rang. 'Hello?'

'Damn. I was hoping to get the answering machine.'

'Hannah? Why, what's up?'

'Er, well. You're not going to be awfully thrilled.'

'You're not coming?'

'Oh, no, we're coming. But Dad's coming too. Now don't go ballistic, Imogen. I couldn't help it. He rang, you see, reminding me it was his birthday—'

'Oh, *shit*.'

'Exactly, and had I remembered that we might meet for a drink, which of course I hadn't, so I said, oh, Dad, I'm awfully sorry, we're going out to lunch. And then of course I put the phone down and felt awful, so I rang Eleanor to say, actually, so sorry, we won't be coming. I've forgotten Dad's birthday, and she said, bring him along.'

'To which you replied, oh, no, I couldn't possibly,' I growled.

'Well, of course I did, but she wasn't having any of it. She said he must come, and bring his girlfriend too—well, what could I do?'

I shut my eyes. 'Well done, Hannah.'

'It wasn't my fault,' she said testily, 'and, if you must know, I'm feeling pretty lousy myself today and would rather stay at home.'

'Sorry,' I said meekly. 'What's wrong?'

'Chronic constipation and stomachache, since you ask. I'll see you later. And don't forget a card for Dad.' And she put the phone down.

Marvellous. Dad never celebrated his birthday for reasons best known to his vanity, yet this year, had chosen to come out of denial and celebrate at the Latimers'. Perfect.

'Aren't you ready yet?' Alex yelled up the stairs.

I grabbed my bag and pashmina and went down. Alex, fresh from the shower, looked like he'd stepped out of the *Sunday Times Style* magazine.

'I've just got to find a card for Dad.' I rifled around in the kitchen drawer—a futile gesture—found a piece of plain white paper, folded it in half and pressured Rufus into making one.

By the time we'd all tumbled out of the cottage—deciding to walk, on the grounds that we could both have a drink—we were late. Actually, I was secretly pleased. If Eleanor had loads of people coming, I reasoned, we could just creep up on the fringes and mingle discreetly, and hopefully Dad and his entourage would do the same. I was nervous, although I shouldn't have been, because actually, I'd decided in the bath the previous night, I was being completely neurotic about Eleanor Latimer. It was my own little crush on Daniel Hunter than had done the trick. Married people *did* have crushes, you see, but it didn't mean anything. Not a thing.

As we rounded the side of the house and approached the back lawn through the rose gardens, it occurred to me that it was all rather quiet. Odd. As the terrace came into view, I saw Piers, sitting up ramrod straight on a bench with Dawn beside him. Hannah was slumped lumpenly in a wicker sofa, and Mum beside her, Eddie was turning sausages on the barbecue, talking to my father, while Eleanor, stunning in salmon-pink T-shirt and denim shorts, buzzed around with a jug of Pimm's.

Alex glanced at me, horrified. 'Your entire family's here!'

'Yes, I . . . forgot to tell you. I thought it was a big bash. Had no idea it was just us. And Eleanor invited them,' I added quickly.

'Christ Alive,' Alex muttered. 'Piers will freak.' It occurred to me that he already had. 'Sweet Jesus, who's the girl with no clothes on?'

'That's Dawn,' I muttered. 'Dad's girlfriend.'

Dawn had dressed up—or down, depending on how you looked at it—in a lot of heavy make-up, a pink crop top, and a skirt, if you counted the white thing round her waist.

'Imogen, Alex, how lovely!' Eleanor did look genuinely delighted. 'And I don't need to introduce you to anyone, because of course you know them all!' she laughed. 'Isn't this jolly?'

'Very,' remarked Alex drily, stepping forward to shake hands with Dad, who came across, beaming with pleasure.

'Happy birthday, Dad,' I smiled, kissing him and handing him the card. 'Sorry I forgot.'

'Oh, don't worry, when you get to my age you stop counting. I say, quite a pad your mates have got here, haven't they, Alex?' His eyes roamed admiringly over the balustrade to the landscaped acres beyond.'

Alex agreed and I moved away to greet Mum, relaxing slightly. At least I could count on her not to let the side down.

'Isn't this marvellous?' she chuckled quietly as I sat down beside her. 'Look at that man. He's about to pass out with shock!'

Piers, it was true, was a picture: veins standing up in his forehead, eyes bulging, as Dawn, tapping his arm for emphasis with a long black fingernail, explained, in carrying tones, about her friend Malcolm who had a big house—almost as big as this—in Peckham.

'He keeps llamas,' she was saying, 'and ostriches.'

Piers blinked. 'Good Lord. In Peckham?'

'Yeah, it's a great little business. You should try ostriches, Piers, wiv all your fields an' that. You sell the meat, see, and you sell the feavers.' She tapped his arm. 'So it's all economically—whatsit?'

'Viable?'

'That's it.'

'But who on earth buys the feathers?'

'Christ knows. But I've got an ostrich pompom G-string, 'aven't I? So someone must! They probably use it to stuff pillows an' that.'

'And . . . where does it go?'

'Pillows go on beds, Piers.'

'No, the pompom.'

'Oh, on the front. Blimey, not round the back. You'd look like the frigging Easter Bunny!' She roared and elbowed him in the ribs. He looked genuinely delighted and roared back.

'Where did he meet her?' Alex bent to hiss in my ear.

I looked up into his furious blue eyes. 'At the opera house, of course,' I said smoothly, getting up to find a drink. I moved on to speak to Hannah. 'How are you feeling?'

'Ghastly. I haven't been to the loo for days.' She looked terrible: pale and slightly damp at the edges. 'I'm banking on getting food poisoning here and then letting it do its worst. Eddie's convinced the sausages are past their sell-by date so he's frazzling them to a crisp.'

'I wondered why he'd taken charge of the barbecue. But is it really just us, Hannah?'

'Piers's mother is knocking around somewhere.'

'Oh God,' I giggled. 'Lady Latimer and *Dawn*!'

'Oh, you missed that floor show. Dawn asked her if she was really a lady, to which she replied, "So my gynaecologist tells me."'

I snorted. 'But no Purple Coat?'

'No, she's got a gig, apparently. Singing at that hotel in town. Oh, and there is someone else here actually, some local chap who lives on the estate, but other than that it's just us.'

'I'm going to kiss my brother-in-law,' I said, getting up.

Eddie paused in his manic sausage turning to greet me. 'Salmonella type C and full-blown dysentery is what we're getting here today,' he informed me *sotto voce*. 'Don't go *near* the pork chops. Warn Rufus.'

'I'll bear it in mind,' I assured him. 'What's up with Hannah?'

'I think she's just been overdoing it. She's started this Weight Watchers thing, and she's exercising as well. Frankly I'm worried she's not fit enough to go to the gym yet. I reckon she's pulled something.'

'Hannah's at the gym?' I boggled.

'Isn't he doing a marvellous job?' Eleanor was suddenly at my shoulder. 'Imogen, you haven't met Piers's mother yet, have you?' I turned to see, in the shadows, just inside the French windows, an older, female version of Piers, complete with long, beaky nose and watery blue eyes. She was talking to someone whose back was to me. I hastened across the terrace with Eleanor.

'Louisa, this is Imogen Cameron, Alex's wife,' Eleanor said in a loud voice. 'Remember I told you? She and Alex have taken a cottage.' At that moment, I realised who her mother-in-law was talking to. I caught my breath. 'And Pat you know, of course. You sat next to him at supper,' Eleanor reminded me.

I took the dry, papery hand the old lady had extended. 'I remember,' I said coldly. 'How do you do, Lady Latimer?'

Pat Flaherty registered my frosty features and dropped his smile.

'He's a vet,' Lady Latimer informed me in sepulchral tones. 'Rather a good one.'

'I know. I mean, that he's a vet,' I added, thereby clarifying, for his benefit, which part of her sentence I agreed with.

'Got marvellous hands,' Lady Latimer said. 'Looks after my fanny.'

'That's Fanny the Yorkshire terrier,' breathed Eleanor quickly.

This was clearly the sort of vet that administered to old ladies' pampered pooches. And he certainly looked the part with his ready smile and easy manner: a twinkly-eyed charmer in a sapphire-blue shirt.

'Eleanor,' hissed Lady Latimer, 'who are those dreadful people on the terrace? I had to pretend it was the heat driving me inside, but they really are beyond the pale.'

'I'm afraid that's my family,' I said smoothly, noticing her nose was very pink at the tip. She looked like a drinker, and I could smell her gin from here. 'Actually, they're perfectly pleasant when you get to know them. Ah, look, the sausages are ready, I must go and feed Rufus.'

I sailed outside, my heart pounding, and went down the slope of the lawn to find Rufus. He was playing with the youngest Latimer on the swings. 'Come on, boys. Lunchtime,' I muttered.

Eleanor came rushing up as I collected the food from Eddie. 'I'm so sorry, Imogen. She's a terrible old snob, I mean—' She broke off.

I grinned, suddenly rather liking her. At least I wasn't the only one whose brain didn't engage before speaking.

'It's OK, I know what you mean. By the way, how come Pat Flaherty's here?' I asked casually.

'Oh, he's renting the lodge house while the builders do up his place, an old rectory in the next village. He's good fun, isn't he?'

'We call it Crumpet Cottage,' remarked Piers, lining up at the barbecue, his plate clamped to his chest, like a small boy at prep school. 'He seems to entertain a never-ending stream of women down there.'

Did he indeed, I thought, going to sit beside Rufus with my hot dog. So he really was the local stud as well as the charming vet, eh? I watched as Pat went to sit next to Hannah on the sofa. Well, that was one female he wouldn't be able to get round. If she wasn't feeling so grim she'd give an obvious charmer like that very short shrift. She'd never had any truck with playboys, and had only really warmed to Alex because I'd married him. Had Alex been a playboy? I thought with a jolt. I looked across at him by the barbecue, and as I did, something terrible happened. I intercepted a glance between him and Eleanor. It was a secret, raised-eyebrow look across a crowded terrace and she gave a quick shrug and a half-smile back. I looked away, horrified. Then I went hot and panicky. Get a grip, Imogen, for heaven's sake. It was probably perfectly innocent. Probably—d'you want a sausage? To which she'd replied with a shrug, 'Yes, I might.'

Luncheon continued. Behind me, Pat's mobile rang and he went inside to take it. I tried not to notice his rather perfect bottom in his jeans as he went through the French windows. Then I decided that if I could notice other men's bottoms, even unspeakably arrogant ones, it was surely a good sign? I couldn't be too suicidal.

Hannah staggered to her feet. 'I think I'm going to go to the loo.'

'Are you going to be all right?' I made to get up, concerned.

'Fine, fine,' she waved me away impatiently as she moved heavily across the terrace, making painful progress.

'She looks terrible,' I hissed to Mum, who'd sat down beside me.

'I think she's pulled something at the gym. It's the same one Dawn goes to, you know, and Dawn says they really make you work out.'

I regarded my mother. 'You get on well with Dawn, don't you?'

'Yes, I do, but not for much longer. She's moving to Newcastle. That's where the best beauticians' course is. But your father's staying put.'

'Well, that'll be the end of that relationship, then. Let's see who he comes up with next,' I grinned.

She grimaced. 'That dreadful Tessa Stanley asked him to dinner at the Hurlingham last week. I do hope he doesn't take up with her.'

I shot her a sideways look. It was odd. Mum was positively gleeful about the likes of Dawn, yet didn't want him consorting with any of their old friends in London. That was her territory.

'Who's that terribly attractive Irishman in the blue shirt?' she asked.

'That's the supremely arrogant Pat Flaherty. He's an expensive vet—'

'Darling, what's wrong?'

I was on my feet. White with shock and fury. For there, through the open French windows, in a dark corner of the drawing room, reflected in the mirror above the fireplace, my worst nightmare was unfolding before my eyes. This image shattered; spun. But even in its disjointed, kaleidoscopic state, a few immutable facts remained. The look on my husband's face as, presuming himself to be hidden from view behind the door, he took Eleanor in his arms; the longing in Eleanor's eyes as he gathered her towards him; the way their bodies melded seamlessly together.

My hand gave an involuntary jerk and my glass let loose a stream of Pimm's, which flew through the air, splashing into Mum's lap. I hurried away without even an apology, across the terrace to the French windows. I flew into the room and spun round. Eleanor was talking animatedly on the telephone, and Alex was on the opposite side of the room on his hands and knees, his head in a cupboard full of glasses.

'Can't find them.' Alex drew his head out and glanced round. 'Oh, hello, love. Eleanor's tasked me off to find some water tumblers before everyone gets too pissed.' He frowned up at me. 'Are you all right?'

I stared down at him, flummoxed.

'Good.' Eleanor put the phone down with a decisive click. 'That was the silk flower company, they're coming with some samples on Tuesday.' She grinned at me. 'Your mother's really enthused me, Imogen.' Then her face clouded over. 'Are you OK? You look a bit pale.'

'Yes . . . no. I'm . . . fine.' I tried to regulate my breathing.

'D'you mean these?' Alex took some tall tumblers from the cupboard.

'Perfect. Grab a few of those, would you. I've put a few bottles of Perrier on the table. Are you sure you're OK, Imogen?'

'Yes. I—I think I'll have a glass of water too.' I picked up some glasses and went back outside in a daze. I went over to the drinks table, then poured myself some water. Suddenly I glanced sharply back over my shoulder at Alex. He'd followed me outside and was talking to Eddie. Eleanor was crouched down in front of Rufus and Theo with a tub of ice cream. Neither of them looked rattled. I put the glass down and raised a hand to my forehead. It was damp. I was actually going mad, seeing things that weren't there, that weren't really happening. Not just imagining the worst, but seeing the worst. Going insane.

I walked shakily back to Mum. 'Sorry about your dress,' I muttered.

'Couldn't matter less. It'll come out in the wash. Are you all right, darling? You look as if you've seen a ghost.'

I picked up my plate of food wordlessly. I'd been so sure I'd seen them together, I thought, but—well, that was classic, wasn't it? The mind playing tricks, the green-eyed monster feeding on whom it preys. And it was very hot. Too hot, for May. Yes, that must be it. The sun had got to me. And the Pimm's.

Behind me, Piers was bellowing with laughter as he teased Pat.

'. . . don't give me that, Pat. You've got no end of fillies trotting in and out. I saw one myself going in only the other day!'

'Nonsense,' drawled Pat, 'that was my great-aunt Phyllis.'

'What, with long blonde hair, dark glasses and pink jeans?'

'Ah, you must mean Cousin Dorothy.'

'Don't believe you for one moment, old boy. My money's on that being some poor, unsuspecting bastard's wife!'

Everyone's at it, I thought feverishly. Was my husband at it too?

'I'm worried about Hannah,' Mum muttered in my ear. 'She's been gone an awfully long time.'

'I'll go and look,' I said, glad of the excuse to go inside.

I went back to the drawing room. As I crossed the threshold I stood for a moment, my eyes darting around; taking in the mirror that had so recently played tricks on me. How pale I looked; how huge and troubled my eyes. I hurried away, and was about to leave the room when my eyes fell on the telephone. Glancing over my shoulder to check I wasn't being observed, I lifted the receiver and pressed redial.

A clear, fluty voice rang out. 'Good afternoon, Marlborough College?'

Marlborough College. Where Eleanor's elder children were at boarding school. Not a silk flower company. I put the phone down, my heart pounding. Well—perhaps they'd rung her. I punched out 1471 then pressed 3, but it was the local butcher in Little Harrington, not a silk florist. I swallowed. My mouth was very dry. Was I . . . not going mad, but being sent mad? By the pair of them? I paused for a moment. No, I thought suddenly, because of course, she'd been using a mobile, hadn't she? Yes, I think she had. So stupid, Imogen, I thought. You saw for yourself how entirely innocent it all was—Eleanor on the phone, husband in a cupboard—your eyes had been deceiving you.

After the bright buzz of the terrace, the house seemed cool and still. For a moment, I couldn't remember what I was doing there. Oh, yes, Hannah. I tried the loo by the front door. No Hannah.

There was another loo down the back passage, but that too was empty. I popped back to the kitchen and stuck my head round. Vera stood with her back to me. 'Vera, have you seen my sister anywhere?'

'Would that be the rather large—I mean . . .' she stopped.

'That's it, in a blue dress.'

'She went upstairs, luv. Someone was in the downstairs one, so I sent her up there.'

I mounted the main staircase. Upstairs was vast, creamy and sprawling, and the first few rooms I encountered looked distinctly pristine and spare. No Hannah. How far into the bowels of this house had she gone? The next landing looked very plush and private, and I guessed I was entering Piers and Eleanor's own quarters. I was just wondering which of the four panelled doors around me would yield a bathroom when I heard a shout of pain coming from one of them.

I tried the handle. It was locked. I rattled it. 'Hannah?'

'Yes!' she gasped back. I heard movement within, and then she unlocked the door, hanging heavily on to the handle, before collapsing in a heap on the cream carpet. I flew to her side.

'Oh my God—Hannah, are you all right?'

She was breathing heavily, holding her side. 'Appendix,' she gasped. 'At least I think so. It's too bloody painful to be constipation!'

'Appendix! Oh God, I'm ringing an ambulance, Hannah! I'll get Eddie up here, but if it's your appendix, you need to get to hospital fast. Just stay there, I'll be back.' Oh joy, a phone. My eyes had spotted it through an open door into what was clearly the master bedroom—huge, with a four-poster bed. I punched out 999 and barked, 'Ambulance! And make it snappy. My sister's got a burst appendix!'

God, had it burst? In horror I beetled back down the stairs to get Eddie, because if it had—well, that was bloody serious, actually . . . I flew outside at racing speed, but only Mum and Lady Latimer were there, chatting quietly. They looked up in surprise as I rushed out.

'Where's Eddie?' I gasped, trying to keep the panic from my voice.

Mum frowned at me. 'Piers took everyone off to look at his aviary, darling. Why, what's wrong?'

'I think Hannah may have appendicitis,' I said, as calmly as I could.

'Oh God.' She stood up quickly.

'I've called an ambulance, but, Mum, I need you to get Eddie.'

'I'll show you.' Lady Latimer, suddenly galvanised, was on her feet. She strode off with Mum hurrying along beside her.

I ran back inside and made for the staircase again, taking the stairs two at a time. Down the long corridor I flew, past the spare rooms, on to the next landing, and into the bathroom. No Hannah. No gasping sister slumped on the floor holding her side, berating me for not getting back quickly enough. Shit. Had she tried to stagger somewhere more comfortable? A bedroom perhaps? I'd *told* her not to move!

'Hannah!' I yelped, spinning about.

At that moment a piercing shriek rang out. It was a primeval sound, full of pain, full of fear, and it went right through me. '*Arghhhhhhh!*'

It was coming from the master bedroom, the door to which was now shut. I burst through. My sister was flat on her back on the four-poster bed, dress rucked up, knees bare and bent, legs wide apart—being forced apart—by Pat Flaherty, who loomed over her, pinning her to the bed, his dark eyes glittering as he ripped off her knickers.

Chapter Seven

'WHAT THE HELL do you think you're doing!' I thundered.

'I'm delivering a baby, what does it look like?' he snapped. 'Your sister's in labour. I was in the downstairs loo and heard her shouts from down there—came running upstairs to find her practically giving birth on the bathroom floor. Somehow I managed to get her in here, which was no mean feat. She's fully dilated. Look, she's pushing already.'

'Oh my *God*, she thought she was constipated!' I gasped, my mind whirring. 'Hannah, you're *pregnant*, didn't you know?'

'Of course I didn't bloody—AARGH!!' she shrieked as another contraction gripped her. 'I want to push!'

'Well, push, next time that happens,' Pat ordered.

'Do you know what you're doing?' I shrieked. 'Have you done this before!'

'I have, as it happens, for complicated reasons, along with countless animal deliveries, but feel free if you think you'd do a better job.' He took his head from between my sister's legs and turned to glare at me.

'No! God. I haven't a clue, but shouldn't she—you know—cross her legs or something, until the ambulance gets here?'

'What, and cut off the oxygen supply and damage the baby? That's about the most dangerous thing you can do. No, this baby's coming. Look,' he stood back to let me see, 'the head's crowning.'

I conquered my qualms and crouched down . . . oh . . . a dark head *was* visible—I could see hair! Black hair!

'Oh, Hannah!' I rushed to seize her hand. 'I can see it, it's a baby!'

'AARRAGGGH!' Hannah gripped my fingers, her head right off the pillow now, eyes squeezed tight, as at that moment, Eddie came in.

He stood there in the doorway, mouth open, blinking. 'What the . . .?'

'She's having a baby!' I screamed. 'She's giving birth!'

Befuddled and mystified beyond belief, Eddie staggered in a few more steps. 'She can't be,' he whispered.

'I bloody am!' hollered Hannah. 'Look at me!'

'Oh . . . my . . . *God*!' Eddie's face went through a myriad of emotions: horror, disbelief, incredulity—then he settled on wonder. He sank down beside her, seizing her hand. 'Oh, darling. But . . . but how?'

'Well, I'm pretty sure you had something to do with it!' she shrieked.

'Oh, my angel!' He kissed her fingers. 'Does it hurt?'

'Does it—AARGH! SHIT! CHRIST!'

'Push,' instructed Pat, crouching down at the sharp end again.

'Yes, and breathe,' enjoined Eddie eagerly. 'You must breathe, I've read that, and you must relax, not tense up, and—'

'AND YOU CAN FUCK OFF!' she screeched, lashing out in fury with her fist, and catching Eddie squarely on the temple. His face lost all of its colour. Then, as blood spurted from his head, he collapsed on the floor.

'Christ! Eddie!' I leapt back in panic. 'Pat, she's knocked him out!'

'Bugger.' Pat hastened round to put Eddie in the recovery position. 'Nice timing, mate,' he muttered. 'Nasty cut you've got there. Oi, Nurse, put a towel on it.' He threw one at me. 'Staunch the flow.'

'WHAT . . . ABOUT . . .ME?' roared my sister murderously.

At that moment, the door flew open. Piers and his mother stood there in the doorway, bug-eyed with amazement as they took in the scene. 'What the . . .?' began Piers, inadequately.

'Hannah's having a baby and she's knocked her husband out,' Pat explained. 'Yes, that's *it*,' he encouraged suddenly. 'Good girl, it's coming!'

'Good grief!' Piers yelped, as at that moment, like something out of a French farce, another door opened, this one in the far corner of the room. Alex and Eleanor stood there, gaping with amazement.

Alex's jaw dropped as he regarded his sister-in-law on the bed. 'Bleeding Ada!' he gasped. 'She's having a baby!'

'Oh, Hannah, it's coming, it's coming!' I sobbed, wringing my hands.

'But shouldn't she be in hospital?' blabbered Piers. 'The bedcover . . . this is the Tudor Room!'

'Oh, for God's sake, Piers, it's too late for that. Can't you see it's coming?' snapped Eleanor, hastening to Hannah's other side.

It was. As Hannah bore down with one final, mighty, primeval moan, suddenly the whole head appeared, bright red and covered in black hair, swiftly followed by a slippery little body, covered in mucus.

'Oh!' we all gasped as Pat caught it expertly in his hands. There was a moment of complete silence, then: 'It's a boy,' he said.

In the gasps of shock and amazement that followed, Pat somehow managed to cut the cord, clean the baby up a bit, wrap him in a towel, move round the bed, and hand him carefully, tenderly, to his mother.

Hannah struggled to sit up and take the baby in her arms. As I flew to help her, propping her up with pillows, she gazed down in disbelief. 'A boy,' she breathed. 'I've got a baby boy.'

Tears fled down my cheeks. 'Oh, Hannah!' I gasped.

In another moment, we heard footsteps pounding up the stairs.

My mother's voice rang out. 'She's up here somewhere. Quick!'

The ambulance crew burst into the room, complete with stretcher and equipment. 'Which one's got the burst appendix, then?'

Later, much later, as I said to Mum that evening, in the hospital cafeteria, it was ironic that in the end it was Eddie who needed the stretcher to the ambulance. Hannah had walked down the stairs—slightly hypnotically perhaps—with her baby in her arms. Eddie told me later that as they were en route to the hospital, he'd come round, and was deemed well enough to sit up and hold the baby. Thus, this brand-new family trundled off to Milton Keynes General with wonder in their hearts, Mum and I following on behind in the car.

'I can't believe she didn't *know* she was pregnant,' Mum insisted.

'But, Mum, she'd been told she couldn't *have* babies. It wouldn't have occurred to her that she was.'

'Yes, but she'd have missed a period!' she squeaked. 'Several!'

'Mum, Hannah thought she was getting the menopause because apparently you got yours early, so when her periods stopped, she just thought, this is it then. And I suppose . . .' I hesitated, feeling disloyal, 'well, if you've always been as big as she was . . .'

'What's a bit more on the tummy? And let's face it, she was getting huge, but—oh God, it just didn't *occur* to me.' She looked distressed.

'Don't,' I said, putting my hand over hers. 'She's fine. She's had a baby, which is what she's always wanted.'

'Yes.' Her face softened as she looked at me. 'And thank God for that marvellous man. What was his name?'

'Pat,' I said shortly, sinking into my coffee.

'Pat. Did you see how he dealt with everything?'

'He's a vet, Mum. It sort of goes with the territory.'

'Hardly,' she snorted. 'He's used to sheep and cows. No, I thought he was absolutely fantastic. And as for Piers—did you see his face?'

'Yes, well, I don't suppose we'll be invited back next Sunday for a barbie,' I said wryly. 'Be surprised if he lets us stay at the cottage.'

'Nonsense. Eleanor was sweet about it.'

Yes, she had been sweet. Had run around finding a clean nightdress and a toothbrush for Hannah to take to hospital and had shooed all the gawping men out of the room and given me a big hug.

I cleared my throat. 'Mum, you know when you went to get Eddie from the aviary? Was Alex there too?'

'No. Eleanor wanted to show him something upstairs. She'd redecorated one of the bedrooms, I think. In the west wing.'

So that explained why they'd appeared through a different door.

'And are you all right, my love?' Mum reached up and took my hand away from my throat. 'You're scratching your neck to bits.'

I nodded. 'Everything's fine. Come on, let's go and see Hannah.'

The doctor was just leaving Hannah's bedside when we got there, assuring Eddie that she was in very good shape. Eddie stammered his thanks, relieved, and hurried to resume his position by her pillow.

'Where's the baby?' I asked as I sat down beside Eddie.

'He's got a bit of jaundice, so he's under a light in the nursery.'

'Rufus was a bit jaundiced too. Oh, Hannah, how wonderful, a baby!' My eyes filled up again. I couldn't help it.

She smiled weakly; looked all in.

'And the proud father.' Mum patted his arm. 'How does it feel?'

'I can honestly say,' Eddie began portentously, his glasses steaming up, 'that aside from the day when Hannah agreed to marry me, this is the happiest, proudest day of my life.'

'Oh, Eddie!' It was no good, my eyes were brimming over now.

'Would you like to see him?' Eddie asked eagerly.

'Oh, *please!*' Mum and I groaned ecstatically.

We stood up as one, and went to follow Eddie, when I glanced back at Hannah. She was staring blankly to one side.

'I'll catch you up,' I said quickly, as Mum and Eddie went on down the corridor. I took her hand. 'What's wrong?' I said.

'Nothing.'

I regarded her anxiously. 'Hannah, this is marvellous, isn't it? The most fantastic thing that ever happened to you.'

'Of course.' Flatly.

'And—and it doesn't matter—'

'What?' she interrupted sharply. 'That I was walking around for nine months with a baby inside me without the faintest idea?'

'Of course not! God, it happens all the time, Hannah!'

'Yes, to teenagers on sink estates, maybe, but not to someone like me. Not a middle-aged teacher, a pillar of the community—albeit a fat one. I feel such a fool!' Tears sprang from her eyes.

'Hannah, so what?' I shook her limp hand. 'Surely it's the outcome that matters, a healthy baby, a *miracle* baby, what you've always wanted! You'll be a proper family now, it'll change your life!'

'But that's just it,' she blurted out suddenly. 'It will change my life, and I'm not sure I want that. Not sure I can cope!'

I was stunned. My bossy, scary sister. . . couldn't cope?

'He's so tiny,' she whispered, 'so fragile—I'm scared to touch him! Oh, Imo, I'm not sure I can do it!' I saw the fear in her eyes. 'It's all so unexpected, and everyone expects me to just adapt, but I'm not sure I can!'

'Of course you can,' I said staunchly. 'Have you fed him yet?'

'No.' She turned her head away, to the window. 'He has to be under the light, you see. I've told the nurses to give him a bottle.'

I nodded. 'Right.' I swallowed. 'Hannah, this is all hormones and— and the shock. You'll be a brilliant mother, simply brilliant!'

'Will I?' she said bitterly. 'I'm not so sure.' She turned back from the window. Her eyes were dead. 'I'm not sure I want him at all.'

I stared at her, dumbfounded. At length, I took a deep breath. 'Hannah, I'll be back, OK? I'm just going to find Mum and Eddie.'

I scuttled away, my heart pounding. I found Mum and Eddie in the day nursery, cooing over the tiny naked baby under a bright light. 'You can pick him up,' a nurse was advising Eddie. 'He doesn't have to be under there all day, just for a few hours at a time.'

'Right.' Eddie wrapped him in a blanket the nurse gave him, and cradled him adoringly in his arms, his eyes shining. 'Hello, son,' he whispered. After a minute, he handed him proudly to Mum for a turn.

'Eddie.' I took his arm as Mum walked across to the window, crooning and soothing. 'Eddie, I'm a bit worried about Hannah.'

'Why?' He looked startled. 'The doctor said she was fine.'

'No, it's not that. It's just. . . well, she should be in here, with him.'

'She's only just given birth, Imogen. Maybe tomorrow?'

I nodded. 'And—and see if you can persuade her to feed. It does make a difference, builds up their immunities, that sort of thing. I think it would help her. Help Hannah.'

He frowned. 'Help Hannah what? I mean . . . surely that's her department, Imo. I can't tell her what to do.' He looked worried.

'I know, but you could encourage her, Eddie. She's had a terrible shock. Her body's in turmoil. She needs you to help her.'

Eddie looked anxious. 'I'll try.'

Mum dropped me back at the cottage later that evening.

'How is she?' Alex asked. 'And the baby?'

'She's fine.' I peeled my coat off wearily. 'The baby's fine too. Healthy, if a bit small.' My shoulders sagged as I looked at him. 'I'm sorry.'

'For what?'

'For my sister giving birth, I suppose. For it all being so awful and embarrassing, in Piers's house. In the frigging Tudor Room.'

'Don't be silly.' He came across and held my shoulders. 'As long as Hannah and the baby are fine, that's all that matters, isn't it?'

'Oh, darling. Thank you for that.'

'What? You think I don't know that? That that's all that matters. Everyone knows that. Everyone was—well, euphoric, almost, after you'd gone. Eleanor rushed off to get some champagne and we all wet the baby's head.'

'Really?' I brightened. Yes, I could imagine Eleanor doing that; taking the lead, saying, 'Isn't this exciting?' Good for her. 'And Piers?'

Alex's mouth twitched. 'Piers's rapture was slightly more modified, it has to be said. Your father was flying, of course. Did a little impromptu waltz with Dawn on the terrace.'

I groaned. 'Will I ever grow out of being embarrassed by my parents?'

'Doubt it,' he said cheerfully, going out to the kitchen where I could smell Bolognese sauce bubbling away on the hob. 'Eleanor thinks they're both terrific incidentally, particularly your mother.'

Oh, so that was all right then. If Eleanor thought so, she must be. Oh, *stop* it, Imogen. God, he's made supper, put Rufus to bed, what more do you want?

We sat down at the table to eat. 'Eleanor thought she might pop in and see the baby tomorrow, if that's OK,' Alex said, twirling spaghetti onto his fork. 'You know, take a present or something.'

'Great,' I nodded. 'Hannah would like that.'

'Oh, and Kate rang, incidentally, while you were out.'

'Oh?' I looked up.

'Apparently I'm moving into their basement flat next week.'

I flushed. 'Oh, Alex, I'm sorry. I asked Kate last week because—well, I thought you'd be so uncomfortable at Charlie's. I know I should have consulted you first, but Kate was going to talk to Sebastian so I thought—well, I'll wait till she gets back to me before—'

'It's fine,' he interrupted, laughing. 'It was just a bit of a surprise, that's all. Kate said to pay whatever I was going to give Charlie.'

'Oh, darling, I'm so pleased, aren't you?' I glowed.

'Of course. The lap of luxury as opposed to a grotty old flat in Chiswick, but—why are you so pleased?' He eyed me beadily.

'I suppose—well, I suppose it means when I come and meet you in town, I get to see Kate too,' I said brightly.

'True,' he nodded. 'And meanwhile I can keep an eye on those pesky tenants of ours across the street.'

'Exactly!' I agreed jovially. Oh, thank you, Kate. Thank you.

'I told her about Hannah. She was staggered. Everyone will be, Imo.'

'I know,' I said. 'And Hannah's really worried about that.'

'I mean, why the hell didn't she know?' He boggled at me. 'I know she was fat, but surely a woman knows her own body better than that?'

'For complicated reasons, Alex, she didn't,' I said shortly, scratching my neck. 'And yes, she is feeling extremely foolish.'

'She could always pretend she knew but wasn't saying anything.'

'What—lie?' I looked at him.

'Well, only a little white one. Just say she wanted to surprise everyone and it came a bit early, that's all.'

'Lie,' I said again. 'That's what you'd do, is it, Alex?'

He laughed. 'Well, if it meant getting myself out of a corner, yes. Eleanor and I were both saying that's what we'd do, just say—*Shit!*'

A plate of spaghetti narrowly missed his ear as it flew past him and smashed on the wall. 'Is it!' I trembled. 'Is that what you'd do?'

He stared at me. 'Jesus, Imo,' he breathed. 'What's with you?'

I stared at his bewildered face. My whole body felt as though it were about to go up in flames. With a strangled sob, I fled upstairs.

About an hour later, when he came upstairs, I was lying way over on my side of the bed, facing the wall, curled up in the foetal position. He got into bed beside me where we lay in silence. I could hear an owl screeching far away in the woods. At length I spoke. 'I'm sorry.'

He slid across and put his arms round me from behind. 'It's OK,' he said softly. 'It's been a long day and you're emotionally strung out.'

'Yes,' I whispered, acknowledging this was true. Even so. Ask him. Ask him now. Outright. Stop this aching inside of you.

'I'm fairly shattered myself,' he yawned. 'Night, darling.'

Ask him, my head screamed. *Ask him now, you coward!* Still my voice wouldn't come. Fear was strangling my vocal cords. I wanted to know, but didn't want to know. Instead, in desperation, I twisted round, held his face in my hands like a precious vessel, and kissed him, tenderly.

'You, my little one,' he murmured in my ear, 'have had a very stressful day. You need to get some sleep.' He turned over and reached for the alarm clock. 'Better set it for six fifteen, I'm afraid. Night, darling.'

I gazed at his hunched form in the gloom; I heard his breathing, heavy and rhythmic; I felt tears fall silently across my face onto the pillow. Clutching the duvet like a child with a comforter, I held on tight as though everything I had was about to slip from my hands.

The following day I found I was almost relieved when he left for London. 'See you on Friday,' he whispered in my ear.

As I opened my eyes, I remembered. Felt sick. Heavy. But then, the weight dropped off me. Yes, go, I thought. So long as he was away from Eleanor, I reasoned, I could breathe again. Take a break from losing touch with reality. And my life was about to get considerably easier, I thought later that morning, walking slowly out to my easel in the meadow. With a weekly boarder for a husband, I could really let things slide. No proper cooking; no bed to make properly, just crawl in under the duvet. Heaven. Odd, wasn't it? I wanted him so badly, but if I knew he was away from her, I was also quite happy without him. The thought brought me up short. But—it was only that I had more time to paint now, I thought quickly.

After I'd dropped Rufus at school that morning, I'd cruised back through the town and drawn up outside the wine bar. Molly was washing the front doorstep like a true Parisian café owner. 'Sold one!' she announced with a grin.

I stared at her. My mouth fell open. 'You *haven't*?'

'Yep, this weekend.' She laughed at my disbelieving face. 'The one of the cows in the water meadow that hung over the archway. You'd better get painting. I need another one for there now.' She picked up her bucket and went inside.

'But . . .' I got out of the car and hastened after her, 'we put four hundred pounds on that, I thought it would be a laugh!'

'So who's laughing now? You get three hundred and I get the rest!'

'Blimey . . .' My mind was still spinning. 'Who bought it?'

She shrugged. 'No idea. I wasn't here yesterday, and Pierre, my new Sunday chap, didn't know. He paid cash, whoever he was.' She grinned. 'What's the matter, didn't you expect them to sell?'

I looked up at her. 'In all honesty, no. Not in a million years.'

She laughed. 'That's how I felt when someone first came in here and ordered a drink. We've got to start believing in ourselves, Imogen.'

Yes, I thought now, raising my brush, yes, I *would*. All bed-making could legitimately be ignored.

Rufus, though, I thought with a jolt some time later, couldn't be ignored, and if I wanted to visit Hannah before I picked him up—I glanced at my watch, one o'clock. *One o'clock, Christ!*—I had to fly.

Hannah was sitting up in bed suckling the baby when I pushed through the ward door, and my heart soared with relief. She looked up briefly to flash me a smile, then gazed down adoringly at her bundle again. I caught Eddie's eye. He winked.

'I saw that wink,' murmured Hannah, keeping her eyes on her suckling child, 'and I know it means you two have been in cahoots, and you,' she cut me a look, 'persuaded him to have a go at me.'

'Nonsense,' I said firmly.

'Told him to tell me to stop squirming with embarrassment and start focusing instead on the most precious thing there is.' She gazed at her baby's downy head. 'And you were right. Who cares what anyone thinks when I've got him?' She looked up at me, slightly appalled. 'How could I ever have thought public opinion mattered, compared to this?'

'Hormones,' I smiled. 'They do funny things to us women.'

Behind me, the door swung open and my parents bustled in, laden with flowers. Dad was beaming from ear to ear. 'Where is he, then?' he boomed in his strongest Welsh accent, causing several babies in the ward to unlatch from their mothers. All six babies wailed mightily.

'Sorry, ladies,' he whispered contritely. 'Ooh, look, there he is!' His eyes lit up. '*Divine!*' He stooped to scoop the baby from his daughter's arms, pausing only to plant a kiss on her cheek. 'Well *done*, pet.'

Happily his grandson was replete and didn't object to the change of venue. Mum and I smiled at each other as Dad cradled him in his arms. Dad had a bit of a thing about babies.

'You're feeding, my love,' Mum observed to Hannah. 'That's nice.'

'Well, I wasn't, but my sister bullied me into it.'

'Oh, Hannah, I hope I—'

'I'm joking,' she laughed. 'Thank God you did. I just needed a push, lacked confidence, you see. Didn't think I could do it.'

God, it was all coming out today, wasn't it? This baby business was certainly revealing. I got to my feet. 'Well, I must go. I've got to go and get Rufus, but I'll pop in tomorrow, Hannah.'

'I'm just waiting for the doctor to sign me off, so come and see me at home. I'd like that. There's so much I don't know, Imo. So much I want to ask you.'

Jeepers. 'I need the loo before I go.' I glanced around.

'That way.' Hannah pointed through the swing doors. 'But you have to come back through the ward.'

'I'll leave my bag then.'

I kissed them all goodbye and nipped to the Ladies. As I went to go back through the double doors to the ward to get my bag, the door was opened for me. Propping the door, looking disreputably handsome and bearing a big smile and a bunch of primroses, was Pat Flaherty.

'What the hell are you doing here?' my mouth said before my brain could stop it.

He looked taken aback. 'Well, it's not every day you deliver a baby, so I thought . . .' he trailed off, embarrassed.

'Oh God, yes, sorry,' I flustered, flushing. 'I—wasn't thinking—'

'Well, helloa, look ye 'ere!' a voice boomed out and my father took Pat firmly by the shoulders. 'This is the man who delivered my grandson, saved my daughter's life—and the baby's too, I'll warrant—marvellous *marvellous* man!' he announced to the ward, clasping Pat to his bosom.

'I'm so very grateful,' said Eddie earnestly. 'Really grateful.'

Pat smiled. 'You're very welcome. But I honestly didn't come here for gratitude. I just popped in to see how the little chap was doing.'

'He's fine,' smiled Hannah from the bed, holding him up so Pat could see. 'Look, *so* lovely, and all thanks to you.'

'Well, he certainly looks in good shape. Oh, I, picked these for you.'

Mum took the primroses from him, smiling broadly. 'You're a dear, sweet man and we don't know how we can thank you enough.'

'I know how I can,' thundered Dad. 'I can take him oot for a pint or ten, that's what. Come on, laddie, let's goa and find a watering hole.'

Pat laughed. 'I'd love to, but I'm operating in an hour.'

'Imogen?' Dad turned to me.

'I've got to get Rufus.' Head down, I made for the door. For some inexplicable reason I found I couldn't look at Pat.

'And I won't linger,' Pat said quickly. 'I just popped in to— '

'Noa, noa, linger away!' roared Dad, pulling up a chair for him. 'Sit down, boyo, sit. We want to hear more, don't we? Imogen said you'd done it once before, like, delivered another babe. Is that right?'

'Yes I . . . well. It was my wife, actually. She gave birth in the back of a taxi in Dublin as we were on our way to hospital.'

I'd got as far as the ward door. Stopped. His wife. Right.

'No!' Mum was exclaiming. 'How dreadful! But you managed?'

'Had to, really. With the taxi driver's help.'

'And what did she have? I mean, what have you got?'

'A girl,' said Pat shortly.

'Lovely! How old?'

'She's twenty-two months. Look, I must go,' he said awkwardly. 'I just wanted to make sure you were OK.'

'Fine,' beamed Hannah.

A moment later I realised Pat was coming up behind me. I moved on through the door. 'Bye!' my family shouted cheerily, and it was at this point that I was about to turn to him, thank him, make polite conversation, but when I turned I realised—he'd gone in the opposite direction.

I drove off to the school, feeling cross and confused. Why had I found it so hard to look at him? I hadn't even thanked him like the rest of my family, but he had rather shot off, hadn't he? *I'd* made him uncomfortable by being so unfriendly.

I shifted in my seat, irritated. Oh, well, what did I care? I didn't even like the man. But I wished I'd at least said thank you.

Rufus and Tanya ran across the village green to meet me. 'Mum, can Tanya come back for tea with us? We want to see if we've got any rabbits.' Disappointed, but not undaunted by the conspicuous lack of foxes in their Heath Robinson trap, Rufus and Tanya had turned their attention to rabbits, and created a contraption that was essentially a salad bar with a trap door.

I glanced over Tanya's blonde head and saw Sheila at the gates collecting her zillions. She saw me and smiled, nodding that she knew.

We drove off, my mind still, ridiculously, on Pat Flaherty. I'd offended him by ignoring him, and now I was ashamed. As I parked in the yard, Tanya and Rufus leapt out, running in the direction of their trap.

I wandered inside to get their tea. Damn, I thought miserably. Now I'd be back to giving him tight little smiles as we passed. Well, so what, I thought with a jolt. Why on earth should that matter?

"Mummy!' I turned to see Rufus running back towards me. 'Mum, come quick,' he panted. 'We've got one! We've got a rabbit!'

I hurried after him to the paddock next to the cows' field. Tanya was in the middle of it, squatting down on her haunches over a large wooden box. 'He's huge!' she squeaked. 'Look!'

I bent down to see. Through the mesh trap door, an enormous grey rabbit with round, scared eyes, his ears flattened, stared back at me.

'He certainly is. And he's lovely, guys, but he's a bit frightened. I should set him free.'

'I know, we will, but we just want to keep him for a little bit. For observation,' pleaded Rufus.

'It's research,' Tanya informed me. 'For a school project. And anyway, we may have to look after him longer, 'cos I think he's limping.'

'Is he?' Rufus bent to see, unused to such ploys to get his own way.

'He is a bit,' she insisted. 'Maybe we should take him to the vet?'

I stared at her a moment. 'Limping, you say?' I enquired softly.

'Yeah, look!' she said, thrilled to bits that her little ruse had been so easily bought. 'I think it's his back leg!'

'Oh dear. Yes. Poor thing,' I murmured. 'Well, maybe we should.'

Without giving myself a moment to question my motives, we piled into the car, the rabbit in his box in the boot. As we drove up the chalky zigzag track, though, my mind was whirring. 'Um, listen, guys,' I called over my shoulder. 'I'm not convinced the vet treats wild animals, so we might have to say that the rabbit's—you know—ours.'

'Really?' Rufus's eyes were huge in my rearview mirror. This was a whole new side to his mother. Not only a pushover, but a fibber too. He beamed and bounced delightedly in his seat.

We pulled up outside the rather smart Victorian house with the brass plaque, which bore the legend 'Marshbank Veterinary Practice'. The children jumped out and ran round to the boot to get the box. I got out and followed them up the path. When he saw that the rabbit was OK—Pat, I mean—I could just—you know—have a dizzy blonde moment. Say—oh gosh, is it? The children were convinced. And he'd laugh at my charming fluffiness and say—don't worry, it happens all the time, and then he'd say—why didn't I have a coffee while I was here? And we'd settle down for a cosy chat, and that would be that. What would be what, Imogen? I wondered. But only fleetingly. I mean, dammit, we were here now.

The pretty blonde receptionist looked up and smiled. 'Can I help?'

'Yes, I'm awfully sorry, we don't have an appointment, but we've got a sick rabbit here and we wondered if the vet could see him.'

'Oh dear, poor thing. I might be able to squeeze you in. Name?'

'Mrs Cameron.'

Her face changed dramatically. It was no longer so friendly and smiley. 'We are rather busy, actually,' she said shortly.

'Oh, but you did say you might be able to squeeze us in,' I said. 'The children would be so grateful.'

The china-blue eyes were cool. She regarded me a long moment. 'Just a minute.' She got up with a flick of her blonde hair over her shoulder and went down the corridor.

In another moment, she had returned. She gave a tight little smile. 'Yes, OK, the vet will see you. But he's operating in five minutes, so you'll have to be quick.'

'Thank you so much,' I gushed disingenuously.

'No problem,' she muttered, sitting down again. 'Now. Name?'

'Mrs Cam—'

'The rabbit's,' she snapped.

Rufus, Tanya and I looked at each other wildly. Then we all spoke at once. 'Bunny.'

'Thumper.'

'Cuddles.'

The receptionist raised her eyebrows.

'Um, yes. That's his . . . full name,' I murmured.

'I see.' She filled in the form, her face inscrutable. 'And how old is Bunny Thumper Cuddles?'

More wild looks. 'He's . . . twenty-two months,' I breathed, for some reason, thinking of Pat's daughter.

'Twenty-two months,' she repeated slowly, writing it down. 'Very precise,' she observed drily. 'And sex?'

'Good heavens, no, he's only a baby!'

'What sex is the rabbit, Mrs Cameron?'

'Oh! Right. He's . . . a—a male. A man rabbit.'

She scribbled some more. 'Right. Well, if you'd like to take this form,' she said sweetly, 'together with your "man rabbit", down the corridor to the first door on the right, the vet will see you now.'

We scurried away down the corridor to the door on the right. He was over on the far side of the room in a white coat, his back to us; but even before he turned, I felt a pang of dismay.

'Mrs Cameron?' A vinegar-faced man with a Scottish accent peered at me over half-moon glasses.

'Oh! I was expecting . . . Mr Flaherty. Is he . . .?'

'Operating, I'm afraid. I'm Mr McAlpine, the senior partner. Will I do?' he enquired scathingly, a quizzical gleam in his eye.

I flushed. 'Yes, of course.'

'Now.' He crossed the room. 'Bunny Thumper Cuddles aged twenty-two months. What seems to be the trouble?'

'Oh, I—I think . . . well, he had a slight limp. But actually, I didn't notice it in the waiting room just now. We'll come back another—'

'Nonsense, you're here now and I've broken off my premed on a Border collie with a tumour to look at him. Come on.' He took the box and put it on the table. 'Now, laddie,' he turned to Rufus, 'would you like to get your bunny out for me?'

Rufus turned terrified eyes to me. I licked my lips. 'Um, the thing is, he hasn't been handled that much, so maybe,' I attempted a fluffy laugh. 'Well, I'm hopeless with animals and you're the pro . . .'

He regarded me scathingly. 'I see. Who mucks him out, then?'

'Who mucks . . . oh! Well, yes, I do. But—not very often. I mean—he's frightfully clean. Hardly any ponky-poos at all!'

'Really. Constipated as well as limping. Well, let's have a look.'

He flicked back the clasp, opened the lid and peered in, at which point the rabbit spun round and, like a kung fu boxer, delivered a powerful kick with both hind legs straight to the vet's face. He caught Mr McAlpine squarely in the right eye, and sent his glasses flying. Then he leapt high into the air and sank his teeth into his finger.

'Jesus Christ!' the vet yelped. The rabbit jumped down to the floor and fled to a corner of the room. Blood pouring from his finger, the vet looked at me aghast. 'That's a wild hare!' he roared.

'Oh!' I gasped. 'Is it?'

'I thought it was big,' volunteered Tanya, in awe.

'What are you doing bringing it in here? It could be diseased!'

'I—I'm sorry,' I stammered. 'I thought it was limping—'

'Limping?' he bellowed, as the hare, desperate to escape, jumped up on the counter, knocking over bottles, sending test tubes flying. 'That hare is no more limping that I'm Olga Korbut!'

The hare was, indeed, looking horribly agile now as he careered round the room, sending jars full of vile-looking liquid smashing to the ground. We watched in horror. 'Get him out of here!' he shrieked, his face contorted with rage.

'Righto,' I croaked. With the children cowering behind me I dithered ineffectually round the room, waving my handbag, bleating, 'Here, Bunny' as I attempted to corner him.

'Oh, for heaven's sake!' Mr McAlpine, exasperated beyond belief, lunged and caught the animal by the haunches, but the hare wriggled free, leapt up and bit him hard on the nose.

'Oh!' shrieked Tanya, her horror betraying a hint of ecstasy.

The vet swore darkly and made another lunge. The animal dodged nimbly, causing Mr McAlpine to bang his head squarely on a cupboard, just as the hare, spotting the open window, sprang out.

'Oh, no!' the children gasped in alarm.

'Best place for him,' panted the vet. '*Jesus* Christ!'

'But he won't know the territory!' said Rufus, running to the window.

'So he'll make new friends,' snapped the vet, 'charm a few locals, a very advisable thing to do when you're new to an area!' He flashed me a look then turned back to glare at my son. 'And anyway, sonny, you should have thought about that before you set about trapping him.'

Rufus hung his head with shame and his eyes filled up.

'There's no need to take it out on a small child!' I snapped. 'Yell at me. I'm the one who suggested bringing him here!'

'Aye, well, you'll think it through a bit more thoroughly next time, won't you? Now, away with you,' he shooed us. 'I've got a surgery to clean up. Go on, be off!'

Needing no further prompting and mumbling effusive apologies, I grabbed the box and backed out, pushing the children ahead of me. We were halfway to the front door when a voice brought me up short. 'Would you like to settle up now?' I stopped. Spun round. 'Only, we always ask emergency calls to settle up on the spot,' the receptionist informed me, handing me a bill for thirty pounds. 'That's our standard charge, Mrs Cameron, but perhaps you'd like to settle your whole account while you're here?'

My whole account. Damn. I looked into her mocking blue eyes and wished I'd thought to cash my cheque for the paintings; put some money in the bank. 'Er, no, just the thirty pounds, for now.'

'So . . .' she murmured silkily as she watched me scribble a cheque. 'Flowers for the headmaster, flirting with the postman, and now wild rabbits for the vet. Whatever will you pull out of the hat next, Mrs Cameron?' I glanced up in horror. Went pale. Rufus looked up at me anxiously. 'Word gets about in a small place like this, you know,' she said softly as she took my cheque. Her eyes were hard and knowing. 'You want to be careful, Mrs Cameron. Very careful indeed.'

A few minutes later found me sitting very still in the car, the children clambering into the back. She'd been telling me in no uncertain terms that I was making a fool of myself. My eyes cut back through the window and I watched as she flicked back her long blonde hair and leaned forward in her pink jeans . . . long blonde hair and pink jeans . . . oh God. She was one of the girls Piers had seen coming out of Crumpet Cottage, one of Pat's girls. How many were there? I wondered. And what was I doing swelling the ranks? I went hot.

'Are you all right, Mummy?' Rufus's face was anxious.

'Yes. Yes, fine.' I gave a bright smile and we drove away.

We passed out of town and into the lanes. The hedgerows flashed by in a riot of late spring colour: red campions and yellow cowslips nodded in the breeze. My mind was racing. This wasn't about me throwing myself at headmasters, or vets. This excuse to see Pat was symptomatic of something much more worrying. It was about being scared, and lonely. About me counting the number of times my husband made love to me, about a vacuum in a marriage. It was a cry for help. And Pink Jeans had pointed this out very succinctly. This was me reacting to a situation I had no control over—and was too scared to confront, for fear of what I might find out.

My breathing became shallow as I raced down the lanes. I hadn't wanted to face this, but now, here it was. And I'd denied it many, many times before.

When love is withdrawn from a marriage, its absence is not felt immediately. After all, the fabric of the union is still there: the house, the mortgage, the child—but slowly you realise the jewel has gone. Everything goes just a little bit darker, but you stumble on in the gloom, taking care not to trip over the evidence, until one day, quite unexpectedly, you're sent sprawling by a crassly stuck-out leg—in my case, with pink jeans on. Me, who was adept at ignoring The Signs.

In London, The Signs had tended to start at the weekend: Alex, sitting in the drawing room in Putney, gazing ruefully into space. Then would come the spurious errands: the nipping to the shops for extra milk when we already had plenty, the trips to check the tyres at the garage, always with his mobile, and then—a less pensive, less reflective Alex: an Alex with an excited light in his eyes, a man with a plan. Finally would come the late night at the office. Never a whole night— he was never that careless—but it would be midnight before he was back, and then, for a day or two afterwards, the excited light would dim to a more contented glow. He'd be very sweet to me, and to Rufus, and very good about the house. There'd be trips out too: but always the three of us, never the two of us in a quiet restaurant for supper with a baby sitter for Rufus—no, Rufus had to come too. And this, a man who was impatient with children; who sometimes treated his son like an irritating friend of mine who'd come to stay. But on these occasions, Rufus was crucial. He was his shield.

But these carefree days wouldn't last and soon he'd be back to the sad, wistful Alex, snapping at Rufus if he suggested a bicycle ride, and then there'd be impromptu trips to the garage, and then the overexcited husband, then the late night—and so the cycle of our lives would go on. He was like a junkie who needed a fix, and the fix wasn't me.

It is to my eternal shame that I never investigated his mobile or went through his pockets. I'm not proud of that. There were no depths to which I would not sink to protect my family, to be innocent of all charges of knowingly living in a faithless marriage. But now this. A well-aimed catty remark from a woman who was intent on protecting her own domestic interests. I took a deep breath. Right. This was it.

I swung the car left down a narrow lane and drove off towards the next village. 'This isn't the way home, is it, Mummy?' said Rufus.

'No, but it's the way to my home,' remarked Tanya, twisting round in surprise as I bumped down the track towards the trailer park.

I drove slowly through the grid of caravans and mobile homes, venturing where the local police daren't, and drew up outside the largest one, surrounded by pansies planted in piles of old tyres. Sheila was hanging rows and rows of grey school knickers out on a washing line.

'Sheila?' I called out of the window. 'Would you have Rufus for me for an hour or so? There's something I need to do.'

'Course, luv.' She bent and peered in at the window. 'You all right?'

'Fine.' I plastered on a smile. 'Really fine. Thanks, Sheila.'

I headed towards Little Harrington and the Latimers' with a remarkably clear head, and for once, something approaching steel in my heart.

The steel didn't waver as I mounted the steps to the heavy front door and gave it a mighty rap with its brass knocker.

As the huge house resounded to the outraged howls of various labradors and lurchers, the door opened cautiously and Vera peered round, frowning. 'Oh. Hello, pet.'

'Is Eleanor in?' I blurted out.

'She's not, I'm afraid, she's gone out to see a girlfriend.'

'Oh.' Damn. 'Will she be long? Can I wait?'

'Well, she's out for the evening, like, but she's going to be ever so cross because she's forgotten her handbag.' She jerked her head across to a quilted Chanel bag, sitting on the hall table.

I looked at the bag. 'D'you know who the friend is?'

''Aven't a clue, luv, but she's renting in the village, I'm told.'

'Well, it's not a big village. She shouldn't be difficult to find. I'll take it.' I reached deftly across to the table and my hand closed on the bag.

'Oh, well, I don't know . . .' Vera faltered, confused.

'Honestly, it's not a problem, Vera,' I said smoothly. 'I'm going that way anyway. And I know Eleanor's car. It's bound to be parked outside.'

Without giving her a chance to stop me, I sped away. The village, in truth, was not that tiny. It sprawled down backstreets and up cul-de-sacs, and I knew I hadn't given myself nearly as simple a task as I'd pretended to Vera. I drove around for a bit without spotting so much as a hint of Eleanor's dark green Range Rover. Damn.

And then I saw it down a lane I'd originally dismissed as being just a farm track. There was a row of cottages at the end, and outside one of them, Eleanor's four-wheel drive.

Which cottage though? I thought wildly. This one—number nine— or the one next door? Blood storming through my veins, I marched up to number nine and leaned on the bell. A huge man, his arms covered in faded army tattoos, swung back the door in irritation. 'Yeah?'

'I'm sorry. I'm looking for a friend of mine, Eleanor Latimer. She's visiting someone who lives in one of these cottages—'

'Never 'eard of her,' he growled, slamming the door in my face.

The lady at number ten, in her yellow dressing gown, was slightly more helpful. 'Well now, that could be number twelve, two doors away,' she said at length.

I thanked her profusely and hurried away to number twelve. I rang the bell but there was no answer. I rang again—still no response. And yet . . . I peered through the small pane of glass in the front door. That was Eleanor's Puffa jacket. She wasn't coming to the door, though, was she? And neither was her friend. Incensed, I squatted down and pushed open the letterbox. *'Eleanor!'* I screamed. *'Eleanor Latimer, I know you're in there! Open the door this instant!'*

I put my ear to the letterbox. Heard voices. My blood boiled. 'ELEANOR LATIMER! COME OUT, YOU TWO-TIMING HUSBAND-SNATCHING HUSSY! YOU JEZEBEL, YOU—*oh!'*

I shrieked as the door flew open . . . and I found myself looking into the unmistakable features of—Daniel Hunter, Rufus's headmaster, wearing a dark green dressing gown.

Chapter Eight

'MRS CAMERON!' He stared at me, astonished.

Behind him I saw Eleanor, at the top of the stairs, also in a dressing gown. 'Shit!' She shot back into the shadows as our eyes met, and in that instant, I understood everything. My mouth fell open.

Eleanor reappeared on the landing. She was pulling on some jeans. 'Wait there!' she ordered fiercely.

'Er, yes. You'd better come in.' Daniel scratched his head sheepishly.

'Oh—no, no! I—I'm terribly sorry, I've made a mistake. . .'

'Imogen, wait!' Eleanor came hurtling down the stairs as I backed down the path, horribly aware that Yellow Dressing Gown and Tattooed Man were now out in their front gardens, watching wide-eyed for the jezebel to appear.

Eleanor didn't disappoint them.

'Don't go,' Daniel implored her. I saw the naked entreaty in his eyes.

'I'll be back,' Eleanor promised in a low voice, and I saw the tenderness in her eyes. 'But I need to explain to Imogen. I must!'

'You don't need to explain!' I squeaked, embarrassed beyond belief but also—also stupendously joyous. Not my husband. Not Alex.

'Listen,' Eleanor hastened after me. 'He *was* married, you're quite right, but he's divorced—or practically divorced—I promise!' Her hazel eyes pleaded with me. 'Come on, we'll go for a drink. I'll explain.'

'Oh!' I stopped in my tracks. 'You mean—what I yelled through the letterbox! Oh, no, I don't mind if *he's* married, couldn't give a monkey's, just so long as he's not married to me!'

'What?' She gaped, and now it was her turn to stop still in the street. I was aware of Yellow Dressing Gown and Tattooed Man walking hypnotically to their front gates to listen, keen not to miss a word.

I hurried to my car. 'Come on, we'll take mine. No, I'm just so happy it's not Alex!' Oh, thank you, God. Thank you!

'You mean,' she got in beside me, 'you thought me and Alex . . .?'

'Yes, and now you're not, and—oh, Eleanor, for heaven's sake, go back and have a lovely time! I'm really sorry I've spoilt your evening.'

'Me and *Alex*!' she gasped, hanging on to the upholstery as we shot off down the road, away from the delighted eyes of the neighbours.

'Yes, but you and Daniel *Hunter*—Eleanor, that's *so* different. I couldn't give two hoots, and I feel dreadful about dragging you away!'

'And I feel dreadful about Piers,' she said firmly. 'And obviously I need to explain.' We drove in silence for a minute. 'We'll go here,' she said eventually, pointing at Molly's wine bar. She picked up her handbag, which she'd found where I'd stowed it in the passenger foot well.

She sat down heavily at a table just inside the door. 'Piers doesn't know. And listen, Imogen, it's really important he doesn't find out, OK? At least, not from anyone but me. Can I count on you?'

'Of course you can!' I assured her, waving at a waiter. Molly didn't seem to be around. 'Shall we have a bottle?' I felt like celebrating.

'Just a Perrier for me, but please say you won't breathe a word.'

'I won't,' I assured her, beaming. I ordered the drinks, feeling sorry for her as she sat back, slumped and defeated in her chair. 'God, I didn't even think you liked each other,' I blurted out when the waiter had gone. 'In fact, when I rang him from London about Rufus and mentioned your name, he was positively rude about you.'

'I know,' she gave a twisted smile. 'We . . . slightly planned that. I didn't want you smelling a rat. We have to be so careful.'

'Has it been going on long?' I asked.

She nodded. 'Three years.'

'But—what about the neighbours in his road? Surely they see you going in and out?' Well, they would now, I thought guiltily.

'Oh, that's not his house. A friend of mine in London rents it. She's in Spain at the moment. Sometimes we go to Daniel's house but it's risky, so it's really just snatched, occasional moments. Precious moments. I love him,' she said simply, and her eyes filled.

I wondered how it had started. Let's face it, Daniel wasn't exactly in her social milieu . . .

'I met him when he first took over the primary school,' she said, reading my thoughts. 'I wanted Theo to go there, thought he'd thrive in a cosy village school. I also thought it would integrate us into the community a bit more, make it a bit less Us and Them. Piers wanted Theo to go to Shelgrove like the others, but I went to see it, anyway. Daniel showed me round. After I'd spent an hour or so with him, I found I couldn't stop thinking about him. He had such soft kind eyes . . .'

I nodded. Yes, I remembered feeling much the same. Those eyes were a killer. I blushed as I remembered the flowers.

'Anyway, I made some pathetic excuse about wanting to go back for a second look and he showed me round again, and we chatted, and by then, it was well into the lunch hour and he suggested a sandwich in the pub. I'm afraid I leapt at it. I felt . . . very isolated, at the time.' She glanced up at me. 'Marriage can be like that, you know.'

I nodded, remembering that I'd thought that too. But not now. Oh God, no, not now. 'He is . . . very different to Piers,' I ventured.

She smiled sadly. 'Yes. And I know what you're thinking. How come I was ever with Piers in the first place?' She sighed. 'Where shall I begin, with Piers? By citing mitigating circumstances, and saying I'd just broken up with a serious boyfriend when I met him? That I was feeling raw and unloved and very definitely on the rebound? That I bumped into someone I thought was strong and protective but turned out to be dull and arrogant? Or shall I tell you that when he drove me out from London in his convertible Aston Martin and we cruised up the long drive to Stockley I fell for his beautiful house, the rolling acres, the whole lady of the manor bit?'

She met my eye. 'If I'm honest, I think it was a little of both. Added to which, all my friends were getting married, I was twenty-eight years old, and suddenly, had gone from being quite a catch—a girl lots of men would like to be seen with—to being horribly available. Suddenly, all those men were with younger girls.' She took a slug of her drink. 'I met and married Piers within three months.'

I nodded, eyes narrowed. 'And was one of those men Alex?'

She sighed. 'Yes, Alex had been a boyfriend. He asked me to marry him once, but I said no.' She shrugged.

I caught my breath. Right. I hadn't known that. That he'd asked her to marry him.

'So . . . when did you realise you'd made a mistake?'

'With Piers? Oh, very early on. But I was too proud to admit it. There's nothing terribly wrong with Piers, Imogen. He's just . . . a bit dull, that's all.' She made a despairing gesture with her hands. 'Naively, I thought children would help. So I had four. Safety in numbers.' She smiled ruefully. 'After Theo was born I realised there was no point having five. It wasn't diluting my husband.' She looked up. 'That's when I had an affair with Alex.'

I nodded, wondering when she'd get to that. 'Tilly's husband,' I said.

'Yes.' She sighed. 'And I'm not proud of it. Not proud at all. We just sort of fell into it, two old friends with problems. It was pain relief for me, and,' she puckered her brow, 'sort of an exorcism for him. Getting me out of his system. The one who'd turned him down. But the moment he knew of your feelings for him, it dwindled between the two of us. You were too much for me. Far too much competition.'

I caught my breath at this. And I'd always thought that of her.

'He was captivated by you,' she said softly. 'Talked about you all the time. But I think he never believed he stood a chance.'

'But he was in love with you,' I said firmly. I wasn't having that, entirely. I remembered Alex's distress when she refused to leave Piers.

She nodded. 'He was, but more so, I think, because he couldn't have me. And when I decided to make a go of it with Piers, he fell so head over heels in love with you that . . . well. That was no rebound, Imo. He adored you. Still does. I can't believe you don't know that!'

She looked at me incredulously and I saw that her eyes were both honest and astonished. How awful. I hadn't always known it.

'I . . . suppose I have, sometimes, doubted it.'

'You mustn't! she insisted, leaning forwards across the table. 'It's only ever been you, Imo, for years now, believe me, and I would know,' she said with feeling.

Yes. Yes, she would. I felt as though my heart might burst with joy and relief. 'I . . . don't really know why I've doubted him,' I whispered. 'He—he has these moods, though. One minute he's a proper loving family man, and the next—well, the next he's distant, irritable, late coming home, and I thought—'

'It's his job,' she said, putting her hand over mine. 'Don't you know that? Don't you know he's terrified of losing his job, of being a failure?'

'But I wouldn't think he was a failure—'

'*He* would, though. And he'd feel it for you too. He was *such* a big shot in the City, and now . . . well, now there are younger, brighter men coming up behind him and he feels threatened.'

'Does he tell you this?' I felt a pang of jealousy. A familiar twinge.

'Yes, because he's too proud to tell you, and also because . . .' she struggled, looked away. 'Well, he says you say it doesn't matter.'

'It doesn't!' I cried. 'I couldn't care if he was a bloody dustman!'

'It matters to him,' she said fiercely. 'Maybe you should talk to him about it,' she urged, 'not just say, "Who cares?" Say, "I care."'

I flushed as it dawned. I hadn't been a very good wife. Hadn't listened to him, had forced him to bottle it up because I'd thought he was bottling something else up . . . 'I've been so stupid,' I whispered.

She stretched across and squeezed my hand. 'No, you've just been barking up the wrong tree. It happens. He loves you very much, Imo. Take it from an old mate who knows.'

I looked at her across the little wooden table, and, for the first time, saw her for what she really was. A good friend; an old friend who, by dint of longevity, was bound to be privy to more information about Alex than I was. But not privy to the beat of his heart, which was mine, all mine. And that was all that mattered. I'd make it up to him, I determined. I'd be a better wife. And—and maybe I'd encourage him to do something else, if work was making him so miserable? Maybe we could farm salmon in Scotland or something, I thought wildly. Maybe he could retrain? Teach, perhaps, like Daniel. Daniel.

I glanced back across the table. 'I've made it so much worse for you,' I said suddenly. 'Shouting in the street like that. In a village this size it'll get around in minutes.' I went hot with horror.

'Let it,' she said quietly. 'It's what I want now.'

'Really?' I was startled.

'Really.' She gave a funny, sad smile. 'One of the reasons I wanted you and Alex to come here, Imo, was because I knew I was going to tell Piers and I wanted friends around.'

I nodded shamefully, realising how stupid I'd been, how I'd maligned her. She'd always tried so hard, and I'd always been so suspicious. Yet . . . 'The other day, when I saw you two together in the drawing room,' I said suddenly, 'I'm sure I saw you in his arms, in the mirror.'

'I was telling him,' she nodded, 'about Daniel. And he was comforting me, and then I saw you come towards us and I leapt for the phone. I thought you might get the wrong idea, I just hoped you wouldn't think it was odd to be ordering silk flowers on a Sunday. And then later, when I pretended to show him the spare room upstairs, I was telling him the rest of it. I just wanted to tell *someone*, I was going crazy with it,' she said desperately. 'I asked Alex not to tell you immediately. Not because I don't trust you or anything,' she said quickly, 'but because I didn't think it was fair on Piers if everyone knew before him.'

'But why now? Why are you telling Piers now, after three years?'

'Because I'm pregnant,' she breathed.

We sat in silence for a moment as the ramifications sank in.

'Right,' I whispered. 'And I suppose I don't have to ask if—'

'Yes. I'm keeping it.' She held my eye. 'I don't blame any young girl

442 | Catherine Alliott

who's never had a baby for having an abortion, but when you've had four like I have, the idea of getting rid of it is—'

'No, I know,' I said quickly. Unthinkable. But for the baby's brothers and sisters . . . oh God. There was real terror in her eyes.

'I know,' she said, going pale, 'the others.'

I licked my lips. For them it would be *so* ghastly. And much as I hadn't always warmed to Piers, my heart went out to him too.

'So you'll leave him? Piers?'

'Yes, I'll leave him. Hopefully he'll give me a quick divorce and I'll move in with Daniel. He's applying for a post in Shropshire. The children are all at boarding school now anyway, apart from Theo, and he goes off in September.' She shrugged miserably. 'And I suppose we'll just share their holidays. After all, other couples manage it, don't they? I mean, look at Alex.'

Yes, look at Alex. Who hadn't seen his daughters for six months, who invited them in the school holidays, but found, increasingly, that boyfriends and parties took precedence. Was he sad about that? Unbelievably, I didn't know, because I didn't ask him. Didn't go there, because in my paranoiac state I'd been afraid that if it *didn't* upset him too much, then my goodness, it could be me and Rufus next, couldn't it? So I hadn't brought it up: hadn't been supportive. Oh, there was *so* much I had to make up for, I thought, ashamed. I glanced at Eleanor. She must know that to Poppy, Sam, Natasha and Theo, Piers was beloved Daddy. He wasn't a cheat, like Mummy, an adulterer, and neither was he having a child with someone else. Eleanor was in for a very bumpy ride, particularly from her teenagers. It seemed to me she was gaining one child and in danger of losing four others.

'I know,' she said quickly, reading my mind, 'it's going to be unutterably bloody, but I want this baby so badly. I got pregnant with the others to cement my marriage, but this baby was conceived through love and I'm having it.'

'How many months are you?'

'Three. So please God I'm over the dodgy stage. But if I miscarry, I'll still leave Piers. This has made up my mind. I can't live a lie any more. Not even for the children.'

That was quite a decision to come to as a mother, and she knew it. She was about to shatter so many lives, just as, I realised with a jolt, she'd once shattered Tilly and the girls'. Only this time it was her own children who'd end up in pieces. I wondered if it could be right to cause so much pain just to achieve personal fulfilment? Did we really have such a divine right to be happy?

'And anyway, I'll have to say something to the family soon, otherwise Piers's mother will do it for me,' Eleanor said darkly.

'She knows?' I said sharply, coming back to her.

'Suspects. She cornered me a few weeks ago, upstairs in my bedroom. Said she had a shrewd idea I was up to something.'

I gazed at her. 'Oh! Was that the day we first arrived?' I said. Eleanor had run down the stairs into Alex's arms, crying.

'Yes, she was absolutely foul. As only she can be.'

Protecting her son. Was that so wrong?

I shifted in my seat. Not uncomfortable but—

'I'll get the bill,' said Eleanor, quickly, noticing. She raised her hand and Molly appeared from behind the bar in a long apron.

'Oh!' I looked up in surprise. 'I thought you weren't here!'

'I was upstairs sorting out my flat. I've got the decorators in.'

'D'you know Eleanor Latimer? This is Molly, the owner.'

Eleanor smiled. 'I've seen you around but I don't think we've met.'

'We haven't, but nice to meet you.' Molly smiled and took away the ten-pound note Eleanor had put on the saucer.

Eleanor leaned across the table. 'I've seen her around, because she's one of Pat Flaherty's visitors,' she hissed.

'Really?' My heart, inexplicably, thudded at this.

'Constantly in and out of his cottage. I've often spotted her creeping in last thing at night and then leaving early in the morning.'

'He seems to lead a complicated life,' I said lightly.

'Just a bit,' Eleanor rolled her eyes, as Molly came back with the change. 'Thanks.'

So. Pat and Molly were an item. Right. I shoved my arms into my coat sleeves. Well, why not? She was a very pretty girl. Tall and slim, and with that shining bob of hair and creamy complexion, she knocked Pink Jeans into a cocked hat. I wondered if they knew about each other. For some reason, I was disappointed. In her, I think.

I drove Eleanor back to her car. When we drew up outside the cottages, she got out. I looked at her. 'Goodbye, Eleanor.' Even as I said it, I felt it had a note of finality to it.

She smiled but her eyes were already somewhere else, darting up to the bedroom window. Daniel was up there, by the curtains, waiting.

'Bye,' she said, before striding away, up the path, head held high, not caring now who saw her.

I drove thoughtfully to Sheila's and picked up Rufus, who bounced out of the trailer with round eyes and vertical hair, full of E numbers and artificial colouring, no doubt. I thanked Sheila and drove away.

'Can we go and see the baby now?'

'Oh, Rufus . . . I'm shattered.'

'Oh, come on, we practically go past their house!'

I sighed. Maybe it would be a good idea; maybe a dash of old-fashioned family values was just what I needed right now, after Eleanor's sledge-hammering of them.

'Well, how lovely!' Eddie hailed us. He scooped Rufus up and swung him round in an arc in the air. Rufus squealed with delight.

'Just practising,' Eddie wheezed as he set him down, 'for when the babe's a bit bigger. Ooh, me back.' He hobbled off to the brand-new pram, rubbing his spine. 'Shouldn't have done that.'

'Still "the babe" then, is it? No name yet?' I peered in the pram.

'Tobias,' said Eddie, straightening up proudly. 'Means gift of God. Tobias Martin Sidebottom, after his grandfather. He's round the back putting the finishing touches to his work of art. Have you seen it yet?'

'No, but I've heard about it, Hannah told me on the phone.' Dad was a whiz at carpentry and was making a cradle for the baby.

'Can we wake him up?' asked Rufus.

Eddie looked shocked. 'Good Lord, no!'

'Maybe he'll wake up later,' I said, seeing Rufus's disappointed face. 'And if he doesn't, we'll come again tomorrow, but, Rufus, it'll be a while before he's playing conkers with you.'

'At least he's a boy,' he said at length. 'At least he'll want to do the same things as me.'

'Course he will!' agreed Eddie. 'Tell you what, Rufus. You can push, and we'll take him to the corner shop for an ice cream.'

'Cool! How fast can I push?'

'Fast as you like, as long as you don't actually catapult him out of it. Hannah's inside, by the way.' He directed this at me as he followed Rufus, who was already off with the pram.

I watched as they went. For all his big talk, Rufus was actually handling his cousin with care. His cousin. Lovely. If only there were more. If only I could *have* more. For a moment I felt a pang of jealousy for Eleanor and her pregnancy.

I sighed and went in to find Hannah. She was on a stepladder, cleaning the windows. 'Should you be doing that?' I asked in alarm.

She looked down. 'Why not?'

'Well, you've just had a baby and—good God, look at this place! You've had a tidy up, and—blimey, the flowers!' I gazed round in wonder. The piles of jumble had all gone, and instead, space prevailed with vases and vases of flowers. 'Who are they from?'

'Oh, all sorts. Locals in the village, teachers, kids at school.'

'Oh, how sweet—sweet of everyone! You see?' I rounded on her. 'Are you still going to teach?'

'Oh, yes, but part time,' she said happily. 'The school's agreed to me doing four mornings a week, and I get all my maternity leave too!' She grinned and I marvelled at how well she looked. Shiny hair, rosy cheeks and *slimmer*. She saw me looking her up and down.

'Breastfeeding,' she said proudly. 'Tobias sucks for England, and after every feed I reckon I lose a couple of pounds. It's the best diet ever.'

'But you're eating?' I said, concerned. 'You've got to, to feed.'

She laughed. 'You sound like Eddie. Yes, I'm eating, but properly. I don't need all that food any more.'

'Because you're happy.'

Tears filled her eyes. 'Because I'm happy. You're right, I was misery eating before. All I ever wanted was to get married and have children. To have the roses round the door, the baking, the babies. I never wanted to be a success.'

'Who says that's not a success?' I said softly. 'And now you are. Now you've got it.'

'Now I've got it!' she echoed, and a big beam spread across her face as she opened her arms to me. I walked into them, my eyes like saucers. Hannah and I never hugged, *never*. Tears sprang to my eyes too. For her, for her hard-won, unexpected happiness, but, I suspect, for myself also. For my peace at last, free from the tyranny of Eleanor.

'You look well too,' she commented, as she led me to the garden.

'I am well,' I agreed. 'Oh golly—look at this!'

Dad straightened up from his carpentry. An immaculate wooden cradle stood proudly on the grass.

'Dad, I can't *believe* you made that. It's fantastic!'

'Isn't it great?' said Hannah, before going back to her windows.

Dad beamed. 'Only the best for the Marmalade Bishop. Haven't you noticed Tobias's hair?' he said gleefully. 'Definite touch of ginger, and that profile: noble yet pious. Made for the ministry.'

I giggled. 'If you say so.'

'And hopefully it's built to last.' He patted the hood. 'Can accommodate any number of grandchildren that might come along.' He winked at me, and although my tummy twisted, I smiled gamely.

It occurred to me that Dad was looking very unlike his usual self today. He had on a pair of ancient beige trousers and a blue sweater. He looked like a regular grandpa. I smelled a rat. 'Dawn gone to Newcastle, yet?' I asked lightly.

'Yes, went Monday. We've called it a day, as you probably know.'

'Well, there was talk you might not go the distance, as it were.'

He glanced up. 'It's not just the travelling. She's too young for me.'

I gaped. Too young? For my dad? He whipped off his jumper, then he dropped his trousers. I didn't flinch, since my father had been taking his clothes off at a moment's notice for as long as I could remember. He reached into a rucksack on the grass and buttoned himself into a crisp, pinstripe shirt; then he pulled on a pair of mustard cords and some brown leather loafers. 'Where the hell are you going?' I asked.

'Out to dinner with Helena Parker. Why?'

Helena was one of Mum and Dad's oldest friends; a lovely, elegant widow now in her late fifties.

'I met up with her at that dinner party Tessa Stanley gave at the Hurlingham a while back. She's a lovely woman.'

Yes. She was. 'Does Mum know?' I asked anxiously.

'I don't see what it's got to do with your mother,' he said as we went back through the house. 'And anyway, she likes Helena. It's Tessa she can't bear. Blimey,' he glanced at his watch, 'better get a wiggle on. How do I look?' He turned at the front door, beaming.

'Terrific.' I swallowed.

'Bye, darling!' he called to Hannah.

'Bye, Dad, and thanks!' she shouted back.

As he went down the front path, Rufus and Eddie were coming back up it. 'Bye, Bishop!' he sang, giving them a jaunty wave.

I walked thoughtfully back inside, chewing my thumbnail. Stopped at the foot of Hannah's ladder. 'Helena Parker!'

'I know, isn't it lovely? Imagine, Dad acting his age for a change, with a suitable girlfriend. Wouldn't it be great?'

'Great,' I agreed shortly.

Later that evening, when Rufus had gone to bed, I rang Alex. His mobile was off, so I tried the office.

'North American Desk?'

'Alex?'

'Oh, hi, darling.' He sounded tired. 'How's tricks?'

'Alex, it's half past nine. You're not still working, are you?'

''Fraid so,' he yawned. 'But nearly finished.'

I felt a sudden rush of love for him; working away late into the night for his family, for me and Rufus, but I felt indignation, too. I resolved once again that I'd persuade him to chuck it in. We'd sell up in London and use the money to start our own business, a joint venture—not salmon farming perhaps; that had been a bit far-fetched—but anything to get Alex out of this loop of misery.

'How's the flat?' I asked.

'Sumptuous, as you might imagine. Why don't you leave Rufus with Hannah and come up for the night? We could see a play or something.'

'I will.'

I put down the phone in a glow of warmth and happiness. Oh, the *relief* to be natural and light-hearted with him, without a shadow lurking over us. Without Her between us. It would have been nice if he'd asked after Rufus, I thought ruefully as I climbed the stairs to bed, but hey, that was being picky, I told myself hurriedly. I got into bed with a smile and turned out the light.

At three twenty, I was woken by Rufus shaking me vigorously.

'Mum. Mum! Wake up! The cows are out of the field!'

I frowned. 'Don't have any cows,' I mumbled.

'MUM!' He shook my shoulders violently. 'Come on, get up!'

He threw back my duvet, and in that instant, stark naked and curled up in the foetal position, I came to. Shit! The cows were out!

I ran to the window. Down below, Marge was casually snacking on a few tea roses in the front garden, while Princess Consuela was busy tap-dancing on the lawn. 'Christ! How the hell did they get out?'

'I think I might have left the gate open,' Rufus cowered.

'Jesus wept! Well, come on, we've got to get them back in again!'

Seizing my dressing gown, I flew downstairs, shoving my arms into the sleeves as I went. 'Wellies on,' I panted.

We flew outside, me waving my arms and shouting like a banshee, whereupon Marge and Consuela lolloped out of the garden, past their open gate, and on down the track.

'You frightened them, Mummy!' yelled Rufus. 'You need to be calm!'

I'd give him calm. 'Get behind them!' I screeched. 'Run round the back and we'll drive them back in a pincer movement!'

'But hadn't we better shut the gate? Otherwise the others will get out? I could stand guard and open it again when you've got this pair lined up to come through!'

Good plan. Wish I'd thought of it myself, although what I really wished I'd thought of was being the gate opener. I was reasonably *au fait* with cows now, but only from the pretty end. Wasn't sure about Going Round The Back. One hand clutching my dressing gown, since it had lost its cord, I nervously nipped round the beasts. Marge and Consuela eyed me with interest as Rufus ran to shut the gate—just in time, before Homer and Bart came ambling out.

'Right. Drive them towards me!' he yelled.

Easier said than done, actually. As I ran to chivvy one, the other one slipped off in the opposite direction. For all their bovine bulk, these beasts were like bleeding quicksilver.

Finally, though, with much swearing and cursing, I'd got them lined up sufficiently to yell, 'Right—open it, Rufus! Open it now!'

He did, and Marge went straight in. Rufus whooped with delight and went to shut the gate but, flushed with success, I yelled, 'No, keep it open! I've got the other one!'

Unfortunately, I hadn't quite, and when Rufus opened the gate, she darted in the other direction. Instinctively we both lunged after her, and as we did, Marge and Bart slipped past Rufus and began galloping joyously after Consuela, who was lolloping down the hill. Rufus and I watched in dismay.

'After them!' I hollered, careering down the chalk track.

'No! Take the car!' called Rufus.

I stopped. Good plan. I came tearing back, ran inside for the car keys, then back to the car. Rufus was already in the front seat.

'If we get the other side of them, we can use the headlights to drive them back in the right direction,' he explained. 'I've seen it in films.'

I nodded, mute with admiration, but also, fear. What would Piers say? His prize herd, his exotics, disappearing into the next county, injuring themselves, dying even—what would he say? He'd say get out.

'Here they are!' Three broad bottoms with whisking tails trotted plumply ahead of us in the headlights. 'Right, I'll drive up on this verge, get round the other—oh shit, SHIT!'

'They think you're racing them!' squealed Rufus. They surely did. As I drew up alongside them, they put their heads down and charged. 'Slow down, Mummy, slow down. They're heading for the road!'

I hit the brakes as the cattle stampeded on. They were heading for the beckoning twinkle of the A41. Oh God, now someone would *die*! And it wouldn't just be a cow, it would be a human being.

'The car's frightening them!' I yelled. 'We'll leave it here and get out!'

As we stopped, the cows, placid, inquisitive creatures by nature, stopped too. Then they promptly put their heads down and grazed. We crept up on them like Red Indians, and there then ensued much scampering about and cajoling, but we were outnumbered.

'It's no good, Mummy, we need someone else! Every time I get Consuela, Bart goes running off again!' Rufus was close to tears. 'Pat's house is just there.' He pointed. 'Why don't I go and get him?'

Panting hard, I hesitated. Things were getting out of control here. I swallowed my pride, which was about the size of a baked potato, and nodded. 'Wait here,' I muttered. 'I'll go.'

I ran down the lane, clutching my dressing gown to me as I threw open his front gate. We'd move, obviously, after this. I rang the bell. He didn't answer. Well, of course he didn't; it was nearly four in the morning. I rang again. Scotland, I decided. Back to the salmon farming.

Eventually there was a shuffling sound, a light went on and the door opened. Molly peered at me, looking dazed.

'Oh, I'm so sorry,' I breathed, taken aback. 'Um, Molly, our cows have escaped and I just wondered—is Pat in? They're almost on the road now and I'm so worried there'll be an accident!' My voice sounded as small and cracked as Rufus's.

'Oh Lord,' she said sleepily. She turned. 'Pat . . . oh.'

A pair of tanned legs in boxer shorts and a bare bronzed torso emerged down the hallway behind her. 'I'm so sorry,' I gasped, 'but our cows have escaped, and there's only me and Rufus—'

'Hang on.'

He reappeared seconds later, thrusting his legs into jeans as he hopped along, a fishing jumper over his head.

'I'd help,' mumbled Molly sleepily, 'but I'm terrified of cows.'

'Such a townee,' said Pat affectionately, ruffling her hair. 'How many are there?' This to me, not so affectionately.

'Oh. Three.'

'Fine. With Rufus we can handle that. Go back to bed, Moll.'

Pat grabbed a handful of walking sticks and a torch and we hurried off down the path. I sneaked a glance at him. Blimey. Quite a coolie, wasn't he? Bedding one beautiful woman after another like that? 'I'm really sorry,' I mumbled as we hurried along in the darkness. 'I didn't know what else to do, and Piers will freak.'

'He will,' he agreed grimly. 'Where are they?'

'Just down the track, over by the water meadow. I told Rufus to stay with them, not to try and move them but—oh!' As we rounded the bend, I swung about in horror. The track was empty. 'RUFUS!' I screamed, terrified now. 'WHERE ARE YOU?'

'I'm here!' an equally terrified voice screamed back out of the night. 'I couldn't stop them, Mum!'

I swung round and as Pat shone his torch, we saw Rufus pointing desperately as the three shaggy Longhorns ambled into the distance. They'd crossed the stream and were heading for the action of the A41.

'Oh Christ, that's exactly what we don't want!' said Pat. 'Come on, we'll have to cross the stream and head them back.' He was fast and much, much more sure-footed than I. As he leapt the stream, Rufus following, I tried nimbly to follow suit—and slipped and fell.

'All right?' he called back over his shoulder, still running, I noticed.

I wasn't at all—my ankle was killing me—but I struggled, soaked to my knees, and scrambled up the bank on all fours. 'Yes!' I bleated, both boots full of water, plastered with mud and pond weed.

'Right. Now we need to take a cow each and get behind it. And then, with arms like this'—he demonstrated a crucifix—'and with a stick in each hand, like so'—he showed us, then handed us some sticks—'we drive them forwards. *Calmly*. Rufus, you take the brown and white one, and, Imogen, that one's yours. I'll take this stroppy madam.'

For a moment I thought he was looking at me, then realised he meant Consuela. Expertly wielding two sticks, he began to head her back across the stream. Rufus got the idea and Bart followed, but Marge, clearly a good-time girl, was still intent on partying, and shot off in the opposite direction.

'Run round her!' yelled Pat, still shepherding his cow, 'and spread your arms out!' I knew exactly what he was demonstrating, but obviously I couldn't do that. My dressing gown had no cord and I was completely naked underneath. I waved a stick feebly with one hand and ran after Marge, but every time I got behind her and tried to drive her forwards, she dodged and doubled back on herself.

'STICK IN EACH HAND!' Pat hollered. 'ARMS OUT!'

'Yes, I KNOW!' I screamed back. Marge ducked round me again, grinning almost, it seemed, and galloped joyously towards the road.

'IMOGEN!' roared Pat, furious. Fuck. Oh fuckity-*fuck*!

Sticks held aloft, I charged after her, zoomed round her rear end, turned her expertly, and with my dressing gown streaming out behind me, came running back towards Pat and Rufus, arms high. 'Happy?' I screeched, as the cow obediently trundled towards them.

Pat's eyes were on stalks. 'Very,' I think I heard him say.

As Marge fell into line with the others, the cows crossed the stream in unison and we followed. I'd managed to clutch my dignity back again too, much to my son's relief.

The cows were stampeding up the track to our cottage now. I struggled up the hill, exhausted, watching as Pat put on a spurt to overtake them—and to swing open the gate. Rufus ran on gamely, but he was going to struggle to get all three in on his own so with one last superhuman effort and a mighty roar, 'GOO ON!' I urged, running up beside him and whacking Marge's backside.

She shot in, followed by the others, and the gate swung shut. The three of us clung to the top bar, panting hard. 'All right?' gasped Pat.

'Yes!' I wheezed.

'Come on,' Pat said, 'let's get Rufus to bed.'

'Yes, bed, Rufus,' I agreed. We staggered up the path to the cottage, and through the front door; Rufus, completely spent, and on automatic now, heading up the stairs with me following. He crawled in under the covers, exhausted. 'Sorry, Mum,' I heard him mutter as I went to shut his door. 'I mean, for letting them out.'

I turned and gave a weak smile in the doorway. 'These things happen.'

When I got back downstairs, Pat was slumped in an armchair. 'Oh— sorry,' he muttered, hauling himself wearily to his feet. 'Collapsed for a moment, there. I'll be on my way.'

'No, no, don't. It's my fault for getting you up in the middle of the night. D'you want a cup of tea? Or even something stronger?'

'Now you're talking,' he grinned. 'Mind if I help myself to a brandy?' He nodded to the sideboard where the bottles were arrayed.

'Do, I'm just going to take off my—well, to change.'

I flushed and disappeared again, flying up to my room. God, I must look a complete fright. A glance in the mirror confirmed my fears. Mud and slime covered my face, my dressing gown was ripped, and my legs were filthy and grazed. I quickly washed my face, pulled on jeans and a jumper, and raked a comb through my hair.

Pat was crouched down by the hearth when I got downstairs. He'd lit the fire. 'It's so bloody cold I felt I had to,' he said, straightening up and handing me a brandy. 'And I thought you could do with some warmth after that dip in the river.'

'Thanks.' I realised I was shivering. I knelt down by the fire, which hadn't really got going yet, trying to absorb its heat.

'I don't usually drink this,' I said, 'but actually, it's quite nice.'

He crouched beside me. 'Ah, well, brandy tastes different under different circumstances. After a shock, it's always very welcome.'

'It was a bit of a shock,' I admitted. 'I don't often wake up with a jolt and run a steeplechase at three in the morning. Not sure I'm fit enough.'

He grinned into the flames. 'You looked pretty fit to me.'

I blushed. 'Yes, well. Thanks to you, it didn't end in disaster. I don't know how I can begin to thank you.'

'Then don't. Anyway, I'm used to getting up at all hours.'

'Yes, I suppose broken nights are an occupational hazard. Not so funny for Molly, though,' I said deliberately, to see what he said.

He grinned. 'She'll live.'

Right. Not much. 'Still,' I went on, 'you could have told me to sod off and gone back to bed. I haven't exactly been a model client, have I?'

He smiled. 'I'm not sure I've ever thought of you as a client, Imogen.'

There was a silence as we both digested this.

'And anyway,' he went on, 'we all have to start somewhere. You're new to the country. I dare say I'd be crap at commuting to the City.'

I smiled. Somehow I couldn't see him in a pinstripe suit trundling off on the misery line to Liverpool Street. I looked at him, leaning back on his elbows by the fire now, at ease, happy in his own skin in that relaxed Irish way. 'Have you always lived in the country?'

'No, I lived in Dublin when I was at university, and then for a couple of years in Belfast. I'm not entirely a country bumpkin. My family are from west Cork though, and that's where my heart is.'

My own heart, inexplicably, stalled at this.

'Is that where you'll go back to, then? Eventually?'

He shrugged. 'Who knows? When is "eventually"?' He stared into the flames. I wanted to say, is that where your wife and child are? But didn't dare. 'At the moment, I'm happy being elsewhere,' he said.

Elsewhere. It sounded as if he was running from something. Ties, perhaps. Responsibilities. I licked my lips. 'My mother always says you can change your skies but you can't change your soul.'

He smiled. 'Sounds like a very wise woman, your mother.'

'And anyway, it's people that make a place,' I went on boldly.

'You're so right. And I think . . . because of that, this place is becoming more than just Elsewhere.'

Ah, I thought. Molly.

'Anyway,' he shifted to face me, 'what about you? What brings you down here to the sticks away from the glamour of London?'

I smiled wryly. 'We couldn't afford to live there any more. I'm a born-and-bred townee, and I never thought I'd take to country life, but actually, I'll be sad to leave this place.'

As I said it, I realised it was true. What, go back to London? To the house I loved, opposite Kate? Surely that would be bliss? But . . . we weren't going to London, were we? We were going to Scotland, salmon farming. Anyway, we were definitely on the move. I swallowed. So, I wouldn't be setting my easel in the buttercup meadow any more, or walking with Rufus to the stream to watch the ducks . . .

'What are you thinking?' He was watching me.

I smiled ruefully. 'That I've let this place get to me.'

'Ah, well, places have a habit of doing that. They creep up on you. Steal into your heart when you're not looking. People too.'

He looked into the fire as he said this, but it seemed to me he looked straight into my soul. I hardly dared breathe. I watched the flames, knowing it was imperative not to take my eyes away from them. And suddenly, I knew too I wanted to bottle this moment for ever—the two of us—Pat, stretched out with fluid grace on the rug, me beside him on the hearth, the firelight flickering on our faces . . . the implications of this thought horrified me. I began to scramble to my feet.

'Where are you going?'

'Well, I just . . .'

'Come here.' And he rolled over and took me in his arms. His weight wasn't constricting: and his lips weren't forceful; they were gentle, tender. I could easily have pulled away. But I didn't. I arched my back into him; felt a flood of uncomplicated passion surge through me, then lost all sense of myself in the utter abandonment of the moment.

Chapter Nine

SECONDS LATER, I was on my feet. 'I can't believe I did that!' I gasped.

He propped himself up on one elbow. 'Joint effort, surely?'

'What must you think of me!'

'Would you like me to tell you?'

'No! You must go,' I breathed. 'Go on, quick!'

'I'm going, I'm going.' He got to his feet in one fluid movement, grinning and still looking absurdly handsome, his eyes twinkling.

'You must think I'm appalling!'

'You said you didn't want me to tell you what I thought of you.'

'No, no, you're right. I—I don't do this sort of thing,' I flustered, hastening him down the passageway to the door. 'What were we *thinking* of?' I breathed.

'Well, I know what I was thinking of.'

'Yes, but I'm *married*!'

'You are. But you're lonely.' The eyes that held me now were steady, less amused. I stared into them.

'Don't be ridiculous,' I spluttered.

'I'm not being ridiculous. It happens. Good night, Imogen.' He reached up and ran a finger lightly down my cheek. 'Take care.'

And then he went sauntering down the path and into the night, or the dawn, actually: a tall, broad figure moving with casual grace.

I slammed the door shut. What on earth had possessed me to behave like that, like—like a *teen*ager, down there on the rug? I went upstairs, my arms wrapped around myself, holding tightly. It was hardly worth going to bed now, I reasoned, but maybe I'd just crawl in under the duvet in my clothes, just for an hour or so. I wouldn't sleep, not after all that drama, but I could just lie down.

I awoke to find bright sunlight streaming through the thin cotton curtains. Rufus was shaking my shoulder. 'Mummy, wake up!'

'Hmm?' I peered at him through bleary eyes. 'Wha's wrong?'

'We've overslept. It's ten o'clock!'

I sat bolt upright and grabbed the clock. He was right, it was. 'Oh God, we're going to be so late, Rufus!'

'Much too late,' he said decisively. 'No point going in now, Mum. Why don't I have the day off?'

I looked up into his wide, innocent brown eyes. Then I flopped back onto the bed. 'Good idea. Why not? God, we've been up half the night cattle rustling. But this is a one-off, Rufus,' I warned. 'We won't be making a habit of missing school just because the cows get out.'

'OK,' he agreed. 'It seems really weird now, to think we were running round the countryside in our pyjamas. Like a dream.'

Wish it had been a dream, I thought darkly as I headed off for a shower. Perhaps Pat, too, could imagine it had never happened?

It was a glorious, bright spring morning, and as Rufus skipped outside to feed the chickens, I resolved to set to in the house. Really get it gleaming.

As hour or so later, I took my head out of the oven, Brillo Pad limp in my hand, shoulders sagging. This wasn't working. No amount of elbow grease was going to exorcise the memory of . . . you know. Well, of course it wouldn't. Painting—that was it, I thought feverishly. Why wasn't I painting? Well, because Rufus was around, that's why, but, on the other hand, I'd managed it in London sometimes, when the evenings had been really bad, so why not here?

When the evenings had been bad. That brought me up short as I went to get my easel. Yes, painting had been a balm there, but I'd been happier here. *We'd* been happier, Alex and I. My chest tightened. Why was I trying to ruin everything then, by grappling with the local stud? Face burning, I hastened to the buttercup meadow and set my easel up quickly. Somehow, though, nothing flowed. It felt all . . . wrong. All disjointed. After a couple of hours, I grimly unscrewed the canvas from the easel and went inside for something to eat. Yes, food. That's what I needed. Hadn't even had breakfast. Rufus appeared to have made himself a sandwich; God, he'd be in care soon. I picked up the loaf and the knife. But I wasn't hungry at all, I realised. Now that was a first. Well, not entirely a first. I'd gone off my food once before, when I'd first met Alex; but that was because I was in . . . oh Lord.

Hands trembling, I reached for the coffee jar. Caffeine would help, and actually, I glanced at the phone—a chat. With Kate. My heart leapt. Yes, *that* was who I needed to talk to, to spill the Pat Flaherty beans to. I took the phone in the sitting room and rang her number, but her answering machine was on. Damn. I glanced at my diary. Thursday. Where was she likely to be on a . . . oh God. I went cold. The play! There it was, in my diary, in red, on the evening of Thursday 25th—*As You Like It*. I'd completely forgotten. What sort of a friend was I?

I rang Alex. My voice was unnaturally high when he answered. I hadn't envisaged speaking to him quite so soon after . . . 'Um, darling, you couldn't possibly scoot along to Kate's play tonight, could you? I completely forgot, it's a charity thing, at that Little Britain theatre in Kensington, near the Albert Hall.'

He groaned. 'Imo, I would, but I've got the ghastly Cronin brothers over from the States. I've got to entertain them this evening. I shall be ploughing through Yorkshire pudding at Simpson's yet again.'

'Oh God, poor you. No, don't worry, I'll leave Kate a message.'

Well . . . Hang on. Why was it impossible for me to go? There was always Hannah. I mean, sure, she'd just had a baby, but Rufus was no trouble. Why didn't I go to Kate's play myself? We could maybe have supper together afterwards. Yes, I thought, my heart quickening, I'd talk it over with Kate, and she'd say, Don't worry, these things happen, heavens, Imo, we've *all* behaved disgracefully in our time.

I rang Hannah, who said she couldn't be more pleased to have Rufus. I dropped him on the way and roared off down the lanes. Yes, this was a *good* plan, I decided.

There was surprisingly little traffic on the roads, and I reached London in record time. I should do this more often, I thought. I parked on a meter behind Kensington High Street and walked off towards the park, ducking down into a side street under the gaze of the Albert Hall, and joined the queue for tickets outside the theatre. Quite a glitzy throng had gathered, I noticed.

We trooped in among much chatter, and took our seats, but because I'd bought a ticket on the night, I was badly placed: right at the back. Damn. I'd need my glasses for this. I rooted around in my bag, but clearly hadn't brought them. Double damn. And when the curtain went up, I realised I'd also failed to buy a programme. I was blowed if I could work out which one Kate was. I leaned across to a pinstripe type beside me. 'Excuse me, could I possibly borrow your programme?'

Smiling my thanks, I scanned the cast list in the dark. No Kate Barrington. She wasn't in it. I frowned, but tried to follow it anyway and laugh at the right bits, but Shakespeare wasn't really my thing. I was glad when it was the interval, and muscled my way pretty promptly to the bar—something I'd got down to a fine art after years of watching Dad's productions—where I ordered a gin and tonic.

'Hello, Imogen.'

I swung round in surprise. A tall, handsome young man with long, poetic chestnut hair was smiling at me. 'Oh, good grief, *Casper*!' I reddened, and he went an even deeper shade of claret as we collectively remembered our first meeting together, ostensibly as gallery owner and prospective artist discussing a forthcoming exhibition.

'What are you doing here?' I said stupidly, for something to say.

'Well, watching the play, like you.' He laughed, embarrassed. 'I saw you when you came in, actually,' he admitted, passing me my drink and ordering a beer for himself, 'but didn't have the nerve to talk to you.'

'Why ever not?'

'Well, you know . . .' He made a face. 'But I wanted to,' he went on quickly, 'to apologise for my appalling behaviour that day.'

'These things happen,' I murmured into my drink. God, I'd forgotten how young he was; how sweet-looking, with his long wavy hair.

'But I also wanted to thank you,' he went on determinedly. 'The advice you gave me that day was spot-on. I did lie low, and I did play the long game, and in the end, it all blew over between Charlotte and Jesus. She eventually got bored with him and came back to me.'

'Oh, Casper, I'm *so* pleased.' I really was. I beamed delightedly. 'So now you're back together? You and Charlotte? With the children?'

'Yes. In fact, I'm watching her tonight. She's in the play.'

'That's why I'm here too. I thought Kate was in it, but I can't see her.'

'Oh, no, Kate left the show a while ago.'

'*Did* she? I didn't know.' I felt awful. God, I hadn't even *asked*.

'She has so much to juggle you see, but she's always got time for her friends. Charlotte and I went to dinner there the other night.'

'Yes, she has always got a lot of time for her mates,' I agreed. 'In fact, she got us together in the first place, didn't she?'

'She did. In fact, she was the one who suggested I go for a little bit more than just lunch with you.'

I blinked. 'Sorry?'

'Oh, no,' he said quickly, 'not—you know—like that. I handled it very badly. She didn't mean for me to jump on you in the restaurant, she just . . .' he hesitated. 'She said she thought you might be lonely.'

I stared at him for a long moment. 'I'm married, Casper.'

'I know,' he said quickly. 'But,' he shrugged, 'well, so was I.'

Lonely. Two people had levelled that accusation against me within the last twenty-four hours. I began to feel hot. I needed to get out, and when the bell went for the second half, I did. I said goodbye to Casper, pretending I was going back to my seat, but actually, slipping out of the side entrance onto the street. It was dark now, and the night air was sharp and cool on my cheeks; welcome. I had a sudden burning desire to see Alex. I was cross with everyone making assumptions about my life, trying, quietly, to make things better for me. A quick bonk by the fire perhaps—or, or a young man estranged from his wife for me to befriend in a restaurant—there, that would do the trick. Poor Imogen, stuck with a busy, distracted husband, with just her small son and her painting for company. The blood rushed to my face as I walked quickly to my car. Did people really pity me?

I glanced at my watch. It was half past nine, and Alex would still be entertaining the Cronins at Simpson's, but he'd be onto the pudding by now. We'd meet up, I decided, getting into the car. Maybe we could go to that piano bar in New Burlington Street; we could have a brandy.

I rang him, but his mobile was off. Annoyed, I left a message, then suddenly, on an impulse, found myself pointing the car towards the Strand. In the direction of Simpson's. Yes, why not? I could leave a message at reception. Or even get one of the waiters to take it in. 'Darling, I'm up in town—long story. Will meet you in half an hour at Romano's.' Yes, that was the name of the bar.

I drew up and parked, rather punchily, right outside Simpson's, on a double yellow line. Leaving the hazard lights on, I nipped through the front door and made a beeline for the supercilious-looking Latin maître d'. 'Excuse me, could you possibly give this to Mr Alex Cameron, please? He's eating here this evening.'

He looked at me a moment, then: 'With pleasure, madam.'

I nipped back to the car and drove off to New Burlington Street. Ah, here it was, Romano's. I approached it slowly and paused for a second, engine still running, to look. I peered in. Through a brightly lit plate-glass window, a bustling bar was getting up a nice head of steam; lovely. I shunted the car into first, about to drive when suddenly, the door opened, and out came Alex. He was laughing, and then turning to smile delightedly at a beautiful girl in a pink sheath dress, with long blonde hair. He took her in his arms and pulled her in towards him, kissing her thoroughly on the lips. It was Kate.

There are moments, often brutal, invariably tragic, when one becomes aware that life as we know it is never going to be the same again. This was my moment. Glimpsed in a second, yet destined to change years. And I couldn't take my eyes off it, frozen like a wild animal in head-lights, by the horror that was unfolding before me.

They crossed the street, yards from my car, and I felt a sharp stab of panic, as if I was the one that shouldn't be seen. I hit the accelerator. I remember hardly being able to breathe. Somehow, I steered the car through the traffic. No coherent thoughts formed in my head; the only thing I knew with any certainty was that I had to get away.

I drove round the streets, anywhere, but eventually found myself driving much too fast through Chelsea going towards Putney, towards home. Eventually I skidded to a halt outside Kate's house, and opposite mine: I turned off the engine, and sat there in the darkness.

I glanced down. My hands were sweaty, clenched tightly in my lap. Alex and Kate. Alex and Kate. I looked at Kate's house. There were a couple of downstairs lights on, but otherwise, it was in darkness. The children would be in bed by now, and perhaps Sebastian too. Did he know? I wondered. Or suspect that Alex and Kate—oh, Alex and *Kate*.

How long? I wondered suddenly. And where? And how often? My mind, up until then a shocked, blank canvas, was suddenly ambushed by questions. I shut them out, squeezing my eyes tight.

My eyes snapped open as I heard a taxi trundle up. It stopped in the middle of the road. Kate got out, her long tanned legs flashing. My stomach gave a sickening lurch. I watched as she went up her path, a spring in her step, and I heard her call out, 'Hi, Maria!' as she went inside. Then Maria came out of the front door: I recognised the elderly Spanish lady who baby-sat occasionally. So Sebastian was away.

A few minutes later, as I knew it would, another taxi drew up. Out got Alex. Like Kate, he looked buoyant, excited even. Suddenly I remembered other evenings, long ago, when I was in that house across the street, in bed, and the same thing would happen. A taxi would rumble up, bearing Kate, and then another would arrive, a few minutes later, with Alex. I used to smile to myself and think how uncanny it was that everyone unerringly arrived back just before midnight. I never put two and two together.

Breathe, breathe, I told myself fiercely. I watched Alex go—not into

the main house, as I'd expected, but down into the basement flat.
Clever. Very clever. Always separate taxis, and always, even if Sebastian
was away, separate entrances, which, of course, was why they'd never
been caught.

As a light went on in the basement, I got out of the car and walked
up the path to the front door of the main house. I rang the bell.

Kate opened the door. 'Imogen! Good heavens. What on earth are
you doing here?'

She had the grace to flush. I laughed. A shrill, unnatural sound ringing out in the still night. 'Oh, it's a long story. Can I come in?'

'Oh! Of course you can.' She collected herself, gave me a quick kiss,
the same one Judas gave, and stood aside to let me through. I went on
down the hallway to the long creamy kitchen. I knew that room inti-
mately. Tears threatened. *Don't* think. Kate was behind me.

'Actually,' I turned, 'I came up to see *As You Like It*.'

'Oh!' Her eyes were wide. Scared. 'Oh, the play! Oh no, I dropped out
of that ages ago.' She fluttered around the kitchen, unable to stay still.

I nodded. 'Yes. Casper said.'

'Casper?'

'Yes, well, I went, you see. And he was there. You remember Casper,
Kate, the art dealer. The one I had lunch with, who jumped me.'

'Oh. Yes, I—' Her eyes were big with fear.

'We had a drink together in the interval. We were recalling our disastrous lunch, which of course you instigated, but not with a view to selling my paintings. I gather you thought I was lonely! Anyone would
think I didn't have a husband of my own!'

'Well, I—I thought you could use a friend, you know . . .' Her voice
was almost a whisper, her face grey, lowered to the counter.

'But I've got loads of friends! I've got you for a start. Tell you what, I
might have a cup of coffee before I drive home. Instant will do.'

She turned, very shaken, but gladly went to the sink to fill the kettle.
I'd seen her seize that kettle so many times, cheerfully, confidently, setting it down on the Aga, which we'd sit either side of on a cold winter's
afternoon, while Rufus and Orlando played. And we'd gossip about all
manner of silly, silly things, whiling away the hours until it was time to
get the boys into their baths, time for our husbands to come home. I
sucked in my breath. Oh God, please tell me this started last week. Not
way back then. But in my heart, I knew.

'I'd forgotten Casper,' Kate was saying as she shakily measured out
the Nescafé. Her face was wretched. She looked about ten years older.

'So had I, until today. There's someone at the back door, Kate.'

Alex had half opened the French windows before he saw me. His face went from delicious excitement to dismay in a trice. 'Imogen!'

'Hello, darling. I came up to see Kate's play. Did you run out of sugar, or something?'

His eyes darted to Kate. She met them briefly, in fright.

'Yes, um, coffee. I fancied one. Hadn't got any. I wondered, Kate—'

'Of course.' Her voice was only barely audible as she passed him the jar of Nescafé, not looking at him.

'Oh, well, have it here, now we're all here!' I smiled. 'Very jolly.'

I reached up to where the mugs were kept and got one down, taking the Nescafé from him and spooning some in. He gingerly came into the kitchen and perched on a stool opposite me, as Kate tried to pour boiling water from the kettle. She kept missing the mugs.

'Here.' I took the kettle from her, so tempted to feel sorry for her, dear, dear Kate, and so, so tempted to pour it on my husband's groin. I nearly did. Would it drop off? I wondered. His penis? 'Milk?'

'No, thanks,' he muttered.

No, of course, he took it black at night, but then I'd forgotten. Hadn't shared a coffee with him at night for so long.

'So, you came up for the play, then straight here?' he said lightly, conversationally, much better than Kate, but then he'd had more practice, hadn't he? With Eleanor, when he was married to Tilly.

'No, I watched the first half, then realised Kate wasn't in it and left. Then I went to Simpson's to see if you wanted to have a drink after your dinner with the Cronins. I left a note with the maître d'.'

He frowned. 'That's odd. I didn't get it.'

Because you weren't fucking there.

'Then I drove on to where I thought we could meet, that new wine bar in Burlington Street. Romano's?'

There was a highly charged silence. Both pairs of eyes swivelled to me. They knew.

'And what should I see,' I went on, my voice trembling with emotion, 'but two people emerging, kissing. My husband and my best friend.'

Kate sank down onto a stool. Tears streamed down her cheeks as Alex struggled to exact damage limitation.

'Now look, Imo, this is all my fault—' he began softly.

'Too right it's your fault. You can't stay faithful to one woman. You couldn't to Tilly and you couldn't to me. You have no moral compass, no notion of honour or duty. I knew you were having an affair, I've known it in my heart for a long time, but Kate . . .'

My voice broke. It was odd. I felt more grief at her betrayal.

Kate was sobbing. 'I'm so sorry. Imo, you have no idea—'

'Of course I had no idea. I had no idea when I asked you if Alex could live in your basement how neatly I'd played into your hands.'

'No!' she shrieked. 'It wasn't like that! I tried so hard! I kept telling Alex it had to stop. It was me who persuaded Alex to move instead. I thought that putting distance between us would help us to stop.'

'You orchestrated my move to the country?'

'Yes, and I told him it was over when you left, finished, but I was so *so* miserable without him, and when you rang and asked about the basement, initially of course I recoiled, but I couldn't resist it.'

Alex was over by the French windows now, his back to us. It was almost as if he were incidental to proceedings.

'I could feel him going back to you, so our plan was working, but it was horrible. I—wasn't strong enough. And I was so unhappy. *So* unhappy,' she said fiercely. 'I panicked. Said yes.'

I remembered how snappy she'd been on the phone when we'd first moved out. I'd thought she was jealous of me being in the country. And I remembered a brief, happy time for Alex and me, when he'd made love to me more frequently. Then the tiredness returning.

Alex had walked out into the garden, literally absenting himself, like a small child who knows the adults need to talk.

'I missed him so much, you have no *idea* how much I love him, Imo,' she hissed, shocking me. As if she were entitled to love him. '*No* idea. I would do anything to keep him, it's all-consuming.'

Her pain was raw, tangible. It brought me up short. Oh, she loved him all right. She was in real trouble. She was in the sort of trouble I'd been in when I'd worked for him, when he was married to Tilly; and it came to me, as a great wave of relief, that I didn't feel that horrible obsession any more, didn't feel my whole personality ebbing away as I forgot everything and everyone I'd ever cared about, my whole existence focusing on him. Because I didn't love him as much as she did. It made me almost feel sorry for her.

'Are you going to tell Sebastian?'

She glanced up, fearful. 'Why would I do that?'

I shrugged. 'Well, I don't want him. Alex, I mean. You have him, Kate. Tell Sebastian, and go live with him. Take your children with you. Tilly and I would advise against it, but feel free, he's all yours.'

She stared at me, shocked. She was trying to work out if I was mocking her, or telling the truth. I was surprised to discover the latter.

'Go on, do it. I've suffered for years, wondering where he is, what he's up to—you have a go. See if you make a better fist of it.'

Yes, OK, I was mocking her now. But I didn't feel bitter. Or angry. I felt pity for how it would wreck her pretty, enviable life, but I knew too that Alex's pull was greater and that she would do it. I looked out to Alex in the garden. That one man could do all this—and such an insubstantial man, at that. Not a man like Sebastian, clever, serious, talented. No, a man who was not clever, but cunning. A man the wrong side of forty, with a mediocre job, precious few assets, slightly on the lanky side, and whose teeth, if we're being picky and I was right now, were not great lately, either. I saw him with brand-new eyes.

Kate followed my gaze. She was looking at him too. And her eyes were ablaze; full of an almost messianic light, that nothing and nobody was going to get in the way of. Not a husband, not three children, and certainly not a best friend.

'Take him,' I said softly. 'He's all yours. Marry him. Here.' I took off my wedding ring and tossed it at her. 'But never forget, Kate, that from his point of view, marrying the mistress only starts another chapter.'

She gazed at me, uncomprehending.

'It creates a vacancy,' I said quietly. Then I turned and walked away.

I drove back to the country in a trance. I felt calm, controlled even. Shock, I decided. Or denial. The tears would come later. Well, they were bound to, weren't they? I'd lost my husband to my best friend, two strikes in one. I held my breath, waited for the floodgates to open. But they didn't. I ransacked my feelings. Why? I *did* feel grief, but it was for Kate, not Alex, I realised with a jolt. I felt her betrayal much more keenly. After all, men did cheat on their wives, we all knew that, and I'd been waiting for Alex to do it for years, but that *Kate* should cheat on *me* . . . It was unnatural, against all the rules; she was my friend, who'd made a farce of my life—that was the shaker. Like a movie shot from two different angles. I was living one version, and all the time another was showing at a different cinema. Same characters, same houses, but spot the difference. There's Kate in her kitchen making a cup of tea for her friend, but—no, on the other screen, she's making a cup of tea for her lover's *wife* as they sit by the Aga together. The deceit was breathtaking.

I wondered how on earth they'd managed it? Obviously Kate's play rehearsals and Alex's late nights at work had been their cover, but what, had they met for supper? No, they'd have gone straight to a hotel. I pictured Kate, getting ready across the road from me while I bathed Rufus, and Sandra bathed her children, aflutter with excitement. Once, I remember, I was at the window as she ran across the road to get a taxi. I'd stuck my head out and called, 'Break a leg!' and she'd called back,

'I'll break Ferdinand's if he still doesn't know his lines!' I was awe-struck by that, now. To lie, so comprehensively. And then, trying to fix me up with Casper, in order to have a clear run at Alex. Did he know about that? Yes, of course he did. The wickedness threatened to overwhelm me. My overriding emotion now was fury. I could feel it oozing over the deep gashes in my heart, flooding me to the core.

And yet, still I hadn't considered Alex's part in this treachery. Well, I'd dismissed him, I realised. What he'd done was so irredeemably dishonest, so disgusting. I'd mentally washed my hands of him. He hadn't been a teensy bit naughty with Old Lover Eleanor—I've bonked her before so perhaps I'll get it past the wife—no, he'd picked Kate. Taken Kate to bed, caressed Kate's—no, don't go there, Imo. I exhaled shakily. There was no decision to be made, no—should I forgive him? Keep the family together? It was a clear, unequivocal *no*. Our relationship had been hanging by a thread, and now that it had snapped, now that I'd finally plummeted to the dark waters below, the ones I'd dreaded, I was finding them surprisingly buoyant. I wasn't drowning.

But my guts wrenched when I thought of Rufus not having a mummy and a daddy who lived together. But Alex and Rufus had never been particularly close . . . I caught my breath. A man who wasn't close to his children? Was this *really* who I'd married? How *could* I?

When I got back to the cottage I mounted the stairs, alone in the quiet house. He'd never come back here, Alex, I mean. I waited for this to devastate me, but . . . it was an oddly liberating feeling. It meant Rufus and I could live where we liked. 'Here, Mummy,' was what I knew Rufus would say firmly. He loved it so, we both did. So, if not in this cottage, then around here somewhere.

The next few days passed in something of a blur. I kept waiting to be shattered. It's true I tottered, rather than strode around our smallholding, and eventually, I did weep. But quietly. Silent tears slipping unexpectedly down my face as I washed up, or read the paper. Nothing violent. By day I painted, but my paintings were darker, I noticed. The world, I discovered, had an extraordinary habit of turning, irrespective of personal fortunes, and I turned with it.

A weekend slipped by. On Monday afternoon, I made Rufus a Nutella sandwich and sat down with him at the kitchen table. I started my preamble with the usual claptrap about people growing apart and blah blah blah. Just as I'd got to the bit about it being better, sometimes, for mummies and daddies to split up, he said, 'Is it because of Kate?'

The saliva dried in my mouth. 'What do you know about that?'

'I saw them kissing in Orlando's back garden.'

'You did?' I gasped. 'When?'

'At Orlando's birthday. You know, the one he had in the conservatory with the funny man. Magic Malcolm.'

I thought back feverishly. Yes, and I'd come across the road with Alex to help Kate and the nanny deal with twenty overexcited children. That had been Orlando's birthday two years ago.

'I needed a pee,' Rufus said, 'and someone was in the downstairs loo, so I ran outside to the bushes. They were kissing down by that chicken house in the orchard, but they didn't see me.'

'Why didn't you say something?'

'Because I thought you'd be upset,' he said simply, brown eyes large.

I gulped. 'Yes,' I whispered. 'Yes, I would.'

'And then I thought, maybe it was nothing. But I kept seeing little things after that. The way they looked at each other, and the way Daddy kept his hand on Kate's waist when he kissed her hello.'

I stood up quickly. My son had known. My nine-year-old son. Seven, at the time. 'And you didn't say anything to Daddy?'

He frowned. 'Like what?'

Yes, like what? But he'd been cool towards his father, hadn't he? I'd seen it, and I'd been upset for Alex. But all the time, my poor boy had been suffering, and I hadn't known. I bent to hug him.

'I'm glad you know,' he said, in a small voice into my neck. 'That was the worst bit. You not knowing. You thinking he loved us.'

I drew back. Held his shoulders. 'He does love you, Rufus. This has nothing whatever to do with you. It's me he's leaving, not you.'

He gave me a wise look. 'I prefer to think we're leaving him.'

The following afternoon, when Rufus was at school, I went to see Piers and Eleanor. I wanted to stay in the cottage, but it was Alex who'd been invited to live there. I was also aware that the rent was due soon and since I didn't have a bean and had spent all the painting money settling my debts, I wasn't entirely sure how I was going to pay it. Would Alex carry on forking out even though he wasn't living here?

Eleanor wasn't there, and Vera took me through to see Piers in his study. Now I really did feel like a forelock-tugging tenant. I outlined the situation in the baldest terms.

Piers took his glasses off. He looked tired. Old, even. 'You and Alex are going to separate?'

'Yes.'

'He's leaving you?'

I smiled. 'That . . . hasn't been discussed yet, believe it or not.' It hadn't. I'd had no contact with him. I think he was waiting for me to make the first move. 'But as far as I'm concerned he's never coming back. I'll change the locks if I have to.'

He nodded. 'But then I'm sure you'll know that my situation has changed too. Eleanor's gone. She went last Friday. She's living with Daniel Hunter.' A muscle went in his face, betraying him.

I took a deep breath. 'Ah. I'd wondered. I'm sorry, Piers.'

He didn't reply for a while. Then: 'I always knew she would, actually,' he said in a low voice. 'Knew in my heart I wouldn't keep her.'

I blanched with recognition. 'That's . . . rather how I felt about Alex. But never really admitted it.'

'No, you don't. You can't believe your luck when someone like that marries you. Just thank your lucky stars and hope it's for ever. But Eleanor was always discontented with me.' He smiled sadly. 'I'm a dull chap, Imogen. Set in my ways, wedded to this house.'

'Yes, but Eleanor loved this house, didn't she?' I said.

'She did. Too much, initially. And my bank balance. But that's never enough, is it? As my mother always says, if you marry money, you pay for it. Luckily for her, my father died relatively young.'

Right. Which was clearly a good thing. Blimey. The family skeletons were clattering out of the closet now, weren't they?

'A house like this, lord of the manor and all that, it's a bit of a poisoned chalice, actually,' he said ruefully. 'Women don't see me at all.'

'Rather like Alex,' I said suddenly. 'He's almost too handsome for his own good. Women fall for it too easily. But actually, there's not much substance to back it up. I don't mean like you,' I said quickly. I was warming to Piers. He didn't seem quite so arrogant and aloof today.

'I've always been rather scared of you, Imogen. You and Alex were such a glamorous London couple, and you're so clever and talented. I thought you looked down on us rough country folk.'

'But I thought you looked down on me for being common!'

'Common?'

'Well, you know, my family and everything.' I blushed.

'Oh, I think they're great fun. Your father's a hoot and your mother's frightfully amusing. My father was a turkey farmer, you know.'

'No, I didn't.' Blimey, that closet door just wouldn't stay shut, would it? All this, via trade, and in only two generations. Three, counting his children. His children.

'Are the children . . .? I mean, is Eleanor . . .?'

'They're staying here,' he said, meeting my eye. 'Eleanor agreed to that. Obviously she'll have them in the holidays, but she and the teacher man are moving to Shropshire. He's got a job up there, and the children don't want to go. We gave them the choice, you see. All frightfully civilised.'

'And they chose you.'

'Yes.' He blinked, surprised. 'They chose me. Well,' he countered, 'they chose their home.'

'Yes, but with you in it. That's quite a vote of confidence, Piers. Even Theo?'

'Even Theo.'

I breathed in sharply. Heavens. Quite something when an eleven-year-old chooses to live without his mother. So she'd gone without any of them. It didn't bear thinking about. I wondered if the children had been told about the baby. Wondered if Piers knew.

'I knew she was pregnant long before she told me,' he said quietly, reading my face. 'You don't live with someone for fifteen years and have four children and not know things like that.'

'And yet you never said anything?'

'No, because I had a vain, foolish hope that it might be mine. I am married to her, after all,' he reminded me, sadly.

We looked at one another, and it seemed to me we'd learned more about each other in the last five minutes than we had in all the years we'd known each other. And I liked what I saw.

'As to the cottage,' he went on, 'of course you can stay. I'd like you to. Theo would like it. And it might be good for the two little chaps in view of their rather similar circumstances.'

'Yes, you're right, it might. Thank you, Piers. But I'm not sure when I'll be able to pay you. Alex and I haven't worked out finances yet—'

'Oh, don't worry about the rent. Pay me whenever.'

I reached up to kiss his cheek. 'Thank you. You've been very kind.'

He looked taken aback, but not displeased. Yes, that's what he was, a kind man. A good man. And what, after all, is a little dullness, set against that?

As I left, his ancient black labrador lumbered up to say goodbye. I patted her. 'She's huge,' I observed.

'She is. About to pop. House is full of pregnant females. She slipped away while she was on heat. No doubt found some rough trade in the village.' This was delivered deadpan. 'Can I interest you in a puppy?'

'No, thanks. I've got enough animals.'

'Well, quite, me too. I'll have to keep one, though, to placate Theo. But Pat will deal with the rest.'

'Oh—you mean . . .?'

'Better than a sack at the side of the M25.' He saw my face. 'It's kinder, Imogen,' he went on more gently. 'A humane injection. They won't know about it. I suggested the same to Eleanor, but she wouldn't hear of it.'

He had a way of delivering these black lines . . .

'Sorry,' he said softly. 'It's my way of dealing with the situation.'

I gave him a hug and, to my surprise, he held on tight. There were tears in his eyes too. 'We'll get through this, Piers, you and I. We could even form a club for abandoned spouses,' I grinned.

'Well, we'd better find some more members, or we'll be the talk of the village. They'll think we're Finding Solace in Each Other.'

I laughed, only a trifle nervously. 'Thank you for the cottage.'

'Ah, yes. Back to the landlord-tenant relationship. My pleasure, wench. That'll be two guineas and a spot of deflowering on the first of every month.'

I giggled and turned to go, tripping lightly down the steps. Gracious. He'd come out of his shell, hadn't he? Positively sparky.

On the road to the village, I flew past the turning to Winslow, where Dad lived. It was a good eight miles away, but I still had an hour to kill before I picked up Rufus . . . Twenty minutes later I was coming to a halt outside Dad's pale blue terraced house. I'd dreaded telling my family, but now that I'd told one person, actually, it wasn't so terrible.

He came to the front door wearing a broad grin and a blue towelling dressing gown. Something in his swagger told me he had company.

'Ah. Bad moment. I'll come back later.'

'Could you, darling? Marvellous.'

I smiled. 'Helena Parker?'

'Well . . .' If he'd had a moustache he'd have stroked it. 'You know how it is.'

I did. You had to hand it to Dad, didn't you?

'You all right, luv?' He gave me a quizzical look as I turned to go.

I took a deep breath. Actually, this would be ideal. Dad only had a few moments before he'd want to get back to ravishing Helena. Why not? I turned. 'Not great, actually. Alex and I have split up.'

'Ah.' He nodded.

I blinked. '"Ah"? Is that it—"ah"?'

'Well, I had an idea it was coming. Rufus told me.'

'Rufus! But when have you seen Rufus?'

'Oh, not recently. But he told me when it happened, Alex and Kate. About two years ago.'

I looked at him aghast. 'I had no *idea*! Why did he tell you?'

'Well, I suppose it was a big thing for a little chap to be carrying around. He had to tell someone. Couldn't tell you, obviously.'

'Right,' I muttered. 'Well. You obviously know. No ground-breaking news here, then. It seems the wife, as ever, is the last to find out.'

'It seemed to me you wouldn't want to be informed. Wouldn't want the truth.'

I thought about this. 'You were wrong, actually, Dad. I wouldn't have wanted to know about Eleanor, who I thought it was, but Kate . . . We all have our breaking point. And that would have been mine. Has been mine. He's gone, Dad. For ever, as far as I'm concerned.'

He nodded. 'And I applaud your decision. There are rakes and there are bounders, but Alex . . . well, he was a bit of a . . .'

'Shit.' I collected myself. 'Anyway, I'll let you go. I've got to get Rufus.'

'Give him my love. He's all right?'

'He's fine. He . . . what are those doing there? Mum's reading glasses. I recognise the case . . . oh my God.' I'd seen his face. He was blushing. 'Dad! I don't believe it. Have you got Mum in there? Mum?' I shoved Dad aside and poked my head round the door. 'Mum, are you in there?'

'Um, Celia, we appear to have been rumbled. I hope you're decent.'

'Perfectly decent, thank you. Hello, darling.'

By now I'd pushed past Dad and made it down the hallway into the sitting room. 'Mum! What the hell are you doing here?'

She tried to maintain her composure but I saw her neck redden. 'Well, what does it look like?'

I sat down, stunned. 'But I thought . . .' I turned to Dad. 'I thought you were seeing Helena Parker! Thought it was all going swimmingly!'

'Oh, it was. It worked a treat.'

'Worked a . . . what d'you mean?'

'I wasn't really seeing Helena Parker, Imo, but when I met her the other week at Tessa's dinner party, it occurred to me she was just the sort of woman to drive your mother crazy. As the others haven't.'

'The others haven't? You mean . . .'

'Imogen, your mother and I split up ten years ago, when, due to a midlife male wobble, I had an affair. A stupid mistake, but your mother chucked me out—quite rightly—and then put the seal on things by moving to the South of France. So that was the end of everything.'

'You never questioned it,' said Mum softly.

'Because you never gave me a chance! You made it very clear from the outset that I would not be forgiven.'

I glanced at her. It was true, she'd never left the door ajar; was far too proud. But no one had thought Dad wanted to come back in.

'You were firmly ensconced with Marjorie,' pointed out Mum.

'Marjorie was a pain in the tubes,' he said irritably, 'as you well know. Anyway, she went back to Derek—after a fairly hefty push from me— and I came out to see you in France.'

'Yes, but you brought that magician's assistant with you! Mandy.'

'Only to make you jealous. I thought if I went younger and prettier it would do the trick!'

'I don't believe this,' I groaned to the carpet.

'Younger and prettier?' Mum gazed at him incredulously. 'But she lasted two years!'

'Well, what was I supposed to do? I was on my own!'

'And then came Audrey, and then Marissa—'

'And all the time,' I turned to her, 'you found it more and more amusing. But when he presented you with Helena Parker . . .'

'An inspired choice?' murmured my father. 'Elegant, sophisticated—'

'Well, I wouldn't be too pleased with yourself,' I snapped. 'It took you ten years to think of it. I can't *believe* you've wasted so much time!' My parents looked down at their feet like a couple of chastened, naughty children. 'And all because you were too proud and stupid to talk to each other.' Further contemplation of the carpet ensued. 'So— then what happened? You broke up with Dawn,' I turned accusingly to my father, 'and pretended you were seeing Helena!'

'And then your mother rang her up!' roared Dad, eyes huge, voice full of awe. 'Gave her an earful about old friendships and how she should keep her hands to herself, until Helena finally managed to get a word in edgeways and told her aside from a dinner party the other night, she hadn't seen me for four years!'

'Yes, that was slightly embarrassing,' admitted Mum, inspecting her nails ruefully, 'but Helena was very sympathetic. She said that if your father could go to the lengths of thinking up such a ridiculous ruse he must care very deeply about me, and wasn't it time we sat down and talked. So we did.'

'Bit more than talked,' grinned my father, unable to suppress himself.

'Thank you, Dad.' I shut my eyes.

'But you're pleased?' said Mum, anxiously. 'You're not too shocked?'

'Oh, I'm *delighted*. Oh God, haven't I said? I'm just so cross you wasted so much time!' I looked at them despairingly. 'I feel so stupid that I didn't sit each of you down and say, Mum, you still like him, and, Dad, you can't want to spend the rest of your life with bimbos. But I was too tied up with my own life, I expect, to notice.'

'You had a lot to be tied up with,' said Mum.

I looked up at her sharply. 'Dad told you?' I said alarmed.

'About what Rufus saw? Yes. And I think he should have told you sooner, but he thought Alex might not be serious about her.'

'Well, *I* never was about Marjorie, or Mandy, or Dawn, so I thought perhaps he wasn't. I've only ever really loved your mother,' Dad said sadly. As he did, he looked across the room at her and his eyes filled. Mum gazed back and hers filled up too. I stood up. Time to go.

'Well, I'm delighted. And so will Hannah be. And now you can both go and tell her.'

'Oh, no!' they both gasped in unison, eyes full of fear.

'Oh, yes,' I insisted. 'But make sure Eddie's there,' I added. Hannah's outrage would be short-lived, though. She too would be overjoyed at having them together again, as loving grandparents for little Tobias, and for Rufus too. Oh, this would go a long way to healing his hurt. I turned at the door in realisation. 'Rufus will be thrilled.'

They both beamed until I thought their faces would crack.

When I picked Rufus up, I had difficulty keeping a foolish grin at bay. Rufus spotted it immediately. 'Why are you smiling so much?'

'I've just had some rather good news. It's about Granny and Grandpa. They're going to get back together again.'

Rufus stared at me, astonished. Then his face lit up. 'Wow!'

We pulled up on the edge of the village. 'That's where your pictures are, isn't it?' He pointed to Molly's bar down the road.

'Yes. That's right.' I realised I'd been avoiding it. Avoiding her. But that was silly. She was selling my paintings, for heaven's sake.

'Rufus, there's an ice-cream shop over there. You go and choose a lolly, and I'll pop in and see if anything's been sold.'

The bar was closed but I could see movement inside. When I rang the bell, Molly came to swing back the door. 'Hello, stranger! Come in, come in. You'll have a quick coffee?'

'I won't, thanks,' I said stepping inside. I'd forgotten how beautiful she was. No wonder he loved her. 'Rufus will be back in a mo. He's just gone to get an ice cream. I just wondered how the pictures were doing.'

'Well, look!' She flung her arms around the bare red walls. 'I was going to ring and tell you—I need more!'

I gasped. 'You've sold them all?'

'Eight out of eleven! Not bad, eh?'

'Not bad? My God—it's brilliant!' All sorts of dizzy emotions jostled within me—excitement, pride—but mostly, an entirely practical one: paying my rent, properly, without going cap in hand to Piers; paying my bills, being independent, which, I suddenly realised, was what I craved. 'Who bought them all? D'you have a list?'

'I do, and they're mostly locals. Even Piers Latimer bought one! We had an opening party for the bar, last week, very impromptu, and I tried to get hold of you, but someone said you were in London. Anyway, he came and bought one, and all three of my brothers came, and one of my brothers even bought three!'

'Good heavens. Well, I'm staggered. Thank you so much, Molly.'

'Don't thank me. You painted them,' she grinned, as Rufus came running in with his lolly. 'Hello, you.'

'Hi.' Rufus smiled politely, then, not so politely: 'Mummy, can we go now? I want to see if Biscuit's had her puppies.'

'The Latimers' dog?' asked Molly. 'She's just about to. Pat was here a minute ago, and he got a call from Piers.'

'Oh! Mum, can we go? Piers said I could.'

'We can, my darling. Thanks, Molly, we'll speak soon.'

'And he said I could have a puppy. Theo's having one. Can I, Mum?'

'I'm afraid I've already said no, Rufus. We've got too many animals.'

We drove up to the Latimers' and I deposited Rufus round at the back door. Back at the cottage, I went straight up to the bedroom where I was forced to keep my paintings in the wardrobe. Maybe I'd earn enough to build a studio, I thought wildly, dragging them all out. I sifted eagerly through them, wondering which ones I should pick to fill the gaps at the bar. What about this seascape above the bar? Or— another Parisian street scene? But they weren't framed, and framing was so expensive. But I had money now, I determined, and I must plough it back in. Fizzing with excitement, I carried the seascape and the street scene downstairs. I'd take them into the framer's tomorrow, I decided— in fact, I'd take six or seven! My heart flipped with excitement, but then I instantly felt sick. There were two envelopes on the doormat, both written in hands I recognised. One from Alex, and one from Kate.

I collected the letters, and also a pen. I carefully readdressed each envelope back from whence it came. No, thank you, Alex and Kate. I don't want your fawning apologies. I'd contact Alex about Rufus in my own time. When Rufus was good and ready too. But Kate? I gazed out of the window. No. Never.

I thought of the hours of agonising that had gone into those letters, Kate's full of, 'You don't know how dreadful I feel'—trying, as if she hadn't taken everything else from me, to steal feeling dreadful as well. And Alex's, full of the same, but with possibly some 'Can you ever forgive me's?' thrown in. No, I couldn't. Couldn't forgive him.

As I put the letters on the hall table to send in the morning, I thought of the expressions on their faces as they received them. I went back upstairs for my next two paintings, feeling slightly less sick.

I made two more trips up and down the stairs until I had seven boards in all stacked in the hall. When the phone rang I picked it up. Rufus's voice shaking with emotion: 'I can't believe you knew they'd be killed! You knew Pat was going to put them down. I'm never speaking to you again. Never!' The phone was slammed down.

I hastily dialled Piers's number but the line was engaged—presumably Rufus had slammed it down, missed and run off. Damn! I thought for a moment, then grabbed my car keys and ran outside.

I roared up the hill and down the back drive to Stockley. I hastened in through the back door, ran down the corridor and pushed open the kitchen door. Piers's lurchers bayed a welcome, but no Biscuit. And no Piers, or Vera washing up, and certainly no Rufus.

I ran on but there was no sign of anyone. Perhaps they were all upstairs? I flew up the back stairs and down the passageway to Theo's room. No little boys. As I was about to leave, I spotted Piers out of the window on the terrace below, admiring his roses. I dashed back downstairs and out of the French windows. 'Piers!' I gasped.

'Oh, hello, Imogen. I've been trying to get hold of you.'

'I'm looking for Rufus,' I panted.

'Yes, that's why I was ringing. I'm afraid I've rather upset him. I told him Pat had taken Biscuit away because she might need a Caesarean section, and then I, you know, told him what might happen to the puppies—and he shot off on Theo's bike after him. I'm terribly sorry, Imogen.' He looked distressed. 'I tried to stop him.'

'OK,' I nodded quickly. 'Not to worry, Piers. I'll find him.'

Piers was still calling his apologies after me, but I waved them aside as I ran off to the car. Cycling into the village alone! At nine!

I sped to the vet's surgery—no sign of him—and parked creatively outside, front wheels on the pavement. Pink Jeans was sitting in reception, looking poised, blonde and bored. Her face darkened.

'Where's Pat?' I gasped, no pride now.

She raised her eyebrows. 'Panting for him now, are we, dear?'

'Just tell me where he is, dear.'

'He's out on a call,' she said shortly. 'Someone's bitch was in trouble. Wasn't you, was it?'

I wanted to slap her. 'Do you or do you not know where he is?'

'No idea,' she said crisply. 'If he's got any sense he's barricaded himself into his home. Away from desperate women like you.'

I glared at her and made for the door. Stopped. 'Oh, by the way, d'you ever change those jeans?' I flashed her a sweet smile and left.

So where the hell was he? I thought. Piers had thought he was bringing Biscuit here for a Caesarean—was there another surgery? I roared back down the lanes, wondering, if, in fact, Rufus had simply cycled home and I missed him. So off the lane I turned and down the bouncy zigzag track—to an empty cottage. Right. Just . . . don't panic. I jumped back in the car because there was now only one obvious place they could be and that was Pat's house. I took a deep breath, braced myself, and headed off towards the lodge.

Sure enough, in the front garden was a red Raleigh. Thank God.

The door swung back, and Pat stood framed in the doorway.

'Oh. Hi.' He looked surprised—and gorgeous. Tall and bronzed from the sun, sleeves rolled up to reveal broad forearms. Suddenly I was aware of the attractive apparition I must present: hot and sweaty, no make-up, grubby old jeans.

A quizzical look came into his eye. 'Looking for your son? He's in the sitting room, along with Biscuit and apparently, HobNob, KitKat and Jammy Dodger.'

'Or Garibaldi,' warned Rufus as I went in. He was sitting crosslegged on the rug by the fireplace, a tiny puppy cradled in his arms.

'Oh!' I sank to my knees beside him. 'She's had them!'

'About twenty minutes ago.' Pat came across and stood over us. 'I picked her up from Piers's, thinking she might need a Caesarean, but she went into labour in the back of the car. I quickly pulled in here and before I knew it, she'd popped out four pups.'

'Four?'

'One died.'

'Of natural causes,' put in Rufus pointedly. 'It was stillborn.'

'Rufus, I'm so sorry, I didn't think. When Piers said he was going to put them down I just assumed that was what country people did!'

'Some country people do behave like that,' agreed Pat, 'and Piers is one of them. But I wouldn't have done it. We can usually find homes for puppies, especially if we put cute photos up in the surgery.'

'And anyway, these have all got homes,' said Rufus. 'Theo's having one, Pat's having another, and I'm having this one, Jammy Dodger. Dodger for short.' He eyed me defiantly.

I swallowed. 'Right.' I glanced up at Pat.

'Apparently I'm not a proper vet if I don't have one. I can't imagine what I've been thinking of all these years.'

I giggled. His knee, as he crouched beside us, was brushing my arm.

It felt as if it was on fire. I was jolly glad to see Rufus safe and sound, but right now, I wished him a million miles away.

'I'm pretty sure they're half collie. Old Geoff Harper has got a very randy sheepdog that's always sniffing around. That's a good cross—there are some labrador crosses you really wouldn't want. A poodle, for example, or a dachshund.'

'Wouldn't that be a bit difficult anyway?'

'What, you mean the copulation?'

I blushed. Oh, splendid, Imogen. You've brought up the problems associated with canine penetration at this spine-tingling moment.

'Oh, you'd be surprised.' He laughed. 'Where there's a will—or a libido—there's generally a way.' He looked at me, quite . . . you know . . . smoulderingly. Intently. His eyes were like two dark, glittering chips of coal. I knew I was pink already, and I felt myself going even pinker. I didn't know where to look, so I glanced at the walls.

'Oh!' My mouth fell open. 'My pictures!' Over the fireplace was the billowing hayfield I'd painted a couple of weeks ago, and opposite, above the sofa, was the same field but earlier on in the year when it was still pasture. They were big pictures. Expensive pictures.

He looked embarrassed. 'Er, yes. I bought them at Molly's. Had to buy both of them because I felt they kind of went together.'

'There's another one in the bedroom,' piped up Rufus. 'In here.' He grabbed my hand. Open-mouthed, I let myself be dragged into the bedroom, where I found myself looking at the very first landscape I'd ever done here, that first day I'd painted, of the weeping willow.

'You bought three!' I said astonished.

'Four, actually. There's one I bought earlier in another room. But yes, I bought three in one go at Molly's party.'

I dragged my eyes away from the picture to stare at him. Three pictures. Molly's party. 'You're Molly's brother,' I breathed.

'Yes, of course I'm Molly's brother. Didn't you know that?'

'Well . . . no, I . . .' I swallowed. 'I knew she was living here.'

'Because she's decorating her flat above the bar.'

'But . . .' I was still gaping openly. 'She's not even Irish!'

He hooted. 'She bloody is! But she did come to boarding school in England when she was twelve,' he admitted. 'Ironed out the accent a bit. I went to All Saints in Dublin and got the brogue.'

'I like it. The lilt.'

'Thank you.' He gave a mock bow. Then looked at me with those dark, sparkling eyes. 'And I like you too.'

I held his gaze for a moment, then cracked. I moved away, twisting my hands about. 'You . . . bought all my latest pictures, I notice,' I said. 'Not any of my London ones.'

'Well, they're not as good. They look as if they've been painted from photographs.'

'They were,' I spluttered.

'And there's no passion in them. These look like you've really been swept away by something. Or someone.'

I was silenced. He seemed to know more about me than I did.

'This one in particular,' he opened a door into an en suite bathroom and there was the cornfield flecked with poppies.

'Oh! That's the first one I sold! Molly said she didn't know who bought it, said Pierre sold it on a Sunday, but he'd have known you?'

'Ah, yes, but I bought his silence,' he grinned.

'Why?' I asked. Couldn't help it.

'Didn't want you to think I was too keen, I suppose.'

A silence hung between us. The room seemed very still. Very quiet.

'All . . . those girlfriends,' I stuttered.

He frowned. 'Which girlfriends?'

'Well, Piers said,' I mumbled, feeling stupid, because of course one of them had obviously been his sister, 'well—you know, Pink Jeans.'

'Oh, Samantha.' He nodded. 'Yes, you're quite right, I did have a quick ding-dong with her when I first came here. She flung herself at me and I was feeling raw and angry so I flung back. Why, should I be celibate? Were you expecting a virgin?'

'N-no! Of course not.' I felt nosy asking, but I really wanted to get back to the raw and angry bit. 'Was it . . . were you feeling that way, because you'd left your wife?' I ploughed on clumsily.

His face changed. A shadow crossed it. He turned, went back into the bedroom. 'I left my wife? Is that what people say?'

'Well, I think Eleanor, or maybe Piers said it.' I followed him.

'Yes, I suppose I did leave her. I could have stayed.'

'You . . . have a child, too? A little girl?'

He turned and smiled an odd sort of smile. 'She's not mine.'

'Not yours? But I thought—'

'Yes, I did too. Well, who wouldn't?' He laughed quietly. 'You marry the girl you love, have a child, assume it's yours. But it wasn't.'

'Oh!' I sat down hard on the bed. My legs seemed to insist upon it.

'She . . . Marina, had been having an affair. With our best man.'

'Crikey.' That sounded rather inadequate. 'How . . . did you find out about the child?'

'Isobel? Marina told me. When the baby was three months old.

Couldn't keep it in any more, I guess. And she wanted to be with him.'

I gulped. 'Did you believe her?'

'I did, actually. I think . . . you can pretend you don't know your other half is having an affair, but in your heart you know.'

I nodded. Lowered my eyes to the carpet. 'Yes. You do.'

'I did insist on DNA, though. I wanted to be sure.'

'So . . . you left?'

'Yes. I left.' His eyes were raw with pain. 'I just couldn't do it, Imo. Bring up another man's child. But it was hard, because I loved Isobel very much.' He gave a cracked laugh. 'As if she was mine.' He sighed. 'But I couldn't even look at Marina. So I left Ireland. Came over here.'

'And they're still together?'

'No, they split up. Marina chucked him out. I don't know why.'

'Right.' I considered this tall, wisecracking man who'd been through so much pain. So much anguish. To lose a child like that.

'That's why I couldn't face the maternity ward when Hannah had her baby. I got over Marina long ago. Getting over Isobel was harder.'

'Will you . . . still see her?'

'I don't know. Marina has a boyfriend now. I wouldn't want to complicate things if he became Isobel's stepfather. It wouldn't be right.'

No, it wouldn't. And we have to do what's right. My own heart lurched for Rufus. I'd make sure he saw as much of his father as he wanted. Actually, I realised with surprise, seeing Alex wouldn't bother me.

'I heard about your own sadness, Imo. I'm sorry.'

'You did?' I glanced at him, surprised. 'Who told you?'

'Rufus. We were tending the puppies, and I—with sheer self-interest—asked if Daddy was coming back this weekend. He said, no, Daddy's not coming back at all. He's gone off with Mum's best friend.'

I gulped. Blimey. Tell it like it is, son.

'There's . . . obviously a lot of it about,' I muttered.

'The best-friend scenario? Oh, it's a well-worn theme. Did you know?'

I looked at him. 'Like you say. You always know in your heart.' We were side by side on the bed. Our elbows were touching. Our legs. Just. 'It . . . won't do the paint any good, you know,' I breathed, looking through the door to my picture in the bathroom. 'The condensation.'

He followed my eyes. 'No, I know. Needs glass. But I like to lie and look at it, you see. When I'm in the bath.'

I caught my breath, imagining that, then frantically tried not to imagine. 'Glass might steam up too,' I managed, in a squeak.

'No more than I do.'

We turned to look at each other. He raised a hand and tucked a bit of hair behind my ear. I almost passed out. I could hear Rufus in the next room. 'Oh, KitKat, *don't* sit on Dodger!'

Pat leaned forward and kissed me, very gently, twice, on the lips.

'Oh, hi!'

We sprang apart. Molly was wheeling her bicycle past the window.

'Oh!' She got the picture. Her face broke into a broad grin. 'Oh, *good*. How marvellous. *Just* what I had in mind.'

'Thank you, Molly,' said Pat evenly, 'for that vote of confidence, and since you've clearly masterminded this whole thing, perhaps you'd like to baby-sit a nine-year-old boy and some puppies. They're in the next room. Imo and I are going for a walk.'

'With pleasure!' She parked her bike against the wall, smiling widely.

We walked out of the tiny garden and on towards the water meadow, through the long grass dotted with cornflowers and buttercups.

'I thought you were going to ravage me on the bed back there.'

'Would you have let me?'

'Certainly not! In front of my son?'

He grinned. Squeezed my hand. I felt weak with longing.

'Anyway, what would be the point? I've seen it all before. First time I met you you fell out of your dress at a dinner party, then you took your knickers off in a flowerbed, then you ran after a herd of cows stark naked.'

I cuffed him lightly on the shoulder. He laughed, caught my hand, kissed it hard, his eyes dancing into mine. As they did, I remembered what it was like to look at someone who looked at you the same way back. A dark, lonely place hidden deep inside that had been sad and dormant for a long time was opening its doors, letting its captive go free, and this man, this lovely, kind, caring, funny man was doing the opening. I had a very certain feeling, one I was almost too scared to identify, but was equally sure I was right about. We turned and walked on, towards the water meadow, the sun sinking into a rosy glow.

'Pat, we appear to be walking off into the sunset.'

'Relax. Thousands have done it before us. As I told you before, there's no new material. It's a well-worn theme, love.'

Love. Ah, yes, that was it.

We moved on together, as one, into the pink light.

Catherine Alliott

'I've always been a mother who writes, rather than a writer who has children,' Catherine Alliott told me, when we met recently in Hertfordshire. Catherine has always fitted writing her novels around her three children and their school day and tried to keep holiday time free to spend with them. From now on, though, it's going to be rather different, as Catherine's youngest daughter, Sophie, has just started at boarding school. 'So, no school runs,' she said, with a slightly sad smile. 'Up until now, my writing day has been governed by drop-offs and pick-ups and without them I feel as though I'm still on holiday. But I'm not, of course. I've got my tenth book to write!'

The house might have become inordinately quiet now that there is only Catherine and her barrister husband, George, in it, but life has hardly quietened down at all for the author. 'With Fred, Emily, and now Sophie all away at school, I've got three horses to exercise and three dogs to walk, including a very naughty black labrador puppy called Slipper. Then there are the cows we inherited from my father-in-law who has a hobby farm. We have seven of them to keep an eye on now, and thirty chickens to feed, and eggs to collect, not to mention the birds in the aviary.' With such an assortment of animals to take care of, how does she find any time at all to write? 'I was just thinking that as I reeled those things off,' she replied, with a laugh. 'No wonder I have to send the kids to boarding school! They always say you should write about what you know, and in *A Crowded Marriage* I guess I did just that.'

Does this mean, then, that Catherine has had the same problems with her cows as her heroine has in the novel? 'Oh, yes. They escape on a regular basis, and then you feel like an extra in an episode of *The Virginian*, because you are quite literally cattle rustling. In the early hours one morning, our cows got out of the field and I had a call from the police to say that someone had spotted them on the road. I woke my son, Fred, but left the girls in bed. We hurried down to find the cows happily out for a stroll and having a wonderful time. The policeman immediately got on his radio and said, "It's OK. The farmer's wife and her son have arrived." And I thought, Oh my God. His words implied a roly-poly farmer's wife and her strapping son, and there was just little old me and my then ten-year-old with a couple of sticks! It took us hours to get them back home.

'Cows are very inquisitive creatures by nature, very friendly. If you go into their field, they come up to you immediately, at which point, people assume that they're being aggressive and run away—and the cows give chase. The best thing to do is just to stroke them and walk on. I love watching them grazing in the fields by the house—they are such restful creatures.'

I asked Catherine if she had planned from the start to write a tale about adultery in *A Crowded Marriage*. 'Oh, no. I began with the idea of what it would be like to be a second wife, inheriting all the baggage of a husband who had been married before. I never really know what's going to happen when I start a new novel. I have a vague idea of the first few chapters, but that's all. I always begin with my heroine—as there is often quite a lot of me in her—and see where she takes me. This time, as the story began to flow, I thought it would be interesting to introduce an old flame into the equation, and explore *her* influence over the new family and . . . um—what's my heroine's name? Oh yes, Imogen.' We laughed as Catherine told me that she is now so immersed in her next novel ('in which my heroine is called Evie, by the way') that she has had to wipe *A Crowded Marriage* almost totally from her mind.

Does Catherine still enjoy writing as much today as when her first novel, *The Old-Girl Network*, was first published? 'Yes, I do. I love it. It's not easy, but it's not that difficult either. Sometimes I have to take a big, deep breath before I start the next one, but I very quickly get caught up in the world of the characters that I am creating. It's like I'm living somebody else's life, I suppose—which is quite nice, isn't it?'

Jane Eastgate